A Single Lion Roars

Book 5

Of The Warrior Series

By

Sandra J Yearman

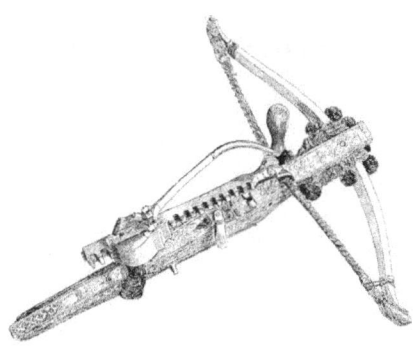

Seraphim Publishing LLC

We Will Bring Light To All The Dark Places

Registered trademark-Sandra J Yearman

Seraphim Publishing
438 Water St
Cambridge, WI 53523
sandrajyearman@gmail.com

Copyright © 2014 Sandra J Yearman

Produced in the United States of America

A Single Lion Roars is a work of fiction. Names, characters, places and incidents are the product of the author's imagination or used fictitiously. Any resemblance to actual persons, living or dead, events or locale is entirely coincidental.

Library of Congress Catalog Number: 2014913977

ISBN: 978-0-9890263-3-8

First Edition

About The Author

Sandra J Yearman is a native of Wisconsin, where she currently resides. She graduated from the University of Wisconsin with a Bachelor of Arts degree in Journalism. Sandra was a member of the United States Army Reserves for over twenty years. She retired from the Dane County Sheriff's Office in Madison Wisconsin as a sergeant.

Sandra is a cancer survivor. And it is on this journey that she says she found her voice and began to write. She established Seraphim Publishing LLC in 2008. Sandra has spent decades supporting and working with rescued domestic animals.

Books written by Sandra:

Novels

Brother Kings
The Scroll And The Sword
Song Of The Second Son
The Faces Of The Damned
A Single Lion Roars
Stand Before The Children
Tyrants, Dictators And Kings

Poetry

This Book is
Dedicated

To The
Rescuers

And To The
Victims

My You Be
Healed

Contents

Contents

Introduction to the World of Nunc

The World of Nunc lies in the Astrum Solar System, which is unique because of its three suns that form a triangle. Seven planets orbit the three suns; Nunc is the third farthest planet from the suns. There are seven continents in the World of Nunc: Anewa, Czarsta, Mayka, Opots, Porto, Salszar and Tansof.

Anewa: lies south of Tansof and is separated from Tansof by the Gaffa Strait. Anewa is southeast of Opots, across the Sea of Grevdt and the Gulf of Caz.

Czarsta: lies to the southwest of Opots; the Schenomi Sea separates the two continents. The Sea of Turnqt separates Czarsta from its northern neighbor Salszar. Mayka lies to the west of Czarsta; the Sea of Ohern separates these two continents.

Mayka: lies to the east of Tansof and Anewa and is separated from these two continents by the Sea of Nepo. Mayka is west of Salszar and Czarsta. The Sea of Wheyt separates Mayka and Salszar while the Sea of Ohern separates Mayka and Czarsta.

Opots: lies east and slightly south east of Salszar. The Phonicha Ocean separates these two large continents on the northwestern border of Opots and the Sea of Talmont separates them on Opots' southwestern border. The Schenomi Sea separates Opots from Czarsta which lies to the southwest of Opots and Porto which lies to the southeast of Opots.

Tansof lies to the northeast of Opots; the Sea of Grevdt separates these two continents. In the series there are several references to creatures that came across the sea and attacked the Kingdom of Lentz. These creatures were warriors from the Dura Tribe of the Continent of Tansof.

Porto: is the smallest continent in Nunc. It lies southeast of Opots and southwest of Anewa. The Schenomi Sea separates Porto from Opots and the Gulf of Caz separates Porto from Anewa.

Salszar: is the largest continent in Nunc. It lies northwest and west of Opots. The Phonicha Ocean separates Opots and Salszar on the northeastern border of Salszar and the Sea of Talmont separates them on Salszar's southeastern border. The Sea of Wheyt borders the western side of Salszar; separating Salszar from Mayka. The Sea of Turnqt separates Salszar on the south from Czarsta.

Tansof: lies to the northeast of Opots; the Sea of Grevdt separates these two continents. The Gaffa Strait separates Tansof from Anewa which lies southeast of Tansof. The Sea of Nepo borders Tansof on the east and separates it from Mayka.

Chapter I
Kidnapped

"Be careful," Shara said and first kissed Sorren then Matthew on the cheek. "Matthew don't worry about anything here, your mother and I will take care of the children. You just find my baby girl."

Rosa hugged her son and Sorren. "I know this is the last thing you want to hear," the Queen said. "But you two have to get some sleep or you will be in no shape to fight. You won't be any good for Angelina and Vivian if you become sick and weak."

"Here," King Mathas said as he handed both Matthew and Sorren several pouches of gold coins. "You don't know what you will be running into and perhaps you will have to pay a ransom."

"The hell we will!" Sorren barked. "Whoever took my daughter will not live long enough to spend any money."

"Well, maybe you use the money to distract them," Mathas said. "I know you are anxious to go but I received a message from Claudius, they will meet you here. They are bringing their children and nurses to stay with us while you search for Angelina and Vivian."

"Are Ingr and Nikki joining us then?" asked Matthew.

"Yes, they refused to stay home. Bella will stay with us and oversee the care of her grandchildren."

"This time the horror ends," Claudius said angrily to Thaos and Stephan as they rode in front of a caravan traveling to Mathas' castle. "This time we stop the forces that Juleta put into motion to destroy our families. And I don't care what we have to do."

"While we are gone, I don't want any of you going anywhere without a military escort," Gabriel said emotionally as he stood before his family and team in the parlor of their home. "Sudfad is having a company of soldiers camping on our land until we find the girls. He said that if you change your minds you are welcome to stay at the castle and to come day or night."

"Calen and Luca you are in charge while we are gone," Gabriel continued. "My family is in your hands. Raphael is afraid that these kidnappings may be a distraction for something else, so he is leaving most of the Patronus priests at the Cicero headquarters. High Priest Joseph will remain in-charge of that facility but you two will be leading any missions or emergency situations which arise in our absence. Please keep the lines of communication open with Joseph."

"Gabriel, Cassandra and I are going with you," Elan said passionately. "She is our friend."

"While I understand your feelings," Gabriel said. "Elan you are not totally healed from your injury. This may be an arduous journey."

"Then I will carry him," Cassandra said. "Gabriel, Vivian brought Elan back from the dead, please don't make him stay behind."

"I won't," Gabriel said with exhaustion. "Matthew and his men should be here sometime after lunch, we will leave then. I know most of you may want to go with us but we need warriors here too. So at this time please tell me who is coming with us."

"Gabriel remember that there are still many Ruala warriors at Sudfad's castle," Maxwell said. "And I hope you don't think I went behind your back but I spoke with Lakin. He and his family are coming here to stay and watch over our family here. Emeral is staying here and I am going with you. Lakin said you need to tell him how many Ruala warriors you want to stay at the castle because they all want to join you."

"That sounds fine," Gabriel said. "I can't say this enough; even if things are uneventful while we are gone we still don't know why those creatures were on this property or why they tied those bodies off our shoreline. Both Raphael and I agree that those of you staying here may come under attack while we are gone." Gabriel looked at his wife and sister. "Hannah and Natasha; please don't make me worry about you while I am gone. I know you both wanted to come along but I beg of you please stay here with the children and don't take any unnecessary risks."

"Honey we will be fine," Hannah said.

"It's you and Raphael that I am concerned about. I don't think he has slept or eaten since Vivian's disappearance and you aren't much better."

Gabriel did not respond to his wife's comment. "So Maxwell, Elan and Cassandra are coming with us; anyone else?"

"I'm going with you," Misha said.

"I think we are all coming with you," said Koby.

"I think at least one of you should stay back here," Calen said. "If this is indeed a distraction I would like a regular member of our team here, someone who knows the property and the house."

After a few moments of silence Koby said, "Bekka and I will stay here, at least for now. We can continue our patrols along the river; since we are familiar with the surroundings."

"Vitomas while we are gone, I don't want you going any place without an escort," Raul said as he was packing. "Simon is telling Annabelle the same thing. It is just too dangerous; both women were taken from their own properties. Who knows what is behind this? We always worry about you two so much when we are gone, please don't take any chances."

"Honey I promise," Vitomas said as she sat on the bed watching Raul pack. "Just find Angelina and Vivian. I can't imagine what Matthew is going through."

"I certainly can," Raul said. "I fell apart when I found out you had been kidnapped. Simon had to take over for a while."

"Raul, I have something to tell you but I am not sure if now is the right time."

"Is anything wrong?"

"No," Vitomas paused. "I am pretty sure I am pregnant again."

A broad smile filled Raul's face as he gently pulled Vitomas to a standing position and kissed her on the lips. "I am glad you told me. I could use some good news."

"Annabelle I feel so guilty leaving you now," Simon said as he was packing. "Laurel and Mother both said they would help you with the children."

"Simon I never like to see you go," Annabelle said as she cradled the infant David in her arms. "But you have to find Angelina and Vivian. Don't laugh but Vitomas and I both said we would go with you if we could; Angelina is like our sister."

Simon stopped packing and kissed Annabelle on the forehead. "I keep remembering what Raul was like when we discovered that Vitomas had been taken. I am glad that Matthew is not traveling here alone."

King Sudfad stood in the front of the Great Hall in his castle. The room was filled to capacity with soldiers from Lentz and Wetpr and warriors from the Nordes, Ruala and Shettee tribes and Enrops. "Because of the nature of this mission we have asked for volunteers and it makes my heart swell with pride to see all of the faces before me," Sudfad said.

"King Mathas and I consider these atrocities that have been committed as acts of war against our kingdoms and we are prepared to send the strengths of our armies to you if you request them. In the past when our men traveled through other kingdoms on missions they did not wear their military uniforms but because this is war you will ride under your flags."

"Mathas and I have spoken at length and have come to some decisions that may anger some of you. Because of the nature of these crimes there are many among you who are overwhelmed with anger and grief. This is not a good way to go into battle. So King Mathas and I have decided that General Claudius will lead this rescue mission. Of course Sorren will be in charge of the Nordes warriors, Raul and Simon will carry out their leadership destinations with the soldiers from Wetpr and Gabriel will head his team which will consist of all the Patronus, Ruala and Shettee warriors but you will all answer to Claudius," Sudfad continued.

"I believe we all agree that these kidnappings could be distractions for other acts of aggression against our kingdoms and families and both Mathas and I are prepared for war. When you leave here you will cross the border into Stordt. I have been in communication with King Hamond and assured him that our armies will merely be travelling through his kingdom but as many of you, I do not trust Hamond so be prepared for anything."

"You will travel through Stordt because it is the fastest way for you to get to Ryed and the Schenomi Sea. The route we have planned for you will take you through Nora; the Sanuri will join you at that point in your journey. Like Stordt," Sudfad explained. "Ryed is a dangerous kingdom that is filled with many dark lords and witches. Once you arrive in Ryed, Gabriel and Raphael will make contact with Vivian's tribe and ask for their assistance."

Sudfad continued, "We all suspect that King Douma from the Kingdom of Ogg is behind these kidnappings but do not close your minds to other adversaries. As you know the Kingdom of Ogg is said to exist on the floor of the Schenomi Sea; hopefully the Sanuri can give you guidance in how to enter this kingdom."

"There are also flocks of Enrops searching the waterways and areas that you will not be travelling. If the Enrops find anything Mathas or I will dispatch troops to those areas so you continue on your course until I tell you otherwise. I will now turn this over to General Claudius and may The Great Ruler be with you."

Later that night as the armies led by Claudius sat around their campfires, there was little laughter.

"I still can't believe the border guards didn't even question us," Archetenus said. "Knowing Hamond that may mean he is up to something."

"I don't know," Stephan said. "Did you see the looks on their faces when they saw all of us approaching? I'm not so sure they were told we would be crossing the border."

"Not to change the subject but why are Gabriel and Raphael sitting alone around a fire?" asked Simon.

"They're trying to learn the language of the Valdees," Misha said.

"The only way I am speaking to those demons is with my sword and battleaxe," Sorren said angrily.

"While I agree with you," said Maxwell. "We may need to get information from some of those creatures."

Matthew had been staring blankly into the fire, now he looked at the faces of his friends and family. "Perhaps I should join them," Matthew said and walked over to Gabriel and Raphael. Silence reigned around the fire for several minutes as everyone was feeling Matthew's pain.

Nikki tried to start conversation, "Archetenus did Jared come too? I haven't seen him."

"He wanted to but now that both of our wives are pregnant one of us needed to stay and take care of them. And honestly I am the one who owes Matthew a great deal," Archetenus said. Then he saw the looks on the faces of Ingr and Nikki. "Is something the matter?"

"I think Nikki and I both had the same thought," Ingr said. "Our babies were huge and you and Jared are so much bigger than our husbands, your wives may have some difficulties with delivery."

"Now don't scare him," Thaos said when he saw the worried look on Archetenus' face.

"That's easy for you to say," Ingr teased. "You're not the one giving birth." This comment brought several laughs from the group.

"Just before we left Vitomas told me she thinks she is pregnant again," said Raul.

"Really," Simon said with a grin. "So you are trying to win that bet?"

"What bet?" Nikki asked.

"We have a bet as to who can have the most children," Simon said with a grin.

"Do your wives know about it?" Ingr asked.

"Oh no," said Raul. "Although they both want big families so perhaps it wouldn't matter."

"Nikki is pregnant now," Thaos said.

"And you let her come along?" Archetenus asked in disbelief.

"It was either she rides with us or she was going to follow us," Thaos said. "Angelina is like her sister."

"Ibula is pregnant and nobody ever tries to make her stay out of battle," Ingr said.

"Oh believe me," said Thaos. "Thedes would prefer she stay home."

Silence once again reigned around the campfire. "I know we are all thinking it," Ingr said after the silence was too much for her. "But both Angelina and Vivian are such powerful warriors they know how to survive and hopefully they are being kept together."

"If those damn creatures spied on us at all they would know to separate those two girls," Sorren spat.

"Whether they are together or not," Dagon said. "We all know they must have been greatly outnumbered to have been taken captive."

"I never was told," Misha said. "Was Angelina near the river when they got her?"

"No," Sorren said. "She was riding on the King's property near the castle. She often goes for morning rides so they must have been waiting for her."

"Did you find anything?" Misha asked.

"Oh yes," Ingr said. "They found an area where the brush was bent and broken and there was blood."

"They followed the blood trail and found one dead creature on the King's property. Then they followed the blood trail to the river which is almost a two hour ride from Mathas' castle; that's when they found another dead creature."

"We're just hoping all the blood came from the creatures and not Angelina," Stephan said.

"We searched the water," said Claudius. "And found nothing. They got away quickly."

Chapter II
War Looms

"Rueben the more I study the outside of that mausoleum the more I believe it is an ancient relic," the Sanuri said to High Priest Rueben, the leader of the Patronus at the Nora headquarters. "But something that old should be covered with vines and brush; there is no plant life within two hundred yards of that building."

"So what do you think that means?" Rueben asked as he poured coffee into their cups.

"The best that I can speculate is that either the mausoleum is emanating so much evil that life cannot be sustained around it or somehow a powerful demon made it suddenly appear here."

"The Lion did tell you it was a trap for us," Rueben said as he placed a plate of eggs and potatoes in front of the Sanuri. "Did he tell you anything else about it?"

"Only that it contains secrets of great importance," the Sanuri replied. "Rueben when Gabriel and the others come for me; I don't want anyone going near that mausoleum until I return. Just have the Rualas watch it as before and notify me of any occurrences."

"With the increasing numbers of Hutas in the area my men may have their hands full," Rueben said as he sat down to eat his breakfast. "I sure would like to know what is drawing those savages here."

"There is an army about a mile ahead of you," Arca, the Enrop told Claudius as he led his men through the Kingdom of Stordt in the early morning hours.

"It must be Hamond," Claudius said. "We don't have time for this. Arca tell me are they together as one group or are they spread out to ambush?"

"From what we could see he has his men together, they are blocking the road you are one," the giant bird answered.

18

"How many?" Matthew asked.

"Maybe two hundred," Arca replied.

"Do they have any scouts or ravens in the area?" Claudius asked.

"No." Arca answered.

"Sorren you take your men and surround them from the east," Claudius ordered. "Raul take your men from the west. We'll surround that bastard and if he wants to play games we will give him what he wants."

"Rueben," Padre Silas called as he ran into the headquarters. "Some of the Rualas saw a large group of Hutas heading towards a farmhouse, the men are saddling up and I sent an Enrop to Fort Nora."

Both the Sanuri and High Priest Rueben jumped up from the table and ran out the door. Fifty Patronus warriors were told to remain at the headquarters while the rest followed Dack, a Ruala warrior, westward. The group rode fast and hard. "If there is such a large group of Hutas," the Sanuri said loudly to Rueben, who was riding at his side. "I fear they are gathering victims for sacrifice."

"I was thinking the same thing," Rueben yelled back.

"There is smoke up ahead," Dack yelled down to the warriors who were following him.

"Stop!" a commanding voice yelled as Claudius and his men rode around a bend in the road and now faced two hundred Taperian soldiers. Claudius was leading the men with Matthew, Simon, Thaos and Stephen immediately to his rear. Archetenus, Gabriel, Raphael, Ingr and Nikki comprised the next line of riders.

Claudius rode forward, "Are you Hamond?" he demanded loudly.

"No, I am Captain Fontaine," the man in the lead roared back. "Why are you in Stordt?"

"King Sudfad has already communicated with Hamond," Claudius said angrily. "Two of our daughters were kidnapped and we are following those who have them. We have no business in this god forsaken kingdom other than travelling through it."

"Hamond is the one who sent us out here, so I doubt if you are telling the truth," Fontaine yelled. Fontaine was a battle experienced warrior who had not seen battle in some time. He was hoping today would be more interesting.

"Are you calling me a liar?" Claudius roared. Archetenus broke rank and now rode up to the two men.

"Fontaine these are good men and he has told you the truth," Archetenus said.

"Archetenus you are alive," Fontaine said with surprise.

"I don't know what kind of bullshit games Hamond is pulling," Claudius said as he aggressively rode closer to Fontaine. "But we don't have time for this. And nothing is getting in our way, do you understand me?"

"Just give us the word," Sorren yelled from behind the Taperian soldiers.

"Hold your ground," Fontaine yelled to his men when they realized they were surrounded. As they turned they saw over two hundred Nordes warriors with their weapons drawn to their right and an equal number of Wetprian soldiers to their left.

"My daughter is one of the girls taken," Sorren yelled out with anger. "Fontaine is mine!"

"Captain look up," one of the Taperian soldiers yelled.

Fontaine's eyes widened when he saw the sky above them filled with Ruala warriors and Enrops.

"Fontaine, you are delaying us," Claudius yelled. "Your choice is whether you want to die today or live, what say you?"

"You may pass," Fontaine said reluctantly.

Now Simon rode up to Claudius and Fontaine, "I am Prince Simon, son of King Sudfad. The agreement between Hamond and my Father is that we are allowing him to sit on the throne here. But now that Roch is dead, this kingdom belongs to our family. You know our armies greatly outnumber yours. If Hamond wants to remain King tell him to stop these games."

"Roch is dead? You know this?" Fontaine asked.

"You'll find his body in the remnants of the Taperian Hotel," Archetenus said. "The Princes killed him; I saw it myself. You might also want to tell Hamond that Roch was hiding in Taperia for some time and he was recruiting men to kill Hamond. If Hamond's spies haven't told him this, well, guess Hamond's got more problems than us."

When Rueben and his men arrived at the farmhouse they found six Ruala warriors shooting arrows down at seventy-five Huta warriors, all of whom were painted for war. Rueben quickly motioned for his troops to divide and circle the Hutas. Rueben and the Sanuri were in the group that charged the Hutas from the front. "I want one of them alive," the Sanuri yelled above the din.

The six Ruala's had done nothing more than to keep the Hutas from entering the farmhouse where a family was hiding. Huta warriors had already set fire to the barn and other small buildings on the farm. The Patronus were well trained fighters who did not falter in battle. Most of the Hutas were on horseback and charged the Patronus priests. The fires from the burning buildings filled the farmyard with thick black smoke. Grunts, cries and screams were heard above the sounds of metal striking metal.

The Sanuri preferred to fight on his feet as opposed to being on the back of a horse. He rode to the front of the farm house and jumped to the ground. He immediately grabbed one of the three Hutas who were trying to force their way through the front door. The Huta quickly turned and the Sanuri ran his sword through the Huta's heart.

The other two Hutas now turned and attacked the Sanuri simultaneously. One attacked the Sanuri from the front while the second Huta grabbed him from behind. This Huta pulled the Sanuri's head back exposing his throat. The Sanuri could not move; just as the second Huta was going to cut the Sanuri's throat he suddenly released his hold on the Sanuri's head. The Sanuri plunged his sword into the Huta in front of him and turned to see that Rueben had crushed the other Huta's head with a battleaxe.

Time changes on a battlefield, as do perceptions. So focused were the combatants on the battle; all the senses in their bodies dedicated to killing the other and to surviving the battle that Huta and Patronus alike did not hear the Horn of Cass blow as the Wetprian soldiers from Fort Nora rode onto the battlefield.

"I know you feel guilty being left behind," Lila said as she brought Luca coffee in Gabriel's study. "But Christopher and I are glad you are with us."

"It's not so much that I feel guilty," Luca said as he unrolled another map of the Kingdom of Ryed. "I'm feeling a little useless here."

Lila sat down on the corner of the desk. "Luca I have been wondering something but I didn't want to say anything in front of Raphael. The families from Lentz believe those horrid creatures took Angelina because of a bounty that Juleta paid but why did the take Vivian?"

"She probably came upon them and the fight was on."

"Then why didn't they kill her, after all they put all of those other bodies on our shoreline."

"Well, that sounds cold," Luca said with surprise.

"No, I didn't mean it like that," Lila said apologetically. "I mean as far as we know those creatures have only killed men. If they are assassins for a demon wouldn't you think they would kill, well anyone? I think the creatures took them because they are both young and beautiful women which means the creatures might keep them alive."

Luca looked quizzically at Lila. "You're thinking they took them for wives?" Luca paused as he considered this motive. "If the Kingdom of Ogg really exists in the ocean they are cut off from the rest of the world. We know they take slaves; perhaps that is also how they keep their bloodlines."

"The only other similarity I could think of," Lila said. "Is that both Angelina and Vivian are fierce female warriors and perhaps they want them to fight in games. I know your tribe is used to female warriors but many tribes have never seen any."

"Lila you have brought up some really good questions," Luca said as he stood up. "I believe I will pay Zoya a visit to see if she can give us some insight; do you want to come along?"

"Fontaine is an ambitious and treacherous man," Archetenus explained after their troops passed the Taperian soldiers and continued their journey to Ryed. "I am not sticking up for Hamond but Fontaine was probably lying to you about Hamond's orders and now that you have embarrassed him in front of his men I would expect retribution."

"So why do you think he confronted us?" Simon asked.

"Fontaine loves battle. If we would not have so greatly outnumbered him, there would have been a fight. But I also suspect he is trying to figure out how to get the throne from Hamond. A victory would elevate his position among the soldiers," said Archetenus.

"So I rather told him how to oust Hamond," Simon said. "By starting a war with us."

"That's right. Roch held the throne because he murdered everyone he suspected was against him," Archetenus said. "Actually tortured and displayed is a better description. Roch liked to make examples of the men and women he thought were traitors."

"Our wives don't want us to take the throne here," Raul said. "They believe our families would be murdered."

"Listen to your wives," Archetenus said. "This kingdom is filled with men like Roch; I should know I used to be one of them."

"You didn't have to bring anything," Zoya said as Luca and Lila walked into her kitchen. "We just enjoy the company."

"It's not much," Lila said and handed Zoya a basket which contained a pie.

"I'll get Jared," Delilah said and walked out of the house.

"We are kind of here on business," Luca said as Zoya placed cups of steaming coffee in front of them. "Have you had any visions about what happened to Angelina and Vivian? Or can you give us any information at all about the creatures that took them?" Luca asked

"Good to see you," Jared said as he shook hands with Luca.

"They brought us a warm pie," Zoya said as she put slices on small plates. "Actually Luca I have been surprised that I have not received information about them. The only thing I have been seeing doesn't make sense to me." Zoya put the freshly cut pie and more coffee on the table.

"Anything you can give us might help," Luca said. "We feel like we are going into this blind."

"Are you talking about the kidnappings?" Jared asked as he sat down at the table.

"Yes," Luca said. "Lila brought up some good questions this morning. All the bodies we found were men. She thinks they may have kept Vivian and Angelina alive for wives or combatants in games. What do you think?"

"Actually I have been wondering why they took Vivian," Jared said. "We expected an attack against the families of Lentz. And I know everyone suspects that Vivian came upon the creatures and fought with them but what if that's not the way it went down. I mean what if they were hunting her?"

"That is definitely a possibility," Luca said. "The more we think about this the more questions we have."

"Zoya what is it you have been seeing?" asked Delilah.

"I have seen the same thing several times and it is so strange that I don't understand if I am seeing it properly. I see great darkness and I can feel fear and for some reason I know it is Vivian's and Angelina's fears that I feel. I believe they are underwater but I can't explain why. Then suddenly there is light in front of them and in the middle of the light is a cyclone cloud but it is upside down. Then I sense that the girls are fighting their captures as they are taken into the cyclone; and that is all I see."

"Do you think that is how the creatures enter their kingdom?" Luca asked Jared.

"If that kingdom is really underwater you would think they would have to have a way to prevent the pressure of the water from destroying everything," Jared said. "Maybe that is the reason for the cyclone cloud. If you have ever been someplace when a cyclone hits you know it changes the pressure."

"I'm not sure how it all works but that would make sense," Luca said as he thought about Jared's words.

"Zoya, I don't understand how your gift works," Lila said. "But Luca told me about the time that Misha's grandmother warned you about Elan. Can you contact spirits and ask for information?"

"I will try and tell you any information that I get."

The battle did not end quickly after the soldiers from Fort Nora arrived at the farm. Hutas were born and bred to be killers. Their true nature was unleashed in the heat of battle, blood and screams awakened the evil within them and the Hutas fought as if the demons were on the battle ground with them.

Through the chaos and the noise the Sanuri heard the screams of a child. The dark smoke from the burning buildings impeded the warriors' sight as well as burning their eyes and throats. The Sanuri had been fighting in the front of the farm house, trying to keep the Hutas from entering. Now he ran around the small structure and saw six Huta warriors dragging the family members from the home. "They have the family," the Sanuri yelled and ran after the Hutas. Only a few soldiers and priests heard the Sanuri's words and of those men only three were able to break free from their adversaries and follow the Sanuri.

The small farmhouse backed up to a steep hill. The Hutas were on foot dragging the family up the hillside. Since the Hutas had not murdered the people in their home, the Sanuri knew the fate that awaited these farmers; they were to be sacrificed to one of the demons that the Hutas worshipped.

Two Wetprian soldiers and a Patronus priest quickly followed the Sanuri as he ran up the hillside. The Sanuri was closing in on a Huta who was dragging a boy of about ten years by the back of his shirt. The boy's body bounced over the rocks and debris along the hillside. As the Sanuri got closer he could see the terror in the child's eyes.

"Release him!" the Sanuri yelled with such authority that the Huta turned. When the Huta saw that an old man was chasing him he laughed and violently threw the boy to the ground. Then the Huta pulled a huge knife from the sheath on his belt and jumped at the Sanuri, who quickly jumped to the right to escape the knife of the Huta. "There are others," the Sanuri yelled as the soldiers and priest caught up to him. The injured boy pointed the way that the Hutas had taken the family and the three men took chase.

The Huta warrior quickly recovered his position and once again lunged at the Sanuri; who was holding a sword in his right hand. The Sanuri swung his sword and sliced the left side of the Huta who was almost upon him. Two of the Huta's ribs were broken but the intense pain did not stop his forward movement.

The Sanuri sidestepped the attack to the left, in the moment that the Huta passed the Sanuri; he felt the Sanuri's sword plunge into his kidneys. The warrior screamed with pain and rage and turned again towards the Sanuri. The Huta was momentarily distracted when the boy threw a rock that hit the Huta in the back of the head. In that instant the Sanuri plunged his sword through the Huta's heart. The Sanuri ran to the boy and picked him up. "Are you hurt?" the Sanuri asked.

"Just a little; they have Mommy and my sisters," the boy cried.

"Hang on," the Sanuri said as he started to run up the hill, carrying the crying boy.

Claudius and his troops had traveled almost an hour towards the southwest, when one of the Ruala warriors flew over Claudius and the Princes. "Those soldiers are back and they are riding hard behind us. They may have increased their numbers: it's hard to tell with the dust clouds.

"Fontaine is mine," Sorren yelled.

"So be it," said Claudius.

"We should be entering the Mangee Forest very soon," Gabriel said. It is better to take a stand there because once we get to where the River Neior crosses the River Nebu there is a tight passageway through some cliffs."

"Once we get to the forest," Claudius barked, "Simon and Matthew lead your men to the east; Raul and Sorren your warriors go to the west. The archers are the first line on both sides of the road. Gabriel and Raphael have the Patronus continue forward for enough distance that those troops believe they are still following us. The Ruala archers will attack from above."

The Sanuri did not have to run far before he found the body of one of the Wetprian soldiers. The young man lay in a large pool of his own blood. Through the centuries that the Sanuri had fought in the world of man he still found such sights greatly disturbing. The Sanuri quickened his pace because he knew the two warriors ahead of him would be facing five Hutas. The Sanuri said a small prayer and soon the sky filled with Enrops. "Stop the Hutas," the Sanuri yelled to the giant birds as he continued to run up the steep hill.

Fontaine's rage overwhelmed him as the captain led his men to their deaths. Never had he felt so humiliated, Claudius and the Princes of Wetpr treated him as a nuisance instead of a powerful force to be reckoned with.

"Disrespect me!" Fontaine yelled out loud. "It will be the last thing they ever do."

Padre Gilbert tackled one of the Hutas who dropped the eight year old girl he was carrying. The little girl rolled to her right screaming as the Huta threw Gilbert off his back. Knifes drawn, both warriors circled each other and each man lunged and was blocked by his opponent. The Huta crouched then threw his weight into Gilbert's stomach, knocking the breath out of the priest.

Gilbert dropped his knife; he stumbled backwards as the Huta tried to take him down to the ground. Gilbert locked the fingers of both of his hands together, striking the Huta hard on the back of the neck with double fists. The Huta temporarily released his hold on Gilbert. Gilbert grabbed the savage's head and used his right knee to repeatedly strike the Huta in the face. The Huta's knees weakened.

"Look out," the little girl screamed.

Gilbert could feel a searing pain in his back. He fell to his knees and was instantly thrown to his side by a powerful kick from the Huta who had stabbed him. Gilbert tried to stand but was kicked again. Sweat burned Gilbert's eyes as he looked up at his attacker. The first Huta grabbed the girl, who was screaming hysterically. The second Huta bent over Gilbert and grabbed his hair, pulling his neck back to expose Gilbert's throat. Suddenly Gilbert's head pushed forward and he saw blackness.

Fontaine's rage overruled his instincts on this sunny morning. Normally Fontaine would have sent scouts ahead of his company of men but he was so focused on retribution that he led his men into the darkness of the Mangee Forest. They continued to follow the well-worn road; Fontaine could hear the horses of the Patronus before him. He never heard the arrow that impaled his skull.

Fontaine was one of the first to fall as arrows reigned upon them. Horses screamed as many of the Taperian soldiers yanked on the reigns in an effort to elude the barrage of arrows. Five Taperian soldiers made it out of the Mangee Forest and headed west towards Hamond's castle.

"I wouldn't let them leave," Archetenus yelled to Claudius. "They will just bring back more men."

"Stop them," Claudius yelled to the Ruala warriors who flew after the soldiers.

Twenty minutes later the Rualas dropped the bodies of the five dead Taperian soldiers on the floor of the forest next to their comrades. So successful was the ambush that few of Claudius' warriors suffered injuries. The wounded were cared for and the march resumed.

By the time the Sanuri thrust his sword through the Huta who was about to cut Padre Gilbert's throat, the Enrops had alerted the soldiers and warriors that the Hutas had the family. While some Enrops led the warriors to the Hutas, other Enrops swarmed and attacked the Hutas, causing them to release their victims. Ruala warriors soared ahead of the soldiers and Patronus priests who had to climb the steep hill.

The Sanuri set the boy on the ground and pulled the dead body of the Huta off from the priest. Gilbert regained consciousness as the Sanuri placed his hands over the stab wound in Gilbert's back and began to pray. Gilbert weakly tried to stand up.

"Hold still," the Sanuri said.

"If I am to die it will not be with my face in the dirt," Padre Gilbert said with determination.

"You will not die my son," the Sanuri said. "But you are making it difficult for me to stop this bleeding."

"I believe I have broken ribs too."

"I realize that," the Sanuri said. "Now hold still."

"The children," Gilbert asked. "Did we save them?"

"The others are retrieving them now," the Sanuri said to Gilbert then he turned to the boy who stood in silence staring at them. "What is your name?"

"Tommy."

"Tommy would you help me heal this priest?"

"Sure," the boy said meekly.

"Sit down over here and hold his hand."

After the fight with the Taperian soldiers, Simon and Raul sent messages to both King Sudfad and King Mathas alerting them of the battle and thus a possibility of war with King Hamond. Claudius and his troops did not make camp until the sun was almost set in the sky. Weary from exhaustion they were driven by their fears and anger to get to Ryed as quickly as possible.

As was becoming habit, Gabriel, Raphael and Matthew made a campfire separate from the rest so they could concentrate on learning the ancient language spoken by the Valdees. Gabriel loved Raphael as his brother and closest friend. Not only did Gabriel feel guilt that one of their family members was abducted from his property when they were all at home but Gabriel was consumed with pain every time he looked at Raphael. Neither Matthew nor Raphael had slept an entire night since their wives had been abducted. Both men had lost weight and had the dullness in their eyes that extreme grief can bring.

Sorren's reaction to the loss of his daughter was very different; he was so consumed with anger and hatred that he could barely speak. He was explosive and greatly on edge. While Claudius and the other leaders in the group understood Sorren's reaction, they knew Sorren's emotions were out of control and watched him closely.

"Stephan, would you mind if I sat with Raphael for a little while after dinner?" Ingr asked as she prepared food over the camp fire. "Every time I look at him it breaks my heart. He doesn't even speak any more."

"Actually I was thinking of doing the same thing," Stephan said. "I know how I felt when I thought you were going to die; I felt like I had died inside." Ingr smiled at Stephan's words and walked over to her husband and kissed him on the forehead.

"It will be a little while for dinner," she said. "Do you want to go over to him now and if you think it will help I will sit with him after dinner?"

A new flock of Enrops circled over the campfires and landed one by one among the warriors. The arrival of these giant birds brought smiles to the faces of many, since they were carrying letters from loved ones. Claudius opened the letters from King Sudfad and King Mathas before he opened the letter from his beloved wife Bella.

"Sudfad has ordered a meeting with Hamond," Claudius announced to the group. "They will meet on the border tomorrow morning. Sudfad says that if any more of Hamond's men attack us there will be a full out war between the kingdoms. And Mathas is standing with Sudfad, so all our kingdoms could go to war."

Matthew, Gabriel and Raphael heard Claudius' words and walked over to his group. "Could I see the letters?" Matthew asked. After Matthew read the letters he said to the group, "While I believe Hamond needs to be taught a lesson I don't think either of our wives would want so many lives to be lost because of their abductions. I think this act would make Angelina and Vivian feel very guilty."

"So do I," Raphael said is a hoarse voice.

"There is much more to this than the abductions of the girls," Raul said. "War between our kingdoms has been looming for a while; I think it is only a matter of time."

"Listen to this," Gabriel said as he read a letter from Luca. "Zoya has been having a vision over and over. She believes in the vision she is seeing what Vivian and Angelina are seeing. They are in darkness; Zoya believes it to be because they are under water."

"Zoya says she can feel the fear of the girls as they look at an underwater cyclone that appears to be upside down. The girls are led to this cyclone. Jared said that the Kingdom of Ogg would need some type of means of preventing the pressure of the ocean from destroying their kingdom and he believes this cyclone is used for that purpose."

"So they are still alive?" Raphael asked as he grabbed the letter. Matthew quickly moved to Raphael's side and the two men read the letter together.

"That would make sort of sense," Sorren said hopefully as he walked over to Matthew and Raphael.

"Gabriel did you read the part about Lila's ideas?" Matthew asked.

"Yes," said Gabriel. "And perhaps she is on to something." Then Gabriel addressed the group. "We have all been wondering why these two girls were taken from two different kingdoms. Lila realized that all of the bodies we found were men and the creatures did not appear to kill women and children. And while we are accustomed to seeing women warriors many peoples are not. Lila thinks that perhaps both girls were taken so they could fight in Gefrey Games or because they are both young and beautiful perhaps that, well, to become wives."

Both Matthew and Raphael gave Gabriel wide-eyed looks. "I know neither idea is good," Gabriel said. "But it would be reasons to keep the girls alive."

With the small hope that his daughter was still alive, Sorren now spoke with his normal authority. "Both those girls are smart and cunning; as well as being well trained warriors. And they know we will come for them. They just have to figure out how to stay alive until we find them."

Chapter III
Blood Moon

The next two days were uneventful for Claudius and his troops; something that surprised them all. From the letters they received from Sudfad, Raul and Simon realized their kingdom was on the brink of war with Stordt. Both Princes realized that the timing of this political conflict could not be worse. The Kingdom of Stordt was the second largest kingdom in all of Opots and their rescue party had many long days of travel ahead of them.

"Of course we can bypass Stordt on the way back but that will probably add an extra month to our journey," Simon said as he passed Sudfad's letter around the campfire. "I hope we can avoid a war until we get the girls home."

"Your father is sending several thousand more troops to Fort Nora," Claudius said as he read the letter. "I'll bet you anything they get attacked between the border and Nora."

"I believe father is counting on that," Raul said. "He is having more trebuchets moved to that fort and another general to help Colter."

"So let's just say your kingdoms go to war," Stephan said. "And you win, which would be likely. Are you or Simon going to claim that throne?"

"That is a sore subject in our households," said. Raul "That is the only subject that we really fight with our wives over. Vitomas and Annabelle say that Stordt is filled with evil men who will try and take the throne from us; they fear greatly for our safety and the safety of our children."

"As I told you before," Archetenus said. "I agree with them. Stordt is very different from Wetpr; it is as if this kingdom breeds and calls to evil. Killing Roch eliminated only a portion of the evil here. Raul and Simon you are good and honorable men. I think you would have to spend some time in hell to fully understand what Vitomas, Annabelle and I are trying to tell you."

"So why don't you just let those men kill each other off?" Ingr asked with disdain.

"Because innocent people get hurt too," Gabriel replied.

"Grandma, we got to ride with the soldiers on their horses," Christopher yelled as he and Nicholas ran into the house the next afternoon.

Emeral walked out of the kitchen and both boys jumped into her arms for hugs. "There's a plate of cookies on the kitchen table, why don't you help yourselves and I will help Hannah bring things in," Emeral said as she kissed the boys.

"Something smells really good," Koby said as he carried groceries and packages into the house.

"There are fresh baked cookies in the kitchen," Emeral told Koby. "If you are going in there perhaps you can help the boys pour some glasses of milk."

"Did you get the gifts?" Emeral asked as Hannah walked into the house with Cerey.

"Yes and they are just beautiful," Hannah said as she handed three small boxes to Emeral. "Where is everyone?"

"Lily had Natasha up all night so they are both napping now. Lakin, Calen and Luca are at a meeting at the castle and Lila, Zada and her children are in Salar."

"Has there been any word?" Hannah asked as she helped Koby with another armload of packages.

"Nothing since we heard they were attacked by Hamond's men."

"Where's Bekka?" Koby asked when he entered the house a third time with packages.

"She and Lakin's two oldest are flying around the river; I think they are searching for any clues that might have been missed," Emeral said.

Padre Gilbert had barely opened his eyes when he heard a boy's voice yell, "He's awake." For just a moment Gilbert didn't know where he was or why he was in bed.

"We've been waiting for you to wake up," a boy's voice said.

"Gilbert turned his head and saw Tommy and his little sister standing next to the bed. At that moment, the Sanuri and High Priest Rueben walked into the bedroom.

"How are you feeling?" the Sanuri asked as he stood over the bed.

"I'm not really sure yet," Gilbert said as he tried to sit up but was overcome with pain.

"Let me help you," Rueben said and gently helped Gilbert to a sitting position and put pillows behind his back for support.

"Tommy and Trina haven't left your side since the attack," Rueben said with a smile. Their family is staying here with us until they figure out where they are going to live."

"So is everyone alright?" asked Gilbert.

"Yes, we saved them all but their home was destroyed," the Sanuri said. "That was three days ago, you have been sleeping all that time. Trina's been waiting to tell you something."

Trina stood on her toes and stretched upwards and kissed Gilbert on the cheek. "Thank you for saving me," the little girl said. Gilbert looked visibly touched by her affection.

"You are most welcome Trina."

"Their father was in Nora buying supplies when the Hutas attacked, just their mother and the five children were in the home," Rueben said. "We saved the family but lost several men. We've already had the funerals; I will tell you more about that when you are better."

"Tommy, Trina why don't you go outside and play," the Sanuri suggested. "You can come back and sit with Gilbert later if you want."

"They're cute children," Gilbert said as he watched them walk out of his bedroom.

"I suspect the entire family will be in to thank you later; that is what they have done with every wounded man," Rueben said. "The Sanuri was able to talk to one of the Hutas before he died, I will let him tell you the rest."

"When Rueben says talk to, he means I looked into the Huta's mind," the Sanuri said as he closed the door to Gilbert's room. "I don't want any of the children to hear." The Sanuri returned to Gilbert's bedside. "The Hutas are gathering people to sacrifice on the next blood moon; apparently they are trying to get hundreds of victims."

"Why? What is the significance of the blood moon?" Padre Gilbert asked.

"As you know this phenomenon has significant meaning for many different types of people. I will be honest I don't know what meaning it has for the Hutas and their demon masters. Perhaps the writing on the mausoleum will shed some light. I am working very hard to translate it," the Sanuri said.

"Why do you think there is a connection between the writing and the sacrifices?" Gilbert asked.

"I can't be sure of the location I saw in the Huta's mind," the Sanuri said. "But I believe the sacrifices are to take place in that mausoleum."

"Do they have other victims?" asked Gilbert.

"Apparently the war party we killed was the first to go hunting for victims."

"How long do we have before the blood moon?"

"Thirty days."

"Where are you going?" Calen asked as he and Luca returned to the house after their meeting at the castle and saw Bekka and Koby packing large packs.

"Bekka and I are going to take gifts and supplies to Gabriel and the others, then we will return," Koby said.

"We've got something for you too," Luca said. "Let me get some paper and write it down."

"Where is everyone?" asked Calen.

"Mostly in the kitchen," Koby said. "You will have to ask Emeral because I just returned from Salar with Hannah."

Calen smiled when he walked into the kitchen and saw Christopher, Nicholas and Cerey drawing pictures at the kitchen table and Emeral, Hannah and Natasha wrapping up hundreds of cookies. "Are those for the troops?"

"Calen, Lily is sleeping over there," Natasha said. "Please keep your voice down."

Calen walked over to a cradle near the far wall of the kitchen. "What is this?" He asked in almost a whisper when he saw an envelope at the foot of the cradle that had *daddy* written on it.

"I don't know," Natasha said. "I guess you will have to open it up."

Christopher and Nicholas stopped drawing on their sheets of paper and watched Calen. Cerey got off her chair and ran over to him. "We made the card cuz Lily is too little," Christopher said and giggled. Calen smiled warmly as he looked at the childish drawings. The card said *a gift for daddy because I love you."

"This is really cute," Calen said without looking down at Cerey who was pulling on his robe.

Christopher and Nicholas both started laughing. "Cerey's trying to give you the gift," Nicholas said.

Calen looked down and saw Cerey staring up at him. She had one hand on his robe and she was holding a small box in her other hand. "I am sorry Cerey," Calen said as he knelt down. Cerey handed Calen the gift then leaned against him as he opened it.

37

"I love it," Calen said as he took his family locket out of the box.

"All of the children wanted to put their hair in it," Emeral said with a laugh. Calen hugged Cerey then picked her up and set her on her seat at the table. He hugged Christopher and Nicholas then walked over to Natasha.

"I didn't even think to get you something like that until I saw you looking at Luca's," Natasha said as Calen kissed her on the cheek. "If you want different stones on it, just let me know."

"No this is beautiful," Calen said then turned the locket over. *To the love of our hearts* was inscribed on the back of the golden locket.

"General Colter just sent word, he is sending troops to every farm outside of Nora and they are taking the families to the fort for protection," the Sanuri told High Priest Rueben.

"That is going to force the Hutas to look elsewhere for their victims," Rueben said. "Do you think there are enough Hutas in the area to attack the city?"

"Or us," the Sanuri said. "We will need to increase the guards."

Ibula was the lone healer with Claudius' troops, an assignment that was keeping her very busy even though they were just days into their journey. Ingr and Nikki often volunteered to help Ibula care for the others.

"Are our wives still working?" Thaos asked as Thedes joined him and Stephan at one of the campfires.

"Yes," Thedes said.

"From the tone of your voice, is something the matter?" asked Stephan.

"Ibula keeps telling me that I worry too much," Thedes said as he shook his head.

"But she is pregnant with the first baby that will be part Ruala and part Shettee, so we really don't know what to expect and she hasn't changed any of her ways since she became pregnant. I think she is doing too much."

Thaos poured some whiskey into a cup and handed it to Thedes. "Well, you should feel at home because Stephan and I are always saying the same thing. Nikki's not as far along as Ibula but she is puking every day. I wanted her to stay home but she threatened to travel by herself if I didn't bring her along."

"And you believed her?" asked Thedes.

"Would you believe Ibula if she said that to you?" Thaos asked then all three men broke into laughter.

A Ruala can fly much faster than a horse can travel and an Enrop can move more quickly in the air than a Ruala. Koby and Bekka crossed the border between Wetpr and Stordt well before dusk the first day of their journey. They were aware of the conflicts with the Taperian soldiers so Koby decided they should travel in concealment. They did not make a campfire their first evening in Stordt, nor did they sleep on the ground. Koby and Bekka slept on large branches of two different trees. They slept in separate trees in case one of them was taken by surprise.

Bekka was almost four years younger than Koby and she was very flattered that such a handsome and courageous warrior wanted to spend time with her. Koby was teaching her a great deal about the world below the Ice Caves and she was an eager student. Bekka liked spending time with him although they were more friends than lovers but for now she was very happy to be both.

"It's too quiet," Claudius said as he led his troops the next morning. "The hair on the back of my neck is standing up, something is wrong."

"I feel it too," Sorren said. "With the problems with Hamond and all of the Hutas in the area we should have seen something."

"Perhaps the sheer numbers of our troops is a deterrent," Simon suggested.

"Oh, I am sure we are being watched," Claudius said as he looked at the winding road ahead of them. "Gabriel send more Rualas out to scout the area, I don't want us riding into a trap."

"The last time we saw a build-up of Hutas in this area is when those priests were trying to raise Omnibus," the Sanuri said to Rueben who sat across from the desk that the Sanuri was working at. "I know these inscriptions hold information I just can't translate the language," the Sanuri said in frustration as he looked at the stacks of books and piles of papers on the desk.

"Maybe you are looking at it in the wrong way," Rueben said. "Sanuri you are an intelligent and gifted man. I cannot believe you have put so much work into finding that language without success. I am beginning to think it isn't a language at all."

"What do you mean?" asked the Sanuri with peaked interest.

"Well, we already know that mausoleum is a trap, I am thinking that writing is perhaps gibberish to keep you distracted or it is some kind of code."

"That food smells delicious," Koby said as he and Bekka landed in the campsite of Claudius and the others. "I hope you have enough for us, we are starving."

"It's good to see you," Gabriel said as he walked up to the two Ruala warriors. Then his demeanor changed. "Is anything wrong at home?" Gabriel asked with much concern.

"No," Koby said. "We come bearing gifts, mail and supplies." As he spoke both Koby and Bekka took large packs off from their backs. People were now gathering around the two Rualas.

"Your packs are so full," Ingr said as she prepared two plates of food for Koby and Bekka.

"Yes, between carrying these packs and sleeping in trees. I might need a backrub tonight," Koby said suggestively and grinned at Bekka who smiled at his comment. "Elan, Cassandra can you help us; there is much to pass out. Sudfad sent fine whiskey and cigars," Koby continued as he handed bottles and boxes to the people closest to him.

"And Emeral and Natasha must have made hundreds of cookies for you," Bekka said with a laugh as she handed out packages. "Here Cassandra can you start handing out the mail?"

"We only brought mail from Wetpr," Koby said. "But we also brought more medical supplies."

"Good," Ibula said and started to sort through the large bag that Koby handed her.

"Ibula I think there is a letter in that bag for you also," Koby said as he continued to hand out packages.

"Well, this is a treat," Sorren said smiling as he grabbed a handful of cookies and a cigar.

"What are those?" Ingr asked Simon.

"Our wives always have the children paint pictures for us when we are gone," Simon said as he and Raul handed several childish paintings to Ingr. "Of course we never know what the paintings are supposed to be but we like getting them."

"Oh they are so cute," Ingr said and showed them to Nikki.

It pleased Bekka and Koby that everyone was so happy with their gifts and letters from home. "Now," Bekka said loudly so she could get everyone's attention. "I was instructed to explain a few of these gifts before we handed them out. As everyone was preparing cookies and letters and things for you, Christopher, Nicholas and Cerey wanted to send things also. Elan would you hand this to Sorren?" Bekka said as she pulled a large pouch out of her pack.

"Me!" Sorren said. "Are you sure?"

41

"Your name is on it," Elan said with a grin as he handed the pouch to Sorren.

"Here's one for Matthew, Gabriel, Raphael and Maxwell," Bekka said as Elan handed out the gifts.

"Sorren are you alright?" Stephan asked when he saw the look on Sorren's face. Sorren didn't speak but handed a card to Stephan.

"Honey read it out loud," said Ingr.

Stephan smiled as he read it, "*Uncle Sorren we are really sad that you lost your daughter. We pray for Angelina and Vivian every night. We sent you one of our toys to make you feel better until you find her. Love Christopher, Nicholas and Cerey.*"

Sorren looked emotional as he held up a stuffed bear for everyone to see. "Mine is similar," Matthew said haltingly. "But I got a horse." Everyone smiled as they could see how the letters touched these two warriors.

Maxwell smiled and tried to bring some levity to the group. "I got a stuffed bear and the card said it was so I wouldn't miss Grandma and the children."

"Mine said pretty much the same thing," Gabriel said with a laugh as he held up a stuffed bear. Now everyone looked at Raphael; who did not say anything.

"Raphael what did you get?" Bekka asked.

"When Vivian was so sick from that potion and we didn't know if she was going to die, Christopher gave her this horse. He wants me to keep it until I can give it to her again."

The group was silent for a moment then Bekka said, "There are more gifts in my bag." And she started removing the last of the packages from the large pouch."

"Elan we got a four page letter from Emeral," Cassandra said. "And it is all questions she wants us to answer. She is starting to work on our chambers."

"That certainly sounds like my wife," Maxwell said as he poured some whiskey into his cup. "Raphael did the children draw you pictures too?"

"Yes," Raphael replied with a sad smile. "They are very cute."

"Are you ready for the rest of the gifts?" Bekka asked as she walked over to Maxwell and handed him a small package. "This is from Emeral." As Maxwell was opening his gift Bekka walked up to Gabriel. "This is from Hannah," Bekka said as she handed him a larger package then Bekka walked up to Raphael. "Raphael this is from Natasha and Hannah."

"I got a family locket," Maxwell announced happily. "Emeral says she just put her and the children's hair in it for now."

"Maxwell your family is so big you'll need more than one locket," Koby joked.

"Simon your wife drew a beautiful picture of my family, everyone should look at this," Gabriel said and handed the picture to Raul who was sitting next to him.

"Annabelle is very talented," Simon said with pride.

"Raphael what did you get?" asked Gabriel.

"They gave me a family locket too," Raphael was speaking very softly. "They put the children's hair into it and they found some of Vivian's hair from her brush." Raphael stopped talking as the tears rolled down his cheeks.

The Sanuri awoke and found that he was still sitting at the desk in the study that once belonged to Hannah's father. The Sanuri leaned back in his chair and looked around the room as he thought about the many visions that Zoya had told him of. Zoya had told the Sanuri and others that the spirit of Hannah's mother was trying to make up for the horror her husband had brought to this world so she told Zoya about the mausoleum in Nora and the temple in Ryed.

The temple that was built inside of a mountain; the opening of which would only be revealed when a full moon aligned with certain rock formations. The Sanuri wondered if the blood moon was significant in revealing the secret passageway to that temple.

He looked around the room with new eyes. Hannah and Gabriel had taken many of the belongings that once decorated that room. After the house had been given to the Patronus for a headquarters, more furniture had been moved in but little else. "If Arthur Marcus was indeed involved with that mausoleum there might be a clue to the code or translation within this house," the Sanuri thought.

The Sanuri looked around the study, then he opened the false wall behind the desk that revealed the hidden safe. He found nothing useful, then he remembered the library that Arthur had. The Sanuri knew that Gabriel, Raul and some of the others had taken many of the books because they were priceless and rare.

The Sanuri walked to the door of the library hoping there would be some text which would help him uncover the secrets of the mausoleum. He was pleasantly surprised to find many shelves filled with large, dusty books. As he looked through the shelves he saw that many of the books had no titles to indicate their contents.

The Sanuri grabbed an armload of books and was about to return to the desk when he spied some scrolls on the very top of one of the bookcases. When the Sanuri picked up the five scrolls they were covered with a heavy layer of dust. As he blew the dust off from the scrolls he realized how old and fragile the parchment was that held the writings. He left the books in the library and took the scrolls to the desk in the study.

"What's all of this?" Misha asked as he and Dagon walked up to the campfire.

"We came bearing gifts," Koby said with a grin. "There's a couple of letters for you two, I think they're from your girlfriends from the wedding."

"I would rather have some of those cookies," Misha said when he spied the many open packages of cookies. "We were out patrolling the area. Everything is really quiet."

"It's too quiet," Claudius said as he opened a letter from Sudfad.

"Have some whiskey and a cigar," Sorren said and handed a bottle to Dagon.

"Claudius you might want to read that letter from Luca first," Koby said as he started to eat his dinner. "Luca said they found out some information just before we left."

Claudius picked up Luca's letter and started to read it. "This is very interesting," Claudius said. "Lakin contacted some of the elders of the Rualas to find out if any of them remembered the Valdees Tribe. A man named Aldron said he remembered reading old texts about that tribe."

"When the Hutas tried to destroy our race they burned everything that held our history," Misha explained. "That is why Lakin went to the elders."

Claudius explained the letter to the group, "Aldron tells a very different story than what we have heard. He says that like the Hutas the Valdees worshipped demons and were known throughout the kingdoms for capturing people for human sacrifice. Aldron says that King Douma was arrogant and consumed with power and he started a war with the demon Fatronas who they worshipped. When Douma lost that battle he turned to the demon Baal who was a longtime rival of Fatronas."

"Douma promised the souls of all his tribe in exchange for Baal's help. Aldron says that Baal opened up the sea from the volcanic mountain of Mount Vue south for ten miles and east and west for twenty miles. Baal told Douma that if he wanted more land for his kingdom he would have to swear everlasting allegiance to the demon. Which apparently he did."

"Aldron goes on to say that Baal held the waters back for two months so that King Douma could build his kingdom. The Valdees Tribe captured many slaves to help them. Aldron said that Douma's castle lies eight miles southwest of Mount Vue."

"On the very southern boundary of that kingdom a prison was built to house the enemies of the demons, it is named the Dungeons of Frey. He says that about three miles east of Douma's castle is a large city named Trapolli. To further protect Douma's kingdom, Baal lined the western shores of the Waste Lands of Manod with quicksand."

"Which is probably why the creatures travel north to Ryed to enter the kingdoms," Raphael said.

"Aldron says that the seas around Mount Vue are treacherous with rocks and a strong downward current."

"That could be that cyclone Zoya saw," said Gabriel.

"Aldron finishes by saying that Baal released the waters on the night of the blood moon and because of that the waters over Douma's kingdom have always remained red."

Chapter IV
Broken

After the gifts and mail were distributed the leaders of Claudius' rescue mission enjoyed their whiskey, cigars and conversation. This was the first night since Vivian and Angelina had been abducted that the members of the group allowed themselves a reprieve from their horror. Matthew was watching Sorren as the older warrior was telling a story.

Matthew found himself envying his father-in-law. Although Sorren was crushed by the kidnapping of his daughter, his rage seemed to help keep Sorren focused. Matthew was responding much differently to the tragedy. Matthew was so overwhelmed with his depression and grief that he was having great difficulty focusing on anything except during the moments when he studied the language of the Valdees.

Matthew was grateful that his father put Claudius in charge of the mission, although he said that to no one. Matthew did not feel he was fit to lead men into battle and into battle they would surely go. Matthew and Raphael had not been close until this nightmare changed their lives. While neither man verbalized their fears; both Matthew and Raphael felt comforted by the presence of the other.

Later that evening as Thaos and Nikki cuddled under their blankets Thaos asked, "Nikki you look so pale are you feeling alright?"

"I'm not going back," she responded adamantly. "If it was me or Ingr who was stolen, Angelina would be doing everything she could to find us and you know it."

"I know," Thaos said as he stroked her hair. "But this is going to be a difficult mission and you are carrying our baby."

Nikki suddenly started to cry. "Thaos that is exactly why I have to be here; we have to stop this madness. Juleta was placed curse after curse upon us because of her own insanity. This is no way to live or to raise our children." Thaos hugged his wife tightly.

Koby and Bekka made their bed away from the others; as they lay under their covers kissing Bekka said, "I am so glad we came here. I think it is the first any of them have smiled for a very long time."

"I know," Koby said. "I can hardly look at Raphael or Matthew they are so broken."

"Koby we know the most direct route for those creatures to follow is the River Nebu." Bekka now whispered in a lowered voice. "If Vivian and Angelina are alive, wouldn't those creatures have to come on shore once in a while? We don't know how they are assisting the girls to breathe underwater but you would think they would have to come up for air once in a while."

"And Claudius and the others are assuming they are ahead of us. But what if they aren't? Juleta was so cunning she always planned for how everyone would react to a situation," Bekka continued with enthusiasm. "And besides if Vivian and Angelina are alive they are probably trying to make the journey as difficult as possible for their captors. When we return tomorrow let's fly over the river."

Koby had been lying on top of Bekka, now he rolled onto his side and propped his head up on his right hand. Koby looked proudly at her. "I was thinking about returning over the river to see if the Enrops might have missed anything. But you have some really good ideas. I think we should brief the others before we leave tomorrow."

The next morning as the troops were eating breakfast, Bekka told Claudius and the others about her ideas. "We were going to check the river again to see if anything had been missed," Koby said. "But I think Bekka has some valid ideas. We just wanted to let you know what we were going to do."

"Bekka has a point," Stephan said. "Juleta spun her webs by predicting our behavior, it's worth looking into."

"Oh I agree," Claudius said. "But I don't want you two doing this alone."

"If you do come across something, well, you never know, we may only have one chance to rescue the girls and I don't want anything to go wrong."

"I'm proud of little sister," Misha said. "I'll go with them."

"So will I," said Dagon.

"We will too," Elan said referring to him and Cassandra.

"If we don't find anything," Misha said. "Koby and Bekka should continue on to Wetpr and we will return to you. There is no need to have them fly back here just to tell you we didn't find anything."

"Let me give you some medical supplies," Ibula said. "If you do find our friends they may be hurt." Ibula went over to her supply bags and started to sort out a few items.

"I have some things to send along also," Raul said as he stood up. "When Vitomas was taken, I was so happy to find her that I didn't even realize that her clothing was torn and filthy. I had wished I would have brought some things for her to wear; so Vitomas and Annabelle packed some clothing for the girls." Raul walked over to his saddlebags and took out two packages.

"I want to say that I was the one who kidnapped Vitomas but I didn't tear her clothing," Archetenus said guiltily. "I think she tore it on the brush."

"No, my girl was leaving us a trail with shreds of her clothing," Raul said with pride.

"Really!" Archetenus said then laughed loudly.

"Did you sleep in that chair all night?" Rueben asked as he walked into the study with two cups of coffee.

"Rueben the more I thought about what you said; the more I think you are right," the Sanuri said as he sipped his coffee. "And further more I think you were correct with both of your ideas. I believe those writings are both a distraction and a code."

49

"I searched this office last night to see if Hannah's father had left anything behind that might be useful to me. I didn't find anything in the study but I found some very interesting books and scrolls in the library. I know Gabriel and the others didn't have time to pack everything from this house but they missed some valuable research materials."

"Have you read all of those?" Rueben asked as he nodded towards several stacks of books on the desk. "Because I am willing to help you."

"Good, pull up a chair," the Sanuri said. "And let me show you what I have found already."

"I wasn't sure if I should have said something," Misha said to his comrades as they flew north along the River Nebu. "When Claudius told Raphael and Matthew they should stay with the troops."

"I know," Dagon said. "I think Claudius was fearful of their disappointment if we didn't find anything."

"Well, they will be disappointed if they are with us or not if we don't find anything," Koby said. "I think he should have let them come along."

These Ruala warriors were flying low to the ground, because the brush and trees hindered their view when they flew higher. "Did you hear what Raul said about Vitomas?" Dagon asked. "If she had the presence of mind to leave a trail that was not spotted by a trained warrior like Archetenus what do you want to bet the girls are doing the same thing. I think we may have to walk along this river because whatever they would leave as a trail has to be subtle enough that the creatures don't realize what they are doing."

"Elan and Cassandra we aren't that far out," Misha said. "Quickly fly back to the others and find out any Nordes symbols or personal clues the girls might leave that would have significance to us but not to the creatures. This is why we should have brought Raphael and Matthew along."

The Sanuri unrolled an ancient scroll before Rueben. "The parchment is breaking apart," the Sanuri said. "But this contains the first writings I have come across about the Grand Masters of the Insidiae. They are the original people from this world who called the demons in, because the demons could not enter this world without the human's opening the doors for them. It is said that these people were given great powers and wealth from the demons as their rewards for betraying the world of man. But little is known about them; I believe even the members of the Insidiae know little about the Grand Masters."

"Some of this writing has so faded with age that I could barely read it. But here," the Sanuri said with a large smile as he pointed to a specific area of the parchment. "Here is listed the original names and the tribe of the first Grand Masters."

Misha and Dagon searched the west side of the River Nebu as Koby and Bekka searched the eastern side. They scrutinized every broken branch they saw. "This is going to take forever," Koby said. "Chances are they wouldn't let the girls get too far from the water so I think we should concentrate close to the shoreline. "Both Angelina and Vivian are strong fighters so they are probably bound most of the time, we might..." Koby did not finish his sentence as he knelt down to closely examine the earth. "Bekka this ground has been swept."

Bekka had been searching an area north of where Koby was standing, she now made her way back towards him. "Bekka I think I found something," Koby said. "Look there is a broken line made with small pebbles, three stones, two stones, three stones. It may be nothing but let's search for more." Koby quickly flew across the river and told Misha and Dagon what he had found. Misha and Dagon returned to the eastern shore but flew farther north along the river to resume their search.

Of the four Rualas Misha was flying the farthest up river, not twenty minutes after he landed on the shoreline he too found a broken line of pebbles, three stones, two stones and three stones. Misha marked the spot and quickly flew back to the others. "I found the same symbol," Misha said with excitement.
"We should look for more and measure the distance in between; that will give us an idea of how far they can travel before they have to come to the surface."

Dagon found the third broken line of pebbles on the shoreline by the time that Elan and Cassandra found them. Ruala warriors Ratri, Paulo, Jael and Ennen accompanied Elan and Cassandra. Ratri carried Sorren, as Cassandra carried Mathew and Jael carried Raphael. The group initially landed close to Koby.

"We think we found something," Koby said excitedly and took the group over to the first broken line of pebbles they discovered. "So far we have found three identical lines like this. All are on the eastern shore. We are measuring the distances to see how often they have to come up for air. And the ground has been swept near each broken line we found."

As Koby was talking Sorren knelt down to examine the stones; he looked up at the others with tears running down his cheeks. "We start warrior training when the children are young, this is the code we teach them if they get lost from the rest of the group. They're alive," Sorren said happily as he stood up. "They're alive."

"Thank you," Raphael said and clutched Koby's shoulder.

Within the next two hours the group found four more broken lines. All seven lines were within an area that was less than four miles. "Whatever means they are using to help the girls breathe it doesn't last long. And the distances between the lines are pretty consistent. We should be able to determine the next stop they will have to make down river," Misha said.

The group flew south along the river until they found the first broken line of pebbles they had discovered. Then they measured off a distance that was comparable to the distances they had measured between the other lines and now they discovered a new one. "They came up for air while we were searching up river," Sorren said. "Let's give them a surprise the next time they come up." The group found two more areas with broken lines. "At least we are on their trail," Sorren said. "Someone should fly ahead and have Claudius turn around."

"I will," Ennen said.

"If those creatures see our troops near the water they probably won't let the girls come up for air," Matthew said. "Make sure Claudius understands that." As soon as Ennen left, the group continued southward along the river bank.

"According to this scroll," the Sanuri explained. "The first humans who sought out the demons came from the tiny Village of Tomar which is now called Eaujr. This village lies in the shadows of the Safer Mountain Range, near the Inlet of Grevtd in the Kingdom of Marba."

"That actually makes sense," Rueben said. "I mean all Hutas worship demons."

"The tribe was known as the Calibanittes, they were the first known cannibals in the continent. Of that tribe there are thirteen names that are first documented in this scroll and one of the names Jared had a vision about as he was fighting the demons that owned him. That name is Emeric."

"This says that Emeric and his sister Banaka both became Grand Masters when they were still in their teens. It lists Emon and his twin daughters Mab and Tahira as Grand Masters. This says Tahira married Aaryan who became a Grand Master as did his father Zadok and his mother Rahi. The others named are Fadil, Xeni, Radnor, Imad and Jerik. I found it interesting that Imad was the shaman of his tribe."

"Why did you find that interesting?" asked Rueben.

"Because most shamans that I have met were healers of their peoples," the Sanuri replied. "Shamans wield great power within their tribes; if he turned to darkness first it would make sense that he could easily influence others."

"If we find them we must separate the girls from the creatures first because once they see us we may not get another chance to free them," Matthew said.

"Koby thinks the girls may be bound," Bekka said. "Because they are such fighters."

"That would make perfect sense," said Sorren.

"Matthew as much as you and I want to see our wives I think the Rualas should grab them first and get them away from the creatures," Raphael said with a renewed spirit. "Misha you are the senior Ruala officer here, pick out two warriors to get the girls while we battle the creatures."

"I would like to volunteer," Bekka said. "I can't explain it but after being a captive myself I would like to free them."

Cassandra was afraid that Misha would keep Elan out of the battle because of his injury so she quickly volunteered. "That's fine," Misha said. "Your primary focus is to get to those girls and get them out of the area. Koby and Elan you two stop anyone who tries to stop Bekka and Cassandra."

"Koby give us the medical pouch," Bekka said.

"There is one more thing," Misha said. "All of you are so emotional and don't misunderstand me I would be the same way. I know you want to kill them all but I believe we should take some captives. Now that some of you can speak the language you may need to find out if other members of your families are also in danger."

Raphael now stopped walking and turned and looked at Misha. "Never in my life have I felt this crippled," Raphael said. "I was so overwhelmed with grief that at times I just couldn't think. I believe Matthew and Sorren have been the same way and because of this we have overlooked many things that we normally would have considered. We owe all of you here a great deal for taking the lead and following your instincts when we were too broken to do the same."

"The boy's right," Sorren said. "When we get the girls home, my tribe will host a celebration in your honor."

Paulo was flying ahead of the small group and now turned back towards them and motioned for them to be quiet. "There is great movement in the water about one hundred yards ahead."
Misha, Koby and Ratri picked up Matthew, Raphael and Sorren and quickly flew ahead.

"For some reason they seem to come on shore on the eastern bank," Misha whispered. "But we should have a few men on the other side, just in case. Jael and Dagon cross the river high so they can't see you."

Within moments the group saw huge ripples in the water as if great fish were jumping. Raphael's heart was pounding and Matthew was fighting an overwhelming urge to run out to the shoreline. The warriors were concealed by the thick brush and trees that lined the river.

Bekka squeezed Cassandra's arm with excitement when they saw bubbles coming to the surface of the water. Soon a creature walked out of the water, he looked up and down the shoreline then said a few words. Two more creatures emerged from the water, they were holding the arms of one of the girls whose hands and feet were bound and her head was covered with what appeared to be a large bag.

Sorren grabbed Matthew to prevent him from running forward. As two more creatures came out of the water with the other captive. The creatures walked a few feet onto the shoreline and pulled the bags off from the heads of Angelina and Vivian; both women were gasping for air.

Sorren held up his hand indicating the others should not attack yet. "They are very close to the water," Sorren said then he whistled as a red Bengi bird would. When Angelina heard the sound she immediately started to roll around on the ground and scream as if she was in pain. The creatures came towards her. "Now!" Sorren said.

Koby and Ratri shot two of the creatures with arrows. The attack took the other creatures by surprise and they quickly looked around to see who was shooting at them. Both Vivian and Angelina rolled to their left to try and hide in some brush. Raphael, Sorren and Matthew fought with the three remaining creatures as Bekka and Cassandra flew to their friends.

"More are coming out of the water," Elan yelled as he flew towards the creatures. Elan swung his sword and severed the head from the next creature that was coming out of the water.

"Cut us loose," Vivian screamed as Cassandra was picking her up. "There are many of them, we will fight."

As Dagon and Jael flew towards their friends they were shooting arrows at the dozens of creatures that were coming out of the water.

"How many are there?" Bekka asked as she was cutting through the robes that bound Angelina.

"Fifty, maybe a few more," Angelina said. "Do you have an extra weapon?"

"Misha there's fifty or sixty of the creatures," Bekka yelled we need to get them out of here."

"Everyone into the air," yelled Misha.

Sorren was rolling on the shoreline with a creature who was trying to stab him. Matthew ran up and kicked the creature in the head, rendering him unconscious. "We've got a captive," Matthew yelled as he dragged the creature off from Sorren.

Dagon, Jael, Paulo and Elan attacked the creatures from the air as the others picked up their friends. When Raphael and the others were safely off the ground, Dagon and Paulo picked up two of the unconscious creatures and they all flew towards Claudius and the rest of the troops.

"Are you alright?" Matthew yelled to Angelina.

"Yes but we have much to tell you."

"Look," Elan yelled as they saw other Rualas who were flying towards them and ahead of the troops.

"Those of you carrying people continue forward, I'm taking these warriors back to the shore line," Misha yelled as he quickly flew towards the oncoming Rualas.

Most of the Valdees were returning to the water when they spotted the second group of Rualas flying towards them. Instead of seeking sanctuary in the depths of the River Nebu the creatures charged towards the Rualas to do battle.

Misha ordered six of his archers to prevent any of the creatures from escaping into the water. The Rualas surrounded the creatures, shooting them with arrows. There was no battle but a massacre. When all of the creatures appeared to be dead, Misha ordered his warriors to search the bodies for information and to kill any of the creatures that might still be alive.

"I'm going to have to land," Paulo yelled. "This one is waking up. Paulo was referring to the unconscious Valdees creature he was carrying.

"We'll all land," Raphael yelled.

Vivian's feet had barely touched the ground before she flew into Raphael's arms. They both cried as they hugged and kissed each other.

"Are you alright?" Matthew kept asking over and over as he and Angelina hugged and kissed. Sorren waited a few moments before he walked up to his daughter and son-in-law. Angelina flew into her father's arms and Sorren cried. The Rualas bound the wrists and feet of both of the Valdees creatures. When one of the creatures tried to bite Koby's hand; Koby punched the creature so hard he lost consciousness again.

Vivian and Angelina took turns hugging each of their rescuers both girls were so emotional they did little talking.

"We have so much to tell you," Angelina said as she cried.

"Let's wait until we are all together," Matthew said. "Then you can tell everyone."

"What do you mean?" asked Angelina.

"There is an army out here searching for you." Matthew replied and kissed Angelina again.

"There they are," Nikki screamed and pointed to the sky as the first group of Rualas was flying towards Claudius and his troops. Ingr and Nikki dismounted and started to run towards the Rualas.

"Thank you," Gabriel prayed when he saw Vivian and Angelina in the arms of the Ruala warriors.

There was another tearful reunion between Angelina, Vivian and the rest of their rescue party. As Angelina was hugging Claudius she said. "We have some very important things to tell you but I can't stop crying."

Claudius laughed with joy. "We might as well make camp here and let the girls get settled."

An hour later, the second group of Rualas which Misha was leading returned to the troops and once again Vivian and Angelina hugged and thanked their rescuers.

"I don't think I have ever been this emotional," Vivian said to Raphael as they stood with their arms around each other. "It wasn't death that I feared; it was the thought that I would never see you again that terrified me." Raphael hugged Vivian tightly and kissed her again and again.

"Vitomas and Annabelle sent along dry clothes for you," Cassandra said as she handed each of the women a package.

"I am not ever letting you out of my sight again," Raphael said and walked with Vivian as she entered a thicket to change her clothes.

"Honey get out of those wet things before you get sick," Matthew said with a laugh as he pulled Angelina towards some bushes. "You have plenty of time to talk to everyone."

"I know I asked you before but I am so upset that I can't remember what you said," Angelina said. "Matthew I was so afraid that I would never see you or our babies again, even after what Miranda told us."

"Miranda! Why didn't she help you?" Matthew asked angrily. "What did she say?"

"Matthew that is what we have to tell all of you."

After Angelina had changed her clothes, Matthew said loudly, "We need to have a meeting the girls have things to tell us."

"Matthew let them eat first," Ingr scolded as she was cooking over a fire. "Vivian said they have had little to eat since they were captured."

"We can talk to you while we eat," Vivian said.

The two creatures had regained consciousness and were both tied to a tree. They made comments to each other about their captors as they watched the troops make camp. Thedes walked into the campsite with an arm load of wood and both of the creatures started to grin and talk. Vivian ran up to the creatures and slapped each one of them across the face as she spoke to them in their native language. Both of the creatures looked shocked that she could talk to them.

"What did they say?" Gabriel demanded.

Vivian turned and looked at Thedes, "Now I understand what Miranda told us. Thedes these swine said they must have missed one, when they saw you. They said they should take you back and you can join the rest of your worthless breed."

"What! They have Shettee captives?" Thedes ran to the creatures and grabbed one of them by the throat. Both creatures laughed. Simon and Raul ran up to Thedes and pulled him away from the creature.

"We brought some of that truth potion along," Simon said. "That will be our best avenue for getting information."

"Girls I believe it is time that we heard what you have to say," Claudius said.

"No ask them about my brethren first," said Thedes.

"Thedes you need to hear this," Angelina said. The group gathered around Angelina and Vivian and everyone grew quiet. "The morning I was taken; those creatures were waiting for me outside of the castle. There were almost twenty of them. I fought but they knocked me out. I awoke when they dragged me under water."

"They put some type of bags over our heads that contained air. I couldn't see anything and I knew I was tied up and being dragged in the water. It was very difficult for me to have a perspective on time."

"I was out riding by the river on Gabriel's land when I heard the sounds of a fight. I rode up and saw Angelina on shore fighting with several creatures. I tried to help her but more creatures came out of the water and they took me too," Vivian said as she held Raphael's hand. "What Angelina said is true, it was very difficult for us to even tell day from night or how long we were in the water."

"Every time they brought us out of the water for air we fought with them," Angelina said. "So they would crowd around us. "I called out to Miranda to help us many times and neither Vivian nor I saw Miranda or heard her voice. "Then one night they brought us onto shore so they could hunt. They tied us to a tree. We watched as they were making camp and suddenly both Vivian and I heard Miranda's voice clearly as if she was sitting with us, but the creatures didn't hear her."

Angelina continued, "Miranda told us that you were looking for us and would find us soon. Then she said that these kidnappings were much larger than just Vivian and me and that we should memorize everything we saw and heard from our captors. She said only two such faithful warriors could go on the journey we were on and after we were saved we had some very important decisions to make. And she told us that no matter how dark the journey seemed we were not alone."

"They spoke freely in front of us because they didn't' realize I could understand their language," Vivian said. "They talked about taking others of you and that includes Vitomas and Annabelle," Vivian said as she looked over at Raul and Simon. "And they have taken many slaves from the kingdoms. If we return home now it will be just a matter of time before they come after us again. They will not stop until the contract is fulfilled. Angelina and I have discussed this and we believe the decisions we have to make are to go to the Kingdom of Ogg and to stop this once and for all and to free the people they have imprisoned."

"Girls why didn't they kill you?" Claudius asked. "Did they want to take you as slaves?"

"They were taking us to be wives of King Douma and his sons," Vivian said.

"I believe it is time to give them the potion," Claudius said.

"I would rather separate them for the interrogations," Simon stated.

As some of the men were tying the creatures to different trees, Misha said. "We killed fifty two creatures today and you girls killed what five or six? Why did they send so many men to grab two girls? I think that is worth asking them."

Chapter V
Contracts

The Valdees creatures had been separated and each tied to a different tree. Simon and Raul wanted them far enough apart that they would not hear each other speak. Ingr volunteered to take notes of the interrogations. The potions had been forcibly poured down each creature's throat.

"Raphael, Matthew and I have been studying the language of these creatures," Gabriel said to Vivian. "We would like to practice our skills. So we will ask the questions but we would like you to help us out, correct us or translate."

Vivian smiled. "I am impressed," she said and squeezed Raphael's hand. The two of them had not let go of each other since her rescue. Vivian looked at the creature sitting before her. "I hope they get as sick from that stuff as I did."

"They won't live that long," Raphael said angrily.

"You might need them to enter their kingdom," Vivian warned. "Don't act too hastily."

"I don't know why I am so emotional," Angelina said. "I am never like this."

"You have been through an awful ordeal," Matthew said as he hugged his wife. "It's normal to be upset. You should have seen your father, Raphael and me; we couldn't even function while you two were missing. Father and Sudfad put Claudius in charge because the rest of us were so emotional. And it was the Rualas who thought you might leave us messages, we weren't thinking that clearly."

"Matthew what scared me most was the idea that I would never see you or our babies again but as much as I want to go home; I think we need to attack Ogg and free those people."

"What is your name?" Gabriel asked.

"Hota."

"Why did you take the girls?"

"There was a contract."

"Tell us about the contract."

"All I know is there is a contract to take many people from Lentz."

"Who are you ordered to take?"

"The children of the ruling families."

"What are you going to do with those people?"

"Bring them back to be slaves."

"Were the girls going to be slaves?"

Hota grinned, "After Douma found out how beautiful the women were he wanted them for himself."

"Are there contracts for people in Wetpr?"

"Yes, many."

"Who are you ordered to take?"

"The two oldest Princes and their wives but then a second contract was made and now we have to get the High Priests and their families."

"Juleta didn't know any of you Gabriel," Claudius said.

As Gabriel interrogated Hota, Vivian translated the conversation for the rest of the group.

"Who put out the contracts?" asked Gabriel.

"Only King Douma makes the contracts; we do as we are told."

"Gabriel ask him about my people," Thedes said.

63

"How many Shettee slaves do you have?"

"I don't know, twenty maybe thirty."

"Tell us about them."

"They are all men what else is there to tell?"

"When did you capture them?"

"Maybe three years ago; they were in the Waste Lands."

"King Neputa was leading a group of warriors, searching for us," Thedes said with both anger and relief.

"Do you have other slaves?"

"Yes our prison is filled," Hota said with a laugh.

"Why did you send so many warriors to steal two girls?"

"We were going to take more but then our orders changed."

"Why?"

"I don't know; I just follow orders."

"Who is giving you the orders?"

"Do you mean since we have been on land?"

"Yes."

"That physician."

"What physician?"

"The one who works for the King of Wetpr."

"Ask him if it is Philip or Gala," Raul said with fear in his voice.

"Is the physician a man or a woman?"

"A man."

"Do you know his name?"

"No, only Court Physician." Simon quickly wrote a note and handed it to an Enrop to take to his father.

"Is the Court Physician a demon?"

"No," Hota replied and laughed. "He works for the demon who made the contract."

"Juleta?"

"I don't know that name."

Gabriel now spoke in his native tongue to the people listening to the interrogation. "Hota already said he didn't know anything about the contracts now he tells us a demon is responsible for them. Can he lie with this potion?"

"Gabriel these creatures do not have high intelligence," Vivian said. "I think he may have been confused by some of your words, may I try?"

"Of course," Gabriel said and moved so Vivian could get closer to the creature. Raphael too moved closer to Hota in case Vivian would be in danger.

"Hota who paid for the contracts for the people in Lentz?"

"A witch."

"Do you know her name?"

"Only that she is the King's daughter."

"What did this witch pay for?"

"We are supposed to take the children and make them slaves. She wanted them tortured and beaten."

"Ask him how Juleta is paying for this," said Claudius.

"How is the witch paying for the contract?" Vivian asked.

"She left a chest of gold coins near her castle for the first payment. That is how Douma makes the contracts. We pick up more payments after each person we capture."

"Did you already pick up the payment when you stole the girl?" Vivian asked.

"No, once Douma sends word that the girls are prisoners then we can pick up another chest of gold."

"Who must Douma contact to receive this payment?"

"I don't know his name."

"Is it the physician?"

"No, some man in Zorta."

"Ask him if the man works for the King of Zorta," Thaos said.

"Does this man work for the King of Zorta?"

"I don't know."

"What do you know about this man?"

"He is the witches' husband."

"Husband!" Matthew repeated. "Vivian ask if the man is old or young."

"Is this man old or young?"

"I don't know."

"Have you ever seen him?"

"No."

"Then how do you know where to get the money?"

"He will tell King Douma."

"How does Douma get a message to this man?"

"We take it."

"Why were two of your warriors travelling across the continent on foot instead of in the water?" asked Vivian.

"Many of them are."

"Why?"

"The demon has promised Douma that our kingdom may return to the land. Douma doesn't know what the land looks like anymore so he is sending warriors out to gather information and to make maps."

"So you won't return to the land you used to live on?"

"No the demon has promised Douma great riches."

"What does Douma have to do to get these riches?"

"Kill the priests and the Sanuri."

"Why?"

"I heard it was because they destroyed the demons Ahriman and Sporos."

"Is this the same demon that is paying for the contract against the Princes of Wetpr?"

"Yes."

"What is that demon's name?"

"Hecate."

"Why has Hecate paid for this contract?"

"Revenge."

"Explain."

"I have been told that she was the wife of the demon Sporos."

"And her connection with Ahriman?"

"Sporos and Hecate were the children of Ahriman."

"Children?" Sorren asked. "What does he mean?"

"I believe he is using that word to mean loyal followers," Vivian said.

"Where are the slaves kept?"

"In the prison."

"How do we get to your kingdom?"

"The sea."

"Yes but once we are in the sea how do we get into your kingdom?"

"Enter the water funnel if you live you will enter the kingdom."

"How do you live through the water funnel?" Gabriel asked.

"Baal has put a mark on us that allows us to come and go as we please."

"What is this mark?"

"It is the symbol of our people."

"Describe the symbol of your people."

"It is the Face of Baal."

"Where do you wear this symbol?"

"On the back of our hands."

"His hands are covered with tattoos," Raphael said.

"Which tattoo is the symbol?"

"The true symbol lies underneath the skin."

"Do all your people wear the symbol on the same hand?"

"Yes."

"Which hand?"

"The left."

"How do you get your slaves through the water funnel?"

"We hang onto them as we go down to the kingdom."

The interrogations lasted long into the night. "Does anyone else have any questions?" Gabriel asked. No one answered him. "Ingr please look at your notes and see if any information is missing," Gabriel said. As Ingr read through her pages of notes Gabriel turned to Claudius. "What do you want to do with them?"

"Kill them and cut off their hands."

"No Claudius," Angelina said as she jumped to a standing position.

"Claudius wait," Archetenus said as he too stood up. "Claudius you have not met any of the Angels that have helped and fought with, well, most of us here. Miranda tells us repeatedly that we must trust her and she has proven herself to us many times."

"Miranda came to the girls and told them the journey they were on is bigger than their kidnappings. For hours we have listened to these creatures tell us about the people they imprison, the people they plan to kill which includes the Sanuri and how they plan to move to land and take over a rich kingdom which will mean more deaths. Claudius trust me; we should not do anything now until we talk to Miranda."

"Claudius, he is right," Matthew said. "You will understand once you meet her."

"I agree with them," said Sorren.

"And just how do we get an Angel to appear to us?" Claudius asked skeptically.

"Call her name," Archetenus said.

"Since this is very important," Gabriel said. "Perhaps we should all call her name. You can say it out loud or to yourself."

As the troops called to Miranda a wind picked up and fanned the flames of the campfires, which drew everyone's attention. As heads were turned to look at the fires Miranda and Daniel appeared in the center of the camp. "I am proud and pleased; you are learning," Miranda said. "For those of you who were not at the battle in Taperia, this is Daniel. Angelina and Vivian you have done well, because of you many lives will be saved."

"Did you have the girls kidnapped so we would learn this information?" Claudius asked incredulously.

"No," Miranda replied. "Claudius think about a road. When you are on a journey there are many paths you can take and each will bring you to a different location. I changed the path they were taking."

"Thank you," Raphael said.

"You are welcome," said Miranda. "Daniel and I have listened to your interrogations and before you ask questions of us I have a question for you. Now that you have heard the words of these Valdees tribesmen what are you prepared to do?"

"We need to go to Ogg and stop Douma and free his slaves," Matthew said as he walked into the center of the camp, closer to Miranda and Daniel.

"It is a dangerous journey that you propose," Miranda said. "Tell me Matthew how are you going to do this?"

Matthew smiled, "Actually I was hoping you will tell us that."

"Archetenus your friends are learning well," Miranda said then she turned to Claudius. "General Claudius you are a brave warrior and a good man. As a strong leader you often see things that others do not. We are not of your world and because of that we see infinitely more than you possibly could. You have three of The Seven Sons and two incredibly powerful priests here."

70

"And you have an army with such incredible faith that it makes us proud to fight beside you. In two days you will meet the Sanuri. He has been trying to disable a trap that was set for all of you; that trap will eventually be disabled but it is no threat to you now because of the choices you have made this night. Because of your choices you have changed the path you were on."

"This is not a trick question," Miranda continued. "I want all of you to think soundly about what I am to ask. Are you willing to walk through hell to save lives, to free the oppressed, to give voices to innocent men, women and children who for too long have been silenced? If your answer is 'yes' then Daniel and I will walk that journey with you; if your answer is 'no' there is no punishment or shame."

"I beg to differ," Sorren said as he walked forward. "There will be shame. I will take that walk with you."

"As will I," rang out voice after voice. "As will I."

It was almost dawn before the Angels left that camp that night and by the time they left Claudius was no longer feeling as if they were disempowering him as a leader. Claudius was born a leader of men, he had seen more death and bloodshed in his life than he cared to remember. He understood the fears, the terror of going into battle and he knew the troops felt safer with a strong leader. In all his years in the military Claudius never let his men see his fears or uncertainty at times. He maintained this iron persona not for his own ego but for the men he led into battle.

Claudius' initial resistance to the Angels was not a response to his beliefs, yet his faith was not as strong as those who stood with him. Claudius was a practical man, a logical man; it was difficult for him to believe in things that he could not see or touch.

This night Claudius learned that the world he knew was only one thread in the tapestry of The Great Ruler. This night Claudius realized the limitations of mankind. This night he pledged to follow the Angels into battle and this night he had an overwhelming feeling to cry, which Claudius did not understand at all.

"Miranda may I ask you a question?" Thaos asked as he walked close to her.

"If your wife stays on this mission," Miranda said softly before Thaos had a chance to ask his question. "She and your son will be fine."

"Do you mean Titus or is Nikki carrying another boy?"

"Nikki will carry this baby in the heat of battle and the significance of what his parents have done will not be lost upon him. He will be a leader among men."

"Thaos you and I have not spoken before although many eyes in heaven have watched you over the years. You were so lost in the darkness of this world; I am proud that you have changed your life. It takes great courage for someone to look into the mirror and see the true image of himself and it takes even more courage to actively change the path you are on. Stay the course you are on and the rewards will be innumerable. But that does not mean that life will always be easy, it is how you respond to the challenges that mold you into the person who you are."

"Come with us," Cassandra said as she and Elan walked up to Raphael and Vivian. The majority of the troops still stood in the campsite, in awe of the visit by the holy messengers.

Hand in hand, Raphael and Vivian followed their friends a short distance from the main campfires and into a small clearing. "We thought you might want some time alone," Elan said as they looked upon a small campsite with a roaring fire and blankets laid out.

"Thank you," Vivian said and kissed Elan on the cheek and hugged Cassandra.

Raphael and Vivian were so completely overwhelmed with their emotions that they were not conscious of their actions of disrobing or crawling under the blankets. They were completely swept up in their love for one another.

"I am never letting go of you," Raphael whispered into his bride's ear.

72

Chapter VI
Traitors among Us

"I can feel you looking at me," Angelina said with a giggle as she opened her eyes and saw Matthew with his head propped up on one arm watching her. "You need to get some sleep Matthew."

"I keep waking up because I can't believe you are really here with me," he said and leaned forward kissing Angelina on the lips. "I always knew how much I loved you. I never realized before how much I need you. It was like I was dead inside while you were gone. I couldn't even think."

Angelina reached up and put her arms around Matthew's neck and kissed him with such intensity they both felt weak. Matthew hugged Angelina so tightly he was afraid he would hurt her. They made love again in the early morning light.

After the Angels left the troops; messages were sent to King Mathas, King Sudfad, King Manu of the Rualas, the Sanuri, Calen and Luca. Since the sun was in the sky, Claudius ordered the execution of the two Valdees creatures and told his troops they would remain at that campsite until the following morning. Many of the people took to their beds, while many others could not sleep after their experiences with the Angels.

The first message that King Sudfad received that morning said only, *Philip, the Court Physician is a spy and helped to orchestrate the kidnappings*. Sudfad and Renya had not yet left their bedroom chambers when the Enrop flew through a window and delivered the message. "Renya, make sure the children are safe," Sudfad said as he jumped out of bed and put on this robe. "Simon said that Philip is a spy and behind the kidnappings."

"Our Philip, the Physician?" Renya asked as she too jumped out of bed.

"Yes, I am going to have him arrested now," Sudfad said and ran out of their bedroom."

"My Lord," said Captain Houser as he entered King Sudfad's study. "We have searched Philip's quarters and his office, there is no sign of him; in fact it appears he has packed up his things and left."

"I am not surprised," Sudfad said with frustration. "Have the men search these grounds, the fort and go into the city; I want that terrorist found."

"Yes, My Lord."

"Captain assign guards to protect Gala, tell her what is happening. Philip was always jealous of her and Hannah."

"Do you want me to put more men at Gabriel's house also?"

"I did send them a message about Philip, but yes that would be a good idea."

"Yes My Lord," Captain Houser said and left the study.

Sudfad quickly wrote a note and gave it to an Enrop, "Nica take this to Jared and tell him they may take shelter in the castle until we figure out what exactly is going on."

"We wondered if you were going to join us," Maxwell said as Raphael and Vivian walked up to his campfire.

"Whatever you are making smells wonderful," said Vivian.

"Maxwell is our resident chef," Gabriel said as he walked over to Vivian and kissed her on the forehead. "It is very good to have you back with us."

"I can't thank you enough," she said as she and Raphael took seats near the fire. "As if being transported underwater wasn't bad enough, Angelina and I knew that there would be no escape once they got us to Ogg."

"What were those things they had over your heads?" Misha asked.

Vivian shuttered, "We think they made those sacks from the lungs they cut out of those men. They smelled horrible."

"Vivian said that those creatures didn't try to harm either of them," Raphael said as he put his arm around her shoulders. "She thinks it's because Douma wanted the girls for his wives."

"Lunch is served," Maxwell said as he handed out plates of food. "Vivian we are all very glad you are back with the family."

Vivian smiled warmly. "All of you are my family and I was thinking. We should go to my tribe when we get to Ryed. First I would like you to meet my blood family," Vivian looked at Raphael and smiled. "But also they could be of great help to us."

"Actually we had planned to go to your tribe and ask them to help us find you and Angelina," Gabriel said. "Even if they don't want to help us fight Douma I would very much like to meet your people."

"I think we all would," Elan said as he was still elated to have his friend back.

"Oh they will be of help," Vivian said. "Once we tell them about the Angels and our plans to attack Ogg they will want to fight also." Vivian now looked at the many Ruala warriors who were sitting around the fire eating. "There are still so many things I want to learn about your ways but what I have already learned is that our tribes have many similarities. I think you will feel at home among my people."

Later that evening when Sudfad received the other messages from Simon, Raul and Claudius he called Luca, Calen and Lakin to the castle for a meeting.

"Thank you for coming at this hour," Sudfad said. "I have received several messages in the last hour and I wanted to share them with you."

"We too have received messages," Lakin said. "And the information is more than disturbing."

"In Raul's last letter he indicated that there was so very much information to pass on that not all of the letters may contain the same subjects," Sudfad said. "I was hoping we could compare what we have received."

There was a knock on the door to the study. "Calen would you open that," Sudfad said. "I believe it is refreshments for you." To their surprise it was the Queen who was carrying a tray of refreshments.

"I would like to sit in on this meeting, if that is alright?" Renya asked.

"By all means," Lakin said as he jumped up and took the tray from Renya's hands.

"My dear since you are still standing would you mind handing some paper and pens to our guests?" Sudfad asked Renya. "We have all received letters but it is likely that not all of them contain the same information."

Sudfad waited until everyone was settled before he began the meeting. "First of all we must thank The Great Ruler that the girls were found alive and unharmed. If they were not such intelligent and well trained warriors we may not have found them. And Lakin it sounds like your warriors were in the forefront of figuring out where the girls might be. We will have a grand celebration for all upon their return."

Sudfad continued, "I am sure your letters tell of the appearances of the Angels Miranda and Daniel after the interrogations of the creatures; all our troops pledged to go to war with them to stop Douma and to free their captives. Did anyone not get that information?"

"Sudfad the Shettees have become our brethren, it fills us with both grief and joy to know that the husbands, brothers and sons of the women and children in the Ice Caves are alive yet slaves of these creatures. Messages have been sent to our King, my father, and although I have not yet heard from him I suspect he will send an army to help with the rescue of these people."

"And I too am sending an army," Sudfad said.

"I am waiting to hear from King Mathas, but I suspect he is also declaring war upon Douma."

"I am a little unclear," Luca said. "Gabriel said there were two contracts made with Douma, Juleta made one to enslave the ruling families of Lentz as well as your family and the demon Hecate put one on the Sanuri and the families of Gabriel and Raphael does that include us as Rualas?"

"We are one family," Calen said before the King had a chance to answer.

"I know that," Luca said. "But think about it. The Valdees are the strongest in water, they cannot fly, which means they may be recruiting other demons or creatures to help them."

"Sorry, that is a good point," said Calen.

"I don't know the answer to that question Luca but since the Rualas have fought in every battle with Gabriel and Raphael I believe you would be included, which means we must be prepared for anything. I have greatly increased the number of troops that will be protecting you and your families. If you would like more troops or if you would like to move everyone into the castle just ask."

"Actually we had a family meeting and talked about that," Calen said. "For now everyone wants to stay in our home but if there is an attack we would like to bring our wives and children here."

"Calen, I will prepare chambers for all of your families so no matter what time day or night they can just move in here," Renya said.

"Thank you that is more than generous."

"The creatures said that they have the Face of Baal under their skin and that it acts as a sort of key to enter the kingdom," Luca said. "Does anyone know how the Angels are going to help our people enter that kingdom?"

"I don't know that answer either," Sudfad said. "Perhaps when they join forces with the Sanuri we will receive more details."

"Did anyone find out why those bodies were in the water near Gabriel's home and near the Nordes Village?" Calen asked.

"Yes," Sudfad said solemnly. "Apparently the creatures or perhaps Philip, we don't know who actually killed those men put their bodies in the water. The number of bodies told the creatures how many people to kidnap."

"There were nine bodies outside our house," Calen said. "And since our home lines up with the castle I am guessing that four of those bodies represent Raul, Simon and their wives. So do the other five represent Gabriel, Raphael, Hannah, Vivian and Natasha?"

"Vivian hasn't even been in this kingdom very long," Luca said. "So perhaps that body represented someone else. But why were the left ears cut off each of the bodies?"

"To tell the Valdees creatures that were doing the kidnapping that these were the specific bodies put in place for them," Sudfad responded. "And remember there were four bodies found near the home of Sorren and two more found in a location north of his village. And no one searched the area that was marked by Claudius' castle."

"I wonder who they wanted from the Nordes Tribe," Lakin said.

"The more I think about this," Calen said. "The bodies that had the lungs removed were greatly mutilated but the bodies used as signals were intact except for where the fish chewed on them. I bet Philip or another human put those bodies in the water. We may have more spies around here than your physician."

That night as Vivian was lying in Raphael's arm he said, "At dinner I was telling Stephan and Thaos and some of the others that we were going to visit your tribe and that you said they would probably join us. Then Ingr and Nikki said that in their tribe when a groom or intended groom meets the woman's family for the first time he should bring gifts or the family is greatly insulted. Does your tribe have a custom like that?"

Vivian propped her head up on her right hand and looked at Raphael, "Yes but I really didn't want to say anything."

"Honey why not?" Raphael asked in amazement. "I certainly don't want to insult your family."

"I just don't feel comfortable asking you for money or to buy things."

"Vivian we are married, the money belongs to both of us. I am very much looking forward to meeting your family and your tribe and I don't want to start off by insulting everyone. When we get to Nora you and I are going shopping for your family. I assume we need to bring your chief something also?"

"That would be a good idea," Vivian said and leaned down and kissed Raphael on the lips. Then she straightened up and looked at him seriously. "There is probably something I should tell you."

"It better not be that you have another husband," Raphael said jokingly.

"No but I had men who wanted to marry me."

"That does not surprise me at all," Raphael said and smiled. "So you are going to warn me about all your old boyfriends?"

Vivian laughed. "I have always been much more interested in my training than in boyfriends; that is until I met you. Our chief has three sons and his oldest, Sampson, has wanted me to be his wife since we were very young. He is a powerful warrior but not a good man. I have never wanted anything to do with him. He asked my father repeatedly for me and my father said I could choose my own husband since I am a Venator. Sampson too is a Venator and if he is in the village when we go there he may cause problems."

"Is your chief a good man?"

"Oh yes, Sampson is nothing like Duncan."

"Well, I am glad that you told me; is there anything else I should know?"

Vivian laughed again, "When you see the shocked look on my parent's faces it will be nothing against you. They thought I would live and die as a hunter and never marry. So you see they will be very happy to meet you."

"I hate feeling like a prisoner in my own house," Natasha said as she was putting plates on the table for breakfast.

"I do too," Hannah said with emphasis as she placed several platters of freshly baked bread on the table.

"It's not that you are prisoners," Calen said as he sat down at the table. "We are just being careful, especially since we have children here."

"It seems like we are prisoners to me," Lila added as she was pouring coffee into cups.

"You too?" Luca asked. "So what do you want us to do?"

"I'm the only one who is not a warrior here," Lila said as she continued to pour coffee. "So I am not the person to ask but since you are asking I think we should treat those creatures like they treat us."

"What do you mean?" Luca asked with a broad smile.

"I think we should set some kind of traps for them," when Lila said these words everyone in the dining room looked at her and smiled. "Alright I know it may sound funny but I think we should try to be one step ahead of them. I mean after all; now we know who they are going after."

"We're smiling," Calen said. "Because for someone who is not a warrior you sure sound like one."

"So you don't think my idea is stupid?"

"No," Luca said. "We've been talking about the same thing. We are just trying to figure out how to trap them."

"Well my husband," Natasha said. "You already know the answer to that; it is simple, use me as bait."

"No!" Calen said sharply.

"You know she is right," Emeral said as she rocked baby Lily. "They are only going to show themselves to grab the people they have contracts on."

"I agree with them," Lakin said. "We could set up traps that would keep the girls safe."

"Girls?" Luca repeated. Fear filled him as he thought Lakin wanted Lila to act as bait also.

"They are after Hannah too, and probably the rest of the family," Lakin said then he turned to Hannah. "Would you be willing to be bait?"

"Of course, but I don't want the children with me," she replied. As Hannah spoke all of the children ran into the dining room. Christopher and Nicholas were chasing Lakin's two youngest children around the room. Cerey ran up to Calen and held up her arms for him to pick her up. "Calen," Cerey said and the room became silent.

"Did Cerey just talk?" Natasha asked with shock.

"She sure did," Calen said with a broad smile as he picked the little girl up and set her on his lap.

Hannah walked towards her daughter and asked, "Cerey whose lap are you sitting on?"

"Calen's," Cerey replied with a big smile.

Hannah rushed over to Cerey and hugged her tightly. "I was really becoming afraid that she couldn't talk," Hannah said with tears in her eyes.

"She stopped talking after Mama and Papa died," Nicholas said as he walked over to his sister and gently touched her hand.

Christopher ran up to Cerey and asked exuberantly, "Cerey what is my name?"

"Christopher," Cerey said then giggled. Christopher got a proud smile on his face.

Tears welled in Emeral's eyes as she said, "Our little girl just realized she is home."

Shortly after dawn, Claudius and his troops resumed their journey heading southwest as Koby, Bekka and twelve other Ruala warriors flew north to return to Wetpr and protect the families who lived in Gabriel's house. Before they had traveled an hour, Enrops were bringing messages to Claudius and his men. After the fourth message was delivered, Claudius ordered his troops to take a short break so he could read the letters. Letters also arrived for Raul, Simon, Matthew, Gabriel, Maxwell, Ibula and Thedes.

"Mathas has declared war against Douma and is sending six thousand troops to assist us," Claudius announced. "King Manu is sending one thousand Ruala warriors, who will meet us at the Patronus headquarters in Nora."

Ibula smiled and touched Thedes arm. "We will bring them all home," she said sweetly. Ibula was referring to the Shettee captives. Thedes was too emotional to speak.

"Sudfad is sending ten thousand men and he wants them to remain at Fort Nora when our mission is completed," Claudius said with a proud smile.

"Do you have any idea how many men Douma has?" Raphael asked Vivian.

"No but if we free the slaves they cannot be used against us."

"All the troops are going to meet us in Nora," Claudius continued. He opened another envelope and started to read it. "Stephan, Thaos this letter is from Bella and she is talking about the babies."

"Are they alright?" Ingr asked nervously as Stephan took the letter from his father.

"Yes," Claudius said then a frown took control of his face which turned to rage. "Fahron had divers search the area near our castle that was marked on the Valdees map. They found ten bodies."

"What!" Stephan screamed. "That would include the children."

"I am going to kill Douma myself," Claudius said through clenched teeth.

"Yes Captain Hauser," King Sudfad said as he looked up at the officer who had just entered his study.

"I have had men searching for the Physician throughout the night and we have had reported sightings of him in Salar. I just sent five hundred more troops to the city to search. Also we are doing extra patrols of Jared's house and Gabriel's house and so far everything is quiet."

"Thank you. Can you tell me where these reported sightings were?" Sudfad asked.

"He was seen in the Bull's Horn Tavern yesterday morning. He got a room in the Main Street Hotel but we searched that room and there was no indication he had even been in there. He was also seen by Jack's Black Smith shop, but he did not purchase anything and nothing is missing from that shop. Might I speak freely My Lord?"

"Of course."

"It's obvious he knows we are searching for him but how did he find out? I mean we started searching as soon as you received that letter and he was already gone. How did he know? And the more I think about it; Philip is a smart man I would think that if he had been planning on running away for a while he would have made better plans than lurking in alleys."

"I too have been thinking about that," Sudfad said. "It is possible that he is a dark lord although I believe the Sanuri would have realized that since he has had many contacts with Philip. The more likely explanation is that we have more traitors among us."

"I agree My Lord, so I am checking into the first officers who received orders to find Philip; I will let you know if I find anything out of the ordinary."

"There is the possibility that if Philip was not warned by one of our soldiers that he is indeed working with a dark lord or demon who knew about the interrogations of the Valdees and if that is the case, Douma might also have been warned. The more I have thought about this, well it is nothing more than speculation now but I believe I will warn Claudius and his men."

Chapter VII
Time

Shortly before Claudius and his troops stopped for a midday meal a small flock of Enrops delivered a letter from the Sanuri. "The Sanuri said to read this the moment that you receive it," the Enrop told Claudius.

"Well, I guess this place is as good as any to stop," Claudius grumbled. "We will take a meal break here," Claudius called over his shoulder.

Vivian called one of the Enrops to her, the bird landed on her arm and Vivian started to pet it. "I just can't get over how intelligent these creatures are," she said to Raphael. "I wish I would have known about them when I was hunting alone, the company would have been nice."

"King Sudfad has given their tribe sanctuary in Wetpr," Raphael explained. "They are greatly honored there. Apparently they were hunted in other kingdoms. If anyone kills an Enrop in Wetpr they will be punished. But so far the people love them so I don't believe anyone has tried to hurt one of the birds."

"I love them too," Vivian said as she continued to pet the Enrop.

"Listen up," Claudius yelled out as he had finished reading the letter from the Sanuri. "Large numbers of Hutas are gathering around Nora. They have been attacking farms to capture people to sacrifice at the next blood moon. General Colter has gathered all of the farm families and given them protection inside of Fort Nora. The farmers are the easiest targets for the Hutas. The Sanuri believes the Hutas will now be forced to look elsewhere for their victims. They believe the Hutas may try to attack the City of Nora or the Patronus headquarters since there are no other areas for the Hutas to gather their victims. He warns us to be careful."

"When is the next blood moon?" Elan asked.

"In about three weeks give or take a few days," said Sorren.

"The Sanuri got information from one of the Hutas," Claudius continued. "They are trying to gather hundreds of people to sacrifice and the Sanuri believes the sacrifices may take place in that mausoleum he has been studying."

"Claudius that letter from Lakin said the waters over the Kingdom of Ogg are always red," Gabriel said. "Has there been any information if the blood moon has special significance for that kingdom?"

"Now that you mention it," Vivian said thoughtfully. "My people have noticed more activity by the creatures before the blood moon. I wonder if they too sacrifice people."

Gabriel wrote a short note and gave it to the Enrops to give to the Sanuri. "I just sent the Sanuri a letter asking him our questions about the blood moon," Gabriel said. "Hopefully he will know the answers."

Late that evening as Claudius and his troops were preparing to retire another flock of Enrops landed in their camp. Some of the great birds brought letters from Lentz while others carried letters from Wetpr. "Claudius this letter is addressed to you, me and Simon," Raul said as he opened the envelope. After Raul read its contents he handed the letter to Claudius and stood up and addressed the group.

"Father said that as soon as he received Simon's message about the Court Physician, which was before dawn, he sent troops to arrest Philip. But Philip had already packed his things and left his quarters. Father has had soldiers searching for him and there have been a few sightings of Philip in Salar," Raul explained. "Father believes Phillip was warned that he would be arrested and had to make a hasty escape. Father has no idea who would have had that information but is concerned that if a demon or dark lord warned Philip that perhaps Douma was warned also and will be waiting for us."

Archetenus stood up and spoke, "If Miranda and Daniel are with us, it really doesn't matter if Douma knows we are coming or not. My concern would be that Douma finds out we are coming and sacrifices the slaves before we get there."

"I was thinking the same thing," Thedes said. "I think we need to act as quickly as we can."

"I would like to know how someone could be listening to our conversations and interrogations," Sorren said. "I mean I understand how the Angels could but they would have known if a demon listened in."

Misha now stood up. "Remember Hota said the Court Physician told them to change their plans at the last minute and to just take the two girls instead of the rest of you. We need to find out what happened that made them change. That is more likely to be the cause for Philip's disappearance than a demon listening to us talk."

"Vivian, Angelina do either of you remember anything that was said or done that might shed some light on this?" Gabriel asked. "Did Miranda say anything else to you that you have not told us?"

Both women sat in silence as they tried to remember every little detail of their ordeal. "If the Valdees talked when we were underwater I could not hear them with that bag over my head," Vivian said. "And we were under water most of the time. They never brought us to land to sleep."

"Didn't they sleep?" asked Elan.

"Maybe they took turns in the water and others carried them," Vivian said. "I don't know. But towards the beginning, I mean after they first took us I remember listening to some of the creatures complaining. They were unhappy that they had to keep bringing us to the surface to breathe. I got the impression from listening to them that they usually did not travel as far as Lentz and Wetpr to take captives. And they were complaining about having to come back and get the rest. I am sorry that is all I can remember."

"Angelina I know you can't speak their language but is there anything that you remember that might help?" Gabriel asked.

"Like I said, they knocked me out and I didn't wake up until they dragged me down into the water but we had to come up so I could get air many times before they grabbed Vivian."

"I fought with them every time we got on land. I knew I couldn't over power that many creatures but I was trying to determine who was the leader. Before they captured Vivian the creatures were fighting among themselves a lot. It seemed to me like they were divided into two groups but I don't know what they were arguing about, maybe it was whether they should kill me, I don't know. But there did seem to be two creatures that took leadership roles, one for each group."

"Well, they have two contracts," Simon said. "Maybe there are some contradictions between the contracts that caused the arguments."

"The arguments got pretty heated a couple of times and I thought some of them would fight," Angelina added.

"I have a thought," Stephan said. "Miranda said that the Sanuri has been trying to diffuse a trap that was set for all of us. Well, all of us would never be in this kingdom if we weren't looking for the girls. That female demon wants some of you dead and our girl Juleta wants the rest of us to be slaves. The Sanuri told us before that there are great wars going on between the demons maybe we are just pawns in some of their power struggles."

"Juleta would know we would search for anyone who was taken," Claudius said. "Are you saying that she has something to do with that mausoleum?"

"From the number of dead bodies in the water it looks like they were meant to take us all," Thaos said. "And if they had kidnapped all of us and were moving us under the water, we wouldn't be able to get caught in whatever trap Miranda was talking about."

"But the River Nebu does flow very close to where that mausoleum is located," Gabriel said.

"Does anyone know if the Hutas and the Valdees are connected in any way?" Ingr asked.

"They could be controlled by some of the same demons," Gabriel said.

"Does anyone know if Douma works with the Insidiae?" Ingr continued.

"We have a lot of questions and no answers," Claudius said. "But I believe we all agree that we could be facing multiple enemies who could be working with each other or against each other. This reinforces the fact that we must be ever vigilant and keep each other informed of even the tiniest thing that seems out of the ordinary."

"I think I found something," the Sanuri said to High Priest Rueben as the two men read through books that had belonged to Arthur Marcus. "This sounds like some kind of demonic prophesy," the Sanuri continued as he moved so Rueben could read the page along with him. "This says that *on the thirteenth night of the blood moon, in the year of Zenus the doors will be opened and the waters will part. The blood that is spilled will rejuvenate the dead and fill them with power. And those who have long defied them will crumble before them.*"

"I really don't like the sounds of that," Rueben said as he reread the passage. "What is the year of Zenus?"

"I have long heard that the demons have a different calendar of sorts from the world of man. Now I need to research that."

"Well, until you find the answer I believe we should assume that this is the year of the Zenus simply because of the activities of the Hutas," Ruben said.

"I am not happy about this at all," Calen said to Natasha.

"Calen do you remember how frustrated you were getting with Raul when he didn't want Vitomas to be used as bait to draw out Roch? Everyone, including Vitomas knew she was probably the one thing that Roch would respond to. Now it is our turn and unlike Vitomas I am a trained fighter. Just set up the same kind of situations that Gabriel did with Roch, have enough warriors around to protect us."

Calen's face was turning red as he listened to his wife speak. "You know she is right," Emeral said. "There are still plenty of our warriors at the castle and you have the Patronus at your disposal as well as Sudfad's troops. The only thing you need is a good plan."

Calen looked at Luca, "How would you like it if we were talking about Lila being bait?"

"I wouldn't like it at all," Luca responded.

"Lila please don't take that as an insult," Koby said. "But Natasha has trained her entire life to be a warrior; it really isn't the same thing."

"Koby I am not insulted," Lila said. "But I would be willing to be bait if it will help to stop this madness. But there is one thing that Natasha, Hannah and I all do have in common. Faith that our brave husbands, who have protected us before will do it again."

Emeral smiled and looked at her sons. "Now if anyone were to ask me," she said. "I have a plan that might work."

"Really," Luca said.

Emeral laughed loudly. "My dear sons; don't forget that your father and I have been fighting in battles since long before any of you were born."

Ingr looked at Nikki, who was riding next to her, and smiled, then she turned to Stephan, who was riding on her other side. "Stephan when we get to Nora can Nikki and I go shopping? We would like to get something for Bella."

Stephan grinned, "Actually Thaos and I had planned to take you girls out on the town. Nora is a large city; Thaos has been there before but I haven't. We thought we could have a nice meal and see the sights." Thaos smiled as he listened to Stephan.

"We had planned to surprise you girls," Thaos said. "But as usual you are one step ahead of us."

"Thaos can we tell them?" Nikki asked.

"You just can't keep a surprise at all, can you?" Thaos asked with a laugh. "Go ahead."

"Thaos talked to Miranda because he was worried about me going into battle since I am with child," Nikki said. "Miranda said we are having another son who would be carried in the heat of battle and that our deeds would not be lost on him and he would become a leader of men."

"Nikki that is exciting," Ingr said.

"You might as well tell them the rest," Thaos said with a grin.

"My father's name was Duran and Thaos' father's first name was Torance. Imagine our surprise when we found out that Stephan and Thaos' father have the same middle name. So this son is going to be named James Duran. We were thinking about naming him Stephan Duran at first."

"You're naming your son after me," Stephan said proudly. "Thank you I consider it an honor."

"Well, he will be a leader of men," Thaos said. "Neither of our fathers were but you certainly are."

Stephan was visibly touched by this compliment which made both Ingr and Nikki smile. "Father," Stephan called out. "Thaos and Nikki are having a son and naming it after me."

"I know," Claudius called out with a proud smile as he turned to look back at his family who were riding behind him. "We will have a drink tonight to celebrate."

"Hutas!" screamed several Enrops as they quickly flew in the direction of Claudius and his men.

"Halt!" Claudius ordered his troops. "How far ahead of us are they?" he asked one of the birds.

"There is a large group of them and they are riding towards you on this road," the Enrop explained.

91

"We killed five ravens but they didn't get close to your group so we don't know how the Hutas know you are here."

"I believe the ravens only talk to dark lords and demons," Gabriel said. "How far out are they?"

"You have about twenty minutes," the Enrop said. "They are riding fast."

"Rueben is the Sanuri with you?" Padre Ezra asked as he quickly entered the main building of the headquarters.

"Yes, he is in the study, what is the matter?" Rueben asked.

"I can tell you both," Ezra answered while he and Rueben walked to the study. The Sanuri was so engrossed in what he was reading that he did not at first realize they had joined him.

"I am sorry to bother you," Ezra said. "But a group of us just returned from Nora. Word is the Hutas crossed the border into Gant and attacked the Villages of Oman and Nerva in the last two nights. General Colter is sending more troops to the Village of Kendra and offering the villagers shelter in the fort."

"Those demons still prefer the easy targets," Rueben said with disdain.

"I should have seen this coming," the Sanuri said.

"You can't be everywhere and protect everyone," Rueben said to his friend.

"I know both of those villages are small," the Sanuri said. "But we know they wanted those people alive and that is a lot of people to move in two nights. Do we have any idea where the Hutas are taking them?"

"Sanuri this entire area is nothing but mountains and hills containing gold mines, they could be anywhere," said Rueben.

"Yes but they were dragging perhaps hundreds of people across the border, you would think that someone would have seen them," the Sanuri said.

"Which makes me wonder if the Hutas are hiding them someplace close to the border." The Sanuri seemed in deep though for a few moments then he added, "I am going to send more Enrops to search that area. When those priests where trying to raise Omnibus, the Hutas hid their victims in caves close to Nora and with the mausoleum being close to Nora I believe we all have been concentrating our energies in that area. Perhaps you were right Rueben, what if the mausoleum appeared here to keep our eyes away from other important locations?"

Claudius and his troops were riding on the eastern side of the River Nebu; for days they had been travelling in heavily forested areas but now they were riding through farm fields as they headed towards the small Village of Kendra which lay north of the Patronus headquarters. If Claudius wanted to conceal his men they would have to cross the river to the forest on the western bank and that was too time consuming.

"They are going to have to cross the River Saz to get to us," Claudius bellowed. "That will slow them down and that is where we will make our stand." Claudius quickly led his troops to the River Saz which intersected with the River Nebu a quarter mile south of Claudius' current location. When they reached the river, Claudius could see that both shores were lined with scraggly brush and tall reeds.

Claudius ordered two lines of archers to conceal themselves in the reeds on the northern bank of the River Saz. The Rualas hid in the brush along the shoreline, Claudius did not want them to attack until the Hutas started to cross the river. "If they want us, they are going to have to work to get us," Claudius said as his leaders were positioning their troops for battle.

Seven of the Enrops flew to Claudius. "We haven't seen any more ravens so the Hutas have not been warned that you are this close."

"I can see their dust cloud," Raul called out.

"Ready the troops!" Claudius ordered as he watched the oncoming dust cloud become more intense. The Hutas were riding in formation and as the leaders approached the southern bank of the River Saz they could see a portion of Claudius' army.

Many of the warriors, besides the archers were hiding in the reeds and scrub brush. Claudius, himself, sat out in the open in front of his troops. Hatred narrowed the eyes of the Hutas as they charged at Claudius, who was waiting for most of their men to get into the water.

"Release!" Claudius ordered and the first line of archers stood up and fired at the Hutas.

"I can't believe they didn't see this coming," Raul said to one of his men as they watched the surprised looks on the faces of the Hutas.

"Release!" Claudius yelled and the first line of archers knelt down as the second line stood up and fired. Claudius had over one-hundred and fifty archers in each line. "Release!" "Release!"

The intense volley of arrows did not deter the Hutas who kept charging towards Claudius. But the archers were greatly thinning out the ranks of the Hutas.

"Rualas!" Claudius ordered as several hundred Ruala warriors took to the sky and rained arrows upon the Hutas who were still charging towards the northern shore. Although Claudius could have let his archers keep firing at the Hutas, he wanted to give the Rualas a chance to fight since the Hutas had almost destroyed the Ruala race.

The Rualas flew over the Huta war party and fired volley after volley of arrows upon their enemy. The few Hutas that made it to the northern shore were immediately attacked by warriors lying in wait in the reeds.

The battle was over. The once blue water of the River Saz turned red from the blood of the Hutas. As Claudius led his troops across the river they dodged the many bodies that were floating in the water. "Keep an eye out in case any of these aren't dead," Claudius yelled.

"I still don't like this," Calen whispered to Luca as they watched Hannah, Natasha and Lila setting up a picnic site and picking armloads of wild flowers.

"Well at least they aren't really close to the water so we can stop the creatures if they grab the girls," Luca said. "And I know exactly how you feel. But Mother is right, they are going to try and grab us anyways; we should control the situation."

"I will say I was surprised when Lila asked for weapons," Calen said.

"I'm not," Luca replied. "The day that I found them, both Lila and Christopher were fighting with two Huta warriors and honestly they were holding their own. I don't think that would have lasted long but they are both fighters and when I landed and told them to leave, Lila wouldn't; in fact she went after one of the Hutas."

Calen chuckled, "And she always seems embarrassed that she isn't a warrior, she has the heart of one."

"The part I am not looking forward to is telling Gabriel we are using his wife and sister as bait," Luca whispered.

"When we tell him that the soldiers found eight more bodies tied near our shoreline, well, I believe he will agree with what we are doing."

"With all the soldiers and Rualas that are patrolling this area I can't believe someone put more bodies down there," Luca said. "The only way they could manage that without being seen is to have dragged the bodies underwater for some distance. Which means we do have more creatures watching us."

"Did I tell you that when I took Mother and the children to the castle, both Vitomas and Annabelle volunteered to be bait also?"

"No, we could probably use them so we don't seen so conspicuous."

"I am still thinking about that," Calen said. "I hate to use them without Raul and Simon knowing, especially after Renya told me that Vitomas is pregnant. I mean think if the roles were reversed."

That night Claudius doubled the guards around the troops. After the battle with the Hutas at the River Saz, there had been no further signs of Hutas or ravens but Claudius and his troops were too experienced to believe they were out of danger.

"I promised that we would have a toast tonight to Thaos and Nikki's son which they are naming after Stephan," Claudius said as he poured whiskey into the cups of the many who sat around a large fire. "And to the many young married couples that we have here, I know you like privacy but I think tonight you should not have separate campsites," Claudius added with a chuckle.

"I think we have all made our camps around the main fire," Matthew said as he helped Claudius in distributing the whiskey.

"Everyone knows that I like my whiskey as much as the next man," Sorren said. "But I think we should drink with caution, I can't get over this feeling that we are being watched."

Just as Claudius was filling the last of the cups, Gabriel and Archetenus walked up to the fire. "Here," Claudius said as he handed them each a cup of whiskey. We are going to have a toast." Claudius walked over to his sons. "For those of you who have not heard the story," Claudius announced with obvious pride. "Thaos talked to the Angel Miranda because of his concerns about Nikki going into battle while she is sick and pregnant. And Miranda told him that the baby is a boy who would be carried in the heat of battle and would himself become a leader of men."

"I am proud to tell you that my next grandson will be named James Duran. James is the middle name of both Stephan and Thaos' father Torance and Duran was the name of Nikki's father. They wanted to name the boy after Stephan, because he is a leader of men." Claudius raised his cup of whiskey and continued, "To Thaos and Nikki may they have long and happy lives and many children and to James Duran may he fulfill his destiny." Everyone in the group raised their cups then drank.

After Vivian had taken a sip of her whiskey she leaned to her right and whispered into Raphael's ear. "I have never thought about having children until I met you and now all I can think about is that I want to give you sons."

Raphael set down his cup and put both of his arms around Vivian and hugged her tightly. "I love you so much," he whispered into her ear then kissed her with great passion.

Misha watched Raphael and Vivian embrace and a pang of jealousy surged through him. Misha both liked and respected Raphael and would never do anything to destroy their relationship yet Vivian was the first woman in a very long time who stole Misha's heart.

After Misha's father was killed in battle his mother was overwhelmed with the task of raising ten children. The grief of losing her husband changed Misha's mother; she took her pain and her anger out on her children. Misha always felt fortunate that he was taken in by Emeral and Maxwell because they gave him the family and life that he so desperately craved. Although Emeral and Maxwell too had a house filled with children, Misha never felt abandoned and betrayed like he felt at home.

Misha often felt conflicted about his relationships with women because although Emeral and Maxwell gave him a loving home and showed him the positive side of relationships, the wounds and scars left by his blood family never really healed. He had decided at an early age that he did not want to be burdened with the responsibilities of a family. But for all of Misha's medals and honors as a warrior sometimes he still felt like that broken little boy who showed up in Maxwell's and Emeral's doorway.

Gabriel waited for a few moments after the toast before he spoke. "Archetenus and I were just checking on our troops on the perimeter. While the men are alright, both Archetenus and I feel that something is just not right."

"Do you feel like we are being watched also?" asked Sorren.

"It's just too quiet," Archetenus said. "We are close to the river yet there aren't any birds or animals. In fact there are few sounds at all. And Gabriel and I both think the air feels thick, the last time I experienced that was when we fought those demons with Miranda when Matthew and many of you helped Delilah and me escape Dieter's men."

"We are close to that mausoleum," Raphael said. "Perhaps the evil from that is affecting nature."

"I thought about that too," Gabriel said. "You know we keep expecting Hutas to attack us but I think we should be prepared for an attack by the Valdees also because it is like something is scaring all the wildlife away from the water."

Claudius turned to the men who were next in command, "Double the guards on the perimeter and station troops along the shoreline; conceal them because if we have visitors tonight we want to surprise them. The rest of us will sleep in shifts."

"I was almost disappointed," Natasha said at the dinner table. "That nothing happened today."

"Even if some of those creatures were in the water they may have been watching to make sure it wasn't a trap," Koby said. "I think tomorrow morning, just one or two of you should go for a ride; we will want to vary the situations."

"I will," Natasha said then looked at Calen, who frowned at her. "Honey I am the logical choice, you know that."

"If the baby keeps you up tonight; I will go," said Hannah.

"What I keep wondering," Luca said as he was cutting Christopher's meat. "Is why the Valdees aren't after any of us, I mean Rualas. After all some of us have been working with Gabriel and Raphael for years and even if it isn't the same crew there are always some Ruala warriors with the Patronus."

"Koby and I were talking about that exact same thing," Calen said. "I wonder if there is more to all of this."

"What do you mean?" Lakin asked.

"Well, is there more to the history of our two tribes, like some kind of treaty or do they have something else planned for us?"

Chapter VIII
Destination

"Here drink this," Vivian said as she handed a cup of a hot steaming beverage to Nikki.

"What is it?" Nikki asked as she took the cup. Nikki's hands were shaking as she put the cup to her lips.

"It's a tea I made from the formalia plant; it will settle your stomach. Last night when Raphael and I were guarding near the river I found the plant. Here I brought you more leaves, just let them soak in boiling water."

"Thank you," Thaos said. "She is starting to worry me. I think Nikki is losing weight from puking so much."

"We should be in Nora by this afternoon," Raphael said. "Perhaps the Sanuri can help."

"This tastes really good," Nikki said with surprise.

"You can drink it hot or cold, but you have to make the tea with really hot water to release the medicine," Vivian said then she turned to Raphael. "Now that the sun is coming up, let's look for more of these plants."

"I want to stay with Nikki," Thaos said. "But will you bring back an entire plant so we can see what it looks like?"

Gabriel was just waking as Raphael and Vivian walked past him. "Gabriel, Vivian and I are going back to the river, last night she found a medicine plant that will help Nikki; we are going to look for more."

"I'll start breakfast," Gabriel said as he stood up.

"I think Maxwell is already cooking," Raphael said. "We shouldn't be gone too long." Raphael took an empty leather pouch out of his saddlebag, then he and Vivian started towards the river. "I don't blame Thaos for being worried," Raphael said. "Nikki doesn't look good."

"But Miranda said the baby would be born," Vivian said then she grabbed Raphael's forearm and stopped walking. Both Raphael and Vivian were experienced warriors and knew that the forest should be filled with life with the dawn of a new day but this morning the silence was deafening. They both drew weapons and proceeded towards the river which was only a few hundred yards ahead of them. As they approached the first Wetprian soldier, Raphael knelt down and asked, "Has it been this still and quiet since the sun rose?"

"Yes," the soldier replied. "Something ain't right here. But we haven't seen anything yet."

"Go back and tell Claudius," Raphael said. "We are moving forward."

Vivian and Raphael silently walked past other soldiers who were hidden in the brush as they made their way towards the river. The rising sun was to their backs. Fog was rising from the water. The tree line ended about fifty yards from the eastern shore. Both Raphael and Vivian knelt down at the edge of the tree line and watched the river. There were no morning birds singing or fish jumping in the water. "Is it usually like this when the Valdees are in an area?" Raphael whispered to Vivian.

"No, they swim with the creatures in the water. I don't know what is happening here."

They heard a sound of wings as Misha, Elan, Dagon and Cassandra landed near Raphael and Vivian. These Ruala warriors too felt an ominous presence.

"Look there is something in the water," Elan whispered and point up stream.

"There is more than one," Vivian said. "It might be Valdees coming to the surface."

They saw no movement other than the fast moving current which was moving towards Raphael and the others. Minutes passed and there was no attack. The objects were moving downstream and now Misha and the others could see there were many objects floating with the current.

100

"You stay here," Misha whispered. "I am going to fly over the river and see what those things are." Misha did not fly far over the water before he landed on the eastern shore and motioned for the others to come to him.

"Elan get Claudius and the others," Misha called as he and Dagon started to pull bodies out of the water.

"There are hundreds of them," Simon said as he squatted down to look at one of the bodies that had been pulled onto shore.

"If there had been a battle between the Valdees and Hutas don't you think we would have heard it?" asked Cassandra.

"This current is strong and moving fast," Stephan said. "That battle could have been a ways up north."

"I wonder if the Valdees thought they could take the Hutas as slaves," Vivian said.

"Or the Hutas could have thought the Valdees killed the men that we did and wanted revenge," Raphael said. "But the most likely answer is that both groups were hunting us and ran into each other."

"There is another explanation," Gabriel said. "Both tribes are working for different demons that want us; perhaps the demons wanted the battle."

"And we are the prize," Thaos said sarcastically as he was looking at bodies. Then he looked up at Vivian and Raphael. "That tea seemed to help Nikki; can you show me some of those plants?"

Vivian and Raphael turned and walked back into the forest, with Thaos a few steps behind them. Vivian was searching through the lower brush for the plants as Raphael and Thaos stood by.

"Raphael, Thaos come here and walk exactly where I walked," Vivian called out from a small thicket. "I found the plants and these," Vivian said as she walked forward and pointed to the ground. "We did have visitors."

"What the hell made those?" Thaos asked as he knelt down and examined the footprints in the soft earth. "They look like bear prints but they are at least twice the size."

"Whatever they were they were close enough to grab our men and didn't," Raphael said as he started to follow the footprints which led back to the river.

"I have tracked many Valdees," Vivian said. "But I have never seen such prints with them."

"The trail stops here," Raphael announced as he came upon a rocky area near the water.

"If they were demons, why didn't they attack us?" Thaos asked. "We need to show these to the others."

"Our men haven't found any sign of those villagers," High Priest Rueben announced as he entered the study in the Patronus headquarters in Nora. "How can that many people just disappear? And you know how brazen Hutas are; they never try to conceal their trails." Rueben paused. "Gilbert what are you doing out of bed?" Rueben asked the wounded priest.

"I have never been much for lying around," Gilbert said. "So I thought I would come down here and help the Sanuri with his research."

"Well don't overdo it," Rueben said as he sat down in a chair near the desk. "Have you found anything useful?"

"I am beginning to wonder just what Hannah's father's role was in the Insidiae," the Sanuri said as he set down a large book. "He has documents in his library that I would not imagine a normal foot soldier to possess."

"Hannah told me that her father was a great collector of things," Rueben said.

"Perhaps," the Sanuri said. "But these are historical documents about the Old Ones and the Grand Masters. I can't imagine there are other copies of this information. I would think these items would be kept in one of their temples."

"Are you thinking he held a high position in the Insidiae?" asked Rueben.

"I don't know," the Sanuri responded. "From what I know about Arthur Marcus he was a cunning and treacherous man. I can't prove anything but I have this nagging feeling that he was conspiring some kind of takeover within the organization when there was a change of events in his life."

"You mean when he stood by and allowed Roch to rape and murder his little girl?" Gilbert asked. "I can't imagine how a father could do that."

"Hannah said that her father was filled with guilt after the girl's death and hung himself but I am beginning to wonder if he didn't have some help," the Sanuri said.

"You mean the Insidiae? But why would they?" asked Rueben.

"Arthur was in possession of the most valuable information of that secret society. He knew the names and locations of many of the members as well as their dirty deeds," the Sanuri continued. "He may have been the only one in the organization with this information and that would make him many enemies."

"We haven't found anything on the bodies of importance," Misha said to Claudius. "There wasn't even a map."

"How many bodies in all?" Claudius asked.

"The soldiers from Wetpr are counting them," Misha said to Claudius then turned and yelled over his shoulder. "Raul what is the count?"

"One hundred and forty two Valdees and two hundred and twenty five Hutas," Raul called out as he walked up to Claudius and Misha. "But I'm not so sure they all killed each other," Raul said. "Some of these bodies are really torn up, like an animal attacked them. And we found bodies of both tribes like that."

"I wonder if whatever creatures made those giant footprints got involved with the battle," Thaos said.

Matthew, Stephan, Angelina, Raphael and Vivian were kneeling down examining some of the bodies. "Father come down here," Stephan called. "The girls may have found something." A group of people now crowded around Stephan and the others.

"Miranda told Vivian and me to memorize everything we could about our captors, because even the little details would be important," Angelina explained. "While at first glance most of these warriors look the same, the ones here have different tattoos than the ones who took us. We think these tattoos have significance other than decoration."

Gabriel and Thaos now crouched down near the bodies. "In many tribes tattoos will signify status within the group or information about the person, like how many enemies they may have killed," Gabriel said.

"The creatures that kidnapped us all wore those vest-like shirts without sleeves," Vivian said. "So we could only see the tattoos on their necks, arms and hands. As you can see these bodies all have tattoos on their chests and backs also but Angelina and I never saw these areas on our captors. Here on the left wrist of each body is three blue bands tattooed around the wrists. Our captors had two red bands around each of their left wrists. And look at the inside of their right forearms, that is writing in their language; we didn't see that on our captors."

"Can you read it?" Claudius asked.

Vivian smiled and turned to Raphael, "Let's see how the student is doing?"

"Unless I am reading this wrong I think it is the name of the military unit they are in," Raphael said because all the arms say the same thing *Tridan One*. And the word Tridan means force."

"I'm impressed," Vivian said with a grin.

"So we are thinking that these guys here are some kind of special fighters?" Stephan asked. "Which would explain why they could kill so many Hutas."

"It also means Douma knows we are here and sent them after us," Gabriel said as he stood up. "I'm beginning to think more and more that we have two different groups here that both want us as prizes."

"So are you thinking they were both coming for us when they saw each other and the fight was on?" asked Simon.

"Yes," Raphael said. "But that doesn't explain those footprints or how torn up these bodies are."

"Do you think the Angels did this?" Claudius asked.

"No," Archetenus said as he stood up from examining a body. "Because I have been in situations where I have asked Miranda questions like that and she said Angels and The Great Ruler don't send demons to attack others and the Angels wouldn't tear bodies up like this."

"So does that mean we have a third enemy that is after us?" asked Raul.

"Looks to me like whatever made those prints were after these guys," Thaos said. "Because they could certainly have attacked us last night."

"We'll be at the Patronus headquarters by noon," Claudius said. "Let's take a couple of these bodies to show the Sanuri, he might be able to figure some of this out. Eat breakfast then we will break camp. And I want everyone to be extra vigilant because we may be riding into a trap."

"I cannot believe my men have not found Philip," King Sudfad said with frustration at his morning meeting with Calen and Luca. "And not only have new bodies been tied off your shoreline but also near the castle of Claudius; I received word this morning. Mathas suspects there are probably more bodies at the same locations in the lands of the Nordes Tribe, but with Sorren gone, Mathas has not sent troops to their land to look."

"Was there any difference in the counts?" Luca asked.

"No," Sudfad said. "Both Mathas and I have troops patrolling the shorelines of the water ways and people are being murdered and displayed right under our noses, I can't begin to tell you how angry this makes me. I am beginning to think more and more that the Valdees are working with a dark lord that walks in our kingdoms."

"Where are they stealing the people from?" asked Calen.

"Both here and in Lentz a lot of the bodies are unclaimed, but so far it's been farmers, miners, fishermen and the likes. Men who aren't warriors and who may be alone when the Valdees find them."

"Natasha, Hannah and Lila have all volunteered to act as bait," Luca said. "And we have set up several traps but so far nothing." Luca paused and looked at Calen.

"Sudfad, Luca and I have been talking; you have had spies infiltrate your military before. Have you considered there might be more?" Calen asked.

"That was my thought from the moment that someone warned Philip," Sudfad said. "I have some of my most trusted officers investigating."

"Bekka do you want to play with us?" Christopher asked when he saw Bekka walk into the parlor.

"Oh Christopher, Koby and I are going on patrol," she said apologetically. "I promise I will play with you when I get back."

"Ok," Christopher said and ran out of the parlor.

"Is he trying to horn in on my girl?" Koby asked kiddingly.

"Your girl?" Bekka asked with surprise. "I thought you just wanted a causal relationship."

"I think we are past that; don't you?" Koby asked.

Bekka didn't say anything which concerned Koby. He took her hand. "I'm not sure I like the look on your face maybe it's time we had a talk," Koby said as he motioned to the sofa. They sat down and Bekka waited for Koby to speak. "Bekka we have spent every day and night together for the past two months, if you aren't interested in having a relationship with me; now would be the time to say so."

"Oh no Koby, I have strong feelings for you, I, I guess I just didn't think you did for me."

"What are you talking about? Whatever gave you that idea?"

"Koby you are every girl's dream. You're handsome and courageous and a wonderful person; I don't understand why you want to be with me. I mean you could have any woman you want. Every day I expect you to tell me that it is over."

"Are you serious?"

"Yes, at first I thought you just wanted to spend time with me because you felt sorry for me."

"I can't believe you are saying these things," Koby said. "Bekka you are a gorgeous woman. You're smart and sexy and funny and you too are a courageous warrior. Don't you see these things in yourself?"

Bekka didn't speak; she shook her head from side to side to indicate she did not see herself as Koby saw her. "Bekka I spend time with you because I care about you not because I feel sorry for you. And I thought we were having a lot of fun together."

"We are Koby, I, well, I am just surprised to hear you say these things because you have said many times you just wanted to be friends."

"I know I did," Koby said then paused. "I don't know if you are going to understand what I am trying to say. Calen, Luca, Misha, Dagon and I grew up together. And I mean we did everything together and none of us wanted to settle down. Then Calen meets Natasha and he is married in less than a week. And Luca wasn't much better."

"Don't get me wrong I love Natasha and Lila but there is a part of me that doesn't think marrying someone you know for a few days is even normal. Then Raphael does the same thing. I guess I didn't want you to expect that of me. I'm not saying that I don't want to ever get married; I just think people should get to know each other first. Does that make sense to you?"

"Koby I understand what you mean," Bekka said. "I care about you very much and I want to be with you but you have been away from the Ice Caves for years. You have done so many things and been so many places. This is my first time in the world below and in a way I feel like I am finding out who I really am. I am not ready for marriage now."

"So what do you want to do?" Koby asked.

"I don't know what you mean?"

"Do you want to keep things the way they are or?"

"Or what?" Bekka asked fearfully.

"Since we spend every night together I was thinking we should move into the same room."

"Really," Bekka said with a rush of relief. "I thought you were going to break up with me."

"Bekka just get those thoughts out of your head. I will be honest, I don't know what the future holds for the two of us but I would like you to be my girl. And if it will make you feel better to keep separate rooms; that is fine too."

Bekka smiled and put her arms around his neck, kissing him on the lips. "So which room should we live in?" she asked then kissed Koby again.

"The Rualas say that General Claudius and the others will be here within the hour," High Priest Amos said as he entered the study where the Sanuri, High Priest Rueben and Padre Gilbert were working.

"Good," Rueben said as he stood up. "I could use a break."

"I am going to make some coffee and get some other refreshments prepared."

"I think we could all use a break and to stretch our legs," the Sanuri said as he too stood up from the desk. "I am going to bring more chairs in here so we can have a meeting right away. I am really interested in hearing about how they rescued the girls and about the Valdees they interrogated."

"I'll help you," Gilbert said as he started to stand up.

"You will do no such thing," Rueben said. "You are already overdoing it by being out of bed so much."

"He's right," said the Sanuri.

"I'm just not the type to stay in bed," Gilbert said. "Besides the children have brought me so many bouquets of flowers my room reeks."

"You could tell them to stop," Rueben said with a grin.

"I don't want to hurt their feelings."

"The children do seem to like you," the Sanuri said. "You should have a family of your own someday."

"I can't really see that happening," Gilbert said. "Besides I wouldn't want to raise a family here in Stordt it is just too dangerous."

"You said you would protect me," Philip yelled accusingly. "Is this protection? I am living in a cave like an animal."

"The King's men have not found you so stop whining," the demon Daegal said with disgust. "You have been paid well for your work."

"I can't spend it if I am dead," Philip bellowed with frustration. "How much longer do I have to stay down here?"

"The streets and roadways are filled with soldiers and great flocks of Enrops are searching the skies; what the hell do you think?" Daegal was clearly showing his agitation with Philip. "You are in the only place that they cannot find you. Just wait for Sudfad to think you have escaped the kingdom and he will return his men to their normal duties."

"Well, I am getting sick of all this," Philip said and kicked some dirt into the small fire he had burning in the cavern.

"Philip perhaps it is time for me to hold a mirror before you," the demon said. "You were of great value to us when you were a spy in Sudfad's castle. You preformed your tasks well, which is the only reason I am protecting you now, because you have lost your value."

Philip had been looking at the ground and kicking at the dirt as Daegal spoke; now Philip's head shot up and he stared at the demon. "What are you saying?" Philip demanded. "I have done everything you have asked of me and you promised me a great deal for my cooperation; I expect you to make good on your word."

"I have paid you for your services," Daegal said. "Now it is up to you to prove your continued value to me; because I am sick of listening to your constant whining and bitching. You betrayed your kingdom and your King for a few bags of gold coins. You knew full well what you were doing. You could have changed your mind at any time."

"You make it sound so easy," Philip said sarcastically. "You're the one who gave me the shartish; now I am addicted to the damn stuff. I thought you were trying to help me; you gave me that drug to control me."

"Philip take some responsibility for your behavior; that is what always amazes me about humans. You make your choices, you take your actions and when things look bad it is always someone else's fault. You are a physician who constantly brags about his great abilities. You knew what shartish was when I gave it to you. I didn't force it down your throat, you took it willingly and you kept taking it until the drug took control of you. You gave that drug your life and now you are throwing blame."

"Don't put this all on me," Philip yelled. "You came to me after my family was killed. The shartish was the only thing that helped me to forget."

"I never forced that drug on you," Daegal said. "You are blaming the wrong demon for your problems."

The study at the Patronus headquarters in Nora was filled to capacity with both the priests and the newly arrived warriors. Angelina and Vivian were asked to start the meeting by telling of their kidnappings, their experiences with the Angel Miranda and their rescue. Then Misha was asked to explain the role the Ruala's played in determining the locations of the girls and their rescue. Gabriel, Raphael and Vivian talked about the interrogations of the Valdees, while Ingr reviewed her notes to remind the speakers of subjects.

Archetenus started explaining the visits by the Angels Miranda and Daniel and many added information. Claudius told of the dead bodies his men pulled from the river that morning and Thaos described the strange footprints that he found. The Patronus priests sat spellbound listening to these warriors talk about their encounters with the holy messengers.

"I believe I know what happened to those Valdees and Hutas that you found this morning and what made those footprints," the Sanuri said. "For I too have come across those same prints while travelling." Then the Sanuri looked over at Archetenus. "Archetenus do you remember the very first time that we met, when I found you wounded?"

"Yes," he replied. "And something was killing my men."

"Something was also hunting the Hutas and tearing their bodies to shreds," the Sanuri explained. "I first came across prints such as you describe a few years ago. I was hunting Hutas who had stolen a powerful gift of The Great Ruler's. The gift was stolen because the dark lords thought it would aid them in raising Omnibus from The Abyss. As I hunted the Hutas, I came across large groups of them who were literally torn to shreds. Then one night I found a wounded Huta warrior, before he died he told me about the demons that had attacked him."

"I thought he was delirious because the Hutas are the pawns of the demons why would the demons attack them. After doing a great deal of research and praying for guidance I learned of a creature called the Teragon which translated from Amark means death terror."

"I found a scroll written in the ancient language of The Great Ruler that basically said when dark ones create evil of grand magnitude they also create the Teragon, rather as a consequence of their evil actions. And the Teragon feed upon the evil that created them. Which would explain why you were not attacked; but now I am concerned as to what the Valdees and Hutas are attempting that has brought the wrath of the Teragon upon them."

Claudius and his army remained at the Patronus headquarters for four more days as they waited for the additional troops sent by Kings Sudfad and Mathas to join them. The army of Ruala warriors arrived at the headquarters on the second night after the arrival of Claudius and his troops.

"Vivian," the Sanuri said as she and Raphael entered the headquarters from a shopping trip in Nora. "I sent a message to Duncan telling him that we would be travelling to your village to speak with him. I didn't want Duncan to think he was under siege when he saw the numbers we are travelling with. And I hope you don't mind but I told him that you were safe and traveling with us. But I did not say that you were married, that is your surprise."

"I am glad you did that," Vivian said. "I was thinking about doing the same thing. Raphael and I have been buying gifts for my family and for Duncan." Vivian squeezed Raphael's hand and said proudly, "My husband is very generous."

"Sanuri I was thinking that perhaps we should bring food and drink for a celebration," Raphael said. "But we would need to carry these things in your boca."

The Sanuri smiled, "I believe that is an excellent idea. Feel free to move everything but my medical bag out of the boca so there is room for your things." Then the Sanuri paused a moment and asked, "Vivian do you expect trouble with Sampson?"

112

"How did you know about that?" Vivian asked with surprise.

"Does your husband know?"

"Yes, I told Raphael but how do you know?"

"Since you have told Raphael I will speak freely," the Sanuri said. "I admire and respect Duncan as a leader and as a man, but his son Sampson is filled with darkness and I rue the day that he takes over leadership of your people. I have maintained communications with Duncan and I know that Sampson has been obsessed with you since you were a child. Did you know that the first time Sampson asked your father for you was when you were only eight?"

"What!" Raphael said loudly. "How old is Sampson?"

"A few years older than you," Vivian said to Raphael then she turned to the Sanuri. "My father only told me that Sampson had demanded that I become his wife several times. You know my father, he is not easily intimidated. Father said the choice was mine and I never wanted anything to do with Sampson."

"You are a smart girl," the Sanuri said. "And I do not mean to meddle in your personal life but I believe that Sampson could be enough of a threat that you should tell Claudius and the others about him. From what I know of Sampson he takes everything he wants by force. The only things he has not taken is the leadership from his father and you. I would not be surprised if he tries to take you and his father's position by force someday."

"When you said Sampson might make trouble, I greatly underestimated the situation," Raphael said to Vivian. "Is there more that you should be telling me?"

"Raphael I wasn't trying to keep anything from you," Vivian said. "I don't fear Sampson but I do not disagree with what the Sanuri has said either."

"Vivian I have known your father for a long time. He is a good man and a fierce warrior. I am inclined to think you should probably send him a message and tell him that you are bringing your husband to meet the family. That way Joshua can be prepared for anything that Sampson might do."

113

"Honey I know you wanted this to be a surprise but after hearing all this I agree with the Sanuri," Raphael said.

"You are right," Vivian said. "I will write the letter now."

"I am going to talk to Claudius and the others," Raphael said. "And if you don't mind I would like to write a few words to your father also."

Chapter IX
Family

"Emeral this doesn't mean we are getting married," Koby said at the breakfast table. "At least not yet. We talked it over and neither of us are ready for marriage yet."

"Is that true Bekka?" Emeral asked.

"Yes," Bekka said and laughed because of the way Emeral was putting Koby on the spot. "Emeral I told Koby that while he has seen and done many things, this is my first experience out of the Ice Caves and there is much I want to see and do."

"Well you can do these things as a married couple," Emeral continued.

"We're not ready to start a family yet," Koby said with frustration.

"You're having sex aren't you?" Emeral asked. "You better be prepared for the possibility that Bekka might get pregnant." The look on both Koby's and Bekka's faces caused Calen and Luca to roar with laughter.

"Apparently they haven't thought about that," Calen kidded then he turned to Koby. "Don't let Mother pressure you into anything; it's your life."

"I'm just being realistic," Emeral said with a grin.

"Whatever choices you make," Natasha said as she took her seat next to Calen. "I think you two make a great couple."

"I am sorry to disturb you," said a soldier as he quickly walked into the dining room. "But King Sudfad wants us to escort your entire family to the castle now."

"What is wrong?" asked Calen as he stood up.

The soldier glanced at Christopher and Nicholas who were looking at him. "I'm not sure that I should say in front of the children. But I need you to gather your things and come with us."

General Orlan was specially chosen by King Sudfad to lead ten thousand troops through Stordt to the Patronus Headquarters in Nora. After the mission in Ogg was completed, Orlan would be assigned to Fort Nora to work with General Colter. Fort Nora was the only Wetprian Military outpost that was located in hostile territory.

The citizens of Nora had been terrorized by King Roch and his men for decades, they had been attacked by bands of Hutas and Rogetts and not until King Sudfad purchased part of their city had these people ever been protected. The citizens of Nora welcomed the Wetprian soldiers and opened the city to them. Besides overseeing the construction of the fort, General Colter found that the people of Nora wanted him to become directly involved in both the operations of the city and the gold mines.

Because King Sudfad now claimed Nora, the citizens were building schools and churches, all of which had been forbidden under the tyrannical regime of King Roch. The Nora City Council looked upon General Colter as the direct representative of King Sudfad and therefore sought Colter's advice and assistance in many areas.

The people of Nora loved General Colter but both Raul and Simon had told their father that Colter needed help. Orlan was a savvy and battle experienced soldier but he was also a kind and compassionate man who liked to talk with people. General Orlan was both proud and excited for the challenges of his new assignment.

General Hurch led the six thousand soldiers from Lentz, to the Patronus headquarters. He had grown up with both King Mathas and General Claudius. These men had fought together in battles since they were young men; they had great admiration and respect for each other. Hurch asked Mathas to allow him to lead the troops for this mission. Claudius was pleased when he was informed that his old friend would join him once again on the battlefield.

King Manu of the Rualas sent his oldest son Prince Gael to lead one thousand warriors to join the Sanuri in Nora. Gael was the older brother of both Princess Ibula and Prince Lakin.

Lakin had remained in Salar with five hundred Ruala warriors to provide protection for the families of Sudfad and Gabriel.

Kings Sudfad, Mathas and Manu decreed that while the leaders they sent to Nora were responsible for the warriors they led, all would answer to General Claudius and the Sanuri. The united forces left Nora and traveled southwest towards the Village of the Clan of Gesmal in the Kingdom of Ryed. The journey was uneventful until the afternoon of the second day when they traveled past the Tar Pits of Dan.

Most of the soldiers had never seen anything like these natural wonders before. The huge pits covered miles and sent great plumes of steam into the air. The army crossed the border into Ryed on the third day and expected to arrive at the Village of Gesmal on the morning of the fourth day of their journey.

Instead of driving his boca, the Sanuri rode a horse next to Claudius as they led the troops through Ryed. One of the Wetprian soldiers drove the boca which was filled with food and gifts for the Clan of Gesmal. Stephan, Ingr, Nikki and Thaos rode directly behind Claudius and next to Matthew, Angelina and Sorren. Raul, Simon, Archetenus, Gabriel, Raphael and Vivian rode in the next line, but the entire group talked among themselves.

"Vivian and Raphael, we are getting close to the village I want the two of you to ride in front," the Sanuri said.

"Can Gabriel ride with us?" Vivian asked. "Because I want to introduce my new family to my blood family."

"Of course," the Sanuri said.

Then Vivian looked up at the Ruala warriors who were flying overhead. "Maxwell, Elan, Cassandra, Misha and Dagon, you too are my family now I would like you to come forward so I can introduce you to my parents when we get there."

"We would be honored," Maxwell said.

"This all has been so exciting," Ingr said.

117

"I have never traveled this far from home before. Nora was so much fun and now we get to meet Vivian's tribe."

"I think you will find you have much in common," Vivian said to Ingr then she looked back at Angelina. "Angelina you have been so quiet is anything wrong?"

"I haven't been feeling well, but it is nothing," Angelina said.

The Sanuri now stopped his horse and turned to Angelina. "Do you not know why you aren't feeling well?" he asked with a warm smile.

Angelina stared at the Sanuri for several moments as did Matthew and Sorren. "Sanuri what are you saying?" Matthew asked.

"That your wife is carrying a future king inside of her."

"I'm pregnant," Angelina gasped as the others smiled. "Now that I think about it, well it makes sense, I guess."

Matthew was elated by the news. "We are having a son?"

"Yes," the Sanuri said happily.

Matthew turned to Angelina, "Tell your father the baby's name.

Angelina smiled, "Matthew and I already picked the name of our first born son; he will be called Mathas Sorren."

"Sorren you are going to be a grandfather again," Stephan said with a grin.

"It looks like we are going to have a lot to celebrate when we get to Vivian's village," Sorren said with a proud smile.

Matthew reached over and squeezed Angelina's hand. "We have company," Misha yelled and pointed to a lone rider coming towards them at a face pace.

"It's Sampson," Vivian said with disgust.

The Sanuri had stopped the troops when he was talking to Angelina. Now they resumed their journey but stopped ten minutes later as Sampson approached them. Sampson was focused on Vivian and rode directly towards her. Raphael moved his horse so he was positioned between Vivian and Sampson, an action which Sampson did not respond to.

Sampson was a large and muscular man. He never wore a shirt just a black leather vest which displayed his powerful arms; that were covered with tattoos. Sampson's head was shaven and also tattooed. As soon as Sampson was near to Vivian he started to yell loudly, "Vivian what is the meaning of this?" Sampson looked past Raphael as if Raphael was not before him.

"Sampson meet my husband Raphael," Vivian said calmly.

Sampson now looked at Raphael with loathing but he continued to yell at Vivian. "Your husband! I was to be your husband, not this stranger." Raphael slowly walked his horse closer to Sampson who appeared oblivious of Raphael's move.

"Sampson I was never promised to you and you never had my heart," Vivian responded still maintaining a calm manner.

"And this stranger has your heart?" Sampson asked angrily. Sampson's face was becoming dark red and the veins were protruding in his neck.

"Raphael has my all, we are one."

"You have your answers," Raphael said to Sampson with a calm but commanding voice. "Now I will tell you this only once. You will never come near my wife again. Do you understand me?"

"No!" Vivian screamed as Sampson grabbed the hilt of a knife on his belt. Raphael too, grabbed his own knife.

"Sampson you have no fight here," the Sanuri said as he rode between the two men. "You may ride with us in peace or leave us." Sampson glared at the Sanuri, who he both feared and revered.

Sampson looked back at Raphael and sneered. "This is not over," Sampson said angrily and turning his horse he sped back towards his village. Raphael now turned his horse and rode up to Vivian.

"Vivian I believe you greatly underestimate him," Raphael said in a stern voice which Vivian had never heard before. "I know it is your village but I want you to stay with me at all times; I do not trust him."

As Vivian listened to Raphael she felt both proud of him and insulted that he was insinuating she could not handle Sampson. She was about to protest but thought better of it and merely said, "I understand." She intended to talk with Raphael about this matter when they were alone. Vivian now turned around on her horse and faced those behind her. "I apologize for this. Please do not judge all of my tribe by this one man. Sampson stands alone in his dark ways."

Stephan leaned towards Thaos and said sarcastically, "This is going to be more interesting than I thought."

As the army neared the Village of the Clan of Gesmal, Claudius ordered the vast majority of the army to make camp, only the leaders and Vivian's new family proceeded into the village. Chief Duncan stood before the majority of his clan as they greeted the Sanuri and others.

"Duncan as always it is good to see you," the Sanuri said.

"Your presence honors us," Duncan said. "Come we have prepared a feast in your honor."

"We too have brought a feast and gifts because of the generosity of Vivian's husband High Priest Raphael of the Patronus. Please allow me to introduce my companions before we proceed to the celebrations. Vivian smiled when she saw her parents in the front of the crowd but she knew it would be disrespectful for her to go to them while the Sanuri was speaking.

"Duncan this is General Claudius, a ruling member of the Kingdom of Lentz. I will introduce the others from left to right. Of course you know Vivian, High Priest Raphael, High Priest Gabriel also of the Patronus."

120

"Prince Raul and Prince Simon of Wetpr, Archetenus, Prince Matthew and his wife Princess Angelina of Lentz, Chief Sorren of the Nordes Tribe in Lentz and father of Angelina. Stephan and Thaos are officers in the Army of Lentz and sons of Claudius; they are accompanied by their warrior wives Ingr and Nikki. Princess Ibula of the Rualas and her husband Thedes the leader of the Shettees, Prince Maxwell of the Rualas, Misha a lieutenant in the Ruala Military, Dagon, Elan and Cassandra are all members of an elite group of hunters who work with the Patronus.

"My people and I are honored by your presence here; but such a group of leaders from so many different origins leads me to believe that your purpose for being here is extremely important. Would you like to have a meeting before our meal?" Duncan asked.

"We have traveled far and my friends are most curious to meet your people," the Sanuri said. "I believe some food and relaxation should come first." The Sanuri turned to Vivian and said, "It is your turn for introductions."

Vivian, Raphael and Gabriel dismounted and walked towards her parents. Vivian walked in the middle and held the hands of both men. When they reached her parents Vivian first hugged her father then her mother then turned to Raphael. "Mother, Father this is my husband Raphael and his brother Gabriel; this is my father Joshua and my mother Iris."

"We never thought our daughter would take a husband," Joshua said smiling and hugged both Raphael and Gabriel. "You are my sons now." Iris too hugged both Raphael and Gabriel and kissed each man on the cheek. Vivian turned back and motioned for Maxwell and the other Rualas to come forward.

"We live in a big beautiful home in Salar," Vivian explained. "Many different people also live there because they are hunters and as the Sanuri said they are members of a very special team. There are husbands and wives and children that live with us and we have become one large family. A few of those people are here now." Vivian proudly took Maxwell's arm and said, "This is Prince Maxwell, he and his wonderful wife Emeral are the parents of several of the members of the team and have adopted the rest of us as their children also."

121

As Maxwell greeted Joshua and Iris, Elan and Cassandra walked forward. "This is Elan and Cassandra; they are engaged to be married soon. Elan recently lost his arm in a battle with many demons. And this is Misha and Dagon. All of them are courageous warriors and noble people; you will be proud to have them as part of our family." As Vivian's parents were greeting these new family members the voice of a small boy was heard.

"Elan tell us about the demons," the boy said enthusiastically which caused everyone to laugh.

"Boys step forward and meet your new family," Joshua said. "These are our sons. Micha is the eldest, second is Thomas, they are both Venatores and they are older than Vivian. Paul and Adrone are our youngest boys." While Vivian was introducing her two families other members of the group dismounted and walked up to Vivian's parents for introductions.

"Father it is the most amazing thing," Vivian said. "All of these people are hunters and even though they come from different lives they are so similar to the people of our tribe; I never would have expected that."

The Clan of Gesmal was just as intrigued by their visitors as Claudius and the others were of the villagers. The feast that was prepared for the Sanuri and honored guests included many activities and competitions which helped to bring all of the people together.

After the initial introductions Sorren and the others emptied the boca of the food, spirits and gifts that Raphael had bought. The food, wine and whiskey were added to that provided by the villagers. Raphael, Vivian and Gabriel presented the many gifts to Vivian's family and to Chief Duncan. Afterwards Gabriel joined the celebration so Raphael and Vivian could talk with her parents.

"Raphael while it is our custom for the husband to give gifts to the bride's family," Joshua said. "You have overwhelmed us with your generosity."

"Honestly I have always been so dedicated to my work that I never thought I would marry," Raphael said.

"For one reason, I never thought I would find a woman who would understand what I do. Then I met Vivian and my world changed. I am very grateful to The Great Ruler for bringing your daughter into my life. And I was anxious to meet her family and tribe." Vivian was holding Raphael's hand and now kissed it, a move that was noticed by both of her parents.

"You and Vivian sound very much alike," Iris said. "Tell us how did you meet?"

Vivian and Raphael both looked at each other, then Raphael said, "I am going to tell your parents the truth." He turned to Joshua and Iris. "As you know we are hunters also and our missions have been so devastating for the demons that they started hunting us and have endangered our families."

"Gabriel was performing a wedding ceremony for a friend at a farm. Most of the people from our team were there as well as the Royal Family of Wetpr. Vivian appeared out of nowhere and started talking with me. I caught her in a lie and walked her over to Gabriel. We believed her to be a dark lord and when we asked her questions she would not answer us."

"The King of Wetpr has a powerful healer who makes a tonic that forces people to tell the truth," Raphael continued. "We gave some to Vivian and she became deathly ill. We had no idea she would be affected like that, for we had not seen it in others."

Vivian now interrupted Raphael, "They took me into their home and cared for me like I was family," Vivian said. "Every time I awoke someone was sitting in the room with me and often it was Raphael. He would sit all night in this tiny little chair next to my bed. Some of the team members went to the Kingdom of Lentz to get medicine to make me better. Everyone felt awful that I became sick from the tonic and they showered me with gifts and affection. By the time I was well I had become part of the family."

"Vivian did not want me to tell you that we almost killed her," Raphael said. "Both Gabriel and I were consumed with guilt. That tonic had only been used a few times and was given to large men who were killed after questioning. We don't know if the dose was too strong for Vivian or if the effects are that devastating for everyone.

"Vivian why were you at the wedding?" Joshua asked.

"I had been hunting two creatures and I lost their trail near Salar. I went into the city to hear if anyone had spotted them and I overheard a couple of women talking about the wedding ceremony they were preparing," Vivian said. "Honestly Father I was sick of being alone and just wanted to have a little fun. As soon as I arrived at the wedding I saw Raphael and couldn't take my eyes off from him. I didn't know anything about Raphael or any of the other people at the celebration and I didn't think they would believe me if I told them I was a hunter."

"Did you find the creatures?" Joshua asked.

"Before Vivian came to the wedding she set traps at her campsite," Raphael explained. "When she felt better we went to the campsite to disable the traps and found the two creatures dead. They had circled around and come after her; which caused me great concern. Joshua, Iris I want you to know that everyone in the household adores Vivian."

"You met Elan. He became very depressed after he lost his arm. He is young and that was his first big battle with demons. Because of his injury Elan lost confidence in himself. Vivian trained with him every day then at our wedding they competed in a sword contest. Elan did very well and all the guests applauded his performance, after that Elan was back to his old self."

"Raphael my heart is so warmed as I watch the two of you," Iris said. "I have never seen our daughter in love before. I am happy that she has found a good man and a loving family. But we will miss her greatly."

"We can visit you," Raphael said. "And perhaps you could come to Salar."

"Raphael why don't you and I take a walk," Joshua said as he stood up. "We have a matter that needs to be discussed."

"Father if you are going to talk to him about Sampson, Raphael already knows. Sampson met us before we arrived at the village and pulled a knife on Raphael."

"He did what?" Joshua asked angrily. "Is that why I haven't seen him since you arrived?"

"The Sanuri stopped us before we fought," Raphael said. "But I did tell Sampson never to come near Vivian again."

Joshua paused for several moments before he spoke. "Raphael do not trust Sampson he is as bad as the creatures he hunts."

"Vivian warned me he would cause problems."

"There may be some things that Vivian doesn't know," Joshua said. "Venatores are trained to kill demons but yet to respect life. Venatores should have honor and integrity as well as courage. Sampson is different from the others. He has no respect for life; he has killed men who did not need to die. And he has a cruelty about him that is not seen in the other villagers. When Sampson was a boy he would torture and kill animals. He likes to inflict pain and his father has caught Sampson torturing others."

"Duncan does not want Sampson to assume the leadership of the tribe but Duncan is afraid that if he names his second son George to be chief that Sampson will kill George."

"Father why didn't you tell me these things before?" Vivian asked.

"I didn't want to scare you and I have always been proud that you wanted nothing to do with Sampson."

"Vivian told me that Sampson wanted her as his wife when she was only eight. Does your tribe marry that young?" Raphael asked.

"No," Joshua said with disgust. "Sampson is ten years older than Vivian and well..." Joshua hesitated.

"Joshua she is a married woman now, tell her," Iris said.

"Your mother and I watched you closely Vivian because Iris found Sampson trying to kiss you one day when you were only five."

"It was more than that," Iris said. "He was lying on top of her. I started beating him with a broom handle and he left."

"Has he been like that with other children?" asked Raphael.

"Not in our village but we have heard stories," Joshua said. "Stories about him raping both women and children." Joshua paused. "I didn't want to tell Vivian this but..."

"But what Father?" Vivian asked.

"Shortly after Thor's and Diana's parents were murdered, I heard screaming and found Thor beating Sampson. Even though Thor was just a boy he was so filled with rage that he was winning the fight. After I pulled Thor off from Sampson; Thor said that Sampson had pulled Diana into the forest and was attacking her."

"What! She was only six. Did he hurt her?" Vivian asked with a mixture of fear, anger and disgust.

"No. You know how protective Thor is of his little sister. Thank The Great Ruler that Thor stopped Sampson in time."

Vivian turned to Raphael and explained, "Thor and Diana are orphans and when they aren't hunting they live with my family. Diana is the sweetest girl and very beautiful." Then Vivian turned again to her father. "Are they hunting now because I haven't seen them?"

"Yes, they have been gone for months hunting in northern Ryed."

"This is disgusting. And no one does anything about Sampson?" Raphael asked incredulously.

"Other than these two incidents, when Sampson was younger he has never raped anyone in our village. If he did he would be put to death," Joshua said. "But he is a great fighter and he loves to intimidate people, I don't know what has happened in other villages."

"Does he have any other wives?" Raphael asked.

"No, we do not believe in that," Joshua replied.

"So he has been waiting around for Vivian?" asked Raphael.

"Yes," Joshua said. "Which is why you must be careful. Iris has prepared Vivian's bedroom for the two of you to stay in while you are here, we don't want you camping out."

"Joshua there is more that we need to tell you," Raphael said. "It is what the Sanuri is going to talk to Duncan about. The Royal Families of both Wetpr and Lentz are good people who follow the ways of The Great Ruler. Our team works to protect them and all of us have been attacked by demons and dark lords."

"A dark lord has put bounties on many of the members of these families and ours also. The Valdees have been paid to attack and abduct these people. Both Vivian and the girl Angelina, who you met, were recently abducted and we rescued them only weeks ago. King Sudfad and King Mathas have declared war on Douma and we will attack his kingdom."

Iris gasped as Raphael spoke. Vivian quickly added, "They did not hurt us because Douma wanted us for his wives. But there is more, the work that Raphael and Gabriel do is very important. Father they work with Angels and I now have witnessed that. The Angel Miranda came to Angelina and me when we were captives and told us that there was much more happening than our abductions."

"Miranda told us we were not alone and would be rescued soon and she told us to memorize everything we could about our captors. Two of the creatures were captured when we were rescued and they were given that truth potion. They told us of their plans but they also told us of all their captive slaves, which include the tribe of Shettees. That is why the Rualas and Shettees are among us, we plan to free the slaves of Douma."

"Angels!" Joshua said in disbelief.

"Vivian is telling you the truth," Raphael said. "The Angels Miranda and Daniel have fought with us against demons before and they said they would help us enter Ogg and free the captives."

"This is rather unbelievable," Joshua said. "Yet I see the truth in both of your eyes. I heard the Sanuri say he wanted his men to relax and eat but I think we should tell him and Duncan to call this meeting soon."

Chapter X
Walking With Monsters

Joshua and Raphael left the house to speak with the Sanuri. Vivian stayed with her mother. "Your father and I like Raphael; he will be a good husband to you."

"Mother I know you were a hunter before you married Father. Did you feel like you were going crazy when you were falling in love with him?"

"I'm not sure what you mean?"

"I pursued Raphael at first, I was just having fun. But when I started to fall in love with him; I was so scared. I couldn't think, I couldn't be away from him for more than a few hours and I often felt weak when I was with him. Mother I have never felt weak before or not known what I was doing, it was awful."

Iris laughed loudly. "What you are describing is part of falling in love and yes I was like that with your father."

"When Raphael asked me to marry him, I was so scared because I didn't want to give up being a Venator, even though he told me we could hunt together. Then I went to a wedding and Raphael was performing the ceremony. Mother he is such a warrior that I had almost forgotten he was a priest too. When Raphael performed that ceremony it was like listening to the Angels sing, everyone was crying, and I don't know, it just made me love him even more."

"He loves you very much," Iris said. "You can see it in his eyes when he looks at you."

"And I love him. Mother you will never believe I am saying this but all I can think about is how I want to give him babies."

Iris laughed again and hugged her daughter, "You are right I never thought I would hear you say those words."

Raphael explained to the Sanuri that he told Joshua everything about the kidnappings and the bounties.

Joshua urged the Sanuri to speak with Duncan and to have the meeting at once. But the Sanuri wanted to wait. "Joshua I know your people, they will want to help us and their help will be welcomed. But your tribe does not often mingle with outsiders and I believe it is important for everyone here to bond first."

"Look around you, the competitions and games are forcing people to interact and work together. You can feel the excitement in the air, there are no hostilities here and that is the way it should be when we go into battle together. We will wait and have the meeting tonight," said the Sanuri.

"You have a point," Joshua said, then he paused. "They told me about Sampson also. While I am not surprised by what he did I believe we should tell Duncan."

"I already have," the Sanuri said. "Duncan sees the same darkness in Sampson that we do but he is a father and it is not easy for him to accept the behaviors of his son. Duncan will have to make some very important decisions one day and the consequences will weigh heavily upon him."

"Have you seen Sampson since you arrived at the village?" Joshua asked.

"No," the Sanuri said. "He is angry and feeling humiliated. I fear that when we see him next we should expect the worse."

"Raphael and Vivian will stay in her room," said Joshua. "I don't want them camping out here."

"I agree," the Sanuri said. Then he turned towards Raphael. "Do not think we believe you cannot defend yourself and Vivian; we want to avoid all problems."

"I understand," said Raphael. "And this is not the way I wanted to meet my new family and Vivian's tribe."

Philip lay on the floor of the cavern writhing in pain. The sweat poured out of his body as his muscles cramped up and sharp pains shot through him like hot irons.

Philip's body so craved the drug shartish that it could no longer function without the intoxicating effects of the poison. The demon Daegal was the only one who knew where Philip was hiding and Philip had not seen him in days.

"That bastard knows I need shartish," Philip yelled out loud as the pain and nausea wracked his body. So great was Philip's physical need for the drug that tremors and seizures attacked him again and again. Philip had lost all control of his bodily functions and now lay in his own human waste.

Philip was a brilliant physician who recognized his own greatness more than anyone else. His arrogance and inflated ego cost Philip not only his friends but also casual acquaintances. Being the Royal Court Physician had many benefits and Philip was constantly invited to balls and parties but as soon as he opened his mouth and started to sing his own praises he was abandoned by others.

The only one who never left Philip was his beloved wife Charlene who died in a boating accident with their two young sons Jack and Horace. Shortly after this tragic accident, when Philip was consumed with grief demons of all manner started to come to him.

Philip had always been a man with many personal demons so the realization that he was walking among the monsters seemed like an evolutionary step for him. Daegal was considerably more cunning than the other demons he was competing with for Philip. It was Daegal who orchestrated the boating accident that killed Philip's family; a fact that Philip was unaware of. Daegal worked for powerful masters who wanted information about the Sanuri and his relationship with the Royal Family of Wetpr.

Daegal had sent other spies to Sudfad's castle but each and every one of them had been discovered and put to death. Daegal then turned his attention to trusted staff who worked for the Royal Family but only Philip possessed the darkness of soul that allowed Daegal to turn him into a spy and betrayer.

It was the arrivals of Annabelle and Vitomas into the castle that started Philip's fall from grace with the Royal Family. Neither of the Princesses liked nor trusted Philip; it was as if they sensed the darkness within him.

The healer Gala was sent to Sudfad by The Lion to give Sudfad information and to save her from being murdered by King Roch. Gala had risked her life on many occasions to help Raul when he was a prisoner in Stordt and then again to help Simon and Raul as they searched for Vitomas. Raul had offered Gala a home in Salar as a free woman. King Sudfad and Queen Renya offered Gala a home at their castle.

Gala took over many of Philip's duties at the castle, not because she wanted Philip's position, but because the Royal Family respected and trusted her. Philip had entertained thoughts about having Gala murdered but then Matthew brought Angelina into the family. Angelina and her mother Shara were both powerful healers who the Royal Family turned to again and again.

Then as the final insult to Philip's ego, Sudfad and Renya adopted the Ruala warrior princess Ibula, whose power as a healer was not of the world of man. Philip found himself assigned to the medical needs of the soldiers instead of the Royal Family and revenge consumed him.

Philip felt great pleasure as he helped Daegal and the Valdees prepare the traps for the Royal Families of Wetpr and Lentz. And Philip became ecstatic when he was told there were now bounties on Gabriel's family, including Gabriel's wife Hannah, a physician with talents that rivaled Philip's. The sweet feeling of retribution that filled Philip's being suddenly crashed when Daegal came to him in the middle of the night and told Philip he was exposed and had to leave Salar at once.

Philip panicked, the paranoia caused by extensive use of shartish greatly enhanced his fears. In Philip's arrogance he had never considered that he could be exposed as a traitor or captured. Philip had no escape plans. He didn't have money hidden nor did he have a safe place to retreat to; so the demon who had promised Philip power and riches beyond his imagination hid Philip in a filthy, damp cave in the bowels of the earth. Philip, once one of the most respected men in the kingdom, shared his hideout with rats and snakes.

"Calen it's been almost a week," Hannah said. "When can we go home?"

"If we didn't have children we could consider the risk," Calen said. "But we don't know if the soldiers have caught all of the Valdees."

"You said they had almost eighty of those creatures in the dungeons didn't you?" Natasha asked as she cradled baby Lily. "When was the last time the soldiers found some?"

"Three days ago for us," Luca said. "But the soldiers in Lentz have been fighting with the Valdees all week and this morning at the meeting Sudfad said that the Nordes Tribe killed six yesterday."

"Thank The Great Ruler that Zoya had that vision; is all I can say," Emeral said. "You can't tell me someone isn't watching over us."

"I'll bet it was Miranda who gave her that vision," Natasha said. "How else would she know so many details?"

Lila entered the room. "I just wanted to check on the children," Lila said as she walked over to Luca and kissed him on the cheek. "Cerey is drawing with Raul's and Simon's boys and Nicholas and Christopher are playing in Petra's room. Have any of you ever seen Petra's room? It looks like a toy store."

"Petra is five years older than those two?" Natasha said. "You wouldn't think he would want to play with them."

"I think there is a little more to it," Emeral said. "Petra's parents were killed by Hutas also; all three of those boys lost their families and experienced horror. I think Petra is taking our boys under his wing like a big brother."

"I think you are right Emeral," Hannah said. "But I sense all the children are getting a little anxious since they aren't allowed to play outside." Hannah stood up. "Well, since Zoya and Delilah are in the castle also I don't have to drive so far to check on my patients. Do any of you want to come along for a visit?"

"I will," said Emeral.

"I would but Lily just fell asleep," Natasha said.

"I swear I never heard of a baby who never wanted to sleep before. She has us up all night and still barely sleeps during the day."

"She's healthy," Hannah said. "She's growing and gaining weight just fine. Maybe she will grow out of it."

"All of our children better not be like this," Natasha joked to Calen, who grinned at her remark.

Lila leaned down and whispered into Luca's ear which made him smile. "Go ahead," he said. "But we don't know for sure."

"I think I am pregnant," Lila said happily. "It's early yet so I am not totally positive. But we are so happy." Everyone in the room smiled and hugged both Lila and Luca.

"So you are going to have the second baby that is part human and part Ruala," Natasha said with a grin. "I'll tell you, when I found out that Calen and I were having the first I was really nervous because I didn't know what to expect."

"They're having the third," Calen said. "I got a letter from Rabi this morning, he and Marcia are expecting too."

"And you didn't tell us Calen, let me see that letter," Hannah scolded. "I can't believe Marcia didn't write and tell me; we were such good friends."

Calen laughed loudly as he handed the letter to Hannah, "Read for yourselves; Rabi's letter is two sentences long."

Hannah laughed and read out loud, *We are having a baby. Marcia's letters are so long I couldn't wait to tell you. Rabi.*

Daegal laughed when he found Philip's cold body. "That arrogant son of a bitch; look at him now," the demon said out loud and continued to laugh. Daegal searched Philip's pockets and took everything of value, then he spit on the body and left the cavern.

"How are you feeling?" Hannah asked as she was examining Zoya. "I am nauseous all the time and Delilah is hardly ever nauseous is that a bad sign?"

"Everyone is different," Hannah explained. "Delilah has had a pretty easy pregnancy so far but that can always change. Are you still feeling so tired?"

"Not all the time," Zoya said. "It's kind of frustrating because I can't get as much done as I want to. But Delilah is a lot of help. I am glad she is staying with us."

"Delilah told me how grateful she is that you and Jared have taken her in while Archetenus is gone," Hannah said. "She didn't want to be alone."

"Hannah don't tell Jared that I told you this," Zoya said and started laughing. "You know what a big, tough man he is; he is so nervous with Delilah and me both being pregnant. It's like he is afraid we are going to break or something. Delilah and I tease him all of the time."

"Jared loves you very much. Did he ever have children with his first wife?"

"No, and I didn't have any with my first husband; so this baby is the first for both of us. We are so excited."

"Well, you certainly seem healthy. I will continue to check on both of you every day but don't wait for my visit if something seems wrong. And if you just want to come and visit us you are more than welcome. I think we are all feeling a little trapped because Sudfad doesn't want us to leave the castle."

"I think it is so gracious of him and Renya to let us stay here," Zoya said. "I was terrified when I started to have those visions of the Valdees."

"Well, thank The Great Ruler you did or they would have attacked us in our sleep," Hannah said then she paused and stared at Zoya. "Are you having a vision now, you have that distant look again?"

Zoya didn't answer for several moments. "Yes, Hannah and I think it was for you. I saw Gabriel, Raphael and the others in a village. I assume it is Vivian's village because the last letter we got from Archetenus said they would be staying there for a day or two. They all looked normal but a voice said to me to tell them that more than one monster walks among them."

"Did you see the monster?" Hannah asked with concern.

"No, I told you everything I saw."

"What was Gabriel doing in your vision?"

"It looked like they were all having a meeting, like they do here," Zoya said. I saw everyone from here but no one else, I mean no strangers."

Just as the grand meeting with the Clan of Gesmal and the leaders of Claudius' army was about to commence a flock of Enrops flew over the group. No one spoke as they watched the giant birds land. Many of the birds carried letters in their beaks. Arca the leader of this flock did not carry anything and was the first to speak. "Great numbers of Valdees have attacked Wetpr and Lentz. But the seer Zoya had a vision and both Sudfad and Mathas had time to prepare."

Raul took a letter from one of the birds and read it as Arca talked. "Our families are all safe and staying at the castle. Father's army killed many and took many prisoners, the dungeons are filled."

"I have a letter from Mathas," Claudius announced. "Zoya warned them about attacks that were to take place at night. She even told Mathas and Sudfad where they could find the Valdees. Mathas says that everything Zoya said came true. Mathas said they killed three hundred creatures the first night and the fighting is still going on. Sorren, your tribe has also been battling the creatures but the numbers attacking your village are much smaller."

"So this is no longer about kidnapping," the Sanuri said.

"If Douma is sending his warriors to attack Lentz and Wetpr he must know that Sudfad and Mathas have declared war against him. And he must also know that we are coming for him."

"I want to know how he is getting this information," Sorren roared. "We must have spies in the kingdoms."

"We know something is watching us," Claudius said. "Because they sent the Hutas and Valdees after us. Sanuri is it possible for a demon to watch us even though we haven't seen any ravens?"

"Yes, if it is a powerful demon."

Thedes jumped to his feet. "Sanuri, I worry that Douma will kill the captives before we can free them."

Angelina stood up, "Thedes we are all afraid of that but think about what Miranda said to us. She wants us to free the captives, so I would have faith that they live."

"Do you have messages for us to take to with us?" Arca asked.

"Duncan can we delay this meeting for an hour while we write letters?" the Sanuri asked.

"Of course," Duncan said. "Everyone can return to the celebrations." As the people left the meeting area Duncan once again looked for his son Sampson in the crowd. Sampson's absence caused Duncan great concern.

After the flock of Enrops left the village headed for the Kingdoms of Wetpr and Lentz, Duncan and the Sanuri met in private. They decided to once again postpone the meeting to allow everyone to partake of the feast. Prior to this, the celebration had consisted of many contests and competitions but now the pigs were roasted and the food prepared.

Before the people ate many toasts were said; to new friends, to victory in battle, to the marriage of Raphael and Vivian, to the unborn sons of Mathew and Angelina and Thaos and Nikki. With every toast Sampson uttered a curse from the shadows of the forest that surrounded his village. So enraged was Sampson that his hands shook violently.

His village would have welcomed him but Sampson chose to isolate himself because he did not want to give credence to Vivian's marriage to Raphael. Years Sampson had waited to take Vivian for his wife. Years he had to put up with the humiliation that her father would not sell her to him. And years he watched as she became a popular and renowned Venator among his clan, a position that prevented him from taking her by force.

Sampson was a strong and courageous warrior, who would someday be chief of his clan. While many women would have been honored to become his wife, there were many others who feared that Sampson would want them; for Sampson had never masked his darkness and cruelty.

Sampson had taken many women; mostly by force but Vivian was the only woman he ever wanted to marry. The fact that he could not control Vivian made Sampson want her more. And now he watched from the shadows as Vivian and Raphael kissed and held hands in front of the other villagers. Sampson turned and mounted his horse, then rode south towards the Tnges Gold Mines.

The feast lasted for two hours after which the Sanuri announced that the meeting that had been anticipated all day would include all the Clan of Gesmal and the visitors instead of just the leaders of that community. The villagers felt honored to be included in such an important meeting so everyone attended except for Sampson and his absence was greatly noticed.

The Sanuri was the first speaker, he told of Juleta and the bounties that were placed on the ruling families of Lentz. He told the Clan of Gesmal about the Royal Family of Wetpr and their battles against the demons and the dark lords. The Sanuri talked about Gabriel, Raphael and their elite team of demon hunters; who also had bounties put upon them by the demon Hecate.

Then the Sanuri changed the subjects and talked about the history of both the Ruala Tribe and the Shettee Tribe. The Sanuri told the people that he was proud that the Rualas and Shettees had found ways to overcome their differences and to blend into a strong and noble culture.

The Sanuri finished his speech by telling the villagers about the bonds that the Rualas and Shettees had made with the ruling families of both Lentz and Wetpr. The Sanuri then asked Archetenus, Matthew, Gabriel and Raphael to speak about their encounters with the holy messengers of The Great Ruler. The villagers were both captivated and skeptical as they listened to these four men speak.

Then the Sanuri asked Angelina and Vivian to stand up and to describe in detail their kidnappings and contacts with Miranda. This was the first that Vivian's brothers or Duncan had heard about the kidnappings because the Sanuri had requested the subject not be spoken of until the meeting. As the two women spoke the villagers became enraged that the Valdees would kidnap a Venator.

Claudius stood up and told the villagers about their journey westward, the battles and the bodies of the Valdees and Hutas that were discovered. Claudius also told the villagers that the army he led consisted of troops from Lentz, Wetpr and the Ice Caves and they were headed to Ogg to overthrow Douma and to free his slaves.

The Sanuri stood up once again, "We have come to you to both warn you about the Valdees and to ask for your help. Our numbers are great yet you possess knowledge which we do not have. Will you speak to the leaders which I have brought before you and give them information which will help in our mission?"

Duncan now stood up and looked around him at the faces of his clan. Then he looked at the Sanuri and smiled. "Old friend of course we will give you as much information as we can but I believe you would dishonor my people if you did not give them the opportunity to fight at your side." Duncan once again looked at the members of his clan who sat in silent anticipation. "The Valdees have been our enemies since we can remember. Who of you here would like to stand with the Sanuri and his friends in this war?"

Venator after Venator stood up and took a knife from their belt and thrust it into the ground; this act symbolized their intent of joining the battle. And those who were no longer hunters because they chose to raise families, such as Vivian's father, now stood up and they too thrust their knives into the ground.

The Sanuri smiled proudly as he watched the Venatores then he turned and looked at Claudius and the others. "My brethren much more has transpired here than you realize. There is an ancient prophesy that brings terror to the hearts of the demons and the dark lords. It is called the Prophesy of The Seven Sons and it foretells of a time when good men and women unit from different cultures and different worlds to stand against the darkness that attacks them. Tonight you are fulfilling that prophesy. The bonds of brotherhood that have been forged here cannot be broken."

Sampson tied his horse before the entrance of a small mine; the opening was barely visible from the road. He grabbed a lit torch that was inserted in a metal ring in the stone wall of the mine and proceeded to walk into the bowels of the pit. Sampson passed several more lit torches as he descended into the earth. The dank smell of decay filled his nostrils and made his eyes water.

"I knew you were coming," a woman's voice said as Sampson entered a well-lit cavern that was decorated with rich carpets and furniture. Sampson put his torch into a metal holder attached to the wall and walked up to the woman. He took her into his arms and kissed her passionately.

"You kiss me yet your heart cries out for another," Hecate said suggestively. "You are a man who is torn between two worlds." Hecate was an ancient demon from a hell dimension in the world of Sidus. She came to the World of Nunc hundreds of years prior to this night. Hecate followed her lover; a demon named Orbus to Nunc but soon left him for another.

Hecate normally took on the form of a human woman when she interacted with the inhabitants of Nunc. Like most demons, Hecate preyed upon the desires and weaknesses of men, the illusion she presented was that of a beautiful seductress; one which few men could resist.

Sampson and Hecate had been lovers for months; he was intoxicated with her beauty and sexuality. But Hecate was not the cause of the darkness that ruled Sampson's soul, she merely played upon it.

While Hecate often changed her appearance, Sampson had only seen her as a shapely woman with long dark hair and blue eyes. He never realized that she took on a similar appearance to Vivian, who had long been Sampson's desire.

Sampson was well aware that Hecate was a demon, a fact he had known since his first encounter with her; when she called to him from the darkness. Sampson had just raped a woman in a neighboring village and was riding back to his home when he heard a woman's voice calling his name. At first Sampson thought it was the wind but the voice persisted until he followed it to a nearby pond.

Hecate took Sampson to her lair that night and he stayed with her for a week. After that first encounter, Sampson visited Hecate on a regular basis. They're sexual relationship was intense and sometimes afterwards Sampson felt as if Hecate was draining him of his life source.

"Tell me my love, what distresses you so?" Hecate asked. Sampson hesitated because he had never spoken to her about Vivian. Hecate handed Sampson a glass of whiskey. "Sampson I know your heart belongs to another and I am alright with that. Is she the cause of your distress?"

Sampson felt uncomfortable talking about his feelings for Vivian to Hecate. "She has returned to the village with a husband," Sampson said softly then his voice loudly raised as did his anger. "I was to be her husband!"

"Was she promised to you?"

"No but I planned to take her."

"And what prevents you from taking her now?"

"She and her husband travel with a great army."

"Why?" Hecate asked.

"I do not know," Sampson replied. "I have stayed away from the village."

"I would very much like to know about this army," Hecate cooed as she rubbed Sampson's back.

"Why?" Sampson growled.

"I have my reasons," Hecate said then she paused. "Perhaps we can help each other."

"What do you mean?"

"If you get me information about that army, I can help you get rid of Vivian's husband."

"How do you know her name? I have never said it to you."

"My dear I am a demon; I know many things. So do we have a deal?"

Raphael and Vivian barely had the door closed to her bedroom before they started making love. "I've been wanting to do this all day," Vivian said as she kissed Raphael again and again. "I hope they can't hear us through the walls." Both Vivian and Raphael laughed at this remark.

"I love you so much," he whispered into Vivian's ear before their desires overwhelmed them."

Archetenus suddenly sat up and listened to the night sounds as every nerve in his body was on alert. He was not sure what woke him and as he looked around at the others sleeping near the campfire, they seemed undisturbed. Archetenus was not a paranoid man, but a man who lived by his instincts and right now he had a very bad feeling. After a moment, Miranda's voice came to Archetenus from the darkness but he did not see her.

"Archetenus wake the others and prepare for battle; the creatures come from the south, from the gold mines."

Gabriel lay closest to Archetenus on his right and Simon on his left. Archetenus woke Gabriel first, then Simon and each man woke others. Archetenus called out to Miranda, "The armies."

"They are awake, although they do not understand that I woke them. But the beasts are not sent after them. You have fought monsters before, the beasts can be slain." Now the warriors who were awake also heard the Angel's voice.

Raphael sat up in bed with such a jolt that he woke Vivian who was sleeping in his arm. "Raphael what is it?"

"I don't know what woke me." Then they heard a blood curdling scream coming from the forest followed by yelps. Both Raphael and Vivian jumped out of bed and grabbed their clothes and weapons.

When Raphael and Vivian ran out of her bedroom they found her parents and brothers up. Joshua, Micha and Thomas were grabbing their weapons when Gabriel knocked on the door. Iris opened the door. Gabriel did not enter but said, "The Angel Miranda warned us that beasts have been sent to attack us. They come from the gold mines."

"Rogetts?" Joshua asked as he appeared in the doorway.

"We don't know," Gabriel said. "But I have never heard Rogetts scream like that."

"We must wake the others," Joshua said.

"We are," Gabriel replied and disappeared into the night.

The Guniar trampled through the forest with great speed for such heavy creatures. Driven by hatred and starvation the hell beasts were not distracted as they followed the orders of their mistress. Sampson followed the creatures on horseback but his horse was so terrified by the monsters that Sampson had to put more distance between them than he would have liked.

Hecate had ordered the Guniar not to harm Sampson for he still had his half of the bargain to keep. Sampson rode with the beasts because he wanted to see them kill Raphael and he wanted to be the hero to save Vivian and some of the others.

As the Guniar approached the village they could smell the foods from the feast and human flesh; these smells prompted them to run faster. The Guniar were large, heavy creatures that ran on four legs. They were not stealthy like a big cat; their advance was more like a stampede of wild bulls. Claudius and the others hid in the shadows as they watched the beasts enter the village. The Guniar resembled giant boars with long treacherous fangs and long hair that hung in matted clumps from their bodies.

The hell beasts went immediately to the campfires where Archetenus and the others had been sleeping. Raul had told everyone to make up their beds to appear they were still sleeping in them. The Guniar stomped on and gouged the empty blankets, then screamed with rage when they realized their meal was missing. The Guniar now turned their attention towards the small houses of the village.

"Release!" Claudius bellowed and torrents of arrows and spears rained upon the hell beasts. The war cries of the Venatores and the other warriors collided in the cool night air with the screams of the Guniar. The sounds of battle were carried on the night wind and Sampson suddenly knew something had gone wrong. He now sped towards his village.

The hides of the Guniar were tough but not impenetrable. The beasts now ran wildly through the village as they were being attacked. The soldiers camped outside of the village now joined the battle, riding up to the Guniar on horseback and stabbing them with their swords. Several Guniar turned and charged at the riders, while the others stampeded through the village trampling anything in their paths.

Many warriors ran up to the Guniar and stabbed them or got their attention to divert the direction in which they were running. The Rualas flew over the beasts and showered them with arrows. The Guniar were aggressive creatures and lunged at every human they spied. Six Guniar had run into the area where the feast had been held which was a large open area with multiple fire pits and long tables. The beasts smelled the food from the feast and were tearing apart the area.

Many warriors followed the Guniar into that area and attacked them. Chief Duncan, Joshua, Vivian, Raphael and Simon were among them. All of these warriors were on foot and stabbed at the great beasts.

Suddenly Sampson rode into the midst of this area and yelled for Vivian to get onto his horse. Vivian continued to fight the Guniar but stopped briefly when she saw how the beasts were acting around Sampson. "Father look at Sampson," Vivian yelled and the eyes of all witnessed the same behavior. Suddenly Raphael pulled Vivian close to him as a Guniar was running towards her. Maxwell landed on top of the beast and plunged his sword through its brain; the monster fell just feet from its intended prey.

Sampson never took a sword against the beasts and when the battle was over his father, Chief Duncan confronted Sampson before all eyes. "My son what have you done!" Duncan bellowed as he walked towards Sampson, who was still mounted on his horse.

"What are you accusing me of?" Sampson yelled back defensively.

"These creatures are not from this world," Duncan said loudly. "Yet they attack everyone except you. And you do not raise a weapon against them. What demons do you consort with?"

"You are a liar!" Sampson yelled.

"We all saw it," Joshua said as he too walked towards Sampson. "The evil within you is worse than we thought."

Duncan grabbed the reigns of Sampson's horse. "You set monsters upon your own people for what; a woman who despises you? You are no leader and you will never þe chief. From this night you are banished from this village and you are no longer a member of the Clan of Gesmal."

Sampson deliberately made his horse rear up on its hind legs and knock Duncan to the ground. Duncan quickly rolled to the left to avoid being struck by the horse's hooves. Joshua and Raphael ran towards Sampson but Misha was the closest.

Misha flew over Sampson and knocked him off from his horse, as Sampson tried to trample his father.

Villagers, warriors and soldiers filled the area where the feast was held. Sampson hit the ground but went immediately into a forward roll and was back on his feet in seconds. One of the soldiers ran forward but Claudius held him back. "Let them take care of their own," Claudius said loudly to his men. Micha, Vivian's older brother threw a knife at Sampson that hit him in his right shoulder.

Sampson cursed and came towards Micha then realized he was encircled by all of the warriors of his village. Sampson quickly ran to his horse and mounted him. "This is not over!" Sampson bellowed and charged his horse through the crowd.

"Let him go," Duncan yelled as he saw some of the villagers start to chase Sampson.

"I do not think that is wise," Joshua said as he helped Duncan to his feet.

"He is my son," Duncan said sadly. "I am not ready to have him put to death."

Chapter XI
Seduction

"You failed me!" Sampson screamed as he ran into Hecate's lair. "Everything is ruined now because of you."

Hecate was standing before a fire with a glass of wine in her hand. She initially did not turn and look at Sampson as he entered the cavern yelling; now she slowly turned as she heard him running towards her. Just as Sampson was reaching his hands towards Hecate's throat she mumbled a few words and the powerful warrior fell to the ground writhing in pain. Hecate smiled as she watched him.

"Sampson I am a demon, not one of those fragile human women that you beat and rape and you will not treat me as such. And it is time you acted like a man and take responsibility for your own actions. I am not responsible for the choices you have made. But I was drawn to you because of them. And from the sounds of it you have failed me also. If you are willing to calmly discuss the happenings of this night I will let you up and offer you a drink."

As angry as Sampson was with Hecate, the pain she inflicted on him was overwhelming. He endured it for a few more moments then nodded his head and said through clenched teeth, "I agree." Instantly the pain that attacked him was gone. Sampson scowled at her as he slowly rose to a standing position. Hecate picked up a glass of whiskey that she already had poured and handed it to him.

"Now that we understand each other; tell me what happened tonight?"

"If you are such a powerful demon don't you know?" Sampson asked sarcastically.

Hecate smiled. "I know I have wounded your pride but you will just have to get over it. I have many powers but being all knowing is not one of them."

"They were waiting for us," Sampson said angrily then gulped down his whiskey.

"What do you mean?" Hecate asked with surprise.

"I mean just what I said. The entire village was in the shadows waiting for us. Your magical beasts were slaughtered like flies and when I rode into the village to save Vivian, they all saw that the beasts did not attack me and I did not raise a weapon against them. My father has now disinherited me and banished me from the village. My brother will be chief and Vivian is still with her husband. Perhaps you aren't as powerful as you think."

Now it was Hecate who became filled with anger. "How could they have known?" she screamed and paced back and forth; then she turned again to Sampson. "Did you find out why that army is in your village?"

"No," Sampson said as he filled his glass with more whiskey. "Seriously you knew they were coming, I thought you knew more about them."

"My spies have been watching them but I know nothing else," Hecate said with frustration. "Someone is interfering with my plans; I sent an army of Valdees against them and all the Valdees were killed by Hutas. Hutas! How could that have happened?"

"There are many bands of Hutas roaming the kingdoms," Sampson said as he again poured more whiskey into his glass.

"You do not understand," Hecate said with frustration. "Hutas are the pawns of demons. Another demon stopped the Valdees from attacking that army; but why would a demon protect them?"

Chief Duncan sat in his home, overwhelmed with humiliation and grief at the betrayal of his eldest son. Duncan's wife Liza and their two other sons George and Ivan sat in silence with their father. Finally Ivan the youngest spoke because the pain he saw in his parent's eyes broke his heart.

"You both blame yourselves for Sampson's actions. You are good parents and Father you are a great chief. George and I have not been filled with the darkness that flows through Sampson. We all know he has been evil since he was a child. It is like he is not part of our family."

"You speak the truth, yet the pain is still very real," Duncan said. "George you will be chief one day which means Sampson may try to kill you; both of my sons, you must be careful."

"Father you are not telling Ivan and me anything we did not already know. We have kept many things from you because we did not want to hurt you but Sampson has already threatened both of us. He said that when he became chief he would banish us from this village," George said.

The burden of his sadness weighed upon Duncan as he said, "Sons it is time for you to tell me everything."

No one returned to bed after the battle. The men dragged the bodies of the hell beasts out of the village while the woman started the fires and breakfast. Matthew, Stephan and Thaos were returning to the village for another body when Sorren passed them. "You boys should talk to your wives," Sorren said.

"Are they alright?" Matthew asked with concern.

"Physically yes, but you need to talk to them," Sorren said then walked over to a couple of villagers to help them drag a Guniar through the street.

"Why the long faces?" Thaos asked as he, Matthew and Stephan found their wives sitting around a fire.

"We really miss our babies," Ingr said as she was about to cry. Stephan walked over to Ingr and put his arm around her.

Nikki quickly swung her head around so she was looking at Thaos, "Don't you miss Titus?"

"Of course I do Nikki," Thaos said and sat down next to her, taking her hand.

Matthew opened his mouth to speak but Angelina interrupted him. "Matthew I know what you are about to say. Nikki and I are both pregnant so we are more emotional but Ingr is just as sad as we are."

Matthew put his arm around Angelina's shoulders. "I was about to ask if you want the Rualas to take you home."

"We have already been thinking about that," Nikki said when Dagon ran into their campsite.

"Angelina come quickly, Ibula is having her baby," Dagon said excitedly.

"Let me grab my bag," Angelina said as everyone jumped up from the fire and followed Dagon. They found Ibula drenched with sweat, lying on the ground with Thedes next to her holding her hand. In moments the entire village knew that Ibula was in labor. Joshua and Iris ran to Ibula and Thedes.

"Vivian is preparing a room," Joshua said. "You're not giving birth in the dirt."

"Thank you," Thedes said and picked Ibula up.

"Thedes I can walk," Ibula said sharply.

"I don't care, I am carrying you," Thedes replied and followed Joshua and Iris.

"The room belongs to our two youngest boys and was a little messy," Iris said apologetically.

"Where will they sleep?" asked Ibula.

"They want to camp out with the rest of you," Joshua said with a grin as he led the small procession to his home.

"Wait just a moment," Vivian said as she finished putting clean bedding on the mattress. Raphael was bringing chairs into the small bedroom. "We have water on the fire."

Simon, Raul, Archetenus and Gabriel had dragged a Guniar to the area where they were to be burned when they saw a crowd gathering around Joshua's house. Fearing the worse all four men ran to the house and pushed through the crowd. "What is going on?" Raul yelled.

"Calm down," Thaos said. "Ibula is having a baby."

Raul and Simon entered the bedroom and walked up to Ibula's bed. "Is there anything we can do for you?" Raul asked.

"Yes," Ibula said with a smile. "Please take care of my husband for me, he is so worried."

"We can do that," Simon said with a grin. "Although we act just the same when our wives give birth."

Thedes now spoke to everyone in the room. "This is the first baby that is half Shettee and half Ruala, we don't know what to expect."

The Sanuri walked into the bedroom, "Joshua, Iris a new race is coming to life in your house this day; I believe that is cause for a celebration."

Joshua smiled broadly and yelled to his two oldest sons, "Micha, Thomas prepare a pig."

"I'll help the boys," Sorren said with a grin and left the house with Joshua's sons.

Angelina was out of her momentary depression and back to herself. "I know Ibula appreciates everyone's concerns but this is a small room and we need some space to move. Vivian I also need some herbs. Do you have any Tinchure plants near here?"

"I know where there is some," Adrone, Vivian's youngest brother said.

"We'll go with him," Elan said and took the boy by the hand.

"Are we going to fly again?" Adrone asked excitedly which made everyone in the room smile.

"Elan and Cassandra have been flying with many of the children," Iris said smiling as she brought an armful of towels into the bedroom. "I don't think any of them will ever be the same again."

"Someone should tell Gael," Ibula said to Thedes. "My brother is a healer too."

"Misha is getting him," Dagon said.

"Really I need most of you to leave this room now because I need to examine her," Angelina said.

As news spread through the village that Ibula's baby would be the first of a new race entering this world, the Clan of Gesmal became proud and excited. The men repaired the tables and fire pits in their meeting area as the women prepared food for a feast to celebrate the birth of Thedes' and Ibula's baby.

Sampson's anger was no match for his desires for Hecate and their fighting seemed to intensify their passions. Sometimes when Sampson made love to her he pretended Hecate was Vivian an illusion that the demon planned. Hecate's lair was so far underground that it was impossible to tell if it was day or night above ground. Sampson and Hecate made love for hours; when he awoke she was not lying next to him.

Sampson left her bed and walked through the cavern without finding Hecate. He left her lair and was almost to the opening to the mine when he heard chanting coming from his left. Sampson walked towards the sound and found Hecate in a smaller cavern; she was kneeling before an unholy altar and praying to demon's more powerful than herself.

Hecate heard Sampson enter the cavern and stopped chanting. "Go back to our bed," she said. "I will be there shortly." Sampson had never taken orders from a woman before but then he had to keep reminding himself that Hecate was not a woman. He turned and returned to her lair. Before he could drink a glass of whiskey, Hecate had returned to him.

"Do not follow me to that room again," she said sternly.

"You do not want me to see you praying?"

"It is not safe for you to be in there."

"Who does a demon pray to anyways?"

"The Old Ones, demons with more power than you can even imagine," Hecate said and sat down on the bed next to Sampson. "I am a powerful demon but I am nothing compared to the Old Ones. To have a human walk in on a ceremony as I was performing could be disastrous. At the very least the demon would kill you."

"And you would not save me?" Sampson asked sarcastically.

"Truthfully I am very fond of you but you and I are not of the same worlds. You act as if you rule all in your world and you have no understanding how dangerous it is for you in my world," Hecate said and kissed Sampson on the cheek. "I was trying to find out what demon is protecting that army and why."

"Are you sure it is not the Sanuri who is protecting it?"

"Oh he is to a point," Hecate said. "But there is much more going on here. Sampson you are a man who desires power. Tell me what it is you want besides that girl."

"I want to be chief of my tribe," Sampson said angrily.

"You have such limited vision, I am surprised."

"What do you mean?"

"You could be so much more than a chief of a tiny village," Hecate said. "You could be a powerful dark lord, a war lord or a king with my help."

"And what price would I have to pay?"

"Everything comes with a price," she said. "But for now I would like you to be the eyes and ears where I cannot go. I will pay you handsomely for your service."

"Angelina I have seen you give this tonic to others but I never realized how wonderful it is. I want to take plants back to the Ice Caves. I feel little pain, yet I am not tired; in fact I feel renewed."

"Mother is making more of it for you," Vivian said. "We had no knowledge of its use. But our people will make it now. There are plenty of Tinchure plants near our village; I will have my brothers dig some up for you."

"Our tribe has been making that tonic since before I was born," Angelina said with pride.

"Where is Thedes?" asked Ibula.

"There is a meeting between the villagers and our people," Nikki said. "The Venatores are telling Claudius and the others everything they know about the Valdees. Thaos said that Raul and Simon took Thedes to that meeting to get his mind off from you."

"I really don't think that is going to work," Ingr said and laughed.

"You girls should go to that meeting, I am fine," Ibula said.

"Our husbands can tell us the information," Nikki said. "We aren't leaving you."

"Ibula besides that you are our friend," Ingr said. "You helped save me when I was stabbed, you helped deliver the twins and you helped deliver Nikki's son. We aren't going to let you go through this alone."

There was a knock at the door. "It's Iris and Joshua," a woman's voice said. Angelina was closest to the door and opened it. Joshua carried a wooden cradle into the room and Iris carried a basket. "We were saving these things for our first grandchild," Iris said. "But I guess we are all family now." Ibula smiled as Iris handed her a basket filled with baby blankets and clothes. Joshua put the cradle on the floor then placed several small blankets inside it.

"These are beautiful," Ibula said as she held up a few of the items for the others to see. "But Iris are you sure you want to give them away?"

"You saved our daughter," Joshua said. "The least we can do is to give you some blankets and clothing for your baby."

Ibula was touched by Joshua's comment. "Thedes and I thank you and appreciate these gifts. I hate to admit it but I brought nothing for the baby. Rualas carry their babies longer than Shettees or humans; I did not expect the baby to come so soon."

"Which reminds me," Angelina said. "I asked your brother to come back when the baby is coming. I have delivered many human babies but if there is something different with your child I do not want to make any mistakes."

"That is probably wise," Ibula said. "Although I feel very good."

"Thedes is worried that the baby will be too big for you because he is so large," Ingr said as she looked at some of the baby clothes Iris gave to Ibula. "Now this is making me miss my babies."

Nikki looked at Iris and Joshua and explained, "We all have babies at home; Ingr has twins. I have a son and Angelina has a baby girl and a small boy they adopted. Now that Vivian and Angelina are safe we are really missing our children."

"You must be wonderful friends to leave your babies to help find Vivian and Angelina," Iris said warmly.

Angelina turned to Ibula, "So we are all going to want to hold your baby because we miss ours," she said and smiled.

Joshua turned to his daughter, "You and Raphael are so much in love, have you talked about a family?"

Vivian smiled then looked at the other girls before answering her father's question. "My parents never thought I would take a husband, I think they are still in shock by all this." Vivian laughed then turned to her father. "We both want to have a baby as soon as we can and he did not talk me into it I want the same thing." Both Joshua and Iris smiled.

"She's right," Iris said. "I never thought those words would come out of her mouth. Both Joshua and I were Venatores but we stopped hunting once we started to have babies. And Vivian told us nothing would ever make her stop hunting."

"I can't go back to my village and spy on that army," Sampson said angrily. "I have been cast out."

"Is there another way you could spy on them?"

"I could follow them," Sampson said. "But Hecate they have Enrops and Rualas in the sky and many warriors on the ground, to say nothing about the Sanuri. I could never get close enough to find out any information."

"Isn't there anyone in that village who would give you information?"

"I tried to kill my father when he dishonored me," Sampson said with shame. "My father is loved by our people." Sampson stared at Hecate for a few moments. "You have told me many times how powerful you are yet you can't find a way to get the information you seek. I don't understand that." Hecate gave Sampson a look of disapproval at his comment. Sampson sat down on her bed and pulled Hecate onto his lap.

"I am not trying to anger you," Sampson continued. "I have never met a demon before and there are many things I do not understand about you."

"I am willing to bet you have met demons before, you just didn't realize it," Hecate said as she realized Sampson was being genuine in his curiosity. "Just like people, there are many types of demons with different levels of power."

"How do you get your powers?"

"Sometimes from more powerful demons like the Old Ones but each of us are created with certain powers and skills just like humans," Hecate could see that Sampson was confused by what she was saying. "Think of it as warriors in your tribe, one might excel in strength and another in running, it is the same concept."

"And can someone take your powers away?"

"Yes, but that being would have to be very powerful."

"Is the Sanuri powerful enough?"

Hecate stared at Sampson for several moments; he could see the anger in her eyes. "Yes," she responded through clenched teeth. "My last husband Sporos was a powerful demon and the Sanuri defeated him in battle and imprisoned him in The Abyss."

"So that is what this is all about," Sampson said. "You want revenge against the Sanuri."

"And there are others within that group that I want. Sampson you have been so consumed with jealousy over Vivian that you have not clearly looked at what is before your eyes. That man she married is a very powerful high priest of The Great Ruler as is his friend Gabriel."

"Many of the people that are in your village were involved in a phenomenal battle in Taperia. The priests' numbers were few yet they battled thousands of demons and won. How can that happen?" Hecate asked angrily. "And when that battle was over one of the Old Ones, Ahriman, a great demon that I was aligned with was imprisoned in The Abyss. That is why I am so curious that those same humans are travelling to your village."

A surge of fear ran through Sampson. "Vivian is part of that group now; do you mean to kill her also?"

"The Valdees had taken Vivian and one other as captives. Even though the Valdees traveled underwater that group, those damn priests reclaimed the girls. But they did not return home after they got their wives."

"This just happened?"

"Weeks ago."

"Hecate you treat me as a fool. The Valdees only leave their world to do the bidding of demons. If they took Vivian and another it was because a demon told them to do so." Sampson's face was red with anger and his voice was getting louder. "You want to destroy Vivian's husband, did you order the Valdees to take her?" Hecate did not answer Sampson. She did not fear that Sampson could hurt her but Hecate still had use for him and did not want to lose her puppet. "Damn you Hecate answer me!"

"Yes I put a bounty on her."

157

"Because of me or because she is married to the priest?"

"She is not only married to the priest but she fights at his side, although I don't believe she was at the battle in Taperia."

"Of course she fights at his side, she is a Venator. You lied to me, you promised me Vivian and all the while you had a bounty on her. Is that bounty still on her?" Sampson demanded.

"Yes."

Sampson quickly stood up, knocking Hecate to the floor. "Take the bounty off Vivian," he said through clenched teeth. Hecate smiled seductively and held her hand up for Sampson to help her stand up.

"I will take the bounty off from your love as soon as you bring me information about why that army is in your village meeting with your chief."

Thedes left the meeting and ran to the home of Joshua and Iris so he could see Ibula. To Thedes' surprise Ibula was sitting up in bed talking to visitors and looking much better than she previously looked. "Has something happened?" Thedes asked with concern as he knelt next to her bed.

Ibula laughed and kissed her husband. "No, Angelina gave me a tonic that has helped me greatly."

"I would like to learn more of that tonic," Prince Gael said to his sister Ibula as he entered the room. "You look much improved."

"We will send plants home with you," Vivian said. "There are many near our village."

"Thedes look at what Joshua and Iris gave us," Ibula said as she pointed to the cradle and the basket of blankets and clothing.

Thedes did not look through the basket but continued to hold Ibula's hand. He turned and looked at Joshua and Iris who were sitting in the room. "Tell me how I can repay you for all of the kindness you have shown to us."

"You helped to save our daughter," Joshua said. "The few things we have done are nothing in comparison."

Suddenly Ibula had another contraction and squeezed Thedes' hand tightly as the pain surged through her. "Is she alright?" Thedes asked frantically.

"Yes," Angelina said. "But she just had a contraction moments before you entered the room. I should examine her again. "Gael would you like to stay?"

Sampson left Hecate's lair in the Tnges Gold Mines and rode north towards his village. He was filled with anger and torn by his desires. Sampson was not a stupid man; he knew Vivian did not love him. Any illusions he may have had about being the desire of Vivian's heart were shattered when he saw her and Raphael together. But Sampson was a controlling man and still planned to take Vivian for himself.

Hecate was everything that Sampson was raised to hate and fear; yet she brought him such pleasure. Hecate knew his desires and offered him great things. Sampson believed that Hecate had the power to give him what he wanted. And the longer he was with her the more he desired her. Sampson had stayed most nights with Hecate since he met her. The sex was like nothing he had ever experienced before but over the months he was forming a bond with this demon.

Suddenly a thought jolted through Sampson causing him to stop his horse. Could he take Vivian and force her to be his wife and still have Hecate as his lover? Would he have to choose between the two women? Sampson had been obsessed with Vivian for so long that he had never thought about taking another for his wife but Hecate could fulfill his dreams.

Raul and Simon had to restrain Thedes to keep him from barging into the bedroom when they heard Ibula's screams. Nikki, Ingr, Angelina, Vivian and Gael were in the small room with Ibula.

"Thedes, both Gael and Angelina are powerful healers," Thaos said as he tried to calm his friend.

159

"I just don't know what to expect," Thedes said. "Ibula is such a tiny woman and look at me; I fear the baby may be too big for her."

"The Sanuri is also here," Sorren said. "Son, she will be alright."

Joshua's small house was filled with people as they came to check on Ibula and Thedes. The villagers were busy repairing the damage done by the Guniars and preparing a feast for the arrival of a baby, a child that would be the first of its kind, a child that would unit cultures.

Just after noon the cry of a baby filled Joshua's house and everyone stopped talking as they listened to the baby cry. Raul stopped Thedes from going into the bedroom. "They will come out and tell you when you should go in," Raul said. "Just give them a couple of minutes." Thedes could not contain himself as the moments seemed like hours to him. Then the door opened and Gael said with a proud smile, "My brother come in and meet your new son."

Thedes ran into the room but stopped and stared at Ibula because he thought she looked radiant. Ibula was lying in bed holding their baby in her arms and smiling. Thedes kissed Ibula and stared in awe at his first born son. Vivian and Ingr were taking soiled linens out of the room as people in the kitchen and parlor asked about the baby.

"He is huge," Ingr said with a smile. "And he looks Shettee but he has wings. He's really cute. Give Ibula and Thedes a few moments then you can go in and see him."

Before the visitors entered the bedroom Thedes walked into the parlor proudly holding his son. "Every one of Ibula's brothers named their first sons after King Manu, their father," Thedes announced. "Ibula and I had planned to name our first son Tamas, after my father, with Manu as his middle name. But we just decided that because of the generosity and kindness shown to us by Joshua and Iris our son's name is Tamas Manu Joshua."

People in the room applauded and walked up to see the baby. Joshua, Iris and Vivian were all surprised and proud that the baby had been named after Joshua.

When word of the baby's name reached the villagers a most remarkable thing happened. With the name of a tiny child the Clan of Gesmal became bonded to the tribes of the Rualas and the Shettees. A bond that would endure wars and hardships; a bond that would last lifetimes.

Sampson reached his village by late afternoon, just as the people were enjoying their feast and celebrating the birth of the baby. He hid in the shadows of the forest and watched his people with great confusion. "Hours ago they were attacked by demons and now they celebrate?" he thought. "What is going on here?" Sampson knew his clan were fighters and the fact that they won the battle against the Guniar would normally not be cause for a grand celebration. He stealthy moved forward, trying to hear people talk. Sampson knew that if he was caught he would be put to death.

He watched as a flock of Enrops landed in the middle of the festivities and proceeded to give pieces of paper to various people, including the Sanuri. After the Sanuri read his letter he walked up to various people and said a few words to them. Every person who the Sanuri spoke to, immediately left the celebration and entered Joshua's and Iris' home. Sampson realized that other than Duncan and Joshua everyone else, who the Sanuri spoke to, was a member of the army he led.

Misha and Dagon were the last two to enter the house. The Sanuri waited until they shut the door before he spoke. The Sanuri chose Joshua's home for the meeting so Ibula and Thedes could also hear what he was to say. "I am sorry to pull you all away from the feast but I want to share with you this letter I just received from Hannah, Gabriel's wife."

"Hannah wrote to you?" Gabriel asked with surprise.

The Sanuri smiled and said, "I am sure she may have sent you the same information. Both Zoya and Delilah are pregnant and Hannah checks on them every day. Hannah said that yesterday morning while she was examining Zoya, Zoya had a vision. Hannah said Zoya described all of you here, in this room and said she saw us having a meeting."

"Then Zoya felt danger and said there were several pairs of eyes watching us but they were unaware of each other. Zoya referred to these eyes as belonging to monsters. Zoya said she saw monsters walking through this village, which she described as human but with great darkness attached to them. Zoya feels we and the villagers are in great danger."

"Who is Zoya?" Duncan asked.

"She is a seer who has proven very valuable to us," the Sanuri said. "Not long ago Zoya had a vision of Valdees soldiers attacking our families in Wetpr and Lentz. She told Sudfad, the attack would come at night and that night the Valdees did attack. Zoya is a humble person who is somewhat afraid of her powers."

"So if I understand her vision," Claudius said. "We have more than one enemy who is trying to figure out what we are doing here. Sanuri do you think our presence poses a danger for this village? Should we leave?"

"Before the Enrops arrived I felt someone watching us," the Sanuri said. "The Enrops described seeing a man who I believe is Sampson watching us from the forest but he is alone. It does not surprise me that Sampson would be spying on us. But the Enrops saw no others, which leads me to believe, the eyes watching us do not belong to humans. While I have no definite answer to your question, I feel that for now our presence is protecting this village."

"I will send our troops into the air," Misha said. "Perhaps we can find these spies."

"Send them in groups," the Sanuri said. "Do not have your warriors fly alone." The Sanuri paused for a moment as if he was listening to a voice no other could hear. "Duncan and Claudius tell your people to stay in groups: I am overwhelmed with a feeling that whoever is watching us is going to abduct people to get information."

Then the Sanuri turned to Duncan. "When Sampson rode out to meet us that first day I saw the darkness within him. He has always been consumed with darkness but what I saw that day was different."

162

"What I saw was the kind of darkness which is not normally attached to a human. Just now in my mind I saw Sampson with the demon Hecate, they have been lovers for some time."

"What!" screamed Duncan with both rage and shame.

The Sanuri now turned to Raphael and Vivian. "Powerful demons can take many forms and appearances. The image of Hecate which I saw greatly resembled Vivian. While I believe this to be part of her scheme to seduce Sampson; I believe Hecate can also use this form to create chaos among us. Be wary."

"That is just disgusting," Vivian said while making a face. "I should kill her just for that."

"Hecate is a very powerful demon' she cannot be killed by a human," the Sanuri said.

"I am just trying to understand what we are up against," Claudius said in his logical way. "If Sampson is spying for Hecate, who are the others watching us? Douma?"

"I don't really know yet," the Sanuri said. "You have told me that Miranda said that mausoleum in Nora was a trap for all of you. I knew it was a trap for me, but only that. I would assume that whoever set that trap is not happy that we did not fall for it. Only a very powerful demon could set a trap like that. And yes, I would guess Douma has spies watching us also."

"So we have two powerful demons and a dark lord king after us," Sorren said with a grin. "It's about time things got more interesting." Everyone laughed at Sorren's comment.

"Sanuri I will have my warriors take Sampson now," Duncan said. "He is too great a threat against us all."

The Sanuri now smiled slyly. "Actually I believe we have the advantage here. Hecate sent Sampson to gather information. I believe we should give her some information."

"What are you thinking?" Claudius asked with a grin.

"Something to cause her chaos and perhaps pit her against the other monsters," the Sanuri answered.

163

After the meeting, Raphael walked up to the Sanuri. "Sanuri I am greatly disturbed by the vision you had of the demon Hecate taking on Vivian's appearance. I fear there is more going on here than Hecate seducing Sampson."

"Hecate does not look exactly like Vivian, but could be mistaken for her from a distance," the Sanuri said. "And I agree with you, although as of now I don't know what her plans are."

"Vivian feels like I am overprotective but I don't want her leaving my side," Raphael said with concern.

The Sanuri looked through the crowd until he saw Vivian. "Vivian would you join us please?" he asked. The Sanuri waited until she was close to him and Raphael before he spoke again. "Your husband and I are discussing your safety. Vivian I know you are great warrior but you have power over things in this world. I know how humble both Raphael and Gabriel are so I doubt either of them have told you just how powerful they are."

"Both men have been tested by The Great Ruler and both men have been rewarded for their courage and faith. Raphael and Gabriel also have power over beings not of this world. Mind you that power has its limits but they are more powerful than any of the warriors here; which is one reason the demons want them destroyed."

Vivian looked at Raphael proudly and took his hand as the Sanuri continued to speak. "Raphael and Gabriel have stood up to very powerful demons, to some of the Old Ones. They both understand the danger here. Your husband is not discounting your abilities; he knows that of all these warriors here only he, Gabriel and I can truly protect you from a demon as powerful as Hecate. You would show your wisdom if you followed your husband in these matters."

To Raphael's surprise Vivian did not argue but asked him, "When Sampson first rode up to us, did you see the same darkness in him that the Sanuri saw?"

"Yes, but I did not want to worry you and spoil your reunion with your family."

164

Vivian stared at Raphael disapprovingly for a moment before speaking. "You can see things that I cannot, so I propose we work out a compromise for the rest of our lives." The Sanuri smiled as he listened to Vivian. "You will no longer withhold information from me and I will listen to you and follow you in these matters."

Raphael smiled and said, "I agree to your terms." Then he bent down and kissed Vivian on the lips.

"I hope the two of you understand by now that it was no accident you found each other," the Sanuri said. "Both of you have denied yourselves much to dedicate your lives to stand up to darkness. Raphael, The Great Ruler sent you the perfect wife and Vivian you the perfect husband. Both of you are strong warriors and strong in your faith, yet combined your strength is magnified greatly. Never forget that."

Chapter XII
Trials

Later that afternoon, after the festivities, Claudius and others from his group and the village worked on strategies for the attack on Ogg.

"The Valdees are merciless creatures," Duncan warned. "We must be prepared that many of their captives will be sick and wounded, perhaps unable to walk."

"Then we will form a rescue group whose only focus will be on getting the captives out of that hell hole," Claudius said. "Thedes I know you want retribution but your tribe will trust you more than us, I believe you should be part of the rescue group as well as those of you who are healers."

"I agree," Thedes said. "But I do not want to lead that group because I fear my emotions may take control of me."

"I think we all had the same idea," Claudius said. "It takes a brave man to make such an admission."

"I would like to lead that group," said Matthew.

"It is done then," Claudius said. "Angelina I want you in charge of preparing medical supplies."

"My family will assist with that," Joshua said.

"While I approve of everything you are discussing," the Sanuri said. "I feel there is a strong threat against this village also, we will need to leave troops here."

"I will volunteer for that and I would like Nikki to remain here with me," Thaos said.

"It is done," said Claudius.

"Thaos, I will be leaving Ibula and Tamas in your hands," Thedes said.

"I know and we will take good care of them," Thaos said.

The door to Duncan's home opened and Misha and Dagon walked in, both men were laughing. "It worked just like you said it would Sanuri. I dropped the letter to Sudfad as I flew and Sampson picked it up. Dagon watched him as he mounted his horse and rode south."

"South," Duncan said. "The Tnges Gold Mines are south of here, do you think that is where the demon lives?"

"Enrops are following him," Dagon said. "So we should have an answer to that soon."

Unaware that he had been tricked, Sampson rode to Hecate's lair with the letter he believed was intended for King Sudfad. Sampson read the letter before he decided to give it to Hecate; he thought she would be pleased with his work. Sampson had felt torn when he was hiding in the shadows of his own village. The only people he knew or cared about lived in that village. It both hurt him and angered him that he had been banned from ever stepping foot into that village again.

Yet there was a part of Sampson that understood why his father took the action he did. As Sampson dwelled upon the events that led up to his expulsion he realized that in Duncan's place Sampson would have had his son put to death. With that realization Sampson was filled with both shame and regret but the darkness of his soul soon turned these two emotions into rage and hatred. As Sampson traveled back to the lair of his demon lover he schemed about overthrowing his father.

"Tell me again how you got this," Hecate demanded.

"Don't use that tone with me," Sampson said as he poured another glass of whiskey for himself. "Do you really think I am stupid?"

Hecate had plans for Sampson and did not want to lose him so she changed her demeanor. "No Sampson I do not think you are stupid. I think you are very intelligent. But I also think the Sanuri and those priests are very cunning. So would you please tell me in detail how you got this letter?"

"I had been watching the village for hours. A flock of Enrops delivered letters to the Sanuri and the others with him. I watched as the Sanuri read his letter then he walked up to different people and whispered something to each of them. As soon as he was done talking, each person left the feast and entered Joshua's house. They were in the house for about an hour, then one of the Ruala warriors walks out and he is holding a leather pouch.

"The Ruala barely gets through the door before the general who was riding with the Sanuri stops him and hands him some paper. The Ruala puts the paper into his pouch and starts to walk away and another man calls to him and hands the same Ruala more paper. The Ruala pushed all of the paper into his pouch and flew into the sky; his pouch must have been open because this letter fell out. I watched as it floated in the air and I grabbed it as soon as it hit the ground."

"Did you read it?" Hecate asked.

"Of course," Sampson said with indignation. "I wasn't going to bring it to you if it was a letter to someone's mother." Then Sampson's voice became less harsh. "I understood the words but I have never heard of the group the letter talks about."

"Sampson it is time you and I had a serious talk," Hecate said as she walked closer to him. "I want to look into your eyes so I can tell if you are being truthful."

"I have always been truthful to you."

"Sampson you and I have been lovers for the last few months and we both have enjoyed our relationship. But since we are just lovers there is much I cannot tell you. I know you have wanted Vivian for many years so this question may be very difficult for you. Do you plan to continue to have a relationship with me?"

"I have been asking myself that same question," Sampson said honestly. "I know you are a demon, which is everything I was raised to hate. Yet I am more satisfied with you than any woman I have ever been with." Sampson paused for several moments. "Hecate I plan to have my revenge on Vivian and her husband but…" Sampson stopped talking and bent down and untied his lamsman and held it out to Hecate.

"It is our custom that when a Venator asks someone to marry him he offers that person his most prized possession which is the lamsman."

Hecate stood in shock, after several moments she stammered, "You are asking me to marry you?"

"I know your last husband Sporos was a human before he turned into a demon, so humans and demons can marry. I don't expect an answer tonight."

Hecate took Sampson's hand and spoke with a sincerity that Sampson had not heard before. "You must understand that while I can walk in your world as a human you cannot walk with me in other worlds. That is one reason that Sporos worked so hard to change himself. And Sampson I am going to be completely honest with you, I can change my appearance, what you see before you is not how I always look. You may not want to see my other appearances."

"So what are you saying?"

"I am saying that you don't know what you are really asking when you ask me to marry you."

"Then is it possible for you to show me?"

"You cannot just walk into other dimensions," Hecate said. "The Old Ones will demand that you go through trials to prove your allegiance to darkness. The trials are horrible and deadly. We could marry without you going through these tests but you would never be part of my world."

"So are you saying you will be my wife?"

"Yes," Hecate whispered. "The choice is yours whether you want to go through the trials, I will not ask you to do so, but if you do, I will try to help you as much as I can."

The meeting continued long into the night. When all the strategies were reviewed and the assignments given, Matthew said. "Sanuri you have not mentioned Miranda or Daniel. We need to talk to them before we proceed any farther."

The Sanuri smiled and said, "These plans and these battles are trials for all of you. I know to call to the heavens for help; you are the ones who need to learn that lesson and I am glad to hear you say those words."

"Miranda used to present herself to just one of us at a time, now she presents herself to our army also," Archetenus said. "If we call to her and she does not come, it might be because she does not want to present herself in front of the villagers. Then we will have to separate and call to her."

"Miranda, Daniel we know you are listening," Matthew called out. "We are preparing to attack Ogg and we need your help."

Suddenly one of the villagers fell to the floor and screamed in pain, the Sanuri walked up to the man and could see smoke rising from his skin. The Sanuri took the man's head in both of his hands and peered through the man's eyes, into the man's soul. "It appears Hecate has seduced more than Sampson," the Sanuri said. The villager fought against the Sanuri but could not break the Sanuri's hold on his body or his mind. "Duncan there is another in your tribe who works for Hecate." As the Sanuri spoke these words a man ran for the door of Joshua's house. Raul and Simon were standing near the door and grabbed the man and wrestled him to the ground.

"Hold him," the Sanuri said to the two Princes. "I will read his mind also. Apparently these two men were unaware of each other's seduction and only learned that Sampson too worked for Hecate when he turned against the village." The Sanuri stared into the first man's eyes for a few more moments then stood up and said. "Duncan he is yours."

Duncan motion to two of his warriors, "Take him out and kill him, then throw his body outside of the village for the animals to tear apart."

"No Duncan, please I am sorry," the man yelled as he was being dragged out of the house.

Raul and Simon pulled the man they were holding to a standing position. The villager was a large and powerful man and fought them greatly.

When the Sanuri placed his hands on either side of the man's head the man screamed and smoke started to rise from his skin. "Sanuri what are you doing to him?" Duncan asked.

"It is not me that is affecting these men," the Sanuri said. "The presence of the Angels is in this room and demons cannot tolerate holiness."

"These men are demons?" Duncan asked in shock. "But I have known them my entire life."

"They were not always demons," the Sanuri said. "Hecate is filling them with her poison."

"The Sanuri once read my mind," Thaos said to the group. "And it was painless."

"Duncan he is yours now," said the Sanuri.

"If they are demons can my men kill them?" Duncan asked.

"Yes, they have no power only darkness," the Sanuri replied and stepped back as two members of the Clan of Gesmal took the villager from Raul and Simon.

"Well, once again Zoya's visions came true," Sorren said.

The Sanuri waited until the four warriors returned from killing the spies. He placed his hands on the heads of each of these warriors, when he had finished the Sanuri walked in front of the group. "Very powerful demons can sometimes see through the eyes of those they turn into vessels, but I believe the Angels prevented Hecate from hearing the information presented in this meeting."

"Sanuri how do you know this?" Claudius asked.

"When a demon sees through the eyes of a human, think of it as looking through a tunnel, then when I look through the person's mind I am essentially looking from the opposite end of the tunnel and will often see the demon behind the mask. I saw walls with both of these men."

"Why did you look into the minds of my men when they returned?" Duncan asked.

"Hecate has to know she lost two of her vessels, I was afraid she would reach through the vessels and touch the men who executed them."

Before anyone else in the house could speak a warm glow appeared to fill every room of the small dwelling. Some people began to cry but they did not understand why. Some people jumped and others knelt when they realized two Angels now stood in their midst.

"Do not kneel before us," Daniel said. "We are not The Great Ruler. We have been listening to you and are pleased with your plans and even more pleased that you have called to us for help. The Great Ruler made your kind with free will which we do not take away from you by imposing ourselves upon you. Miranda and I will help you enter the Kingdom of Ogg, a place where no one calls to Angels or to The Great Ruler. We will help you find the captives and we will help you leave that hell dimension but you must be prepared for what you will encounter there."

"Have we overlooked something in our plans?" Claudius asked.

"No," Miranda said as she walked around the room and looked into the faces of those in attendance. "You are courageous and faithful warriors who are planning to risk your lives to enter hell to save the victims there. Do not take our description of the Kingdom of Ogg lightly. While you all have seen battle and the horrors that man can inflict upon his brethren, besides the Sanuri there are but three in this room who have seen a hell dimension and live to talk about it. Archetenus, Gabriel and Simon, in your experiences you were fighting for your lives. In two days you will be fighting for the lives of many and what you will see will never leave you."

"Claudius, Sorren," Miranda said as she now stood before these two seasoned warriors. "You have led warriors in battle for most of your lives, yet even for men of your strength and endurance your knees may weaken and your hearts break at what you will see. I do not tell you these things to scare you or to discourage you on this mission of Mercy. I tell you these things to prepare you so you do not falter in battle."

"Duncan," Miranda said and walked up to the chief, who was so overwhelmed in the presence of the Angels that he was visibly shaking. "Before Claudius and this brave army arrived here I told them the things I will tell your people now. There are many victims in the Kingdom of Ogg whose voices can no longer be heard, who have been in darkness so long that they can barely remember the light."

"Men, women and children who were abducted and carried into hell. This may be one of the most dangerous battles you will ever fight but Daniel and I will be with you. But the choice is yours; we will not force anyone to descend into this world of horrors. If you choose not to join us there will be no punishment or loss of honor."

Before Duncan could speak, Vivian walked up to Miranda and taking her sword from its sheath, Vivian thrust it into the floor and took her place next to the Angel. Duncan watched with pride as villager after villager preformed the same feat, symbolizing their loyalty to The Great Ruler. When every villager in the house now stood with the Angels, Duncan walked forward.

"Our friends here have spoken of both of you with love, honor and awe. Never in my life did I think I would be blessed in such a manner as to set my eyes upon Angels, my legs can barely hold me up." Duncan drew his sword and thrust it into the floor. "From this day forward the Clan of Gesmal will be at your bidding; we surrender our swords and our lives to The Great Ruler."

Daniel walked up to Duncan and placed his hand on the chief's shoulder. "Your heart is broken and the oath you just swore to The Great Ruler will increase the distance between you and your son Sampson."

"My son serves another master," Duncan said as tears rolled down his cheeks. "He has made his choices as I have made mine." The room stood in silence for several moments before Miranda spoke again.

"As Daniel said we are very pleased with your plans but we would like to add some input. First of all the Sanuri is correct in his feelings about the vulnerability of this village. It will be attacked by both Hutas and King Hamond's army from Stordt."

173

"Hamond!" Claudius said. "He is crossing his border to attack us?"

"Yes," Daniel said. "He believes he can destroy you and blame your deaths on others so as not to incur the wrath of King Sudfad."

"Claudius you are in charge of these men," Miranda said. "But I would suggest you leave Archetenus here with Thaos to lead the troops. Archetenus is more than prepared to recognize the ruses of Hamond's men. And you should leave at least two thousand men here also," Miranda now turned to Duncan. "You will need to turn your village into a hospital for all of the captives who will be brought from Ogg. What do you say?"

"Miranda just tell us what you want and it is done," Claudius said.

Miranda smiled warmly, "Claudius you have come far in your faith on this journey, I am pleased."

"I stand with Claudius," Duncan said.

"You have two days to fortify this village, to prepare for the many wounded and for part of your army to reach the coast. Miranda and I will be with you and unlike demons we are powerful enough to expand our presence to more than one location. We will both be in Ogg and in this village at the same time," Daniel explained.

"In Stordt, you touched our swords with holiness so we could fight against the demons," Raul said. "Will you help us in such a manner again?"

"Gabriel and Raphael you and I fought back to back against thousands," Daniel said. "Do you remember how you felt?"

"We felt like we had become one with you," Raphael said.

"And our swords felt light and we did not tire," Gabriel added.

"Pull out your swords now," Daniel said.

Both Gabriel and Raphael smiled, then Raul, Simon, Sorren and the others pulled their swords from their sheaths. "They are light again," Gabriel told the group.

Daniel now turned to the villagers who still stood near him and Miranda. "Pull your swords from the floor and return them to their sheaths," Daniel said.

"Father my sword feels different," Micha exclaimed to Joshua.

"A demon cannot stand up to holiness," Daniel said. "You now have the power to fight both man and demon."

"Is this what I will need to stop Sampson?" Duncan asked sadly.

"Duncan do you want the answer before the others here or in private?" Daniel asked.

"He is a threat to us all; I will not hide his darkness," Duncan said as his heart filled with grief.

"Your son has taken the demon Hecate as his wife," Daniel said as a collective gasp permeated the room. "While he still plans revenge on all of you, for now he is distracted. He has chosen to undergo the trials of the Old Ones. If he passes these tests he will be able to walk in hell dimensions with his bride."

"Are you saying he will be a demon?" Raphael asked.

"Yes but not powerful like Hecate."

The color drained from Duncan's face as he looked at his two sons who stood with the Angels. "Let me tell your mother this news; it will break her heart. My son's you two have made me very proud this day; and before the Angels I want you to promise that you will uphold the covenant I just made between our people and The Great Ruler."

"Our soldiers killed fifteen more Valdees last night," Sudfad said the next morning at a meeting in his study. "And we captured twenty more. We now have one hundred and sixty-two Valdees soldiers in the dungeons."

"And honestly I feel like we are capturing them too easily. I am beginning to think this is some kind of plot."

"Well, I am glad to hear you say that," Lakin said. "Just this morning we were discussing the same thing. Sudfad there are other kings who would have executed those prisoners, you are known for your kindness; don't imperil your kingdom because of it."

"How many Valdees prisoners does Mathas have now?" Luca asked.

"Last I heard about one hundred and forty," Sudfad said, then he paused. "I will order their executions today and send Mathas word of our concerns."

There was a knock at the door and without waiting for someone to open the door Queen Renya and Hannah entered the study. "Forgive us for barging in," Renya said. "But Hannah just received a letter from both Gabriel and the Sanuri and I feel we need to discuss it." Renya turned to Hannah and said, "Show Sudfad the letter."

"What is wrong?" Calen asked with great concern.

"The Enrops flew all night to get this letter to me," Hannah said. "The Angels, Miranda and Daniel are in the village with everyone. They, that is the Angels want to attack Ogg, oh I guess it would be tomorrow. The Angels said that there are so many injured captives that they want Vivian's entire village turned into a hospital. And the Angels said that both Hutas and Hamond's men will attack the village. Gabriel is asking that we send medical supplies."

"Our warriors would have to take the supplies to get them to the village in time," Lakin said as he stared at Hannah. "Hannah we have been friends for a long time. I have seen that look on your face before."

"Lakin, Ibula is a powerful healer but she just gave birth and your brother cannot tend to all of those patients. They have no physicians and few healers, I am going." There was silence in the room after Hannah's statement. "What no one is going to argue with me?" she challenged.

176

"Hannah you just said what we were thinking," Luca said, then he turned to Sudfad. "Sudfad all of our families are in the castle and under the protection of your army. Calen and I promised Gabriel we would watch over Hannah, I am going to fly her to Ryed."

"Sudfad do you really need us here?" asked Calen.

"No," Sudfad said with a smile.

"Then I am going to Ryed also," Calen said. "I feel useless here while our family is going into battle."

"Hannah and I make a great medical team," Lakin said as he started to stand up. "I need to purchase supplies."

Renya smiled, "I have already sent soldiers out to buy the supplies. Hannah gave them a long list, so you will need many warriors to carry everything."

"We have the warriors here and I believe they will be glad to join the others," Lakin said.

"If your troops have room I have a few things I would like to send along," said Renya.

"You all should read this letter before you leave," Sudfad said as he handed the long letter to Calen. "Chief Duncan's son took the demon Hecate for his wife and now he is going through some tests to become a demon. I have not had as much interaction with the Angels as Archetenus, Matthew, Angelina and some of the others; but it is my understanding that the Angels make an appearance and leave."

"Gabriel says the Angels have not left them, which is making everyone wonder if there is more going on than what the Angels have told them. I will send Claudius a note and tell him I am sending another ten thousand troops to Nora and they will be at his disposal. But you will reach Claudius before the troops do so be careful."

Calen read the letter then handed it to Lakin. "Renya how long will it take to get the supplies here?"

"The troops left for Salar about an hour ago, I would expect them back this morning."

"Hannah how long before you are ready?" Calen asked.

"I already talked with Emeral, Natasha and Lila and they will take care of the children. Natasha is packing food and medical supplies while I am here."

"So we could leave this afternoon?" Calen asked but no one answered. "Luca, Lakin what do you think?" After Lakin read a page of the letter he handed it to Luca and both men were engrossed in what they were reading.

"I think we should try for early afternoon," Lakin said. "I am going to prepare our warriors as soon as I finish this letter."

"I am leaving three thousand troops with you," Claudius said to Thaos and Archetenus. "They are all soldiers of Lentz. Can the two of you work out your responsibilities or do you want me to make assignments?"

"Already done," Thaos said with a laugh. "Archetenus used to be a captain in the Army of Stordt. I am dividing the troops into two contingents; I will command one and Archetenus the other." "Nikki is not happy with me but I have assigned her to personally guard Ibula and the baby. She thinks I am trying to keep her out of battle."

"You are," Archetenus said with a grin.

"I know," Thaos said and laughed again. "But if things get as bad as the Angels are saying, both Nikki and Ibula may be fighting."

"I know all of the wives here are warriors and I don't mean to insult anyone," Archetenus said. "But I would not be able to concentrate if Delilah was fighting in battle with me."

"You try telling our wives that," Thaos said.

"Papa and Uncle Raphael and the others are trying to save some people who are very injured and sick," Hannah said as she had her arms around both Nicholas and Cerey. They don't have any physicians so Uncle Lakin and I are going to help them. Grandma Emeral and Natasha and Lila will take care of you. I want you both to do what they say."

"How long are you going to be gone?" Nicholas asked.

"I don't know Honey but Papa and I will come back as soon as we can. You know we both love you two very much," Hannah said and kissed both of her children while tears filled her eyes.

"I can't believe you aren't mad at me for leaving," Calen said as he helped Natasha pack supplies. Natasha turned around and looked at him.

"Calen, this is exactly the kind of mission I would want to go on. And when Lily is older I will go with you. Just save those poor people and come home."

Calen put both of his arms around Natasha and hugged her tightly. "I love you so much," he said and kissed Natasha on the lips. "I am going upstairs and pack a few things."

"I already packed your things," Natasha said. "As soon as Hannah told me she was going I knew you and Luca would go too. There are a couple of small gifts in your bag from Lily, one is for you and the other for Maxwell."

"I don't want you to go," Christopher said as he hugged Luca.

"Christopher remember when I helped you and Lila fight those Hutas? Christopher looked at Luca and wiped the tears from his eyes but did not speak, so Luca continued. "Both you and Lila were fighting those Hutas like warriors. I know you will be a great warrior someday and true warriors defend others. The people we are going to help really need us, there are little children too who are captives."

"I don't know if I am explaining this to you very well, but Calen, Hannah and I cannot stay in this beautiful place with all the food we can eat while those people are suffering. Does that make any sense to you?"

Christopher hugged Luca again, "I want to be just like you," Christopher whispered, as the tears ran down Lila's face.

Chapter XIII
Man's Curse upon Nature

"Ibula what are you doing out of bed?" Iris asked as Ibula walked into the kitchen.

"I have never been one to lie around and I know you need help," Ibula said as she sat down at the kitchen table. "I am a healer I can at least help prepare for wounded."

"Ibula, you just had a huge baby," Iris said as she walked over to Ibula and felt her forehead. "You are very pale; how do you feel?"

"Weak and shaky. Perhaps I should have some more of Angelina's tonic."

"I was thinking the same thing," Iris said. "But you are having it in bed. Now come." Iris put her arms around Ibula and gently pulled her to her feet.

"Gabriel told me he sent a letter to his wife asking for medical supplies," Ibula said as Iris helped her walk back to bed. "His wife is a great physician; I wish she was here now."

"Ibula, you are not the only one who knows how to care for wounded," Iris scolded. "The entire village is preparing for both war and wounded, everything will be alright."

"I feel so guilty leaving Ibula and the baby," Thedes said to Raul and Simon as they rode westward towards the coast of the Schenomi Sea.

"We understand how you feel," Raul said. "But she is well cared for and you know that Thaos and Archetenus will protect her."

"Besides," Simon said. "You are needed to help rescue the Shettee captives."

"I know all of these things yet I do not feel better," Thedes said.

"Thedes do you think your people will want to join you in the Ice Caves?" Gabriel asked.

"What was our kingdom is destroyed and Hutas control the lands. From what the Angels have said I fear the brethren we find will be in no shape to take back Xepoltr. I would like to take them to the Ice Caves to heal and after that they can choose where they want to live."

"There is plenty of room in the Ice Caves for all our people," Misha said as he flew overhead.

"Misha do you remember what I was like when we first met?" Thedes asked. "Our tribe kept itself isolated from others because we trusted no one. We were wrong in our thinking; I understand that now. But the Shettees that have been tortured as captives may be more untrusting; who knows what they will want?"

"But their families are living happily in the Ice Caves," Raphael said. "Do you think that will greatly influence them?"

"I do not know what to expect," Thedes continued. "Just a few years ago I would never have believed that I would have family and friends who were Ruala and human. I believe it will be hard for some of the others to accept."

"What will be hard for them to accept?" Angelina asked.

"That we are much more alike than we are different," Thedes answered; causing the Sanuri to smile.

Thaos rode up to Archetenus and said, "It's too quiet, I don't like it."

"I was thinking the same thing, but the Enrops and Rualas haven't seen anything," Archetenus said.

"Well, if anyone is watching us they know that most of the army and part of the village left this morning,"

"We still have over three thousand men. Our numbers might be a deterrent."

"Perhaps for Hamond's men but I don't think anything deters demons."

Both men turned as they heard a horse approaching. "Is something wrong?" Thaos asked as Nikki rode up to them.

"Here Iris sent this for you," Nikki said as she handed a basket to Thaos.

"For me?"

"It is food for both of you," Nikki said. "Some of the men said neither of you have eaten. You can dismount long enough to eat. I'll stand watch."

"Whatever it is it sure smells good," Archetenus said as both men dismounted and sat on the ground.

"How's Ibula?" Thaos asked as he took two plates out of the basket, each plate was covered with a cloth. "There is pie in here too," he said with surprise."

"The baby was so big she lost a lot of blood," Nikki said as her eyes searched the horizon. "She is weak and shaky but otherwise fine. She wants to help prepare for the battles and captives but she's not ready yet."

"I can never get over how much Vitomas and Ibula look alike," Archetenus said. "I mean have you ever seen anything like that for people who aren't related?"

"There are Enrops flying this way," Nikki said. Thaos and Archetenus quickly devoured their food as the birds approached them.

"Soldiers from Stordt are heading this way," Arca one of the Enrops said. "You have about a half hour before they get to the village."

"How many are there?" Thaos asked as he stood up.

"Maybe five hundred," Arca replied. "But they aren't tracking you, they are riding quickly."

"So they know we are here," Archetenus said. "Who the hell told them?"

"Do they consort with demons?" Nikki asked.

"Roch was the only king that I knew of who allowed demons in the castle but who knows what Hamond does," Archetenus said as he mounted his horse.

"Nikki, thank Iris for the food and tell the village to get ready," Thaos said and rode towards his contingent of men.

Lakin led over five hundred Ruala warriors to Ryed. Hannah was their only human passenger. All of the warriors carried large packs on their backs that contained not only their supplies but medical supplies for the freed captives and the wounded. They took few rest breaks, only what was necessary to maintain their strength and vigor. Everyone was anxious to reach their destination. The group left Salar hours sooner than they had originally planned. A flock of Enrops flew with the Rualas.

Archetenus and Thaos wanted to keep the battle out of the village. They knew that the Army of Stordt had traveled from the north, probably to bypass Fort Nora, then turned southwest once they crossed the border of Ryed. From that angle the army would have to travel through a forest and climb a series of small hills to reach the Village of the Clan of Gesmal. Thaos' men took a position of power near the tops of the hills, while Archetenus positioned his men in the forest. The troops from Lentz were well concealed in the natural surroundings.

While many of the Venatores traveled with the Sanuri and Claudius, the majority of warriors stayed behind to protect their village and families. Duncan stayed with his people and now prepared their defenses for an attack. Elan and Cassandra were among the Ruala warriors who stayed to protect the village. Thaos wanted the Rualas to remain closer to the village in case Hecate orchestrated an attack while the soldiers of Lentz were fighting on the front lines.

Thaos stood on top of the highest hill which afforded him a great view of the land in all directions.

He saw the dust produced by the horses of the Army of Stordt. As Hamond's men started to come into view, Thaos said out loud, "What drives these men; they are riding as if demons are chasing them?" Thaos sent an Enrop down to Archetenus; the message was only, *ten minutes*.

The army from Stordt, the Taperian soldiers, were led by Captain Sobre, an ambitious man who wanted to prove his worth to King Hamond. The King did not want to alert the troops at Fort Nora so he ordered Sobre to take a small contingent of battle experienced soldiers and attack Claudius and his men from the north.

Hamond told Sobre he would find Claudius in the Village of the Clan of Gesmal as well as telling Sobre the location of this small village. Sobre had no idea where Hamond obtained his information nor did he care. Although Sobre knew he was outnumbered he had no idea of the size of the army which Claudius led. Sobre believed the element of surprise would balance out the battle.

"Make Ready!" Archetenus ordered his archers.

"Make Ready!" Thaos called out to his men.

As the army from Stordt drew close Archetenus could feel the earth shake and he wondered if the Enrops were wrong and there were more than five hundred men riding towards them. Thaos too, felt the vibrations. He once again searched the horizons on all sides; something felt very wrong to him. A strange smell started to fill the air, unrecognizable to all. Enrops continued to fly overhead; both Thaos and Archetenus looked up at the giant birds for any indication that something was amiss.

As Captain Sobre was about to lead his men into the ambush he stopped and stared at the sight before him. Thaos was watching from the hill and wondered if Sobre had seen one of Archetenus' men.

Thaos continued to watch as Sobre appeared to be yelling to someone. Thaos could not make out any voices as he strained to hear what the leader of the Taperian soldiers was yelling.

The smell continued to grow stronger, a rancid, disgusting smell that burned the eyes and noses of the soldiers. Duncan and the villagers too smelled the putrid air. "Elan, Cassandra quickly," Duncan yelled as the two Ruala warriors now flew to him. "Warn Thaos and Archetenus there are creatures in the area, that smell it is the Grogs."

"What are Grogs?" Elan yelled.

"They are the tar creatures, they live in the pits. They eat humans, hurry warn them," Duncan said.

"How do you kill these creatures?" asked Cassandra.

"Fire is the only way," Duncan said as he handed each of them a burning log. "Grogs," Duncan yelled to the villagers.

Just as Elan found Thaos they heard the Taperian soldiers screaming but they could not see what was happening because a dense fog was filling the air. "Duncan said there are creatures from the tar pits in the area that is causing that smell. They eat humans and the only way to kill them is with fire."

"But the tar pits are not close," Thaos said out loud, then he said to Elan, "Tell this to Archetenus."

"Cassandra is warning him and taking him fire."

"Elan have the Rualas bring us oil for our arrows," Thaos said then motioned to the Enrops flying overhead. Elan quickly returned to the village. "Tell Archetenus and the others that the creatures fighting with the Taperians are creatures from the tar pits and can only be killed with fire. The Rualas will be bringing us oil for our arrows." Thaos was holding the burning log that Elan had handed him. "Gather brush and wood," Thaos yelled to his men.

Before Elan reached the village he met other Rualas who were flying to the front lines, carrying crocks of oil from the villagers. Elan joined this group and returned to the front lines.

Neither Archetenus nor Thaos ordered their men to help the Taperian soldiers. Both captains believed the creatures would kill the Taperians then turn and come towards the village, Archetenus and Thaos planned to stop them.

The sounds of frightened men and horses could be heard in the cloud of fog as well as the sounds of battle. "When the screams stop they will come for us," Thaos yelled. "Dip all of your arrows into the oil." The soldiers from Lentz had built hundreds of small fires on the hills and in the forests so they could ignite their weapons. "Arca," Thaos called to one of the Enrops, who landed near him. "How is it you could not see these creatures?"

"In a way we did," the Enrop replied. "They appeared as pools of mud on the ground and started to take form when the Taperians approached them; then as they grew the fog formed."

"Let us attack them from the sky first," Ratri said to Thaos.

Although the screams were stopping; the soldiers from Lentz and the Rualas could hear hideous sounds coming from the fog as the creatures devoured their kills. Thaos nodded and Ratri led the Rualas forward. The fog was thick but the Rualas shot flaming arrows into it. They could barely see movement inside of the fog but when the first flaming arrow struck a creature great flames shot into the air. The Rualas showered the fog with flaming arrows for they had no idea how many creatures were hidden inside. Neither Thaos nor Archetenus ordered their men to fire for fear they would hit the Rualas.

Giant flames shot up from the fog as the Rualas destroyed the creatures but the fog did not dissipate. The Rualas had no idea how many creatures were still inside. Archetenus could no longer stand by. He ordered his men to move forward and to shoot low into the fog. "Ratri we are firing too," Archetenus yelled and the Rualas flew higher into the sky.

When the creatures were hit with the flaming arrows their bodies burst into flames and continued to burn until the tar like substance had disintegrated. The demonic fog soon appeared as a giant fireball. The Rualas flew higher in the sky to escape the heat.

The creatures bellowed as they were being attacked. They could not reach the Rualas but as the creatures realized they were being attacked by soldiers in the forest they ran into the trees. Although Archetenus and his men could not see the creatures clearly, they could see the fog that was emitted from the beings.

"Release! Release! Release!" Archetenus ordered. As the creatures burst into flames they now set some of the dry brush on the floor of the forest on fire. The fires spread quickly and Archetenus ordered his men to retreat. The creatures were not willing to brave the fires to follow Archetenus and his men. The creatures turned, leaving the forest and running back towards the battlefield, in an attempt to flee the flames of the forest fire. The Rualas continued to shoot into the fog which was now mostly black smoke.

Thaos and his men held their ground in the hills. Archetenus sent his men back to the village while he joined Thaos on top of the hill. "I sent my men back to the village to cut down trees and brush so this fire doesn't destroy it."

"Good idea," Thaos said as his eyes constantly searched the horizons. "The Enrops said these creatures appeared as nothing more than pools of mud that suddenly took shape when the Taperians approached them. I'm putting my money on Hecate being behind this. She must know we have Enrops and Rualas in the skies."

"I'm not really sure how this thing works with demons," Archetenus said. "But if she is so smart wouldn't you think she would know the Taperians would encounter the creatures first?"

"You think this was a diversion?" Thaos asked. "Why don't you return to the village and we will watch for more invaders. Send word if you need help."

"The way that fire is spreading you may not be up here long," Archetenus said as he pointed to the area where he and his men had been hiding. "There aren't many trees up here but that smoke is rising."

"I know," Thaos said. "I can't explain it I just have this nagging feeling that something is wrong and I just can't see it."

"A lot of times Miranda would plague me with feelings like that, it was always a warning."

"Well how about you? Are you feeling it?"

"Hell I've been feeling like we are sitting ducks since we arrived at the village," Archetenus said. "I still can't figure out how all these spies can be watching us. We haven't seen a raven since we got here and I think the Angels weeded out the villagers who were spies."

"If some other type of bird was being used by the demons, wouldn't the Enrops know it?" Thaos asked.

"Not sure," Archetenus replied. The two warriors watched as terrified animals ran out of the forest to escape the blaze.

"What is that?"

"What?" Archetenus asked.

"Over there, to the right by the battlefield, is that an animal?" Thaos asked then he looked up into the air and called to the Rualas. "Ratri there is a creature near the battlefield, stop it and bring it here."

Now Archetenus could also see the creature running on two legs, but it was much smaller than a normal human. The creature was dark and its color blended in with the smoke. Thaos and Archetenus watched as two Ruala warriors chased the creature which was running back and forth like a scared rabbit. One of the Rualas swooped down and grabbed the creature.

"What the hell is that?" Thaos asked as several Rualas landed on the hill top. The creature's color now changed to the same green as the grasses and vegetation on top of the hill. "Did you see that?" Thaos asked in disbelief.

The creature somewhat reassembled a human but was only three feet tall and its skin was gnarled like the bark of a tree. The creature hissed at the Rualas. "Wait," Ratri said and he took off his crystal necklace and touched the crystal to the arm of the creature, who screamed in pain. "He's some type of demon," Ratri said. "The crystals are blessed with holiness."

189

"I think we found our spies," Archetenus said.

"Ratri, send someone to bring Duncan up here," Thaos said. "I don't want to take that thing into the village."

"Who do you work for?" Archetenus asked the demon, who just hissed.

"The Sanuri said that some demons can see through the eyes of their vessels," Thaos said. "Maybe if we look into its eyes we can tell."

"I'm not sure I would get that close," Ratri said. "We still don't know what kind of demon it is?"

"What are you called?" Archetenus asked the demon. The demon did not answer but his behavior was changing. The little demon had been staring at the men and Rualas who stood before him, now the demon was looking around. "Think he is trying to figure out how to escape?" Archetenus asked with a grin.

Thaos dismounted and grabbed a small burning log from one of the fires, then he walked up to the demon. As Thaos lowered the flame towards the demons arm it pulled back and looked fearful. "It's afraid of fire," Thaos asked. "What kind of demon is afraid of fire, I mean isn't hell full of fire?"

"I didn't see any when I got pulled down there," Archetenus said.

"Here they come," Ratri said as he pointed to two Ruala warriors who were carrying Duncan and Joshua."

Enrops were landing on the hill top and looking at the demon. "We have never seen his kind before," one of the giant birds said as it walked around the demon. "The demons are different in Ryed."

"That's not really a demon," Duncan said. "It's a Half-Man. They live in the forests."

"Well, he screamed when touched with a holy crystal," Ratri said. "So he has something to do with demons."

"He changes color to blend in with his surroundings," Thaos said. "We think he is one of the spies watching us and your village. He isn't answering our questions."

"They don't speak your language," Joshua said as he walked up to the creature and spoke in what sounded like gibberish to the others. The Half-Man growled and hissed at Joshua but also spoke to him.

A female Ruala warrior landed on the hill top, "There are other creatures like this running from the fire, do you want us to capture them?"

Joshua again spoke to the Half-Man then turned to the Ruala and said, "No, it is his village. The fire is destroying their home. They are mad at us for burning the forest." Joshua spoke with the Half-Man for a few more moments then looked at the Rualas.

"Let go of him," Joshua said. "These creatures have a limited language. They talk through their drawings. He is going to show us what is spying on us." As soon as the Rualas released the creature, the Half-Man talked a great deal and moved his arms with great exaggeration, then he picked up a small stick from the ground and started to draw. As he drew he kept pointing to the burning forest.

"He said that snakes followed your army here," Joshua said. "While your men were camped the snakes took refuge in the forest and started killing all the creatures. Everything in the forest was scared of these giant snakes because they were evil. He says the snakes were climbing trees and killing the birds and going into the burrows and homes of other creatures. He says the only good thing about the fire is that it is killing the snakes."

"We haven't seen any snakes come out of the forest," a Ruala warrior said.

"I wonder why they don't escape the flames," said Archetenus.

"So did Hecate send the snakes or whatever that was, that was going to trap us in the mausoleum?" Thaos asked. Joshua turned back to the Half-Man and asked him if he knew who sent the snakes.

The Half-Man once again became very animated as he talked. Thaos and Archetenus were trying not to grin as they watched the creature. "He says that the first night that the snakes entered the forest demons walked among them. Demons like he had never seen before, they walked through the woods and whispered. He is wondering why your army brought such awful beings here. I told him you fight demons and the demons are trying to stop you. He says every living creature around our village has been scared because of the darkness that follows your army."

"Raul and Simon talked about shadows that whispered after the great battle near Nora," Thaos said. "Ask him if they are the same as in the forest."

Joshua spoke to the Half-Man again who now looked at Thaos like he was stupid. Joshua laughed and said, "He can't understand why you don't know more about the creatures that follow you, but they sound the same."

"Joshua tell him that we will give them baskets of food, since we burned the forest," Duncan said. "Ask him if his tribe wants to come to the village and if they don't, ask him where they want us to put the food?"

The Half-Man looked at both Joshua and Duncan with surprise, then he started talking quickly again. "He is both pleased and shocked that we will give them food. He doesn't trust us enough to enter the village so he said this hill top would be fine. He wants us to get rid of the snakes and demons. I told him we will if we know about them. I made a deal with him, we will keep giving them food if they come and tell us when they see the snakes and demons."

The flock of Enrops had been standing on the hill top listening to Joshua and the Half-Man speak. Now Arca the leader of the flock stepped forward and started to speak to the Half-Man in his language. The Half-Man like the others looked surprised at the bird's ability, but soon everyone noticed that the Half-Man seemed more at ease speaking with the bird than the humans.

"I told him that if his kind was afraid to come to you they should call to us when they see the snakes and demons."

"He says his tribe is running towards the river and will stay there for a while, so they won't be so close to your village."

"Ask him if he wants us to carry the food to his tribe?" Ratri asked. "Tell him we will not hurt them."

Both Joshua and Arca spoke with the Half-Man. "Then Joshua turned to the others. This creature is more wild than human, he trusts the Enrops more than us," Joshua said. "Arca will wait here with the Half-Man while we get food, then the Enrops will fly with the Rualas when they take the food and Erwat home to his tribe."

"Erwat?" Thaos asked.

"That's his name," said Joshua.

Suddenly the sky filled with dark clouds and rain poured upon them. "Thank you Miranda," Archetenus said out loud.

"Do you think she sent the rain to put out the fire?" Duncan asked.

"It certainly is something she would do," said Archetenus.

Duncan returned to the village and had his people fill baskets with food for the Half-Man Tribe. Joshua stayed on the hill top with Thaos, Archetenus and Erwat.

"Joshua ask Erwat if he has seen a female demon near the village," Thaos said.

"He said no," Joshua replied. "But he says the ones that whisper are very dangerous because they work for the Old Ones." Suddenly Joshua's face paled as he continued to listen to Erwat.

"What did he say?" Archetenus asked.

"He said the shadows that whisper may not be after us because they followed the army when it left the village this morning."

"Arca have some of your tribe warn the Sanuri," Thaos said. "Tell him about the Grogs and what Erwat has said."

Arca spoke to some members of his flock in a language the humans did not understand then a dozen birds took to the air.

"What about the snakes?" Archetenus asked. "Are they still here?"

"Erwat said it looked like they were burning in the fire," Joshua said. Erwat continued to talk then he spit upon the ground. Joshua turned to the others. "He is angry. He says that man brings so much destruction to nature; he is wondering why we do not learn from our mistakes."

Chapter XIV
Miracles

Ratri and eleven other Rualas flew Erwat to his tribe who were hiding in vegetation on the western bank of the River Cheban. As they were landing Arca said, "Erwat says his tribe will not come out of hiding while you are here." Ratri set Erwat on the ground.

"Tell him we understand," Ratri said. "Does he want us to just put the baskets here because everything will get wet?" The packs that the Rualas carried on their bags were water resistant. The storm had taken on terrible proportions and appeared to be getting worse. Arca spoke to Erwat who turned and yelled. Suddenly dozens of Half-Mans appeared from the vegetation and grabbed the many baskets. A lightning bolt struck a nearby tree causing a huge branch to fall just feet away from the Rualas.

"Erwat said he will show you a place to take shelter," Arca said. "The Rualas followed the tiny Half-Man to a small cave near the river bank.

"There's dry wood in here," Cassandra said. "We can make a fire."

"Why don't Erwat and his tribe take shelter?" asked Ratri.

Arca spoke again to Erwat. "He says there are other small caves and burrows."

"But they were hiding in the vegetation," Ratri continued.

"The Half-Mans we saw are warriors," Arca said. "They were prepared to fight you." The Enrop's comment made everyone smile.

"Tell him we appreciate this," Ratri said.

Elan was making a fire while Ratri talked with Arca and Erwat. After the Half-Man left the cave, Elan asked, "Arca how do you know his language?"

"I didn't before today," Arca said. "As I listened to Joshua and Erwat talk I suddenly understood what they were saying."

"Hundreds of years ago my ancestors promised The Great Ruler that our tribe would always work on His behalf. After that a miracle happened, they could speak and understand many languages. That gift has been passed down to us for generations."

The blinding rain and intense lightening forced Thaos to pull all of the soldiers back to the village. Many of the villagers gave the soldiers shelter in their homes. And the women brought hot food to the soldiers who were guarding the perimeter of the village. Both Archetenus and Thaos kept saying that they felt uneasy so they continually took turns walking the perimeter and checking on their men.

Vivian's two younger brothers, Paul and Adrone had become very attached to Elan and Cassandra. The boys kept running to the windows and peeking through the shutters. "Father do you think they will make it home in this storm?" Adrone asked with concern.

"That is the fifth time you have asked your father that question," Iris said with a smile.

"They are experienced warriors I am sure they took shelter some place," Joshua said with a grin.

Paul walked up to Joshua who was sitting at the kitchen table. "Father, Raphael said we could come and visit them whenever we liked. Do you think we can go someday?" asked Paul.

"Your mother and I were discussing that earlier," Joshua said. "It is a very long and dangerous journey to get to Wetpr. But we too would like to visit them."

Adrone turned from the window and ran up to the kitchen table, "Elan said that if you send Raphael a letter and let them know when we are coming, some of the Rualas can come and get us so we don't have to fight with Hutas. Can we go Father? Please."

"Dear I think you are the only one in the family who has not flown with the Rualas," Joshua said to Iris. "Do you think you would be up for such a journey?"

"Oh Mother it is really fun," said Paul.

"I can fly with her here," Ibula said as she and Nikki walked into the kitchen. Ibula was carrying her baby. "That way Iris can see if she likes it."

"Well, is sounds much safer than travelling across land with two small children," Iris said. Then she paused and looked at Ibula. "Does anyone ever get sick when you take them flying?"

"Sometimes," Ibula replied with a laugh.

Lakin and his warriors were still too far east to be affected by the storm. They traveled late into the night. Lakin, Calen, Luca, Hannah, Bekka and Koby shared the same campfire. Hannah cooked their meal as the others set up the campsite.

"Hannah I will say it is a treat having you do the cooking on this journey," Lakin said.

"I love to cook," said Hannah. "Remember when I first met all of you? Marcia and I never realized how lonely we were living in that big house until all of you came to stay with us. It was so much fun having you there. I love having a house full of people."

"Do you think Gabriel is going to get mad when he sees you?" Bekka asked.

"He might, that is why I didn't send him a message," Hannah said. "I didn't want him telling me to stay home."

"If he gets mad it's just because he doesn't want to put you in danger," said Calen.

"Actually I think he will be happy to see her," said Luca. "Hannah whenever you and Natasha aren't with us all Gabriel and Calen talk about are you two girls."

"Really?" Hannah asked then smiled. Hannah was putting steaks, fried potatoes, beans and biscuits on plates and handing them to each of the warriors.

"This really smells good," Koby said.

197

"There are still plenty of Emeral's cookies for desert," Hannah said. "I hope all of you realize I am not going to Ryed to be defiant. Ever since I can remember I wanted to heal things. When I was a little girl I would take in every wounded animal and bird I found. Pretty soon other people started to bring injured animals to me, then injured people."

"That is why Father sent me away to school; he knew how much I love medicine. Then when I read Gabriel's letter, I mean there will be plenty of wounded from the battles; but when Gabriel wrote about the captives, it broke my heart. If I would have stayed home I never would have forgiven myself."

"If Gabriel does get mad," Lakin said. "Tell him what you just told us."

"Hannah I think you should have a weapon," Koby said. "If you didn't bring one, I have extras." Both Calen and Luca grinned at Koby's suggestion.

"I have my small crossbow and arrows in my medical bag and Natasha has been teaching me how to throw knives, so I made a jacket like hers."

Koby roared with laughter, "You mean the jacket that had all the small knife sheaths in it?"

"Yes," Calen said. "And Natasha has been teaching Hannah how to pick locks and open safes. The skills every demon hunter needs."

"Natasha's skills were very useful," Luca said with a grin.

"I know, I was actually being serious," Calen said. "I just want to watch when Natasha teaches her how to use the bullwhip."

Claudius and the Sanuri had the army make camp when the blinding rain made it impossible to see. They were travelling south of the Village of Gesmal, which was an area filled with large hills and gold mines.

"I am sure Hecate is watching us," Stephan said. "We must be in her back yard."

"I think she has been watching us for a very long time," the Sanuri said as they huddled over a campfire in a cave.

"Sanuri did the Angels tell you how we are to cross the Schenomi Sea?" Claudius asked.

"No but they were detailed in telling you what to prepare for; if we needed something to cross the water I am sure they would have told us," the Sanuri replied.

"Remember when we were going to Ganz to save Archetenus and Delilah?" Angelina asked as she prepared food over the fire. "The river was very swollen so we couldn't cross. As soon as Matthew called out to Miranda a barge appeared and the men took us across the river." The Sanuri smiled as he listened to Angelia. "Miranda wants us to save those people; she will have something for us."

The storm raged through the night and stopped when the first rays of sunlight appeared in the sky. Ratri and the others left their shelter as soon as the storm subsided and headed back to the village. "I still have to smile when Arca said those Half-Man warriors were going to fight with us," Elan said.

"I asked Erwat what they used for weapons," Arca said. "He said they use poison darts on humans and large animals."

"Well, I am glad we didn't fight with them," Ratri said as they all laughed.

"I think that storm did a lot of damage," Cassandra said as they flew over fallen trees.

"Look you can see the black spots on the ground where the tar monsters burned," said Tort, one of the Rualas. They were all looking at the battleground and the damage done by the forest fire.

"At least the rain stopped that fire before too much was destroyed," Elan said as they all flew westward over the hills that Thaos and his men had hidden in the day before.

"Ratri look," Tort yelled and pointed to the ground immediately west of the hills. The Rualas flew lower as they inspected the scene below them.

"They look like they are dead," Ratri said. "Land but be careful, remember what happened to Bekka and Fala."

"What do you think killed them?" Bekka asked as they walked around hundreds of Huta bodies.

"Many of them look like they were struck by lightning and so many of them have trees on top of them," Daz, a Ruala warrior said.

"Whoever heard of a storm killing an entire army?" Ratri asked.

"I think the Angels were watching over the village last night," Elan whispered.

Being cold and wet prevented many in the army of Claudius from sleeping through the night. Almost everyone was up before the sun, trying to make fires and dry out their gear. A small group of Enrops entered the camp of the Sanuri as the sun was rising. They gave him the verbal message from Thaos. Claudius and the others listened in silence as the Enrops talked about the Grogs, the Half-Man, the demon snakes and the whispering shadows.

Vivian adored the Enrops and took food out of her saddlebags to feed them. When the birds finished talking Claudius asked the Sanuri, "What does this all mean? Do you know who is behind this?"

"Actually we learned a great deal this morning," the Sanuri said as he poured himself a cup of hot coffee. "At least one of the Old Ones is behind the mausoleum trap. Although most demons can call up the snakes only the Old Ones can call forth the whispering shadows. I am assuming the Old Ones are behind the Huta attacks while Hecate is using the Valdees."

"So basically Hecate and the Old Ones are competing against each other for us," Stephan said. "That's a welcoming thought."

200

"Oh it is much more than competing," the Sanuri explained. "Most demons, even ones as powerful as Hecate dare not go against the Old Ones. But many of the demons are at war with each other. I don't believe Hecate is stupid or has a death wish which means she must have one of the Old Ones backing her. I would not be surprised if they all didn't go to war with each other, because of us."

"Now I understand why the Angels have been so close at hand," Maxwell said as he was cooking breakfast over the fire.

"Sanuri I didn't want to say anything in front of Duncan," Vivian said. "But I am greatly disturbed about what Sampson is doing."

"You mean that he wants to become a demon?" asked Raphael.

"Yes, I mean that is a horrid thought for anyone, but, well, the Sanuri knows how we are raised. From the first moments I can remember we are taught that our mission in life is to stop the demons and monsters from hurting others. It is ingrained in us. How can someone so blatantly go against all of that?" Vivian asked.

"You choose to uphold the teachings of your tribe," the Sanuri said. "Sampson does not. He has freely made his choices through life and each choice filled him with more darkness. Now he has taken a demon for his wife and is trying to give up his humanity."

"I can't imagine the trials he must endure are easy," Gabriel said. "Chances are good that he may not survive."

"But don't you think Hecate would help him?" Ingr asked. "I mean if she cares about him at all."

"Well, that is what is curious about all of this," the Sanuri said. "Hecate is known to be a seducer, I am sure she can control Sampson without marrying him. And I know of one other human who she married and he later turned into a demon. It is possible that she does have feelings for Sampson."

"Then she will help him through the trials and he will become a demon and come after us," Vivian said then she looked at Raphael. "It is my family and the villagers that I fear for."

"Your family is welcome to come home with us," Gabriel said. "Although that does not solve the problem."

"I thank you for your generosity," Vivian said. "But I believe that Sampson's hatred and anger is directed at me. I think we should set up a trap for him and use me as bait."

Maxwell spoke before anyone else could. "Vivian while what you say is true, this situation is much more complicated. Sampson will want to take revenge against his father for disinheriting him and against his brothers who are next in line for the leadership of your clan. And I am speculating on this but after hearing about how your clan raises their children, I suspect that even though Sampson makes his own choices there is a part of him that hates himself. This type of self-loathing fills people with anger and hatred which they often direct at others. I believe he will try to destroy your entire village."

Everyone listened to Maxwell intently but did not speak so Maxwell turned to the Sanuri, "Tell me is this just the ramblings of an old man?"

"Maxwell you are as keen of mind as you are quick of sword," the Sanuri said. "Your age has allowed you to understand human nature."

"Sanuri we cannot allow him to destroy that village," Raphael said. "Can we get to him while he is taking the tests?"

"You would have to go into the hell dimensions of the Old Ones," the Sanuri said.

"How long do the tests take?" Vivian asked.

"You seem to have forgotten that Duncan has made a covenant with The Great Ruler, a covenant his sons and their sons will honor. That tiny village of people is the only light in a very dark kingdom. I do not think it is fate that the Clan of Gesmal lives in Ryed; they are the only ones here who call in the Spirit of The Great Ruler and His emissaries. I believe you will need to address your concerns with Miranda and Daniel."

202

"Speaking of them," Claudius said. "We should reach the shore of the sea by noon today, any word yet on how we are going to cross the water?"

"We'll call to them when we get there," Angelina said. "They always come when we call."

"Sorren, Matthew you both have been awfully quiet since we left the village," the Sanuri said. "What is bothering you?"

"I am worried about how we are going to get all of the captives out," Matthew said. "From the way Miranda and Daniel talked, some of them might not be able to walk, then once we get them out of Ogg we still have to get them to the village."

"The Rualas will fly the captives to the village," Claudius said.

"I know that is the plan," Matthew said. "I guess I don't really know what is bothering me, maybe I am worried that we only have one shot at this and we have to make it good."

"First of all you are working with Angels," the Sanuri said. "So we don't really know if we only have one shot at this. You are used to going into battle and fighting enemies, not rescuing poor souls. I believe you are worried because this is the first mission like this you are leading."

"Perhaps you are right," Matthew replied.

"I'll tell you why I am quiet," Sorren said. "I am damn mad. I really like Vivian's people; in fact they seem like an extension of my tribe. But their clan is small and they are surrounded by demons. In fact there seems to be damn demons everywhere. Has it always been like this and I just never realized it or has the world changed? I've got another grandchild coming into this world and do I want him walking in a world filled with demons?"

"Both," the Sanuri replied. "This world is mostly populated with humans. The demons would not be here if the humans had not called them in. As long as there is weakness and dark desires in man, there will always be demons walking among them. But, there are times in the history of every world when darkness becomes more prevalent; and this is such a time for the World of Nunc."

"Demons become empowered by fear so for example, just think of all the fear that Hutas create in every kingdom. Demons thrive on chaos, because chaos causes fear. Wars cause fear."

"While you are talking I keep thinking about the people of Nora," Raul said. "All Roch did was to create fear and chaos among his people. At first we thought all of the people in Nora were evil but they were paralyzed by their fears."

"And they were without hope," Simon said. "Remember that is what the members of the City Council kept saying to us, that our Father was giving them hope."

"Think about the captives," Thedes said. "They probably lost all hope of ever being rescued."

"What!" Thaos yelled when Ratri and the other Rualas told of the dead army of Hutas just outside of the village.

"Look for yourselves," Ratri said. "And it appears they all died in the storm."

"Both Archetenus and I had a bad feeling all night," Thaos said.

"Thank you Miranda," Archetenus said with a grin. Thaos and the villagers looked at him. "Oh come on, do you really believe a storm destroyed an army of Hutas?" Archetenus asked. "When I first met Miranda I was skeptical too," then he laughed. "Actually I was a whole lot worse than skeptical now I believe in the impossible."

"I think some would call that miracles," Joshua said with a grin.

"Well, then I believe in miracles," Archetenus said. "Did I ever tell you the story about the army of demons that surrounded Jared's house? There was just Jared, me and both of our wives." "Delilah called to Miranda and Miranda told us just to stay in the house. Jared and I both argued because we didn't like feeling like sitting ducks, we wanted to fight. All night we could hear the demons trying to get into the house. Damn, the next morning Miranda tells us to come outside and not only is the ground littered with thousands of dead demons but not one building was damaged and none of the farm animals were killed."

Chapter XV
When Angels Cry

Although Claudius and his troops were aware they were being followed by demons, nothing tried to stop the army from its march to the Sea of Schenomi. There were signs everywhere showing the destructive forces of the previous night's storm. Several times the army had to stop to remove fallen trees from blocking its path; and each time Claudius and the others were prepared for attack, but none came. Even with these unexpected delays the army reached the shores of the great sea just after noon.

"Well I'll be damned," Claudius said with a huge smile on his face. Sorren let out a war cry and the soldiers and warriors followed in kind as they looked at the fleet of ships docked at the shore. Miranda and Daniel stood before the ships and smiled at the reaction of the army.

"Miranda I told them you would have a way," Angelina said as she rode up to the Angels. "Matthew worries too much." Both Miranda and Daniel laughed at her comment.

"Is that a pirate flag on one of the ships?" Stephan asked.

"Where did you get these ships from?" Raul asked in disbelief.

"Yes, there are pirates here," Daniel said with a grin. "There are also merchants of all sorts and fishermen. The Valdees have been attacking them all for years, stealing their cargos and taking their sailors for captives. When they heard we were going to attack Ogg and free the captives; ships kept volunteering their services."

"And how did they hear these things?" Simon asked with a grin.

Miranda smiled but did not answer Simon's question. "You will need to leave your horses on shore. The crews of these ships will transport us to Ogg and bring everyone back to shore. They will fight with us in the battle and they can reclaim their stolen cargo and crews. But most of these men are just hoping to find their friends and relatives still alive. And they are hoping that after today, the Valdees will no longer be a threat to every ship at sea."

"What about the Valdees women and children?" Matthew asked. "We will not kill them."

Daniel said, "Of course not. We will give them a choice. They can remain in their underworld home or start new lives on land."

Claudius left one hundred soldiers behind to care for the horses as they prepared to board the ships. "I'm not sure I want my wife riding in a pirate ship," Stephan commented.

"They will be safe from the crews," Daniel promised. "And Miranda and I have already planned which ships you will sail in." Claudius and his troops gathered around the Angels as Miranda and Daniel explained the plans for entering and leaving Ogg.

"This is exciting," Ingr said. "I have never been on a ship like this before."

"Well, just make sure you stay close to me," Stephan said. Then he looked at Raul who was standing next to him. "Raul if something happens to me, watch over Ingr."

"Of course I will," Raul said.

"Stephan don't even talk like that," Ingr scolded as she took Stephan's hand in hers.

"Look, there's the volcano," Simon said as he pointed at the top of Mount Vue. "Ogg lies just on the other side of that."

The majority of Nordes warriors were assigned to the rescue team because they all could do some level of medical care. Sorren was elated to be on the ship as he stood next to Angelina and Matthew. "We are going to have great stories to tell the children," Sorren said. Angelina laughed at her father's comment and enthusiasm.

"Son, what worries you so?" Sorren asked. "This is not like you."

"I don't know," Matthew said seriously. "Maybe the Sanuri is right and it is just that I am not used to this type of mission."

"It should be any time now," Angelina said. "We just passed the volcano."

Suddenly a great wind came up causing huge waves to rock all of the ships violently. There were no storm clouds in the sky, nor rain or lightning. Everyone grabbed for things to cling to since they were losing their footing with the rocking of the ships.

"I don't understand this," one of the sailors yelled who was standing close to Matthew. Deafening sounds like explosions filled the air and now the ships started to spin in circles.

"What is happening?" Angelina yelled as she clung to Matthew.

Sorren laughed, "I think the Angels just busted down the doors to hell. Hang on."

The ships spun like tops as they descended into the cold waters of the Schenomi Sea. The castle of King Douma was slightly southwest of Mount Vue, while the City of Trapolli was directly east of the castle. The Dungeons of Frey, where the captives were kept were south of both the castle and the city. Miranda led the rescue team into the dungeons as Daniel led the team that attacked Douma's castle; a third team led by the Sanuri attacked the City of Trapolli.

King Douma had been warned by demons that the humans planned to attack his kingdom but in his arrogance Douma did not take the warnings seriously. Not until the doors to his castle flew open and hundreds of armed warriors charged inside.

The Valdees were taken completely by surprise but it did not take them long to call forth their troops. There was no water inside any of the buildings. The Valdees and the attacking army were breathing air. Claudius, Stephan, Ingr, Gabriel, Raphael, Vivian, Simon, Raul and Misha were among the group that burst into the castle, killing every Valdees soldier they encountered. The Ruala warriors flew over the combatants and shot arrows into the Valdees.

Douma did not show himself but ran to the inner sanctum of his castle were his unholy altar was located. As the sounds of battle grew closer, Douma called upon the Old Ones for help.

Simon and a Valdees soldier were rolling on the floor, gouging at each other's eyes. The skin of the Valdees was slippery and Simon was having difficulty grasping his opponent. The Valdees shifted his weight and rolled to his side, pinning Simon underneath him. The Valdees pulled a large knife from the sheath on his belt and tried to cut Simon's throat.

Simon grabbed the knife welding arm of the Valdees with both of his hands, but his hands were losing their grip when the Valdees suddenly fell on top of Simon. He quickly pushed the dead soldier off from him; as Ingr pulled her spear out of the back of the Valdees.

Gabriel was chasing a Valdees soldier up a flight of stone stairs when a small army of Valdees appeared; coming down the stairs. Greatly outnumbered and in a bad tactical position; Gabriel jumped over the railing and grabbed a large metal candelabra which was hanging from the ceiling. The candelabra immediately crumbled under Gabriel's weight. He crashed onto the stone floor as hundreds of Valdees soldiers ran down the stone steps.

The City of Trapolli was surrounded by a large stone wall with wooden gates. The gates literally exploded from the power of the Sanuri. There were no guards on the top of the wall to the city but as soon as the Sanuri led his army inside they encountered great numbers of Valdees who came running towards the sounds of the explosion. The fighting started in a stone courtyard.

Screams and the sounds of metal hitting metal were deafening. The stones of the courtyard became slippery from the blood that was flowing, causing combatants on both sides of the battle to slip and fall. Trapolli was a large city; the Sanuri knew this battle would not end quickly.

Without saying a word, Miranda blew the doors off the large stone wall that surrounded the Dungeons of Frey. Matthew led the charge with Sorren immediately behind him. There were only a handful of Valdees soldiers at the front gate, many of them were killed before they realized they were being attacked. Matthew and his troops only traveled two hundred yards before their way was blocked by another locked gate.

Miranda waved her hand and the chains fell off the handles and the two heavy doors opened on their own. The smell of death filled the nostrils of Matthew's army; causing many to fear the captives had been killed. There were lit torches on the walls but they did little to dispel the darkness of the massive arena they had just entered. "Miranda we need light," Angelina said, then stood horrified as the light revealed the scene before them.

Matthew and his entire army stopped in their tracks and stared with disbelief at the emaciated bodies that were locked in cages and chained to walls throughout the arena. Many of the captives resembled skeletons with bulging eyes and bloated stomachs. With their minds and eyes dulled from starvation the captives watched the approaching army, not realizing they were being rescued.

"Do not fear," Matthew yelled when he composed himself. "We are here to take you home." The captives who could walk to the doors of their cells only stared in silence.

"Miranda these doors are chained," Sorren yelled.

Miranda now walked before the army of rescuers and although she spoke in one language it was understood by all. "The Great Ruler has sent us to save you. We are taking you home." With her words all of the chains and locks released and the doors opened.

Angelina ran to the nearest door and an emaciated child fell into her arms. Filled with anger, Angelina screamed. "Miranda why? Why have you not come here before this?"

"Because only you asked us in," Miranda said. Angelina ran up to the Angel to show her the dying child. Miranda placed her hand gently on the child's forehead and Angelina saw tears running down Miranda's cheeks.

Thedes threw his massive head back and emitted a mournful bellow that did not sound human. Soon another similar sound was heard from one of the cages, then another and another. Thedes yelled out in his native tongue, "I am Shettee; we are taking you home to your families." Thedes ran to a cage where he heard his brethren and his knees weakened as he saw a dozen emaciated Shettee warriors crammed inside a small cage.

"Come, these people are our friends," Thedes said as the captives simply stared at him. "I will carry you." Thedes picked up a warrior who was lying on the ground and started to walk out of the cage when he heard a weak voice call his name.

"Thedes is that you?"

Thedes watched as a man feebly moved through the crowded cell. Thedes at first did not recognize his friend and his King. "Neputa is that really you?" Thedes asked.

"Yes," Neputa said as he started to both laugh and cry.

"My friends, your families are safe we will take you to them," Thedes said.

"Our families are alive?" Neputa asked in disbelief.

"Yes, they all survived," Thedes said. "I will explain later but now we must get you out of here."

"Move to the side son," Sorren said as he entered the cage and picked up one of the Shettees. When Thedes walked out of the cage he could see that many of the captives were being carried and the captives who had any strength were helping others to escape.

"Prince Matthew there are Hutas in here," one of the soldiers yelled. Matthew walked to the cage and saw eight wounded and emaciated Huta warriors lying in their own filth.

"Bring them too," Matthew said. "They are in no shape to cause problems."

The horror of the rescuers was compounded when one of the captives yelled, "There are more dungeons below."

"Raphael," Vivian screamed when she saw him leaning against a wall and his side covered with blood. Vivian ran to her husband and opened his shirt, which revealed a deep gash in his side. "I have to stop that bleeding," Vivian said to Raphael.

"Misha help me," Vivian screamed as she saw her friend flying overhead. With one mighty swing of his sword, Misha cut the head off from a Valdees soldier who was coming up behind Vivian. "Misha can you hold him while I burn it?" Vivian asked.

Misha suddenly grabbed Raphael as he lost consciousness. Vivian heated the blade of her sword in the fire of one of the torches attached to the wall. She cried as she pressed the hot blade against Raphael's skin. "Misha will you take him to the ship?"

"Of course," Misha said. "Then I will come back for you." Suddenly Vivian grabbed a knife from her belt and threw it behind Misha, hitting a Valdees soldier in the heart.

"Misha please get him to safety," she begged.

"I will be right back," Misha said as he picked Raphael up and ascended above the battling crowd.

Vivian quickly turned as a knife sped past her head and struck the stone wall. Vivian grabbed the knife and plunged it into the stomach of the Valdees who was trying to grab her.

Blood was running into Claudius' eyes from a large gash on his forehead. He was facing three armed Valdees soldiers. One of the soldiers charged at Claudius with his sword drawn. Claudius side stepped the attack and quickly grabbed the Valdees and thrust the soldier in front of him as a second Valdees was about to stab Claudius.

The second Valdees killed his comrade that Claudius was using as a shield. Claudius pushed the dead Valdees into the second attacker as he stepped to the right and thrust his sword into the third Valdees soldier. Claudius quickly pulled his sword out of the Valdees warrior. As Claudius swung to his left, he lowered his center of gravity and thrust his sword into the second attacker.

Hundreds of Ruala warriors flew over the streets of Trapolli and shot arrows into the Valdees soldiers. The Sanuri and his troops were pushing the Valdees back from the front courtyard of the city.

The Sanuri suddenly heard a horn blow and turning to his right he saw Valdees soldiers riding through the streets on gigantic creatures which the Sanuri had never before seen.

The Uthan were an ancient breed of giant sea horse, only found in the extreme depths of the Schenomi Sea. Their appearances seemed benign at first, until the Sanuri saw the giant fangs protruding from their mouths and the barbarous balls on the tips of their tails.

"Be wary of these creatures," the Sanuri called out with his booming voice and charged at his new adversaries. Hearing the Sanuri's voice, many of the Rualas turned their attention to the Valdees who were riding on the Uthan. The sea horses hissed at the Rualas and tried to pull them from the air. The Sanuri plunged his sword into the chest of one of the beasts as another tried to bite the Sanuri's shoulder. The blood of the Uthan was green, thick and foul smelling.

The streets of the city were all made of stone, most were narrow and winding. While the designs of the streets proved advantageous for the Ruala warriors who were trapping their prey, the soldiers on foot were also being trapped in the narrow lanes. The crews from the ships fought savagely at the sides of the trained soldiers and warriors; war cries filled the air as well as intense smoke. The pirates were burning the city.

Of the six ships docked outside of the Dungeons of Frey, three were designated for the captives. Nordes warriors provided medical care and gave the captives all of the food and water they could find. There was not one warrior of the fierce Nordes Tribe who was not affected by the condition of the captives. Some of the warriors became angry while others could barely contain their tears.

The captives appreciated even the smallest act of kindness; many of them were too weak and sick to eat the food that was given to them. As the dungeons were being emptied, Angelina boarded one of the ships so she could help care for the patients. Her emotions were running high; Angelina was filled with anger at the horrors that man can place upon his kind.

"Miranda help us!" Angelina screamed with frustration. "They cannot eat or drink; have we come this far not to save them?"

Miranda suddenly appeared next to Angelina. "Angelina you will be a queen one day of one of the most powerful kingdoms in Opots. Never forget what you have seen here and never lose your compassion." Miranda disappeared but a warmth filled the ships. Both the captives and their rescuers felt as if they were babies being held in the arms of their parents. No one understood what was happening to them; no one realized they were being healed by holiness.

Stephan and Ingr were fighting back to back as they were surrounded by Valdees soldiers. The two had chased three Valdees into a side room only to discover they ran into a trap. Stephan feared for the safety of his wife. He almost lost her once he was not prepared to lose her again.

"Daniel we could use some help in here," Stephan yelled as he stepped forward and plunged his sword into the stomach of a Valdees soldier. The Valdees were not rushing Stephan and Ingr all together which Stephan found curious until he realized that he and Ingr were not alone. Daniel suddenly appeared in the small room and stood with Stephan and Ingr so they formed a triangle. What humanity that was left in the Valdees sought to flee at the sight of the Angel but these creatures had sold their souls to demons and the darkness within them relished the fight.

Now the room full of Valdees attacked the three in one move. The presence of Daniel greatly intensified the abilities of both Stephan and Ingr; the battle took on incredible proportions. Stephan would later describe what he remembered of the fight as being similar to watching two wild cats fighting with each other; where they become one ball of flying fur and claws. Daniel, Ingr and Stephan did not break the triad they formed and the demons did not survive the battle.

An Uthan grabbed a Wetprian soldier, who threw a spear at it. The soldier screamed in fear and agony as the demonic beast crushed his chest with its great fangs. Ruala warriors throughout the city now focused their attention on this new threat and showered their arrows on the Uthan and their riders.

The hides of the Uthan were thick and seemed impervious to the arrows. The Uthan continued their attack after their riders had fallen dead onto the streets.

"Everyone back," yelled the Sanuri as he sized up these new opponents. The Sanuri waved his hand and the stone buildings on either side of the street began to tremble, the movement of the buildings became more and more intense until their foundations could no longer hold them. The buildings collapsed on the army of Uthan; while many of the creatures were crushed by the tons of stone others continued their advance.

Daniel disappeared as quickly as he had appeared in the small room; leaving Stephan and Ingr somewhat dazed as they stared at the piles of bodies on the floor. Daniel could hear the voice of King Douma as he beseeched the Old Ones for help. Daniel could feel the presence of powerful evil entering in. Daniel grasped his sword and prayed, "Great Ruler be with us."

"Vivian," Misha yelled as he swooped down and picked her up from the floor of the castle. Misha flew his friend to one of the two ships that had been designated for the wounded warriors. Prince Gael was placing blessed crystals on Raphael's wounds when Vivian and Misha arrived. Vivian started to cry when she saw how pale Raphael was.

"Gael will he live?" Vivian could barely stammer out the words.

"He had more wounds than the one you burnt," Gael said. "He was attacked from the side and the back and he has lost a great deal of blood."

"Can you give him my blood?" Vivian asked.

"Misha leave us," Gael said. Prince Gael was the oldest son of King Manu and Queen Delilia of the Rualas. He was a powerful warrior and an even more powerful healer. Gael had received his medical training from the Ruala Chief Healer Mateo and Gael had received his spiritual training from the Sanuri himself. "Vivian you have spent enough time with my people to know that our medicine is not of the world of man. Your husband is dying are you willing to give of your life force to save him?"

214

"Of course, how can you even ask?" she asked tearfully.

"What if he needs all of your life force?"

"Then I will die to save him, please tell me what I must do?"

"Then give me your hand," Gael said. Gael held Vivian's hand in his left hand. With his right hand, Gael opened Raphael's mouth and blew into it for several moments. Vivian did not understand why, but she suddenly felt dizzy and weak. Then Gael took his right hand and placed it over one of Raphael's wounds and began to pray.

The Sanuri sensed the increasing presence of malevolence in the city as he watched the army of Uthan advance. "Old friend," the Sanuri whispered. "I think the Old Ones are driving these creatures, I do not have the power to stop them alone. Please help us in this mission." The Sanuri had not finished his request before the image of The Lion appeared at his side.

"Douma has called the Old Ones in," The Lion said. "Tell your soldiers to retreat; this is not a battle of their world anymore."

In a rare instant the image of The Lion was seen by others besides the Sanuri. Although the pirates, sailors and many of the soldiers did not understand the significance, the Rualas and Venatores did.

"Retreat! Retreat!" the Sanuri yelled. His voice amplified over the chaos of war and was heard throughout the city.

Micha, the oldest son of Joshua and Iris ran up to The Lion and bowed before him. "We will not let you fight this evil alone. The swords of the Venatores are yours."

"As are the swords of the Rualas," said Prince Hadar, the younger brother of Gael, as he too bowed before the Angel.

"Give them a choice," The Lion said to the Sanuri.

"The most powerful Angel warrior in the heavens is in our midst," the Sanuri yelled and his voice echoed throughout the city.

"It is your choice to retreat or to fight at his side. Will you stand with the Angels?"

Men and women of all manner; momentarily stopped as they made one of the most important decisions of their lives. The number who ran to The Lion greatly outnumbered those who chose to retreat. The battle now took on new dimensions.

Douma was kneeling before his unholy altar and now jumped to his feet at the sound of Daniel's voice. "Douma the atrocities you have committed against The Great Ruler and His children are great. You not only sold your soul to the demons but the souls of others. You have raped, murdered and tortured in the name of darkness and now you call the Old Ones into this place."

Douma laughed, "And you are going to fight all of these demons?"

Daniel could see the demon behind Douma's human mask. "Demon be gone," Daniel ordered. And with his words the demon was vanquished leaving the shell of humanity standing before the Angel. Douma had given himself over to his demons so long ago that he had forgotten what it felt like to exist without them. Daniel now gave Douma back his conscience which had been eradicated by the darkness of his soul.

With this act all of Douma's transgressions flooded his mind. Douma screamed with horror at the monster he was. He quickly turned and grabbed the sacrificial knife that lay on the altar and thrust it into his own heart. But Douma's spirit suddenly realized that while his body had escaped the penalties of his actions, his soul had not.

Daniel's presence grew and filled the demonic chambers. The altar exploded and burst into flames and the demons appeared.

Every bed that had been prepared for the captives was filled. Miranda walked through the three ships and blessed the patients and those who cared for them. "Miranda," Matthew said breathlessly. "I have been looking for you. We have all of the captives out of the dungeons. Are we needed in battle?"

"Douma has called the Old Ones in," Miranda said. "They are in the city and the castle."

"Send us where you need us," Matthew said. Faster than he could blink, Matthew found himself in the castle of Douma; as he looked around Matthew heard Miranda's voice in his head. "Now three of The Seven Sons are in the castle, Daniel is alone with Douma's altar and the Old Ones."

"Raul, Simon," Matthew yelled as he pushed through the battling crowd.

"They are up stairs," Gabriel yelled as he hit a Valdees over the head with a battle axe.

"Gabriel come with me," Matthew yelled. "Daniel is fighting the Old Ones."

"Miranda show us where we need to go," Matthew yelled as he and Gabriel ran up the stone steps.

"To your right." Matthew and Gabriel heard Miranda's voice. They ran into a large room on the second floor and saw Raul and Simon among the many who were battling Valdees. Matthew and Gabriel ran up to their friends. Gabriel grabbed a Valdees who was trying to stab Simon and ran his sword through the creature; while Matthew stabbed one of the two Valdees who Raul was fighting against.

"Come," Matthew yelled. "Miranda wants us to help Daniel; he is fighting the Old Ones."

"Where are we going?" Simon yelled as the four warriors ran out of the room.

"Miranda will tell us," Gabriel said.

"Up two more flights of stairs," Miranda instructed. "You will be entering the chambers of Douma go straight back; past his bedroom chambers is the unholy room."

To the horror of many the entire City of Trapolli started to shake as if hit by a great earth quake.

Some of the warriors thought it was the Sanuri or The Lion who was causing the quake; until they saw the dark clouds filling the streets. The smell of death filled the nostrils of all as the legions of demons took form.

"Where is your leader?" The Lion called out. There was no answer.

"For all the fear you create, demons are nothing more than cowards," The Lion said mockingly. "The Valdees may have called you but this army stands against you. Who among you has the courage to come forward?"

A great wind developed in front of The Lion and the Sanuri. Many of the soldiers were blown off their feet and the Rualas had difficulty staying in the air. A funnel cloud of great proportions appeared in the city."

"Stand your ground," the Sanuri ordered the troops. "The demon is trying to instill fear; it is nothing more than a show."

"And what do we do for a show?" Sorren yelled as Miranda had suddenly transported him and others into the city. In a deliberate act to mock the power of the demon, Sorren started to clap his hands and to laugh. Others stared at Sorren in disbelief but as the old warrior walked towards the funnel cloud, others joined in. One by one the soldiers broke into laughter and clapped their hands. Both the Sanuri and The Lion smiled for the laughter was dissolving the fear and thus disempowering the demons. "What else have you got?" Sorren yelled out boldly.

The funnel cloud quickly took a different form and the eyes of all watched as the powerful demon Bentra grew before them. Bentra was one of the Old Ones; he was in the second group of thirteen who had descended on the World of Nunc. "Who are you to mock me?" the demon screamed with such rage that buildings tumbled from their foundations.

"Who are you?" Sorren asked mockingly.

"I Am The Darkness Within Man! I Am Fear Itself!"

"You aren't the first demon we have heard say that, don't you have a name?"

218

Sorren's boldness and lack of fear was driving the demon into a frenzy. "My name is imprinted in the hearts of mankind, I am Bentra!"

"Sorry, never heard of you," Sorren said as he now stood next to the Sanuri and The Lion.

The Sanuri turned to Sorren and said, "Mankind called him in, sometimes it only takes one voice to send him away." Sorren gave the Sanuri a quizzical look for just a moment, then suddenly Sorren knew what he had to say.

Sorren took three steps forward and thrust his sword downward with such force that it became impaled in the stone floor of the city. "We claim this city, this kingdom in the name of The Great Ruler and we call Him in." In that instant legions of Angels appeared in both the city and the castle.

When Matthew, Gabriel, Raul and Simon found Daniel he alone was doing battle with thirteen Old Ones. Matthew would later say that he never remembered entering that room because as soon as the four men made the choice to fight for the Angel something happened to them; something they never understood. The four human warriors felt lighter and stronger, they literally flew through the air and attacked some of the most powerful demons of all the worlds.

Some of the Old Ones stood in amazement as they realized the powers of their new opponents and in their hesitation they opened themselves up for attack. All four of the men thrust their swords as one into the demon Moloch; the holiness attached to their swords surged through the great demon like electrical energy.

Moloch screamed in agonizing pain and tried to dislodge the humans from him. But they stabbed him again and again. The screams of Moloch distracted the other Old Ones, who had never seen humans inflict pain upon their kind before. The holiness so weakened Moloch that he ran from the battle and tried to return to his hell dimension as quickly as he could; for Moloch thought he would regain his strength there.

Matthew, Raul, Simon and Gabriel now jumped onto Ipos, as he screamed in pain the demon Chaladrone tried to attack the humans but Daniel prevent the attack. Ipos too, retreated to his hell dimension. It was only then, when the four turned to attack another demon that they realized the room was filled with Angels and the Old Ones were trying to escape. Within moments these four men found themselves back on one of the ships with their comrades.

The fleet's exit from the underworld Kingdom of Ogg was not as dramatic as their entrance. Claudius and his troops suddenly found themselves aboard the ships which were now sailing on the water, heading towards the Kingdom of Ryed.

"What happened?" Sorren asked as he was disappointed to be taken out of the battle.

"The Angels took over that battlefield," the Sanuri replied. "You did well Sorren, do you realize the power you possess? Most humans never realize they can do what you just did."

Before Sorren could speak, Miranda appeared before him. "Sorren do you remember when Daniel and I came to your camp after you rescued Angelina and Vivian? We told all of you of the plight of the captives and the intents of the demons. We also told you about the dangers of this mission and gave you a choice. I said there would be no punishment or shame for those who did not go to Ogg."

"You stood before the others and as I listened to your words I also read your heart. You were prepared to perform the mission alone and your courage and faith led the others around you to join you. Daniel and I wanted the others to see what we saw in you that night. That is why I sent you to the city."

"So you gave me the power to call forth that army of Angels?" Sorren asked as his voice shook with emotion.

"No, you already had the courage and the faith; we just helped you with the words."

Chapter XVI
Healing

"We're glad to see you," Thaos said as Lakin led his small army into the Village of the Clan of Gesmal.

"We saw all the dead Hutas," Lakin said. "We brought medical supplies; do you have wounded who need to be cared for?"

"We didn't kill those Hutas," Thaos said. "It appears a storm did, if you can believe that. We are expecting lots of wounded as soon as the others return."

"Hannah," Cassandra said loudly and walked up and hugged her friend. "I didn't know you were coming?"

"No one did," Hannah said. "As soon as I got Gabriel's letter I couldn't stay home. All of these warriors are carrying medical supplies, where should we set up?"

"Why don't you let me introduce you to Chief Duncan and Vivian's family first? They have been in charge of setting up the hospital areas. Everyone here is so nice, you will really like them. Ibula had her baby, it's a boy."

"I heard," said Hannah.

"Lakin, Calen, Luca come with us," Cassandra said. "I want to introduce you to some people." Cassandra led her friends towards the only large meeting hall in the village."

"Are they building homes?" Luca asked as he watched the activity all around them.

"Not homes, places for the wounded," Cassandra replied. "Miranda and Daniel said we would need them. Elan look who is here." Cassandra called when she saw her fiancé dragging a small log. Elan immediately stopped and walked up to the group and hugged Hannah.

"Gabriel didn't say you were coming," Elan said.

"He doesn't know," Hannah replied. "I was afraid he would tell me to stay home."

"Well, we are glad to see all of you," Elan said. "It sounds like we are going to have our hands full."

The group walked about one hundred yards and entered a large log building. Men were busy building bed frames while women were bringing in bedding. No one seemed to notice as the group entered the building. "Duncan, Joshua," Cassandra called. "We have a wonderful surprise."

Both men put down their tools and walked up to the group. "This is Chief Duncan and Joshua, Vivian's father and this is Prince Lakin, Ibula's brother and his cousins Calen and Luca. And this is Hannah, Gabriel's wife, she is a great physician and Lakin is a powerful healer. They brought lots of medical supplies."

"We also brought many blankets," said Hannah.

"We are very glad you are here," Duncan said as he shook hands with the Rualas. To Hannah's surprise Joshua hugged her.

"Both Raphael and Gabriel are my sons now," Joshua said with pride. "So you are my new daughter. I must take you to the house to meet Iris." Then Joshua turned to Lakin, Calen and Luca, "Please come to my home, Vivian and the others have spoken a great deal about all of you. My family is honored to have you here."

"Before we go," Lakin said. "I brought five hundred warriors and they are all carrying medical supplies, where do you want them?"

"We'll take care of that," Elan said as he and Cassandra walked out of the building.

"Duncan join us," Joshua said as he led the small group to his house. "My two youngest sons are so attached to Elan and Cassandra that it will be very difficult for them when you leave." This comment made everyone smile.

"When do you expect the others back?" asked Luca.

"We really don't know," Duncan said. "Tomorrow or the next day. We still have much to do."

"My warriors can help," Lakin said. "But we have rested little since we left Wetpr."

"There are many soldiers helping us," Duncan said. "Let your men get some sleep."

Joshua's house was filled with people who were both working and visiting Ibula. Joshua proudly made introductions and made an announcement about the medical supplies. Iris hugged Hannah as Lakin, Calen and Luca gathered around Ibula. "Thank The Great Ruler you came," Iris said. "We have been so worried about how we were going to care for all those poor captives. Now Hannah you are family, I will put you in the room of our two oldest boys, just give me a little time to straighten it up."

"I don't want to be any trouble," Hannah said. "But thank you. You both should know that Gabriel doesn't know I am here. I was afraid he would tell me to stay home; but his letter made it sound like you badly needed help."

"I am sure he will be glad to see you," Iris said kindly. "He talks about you and the children all of the time."

"Hannah you have to see the baby," Calen called out proudly. "Like Lily he is the first of his kind."

When Vivian awoke she found herself lying on a cot. She didn't recognize her surroundings and attempted to sit up but the pounding pain in her head forced her to lie back down. "Vivian take it easy," Misha said. She opened her eyes to look at Misha but closed them immediately.

"Misha I am so dizzy I can't even look at you, what happened?" Suddenly Vivian's eyes shot open and she sat up, "Oh my god, Raphael, where is he? Is he alright?"

"He's right here," Misha said as he was sitting on the floor between the two cots. "Gael said he will be fine but he has a lot of healing ahead of him. He was stabbed many times and mostly in the back. You saved his life."

"Oh thank you," Vivian said weakly as she grabbed her head. "I don't remember much."

"Does your head hurt?" Misha asked. "I will get Gael."

"No stay here and tell me what happened first."

"You gave your life force to save Raphael. Gael said that you will be weak for several days."

"I am trying to remember," Vivian said as she continued to cradle her head in her hands. "I remember Gael taking my hand and blowing into Raphael's mouth, then I remember hearing Gael pray, I must have blacked out. Misha what happened? Did we get all the captives? And the battle?"

"We are on the ships and returning home. I have much to tell you."

The ships docked at the shores of the Kingdom of Ryed just hours after leaving the Kingdom of Ogg. All of the people who had been captives were now gently unloaded from the ships. The crews from the ships walked among the captives and found their friends and family members. For those who were seeing the captives for the first time, it was a very emotional reunion.

"Everyone who is not claimed by the crews of the ships will be taken to the village," Matthew said.

"Even the Hutas?" asked Angelina.

"Yes," Matthew said. "I would not leave an animal in such condition."

As soon as the ships docked, Misha took Raphael and headed towards the village, Dagon followed carrying Vivian. It was several hours before the rest of the Ruala army left the ships. Each Ruala warrior carried either a former captive or a wounded warrior. Many of the wounded were also transported on horseback. Claudius and his army did not leave the ships until arrangements had been made for all of the wounded.

224

There were few among the army who had not suffered some type of injury. "I don't know how those villagers are going to take care of all these wounded." Claudius said with great concern. "Sanuri is there some way we can get more help?"

The Sanuri smiled and now looked behind him at Gabriel. "Gabriel already did."

"What do you mean?" asked Gabriel.

"Your letter to Hannah stirred the hearts of many," the Sanuri continued. "Sudfad and Renya sent large quantities of medical supplies and blankets for the wounded. Lakin and five hundred warriors just landed in the village with the supplies and with the new Court Physician."

"Who, wait is Hannah here?" Gabriel asked with both excitement and concern.

"You should know by now that your wife cannot stand idle when there is such need," the Sanuri said smiling. "We now have Lakin, Gael, Hannah and Angelina as healers; and of course me."

"Hannah is now the Court Physician?" Gabriel asked.

"It's about time," Raul said. "The girls hated Philip and that was before we discovered he was a traitor."

"Looks like you may be spending more time in Salar, than you originally expected," Simon said to Gabriel.

"I believe Salar has become home to my family and my team," Gabriel said. "And now that Maxwell and Emeral are living with us I don't think Calen and Natasha will be moving to the Ice Caves any time soon."

"Maxwell was telling us how much he and Emeral love their lives with all of you," Ingr said. "Emeral feels needed again and Maxwell feels alive again helping with the missions."

"Have you seen Emeral and our mother together?" Raul asked. "They are so much alike and it's like they bring out the wildness in each other."

"Just be glad they didn't meet when they were young," Sorren said with a laugh. "Or you boys might not be here."

"When Natasha and Calen told us that his parents were coming for a visit, well, I will be frank we really didn't know what to expect," Gabriel said. "Actually we thought we would have to babysit them. And I think Calen was a little concerned about how we would react to his family. Well you've met them. By the end of the first week it was like they had adopted everyone in the house; in a way they take care of all of us. We all love them, especially Hannah and Natasha since they don't have parents."

"Gabriel you have quite the home now," the Sanuri said. "For years most of you were such lone warriors, now look at you, husbands, wives and children and everyone is happy living together."

"I know, Natasha and I have talked about that same thing," Gabriel said. "What are the odds that many people could live under one roof and get along?"

"Gabriel we have worked with you," Simon said as he winced with pain. "You and your team are very good at what you do but it is a lonely and dangerous life; that is why you all became so close. Whether you want to admit it or not, I think all of you craved a normal family life too."

"Simon you are right," Gabriel said. "But none of us ever believed we would find wives and husbands who would understand what we did, much less help us and fight by our sides."

Since Lakin and Hannah were quite experienced in administering to large numbers of seriously wounded warriors, Duncan allowed them to sit up the medical areas as they wanted. Hannah and Lakin set up a series of medical stations and each station was manned by two people with some level of medical training. Each area was numbered and indicated the level of care that could be provided there. The most serious injuries would go directly to Hannah and Lakin, so their stations became surgical areas.

Joshua and Elan were put in charge of forming transportation teams. The people on these teams would determine the level of care the patient needed and make sure the patient was transported to the appropriate area. Since Miranda had told the villagers that many of the captives had been deprived of both food and water, the woman of the village were busy making soups and more substantial foods.

Nikki and Cassandra took over the kitchen in Joshua's home and were making large kettles of tonics. Joshua's two youngest sons took other children into the woods and they picked the herbs needed for the tonics. All soldiers who were not guarding the perimeter of the village were helping prepare for the wounded. People worked quickly and diligently as they expected the worst when the army returned.

Although Lakin had ordered his warriors to rest; most did not and chose instead to help set up the medical areas. It was towards evening when some Enrops flew into the village. "Misha and Dagon are bringing the first two patients, they will be here within the hour," the birds told Lakin and Hannah. They said they don't know how far behind them the rest of the Rualas are."

Lakin glanced at Hannah to see if she understood the significance of what the Enrops were saying. "Do you know who the first two patients are?"

"Raphael and Vivian," Neeko the Enrop replied. "We are supposed to tell you that Raphael almost bled to death from multiple knife wounds. Gael preformed a ceremony and Vivian gave her life force to save Raphael. They are both healing now."

Tears ran down Hannah's face as she listened to Neeko. "My husband Gabriel is he alright?" she asked fearfully.

"We have not seen them; but Misha said everyone is wounded but alive," Neeko replied.

"We need to find Iris and Joshua," Hannah said and stood up. Lakin grabbed her hand because he could see how upset she was.

"I will come with you," said Lakin.

They found Joshua first and told him the news. The three of them walked to Joshua's home, where they told Iris the news. Iris started to cry, then tried to control her emotions. "Can we put them both in the same bed?" she asked.

"I would think so," Lakin replied.

"Then I am going to prepare her room," Iris said and left the kitchen.

"I will help you," Nikki said and put her arm around Iris.

As Hannah and Lakin turned to leave the house, Ibula called to them from her bedroom. "I need to help, what can I do?" Ibula asked.

"I am not sure that is wise," said Lakin.

"I am doing much better," Ibula said. "I tire easily but I am getting stronger and no longer bleeding."

"Perhaps she can help determine the needs of the patients," Hannah suggested. "There are chairs in that area and we can have Elan watch over her."

"I can do that," Ibula said. "Iris told me how you have set up the areas."

"You can help only if you promise to take care of yourself Ibula. If you feel weak or faint, stop and sit down," Lakin said then he smiled. "I don't want anything happening to my little sister."

Dagon and Misha bypassed the medical areas and flew directly to Joshua's house. Both Raphael and Vivian were unconscious and put side by side in Vivian's bed.

"Get Hannah and Lakin," Joshua said to Paul and Adrone. The two boys ran out of the house.

Ibula walked into Vivian's bedroom and examined both Raphael and Vivian. "They are alright but will need a great deal of rest to heal," Ibula explained to Iris and Joshua.

"I have to admit that I don't understand what Vivian did to save Raphael," Iris said as tears ran down her cheeks.

"It is a ceremony that the Sanuri taught us," Ibula said. "It is a great act of love for one person to give up their life energy for another."

"Misha, Dagon I have fixed plates for you," Nikki said. "Come tell us what happened."

It was almost midnight when the Ruala army arrived with the wounded and former captives. Duncan had his people build great fires throughout the village to provide light. Even though the medical areas were set up efficiently, over one thousand patients arrived within an hour. Everyone in the village was awake and helping in some way, whether it was to care for the patients, maintain the fires or feed the warriors.

"They say there are many more wounded coming on horseback," Ratri said as he helped to carry a wounded soldier to Lakin's medical station.

"This is going to be a long night," Lakin said to Hannah as she cut the bloody shirt off from the soldier.

Iris stayed in her home and watched over Vivian, Raphael and Ibula's baby, as the others helped the wounded. Her two youngest sons burst into the kitchen and each grabbed crocks from the table.

"Nikki said to bring more tonic," Paul said. "Mother these people don't look real, the captives I mean."

"What are you saying?" Iris asked.

"They all look like they have been dead for a long time," Adrone said. "They are only bones."

Both Archetenus and Thaos came in from the perimeter to help with the wounded. Even these two experienced warriors were horrified at the condition of the patients.

"Hutas," a woman yelled and Archetenus and Thaos ran in her direction with swords drawn. Then they saw the emaciated, injured Hutas lying on the ground.

"I can't believe they brought these things here," Thaos said with disgust.

"If they didn't kill them there must be a reason," Archetenus said. "Maybe the Angels wanted them saved."

"Hannah," Thaos yelled as he saw her running past them with an armload of bandages. "Hannah come here a moment."

"I really need to get back to Lakin," Hannah said. "What is it?"

"They brought us Hutas," Thaos said and pointed to the men who were too weak to stand.

Hannah bent down and examined a couple of the men who did not act aggressively towards her. "Elan," Hannah yelled. "These men need soup and water right away."

"You're going to take care of them?" Thaos asked.

"They may be monsters but tonight they too are victims," Hannah said. "And yes we will take care of them. When they are healed, well, I guess you can do with them as you want."

"Seems like a waste of time to me," Thaos said.

"Thaos saving a life is never a waste of time," Hannah said. "Now I have to get back to Lakin."

Few slept in the village for the next day and a half. Archetenus, Thaos and Lakin made their warriors sleep in shifts, so they would not be exhausted if the village was attacked. Teams of Rualas were constantly flying around the village watching for enemies and the fact that none came, made everyone in the village uneasy.

"With all these wounded we are very vulnerable," Archetenus said to Thaos and Duncan. "I would expect this is when an attack would be launched. Something just doesn't seem right."

Six Rualas flew over the village calling for Joshua. "They're carrying Half-Mans," Archetenus said. "We better see what this is about." Joshua walked out of one of the medical buildings and looked around when he heard his name called.

"The Rualas have Half-Mans," Thaos said as he, Duncan and Archetenus walked up to Joshua. When the Rualas landed Erwat walked up to Joshua, while his five comrades stood back because they did not trust the humans. As Joshua spoke with Erwat, Paul and Adrone walked up to the Half-Mans and handed them cookies. The Half-Mans were reluctant to take them until Paul bit into a cookie and smiled. Then each Half-Man took a cookie and suspiciously bit into it. Paul and Adrone grinned as the Half-Mans devoured the cookies.

"They like them," Adrone said and walked up to Erwat and handed him a cookie.

"Erwat says the snakes are coming back to the forest," Joshua said.

"He is sure they aren't the same snakes from before?" Archetenus asked.

"He says these snakes are different, they are talking. Erwat thinks they are demons in disguise," Joshua said then turned back to Erwat and spoke in his language.

"He says there are lots of snakes and they just appeared out of nowhere," said Joshua.

"Ask him if his tribe wants to take refuge here," Duncan told Joshua.

"Erwat says they are safer where they are because the snakes are circling the village."

"Calen, Luca, Misha," Archetenus yelled. Calen was the first to reach the group.

"What are those?" Calen asked when he saw the Half-Man's.

"They are creatures that live in the woods," Thaos said.

231

"Duncan and Joshua give them food in exchange for information. They said a bunch of giant talking snakes are circling the village, the Half-Mans think they are demons in disguise."

"I hope we can kill them," Archetenus said as they all ran to their posts on the perimeter of the village.

The Rualas returned the Half-Mans to their tribe, with additional food that Duncan provided. As the Rualas were returning to the village they saw movement below.

"Let's see if we can kill some demon snakes," Barto said as he flew downward towards the ground.

"Those can't be snakes," Apel said. "They have to be thirty feet long.

The six Rualas flew over three snakes and repeatedly shot the demonic reptiles with arrows. "We need to get back and warn the village," Barto said and ascended into the air. Moments later they heard screams and turning they saw the tongue of one of the snakes wrapped around Jars, a Ruala warrior.

Quickly the five Rualas drew their swords and flew to their comrade, who was being pulled out of the sky. Three of the Rualas were trying to cut the snake's tongue with their swords while the other two were trying to pull Jars from the grasp of the reptile.

"We've got it," Apel yelled as they severed the upper part of the tongue from the monster. But the tip of the tongue was still wrapped tightly around Jars. "Take him back to the village," Barto yelled.

Moments later the Rualas landed in the center of the village, yelling for Lakin and Gael. Jars was still alive but barely breathing. The Rualas placed Jars on the ground and tried to remove the tongue that was choking the life from their friend.

"What is that?" Calen yelled as he ran up to his friends.

"The tongue of one of those giant snakes," Barto replied as he was trying to loosen its grasp on Jars.

"Give me your crystals," Luca yelled as he came upon the scene. As warriors were tearing off their crystal necklaces Luca yelled, "Cut a hole in the tongue and hold it open." A large group was now gathering around Jars and trying to help. Two Rualas were holding part of the tongue while others cut into it. Luca dropped the crystals into the incision and held them in place. The tongue started to smoke and jerk as it tried to release itself from the crystals.

The movements of the tongue became more exaggerated and erratic, Luca used all of his strength to keep the crystals in place as the tongue started to thrash around, loosening its grip on Jars. Calen and Ratri were grasping Jar's shoulders and pulled him free of the tongue. Calen picked Jars up and ran to Lakin's medical station.

The tongue was jumping wildly and now several other Rualas were trying to restrain it so Luca could maintain pressure on the crystals. Plumes of smoke rose from the tongue as the holiness of the crystals were destroying the darkness of the beast. Suddenly the tongue burst into flames and the Rualas jumped off.

"That's the damndest thing I ever saw," said Archetenus.

"We saw three snakes, they were at least thirty feet long," Barto said. "We shot them with arrows but couldn't kill the beasts. When we started back here, one of the snake's tongue pulled Jars from the sky. We cut the tongue off, well you saw the rest."

"The snakes are demons," Luca said. "We need to figure out a plan."

Nikki rode out to Thaos who was on the perimeter of the village. "Did you hear about the Ruala who was attacked by the demon snake?" she asked.

"Yes," Thaos said. "Archetenus stopped by and told me."

"How are you going to kill them?"

"Not sure yet," Thaos said. "And you should get back to the village."

"Don't you think now would be a good time to call Miranda or Daniel?" Nikki asked as she saw the concern on her husband's face.

Thaos hesitated, "I suppose so but I hate to bother them. We can probably kill the demons ourselves."

"Why are you men so hesitant to ask for help?" Nikki asked with frustration. "We have a village full of wounded to protect." Then Nikki looked at the sky and called, "Miranda, Daniel we need help down here protecting the wounded. How do we kill these demons?"

"We are right here," Daniel said with a smile and both Nikki and Thaos turned around and saw Miranda and Daniel standing behind them.

"I didn't want to bother you," Thaos said somewhat embarrassed.

"Thaos you are an extremely intelligent and capable man," Daniel said. "Some would say you are truly remarkable. One day you looked in the mirror and decided to change the person you were and your life and you did successfully; a feat not achieved by many. But you and the others must understand; you do not have power over things not from your world."

"There are some demons that we can kill," Thaos said defensively.

"Yes but none of you in this village know enough about demons to be able to tell the difference. And once you are in the heat of battle is not the time to find out you don't have the proper weapons. All you have to do is ask us for help or information. Those are not demon snakes they are powerful demons momentarily disguised as snakes. You cannot defeat them without the help of The Great Ruler." Thaos did not respond.

"Thaos," Daniel continued. "I begged The Great Ruler to allow me to help Miranda with her missions not because of the need, because there is need everywhere. But because of the extraordinary people she is helping; the ruling families of Lentz and Wetpr, the Rualas, the Clan of Gesmal, Raphael and Gabriel."

234

"The reason the demons have targeted all of you is because many times you are the only light in a very dark world. The courage, faith and integrity you all bear have affected others in ways you will never realize. Every one of you has the courage to stand up to darkness in the name of The Great Ruler and all of you are leaders in varying degrees. So it is challenging for us to help you without making you feel disempowered. Don't ever think you are bothering us."

Thaos appeared more relaxed, "So how do we stop them?"

"These demons were sent by the Old Ones, who set the trap for you at the mausoleum," Miranda said. "The Sanuri and the army that Claudius leads will be here in a few hours, but the snakes know that and will attack before the army gets here."

"You do realize that we wanted you to rescue those captives and all of you have done everything that we have asked of you," Daniel said. "We had no intentions of leaving you to fight those demons alone. Thaos what creature in your world is powerful enough to kill normal snakes?"

Thaos thought for a moment, "Eagles?"

"Look in the trees," said Daniel.

"Blue Hengers," Nikki said excitedly. "There must be hundreds of them."

"Thousands," said Miranda.

"Thank you so much," Nikki said.

"Just tell the Rualas to stay out of the sky when the battle begins," Daniel said.

"Those little people that told us about the snakes, the Half-Mans; will they be alright?" Thaos asked.

"They will be safe from these demons," Miranda said. "And I foresee a unique relationship developing between them and the Clan of Gesmal. But they are part of nature and humans are the caretakers of that gift."

Chapter XVII
The Ground Shook

"What the hell is that?" Claudius yelled as the earth shook underneath them.

"It's coming from the direction of the village," Stephan yelled. "We need to hurry."

Claudius and the army sped towards the village which was less than a mile to the northeast. Thunderous sounds came from the village but there were no storm clouds in the sky. The shaking of the ground greatly increased the closer they got to the village.

"What is that?" Matthew yelled. "What is over the village? What are we riding into Sanuri?"

"There are Hengers," the Sanuri yelled over his shoulder. "The sky is filled with Blue Hengers. The Angels must have called them in to fight the demons."

"Those carrying wounded, slow down," Claudius ordered. "The rest of us will move forward."

As the army drew closer they could see that the village was completely surrounded by giant snakes that were embroiled in a vicious battle with thousands of Blue Hengers.

"Hannah," Gabriel gasped loudly and started to leave the formation.

"Gabriel stop!" the Sanuri said. "The Angels are in the village and the Blue Hengers are killing the demons, Hannah is safe but you are in no condition to ride onto that battlefield, you can barely stay on your horse.

"You are sure she is safe?" Gabriel asked fearfully.

"Yes, we will enter when the Hengers are done."

The ground shook with such force from the battle between the ancient creatures that tables were overturning and belongings were falling from the walls of the village homes. The soldiers stood ready to enter the battle, while the villagers sought to protect and calm the terrified patients and children. Both the Hengers and the demons screamed and screeched as they fought and these deafening sounds only added to the din.

Lakin and Hannah were trying to work on Jars, who was critically injured by the demon snake. The small building they were in had been built hastily in preparation for the wounded. Hannah threw her body over Jars as boards started to fall from the ceiling. "Hannah!" Lakin yelled when he saw a large board hit her on the back.

"I'm alright," she said as she pushed the board to the floor.

Lakin ran to the door and saw Luca and Ratri standing a short distance away. "We could use your help," Lakin called to the two Ruala warriors; who immediately ran to the building. "The ceiling is caving in, we need help moving Jars."

"Hannah are you alright?" Luca asked. "There is blood on the back of your blouse."

"Really I am fine," Hannah said. "But we need to get him to a safer place."

"She shielded Jars with her body," Lakin said. "Let me run to the next building to see if it is withstanding this shaking any better."

"We can move him next door," Lakin said a few moments later when he reentered the building. Luca and Ratri picked Jars up and started to walk towards the door. The earth shook violently and the ceiling above the cot Jars had been lying on came crashing down.

"Oh my god!" Hannah said. "That would have killed him." Hannah ran around the room grabbing the medical supplies, then followed the men to the next building.

"Grandma, what is that sound?" Christopher yelled as he ran to the window in the parlor of their chambers in the castle of Wetpr.

"I don't know," Emeral said and quickly followed the boy.

"What is happening?" Natasha asked Emeral as Natasha burst into the parlor holding baby Lily. "Is it an earthquake?"

"I don't know," Emeral said as she looked out the window. "Where are Nicholas and Cerey?"

"Taking naps in the next room," said Natasha as she too walked over to the window.

"Stay with Christopher," Emeral said. "I'll get Cerey and Nicholas. I don't have a good feeling about this." As Emeral was leaving the room she turned to Natasha and asked. "Where is Lila?"

"I'm not sure," Natasha replied. "I think she went into Salar."

The frightened horses jumped and screamed as Claudius and the army watched the battle around the village. "I don't like sitting here," Claudius bellowed.

"You have no power against those demons," the Sanuri said. "They are being dealt with."

"Can we at least move closer?" asked Raul.

The scene in Salar was chaotic as people ran for shelter while the ground trembled beneath them. Troops from Fort Salar were riding to the city as well as to Sudfad's castle.

"You two go in with Emeral and the others," Jared yelled to Zoya and Delilah. "I'm going to find Sudfad."

Annabelle and Vitomas each carried a baby as they ran to the children's play room, where the nurses were gathered with the royal grandchildren. "Let's get everyone to the main parlor," Vitomas said. "Perhaps Sudfad and Renya can tell us what is happening."

The children cried at the loud noises as they were hurried down the long hallway.

"What the hell!" yelled Sorren. "Where is the Sanuri?"

"Did anyone see him get off his horse?" Claudius asked as he looked at the riderless horse standing next to him.

"Sanuri, Sanuri," Simon yelled; no answer came.

"Do you think the Angels took him?" asked Stephan.

"For his sake, I hope it was the Angels," Claudius replied.

"Girls I was just coming to get you," Renya yelled as she ran down the hallway towards Vitomas, Annabelle and the children. Renya had a sword in her hand.

"Are we being attacked?" asked Annabelle.

"We don't know yet," Renya said as she turned and led the group to the parlor, where they found Alexander, Laurel and Petra. As soon as they entered the room, Vitomas pulled Renya aside.

"Renya there is something I must tell you," Vitomas whispered.

Renya and Vitomas who was holding Ariel burst into Sudfad's study. Sudfad and Jared were talking with several military officers. "I am sorry to burst in like this," Renya said. "But Vitomas has something to tell you."

"Zoya, Delilah," Natasha said as the two women entered the parlor of the chambers where Gabriel's family was staying in the castle. "Have you seen Lila anywhere?"

"No," Delilah said. "Do you want us to look for her?"

"I think you should all stay here," Emeral said as she walked into the room with Cerey and Nicholas.

"Jared's down looking for Sudfad," Zoya said.

"Have you had any visions? Do you know what this is?" Natasha asked.

"No," said Zoya.

"You two play with Christopher," Emeral said as she led the children to the middle of the parlor. "I will get you some cookies." Emeral turned and walked up to an armoire that stood against the far wall of the parlor; she opened the door and took out a sword and a dagger.

"I didn't even know there were weapons in there," Natasha said. "Let me look." Then she turned to Zoya and Delilah. "We might need you to help with the children," Natasha said.

"Of course," Delilah said. "Why don't you give me Lily?"

"All I am saying is that when we were in that hotel in Taperia, the ground shook like this when we were battling all those demons," Vitomas said. "Demons were coming from everywhere. I am sure Raul and Simon told you." Then Vitomas looked at Jared. "You were there, don't you remember?"

"She's right," Jared said.

"We've never had an earthquake here," Sudfad said. "Nothing would surprise me."

"Well, if its demons we are going to need help," Renya said. "Have you called to the Angels yet?"

"Yes, a few minutes ago," Sudfad responded.

General Hoff, who was standing in front of Sudfad's desk growled, "Angels, My Lord you have the most powerful army in Wetpr here."

Jared laughed, "We've kinda learned the hard way that demons aren't that easy to destroy. Guess you haven't seen the Angels in action yet."

"I don't believe in Angels or demons," Hoff announced irritably.

"Then you are a fool," Renya said and grabbed Vitomas' hand and the two women left the room.

Both Emeral and Natasha quickly changed their clothing. Emeral put on her warrior's robe and Natasha changed into riding pants and a shirt. Emeral smiled as she and Natasha put sheathed weapons onto their belts. "Natasha my three blood daughters have never fought at my side," Emeral said. "You make me proud."

"And you are the mother I never had," Natasha said and kissed Emeral on the cheek. Then both women returned to the parlor where Zoya and Delilah were playing with the children.

"Christopher, Nicholas and Cerey," Emeral said as she knelt down on the floor with the children. "We don't know what is happening with the loud noises and the ground shaking but Lila is out there and may need our help. Natasha and I are going to look for her; I want you to be good for Zoya and Delilah. Will you do that for me?"

"Yes Grandma," Nicholas said sweetly.

"Can I help?" Christopher asked as he was now becoming scared that something might have happened to his sister.

"You and Nicholas can help by staying here and protecting Lily and Cerey, will you do that?"

"Yes, Grandma but there is something I have to tell you," Christopher said earnestly. "Lila and I had this game, when we were in the forest if one of us got lost we would whistle like a yellow bird until we were found. It worked."

"Thank you dear, that is very helpful," Emeral said and the two women left their chambers to find Renya.

Ibula was trying to comfort her baby who was frightened by the sounds of battle.

241

Nikki, Elan and Cassandra were all in Joshua's house. Thaos had ordered them to protect Joshua's family and Ibula. Neither Raphael nor Vivian had regained consciousness and Thaos was particularly concerned that the demons were looking for Raphael. The door to the home opened and Misha and Dagon entered. "Lakin wants us in here to help protect the others," Misha said. "At least for now the Angels want us to stay out of the fight."

"Have Raphael and Vivian awakened yet?" Dagon asked.

"No," Ibula said. "But that is normal for what they have been through."

Vivian's two younger brothers were in the house; her two older brothers had fought with Claudius' army in Ogg. Joshua was helping Hannah and Lakin care for the wounded. "Dagon did you see the demon snakes?" Paul asked.

Dagon picked the boy up and set him on his lap. "Yes, they are huge. But so are the Hengers who are fighting with them."

"Father says we can't go out there," Adrone said as he too climbed onto Dagon's lap.

"Your father is a wise man," Dagon said. "It is good that you listen to him."

Suddenly it was quiet, an almost eerie, surreal lack of sound. "All of you stay here," Misha said. "I am going to find out what is going on."

"Renya," Emeral said as she and Natasha entered the parlor of the King and Queen. "Do you know what is happening?"

"Not yet," Renya said. "Why are you two dressed like that?"

"Lila has not returned from Salar, we are going to find her," Emeral replied.

"And if she is hurt?" Jared asked as he stood in the doorway. "You can't carry both the girls and stay in the air."

"Emeral can come back for me," Natasha said. "Besides someone has to drive the horses; I think Lila took a small boca into the city."

"Are Zoya and Delilah in your chambers?" Jared asked.

"Yes, they are watching the children," Natasha said.

"Annabelle why don't you go up there and bring them all down here with us?" Renya suggested.

"I'm going with you two," Jared said to Emeral and Natasha. "I'll ride my horse and one of the girls can ride with me."

"Is it over?" Misha asked as he flew up to Archetenus.

"Not sure," Archetenus replied. "It sounds like it but no one can see through this fog. And damn doesn't something feel strange?"

"Where are the Angels?" Misha asked as he strained his eyes to see through the fog.

"Haven't seen them in a while," Archetenus replied. "We had this same damn fog with the tar creatures, think they joined the snakes?"

The shaking of the ground terrified Jared's horse. Although Jared was an experienced horseman he was having difficulty because the horse kept rearing up. Emeral flew overhead, holding Natasha by the waist.

"Jared," Emeral called out. "I am going higher; there might be more than the shaking that is scaring your horse." Natasha caught her breath as Emeral quickly ascended into the air.

They had barely risen above the tree tops when Natasha screamed, "Look!"

"Jared," Emeral yelled. "Stop and turn back. Tell Sudfad the ground has opened up and creatures are coming out, hundreds of them."

"What about you?"

"We're going to find Lila."

Jared traveled the short distance back to the castle; he burst through the front door and ran past the parlor and down the hallway to Sudfad's study. Renya left the parlor and ran after him.

"Sudfad we're being attacked," Jared said as he ran into the study. "Emeral saw the ground opening up and hundreds of creatures coming out. I suspect they are demons."

"Where?" Sudfad asked as he unrolled a map.

Jared marked the area on the map as Renya entered the room. "Renya call the soldiers in here, then take the family to a safe place in the castle," Sudfad ordered. Renya screamed as she turned and bumped into the Sanuri who had just materialized in the doorway of the study.

"When did you get here?" asked Sudfad.

"The Lion just brought me from Ryed. Our forces are being attacked there but the Angels are with them."

"Well, it sounds like the demons are attacking us too," Sudfad said.

"Renya gather the children and staff," the Sanuri said. "Take everyone down to your wine cellar. Take food, water and blankets because you may be there a while. Stay out of the castle towers because Talmuth have been called forth."

Instead of leaving the room, Renya ran to the weapon's closet and started to take weapons from the wall. "Jared do Zoya or Delilah know how to use weapons?" Renya called out.

"Zoya does, I don't' know about Delilah."

"I may be back for more," Renya said as she quickly left the study with an arm full of weapons.

"The Lion is not leaving you in this," the Sanuri said to Sudfad. "But he wants you to follow his directions."

"What the hell is that smell?" Archetenus asked as the air filled with a putrid odor. "I've smelled that before," Archetenus said as his eyes widened. "Miranda where are you?" He called out loudly.

"What is it?" Misha asked.

"I smelled that same odor when I was pulled into hell," Archetenus said. "Miranda," he called again.

Suddenly Miranda's voice was heard by all the soldiers on the perimeter. "Archetenus, Thaos pull all your men from the perimeter and return to the village. Claudius will try entering your village in just minutes and he has many wounded with him. Just take care of the wounded and everyone must stay in the village."

"Miranda we will fight with you," Archetenus said. "I can smell the odors of hell."

"You and the others have proven your faith and courage to the heavens, there are few among you who are not wounded. Daniel and I said we would not leave you on this journey, have faith in us."

"I'll tell the others in the village," Misha said and turned and flew back to the village.

Both Archetenus and Thaos hesitated; it was not easy for them to fallback when they knew they were surrounded by demons. "Fall back," Archetenus ordered. "You heard her, fall back to the village."

"What are they?" Natasha asked as she looked down at the demons that were pouring out of the giant crevice.

"I don't know what type of demon, if that is what you are asking," Emeral said. "But look back towards the castle."

"Talmuth," Natasha gasped. "They're circling the castle."

245

"Dear, I am going to increase my speed, it may take your breath away," Emeral said as she sped towards Salar.

"Claudius," Daniel's voice called out as the army was approaching the village. "I will make an opening in the fog, only travel in the opening lest your men fall into a hell dimension."

"What!" yelled Claudius. "We will fight."

"You cannot go where this battle ground exists," Daniel said. "Now take your warriors into the village and stay there, do not come near the fog."

"Is that what hell smells like?" Sorren yelled as the putrid odor attacked their noses and eyes; causing many to choke and cough.

Suddenly a doorway opened in the wall of fog. There was enough room for the army to ride six abreast. Claudius led his warriors through the ring of hell.

"What has happened?" Misha asked as he landed near the medical area of Lakin and Hannah.

"We couldn't save him?" Hannah said with tears in her eyes.

"Who?" Misha asked.

"Jars," Lakin said sadly. "He was too badly injured even for our medicine."

"He was my friend," Misha said sadly. "But I will have to mourn later. The Angels are sending everyone back into the village as they fight the demons. Miranda said that Claudius' army will be here in minutes and they have many wounded. Everyone is to stay in the village."

"Gabriel," Hannah gasped and started to run towards the center of the village.

Hundreds of Wetprian soldiers had entered the City of Salar to help the citizens when the ground started shaking violently. The demons had not yet surfaced.

Great chasms were opening around the city cutting these soldiers off from the castle and Fort Salar. Thousands of Amulth, the demons created for the Insidiae, rose from the depths of hell and entered the World of Nunc. These attacks took place simultaneously in Wetpr and Ryed as the Old Ones united in an attack against those who they believed to be working for The Great Ruler.

The stench and heat from the hell dimensions intermingled with the air of Nunc causing a thick putrid fog to cover the chasms. Like the Village of the Clan of Gesmal, the City of Salar, Fort Salar and the castle of Sudfad were now surrounded with the surreal murkiness. "How can you see through this?" Natasha asked as she coughed.

"After so many years of flying one can just sense things," Emeral said. "But I must admit it is difficult."

Both women felt the rushing of air as something flew past them. "If that was a Talmuth," Natasha said. "Aim for under its throat or its eyes."

"I'm going to try and get above this fog," Emeral said and started to ascend when her back suddenly hit something and Emeral fell forward loosening her grasp on Natasha.

"I got your robe," Natasha yelled. "Are you alright?" The two women fell almost ten feet before Emeral regained her balance.

"Yes, I hit something hard," Emeral said as she grabbed onto Natasha. "If it was a Talmuth I can't understand why it didn't attack us."

"What else do you think is flying around up here?" Natasha asked as she strained to see through the thick vapor.

Gabriel was off from his horse as soon as he entered the village which had changed in appearance since the army left for the Kingdom of Ogg. There were now dozens of hastily built wooden buildings crammed into the village to provide shelter for the wounded. And in between the buildings patients were lying on all manner of bedding. While the thick fog created a wall around the village; it had not yet entered the village.

"Hannah, Hannah," Gabriel called as he ran between the buildings.

"She's down that way," a woman from the village said and pointed to the north. Gabriel turned and ran north as he continued to call Hannah's name.

"Gabriel," Hannah yelled when she heard her name called. Her heart jumped as she realized her husband was alive. "Gabriel keep calling I will find you." The village was so crowded with soldiers and patients that it was difficult for Hannah to see through the crowd because of her height. Suddenly someone grabbed her left arm; Hannah quickly turned and started to cry when she saw Gabriel. She was going to jump into his arms until she saw that he was covered with bloody bandages and his left arm was in a sling.

"Oh Gabriel you are alive," Hannah cried as tears ran down her cheeks. "But look at you. I want to hug you but I am afraid I will hurt you." Gabriel laughed and put his right arm around his wife; he bent down and kissed Hannah on the lips over and over. Hannah started to laugh. They laughed and kissed for several minutes then Hannah said. "Let me take a look at your wounds." Hannah took Gabriel's hand and they walked to her medical station.

"There are others who are in worse shape than me," Gabriel said.

"Honey I won't be able to concentrate on helping anyone else until I check you over." They entered a small wooden building that Hannah had set up for her medical station. "Do you have another shirt with you?" Hannah asked as she started to examine Gabriel's wounds.

"Yes," he said and laughed.

"Good, I am cutting this one off from you. There is so much caked, dried blood that I don't want to reopen any wounds." Gabriel kissed Hannah several times while she was examining him which made her laugh. "I was afraid you might be mad that I came," Hannah said. "You understand that I had to come don't you? I couldn't stay home after I got your letter."

"I didn't get mad," Gabriel said. "Actually when the Sanuri told me you were here I was really happy but worried for your safety."

"Who put the crystals on you?" Hannah asked as she examined a deep wound on Gabriel's arm.

"Gael."

"I'm glad. Your wounds are clean and starting to heal," Hannah said. "But as you know you have many wounds and will need some rest. Joshua and Iris gave me a room in their house, next to Raphael and Vivian. Do you know where they live?"

"Yes," Gabriel said as he kissed Hannah's hand. "Although the village really looks different now."

"We aren't that far away," Hannah said. "I'll take you there and you get some sleep."

"I can't sleep, we're surrounded by demons."

"And the Angels are taking care of them."

"I can help with the wounded."

"Gabriel you aren't in any shape to do anything," Hannah scolded. "And I am saying that as your physician not as your wife. Now I am going to put you to bed and I want you to stay there."

"Oh my," Iris said as Hannah and Gabriel walked into the house. Gabriel was not wearing a shirt, so his many bruises and bandaged wounds were exposed.

"Iris I am putting him to bed," Hannah said. "Gabriel thinks he is in better shape than he is."

"I'll make sure he stays there," Calen said with a grin as he entered the house."

Chapter XVIII
Ring of Hell

"This is outrageous," General Hoff complained as Sudfad gave him his orders. With both Raul and Simon gone, Hoff was acting Commanding General at Fort Salar. A savvy and battle experienced man, Hoff was very black and white in his thinking and extremely set in his ways. His normally rigid personality became more brittle with age.

"General Hoff, you will follow my orders or I will replace you with someone who will," King Sudfad said sternly as the Sanuri stood by.

"My Lord it is about time that someone reminded you to use your logic instead of believing in all this hocus pocus."

"You believe The Great Ruler is hocus pocus?" the Sanuri asked.

"Well, I don't believe in Him, if that is what you are asking," Hoff responded irritably. "Sudfad you have some of the best military minds in the world at your disposal and you listen to him," Hoff said with disdain as he pointed at the Sanuri. "I think you are putting your kingdom at risk."

"General Hoff I cannot have you in charge if you refuse to acknowledge the existence of the enemy that is attacking us. You are relieved of your duties."

"I protest," Hoff said and slammed his fist down on Sudfad's desk.

"Sudfad, perhaps the General should take a walk with me," the Sanuri said, then he turned to Hoff. "Are you willing to come with me?"

"Where?" demanded Hoff.

"If you want to keep your position you will go with him," growled Sudfad.

The Sanuri walked up to Hoff and touched the sleeve of his uniform jacket. Suddenly the two men were outside of the castle standing on top of one of the stone towers. "What the hell!" Hoff said as he looked around but within seconds his eyes widened as he saw great outlines in the thick fog. "What are those?" Hoff asked.

"Those are some of the things you do not believe in," the Sanuri said mildly. "They are Talmuth, an ancient species of war that can only be called forth by demons or very powerful dark lords. And because they are created by dark magics they are not easily killed by the fragile power of humans." A Talmuth dove at Hoff and the Sanuri.

Hoff could see the red face of the monster and feel its breath. He pulled his sword and just as the dragon-like creature tried to grab him with its mouth; suddenly a giant Blue Henger appeared out of the fog and hit the Talmuth on the left side with such force that the beast started to fall from the skies. Hoff did not speak he just turned and stared at the Sanuri.

"That creature that just saved your life is a Blue Henger; an ancient species of war that is called forth by The Great Ruler. You may not believe in him, but you owe him your life. This strange fog is caused because the ground is opening up and the noxious vapors from hell are being released and mixing with the air of this world. Come."

Before Hoff could speak, he found himself standing on the road between the castle and the City of Salar. "Explain that," the Sanuri challenged as the two men watched as hundreds of Amulth were climbing out of one of the giant chasms only to be attacked by thousands of Blue Hengers.

"I must be dreaming," Hoff exclaimed as he was unwilling to believe what was before his eyes.

"General your soldiers do not have the power to kill those demons, yet you would send them to their deaths because you have such a closed mind and steel heart. If you do not believe me, by all means go over there and attack those monsters." Hoff grabbed the hilt of his sword and took two steps forward then he turned and looked at the Sanuri.

"But how can this be?" asked Hoff.

"Humans are unique among all of The Great Ruler's children," the Sanuri said calmly. "You are so powerful yet so frightened at the same time. Humans feel safe and in control when they think they have all knowledge but the truth is General there is so much more to life than you can see with your eyes. There are other worlds and other beings and truths you have yet to be aware of. Whether you choose to accept it or not you have been given a great gift this day, for one moment in time you transcended the boundaries of your existence."

Emeral and Natasha felt a great wind speed past them but they could see nothing. Emeral clutched her daughter-in-law as she tried to see through the murky fog. "Great Ruler help us," Emeral whispered under her breath. Suddenly the fog became less dense around the two women.

"Oh my god!" Natasha exclaimed. "We're surrounded by Blue Hengers. Emeral they're protecting us."

The older woman cried.

Archetenus and Thaos met the returning army. Claudius, Raul, Simon, Sorren, Matthew, Stephan, Ingr and Angelina dismounted and the group walked a short distance from the rest of the troops.

"This is worse than I first thought," Archetenus said. "That stink that you smell, well I smelled that before, when that demon pulled me into hell. Something pretty damn powerful opened up the doors and the demons are escaping."

"The villagers?" asked Raul.

"Everything in the village is fine," Thaos said. "The fog hasn't even entered. There is just so many wounded to care for and honestly all of you look awful too."

"We heard the voice of Daniel," Claudius said. "He cleared a path for us to enter the village. He ordered us to stay in the village and away from the ring of fog."

"Miranda told us the same thing," Archetenus said. "But we have much to tell you." He paused. "But it can wait you all look like you need some care."

"Claudius, Raul and Simon, this may not be the best time but I may have been the only one who didn't know that Archetenus was raised in the military and held the rank of captain. Whichever kingdom he decides to live in, we would benefit from having him in our military," Thaos said.

"Is that something you would consider?" Claudius asked Archetenus.

Archetenus was obviously surprised by Thaos' comments. "Delilah wants to live on a farm. I don't know how to be a farmer; I've been a soldier my whole life. The answer is yes, I would like to be in the military again."

"If you decide to live in Lentz, you will have a position and retain your rank of captain," Claudius said.

"Thank you," Archetenus said.

Simon and Raul looked at each other; the closeness of these two brothers often allowed them to communicate without words. "Archetenus, our father has to make that decision but both Simon and I would support it," Raul said to most everyone's surprise.

"I will have to say that Delilah has become close with many people in Wetpr and may want to stay there," Archetenus said. "But I would be proud to serve for either kingdom."

"Understandable," Claudius said. "After the wounded are cared for and we have some food, I want to call a meeting of all the leaders."

"Ibula do you feel strong enough to help with the wounded?" Elan asked as he entered the home of Joshua. "The army has returned and there are so many."

"I can watch the baby," Iris said. "If you feel up to it."

"Thank you," Ibula said. "He is sleeping in his cradle." Ibula grabbed her medical bag from her bedroom and quickly followed Elan out of the door.

Nikki knocked on the door to Gabriel's bedroom. "I have some food if you are up to eating." Calen opened the door to the small room, and Nikki saw that Gabriel was sitting up in bed. "I thought you were supposed to be resting," Nikki said with a grin as she set a tray down on the small table next to Gabriel's bed.

"Calen was just telling me about everything that happened here," Gabriel replied. "Whatever that is, it sure smells good."

"Iris is a wonderful cook," Nikki said. "She and Joshua have taken us all in as family. We owe them a great deal."

"Gabriel was just about to tell me about the Kingdom of Ogg, do you want to hear too?" Calen asked.

"Yes," Nikki said with enthusiasm. "Can I ask Iris and the boys if they would like to hear also?"

"So what do you have to say?" Sudfad demanded of Hoff when the Sanuri and the General reappeared inside of the King's study. Hoff was visibly pale.

"It is as you have said My Lord," Hoff said. "Everything. I would not have believed it if I had not seen it with my own eyes. And honestly I am still not sure I believe it."

"Be that as it may," Sudfad snarled. "I am the King and I will not have you leading men if you refuse to follow my orders. Do you understand me?"

"Yes," Hoff said sheepishly; he was not the kind of man who liked being wrong.

"This kingdom follows The Great Ruler if you cannot accept that I would suggest you resign your position," Sudfad continued. "I will give you two days to consider your options. In the mean time you have your orders."

"Yes, My Lord," Hoff said.

"You're dismissed," Sudfad snapped. Hoff turned and left the room.

"I think there is more to Hoff," the Sanuri said.

"Do you think he is one of the spies?"

"I am not sure but he genuinely seemed shocked and frightened when he saw the demons and the Hengers."

"I will not tolerate his insolence," Sudfad said. "Find out what you can about him."

"I believe he is loyal to the kingdom," the Sanuri said. "But he thinks your faith in The Great Ruler is a sign of weakness. His loyalty to you is the question."

"I think we are over the city," Natasha said. "I can hear people yelling." The ground was still shaking violently and causing great havoc in the city. Emeral slowly descended as her visibility was greatly compromised by the fog. Unlike the Village of the Clan of Gesmal, the fog had infiltrated the city, making travel hazardous. The shaking of the ground caused damage to many of the buildings in Salar, resulting in at least two building fires. The smoke from the fires only intensified the fog.

"Do you know what stores Lila intended to go to?" Emeral asked.

"I know she mentioned the General Store but she also wanted to find a gift for Luca. I would guess she would get him jewelry or weapons," Natasha replied as the two women landed on a road in Salar. "We should get on the sidewalk," Natasha said as she grabbed Emeral by the hand and felt her way through the fog.

Salar was a large and highly populated city. Many people were running blindly in the fog, spurred by their fears. As soon as Natasha stepped onto the wooden sidewalk she was almost knocked over by a man hysterically running for shelter. "Let's just call her name," Natasha said. "We are never going to see her in this."

"With all of this noise she may not hear us either," Emeral said. The two women held hands and felt their way along store fronts, yelling Lila's name.

"The Hengers must be attacking the demons," Natasha whispered into Emeral's ear. "Or they would have been here by now."

"They could be and we just don't know it."

"Oh, I think there would be a lot more screaming," Natasha said.

After almost twenty minutes Natasha said. "I think we are in front of the General Store, I can smell the spices and leather."

"Lila," Emeral called loudly. The women heard a click and they were both pulled inside of the General Store. All of the doors and windows were closed so the demonic fog had not entered the building.

"What are you two doing out in this?" Lila asked as she hugged both Emeral and Natasha.

"Looking for you my dear," Emeral said kindly. As Emeral looked around she could see that the store was filled with frightened people, so she did not want to tell Lila about the demons. "I can only carry one of you at a time and I don't want to leave either of you behind, so let's sit it out here for a while."

"Natasha why don't you make sure the back door is locked," Emeral whispered in her daughter-in-law's ear. Lila heard what Emeral said and gave both of the women a serious look.

"What is happening?" Lila whispered.

"I don't want to say in front of the others," Emeral said. "They already look terrified. But it isn't good. Do you have a weapon?"

"No."

"Why don't you calmly buy a few things," Emeral suggested.

256

Cassandra and Ratri carried another wounded soldier into Hannah's medical station. "Cassandra I am going to need more bandages and towels," Hannah said as she unbuttoned the soldier's uniform jacket.

"Hannah we are running out of supplies and food," Cassandra said frantically. "There are just so many wounded."

"Are there any cities or villages near here?" Hannah asked Cassandra then turned to the soldier. "I am going to clean out the wound on your chest first, it might hurt a little. Thank god most of these wounds were tended to on the ship."

"Hannah there is a large village to the west and another northeast of here," Ratri said. "But we can't leave here."

"Gabriel is in our room in the home of Joshua and Iris. I am sure he is not sleeping like I told him to," Hannah said. "Ask him to ask the Angels if some of you can go for supplies. On the floor of the bedroom is a pouch containing my clothes, inside of that is a leather purse with money. I brought extra money in case we needed more supplies. I can't leave here; can I trust you two to organize everything?"

"Of course," said Ratri.

"I'll make lists of what we need and meet you back at the house," Cassandra said to Ratri.

Hannah turned to the soldier, "Now I need to see the wound on your leg."

When Ratri entered the home of Joshua and Iris he found Gabriel's room filled with people who were listening to the details of what happened in Ogg. Ratri laughed. "Your wife said you wouldn't be sleeping."

"Ratri you should listen to this," Adrone said.

"I can't; Gabriel, Hannah sent me here. We are quickly running out of medical supplies and food. Hannah said she has a bag in here with money that she brought to buy supplies."

"Hannah wants you to ask the Angels if some of us can leave the village to get these things."

"Of course," Gabriel said as he sat up straighter in bed.

"Is this the bag?" Calen asked as he picked one up from the floor.

"She said her clothes are in there and a leather purse with money," Ratri said.

"I don't want to dig through your wife's clothes," Calen said and handed the bag to Gabriel but Nikki grabbed it and with a disapproving roll of her eyes she opened the bag and found the purse, which she handed to Gabriel.

Gabriel opened the purse and pulled out two large pouches of gold coins, "Will this be enough?" he asked.

"I don't know," Ratri said. "Cassandra is making lists of what we need."

"Can one of you find my horse?" Gabriel asked. "There is money in the left saddlebag; bring it all."

"I'll find it," Calen said and left the house.

"Do you want us to leave?" Nikki asked.

"No, they have appeared to all of us before," Gabriel said. "I know it sounds crazy but I don't feel right calling upon Angels when I am only half dressed. Can someone grab one of Raphael's shirts for me?"

"I will," Adrone said and started to run out of the room.

"I'll go with you," Nikki said with a laugh. "In case they are awake."

"Iris make a list of what you need too," Gabriel said. "You have taken us all in and we haven't begun to repay you."

Adrone ran up to Gabriel and handed him a red shirt. "I liked this one the best," the young boy said eagerly.

Gabriel put on the shirt and got out of bed. "Miranda, Daniel we need your help. We are running out of food and supplies for the wounded. Can some of the warriors leave to get more?"

The Angels did not appear but Miranda's voice filled the small home. "Have the Rualas go, they will have safe passage."

"I'll get more warriors," Ratri said and quickly left the room.

Almost twenty minutes later, Calen returned to Gabriel's room. "Raul, Simon and Claudius gave me money too," Calen said as he placed the bags of gold coins on Gabriel's bed. "What did the Angels say?"

"To send the Rualas that you would have safe passage," Gabriel answered. "Ratri is getting warriors and I am still waiting for Cassandra with the lists."

"I'm going," Calen said.

"Well, then take the money and here is a list from Iris," Gabriel said. "Calen if there is some money left over why don't you get some candy for the children."

Calen laughed but before he could answer, Cassandra came into the bedroom. "We need a lot of things, I have the lists here. And Lakin and Gael gave us money when I told them what we were going to do."

Ratri entered the house moments later. "Matthew, Stephan and Thaos just gave us money and I have several hundred warriors ready to leave."

Misha led the Ruala warriors as they headed west towards the Village of Benfax which was on the coast of the Sea of Talmont. The Sea of Talmont was the western border for the Continent of Opots and separated Opots from the much larger Continent of Salszar. The large City of Rubar had always been the main port city of Ryed. But the Clan of Teivel, which owned most of the kingdom, was extorting protection money from the ships that docked in Rubar. Many savvy sea captains now traveled farther south down the coast line to the Village of Benfax to sell their goods.

The people of Benfax welcomed the trade ships with open arms because of the boost they gave to the economy of the village. Word spread among the sailors that Benfax was a safer and much friendlier port than Rubar which greatly increased the activity at the small port of the village. The Rualas thought they had a greater chance of purchasing all they needed in Benfax than in the smaller Village of Marlas which was northeast of the Village of Gesmal.

"Keep ascending you will rise above the fog," Daniel's voice rang out to the Ruala warriors. Each warrior carried a large back pack for the supplies.

The people of Benfax gathered in awe as the Ruala warriors landed in their village. "We come in peace," Misha called out. "We are Rualas and we have many wounded to care for. We need food and supplies."

The villagers looked upon the Rualas suspiciously. "Please," Calen called out. "We have money; we need to buy medical supplies, where is the store?" No one in the crowd answered or moved out of the way of the Rualas.

"Don't you know who these boys are?" a voice yelled from the crowd. An old sailor who wore a wooden peg in place of his lower right leg pushed through the crowd until he came up to Misha. "You're the boys who freed the captives from Ogg, ain't ya?"

"Yes and that is who the supplies are for," Misha said. "And our warriors who were wounded in that battle."

There were whisperings among the crowd, then the voices grew louder. Suddenly the crowd started to applaud the Ruala warriors, who became quite embarrassed.

A middle aged, rotund man walked up to Misha and said in a very loud voice. "I am the mayor of this village, you can call me Fred. We couldn't be more honored to have you here; follow me, we will get you all that you need."

Within moments after Emeral and Natasha arrived, there was loud knocking on the front doors of the General Store.

Maggie the store owner opened the door and gasped as she saw two bloody men standing before her. One man was holding up the other. "Charlie, Hank, get in here," Maggie said "What happened?"

"I think Hank is hurt pretty bad. Stones fell on us from one of the buildings. You can't see a damn thing out there," Charlie said angrily.

"We can help," Lila said as she and Natasha ran up to the men.

"Grab some of those blankets and make a place for him on the floor," Maggie ordered some of the people who were standing in the store. Lila and Natasha helped Charlie lower Hank to the makeshift bed.

"I'll get you girls some water," Maggie said and disappeared into the back of the store.

Emeral guarded the front door of the store as she proudly watched her two daughters-in-law tend to the wounded man.

"Maggie he is going to need some whiskey," Natasha said. "His leg is broken." Hank drank half a bottle of whiskey but it did not numb him enough. Hank yelled as the girls set his leg and cleaned and stitched his wounds."

"Are you two girls physicians?" Charlie asked.

"No our husbands are warriors and they get hurt a lot," Natasha said with smile.

"Our sister-in-law is Hannah, she is a physician," Lila said. "Perhaps you have heard of her."

"I know Hannah, and a sweet girl she is," Maggie said. "Then you are all friends of the Royal Family," Maggie commented loudly. Emeral watched the faces of the people taking shelter in the store as Maggie spoke; for Emeral feared that the revelation that they were friends of the Royal Family might be a dangerous thing considering the city was under attack.

Most of the people in the store had been quiet and watchful. Emeral noticed the look on one man's face as Maggie spoke.

261

The man stood in the very back of the room. He had dark curly hair and was staring intensely at Emeral, Natasha and Lila. "Natasha dear, will you come here for a moment?" Emeral asked sweetly.

Natasha could sense that something was wrong. She walked up to Emeral and faced the door so her back was to the people in the store. "The man in the back with the dark curly hair bears watching," Emeral whispered.

"He's been staring at us," Natasha replied in a low voice. "Why don't I take a walk back there?" Natasha slowly walked around the store looking at the goods that were piled on tables and shelves. She took two blankets from a pile and covered Hank with them then she walked over to a shelf which contained jars of dried herbs.

Natasha literally grew up performing covert operations with her brother Gabriel and she had mastered many skills. Natasha talked to Emeral and Maggie as she walked through the store looking at items, but all the while Natasha was watching the man in the back of the store with the dark curly hair. Natasha was piling the items she intended to purchase on the front counter of the store.

Many of the other people in the store started to relax and talk among themselves; several followed Natasha's lead and started their shopping. Natasha walked to the back of the store and looked at leather goods; she quickly turned and purposely bumped into the suspicious man.

"Oh I am so very sorry," Natasha said in a sweet and flirtatious manner. She gently touched the man's forearm but he did not flinch when the crystal in the palm of her hand touched his skin. Now that Natasha knew that he was not a demon or dark lord she struck up a conversation with the man.

Although he spoke in a friendly manner to her, there was something about the man that Natasha did not trust. She noticed that the man's face smiled in a friendly manner but his eyes were piercing through her as if he was trying to read her motives. "The saddles are in back," Natasha said. "Would you be so kind as to help me?"

"There was one I wanted to look at for my husband. Emeral watched as Natasha led the stranger behind some thick curtains into the back room of the store. Lila was sitting near Hank and watching both Natasha and Emeral. Lila sensed that something was wrong and she slowly stood up and followed Emeral out of the main area of the store.

"I didn't know Ruala's needed saddles," the man said letting Natasha know he knew she was tricking him.

Natasha quickly spun around and stuck the point of a dagger into the man's stomach. "How do you know my husband is a Ruala? And why have you been staring at us?"

The man laughed. "I could say it is because you are such beautiful women."

"And that would be a lie; answer my questions. If you know anything about me you know I am not afraid to use this."

Emeral entered the back area without speaking. "Emeral he already knows Calen is Ruala which means he has been spying on us," Natasha said without turning her gaze from the man.

"Young man, we are very protective of our family," Emeral said sweetly but with an authority to her voice. "I would strongly suggest that you answer my daughter's questions."

"I now have three beautiful women prepared to attack me," the man said with a hearty laugh when Lila entered the area.

"I am going to ask you again, who are you and how do you know us?" Natasha asked.

"Well, you know I am not a demon because of your trick with the crystal," the man said and grinned.

"Most men would not understand the significance of the crystal," Emeral said suspiciously. "What is your name?"

"My name is Edward and if you will allow me to remove some papers from my breast pocket, I will show you who I am," the man said all the while smiling. He seemed to genuinely enjoy the encounter with the women.

"I'll get it," Natasha said. "Which side?"

"Right," Edward answered.

Natasha still grasped the dagger with her right hand but now she put her left hand inside of the man's right shirt pocket and pulled out some folded papers. Emeral stepped forward and took the papers and unfolded them.

"This is a letter to King Sudfad," Emeral said. "Why have you not presented it to him?"

"I believe you know," Edward said as he lowered his voice. "I arrived in the city last night. This morning as I was riding towards the castle I saw that army of demons climbing out of hell. Then the Hengers started to attack them and I came back here to sit it out. I suspect you are doing the same thing since you have been guarding the doors to this store. Read the letter in its entirety."

As Emeral read the letter Edward said, "You can tell the girls what it says then maybe Natasha will take this dagger out of my gut." Edward winked at Natasha when he spoke. But before Emeral could speak Edward continued talking. "Queen Tasha is sister to Queen Renya and King Mathas. King Tobias is loyal to The Great Ruler and a friend of the Sanuri's."

"Dear, you can lower your weapon," Emeral said to Natasha. "This is a letter from King Tobias of Puntd. Apparently he sent Edward here with information for Sudfad and to help us."

"I still don't trust you," Natasha said.

"Good, you should trust few these days," Edward said. "That is why I am here."

"Well, we can't leave here for a while so tell me how do you know us?" Natasha asked.

"Natasha I have seen you before although we were not introduced. King Sudfad and King Mathas correspond regularly with King Tobias. When Sudfad sent the Patronus to Malga to take over the monastery from the dark lords, King Tobias created his own special army; of which I am a member."

"I am a major in the military of Puntd and volunteered for this assignment. Tobias sent us to the monastery to be trained by the Patronus. High Priest Raphael started our training and High Priest Philetus finished it."

"The members of the Patronus speak often of you and Gabriel and that is how I heard that you married one of the Ruala warriors who is part of Gabriel's team. As you know the vast majority of forces who fight the dark lords are men; you are a talented woman with many useful skills; so you are talked about a great deal. I have also heard about Hannah. Gabriel is a fortunate man to have both a wife and a sister who fight alongside of him."

"Neither Gabriel or Raphael are in Wetpr," Emeral said as she handed the letter back to Edward.

"I know, the Sanuri sent a letter to King Tobias telling him about the abductions and the army that was looking for the girls."

"You look awfully young to be a major," said Lila.

"What can I say, I am good at what I do," Edward said with the grin that had not left his face. "Now ladies would you be kind enough to introduce yourselves. Natasha is the only one I know."

"This is my mother-in-law Emeral, wife of Prince Maxwell," Natasha said. "And this is Lila, the wife of Luca who is also a member of the team and my husband's brother. My husband's name is Calen."

"I must say I have never been accosted by three such beautiful women before," then Edward laughed. "Actually I have never been accosted by women before. So tell me, why out of this store full of people did you suspect me?"

"Your eyes," Emeral said. "You watched us like you knew more than the others."

"As soon as it is clear I will go to the castle," Edward said. "Would you like me to see you home first?"

Natasha gave Edward such a disapproving look that he roared with laughter. "After the last attack by the Valdees we are also staying at the castle," Emeral said. "We will travel with you."

"The Valdees have already attacked?" Edward asked with concern. "Has Sudfad taken captives? How have they disposed of the bodies?"

"Why?" Natasha asked.

"That is some of the information I have for King Sudfad. There are so many spies everywhere that King Tobias did not want to send a letter. Ladies it has truly been my pleasure but I need to speak to King Sudfad at once."

"You can't go out in that," Natasha said.

"My dear, the threat to your kingdom is worth the risk."

"I will fly you," Emeral said. "Girls I will come back for you."

"Emeral we are fine," Natasha said. "Do not try to fly back in that demon fog. When it clears we will come home."

"Lock the door behind us," Emeral said as she and Edward walked out of the back door of the store.

Chapter XVIX
The Demon Link

Once the inhabitants of Benfax realized the Rualas were not an invading army their attitudes changed. The old sailor with the wooden leg was loudly telling stories of how the Valdees had terrorized ships and villages for centuries. While many of the villagers knew the old sailor was greatly exaggerating some of his stories, no one cared; they were feeling honored to have heroes walk among them. People poured out of stores and homes to meet the Ruala warriors who had defeated the tyrant of Ogg.

Misha was overheard telling a store clerk that the captives were so starved their stomachs could only tolerate soup. The horror of this statement went through the village like a wild fire. Soon people were bringing baskets of vegetables from their gardens and giving them to the Rualas. The local butcher had lost his youngest son to the Valdees and gave the Rualas most of the meat in his shop. The Rualas literally emptied shelves at several stores but found that most of the store owners did not charge them full price for the items.

Calen walked up to the owner of the largest store in Benfax and handed him three pouches of gold coins. "Please tell me how much more you need," Calen said as the owner poured the coins onto the counter. "If there is money left can we have some candy to take back for the children. We are at the Village of Gesmal and all of the children are helping take care of the wounded." The store owner stared at Calen for a moment then yelled over his shoulder, "Martha did you hear?"

"I sure did," a female voice called out from the back room of the store. Soon a short, stout woman with spectacles came out of the back room with three huge cloth bags and handed them to Calen. "Art don't you dare charge him for this candy," the woman said and returned to the back room.

Emeral's and Edward's journey to the castle seemed long since they were still blinded by the fog. Edward had never flown before and was filled with excitement which made Emeral laugh.

"Those are Hengers flying past us," Emeral explained as the two felt air rushing past them. "They protected Natasha and me before, I am sure they are doing the same thing now."

"What are they protecting us from up here?" Edward asked.

"Talmuth."

"I don't know what that is?"

"Have you ever heard of the large red snakes that are the Mark of Satin?" asked Emeral.

"Yes, in fact I saw one."

"The Talmuth look like a cross between those snakes and dragons. They have wings and are very powerful. They also have claws and teeth."

"Then they are creatures from hell," Edward said. "So that must mean that if the Hengers are flying close to us so are the Talmuth."

"You are a smart boy," Emeral teased. "I can see why you made major at such a young age."

Edward roared with laughter then said with honest conviction, "Emeral I really like you."

As the small army of Rualas neared the Village of Gesmal they heard screams, howls and thunder among other sounds. Misha increased the speed of the group since they all feared the village was under attack. As they neared the village they saw that the fog had not only gotten thicker but was now covering more land.

"You have safe passage," Daniel's voice rang out. The Rualas flew through the fog which made many of them cough and choke. But none of the toxic fumes had entered the village. There was great fanfare when they entered the village for many had feared for the safety of the Rualas.

"Duncan our packs are filled with food and supplies," Misha said as the chief walked up to them.

"How do you want them handed out?" Duncan called to several members of his clan and told them to divide the food among the villagers.

"We can hand out the medical supplies," Calen said. "Also I have a list for Iris."

"We were fearful the village was being attacked," Misha said.

"The Angels are doing battle," Duncan said. "We asked again if they wanted our help and they told us to stay in the village. The sounds are scaring the children."

Calen smiled and took off his back pack. He opened it and handed the three bags of candy to Duncan. "This is candy for the children, not sure how you want to hand it out."

Duncan laughed and called to his wife, Liza. "I better take some for Adrone and Paul," Calen said as he reached into one of the bags and grabbed a large handful of candy.

"Liza besides everything else they brought candy for the children," Duncan said. "Do you want to hand it out?"

"Oh bless you," Liza said. "You are going to make them so happy."

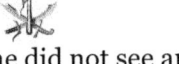

Emeral was surprised that she did not see any members of the Royal Family as she walked Edward down the long hallway to Sudfad's study. She knocked on the door and was surprised when it was opened by the Sanuri. "Is everyone back?" Emeral gasped.

"No, The Lion sent me back here," the Sanuri said and smiled when he saw Edward.

Edward reached out his hand to shake with the Sanuri. "Sanuri it is good to see you."

"You know him?" Emeral asked.

"Yes," the Sanuri said. "He is one of Tobias' men."

269

Emeral turned and looked at Edward and said sarcastically, "I am glad you aren't a dark lord, I rather like you."

"Are the girls alright?" Jared asked. "I felt guilty leaving you."

"They are in the General Store with many other people," Emeral said then she turned to Sudfad. "King Sudfad my daughters and I mistook this man for a dark lord, but he has a letter for you from King Tobias. Edward may I introduce King Sudfad and Sudfad this is Edward he is a major in the military of Puntd and now part of some special team. He says he brings important information."

Edward handed the letter to Sudfad, as the King read it Emeral introduced Edward to Jared. "Well, I will leave you men to talk," Emeral said. "I am going back for my girls."

"Emeral I think it is too dangerous for you to be alone," Edward said quickly. "I will go back with you after the meeting."

"I believe those girls are safe," the Sanuri said. "And Sudfad I have a strong feeling that Emeral should join this meeting, after all she is the head of her family here."

"Yes of course," Sudfad said. "Please both of you take a seat." Sudfad waved his hand towards several empty chairs in the room. "First, Emeral why did you tell us you mistook Edward for a dark lord? What happened?"

Edward laughed loudly. "Emeral, Natasha and Lila should make you all proud. They were protecting the people in that store as well as providing medical care. I recognized Natasha and they told me my eyes betrayed that I knew more than the others in the store so," Edward laughed again. "Natasha took me into the back room and pulled a dagger on me. I have heard stories about that girl, now I believe them all."

Edward's laughter was infectious and soon everyone in the room was laughing. "But now My Lord, the rest that I have to tell you is no laughing matter. King Tobias did not want to send what I am to tell you in a letter for fear it would be intercepted. I think I should start at the very beginning so you understand the complete picture."

"King Sudfad, I know my King communicates with you often so you may already know some of this information." Edward sat up straighter in his chair and started his story. "When King Sudfad sent the Patronus to the monastery in Malga and they found demons and dark lords there, well, that shocked King Tobias greatly. He couldn't understand how something like that could happen under his rule so he went to the monastery and met with High Priest Raphael."

"I don't know if it was during these meetings or from your letters that Tobias found out about the threats and attacks against your family, which is also his family. King Tobias was very impressed with the Patronus and upon returning to his castle he created a somewhat similar organization," Edward said.

"We are called the Guardians," Edward continued. "As I said, King Tobias is very impressed with the Patronus, that group as you know are all warrior priests. But King Tobias felt there was such an urgent need for our group that instead of having us study to be priests he sent us to the monastery at Malga to be trained by the Patronus."

"King Tobias personally selected the members of our group because he doesn't want others to know that we exist. There are almost five hundred of us now. My King has not outwardly aligned with King Sudfad and King Mathas in hopes of obtaining information. Our kingdom is near to both Stordt and Ryed and we have many travelers. The Guardians do not wear our military uniforms, which greatly helps us in obtaining information. Now that you know our history I will tell you why I am here."

"A few weeks ago," Edward said. "One of our men was in a local tavern that is often frequented by travelers; he was listening to conversations when a fight broke out. At first the fight involved just two men but soon the entire tavern was involved. Our man did not join the battle but watched as a man wearing the robe of a priest entered the tavern and grabbed a package that was on one of the tables then quickly left. The Guardian ran after the man in the robe and grabbed him."

"The man wearing the robe was no priest; in fact he didn't look human. They fought and the Guardian was greatly injured. Just as the creature was about to plunge a dagger into the Guardian's heart, a lion roared."

"The creature fled into the forest leaving his stolen package on the ground. The Guardian was able to make it back to the castle and gave the package to King Tobias." Edward reached inside of his shirt and removed a leather pouch from which he took out a letter and handed it to Sudfad.

"That is a letter from the demon Hecate to someone named Daegal," Edward explained. "Hecate is telling Daegal to have Philip your Court Physician poison your family and the families of the High Priests Gabriel and Raphael. She tells Daegal to kill Philip after the crime is committed. Hecate instructed Daegal to use the contents of these envelopes as the poison," Edward said as he removed six small envelopes, each with written instructions on the outside. Edward handed the envelopes to Sudfad.

"Hecate tells Daegal not to have the Sanuri poisoned because she has other plans for him. But she warns that the Sanuri might foil her plans so she tells Daegal that she is sending more Valdees to Wetpr and Lentz but that Daegal does not need to mark areas for them as he had done before, I am not sure what she is referring to with that sentence. But she continues that the Valdees are instructed to attack your troops and to lose the battle so they will be taken as captives. Each Valdees has a Mark of Satan tattooed on them. Hecate says that those marks will take life and attack your forces from inside the walls of the fort."

"Both Mathas and I had many Valdees prisoners in our dungeons which made us both suspicious that these warriors were so easily captured. We killed them and burned the bodies," Sudfad said. "In the last paragraph of this letter, Hecate warns Daegal that Moloch and Ipos may have discovered that she is sabotaging their plans for the Sanuri and The Seven Sons but she has been in contact with Baal and Thanatoes for protection. "

"Hecate reminds Daegal that if she can kill us first she will be greatly rewarded and so will Daegal." Sudfad turned and looked at the Sanuri. "I recognize some of these names as the Old Ones; it sounds like they are competing for us. Why are the Old Ones involved; is it because of what The Lion did to Ahriman?"

"Miranda can't we help you?" Archetenus called out. "Warriors do not stand by and let others fight their battles."

The sounds of battle were making many in the camp feel anxious; as exhausted and wounded as they were, many felt the need to join the battle. Claudius, Sorren, Raul, Simon, Thaos, Stephan and Matthew stood with Archetenus waiting for an answer but none came. After a few moments Matthew stepped forward. "Miranda if you think we are too wounded to help you, then heal us and we will fight at your side."

Suddenly both Daniel and Miranda appeared before the small group. "I see what you mean," Daniel said to Miranda with a smile. Then Daniel turned and looked at the men. "Miranda speaks of you often with pride; you are worthy of the responsibilities that have been placed upon you. These great chasms that have opened around the village are openings to a hell dimension; that is where this battle is taking place. Would you follow us into hell?" Daniel asked.

"I think you already know the answer to that question," Sorren said gruffly.

"We will not force anyone to take such a journey," Daniel said. "Go back to your men and ask for volunteers but remember many need to stay behind and take care of the wounded. We will return in one hour, those who want to join us will have what they need." When Daniel finished speaking both Angels disappeared.

The Sanuri looked thoughtfully at Jared, Emeral and Edward before he spoke. "There are many reasons that the demons and dark lords have targeted the people you mentioned Edward; for those intended victims harbor many secrets. Secrets that I have told them to keep. The families of Sudfad, Mathas, Claudius, Gabriel and Raphael have been fighting alone in a battle beyond your comprehension."

"Emeral your sons and daughters know the secrets I am about to reveal and because of that there are bounties put upon them. The Great Ruler in His wisdom is sending more of His children to help in this battle. But I will give you a choice. To know these secrets will put you in more danger than you are already in. If you do not want the secrets revealed please leave this room."

Hannah left her medical station and ran to the home of Joshua and Iris. "Gabriel are you insane?" Hannah yelled as she entered the house.

"Probably," Gabriel said as he was getting dressed.

"You can barely walk and you are going back into battle. Do you really want to die?" Hannah yelled. None of the other warriors in the home had ever heard Hannah raise her voice before; now they just stood and stared at Gabriel and Hannah.

"The Angels said we would have what we needed," Gabriel said. "Which in my case would be healing. They have taken care of us this far, Hannah. Don't you think they will continue to?"

"Gabriel I love you so much I don't want anything to happen to you," Hannah said and started to cry. "And now we have children, you have to think about them too."

"I'll tell you what," Gabriel said as he put his arm around Hannah and kissed her on the forehead. "I will ask the Angels if I should go."

"Why don't you ask them if you are going to come back to us?" Hannah cried angrily as she wiped the tears from her face.

"Hannah if it makes you feel better I will watch out for him," Maxwell said.

"You're hurt too," Hannah cried. "You all just make me so mad." Hannah stormed out of the house and slammed the door.

"Felt like I was home with Natasha for a moment there," Calen said jokingly as he tried to ease the tension in the house.

"I know you are warriors and although I am proud of all of you," Iris said. "You have to understand that Hannah has not slept one wink since she arrived here. She has been tending to the wounded and dying and she is wearing their blood and crying their tears. Gabriel your wife is a good woman and she too has a point to make."

"I know," Gabriel said softly and walked out of the house.

"Many generations ago," the Sanuri explained to Emeral, Jared and Edward. "The Royal Family of Wetpr made a covenant with The Great Ruler. Every new generation is told of the covenant and asked if they will honor it and every generation makes the right choice. The Royal Family of Wetpr are The Keepers of The Scrolls, which means they risk their lives to protect the gifts that The Great Ruler has given to His children. Most of these gifts are highly coveted by the demons and dark lords, who suspect the role of Sudfad's family.

"In addition," the Sanuri continued. "There is an ancient prophesy about Seven Sons of Light who battle the darkness. This prophesy terrifies the dark ones who have spent centuries trying to discover who these Seven Sons are. The prophesy is now unfolding and Ahriman had discovered some of the identities of the Seven. This prophesy refers to Seven Sons of The Great Ruler; not of one man. So far the identities of six are known to us. Sudfad, Raul, Simon, Matthew, Petra and myself make up the six. Gabriel's and Raphael's families have sworn covenants to protect and serve with us."

No one in the room said a word so the Sanuri continued. "Sudfad now to answer your question. For years you have asked why you were not allowed to kill Roch, even though he brought great pain to this world. I too had asked The Lion that same question and only recently was the answer revealed to me."

"During Roch's life many holy messengers appeared to him and warned him of his destiny and gave him the choice to return to The Great Ruler. As you know Roch chose to align himself with Ahriman. Because of his choices Roch would have been an evil man even without the Insidiae trying to make him a vessel for the demon Omnibus."

"Part of the initiation rites of the Insidiae is to take a blood oath, with each other and with the demons they worship. This blood oath links them together. Members of the ruling families of Lentz, Wetpr, the Nordes Tribe, Gabriel's team, Jared and Archetenus among others were told that Roch was transforming into a very powerful demon and went to Stordt to stop that transformation."

"Although they could not stop Roch from turning into a demon, this faithful army fought thousands of demons and with the help of the Angels they won that battle. But I believe you all know this. But what you did not know is three of The Seven Sons acted as one and destroyed the demon Roch; as the three plunged their swords into him holiness surged through Roch and all those who he was connected to," the Sanuri said.

"Darkness cannot withstand holiness, so think of this act as similar to a great disease ravishing a village. The effects of that single act are still crippling the demons and dark lords and that is why they are banding together to inflict revenge and to destroy the power of The Seven Sons. The energies are in motion and there are forces beyond the comprehension of man that will affect the destinies of mankind." The Sanuri now looked at Edward. "Your King does not know the things I have told you this day. It is not your role to tell him."

"Sanuri why did you tell us?" Edward asked as he was humbled by the responsibility he now assumed.

"Because of the choices you have made."

Hannah was changing the bandage wrapped around a soldier's ribs when Gabriel entered her medical station. Although she was aware of Gabriel's presence she did not acknowledge him.

"Hannah I don't want us to part like this," Gabriel said. She did not answer or look at him. "Hannah you know how much I love you and the children. I am not doing this to hurt you."

The soldier did not speak as he watched the tears running down Hannah's cheeks. Gabriel turned and walked out of the building. He had only taken three steps when he heard Hannah's voice.

"Wait," Hannah called as she ran towards him. Hannah stopped when she was next to Gabriel. "You better come back to us," Hannah said. Gabriel leaned down and kissed his wife passionately.

"Edward where are you staying?" Sudfad asked.

"I got a room in town, my horse and all of my gear are in Salar."

"I want you to move into the castle," Sudfad said. "If the Sanuri shared with you such important information I believe you have a role to play in all of this."

"Sanuri when can I go after the girls?" asked Emeral.

"Truly they are safe," the Sanuri said. "They are bringing strength and comfort to the frightened people huddled in that store."

"I'll take Edward into Salar to get his things and we can pick up the girls," Jared said.

"Wait until the battle is over," said the Sanuri. "In the meantime Jared and Emeral why don't you fill Edward in on all that has transpired here. And that includes the lives of Jared and Archetenus. Sudfad and I have some things we need to discuss."

Miranda and Daniel smiled when they saw the army lined up behind Claudius. "You are a rather sorry looking lot," Miranda said warmly. "Are you sure you want to do this?"

"We are ready," Claudius said.

"Nikki go back to the house," Thaos yelled when she ran up to join the army.

"Thaos now is the time she should be at your side," Miranda said. "This is the battle that will form the destiny of your unborn son." Thaos took Nikki's hand in his.

"You are following us to a different world," Daniel said loudly. "It does not have the same air that you breathe or the same surface you are accustomed to walk on. But do not fear; we will give you what you need."

Claudius and the other warriors never remembered leaving the Village of Gesmal. Nor did they remember the journey to the hell dimension. The acidity of the toxic air burned their faces and made them cough.

As one they realized they could see through the putrid haze because of the light that was emitted from the Angels. There was a strange color to this world, not seen in the world of man. Archetenus was the only one who recognized the color for he had been shown it many years before.

"This is the color of hell," Archetenus said as he grasped the hilt of his sword.

"Where are the demons?" Claudius asked. "We can hear the sounds of battle yet you stand before us."

"We are not the only Angels here," Daniel said. "Proceed before us and each of you touch either Miranda's or my robe as you pass. And you will receive what you need."

"By god Claudius you are glowing," Sorren said in amazement as Claudius was the first to touch the Angel's robe. Claudius looked at himself and his sword which was also glowing.

"I feel," Claudius stammered. "I have never felt like this before. It is incredible."

"Claudius lead your army straight forward," Miranda said. "You will find the demons. The demons you will be fighting are very powerful but you have the power to destroy them."

As in Ryed, there was an army of Angels doing battle with the demons that were trying to attack Salar. And as in Ryed, it was difficult for the soldiers to listen to the sounds of battle and do nothing.

"Sanuri if this is some type of test of faith, well I guess I can understand that," Sudfad said with frustration. "But we should be fighting also."

"Perhaps it is not your faith that is being tested," the Sanuri said.

"So there is nothing I can do?" Sudfad asked anxiously. "I know the Angels can protect us I just don't feel right having them do all of the work."

"Sudfad it is time for you to do something you have never done before," the Sanuri said gently. "Call upon The Lion and ask him how you should proceed."

"The Lion," Sudfad said humbly. "But why would he appear to me?"

"You can ask him that question; it is time," the Sanuri said and walked out of the study.

The King of the most powerful kingdom in Opots got down on his knees. "Lion I do not feel worthy to ask for an audience but I need some guidance."

"Sudfad you have devoted your life to working on behalf of The Great Ruler why did it never occur to you to call upon the Angels?" The Lion asked as he appeared before the King.

Sudfad stared in awe at The Lion. "I never thought that I was worthy," the great king stammered.

"And you relied on the Sanuri to give you our messages. When will men learn they do not need intermediaries to talk to the heavens? Every prayer is heard, no matter who you are. Sudfad you do not need to bow before me, I am not The Great Ruler," The Lion said. Sudfad stood up although his knees were weak.

The Lion continued, "Sudfad a time of great darkness is coming to this world, a darkness like it has never before experienced. You and Renya proved that you were willing to stand alone against the darkness but now things will change. You will have to amass an army with incredible faith to fight in this war. That is why your troops are not doing battle for they will see the results when this battle is over. They will learn that there is more to their lives than they can understand and they will learn that The Great Ruler will send messengers to protect them."

"Sudfad at this very moment your sons and most of the army that Claudius leads just followed two Angels into hell to fight at their sides. That is the kind of faith your army must possess. You are a courageous man and a shrewd military leader but you cannot instill this type of faith in your army without our help. If you truly want to lead this fight you must get into the habit of calling to us, we will answer you."

"I have not come this far to fail you now," Sudfad said. "Tell me what I must do."

"When this battle is over have all of the soldiers from Fort Salar view the battlefield. And tell them that The Great Ruler sent Angels to protect them because the adversaries could not be killed by mortal men. Tell them they have received a great gift this day for they have seen with their own eyes that miracles are real. When you say these words the traitors among your men will be exposed."

Time appeared different in the hell dimension. As soon as each warrior touched the robe of an Angel they found themselves on a battlefield and each warrior was whole again. The sons of Chief Duncan, George and Ivan joined the invasion into hell, as well as Micha and Thomas the two oldest sons of Joshua. The terrain was barren for there was no life in hell; the mountains rose up menacingly in the dark haze. Everything appeared to be covered with a thick tar-like substance.

The army could feel eyes upon them as they made their way through a narrow crevice in a mountain. "The hair on the back of my neck is standing up," Sorren said. "Where are those bastards?"

Claudius was in the lead and said, "I am sure we are walking into some type of trap."

"This reminds me of that time that Ahriman pulled me into hell," Gabriel said to Raul. "It looked just like this."

The group suddenly heard the flapping of wings and saw five enormous flying creatures. They looked like the skeletons of birds with elongated heads and bodies. The creatures screeched and exposed the many rows of long fangs in their mouths. "I have fought those birds before," Luca said. "They are Durisks; I stabbed them and stuck my crystal in the wound. The Sanuri said only holiness could destroy them."

The Durisks did not attack the army but kept circling over it. "I think our glow is keeping them away," Simon said.

Claudius stopped abruptly. "Gabriel bring the boys from Gesmal up here," Claudius called out. Gabriel pushed through the crowd with the sons of Duncan and the sons of Joshua. When they reached the front of the army Claudius pointed up to a small cliff on the left side of the crevice. "Is he one of yours?" Claudius asked. The body of a man was hanging from his wrists, his chest and stomach had been torn open exposing his organs.

"Sampson," yelled George. "That is our brother." Both George and Ivan started to climb towards the body but Sorren and Stephan pulled them back. "Let go," Ivan yelled.

"Son this is some kind of trap; we aren't letting you run into it," Sorren said.

A malicious laugh echoed off the rock walls. And the body of Sampson started to move. "Look," Micha gasped as they watched Sampson's body transform into a creature from hell. Sampson grew considerably larger, his body was covered with long hair and his eyes were ablaze. Sampson broke the chains which had secured him to the mountain. He started to growl and to foam at the mouth as he looked at the army below him.

A loud voice rang out but it did not come from Sampson's body. "Sampson you know what your final test is." Then the voice laughed loudly.

"Who is speaking?" demanded Claudius.

"I am offended that you don't know me."

"All you damn demons are so arrogant," Sorren yelled. "If you don't tell us your name, guess we will just have to give you one."

"You insolent worm," the voice bellowed. "Who are you to talk to me that way?" Lightening shot down at Sorren but it could not penetrate the aura of holiness that surrounded him. Sorren had jumped to the side and pulled his sword but when he realized the lightning could not touch him; Sorren broke into laughter. "No!" screamed the voice with such power that rocks started to fall from the mountain. But as the army moved to escape the boulders, the avalanche suddenly disappeared. The voice was consumed with anger and screamed and cursed the army of mortals. "Sampson kill your brothers," the voice yelled angrily.

Sampson started to howl and snarl. Micha and Thomas ran in front of George and Ivan. "What are you doing?" George asked angrily.

"No man should have to kill his own brother," Micha said and readied his sword for the attack.

Sorren and Stephan grabbed George and Ivan again and held them back. "He's right son," Sorren said as the creature Sampson jumped down from the cliff.

"Sampson keep killing them until you get to your brothers," the voice bellowed. Micha had a shield in his left hand and a sword in his right; he crouched down and started to circle Sampson. Sampson's claws and fangs grew longer as he watched Micha. Sampson lunged at Micha who did a forward roll to his right and came up on his feet. Sampson lunged again and this time Micha moved backwards. Micha was studying his opponent. Sampson started to grow larger and larger before their eyes. Micha was soon dwarfed by the demonic giant.

"We need to help the kid," Raul said.

"Like with Roch?" asked Archetenus.

"Exactly," Simon said.

Raul, Simon, Matthew and Archetenus ran forward and started to climb up the creature by holding onto Sampson's long hair. As they climbed they stabbed Sampson repeatedly. The holiness on the swords of these four men surged through the demon's body causing Sampson to scream in pain. When Micha saw what they were doing he too hoisted himself up the monster as did his brother Thomas.

The voice started to laugh, "You look like ants do you really think you can kill a demon?" Sampson was grabbing at the men but each warrior was encircled with an aura of holiness which not only protected them but caused the body of the demon to burn and smoke. Sampson pulled Raul off from him and was about to crush Raul between his fingers when Matthew plunged his sword into Sampson's hand. Sampson dropped Raul who broke his fall by grabbing onto a tuff of Sampson's hair.

"Baal stop this!" Hecate's voice rang out. "They will destroy him."

"Hecate your husband is covered in ants nothing more," Baal yelled then laughed loudly.

"If you don't stop this I will," Hecate yelled. "Don't you know who those men are?"

"It doesn't matter," Baal bellowed. "He has to complete his tests."

"He will not live through this," Hecate screamed.

"That really is not my concern," Baal yelled back. He was becoming angry with Hecate for challenging him.

Sampson screamed in pain as Archetenus plunged his sword into Sampson's left eye. Archetenus stabbed Sampson again and again as Simon plunged his sword into Sampson's right eye. Raul and Matthew were climbing up Sampson's back, heading towards his head. Micha and Thomas were climbing up Sampson's face. "Keep stabbing him in the eyes," Simon yelled as he climbed upwards towards the top of Sampson's head.

"No!" screamed Hecate and the ground began to shake. Suddenly a strong wind started to blow making it difficult for Raul and the others to maintain their holds on Sampson.

"Hurry," Raul yelled to the others as he tightened his grasp on Sampson's hair.

"The tests are done," screamed Hecate.

"You dare defy me!" Baal yelled.

Sampson kept screaming from the holiness that was surging through his body. He started to gyrate violently in an attempt to dislodge the men who were climbing on him. Sampson was stomping his feet and shaking his head. "We need to get to his brain," Simon yelled as he was barely hanging on to Sampson's fur.

The world became black as a thick and clammy darkness fell upon them like a cloak. But the auras maintained their light in the darkness. "I demand that you stop this!" Hecate screamed as she suddenly appeared behind Sampson. Hecate appeared larger than Sampson. She did not present her earthly appearance because she did not need to project those illusions in hell. Hecate's long hair was ablaze and illuminated her gaunt and pock marked face. Her body was covered in lesions which emitted a foul smelling pus that was dripping down her body.

"So this is the girl friend," Sorren said sarcastically which made the warriors laugh.

"You dare laugh at me; you minions. You dare enter our realm."

"Seems only fitting cause you enter ours," Sorren yelled back as Claudius readied the troops for attack. Sorren was trying to distract the great demon as some of the warriors were sneaking around her. "I'll tell you what, pretty lady. You stay out of our world and we'll stay out of yours."

Hecate was blinded by her rage. She quickly shot her tongue out which maneuvered around Sampson and headed towards Sorren. When the long, muscular organ was within feet of Sorren, Claudius ordered, "Now!" Hundreds of warriors attacked Hecate's tongue as warriors climbed up her body and stabbed her with their swords. Hecate was not covered in fur like Sampson so climbing was more difficult for the warriors, who were also dealing with the slippery pus on her body.

Hecate screamed with pain as holiness was weakening her dark powers. Hecate heard Baal laughing which jolted her out of her blinding rage, she looked at Sampson and saw that Raul, Matthew and Simon were about to plunge their swords into Sampson's brain. "No!" Hecate screamed and both Sampson and Hecate disappeared. The warriors who were climbing on both demons fell to the ground but were not hurt.

"Baal you're next, show yourself!" Claudius ordered.

The ground began to shake and smoke. Screeches and war cries filled the toxic air as thousands of demons descended on the army of mortals.

Chapter XX
Between Worlds

"I'm not sure I like this," Joshua said as he watched Ibula feeding the Hutas who had been captives of the Valdees. "It is like bringing a poison into our village."

"Joshua look at them," Ibula said. "There isn't one who can hold a spoon by himself, what are they going to do?"

"What are they going to do when they are healthy?"

"Well, then maybe we will have to fight them but for now there is no honor in slaying a man who can barely move."

"It's not honor I am worried about," Joshua continued. "It's the safety of our children."

"When the Angels return we will ask them what we should do," Ibula said. "They were not against us saving the Hutas."

"Just the same, I am going to have a cage built to contain them as they improve."

Soon after The Lion left Sudfad the demonic fog started to clear in his kingdom. Sudfad went down to the wine cellar and told his family to come out of hiding. Then he brought Renya into his study and told her everything The Lion had said. Sudfad told Renya about Edward and the Guardians and everything that had been discussed at the meeting between the Sanuri, Jared, Emeral, Edward and Sudfad. But before he could finish there was a knock on the door.

"Sudfad, Edward and I are going into Salar to get the girls and Edward's gear," Jared said as he popped his head into the study.

"Is Edward with you now?" Sudfad asked.

"Ya, he's in the hallway."

"Have him step in here so Renya can meet him."

A few moments later the door opened and Edward entered the study of King Sudfad. Edward was not accustomed to the informal behavior that Sudfad preferred in his household. Edward entered the study in a professional manner and bowed before the Queen.

"Edward my husband tells me you will be living with us for a while," Renya said sweetly. "We prefer more of a family atmosphere here."

"I will admit that will be difficult for me to get used to," Edward replied. "But My Lady I do have something for you." Edward reached inside his military jacket and pulled out a thick envelope which he handed to Renya. "This is from Queen Tasha."

Renya took the envelope with excitement. "Edward I have not seen my sister in years. After you get settled in I want you to meet with me and tell me all about her family. That is unless Sudfad has something for you."

"He is all yours my dear," Sudfad said. "I will be spending time with the troops."

"What is it Iris?" Hannah asked as she ran into the house. "Adrone just told me to come quickly."

"Paul is getting Ibula also," Iris said. "I went in to check on Vivian and Raphael and well, they aren't awake but they are both moaning and thrashing around."

Hannah entered the bedroom and examined Raphael first since he was the closest to the door. Ibula entered the room a moment later. "They are both unconscious," Hannah explained to Ibula but look at them. They are both acting in the same manner; is this normal for someone who has had that procedure?"

"No," Ibula said and knelt down next to Vivian.

"Ibula," Hannah said fearfully. "I have seen something like this before when Gabriel was pulled into hell." Hannah turned towards the doorway. "Iris have the boys get Lakin quickly."

286

"The passage widens farther up," Calen said to Claudius as his army was surrounded by demons and fighting in the narrow crevice in the mountains. While the auras around the warriors seemed to give them more power against the demons, the battle was intense. Warriors were being wounded and exhaustion was affecting many of them. The toxic air was becoming thicker as the bodies of the dead demons smoked and burst into flames from the holiness of the swords of the warriors.

Claudius did not like the tactical position his troops were in but the battle was too heated to order their movement. For the first time Claudius called to the Angels. "Miranda I need to move my men, we are trapped here and the army of demons is unending. What would you have us do?"

"Do you want to come back?" Miranda's voice asked.

"Of course not," Claudius barked. "But we are in a bad position here."

The intense darkness of the hell dimension was filled with a white light that blinded the demons, which ran and hid from the holiness. "You may return or move forward now," Daniel's voice said.

"Forward!" Claudius yelled.

"I'm glad we didn't take a boca," Jared said as he and Edward maneuvered their horses around the dead bodies of thousands of demons. Edward stared in awe at the gnarled and hideous bodies that littered the ground. "First time you've seen demons?" Jared asked with a grin.

"Yes," Edward replied.

"Well get used to it," Jared explained. "But you can't always see them. Sometimes you can just feel their presence. But you can always smell them. Take a good whiff so you remember that smell."

"I'm surprised these openings haven't closed up," Edward said about the huge crevices in the ground. "Do you think they will stay this way?"

"Can't imagine the Angels would let the doors to hell stay open, unless of course they want us to go down there and fight."

"And you have seen these Angels?" Edward asked skeptically.

Jared laughed at the tone of Edward's voice. "You know Miranda once asked how people could so easily believe in demons and not Angels. It was hard for me to believe what the others were saying too. But I have not only seen them, I have spoken to them and fought alongside of them. You think seeing these demons is something wait until you see the Angels."

"Don't get me wrong," Edward said. "I'm not saying anyone is lying it is just difficult to believe."

"Wait until I finish telling you about King Roch," Jared said with a laugh. "You're gonna think I made that whole damn thing up."

"How long have they been like this?" Lakin asked as he examined Raphael and Vivian.

"I came in about half an hour ago and saw them like this," Iris said. "Don't know how long it had been going on."

"Iris why don't you take the boys out of here and close the door," Lakin said as he opened his medical bag. Only Hannah and Ibula remained in the room with Lakin and the patients. Raphael and Vivian were lying side by side in bed; both bodies were gyrating with spasmodic movements. Raphael and Vivian were groaning and appeared to be trying to talk.

"Do you think this is related to the others fighting in hell?" Ibula asked.

"I don't know," Lakin said. "Now both of you stand back." Lakin poured blessed water on the heads of both Vivian and Raphael with the same results, their skin started to smoke. "Demons are trying to take them over," Lakin said. "Since we have two victims here I am going to try something different. Ibula soak these crystals in the blessed water to increase their strength. Hannah take this vial of blessed water and make a circle around the bed, make it close to the bed."

288

As the women preformed their tasks Lakin started to pray over Raphael and Vivian.

"I'll get the girls," Jared said as they stopped in front of the General Store. "Get your gear and meet us back here." As the fog was lifting Jared looked up and down the main street of Salar where every building had sustained damage from the powerful quakes. He dismounted and tried to walk into the General Store but the doors were locked.

"It's Jared," he yelled as he knocked at the door. "I'm here to get Natasha and Lila."

Maggie the store owner opened the doors, "Is it safe to come out now?"

"Yes," Jared said. "The demons are all dead."

"Demons!" Maggie gasped. "Is that what was attacking us?"

"Yes, where are the girls?"

"Why they are gone, they left a while ago," said Maggie.

The light that invaded the hell region gave Claudius enough time to move his troops out of the passageway between the mountains. They found themselves in a large open, exposed area at the base of a mountain which was to their right. They heard Baal's voice laughing again.

"Show yourself," Claudius demanded. "Does the powerful demon hide from mere men?"

The army heard screams, but these were not from demons but voices familiar to them all. "No," screamed Gabriel as he saw Raphael and Vivian appear. They were chained by the wrists to the wall of the mountain. Raul grabbed Gabriel to prevent him from running to his friends. "Wait," Raul whispered. "This is a trick."

"Cover their bodies with the crystals," Lakin instructed Ibula.

"When both of you are done come next to me and pray."

"What should we say?" Hannah asked as she saw blood running from the eyes and noses of Raphael and Vivian.

"Just repeat what I say," Lakin said. "Great Ruler save them from the darkness that is trying to devour them. Give them what they need to fight the powers of evil. Help them to return to us."

"And you dare question my powers," Baal yelled. "I Am The Originator Of Man! I Am The Death That Walks Among You! I Am Fear Itself!"

"Let them go and take me," Gabriel yelled.

"So the priest would sacrifice himself for his friends, how noble of him," Baal said sarcastically. "But you are in hell now, there is no nobility here. Have The Seven Sons nothing to say?" With Baal's words the army now understood the trap. Calen and Luca flew to Raphael and Vivian but were knocked out of the sky by an unseen force.

"Great Ruler save our friends, bless them and help them to conquer this dark journey they are on," Lakin, Hannah and Ibula prayed in unison. "Disempower the darkness and its hold on mankind. Let your presence fill the dark places, help our friends to conquer the darkness; please save them."

Raphael and Vivian thrashed around more violently. Sweat was pouring out of both their bodies. Suddenly Hannah was filled with fear as Raphael yelled, "Gabriel stay back!"

Simon and Raul started to step forward but Archetenus and Thaos held them back. "It's you he wants," Archetenus said. "But you are surrounded by holiness; I don't think the demon can grab you."

The army could see Raphael and Vivian fighting against the chains that bound them. The spirits and bodies of Raphael and Vivian were being torn between two worlds; they were not whole in either world.

Suddenly Raphael's voice rang out, "Gabriel stay back!"

Archetenus stepped forward. "This is not my first time in hell Baal, nor is it the first time for several others here. We have escaped you before and we will do it again. You play your games because you really don't have enough power to stop us; not as long as we walk with the Angels. How do we know what we are looking at is real?" Baal did not speak.

"Miranda did you take the tongue of the demon?" Archetenus called out sarcastically.

"He has no power if you all denounce him," Miranda's voice said. "Even in his realm he must have fear to thrive. Gabriel knows the words."

Gabriel now pushed to the front of the army, "Demon be gone; you have no power here. Demon be gone, you have no power here." As Gabriel repeated the words the others joined in. The entire army chanted the words over and over causing Baal's power to fade.

"They are gone," Sorren yelled and everyone saw that the illusions of Raphael and Vivian were no longer chained to the side of the mountain. The army kept chanting.

"You fools you have no power against me," Baal screamed.

"Then show yourself," Claudius yelled. "If you are so powerful why do you hide behind others? Why do you hide your face? You say there is no nobility in hell; well, there aren't any warriors here either."

"It's changing here," Ingr said as she realized the air was getting lighter and the darkness was diminishing.

"I curse you all!" Baal screamed.

Both Raphael and Vivian sat up in bed and stared wildly for a moment as their spirits returned to their bodies. Raphael turned and grabbed Vivian and hugged her tightly and kissed her again and again.

"Are you alright?" Hannah asked fearfully.

"Where were you?" Lakin asked before either Raphael or Vivian had a chance to answer Hannah's question.

"We were in hell with the others," Raphael said. "Baal was trying to use me and Vivian to draw the others away from the group so he could kill them."

"Gabriel is he alright?" Hannah asked as she started to cry.

"Yes," Vivian said. "I think they all are because they figured out what Baal was up to."

"Tell us what happened," said Lakin.

"Baal chained Vivian and me to the side of a mountain, he made our bodies look like they were cut open but our bodies were here, so we felt no pain. The entire army is surrounded with light, like the Angels always are. Baal wasn't strong enough to go against them all because of the Angels; so he was trying to separate Gabriel, Raul, Simon and Matthew from the group so he could kill them."

"Why Gabriel?" Hannah asked as tears ran down her cheeks.

"Because he knows how to take the power from a demon," Raphael said. "Gabriel started to chant the words and the others joined in. Baal lost his hold on us and we are here now."

There was noise outside of the bedroom door which flew open as Gabriel, Calen, Raul, Simon, Luca and many others filled the room. "You're alright," Gabriel gasped with relief. Micha and Thomas pushed through the crowd and hugged their sister Vivian.

"How did you get back?" Raphael asked as Gabriel and Hannah embraced.

"We kept chanting and suddenly we were back in the village," Simon said. "I'm still not really sure what all happened down there."

292

"I think that journey was more for us," Sorren said. "Then to actually stop the demons."

"Where is Thedes?" asked Raul.

"He is caring for the other Shettees," Ibula said. "He has not left them since you brought them into the village."

"Micha, Thomas you need to find the other two boys and meet with your fathers," Claudius said. "I will go with you. Miranda said you had to tell them everything."

"Mother where is Father?" Micha called out.

"He is building a cage to put the Hutas in for when they are healthy," Ibula said.

"You should have let them kill me," Sampson screamed as he writhed in pain on the bed in Hecate's lair. Both Hecate and Sampson were bleeding from wounds they received when they were in Baal's hell domain. "My insides are burning," Sampson screamed as he rolled back and forth.

"That's the holiness," Hecate said as she was chanting over her husband. "And I wasn't going to let them kill you."

"Hecate what is happening?" Sampson cried as he doubled up in pain.

"I am trying to heal you, but every spell only seems to make your pain worse," Hecate said. "Here drink this," Hecate said as she helped Sampson to raise his head and drink out of the goblet she held to his lips. "It will make you sleep, while I figure out a way to heal you."

"What do you mean the girls are gone?" Edward asked. "Wouldn't we have passed them on the road?"

"Maggie said she thought they returned to the castle," Jared said. "But maybe they stopped someplace else. Let's look around a little before we head back."

Edward dismounted and the two men started to walk down the main street of Salar. People were running around frantically as they were still filled with fear from the strange attack although most did not understand what had happened.

"Help me," a voice yelled out as Jared and Edward walked past an alley. Both men turned and saw a man lying on the ground; the lower half of his body was covered with sheets of wood from the roof of the building he lay next to. As Jared and Edward lifted the wooden sheets from the man's body they saw that the sheets covered a huge wooden beam that was crushing the man's legs.

"I can't feel my legs," the man kept saying.

"What is your name?" Edward asked.

"Arnold."

"Well, Arnold you lay still and we will get this off from you," Edward said as he tried to reassure the man. Jared gave Edward a worrisome glance because both men could see how mangled Arnold's legs were. Edward was a big man, although not the giant that Jared was. Both men strained to move the beam from Arnold's legs. Edward and Jared tried two, three, four times before they could lift the beam enough to move it away from Arnold.

"He's getting awfully pale," Edward said. Jared picked Arnold up and carried him out of the alley as he looked for a physician's office.

Sorren and Claudius both met with Duncan, Joshua and their sons. Both George and Ivan were reluctant to tell their father about Sampson because they did not want to break his heart.

"What is so awful that you cannot tell me?" Duncan asked as both his sons looked down at the floor of their home.

"Your sons are afraid that what they have to say will hurt you greatly," Claudius said. "And it will but you have to be told."

"Go on," Duncan said hesitantly.

"Perhaps this would go better if we all had a glass of whiskey," Sorren offered.

"Very well," Duncan said and took a bottle out of a cupboard. He poured the whiskey into cups and handed one to each man.

"We are all fathers here," Sorren said. "And first of all your sons all acted bravely, you should be proud of them."

"Then what is it you must tell me?" Duncan demanded.

"We were walking through a mountain range, I was in the lead," Claudius said. "We came around a bend and I saw your other son Sampson hanging from a mountain wall. He was chained by the wrists and covered in blood; he looked like he was disemboweled. I call all your sons forward to identify Sampson for there was much blood on his face also."

"When George and Ivan recognized Sampson they tried to run to help him but the others held them back because we knew it was a trap. Soon we heard the voice of a demon, who we latter found out was Baal. The demon told Sampson he knew what his final test was. All of a sudden Sampson turned from a human into a big hairy creature. The demon told Sampson to kill his brothers." Duncan was becoming pale as he listened to Claudius.

"Micha and Thomas jumped in front of your boys, so they would not be forced to kill their own brother. As Sampson was fighting with Micha he kept growing larger, he must have been fifty feet tall when Raul, Simon, Matthew and Archetenus started to climb up Sampson's body and stab him with their swords. They had fought another demon in such as manner."

"Micha and Thomas joined them. Suddenly we hear Hecate and Baal fighting over Sampson. She wanted Baal to stop the tests. Baal would not so Hecate came out to defend her husband. We all attacked her and suddenly she and Sampson just disappeared," Claudius explained then he took a large gulp of his whiskey.

"I don't understand how you could do damage to the demons," Joshua said.

"Well the Angels did something to us," Sorren explained. "I'm not sure how to describe it. They healed us all from our wounds and we all glowed like they do. They touched our swords with holiness so we would be stronger against the demons."

"The Angel Miranda told your sons that they must tell you everything because you will still have to protect the village after we leave," Claudius said.

The pain in Duncan's eyes was obvious to all. "So my eldest son wants to be a demon so badly he would be tortured and kill his own brothers. What did I do wrong? How could he turn out like this?"

"Father it's not your fault," George said as he put his arm round his father's shoulders. "You are a great father and a great chief. It is Sampson who is evil."

"And there is more that we must tell you," Micha said as he looked at Joshua.

Jared and Edward left Arnold in a physician's office which was already filled with injured patients.

"Natasha and Lila might be helping to take care of injured people," Edward said. "That's what they were doing in the General Store. The two men continued down Main Street looking into stores. "Emeral said that Lila brought a small boca to town, any idea where she would tie the horse?"

"I would have thought in front of the store she was shopping in," Jared said. "Let's turn around and if'n we don't see them we will return to the castle."

Raul and Simon found Thedes sitting amidst a group of Shettees. Thedes seemed immense compared to his emaciated brethren. "Raul, Simon," Thedes said happily. "Let me introduce you to my friends. This is King Neputa," Thedes said proudly as Simon and Raul shook hands with Neputa. "And his brothers Balius and Orcus. This is my nephew Pallas. My old friends, Cronos, Dymas, Nelpus, Aetes, Muhar, Bode, Aloeus and Eachann. We were all in the same unit in our military."

Thedes faced the other Shettees. "This is Prince Raul and Prince Simon of the Kingdom of Wetpr and my adopted brothers."

"Thedes has been telling us about you and your family," Neputa said. "We owe you greatly for pulling us out of hell. It is unimaginable to us that complete strangers would risk everything to save us. We had long ago lost all hope."

"Did Thedes tell you that he and Ibula saved our lives?" Simon asked. "And they were complete strangers then."

"Thedes is well respected as a warrior and a good man," Raul said. "He has many friends and many of them helped to rescue you."

"He has been telling us about the Ice Caves, and our families," Aloeus said. "It sounds like a wonderful world."

"You will be amazed at its beauty," Simon said. "We couldn't believe our eyes."

"You have been there?" asked Neputa.

"The Sanuri sent the Rualas to save us when we were almost killed by Hutas," Raul said. "Thedes and Ibula took us into their home and treated us like family. Ibula even wrote to our family so they wouldn't worry. Thedes would take us on outings to help us regain our strength. Simon and I had heard about the Ice Caves but we were not prepared for what we saw. These are not like the caves we are used to here. They are like beautiful worlds within worlds. And the Shettees and Rualas live very happily together."

"We were surprised you saved the Hutas too," Cronos said. "But as much as we hate them, the Valdees were even worse to them than they were to us. It is amazing that any of them are alive."

"I think it is amazing that any of you are alive," Simon said. "It must speak to the strength of your character."

"It was the decision of my great, great grandfather that our tribe should not intermingle with those who were not Shettee. He did this to protect our families and our way of life," Neputa said.

"But Thedes is convincing me that should no longer be our way. He believes we should live in the Ice Caves instead of Xepoltr."

"I think once you see the Ice Caves you will not want to leave," Simon said. "Xepoltr has been taken over by the Hutas, do you really want to put your families through that kind of life again. You have been through so much; enjoy the life you have left, enjoy your families."

"I don't know why I can't stop crying," Hannah said. "I am just so happy you are safe."

"And we'll be going home soon," Gabriel said as he hugged Hannah inside of their room in Joshua's home.

"Raphael said the demon singled you out," Hannah said. "Gabriel that means he knows who you are."

"Don't think about that now," Gabriel whispered. "Iris said you haven't slept since you got here. We are both exhausted. Let's take a nap for a little while."

"But Vivian and Raphael," Hannah said. "I should check on them."

"Iris is feeding them and Ibula and Lakin are still here," Gabriel said and kissed Hannah. "You don't have to take care of everyone."

"I miss the children," Hannah said sadly.

"So do I," Gabriel said as he gently pulled Hannah down on the bed.

While Sampson slept, Hecate prayed before her unholy altar. She had defied Baal and now expected retribution. Hecate was not praying as much as soliciting protection. Hecate knew she would have to pay a high price to whichever Old One agreed to help her. Although the Old Ones constantly fought with each other they expected unquestionable obedience from their subordinates. Even the enemies of Baal would not look favorably on Hecate's behavior.

Hecate knew she had to be shrewd in her attempts to get another benefactor. It was known by many in the underworlds that she was challenging Moloch and Ipos for the souls of The Seven Sons, the high priests and the Sanuri. Hecate was ambitious and driven. But she was a seductress of the demons as well as other species.

Hecate was used to getting her way, but now she had herself in a very dangerous position. She was defying three of the Old Ones and Ahriman was no longer able to help her. She knew she had to come up with a plan that would provide her and Sampson with protection. Hecate rubbed her stomach and smiled, her first child. Then her thoughts returned to Baal and Hecate prayed more earnestly at her altar.

Chapter XXI
Mysteries

"Are you sure they aren't here?" Jared asked Zoya and Delilah.

"Honey we would know if they were here," Zoya said. "Lily has been crying so Annabelle fed her. Natasha is a good mother; she would have taken Lily as soon as she returned.

"Where is Emeral?" Edward asked.

"She's with the other children," Delilah said. "I'll get her."

A few minutes later Emeral entered the room. "What is wrong, you both look worried?"

"We can't find the girls," Jared said. "Maggie said they left before we got there. We didn't see them on the road and we wandered around the city for a while looking for them. Is there any place they would go?"

"Maybe home," Emeral said. "Why don't the two of you go back to Salar? There are a few other Rualas here; we will search our house and the roadways if we find them we will find you."

Although the demon attack in Wetpr ended hours after it was launched; the battle surrounding the Village of Gesmal lasted for several more days. The demon fog continued to surround the village and the sounds of the battle between the forces of light and darkness were at times deafening. Claudius asked Miranda if she wanted his army to help the Angels. But Miranda wanted them to concentrate on helping the wounded and dying who filled the small village.

"It's been three days," Emeral said to Sudfad, Edward, Jared and Renya. "I would think the Enrops will be arriving in Gesmal very soon. I just don't know how they could have disappeared without any trace." Emeral started to cry and Renya got out of her chair and put her arms around Emeral. "Telling my sons what happened was the hardest thing I ever did," she sobbed.

300

"Emeral I hope you aren't blaming yourself," Sudfad said. "You didn't do anything wrong. Why even the Sanuri said they would be alright."

"The Sanuri," Emeral said. "Why I haven't seen him in days is he missing too?"

Calen burst through the door of Joshua's house. "Where are Luca and Gabriel?" he asked loudly and frantically.

"Calen you are crying, what is wrong?" Iris asked. She ran across the kitchen to Calen. "Adrone get your father quickly," Iris said. Calen's hand shook as he handed Iris the letter. The color drained from Iris' face as she read Emeral's letter. "Honey drink this," Iris said as she handed Calen a cup of whiskey.

Joshua and Sorren ran into the house. "The boys are looking for Gabriel and Luca," Joshua said. "What is wrong?"

Calen could not speak so he handed the letter to Sorren, who was standing the closest to him. "The demons attacked Wetpr like they did here but the Angels and Hengers ended the battle quickly but afterwards, well, Natasha and Lila are missing," Iris explained.

"Joshua stay with the boy, I am going to get the others," Sorren said and quickly left the house. Joshua sat down at the kitchen table and read the letter.

"This really doesn't make sense," Joshua said. "If the Angels stopped the attack who took the girls? Do you think it was the Valdees?" Calen swallowed hard and just stared blankly at Joshua.

Within minutes the small house filled with people. Hannah ran to Calen and put her arms around him. Calen started to cry on Hannah's shoulder. "Has anyone found Gabriel or Luca yet?" Hannah asked as tears ran down her face.

Gabriel and Raphael entered the house but stopped abruptly when they saw Calen crying in Hannah's arms. "Hannah what has happened?" Gabriel asked fearfully.

"Natasha and Lila are missing," Hannah cried.

"The details are in this letter," Joshua said and handed it to Gabriel who looked stunned.

"Raphael I, I can't read it," Gabriel stammered and handed the letter to Raphael. "We have to find Luca," Gabriel said in a dazed manner. Hannah walked over to Gabriel and hugged him tightly. Luca, Elan, Cassandra and Vivian pushed through the crowd.

"Adrone told us to come at once," Luca said. "What has happened?" As Luca spoke he saw his brother and Hannah crying and the looks on Gabriel's and Raphael's faces. Maxwell entered the small kitchen as Luca was speaking.

"Our wives are missing," Calen said to Luca in a halting voice.

"Lila and Natasha?" Luca asked. "How?" What happened?"

"Your mother sent this letter," Raphael said and handed it to Luca.

"Raphael why don't you just tell us all what it says," Maxwell said as he walked up to his sons.

"Emeral describes a similar demon attack in Wetpr," Raphael started to say but was interrupted by Raul, Matthew and Simon who ran into the house.

"An attack in Wetpr?" Raul asked loudly.

"Let him finish telling us," Maxwell said.

"The ground opened up and there was the same fog as here. Emeral and Renya gathered all the families together when they realized Lila had not returned from Salar. Emeral and Natasha went into Salar and found Lila taking refuge in the General Store with many other people. While they were in the store they, well, you can read about it in the letter but basically they meet a man named Edward, who works for King Tobias and was trying to get to the castle to give Sudfad a very important letter about the Valdees attacks. Emeral flew Edward to the castle and the girls stayed at the store," Raphael continued.

302

"Natasha told Emeral they would return to the castle when the fog cleared. The Sanuri was at the castle and told Emeral not to go back out in the fog because the girls would be alright. As soon as the fog started to clear, Jared and Edward went into Salar to bring the girls home. People at the store said the girls left but they didn't know where to. People have been searching for almost two days and there is no sign of the girls."

"Lila's pregnant," Luca whispered as his knees gave out and he sat down on a kitchen chair. "Raphael does Mother say why Lila went into the city by herself, that's not like her?"

Raphael hesitated, "She was getting you a gift."

"We'll talk to Miranda," Raul said. "Everyone just stay here until we return."

"I know how they feel," Matthew said to Simon and Raul as they walked from the house. "When Angelina was kidnapped I couldn't even think."

Sudfad stared at Emeral for a moment. "Has anyone seen the Sanuri since that meeting?" Sudfad asked. No one in the room answered. "He always tells Renya and me that he is leaving, something must be wrong."

"I'll go and look in his room," Renya said and quickly left the study.

"We have been so focused on the girls," Sudfad said. "Is anyone else missing? Jared and Edward would you talk to the staff and find out if everyone is accounted for and if they have seen anything suspicious? I am going to send letters to Mathas and Claudius. Oh and can you tell the guards outside of the door that I need to see General Hoff at once; perhaps some of our men are missing too?"

"Miranda, Daniel," Matthew called out. "Please we need to speak with you. The wives of Calen and Luca..." Both Angels appeared to the three men before Matthew completed his sentence.

"Thank you for coming," Simon said. "The demons attacked Wetpr like they did here, now the wives of Calen and Luca are missing. Can you help us find them?"

Hecate performed spell after spell for three days before she saw any improvement in Sampson's condition. During this time she kept him drugged to ease his pain and to prevent him from looking in a mirror. Sampson was under Baal's power when Hecate removed him from the hell dimension. As a true demon, Hecate could change her appearance as she moved between worlds but Sampson had not completed the trials.

When Hecate and Sampson first returned to the World of Nunc, Sampson still maintained the appearance of the giant demon that appeared before the army of mortals. Because of Hecate's spells, Sampson had returned to his normal human height but his body was still covered in long hair with long fangs and claws. Now, after three days, Sampson's human face was starting to show through the demon mask. Hecate was getting frustrated and knew she would need the help of an Old One to complete Sampson's transformation.

Miranda disappeared as soon as Simon finished speaking. "That is The Lion's assignment," Daniel explained. "Miranda and I didn't know anything about what happened in Wetpr but she left to get information. Tell Gabriel to gather his family and team and we will take them home. But the rest of you still have work that must be done here."

The news about Natasha and Lila spread through the small Village of Gesmal quickly. A small crowd had gathered around Joshua's house.

"Where are they?" Raul asked as they walked into Joshua's kitchen but did not see Gabriel's family.

"They are all packing," Iris said.

Gabriel ran out of the bedroom when he heard Raul's voice. "What did they say?" he asked fearfully.

"They said Wetpr is The Lion's assignment and they did not know anything about Natasha or Lila. But Miranda is trying to find out information," Raul explained. "But in the meantime Daniel said for you to gather your team and the Angels will take you home."

"Calen and Luca and the others will be back here shortly," Gabriel said.

"Will I need to pack food if the Angels are taking you?" Iris asked.

"I don't think so," Matthew replied.

Hannah came out of the bedroom carrying her bag, which she set on the floor. Hannah walked over to Iris and hugged her. "Thank you so much for everything," Hannah said.

"You are our family now," Iris said as tears came to her eyes.

As Vivian and Raphael packed, her father and brothers were in the bedroom saying their goodbyes. "If you can talk your mother into flying with the Rualas we will come and visit," Joshua said loudly.

"Oh Iris you will love flying," Hannah said. "And we would love to have you visit."

"You've talked me into it," Iris said as she walked up to Vivian and Raphael and hugged and kissed them both.

"Archetenus is coming back with us," Calen said as he walked into the house.

"The Angels are taking us home," Raphael said.

"How?" asked Calen.

"We have no idea," Gabriel replied.

"Did they know what happened to our wives?" Luca asked as he and Dagon entered the kitchen.

"No," Matthew said. "They said Wetpr was The Lion's assignment but Miranda was going to try and get information."

"Is everyone here?" asked Gabriel.

"I don't think so," Luca said. "But they should be here shortly."

Gabriel, Hannah, Raphael, Vivian, Koby, Bekka, Elan, Cassandra, Dagon, Misha, Maxwell, Luca, Calen and Archetenus gathered outside of Joshua's house with their belongings. "Daniel, Miranda we are ready," Gabriel called. Both Angels appeared in an instant.

"Miranda is it alright if I return with them?" Archetenus asked.

"Of course," Miranda said. "You will leave your horses here, I am sure your friends will bring them back. Grab the belongings you want to take."

"Miranda did you find out anything about our wives?" Calen asked. His fears were increasing because Miranda had not already mentioned anything.

"Very little," she said. "But I do know that the Sanuri is missing also."

"But I thought Angels knew everything," Luca said. "Are you just not telling us?"

"Only The Great Ruler knows everything," Miranda said warmly. "Angels know infinitely more than men but often like with you, The Great Ruler reveals things to us only when we need to know."

"If the Sanuri is with your wives he will protect them," said Daniel.

"But it would have to be something very powerful to take the Sanuri too," said Elan.

"Because you have been so faithful and diligent in your duties Daniel and I are giving you a gift."

"You will feel like you have fallen asleep; when you wake you will be in Wetpr," Miranda said.

"Thank you," Hannah said to the Angels.

"General Hoff," Sudfad said professionally as he did not care for the man. "What do you have to report?"

Hoff looked at Jared and Edward who were seated in the King's study and a pang of jealousy surged through him as he realized these two strangers held the King's favor.

"General Hoff," Sudfad repeated.

"All the soldiers at Fort Salar are accounted for My Lord," Hoff said stiffly.

"Thank you, that will be all," Sudfad said as he dismissed the General.

"Actually King Sudfad there is one more thing," Hoff said. "It might be of such little significance that I didn't want to burden you with it. But as you know our troops routinely patrol the homes of Gabriel and Jared. Earlier this morning one of my men reported seeing a door in Gabriel's house open. He walked inside of the house and did not find any intruders but he did find this." Hoff took an item out of his pocket and handed it to the King. "The soldier said it was hanging outside of the opened door. Do you know what it is?"

"Unfortunately I do," Sudfad said. "And this is worse than I thought."

Hecate was again praying at her unholy altar when she heard Sampson screaming. She ran out of the room and to her main living quarters in the cavern. "Hecate am I having a nightmare? Tell me what do I look like?" Sampson was standing before the large mirror which hung near Hecate's bed.

"I will fix this," Hecate said soothingly. "Now sit down we need to talk."

"I look like a monster, am I still a man?" he shrieked.

"Tell me do you remember anything of your trials?"

Sampson was quiet as he tried to remember his ordeal in hell. "Some of it, I think," Sampson said.

"Your trials were grueling," Hecate explained. "Baal, a very powerful Old One was performing the tests. While you were being tested that army that was at your village, attacked the Kingdom of Ogg. It is completely destroyed and all of the captives are in your village being cared for. Baal was irate because he owned the souls of Ogg. When a demon owns souls it makes him more powerful, so losing Ogg greatly weakened Baal."

"I don't..." Sampson started to say.

"Let me finish," Hecate said. "Baal consorted with Moloch and Ipos and the three Old Ones tried to attack your village as well as Sudfad's castle in Wetpr. It took a great deal of power but these Old Ones opened the doors between the worlds. The ground opened up and armies of demons were unleashed."

"My village," Sampson gasped.

"Your village was unharmed," Hecate said. "Both attacks were stopped by The Great Ruler who sent Angels and Hengers to battle the demons. Armies of Angels invaded the hell domains. The Old Ones were greatly losing their power, then to add to the insult that army of humans descends into hell and challenges Baal. The Angels were protecting the humans from Baal's wrath."

"Baal turned you into a version of what you see now and told you to kill your brothers, which was your final trial. But the others attacked you and were killing you. I argued with Baal but he would not stop the tests. I tried to protect you but they attacked me also so against Baal's orders I pulled both of us out of that world. That is why you still resemble the demon you were."

Sampson stared at Hecate. "Will I change back?"

"I am working on it, but yes."

"What I don't understand is how those men could hurt us if we were demons in hell?"

"Those were not just any men," Hecate said. "That is why I have been trying to destroy them. Those men destroyed the powerful Old One Ahriman, who was my benefactor. They work on behalf of The Great Ruler and possess powers that other men do not."

"Didn't Baal stop them?"

"I don't know what happened after we left but the army returned to your village."

"So are you telling me that The Great Ruler is more powerful than all the demons in hell?"

Cerey screamed with delight when she saw Gabriel, Hannah and the others suddenly appear in the front foyer of Sudfad's castle. "Mama, Papa," the little girl screamed and ran to Hannah. Nicholas and Christopher had been playing on the floor of the main parlor with Cerey, both boys now looked up and got bright smiles on their faces.

"Papa, Mama," Nicholas yelled and ran to Gabriel.

"Luca," screamed Christopher and with a running start jumped into Luca's arms. Luca and Christopher hugged tightly.

"Where are Simon and Raul?" Annabelle asked as she stood up from her chair.

"The Angels only sent us back now, but everyone else is fine," Raphael replied as he watched Gabriel and Hannah hugging and kissing their children.

"Where is Delilah?" asked Archetenus.

"She's upstairs taking a nap," Annabelle said. "Fourth door on the right." Archetenus dropped his bag and ran up the stairs.

Laurel walked up to Calen with a big smile on her face. "Would you like to see your daddy?" Laurel said to baby Lily. Tears came to Calen's eyes as he took his daughter.

"Luca, Lila and Natasha got lost in the fog," Christopher said. "Grandma is out looking for them."

"I know Christopher, that is why we came back before the others," said Luca.

Renya came out of Sudfad's study and walked down the hallway when she heard the children scream. "Thank god you are alright," Renya said as she looked at her friends. "But where are the others?"

"They are still in Ryed," Gabriel said. "The Angels transported us back here because of Natasha and Lila."

"I know you want to talk to Sudfad but you all look exhausted," said Renya. "Come I will get you rooms, then some lunch. You can talk business later."

"Calen," Annabelle said as she walked up to him. "Whenever Simon and Raul are gone, I move in with Vitomas. She and I are both nursing and have been taking care of Lily. You are welcome to stay in one of the spare bedrooms, if you want to be closer to her."

"Thank you," Calen replied in a whisper.

Jared and Edward entered the castle as Renya was taking her guests up the front stairs. She turned when she heard the door. "There is so much we all have to talk about," Renya said. "But for now, everyone the man with Jared is Edward, he was sent here by King Tobias. You can all get acquainted after I get you rooms.

"Luca, Calen we should talk with you," Jared said.

Gabriel was half way up the staircase when he heard Jared's words. Gabriel set Nicholas down and said to him, "Why don't you go with Mama; I will be up in a little bit."

As Gabriel started to walk down the steps Jared said. "Maybe Christopher should go with Hannah too."

"I don't want to," Christopher said as he held tightly onto Luca's neck.

310

"Christopher what he has to say might help us find Lila," Luca said as he set Christopher down. "Why don't you play with Nicholas and I will come up and get you in a little while." Christopher reluctantly ran up the steps to Nicholas and Hannah.

Suddenly Christopher turned around and yelled, "Luca can I sleep with you tonight?"

"Yes," Luca said with a grin. And Christopher ran up the stairs.

Raphael put his bags in the bedroom Renya had assigned to him and Vivian, then Raphael met with the other men at the bottom of the staircase.

"Have you found anything?" Calen asked.

"We have been searching everywhere," Jared said. "Without so much as a trail. The girls were driving a small boca. This morning one of the soldiers patrolled past your house and saw a door open. He looked inside and didn't see any intruders but found a demon thing hanging over the door. Sudfad has it, he says it's an aboultis. He said it is some kind of calling card that a demon is taking credit for collecting a bounty. Edward and I just came from your house. Nothing was messed up but I haven't been in your place enough to know if anything is missing. You should come back there with us."

"Let me see that aboultis first," Raphael said. "Different demons have their unique marks."

"Annabelle can you take Lily?" Calen asked.

"Of course," Annabelle said. "Do you know that the Sanuri is missing too?"

"The Angels told us," Luca said. "But that is all they told us." Maxwell and the other Rualas now came down the stairs.

"What is going on?" Maxwell asked.

"This morning a soldier found one of the doors to our house open and a demon's calling card hanging over it," Gabriel said.

"Jared and Edward walked through the house and didn't find any more calling cards but they don't know if anything is missing. We're going back to the house now to look around."

Hannah and Vivian appeared at the top of the stairs. "Gabriel have you any news? Do you need us to help?"

"No," Gabriel said. "You two get some rest; we are going out to search for a while."

Shortly after Gabriel's team was transported to Wetpr, Daniel and Miranda returned to the Village of Gesmal. "First we would like to meet with the leaders," Miranda said.

"Please come to my home," Chief Duncan said. "Our meeting lodge is filled with patients."

Claudius, Stephan, Thaos, Matthew, Sorren, Angelina, Raul, Simon, Thedes, Ibula, Lakin and Gael entered the home. "Duncan your sons should be here as well as Joshua and his two oldest sons," Miranda said. When everyone was accounted for, Miranda started to speak.

"Duncan you now know the true nature of your son Sampson. You still love him but understand that he is a threat to your family and to your tribe," Miranda said then faced the group. "All of you have done very well and we are pleased but your work is not done. Months ago when we were in Taperia much more happened than you realized."

"Once Roch fully became a demon he was intertwined in a web that connected all of the Insidiae and other demons. When Matthew, Raul and Simon combined their powers as three of The Seven Sons, not only did they destroy Roch but they sent waves of holiness through that demonic web. Claudius you and the others saw how weakened the demons are by holiness. The waves that were sent through Roch were so powerful that they weakened every demon and dark lord connected to this world."

"Baal, the demon that you faced in the underworld, owned all of the souls of the Valdees," Daniel explained. "When we destroyed Ogg it not only enraged Baal but weakened him."

312

"When we were fighting in Ogg other Old Ones appeared, the Old ones normally do not get involved in battles. Among that group were the demons Moloch and Ipos, both very powerful demons. These are the same two demons who laid the trap for you in that mausoleum. They are seeking revenge for Ahriman's fall and the holiness that weakened them all. And they are trying to stop the forces that work on behalf of The Great Ruler."

Daniel continued, "This ring around your village is the combined work of Baal, Moloch and Ipos. They opened the doors to hell to kill the Sanuri, The Seven Sons and many others. But this move was not for revenge."

"There is an ancient prophesy about the blood moon, which predicts that on the thirteenth night of the blood moon in the year of Zenus the doors will be opened and the waters will part. The blood that is spilled will rejuvenate the dead and fill them with power. This prophesy is talking about the doors to hell being opened and the demons freely entering other worlds. The Old Ones want to kill you so you can't interfere with this prophesy being fulfilled."

"You mean it can happen?" Claudius bellowed.

"Yes," Daniel said. "Baal, Moloch and Ipos opened some of the doors to hell here and in Wetpr hoping to stop you. But they were unsuccessful. For weeks Hutas have been capturing innocent people from farms and villages and imprisoning them to be sacrificed on the thirteenth because the blood of those victims will be some of the blood that empowers the demons."

"The Sanuri was trying to figure out where these victims were being hidden," Raul said. "Did he figure it out?"

"No," Daniel responded.

"I am assuming this is the year of Zenus," Claudius said. "How long before the thirteenth night?"

"Tonight is the third night," Daniel said.

"Ten days," Stephan said. "We heard you tell Gabriel and the others that the Sanuri is missing too. Does that have anything to do with this blood moon prophesy?"

313

"We honestly don't know the answer to that," Miranda said. "But if I had to guess I would say yes."

"How do Natasha and Lila figure in?" Ibula asked.

"I don't know if they do," said Daniel.

"What do you need us to do?" Claudius asked.

"For the next ten days all of you are in great danger," Daniel replied.

"That is not what I asked," Claudius said.

Daniel smiled. "Will you work with us to stop this prophesy from coming to fruition?"

"Of course," Claudius said.

"I'm guessing we need to find those poor bastards that the Hutas have," Sorren said.

Barely had Gabriel and the others walked down the front steps of the castle, when Emeral flew up to them. Her face was flushed. "Emeral what is the matter?" Maxwell asked as he ran to his wife.

"Please you have to come with me," Emeral said. "Carry those who cannot fly." Before anyone could speak Emeral ascended into the sky and flew northeastward towards the forest that separated Sudfad's castle from the River Toba. They flew for several miles before Emeral started to descend into a thickly wooded area.

As the others descended they found Emeral standing near a small boca. The two horses were tangled in their reigns. "This is the girls' boca," Emeral said as tears came to her eyes. "Look at these poor horses, something must have scared them and they ran until they got so tangled up they couldn't move."

Gabriel and Raphael searched the inside of the boca, while Bekka and Cassandra freed the horses. The others were searching the ground for tracks or any sign of Natasha and Lila.

"Your mother has been filled with guilt," Edward said to Calen loudly. "I keep telling her it is not her fault."

Maxwell walked up to Emeral and put his arms around her. "Maxwell I don't know where our babies are," she said and started to cry.

"Honey we'll find them," Maxwell said soothingly.

Jared was examining the horses for injuries, "I'll drive the boca back," he said. "Gabriel are these your horses or Sudfad's?"

"Mine, why?"

"Come over here and look at this," Jared said. "These scars look pretty fresh; did the horses have them before?"

"No," Gabriel said as he saw large claw marks on the leg of one of the horses.

"As tangled up as these horses were they would be defenseless if something attacked them here," Jared said. "Maybe this is why the horses started running."

After the meeting, Claudius and the others followed Miranda and Daniel out of Duncan's home. The Angels were headed to the areas were the wounded were being treated.

"The fog is gone," Thaos said as soon as they stepped outside. "Does that mean the doors to hell are closed?"

"For now," said Daniel.

"Well it's good to see the sun again," Stephan said as he looked up into the sky.

The Angels stopped first at the location where the eight Huta warriors were being treated. All of these men were still so weak that not one among them could stand without assistance.

"Adrone come here," Joshua called angrily when he saw his young son sitting next to Nikki who was changing the bandage on a Huta.

315

"I haven't done anything wrong," Adrone said as he walked over to his father. It had been decided when the Hutas were first brought to the village that only warriors would tend to them as the Hutas might be a danger to others.

Nikki bowed before the Angels and said, "A rather remarkable thing just happened. Adrone gave half of his cookie to this warrior and I swear the man got tears in his eyes. Guess I never thought of a Huta as having feelings."

"Nikki we have told you that you do not need to bow before us," Daniel said gently.

"I know, but it is my way of honoring you." As Nikki and the Angels talked a small crowd started to gather around them.

"Nikki your services are not needed here anymore," Daniel said.

"Are you going to kill them?" Ibula asked with surprise.

"Would you have us save them?" asked Daniel.

"I know they are Hutas but look at them," Ibula said compassionately. "To kill a man when he is too weak to even move; does not seem right to me."

"We agree with you," Daniel said.

"What are you going to do?" asked Sorren.

Daniel did not answer the question. All eyes were upon Miranda as she walked up to the eight wounded Hutas. Miranda spoke in one language but it was understood by all. "Look about you and remember this scene," Miranda said as she pointed to the thousands of wounded people. "This is the face of fear, the face of hatred and the face of ideas of racial superiority. Tell me what human dare judge which of The Great Ruler's children are worthy. They are all worthy in His eyes; He created them." The Hutas looked upon the Angels fearfully.

"These people who you regard as your enemy, who you believe are inferior races have shown you mercy, a word not understood by your tribe."

"The love and compassion they have shown you are not signs of weakness just the opposite. The goodness and faith within them makes them strong. They have fought the demons you worship and these people win their battles." The crowd around the Angels and Hutas grew larger as the patients who could walk now joined the warriors and villagers.

"Stand now," Miranda ordered. "You are healed." Listening to her words the crowd started to whisper. The fearful Hutas did not move. "Rise," Miranda ordered. The Huta who Nikki had been tending was the first to stand. The other Hutas slowly stood one by one as the crowd stared in disbelief at the transformations taking place before their eyes.

"Go now," Miranda said. "And know these people; this village is protected by Angels." The Hutas were so shocked by the miraculous changes that were occurring within their bodies that they did not move."

"You're letting them go?" Duncan gasped. Daniel held up his hand for all to be silent.

The Huta who Nikki was caring for walked boldly up to Miranda, when he got within feet of her, he did something that made the entire crowd gasp. The Huta bowed before the Angel. "What is your name?" Miranda asked.

"Tetro," the Huta replied.

"Tetro stand, you are free to go," Miranda said. "Your men think this is a trick, it is not."

The Hutas turned and started to walk away but after a few steps Tetro turned back and walked up to Joshua. Tetro took off his necklace which contained a large ruby stone and handed it to Joshua. Tetro spoke and Daniel translated. "He is telling you it is a gift for Adrone. He too has a young son." Joshua took the necklace and nodded to the Huta. Joshua then handed the necklace to Adrone, who became very excited.

"Are you really doing this?" Thaos asked as Tetro turned and joined his men.

317

"Sometimes the biggest miracles are the ones most difficult to understand," Daniel said loudly. "The kindness and mercy you have shown these men will affect them the rest of their lives; they will not return as your enemy. And that light which has now been ignited within them will slowly grow and affect the others of their kind. You will not see big results in your lives but know that the choices you made here have changed the future of this world."

"For the better?" Sorren asked incredulously.

"Yes," Daniel said with a smile.

"Miranda tell them to wait," Thaos said as he pulled a knife from his belt.

"Why?" the Angel asked.

"They have no food, they will at least need a weapon to hunt with," Thaos said.

"Wait," Miranda called. The Hutas stopped and turned towards the village.

By the time Thaos reached the men he was carrying six knives and two bows with arrows. "I can't believe I am doing this," Thaos said out loud as he handed the weapons to the Hutas. Not one Huta thought about turning the weapons on Thaos, in fact they didn't know what to think about any of the things that were now happening to them.

Tetro spoke to Thaos but Thaos motioned that he could not understand what the Huta was saying. Thaos turned and walked back to the crowd and the Hutas walked away from the village.

"He said, 'plet,'" Thaos said. "Does that mean thank you?"

"No," Daniel said. "He asked you, 'why?'"

Chapter XXII
The Death Vow

Misha, Dagon, Koby, Elan, Calen, Luca and Edward, returned to the boca where the others were still searching the area. "The horses were running wild," Calen said to Gabriel, Raphael, Emeral, Maxwell, Jared, Bekka and Cassandra. "So they made a good trail which leads to our house."

"We're thinking the girls stopped there to get something," Luca said. "Either something was waiting for them or the girls surprised them."

"They didn't say anything about going home," said Emeral.

"Did you find anything?" Misha asked.

"Jared found these claw marks on one of the horses," Gabriel said as he pointed to the injuries on the horse. There isn't any blood on the boca but we found one of Natasha's throwing knives on the floor in front."

"We searched the ground and the bushes and there isn't anything," said Bekka.

"We need to go back to the house," Raphael said. "Jared, Edward were you told which door that soldier found open?"

"The back kitchen door," Edward said. "He found the aboultis hanging on that flower trellis you have by the door."

"It might be a challenge getting this thing out of here," Jared said as he climbed into the front of the boca.

"I'll ride with you," Edward said and climbed into the passenger's seat.

"Cassandra and I will fly with you," Elan said. "In case you have problems."

Everyone's attention was focused on the Hutas that were walking away from the village, when a voice cried out.

"I am healed." People cried and rejoiced when they realized that Miranda had healed everyone with her words.

"You are all free to go," Miranda said. Now many of the former captives stopped cheering because they didn't know where to go.

Prince Gael and Prince Lakin walked up to the large group of Shettees. "Our warriors will take you to the Ice Caves to be reunited with your families. We hope you are still there when we return," Gael said.

"You are not coming?" Neputa asked with surprise.

"Our work is not done," Gael said. "The Angels just told us of a demonic plot that threatens all of us. And to initiate this plot the demons need the blood of countless victims. The Hutas have been gathering people to be sacrificed and we are going to find them and free them."

One of the former captives walked up to the Ruala Princes. "I don't really have a home cuz the Hutas killed everyone. I came to Ryed to get work and the Valdees got me. I know how to use weapons; I would be willing to help you."

"What is your name?" Lakin asked.

"Ted. I was a soldier before I got married, so I do know how to fight."

"Raul, we got you another soldier," Lakin called out. "He needs a horse and weapons." Lakin turned to Ted and pointed out Prince Raul. "Go to him and he will get you what you need." As Lakin and Gael turned to walk away, Neputa called to them.

"We desperately want to see our families but we owe all of you so much," Neputa said. "We will join you. And we will all return to our families together."

Renya walked into Sudfad's study and closed the door behind her. "Did he appear to you?" she asked.

"Yes," Sudfad said as he was still shaking from his experience with The Lion.

"I asked him if the Sanuri was in danger and The Lion said yes, but that my men could not follow the Sanuri where he was going. Which I assume is some kind of hell dimension. I asked what could be powerful enough to capture him and The Lion said that the Sanuri wasn't captured but had gone after Natasha and Lila. Renya I don't know if I should tell Gabriel and the others what The Lion said."

"Sudfad it will terrify them but you have to tell them," Renya said.

"You're right," Sudfad said sadly. "Tell me when they return."

"At first glance it doesn't look like anything was disturbed," Raphael said as he led the group inside of the house.

"Bekka and I will search the stable and buildings," Koby said.

"Here's Lila's purse," Luca said as he picked a small bag up from the floor.

"If that was on the floor, I am guessing they were grabbed in the kitchen," Maxwell said.

"If they came home it was probably to get something for the children," Emeral said. "We need to keep looking."

Luca poured the contents of Lila's purse onto the kitchen table. It held little, some gold coins, a shopping list and a small pouch. Luca opened the pouch and took out a man's ring which was yellow gold with a large emerald stone that was surrounded with diamonds. Luca held the ring for several moments then he said haltingly, "This makes me feel worse, this is why she was in Salar."

"She loves you," Dagon said as he looked at the ring.

"We found a pile of Lily's clothes on the floor," Maxwell said as he and Emeral entered the kitchen. "That's why the girls came home."

"While we are here I am going to get more clothing for all of the children," Emeral said and left the room.

"You need to come out here," Bekka said as she appeared in the doorway.

Hecate returned to her unholy altar leaving Sampson in their bedroom. Sampson stood in front of the large mirror by the bed staring at himself and thinking about what Hecate had told him. Sampson felt no remorse about his actions in Baal's hell domain. He felt no remorse that he tried to kill his brothers and others from his village. Sampson felt only anger.

Baal still had a hold on Sampson, who had not completed his trials. Neither Hecate nor Sampson understood exactly what Sampson was now. Was he a demon, was he a human or a hybrid. Did he have any powers? And regardless of what he was did the holiness damage him? As Sampson stared at the mirror he became more and more irate. Sampson was an arrogant, self-centered man who took great pride in his muscular physic and appearance. He did not want to walk around in the body of this monster. Sampson left the bedroom and marched to the room where Hecate was trying to negotiate with the Old Ones.

"Sampson I told you to never come here," Hecate said angrily.

"I don't know if I am a demon or not," Sampson yelled. "I need to finish the trials."

The room filled with laughter. "Hecate your boy wants to be a demon."

"I am her husband," Sampson yelled angrily at the voice.

The voice laughed again then said, "Hecate I will never understand your weakness for human men. But your last husband turned out to be an asset to us; perhaps this one will also." The voice now took on a serious tone. "If I agree to be your benefactor I expect total obedience. I will not tolerate the games you have been playing. Do you understand me?"

"But Raum, the Sanuri and the others destroyed Ahriman and Sporos," Hecate said defensively.

"And we will get them," Raum said. "But you subverted the trap that Moloch and Ipos set. And did it do any good? You all lost."

"And now you have a husband who is trapped between two worlds. We will get the Sanuri and the others, but not if we sabotage each other."

"I understand," Hecate said.

"Do you? Do you really?" demanded Raum.

"Yes," Hecate said. "I will follow only your orders."

"Good," Raum said solemnly. "Now tell me, if I help your husband does he swear allegiance to me also?"

"Misha, Raphael," Luca called as the others followed Bekka out of the kitchen door of the house. Koby was standing near the stable.

"Stop where you are," Koby said and flew the few yards to his friends. Misha and Raphael now joined the group. "You can see all of the horse tracks here from the soldiers and probably Jared and Edward," Koby said. "The ground is covered with them obliterating anything else. So Bekka and I started to look around the house and buildings. Come over here," Koby said and walked towards the opposite side of the house.

"The grass is smashed down and broken like something was setting here for some time. Then look at this," Koby said as he pointed to claw marks on the side of the house. "I think something was waiting for one of us to come home and whatever it was clawed the house as it stood up."

"You know what fighters those girls are," Misha said. "There had to be more than one creature to overpower them."

"Exactly," Koby said. "Bekka found claw marks on the doors to the stable.

"Did they take the horses?" Gabriel asked.

"We took all of the horses to the castle before we left," Calen said. "Sudfad didn't want anyone coming back here to care for them."

"So you think they were hiding in the stable too?" Luca asked.

"Yes," said Koby.

"Well, it looked like Lila might have been grabbed in the kitchen," Emeral said. "And Natasha in her bedroom."

"Was there any blood in the house?" Bekka asked.

"No," said Gabriel.

"We found some," Koby said and walked to the outside rear of the stable. "Look at how these branches are broken," Koby pointed out. "And there is blood on the side of the building and the ground and a blood trail back to the house."

Both Luca and Calen stared at the blood in horror. "I hope that is from one of the creatures," Calen whispered.

"I'll bet the girls fought with them here and got away," Koby said. "They ran back to the boca. Natasha was probably pulling out one of her throwing knives when whatever these creatures were grabbed the girls again. The horses got scared and ran off."

"The girls are going to know we will come after them," Dagon said as he stood up from looking at the blood trail. "They will try to leave us some signs. I think we should all walk through this area carefully and look for a trail."

"Emeral do you remember what the girls were wearing?" Maxwell asked.

"Natasha had on brown riding pants, boots and a white blouse," Emeral said thoughtfully." She changed before we went looking for Lila and I know Natasha was wearing several weapons. Lila had on a light blue dress with a white ruffle. I don't remember if either of the girls was wearing jewelry, oh but Lila had some blue ribbons in her hair."

"Well now that wasn't so bad," Raum said to Sampson. "All I demand is that you worship and obey me."

"I don't feel any different," Sampson said. "I thought it would feel different."

"You sold your soul to darkness so long ago Sampson, that this is of little change for you," the Old One said. "Now you are more use to me as a demon that can change appearance. I have plans for you and I want you to get your former appearance back."

"Will the trials be the same?" Sampson asked.

"No," Raum said. "The Angels know you intended to kill your brothers, they will be protecting them now. I have other plans. Hecate while your husband is going through the trials I expect you to be gathering tribute not only for me but also for Baal, Moloch and Ipos. It will make it easier for me to talk them out of killing the both of you."

"What sort of payment?" Sampson asked Hecate.

"There are things that he wants me to steal from the monastery at Rubar."

"Can a demon go into a monastery?" Sampson asked.

"Not unless a human invites them in," Hecate said. "Don't worry I can do this."

"Raum, I am not a demon yet," Sampson said. "Can you give me back my appearance and I will steal the things you want?"

"Hecate, I believe you brought us another good one," Raum said approvingly. "It is done."

Hecate hugged Sampson as he returned to his human form. "Hecate don't keep the boy, Rubar is a distance and he has to be back here by the thirteenth night of the blood moon."

The Villagers of Gesmal prepared one final feast for their friends from Wetpr, Lentz and the Ice Caves. While the members of Claudius' army were glad to be leaving Ryed, many had bonded with the villagers and were sad to leave them. Since Ingr was the artist among them, Claudius asked her to draw maps of Wetpr and Lentz to give to Duncan, Joshua and others.

The Angels called out for a flock of Enrops to live with the villagers. Within the hour a flock led by Odo arrived at the village. The villagers of Gesmal were delighted to have these unique creatures live among them.

Since it was a long and arduous journey from Ryed to Wetpr, Lentz or the Ice Caves, Prince Gael and Prince Lakin told Duncan to have his people send messages via Enrops. "If any of your people want to come to our kingdoms, we will have our warriors fly them," Gael said warmly. "Our tribes are united now."

By late morning a second flock of Enrops arrived at the Village of Gesmal, these birds carried letters from Lentz and Wetpr. Simon and Raul sat next to each other on the ground and read the letters from their wives. "Annabelle and Vitomas are taking care of Lily so they can nurse her," Simon said. "I didn't even think about that."

"Annabelle is probably doing most of the work," Raul said with concern. "Vitomas said she is pretty sick with this pregnancy. They want to know when we are coming home."

Angelina, Ingr and Nikki walked around the village until they found their husbands who were meeting with Claudius and Sorren about the security of the village after the army left.

"Can we talk with you?" Angelina asked.

"Is something wrong?" Stephan asked fearfully when he saw that Ingr's face was red and swollen.

"We need to go home," said Nikki. "We have been away from our babies too long."

"But we don't want to leave you either," Ingr said and started to cry.

Stephan stood up and put his arms around Ingr. "I think that is a wonderful idea," he said happily.

Thaos pulled Nikki down on his lap and hugged her. "We'll have the Rualas take you home this morning."

Matthew was not used to seeing Angelina upset. He put his arm around her as she cried. "I think I am more emotional because I am pregnant," Angelina sobbed. "You all seem awfully anxious to get rid of us." Her comment made everyone laugh.

"Honey you know we just want you to be safe," Matthew said as he kissed his wife.

"What upset all of you?" asked Claudius.

"Bella's letters," Ingr said and handed one to Claudius.

"Are the babies alright?" Sorren asked.

"Yes," Nikki said and handed Sorren a letter. "Bella tells us every little detail about the children so we don't miss out on their growing up; and we just miss them so much."

"Do you want to leave now?" Stephan asked.

"Maybe we should wait until after the feast so we can say goodbye to everyone," Angelina said as she looked at Ingr and Nikki, who both nodded their heads.

Claudius smiled. "I was going to wait for the feast but maybe you girls should do this now," Claudius said as he pulled a letter from the breast pocket of his uniform. "Bella said you girls were writing about how good Iris and Joshua were to you, so she sent them gifts. Of course they had to be small so the Enrops could carry them."

Ingr opened one envelope and took out a ruby necklace and earrings. "Oh these are beautiful," Ingr said as she handed them to Angelina to look at. Nikki opened the second envelope which contained a man's ring; it was yellow gold with a dark blue sapphire stone.

"This is very nice," Nikki said as she showed it to Thaos.

"The gifts are from all our families," Claudius said. "Why don't you girls give Iris and Joshua their gifts and pack your things. I will talk to Gael and Lakin about getting you home."

327

"I forgot what it was like to feel healthy and strong again," Neputa said to Thedes as a small group of Shettees walked to the home of Joshua and Iris to visit Thedes' son. "Tell me Thedes what does it feel like to know that you have done something that none of the rest of us could do; reunite our people."

"I didn't do it," Thedes said. "Although I am so incredibly grateful my heart could burst. The Great Ruler saved us all and is bringing us together. We would never have been able to get you out of Ogg without the Angels."

"Have you seen The Great Ruler?" asked Neputa.

"No," Thedes said. "But He is the one who sends the Angels and the Sanuri to help others."

"We have seen the Angels and the Sanuri," Neputa said. "But if you haven't seen The Great Ruler how do you know He exists?"

"I asked those same questions when the Rualas saved us," Thedes said. "I didn't trust the Rualas and thought we were being led into a trap. But after a while," Thedes paused. "It is very difficult to explain. You know how you feel when the Angels are around; I don't really have a word to describe it."

"We know what you are talking about," Orcus said. "We felt it when Miranda entered our prison. We felt her before we saw her."

"Well, Ibula taught me that when you talk to The Great Ruler you feel the same way but sometimes the feeling is even more intense," Thedes said. "It took me a long time to understand what she was talking about; but when I felt it I knew He was real."

"It is difficult to believe in something you can't see," Neputa said. "But it is also difficult to explain everything that has happened since you rescued us."

"I believe in The Great Ruler," Thedes said. "But I am not very good at talking about Him. The Rualas are much better at explaining things." When Thedes and the others entered the house, they found Joshua and Iris in the kitchen with Ibula, Angelina, Nikki and Ingr.

They were all hugging each other and some of the women were crying. "Is everything all right?" Thedes asked.

"The girls are going home to their babies," Joshua said. "And their families sent Iris and me beautiful gifts. Look." Joshua said as he proudly showed off his new ring.

"All you girls have become family to us," Iris said as tears filled her eyes. "Now you write, especially when the babies are born."

"Babies," Orcus said with surprise.

"Angelina and Nikki are both pregnant," Ibula said and they all have small babies at home.

"Forgive my brother for staring," Neputa said. "Thedes has explained to us that all your tribes have female warriors who are just as fierce as the men. But until we came here we have never heard of such things. And now to hear that you are pregnant and mothers it is new for us."

Ibula laughed at Neputa's words. "I am sure that my husband has many good stories to tell you."

"Not all women are warriors," Angelina said. "Some cultures don't have any women warriors. In our tribe the women can choose to be a warrior or not. But just because you are a warrior doesn't mean you can't be a wife and a mother."

Now Neputa laughed and shook his head. "We have many new things to learn." While they were talking Thedes walked out from the bedroom holding his infant son. "This is Tamas Manu Joshua," Thedes said as he was bursting with pride. "He is the first child born that is Shettee and Ruala. Tamas this is your King, Neputa."

Neputa took Tamas from Thedes, "It has been too long since I held a baby," Neputa said.

"He is named after my father," Thedes explained. "Ibula's father who is the King of the Rualas and Joshua. Iris and Joshua did not know us but when they heard that Ibula was having a baby they brought us into their home and treated us like family. This child binds our tribes."

"I found a trail," Calen yelled excitedly as he searched the wooded area behind the horse stables. "I'm in the thicket behind the stables," he called out as the others ran to his location.

"Look, these branches are broken all along this area. And they are all broken in the same manner, not like they were bumped into." Calen pointed out.

"You think the creatures are carrying the girls over their shoulders?" Gabriel asked as he examined a branch. "Because this is too high up for them to reach otherwise." The family carefully followed what they thought to be a trail, as they looked for more signs.

"I found a footprint," Luca yelled as he pointed to an area of the ground that was lower than the surrounding area and had mud in it from the last rain.

"What is that?" Misha asked as he bent down to examine the giant print. "It looks like some kind of animal, look at those claws."

"Look how deep it is," Raphael said. "Whatever these creatures are, they are big."

Everyone's hopes rose when Dagon yelled that he had found a small blue ribbon. "Look," Dagon said as he pointed to a ribbon hanging from a branch.

"Now we know for certain that the girls are leaving a trail," Maxwell said. "But Lila only has so many ribbons so we have to be clever in our search."

The group followed the trail northeast until it stopped at the western shore of the River Toba. "I'm going to look on the other shore," Dagon said and Koby and Bekka followed him.

"We know they aren't Valdees," Gabriel said. "So they must have had a boat waiting. Look for any signs along the shoreline."

Jared pulled the boca up to Gabriel's house. "Looks pretty quiet here," Edward said. "They might be gone."

"They might be searching the area too," Elan said. "Stay here until we return." The two Rualas flew towards the wooded area behind Gabriel's house.

"Well, these poor horses need some food and water," Jared said. "I'm going to take them over to the stable."

Gabriel and the others left the doors to the stable open after they searched inside, so Jared and Edward did not see the claw marks on the doors. The men unhitched the horses from the boca and put them inside of stalls to eat. "I need to work on that horse's wounds," Jared said. "Wonder what they got in here for medicines." The two men started searching the stable when Edward said loudly, "Well hello there, what have we here? Jared look at this."

"What the hell is that?" Jared asked as he stared an object that was attached to one of the beams in the stable. "That thing in the middle is one of those Mark of Satan snakes. But this damn thing looks like it is alive." Edward pulled out his knife, but Jared said, "No, why don't we wait until the priests see this thing."

Gabriel and the others were already heading back towards the house when they encountered Elan and Cassandra. While Jared and Edward were examining the mysterious thing they found in the stable they heard the voices of their friends returning to the house. Edward walked out of the stable and yelled, "Everyone come here we found something."

"We already searched here," Calen said as they all walked inside.

"Well, you missed this damn thing," Jared said. "What do you make of it?"

Calen looked at the object and yelled to his friends, "Gabriel, Raphael I think this needs your expertise." Raphael and Gabriel were just entering the stable.

"We know it's one of those Mark of Satan snakes," Jared said. "And the damn thing is moving."

"I think I know what this is," Raphael said as he and Gabriel examined the object. "I can't remember what it is called, but the Sanuri talked about finding something like this once. Some demons wanted a man so they put something like this on his door. When the man came home the snake came alive and let the demons know the man was there."

"So we may be getting some company," Gabriel said. "Let's surprise them. We have extra weapons in the house."

"Mother you should go to the castle," Calen said.

"I will pretend I didn't hear that," Emeral said as she gave her son a disapproving look. Maxwell winked at Calen and grinned.

Hecate had written down the list of items that Raum wanted from the monastery at Rubar. She also wrote down descriptions of what the items looked like. Hecate now gave the list and some empty leather pouches to Sampson.

"Did you pack food and water?" Hecate asked.

"Yes," Sampson said and pulled her to him. Sampson leaned down and kissed Hecate passionately. The two embraced for several minutes before Hecate said, "You must go now. If you are late returning with those items the wrath of Raum will be upon you."

"I won't be late," Sampson said and leaned down and kissed Hecate again.

Gabriel and the others did not have to wait long for the demons to arrive. All of the Rualas were hiding on the roofs of the house and other buildings on the property. Jared and Edward were hiding in the stable and Gabriel and Raphael were inside of the house. The plan was for the demons to see Gabriel and Raphael so the demons would not think the situation suspicious.

Ten creatures slowly crept out of the wooded area behind the house. It was almost noon; the demons could not hide in the shadows so they moved from tree to tree trying to stay concealed while they spied on the house. Once the demons were convinced that the only people home were in the house they quickly moved forward.

The creatures walked on two legs like humans but they were considerably larger and stronger than a human male. Their bodies were covered with long hair but their faces, hands and feet looked like old tough leather. They had huge jowls which were wet from the constant drool that was dripping from their mouths. Their faces were emphasized by large rounded tusks that turned back towards their eyes.

Four demons ran to the front door and pulled it open which released an arrow from a crossbow that ran through the heart of the demon in front. Gabriel had poured blessed water over the arrow so smoke was rising from the demon's wound. This momentary distraction allowed Koby, Dagon and Bekka to come out of hiding and shoot arrows at the three remaining demons in the front doorway. One of the demons yelled and alerted the two demons that were waiting in the yard. Edward and Jared ran out of the stable and attacked these demons from behind.

The four demons that were entering the back door of the house, never heard the warning their comrade yelled. The first two that entered the kitchen were shot by Raphael and Gabriel who were standing in front of the door with crossbows. After the first shot both men dropped the crossbows and pulled out their swords.

Calen, Luca, Maxwell and Emeral helped Jared and Edward subdue the two demons they were fighting with, so they could be taken captive. Misha, Elan and Cassandra flew towards the river looking for more demons. As soon as Koby, Dagon and Bekka killed the three demons at the front door they flew after Misha and the others because they feared there would be more demons with a boat.

Gabriel lunged at one of the demons that were entering the kitchen. The demon carried a huge knife with a curved blade. He wielded the knife with such force that when the demon missed Gabriel he hit the kitchen table, breaking it in two.

333

The demon quickly recovered and lunged at Gabriel again, who jumped backwards as the blade barely missed cutting open his stomach.

Meanwhile Raphael was fighting with a demon that carried a battleaxe. Raphael lowered his center of gravity and rolled forward as the demon swung the axe at his head. Raphael came up and stabbed the demon first in the left thigh then in the stomach, blood gushed from both wounds but the demon did not falter. The demon grabbed Raphael's belt and started to pull him upwards but dropped Raphael on the floor when Maxwell cut the demon's head off.

Gabriel was barely holding his own with the demon he was battling when Calen and Luca both jumped the demon from behind. Calen slit the demon's throat.

"Throw those beasts outside," Emeral shouted. "We can't let the children see all this blood." Emeral filled pots with water and put them on the stove; then grabbed scrubbing brushes and soap.

"We found the boat but didn't see any more demons," Misha said as he entered the house. Gabriel grabbed a bottle of blessed water and a crystal, he and Raphael ran to the stable while the others removed the demon bodies from the house. The priests ran past Edward, Jared, Koby and Dagon as they guarded two demons that were tied to trees.

"We'll be right back," Gabriel shouted. "We are going to destroy their alarm." Gabriel and Raphael started to pray as soon as they entered the stable. The two horses were agitated by the presence of evil in the building. Once they reached the unholy icon, both priests stood and prayed in unison for several minutes before Gabriel poured blessed water on the Mark of Satan.

The snake started to gyrate and smoke, when the snake was soaked in the water, Raphael pushed a blessed crystal into it, causing the snake to explode. As the icon exploded, Raphael and Gabriel heard voices screaming. At first they thought the voices were coming from outside, then they realized that the voices came from hell.

Chapter XXIII
Preparations

Sampson left Hecate's lair in the Tnges Gold Mines and headed northwest towards the coast. Rubar was at least a week's journey north. It was the second largest city in Ryed and was built on the coast of the Sea of Talmont. The monastery was at the southern end of city. There were several routes that Sampson could have chosen that would take him to his destination. He chose the route that would take him close to the Village of Gesmal.

Once Gabriel and Raphael disabled the demonic icon they turned their attention to the two demons that were taken captive. Although both Raphael and Gabriel had majored in studies of ancient languages at the monastery, they spent over an hour trying to communicate with the demons.

"Are you sure they really don't understand you?" Calen asked skeptically.

"We are watching their eyes," Raphael said. "If they really do understand us they are good actors."

"We could try to beat it out of them," Luca said with frustration.

"And if they really can't communicate with us, what good does that do?" Gabriel asked.

A small flock of Enrops landed in the yard. Nica the leader of the flock that protected Sudfad's family stepped forward. "The King wanted us to check on you," the bird said.

"Ten of these demons attacked us," Gabriel explained. "We believe they are the same demons responsible for taking Natasha and Lila but we can't find a language they can understand."

"I have seen these demons before," Nica said. "Years ago when I was travelling with the Sanuri, he stopped demons like this from attacking a family. They are called Quatars; the Sanuri said they are very strong but not very smart. They probably don't speak a language as you know it."

"Did the Sanuri speak to them?" Raphael asked.

"No, he looked into their eyes and read their minds," Nica replied.

"Nica look how focused the demons are on you," Koby said. "Do you think they understand what you are saying?"

"Probably not, but they may know that Enrops work for The Great Ruler," the bird replied as he walked closer to one of the demons, who grunted and tried to move away from the bird.

"How can he be afraid of you and not us?" asked Calen.

Nica took a few more steps towards the demon; that again pulled at the ropes that bound him and tried to move. "Nica do you have some powers that we don't know about?" Luca asked.

"Actually I find his behavior strange also," the giant bird remarked. "But did you notice that he grunted instead of speaking?"

"Do you know a language to communicate with them?" Gabriel asked.

"No," Nica said then paused and looked dazed for a few moments.

"Are you alright?" Maxwell asked. "Are the demons doing something to you?"

"I hear the Sanuri's voice in my head," Nica said. "He often communicates with us in such a manner. He is going to look through my eyes to see inside of the demon. He said you must hold the demon's head very still."

The demons had been separated and tied to different trees in front of the house. Misha and Dagon both grabbed the massive head of one of the demons and held it tightly. Nica flew close to the demon's face and stared into its eyes. The demon started to thrash around, so Edward and Jared grabbed the demon to stabilize him. The demon looked fearfully at the Enrop. Nica did not say a word as he stared into the eyes of the beast.

336

After several minutes Nica said, "The Sanuri says, 'Now the other one.'" The men walked over to the second demon who acted in the same fearful manner around Nica. No sooner had Jared, Edward, Misha and Dagon put hands on the second demon, when they all heard a blood curdling scream.

"He just burst into flames," Elan said of the first demon.

"Quickly," Nica said. "But the second demon also burst into flames causing the men and Nica to quickly jump away from him."

Sampson dismounted and crept close to the Village of Gesmal. He could smell food cooking and watched the villagers preparing a feast. "I wonder what they are celebrating now." He thought to himself. Sampson moved quietly in the woods as he changed his position for a better view. He smiled when he saw soldiers packing up their campsites and realized the army was leaving. "Now I can finish my trials," He thought with satisfaction and turned to return to his horse.

Suddenly Sampson saw the slightest movement in the corner of his eye. He turned his head and stared in the direction of the movement but he couldn't distinguish the Half-Mans since they had taken on the color of the brush they were hiding in. Before Sampson's brain realized what he saw, three Half-Mans shot him with blow darts.

"Is everyone alright?" Maxwell asked.

"I am," Edward said as he wiped dirt from his pants.

"We all are," Misha replied. "I can't believe how they stink."

"Nica did you see anything?" Gabriel asked.

"It wasn't really me seeing it," Nica explained. "It was the Sanuri, but he is telling me, wait. He says there is another of those things you found which call to the demons; it is behind the trellis near the kitchen door."

Koby ran over to the trellis and tore the climbing flowers down. "Found it," he yelled.

"Don't touch it," Raphael said.

"We are going to be getting more company," Jared remarked.

"Not now," Nica said. "They think the Sanuri is here, that is why the demons seemed afraid. The demon that sent these could see the Sanuri's face through my eyes; that is why he killed them before they could give us much information."

"Do you know who the demon is?" Gabriel asked.

"His name is Daegal. The Sanuri says he hires out to do work for other demons."

"Who is he working for now?" asked Gabriel.

"The Sanuri says he saw several faces, one was Hecate, but there was also Moloch and Ipos," Nica explained.

"Please tell us you saw something about the girls," Luca said earnestly.

"The Sanuri said for you not to worry, that he has your wives and they are safe."

"Oh, thank The Great Ruler," Maxwell said. "I have to tell Emeral."

"Where are they?" Calen asked. "When is he bringing them home?"

Five Half-Mans ran into the Village of Gesmal, they were talking loudly and waving their arms. Micha, Joshua's oldest son was the first to see them. "Father come quickly," Micha yelled and ran towards the Half-Man's. Others followed Joshua. Micha was already talking to the Half-Man's when the others arrived.

"Erwat says they found a demon spying on us and they shot him with their darts. They said we should come quickly," Micha explained.

A small group of men followed Erwat and his tribesmen into the forest where they found Sampson doubled over on the ground and unconscious. Three Half-Man's were standing near Sampson ready to shoot him again if he moved.

"Sampson," Joshua gasped. Then without turning Joshua ordered Micha to get Duncan. "Is he dead?" Joshua asked as Simon was examining Sampson."

"No, ask them what they put on their darts," said Simon.

Joshua talked to Erwat for a few moments then turned to Simon. "He says they use a poison from the belacor plant. They have only shot large animals and humans with it before never a demon. He said it kills instantly."

"Well then Sampson is a demon," Simon said because he has three darts in him and he is still breathing.

Raul started to search Sampson's pockets when he yelled out that someone should find Sampson's horse and search it. Raul pulled a folded paper from Sampson's vest pocket and unfolded it. "Look at this," Raul said seriously as he handed the paper to Simon.

"What is it?" Duncan asked as he had just joined the group.

"It's a list with names and descriptions of holy items," Raul said. "Hecate must have sent Sampson to get these things. But where would he get them?"

"There is a monastery in Rubar," Duncan said as he now took the paper from Simon. Both anger and sadness consumed Duncan as he read the list. "Sampson will be executed," Duncan said.

"You may not be able to do that," Simon said. "The Half-Mans shot him with poison that would normally kill a man and Sampson is not dead. We're going to have to call the Angels on this."

Nica was quiet as he listened to the Sanuri's voice in his head.

The fact that Nica was not immediately answering Calen's questions filled the others with fear. "Nica what is he saying?" Luca asked frantically. "Is something wrong?"

"I am trying to understand what he is showing me," Nica said. "The Sanuri saved your wives almost immediately. But the Angels are helping him do some kind of trick on the demons. They believe they still have the girls as captives. The demons are seeing things that aren't real. But the illusions can't talk, so your wives are with the Sanuri helping him to keep up this trick."

"Why?" Calen asked.

Nica was quiet again. "The demons were taking your wives to be sacrificed for the blood moon ceremonies. The Sanuri wants to find out where all the victims are hidden so he can stop the sacrifices. Your wives are helping him."

Everyone stared at the bird in silence. After a few moments Gabriel asked, "Will Natasha and Lila be safe?"

Nica again was quiet as he communicated the question telepathically to the Sanuri. "He says they will be safe and that they wanted to help."

"Of course they did," Calen said. "But why are we just finding out now?"

"The Sanuri says the demon Daegal has many spies watching the castle. He says that soon after the Angels exposed the spies among the soldiers of King Sudfad, Daegal put more in place. The Sanuri says you have to pretend you are still worried about your wives or the demons might learn of the trick. He says be careful of who you tell." Nica paused for a moment then he added, "The Sanuri says the old Court Physician is dead and is no longer a threat."

"Is there some way that we can help?" Gabriel asked.

"Not yet, just be careful who knows the truth."

The Half-Man's fell to the ground and bowed as Miranda and Daniel appeared to the small group.

Daniel spoke to the Half-Man's who reluctantly stood up then got broad smiles on their faces. "I told them that they did more than capture a demon, they stopped a diabolical plot."

"Don't they have some demon in them?" Thaos asked. "Erwat's skin started to smoke when Ratri touched him with a crystal."

"No, they were all covered with small fragments of tar. The tar monsters were exploding as your men destroyed them."

"Is Sampson a demon?" Joshua asked because he knew Duncan could not say the words.

"His transformation is not complete," Miranda explained. "But he has sold his soul to Raum which is now Hecate's benefactor. Raum will complete Sampson's trials." Miranda turned to Duncan. "We know this is breaking your heart but Sampson has been waiting for the army to leave so he can complete his trials by killing his brothers." Duncan's knees weakened as he listened to the Angel's words.

"I have ordered his execution," Duncan said. "But we don't know if it is possible for us to kill him."

"It is complicated," Daniel said. "Sampson is not really a demon so men should be able to kill him but he is being protected by both Hecate and Raum. The items he was sent to steal are needed by the demons for their blood moon ceremonies. The demons believe those holy items will give them more power to open the doors of hell permanently."

After Nica flew off, Gabriel and Raphael destroyed the second demonic alarm while the others went inside of the house, where they found Emeral, Cassandra and Bekka cleaning up blood stains. Maxwell told the women what Nica had said, which made Emeral cry. "Oh I am so thankful," she said as she hugged Maxwell.

"There is something that really bothers me about Nica's messages," Raphael said. "There must be spies inside of the castle for the Sanuri to warn us more than once about being careful who we told the truth."

"Perhaps he is afraid the children will give it away," Bekka said.

"Possibly," Raphael said. "But after you have been working with the Sanuri for a while you learn to read between the lines."

"Raphael is right," Gabriel said as he picked up the pieces of the broken kitchen table. "We need to plan who we will tell."

"Well obviously Sudfad and Renya," Emeral said. "We will just be careful not to say anything in front of their staff or soldiers."

"I feel like we should tell Vitomas and Annabelle," Calen said. "They are close friends with the girls."

"And how about all our wives?" Jared asked.

"First we all agree that none of the children in the castle can know," Emeral said then she looked at Luca and added. "That will be hard on Christopher but you know he can't keep a secret for more than a few minutes."

"I think everyone that you have mentioned is safe to tell," Dagon said. "But they will have to understand that they must keep up the pretense."

"And don't send anyone messages with that information," Edward advised. "There are just too many spies."

"That just seems so strange to me," Raul said. "That demons think they can get more power from holy items. I mean they can't even touch something that is holy can they?"

"And that is why Sampson is not a true demon yet," Daniel said.

"Well what do you want us to do with him?" asked Thaos. "Kill him or can we play some kind of trick on the demons with him?"

"What are you thinking?" Daniel asked.

"I'm not really sure," replied Thaos. "But we all have been worried about the safety of this village after we leave."

"Is there a way we could have him give the demons something that would sabotage the blood moon ceremonies?" Simon asked.

"Or tell us where the victims are?" Raul asked.

Gabriel and the others did not return to the castle until dinner time. Renya had set up a second table in the family dining room for all of the children to eat at and was helping her grandchildren into their seats.

"I'm glad you made it," Renya said and walked into the front foyer as Gabriel and the others entered the castle. "Please be seated; dinner will be served soon.

Gabriel walked up to Renya and acted like he was going to kiss her on the cheek but he whispered into her ear, "We would like a private meeting with you and Sudfad after dinner."

"Of course," Renya said.

"Papa," Cerey yelled and ran down the stairs, jumping into Gabriel's arms.

"I can't get use to her talking," Gabriel said as Hannah was walking down the stairs towards him.

"Did you find out anything?" Hannah asked after she kissed Gabriel.

"We'll tell you later," he said quietly. He now bent down and picked up Nicholas. Gabriel carried both of his children into the dining room.

"Grandpa," Christopher yelled and ran to Maxwell. "I didn't see you before."

"Well, it's about time you two left the bedroom," Annabelle said kiddingly to Archetenus and Delilah as they walked down the stairs smiling and holding hands.

"I can't stop crying, I'm just so happy to have him home," Delilah said.

Sudfad and Vitomas were the last two to enter the dining room and take their seats. "We have much to catch up on," Sudfad said. "I would like to have a meeting after dinner."

"We agree," said Gabriel.

"But for now let's have a toast," Sudfad said and stood up, raising his glass of wine. "To your safe return and the safe return of the rest of our families, friends and armies." After everyone had taken a drink of their wine Sudfad said. "Archetenus, Raul and Simon asked me to offer you a position in our military. They are impressed with your training and leadership skills."

"They said Claudius has already offered you a position as captain in the Military of Lentz but you wanted to talk things over with Delilah first. Vitomas and I just discussed the matter and if you and Delilah want to make your home in Wetpr I will make you the same offer as Claudius."

"Thank you," Archetenus said as he looked at Sudfad then at Vitomas. "Delilah and I were discussing our future this afternoon. She would like a little farm like Jared and Zoya have but I know nothing about farming and would prefer to be a soldier. We have both made good friends here and would like to remain in Wetpr so I will accept the offer. I would be proud to work in your service."

"Good," Sudfad said. "Raul and Simon will train you in our procedures when they return. Tomorrow I will send you to the tailor to get uniforms fitted."

Delilah smiled and kissed Archetenus on the cheek. "Oh, I am so happy," Zoya said. "I didn't want you to move."

"Can't you still get a little farm and be a soldier?" asked Bekka.

"We certainly can," Archetenus said as he looked at Delilah. "But I will hire some men to work on the place."

"And Delilah can stay with us, if you have to leave the area," Jared said. "You should have Alexander help you find a place and get set up. He worked miracles for us."

344

"I would be happy to," Alexander said. "You know there is land for sale on the other side of that creek that borders Jared's property. But there aren't any buildings. You would have to have a house built.

Delilah looked at Archetenus and her eyes were filled with excitement, which warmed his heart. "Let's take a ride out there tomorrow," He said to Alexander then Archetenus looked at Jared. "Want to come along?"

"Hell, I mean yes," Jared caught himself from swearing when he remembered the children in the room. "Bet the girls want to come too."

Sampson awoke and immediately started retching from the poison of the darts. His head was pounding and his stomach felt like it was on fire. As Sampson lay on the ground he was trying to remember what happened to him. He raised his head and tried to look around but the severe dizziness forced him to lay his head back down. Nothing around him looked familiar. Sampson lost consciousness a few minutes later.

"Calen did you want Vitomas and me to prepare you a room by us?" Annabelle asked as they ate dinner.

Calen looked at both women sheepishly, "I very much appreciate everything you both are doing for my family but honestly I don't feel comfortable staying with the two of you while your husbands are gone."

"He's afraid," Luca said and started to laugh.

"He just doesn't want to be stuck with us and eight small children," Annabelle said with a chuckle.

"It shows he is a smart man," Vitomas said with a grin. "Sometimes things get a little crazy and we really don't sleep a lot."

Calen looked embarrassed which amused many at the table. "Why are they asking you to stay with them?" asked Misha.

"They are nursing Lily and wanted to know if I wanted to have a room near her," Calen said. "And really I do appreciate the offer."

"Calen I hope you know you owe those girls a great deal," Emeral said in almost a scolding manner.

"Oh I know," Calen said. Luca and Misha kept staring at Calen and grinning. "I think it's that I remember how jealous I got when Simon and Natasha were working together. I knew I could trust them both but I still got jealous. I just don't want the same thing to happen with Simon and Raul."

"Well, I think it will be good practice for when you have more children," Luca teased.

"Believe me, our husbands know what it is like when we combine both our families," Annabelle said as she too enjoyed Calen looking so uncomfortable. "They would probably give you a medal instead of becoming jealous."

"Why Calen, I think you are shy," Bekka said with a grin which made everyone at the table laugh.

The feast in the Village of Gesmal lasted longer than Angelina, Nikki and Ingr had expected. All three of the women were emotional as they kissed their husbands, family and friends goodbye.

"I really don't want to leave you," Nikki said to Thaos.

"I know Honey but this really is for the best. We will come home as soon as we can," Thaos said and kissed Nikki again.

"I'm sorry, I just can't stop crying," Ingr said and put her arms back around Stephan's neck. "I don't want to leave you here and I don't want to be away from the babies any longer."

"You're doing the right thing," Stephan said as he caressed Ingr's long hair. "You know I am going to miss you but I would rather have you at home."

"I have the gifts for Bella in my bag. Do you want me to wait until you come home to give them to her?"

"No, give them to her when you get home." Stephan picked Ingr up and hugged her tightly.

"Don't wait for me to come home to tell my parents about the baby," Matthew said as he hugged Angelina. "The news will make them very happy. And tell Jacob and Alexas that I love them and miss them." Angelina didn't say anything but looked at Matthew and started crying again.

Immediately after dinner, Gabriel and Raphael met with Sudfad and Renya in Sudfad's study. They told the King and Queen about the demons that had attacked them and the words of the Sanuri. "We haven't even told our wives yet," Raphael said. "Both Gabriel and I feel there was more to the Sanuri's message then Nica said. The fact that he repeated the warning for us to be careful about who we told the truth, made us feel that the Sanuri was trying to warn us there were more spies and possibly close at hand."

"Well, thank The Great Ruler the girls are alright," Renya said with a sigh of relief.

"I think you are right in your assumptions," Sudfad said. "But did he give you any indication who might be spies?"

"No," Gabriel said. "We talked among ourselves before we left the house and thought it would be safe to tell all our wives, Vitomas, Annabelle and Archetenus. But anyone we tell must continue the ruse. We can't trust the children, so we will have to be careful about talking in front of them. But we didn't want to tell anyone until we spoke with you."

"I'm inclined to think we should just bring all of you in here and have one large meeting because there are other things we must discuss also," Sudfad said." Of course it will be a little crowded."

"I'll have the nurses take all of the children," Renya said as she started to stand up.

"Renya I am sure you will have refreshments brought in here but I don't want the staff interrupting us, so have the things brought in right away."

"You don't suspect Marie do you?" Renya asked in astonishment.

"No but honestly the way things are happening I just don't know who we can trust anymore."

"I hate living like this," Annabelle said as she and Vitomas were preparing their children for bed, later that evening.

"You mean staying with me and all of these wild children?" Vitomas joked.

"No," Annabelle said and laughed. "Having to be suspicious of everyone; it's like we are back in Roch's castle."

"How you exaggerate," Vitomas laughed. "But I do know what you mean. It such a relief to hear about..." Vitomas stopped herself from saying Natasha's and Lila's names. "To hear that they are alright."

"Wasn't that funny how embarrassed Calen got tonight," Annabelle said. "I think he is shy to be around us."

"That's why he brought us," Luca said loudly.

Both Annabelle and Vitomas quickly walked into the kitchen and found Calen, Luca and Misha sitting at the table. "How long have you been here?" Annabelle asked and laughed.

"Just a few minutes," Calen said. But before he could finish his sentence, little Sudfad, Samuel, Anthony and Alexander all jumped out of their beds and ran into the kitchen to greet their visitors.

"Well so much for putting them to bed," Vitomas said with a grin. "I swear these boys never want to sleep. It's worse when all four are together."

"That's how we all used to be," Misha said. "Sometimes I wonder why Emeral and Maxwell took us all in."

"Do you want whiskey or wine?" Vitomas asked as Misha, Luca and Calen played with the boys.

"We'll all have whiskey," Luca said. "I would have brought Christopher if I had known your boys were up."

"Calen, your sleepy princess," Annabelle said as she brought Lily from the bedroom and put her into Calen's arms. "She is such a pretty baby."

"They really like to wrestle," Misha said as he played on the floor with the boys.

"Raul and Simon wrestle with the boys a lot, especially before bedtime," Vitomas said. "The boys miss their fathers, so it is nice that you came over."

"I guess we never thought about that," Calen said. "We can certainly come over more and play with them."

"That would be really nice," Vitomas said. "Even though all the children play together during the day, well, it's different when they spend time with their fathers."

"Did I tell you that Lila and I are going to have a baby?" Luca asked proudly.

"No," Annabelle said with a big smile.

"I am happy for you," Vitomas said. "You know I think we will have enough children for Sudfad's school."

"What school?" asked Calen.

"When Petra was kidnapped our family fell apart so Sudfad came up with a wonderful idea to keep us busy. We are building a learning center on the grounds. It will be a school for children of all ages. He even plans to build a university," Vitomas said.

"We all helped with the planning and design," said Annabelle. "And it is being constructed now."

"Why is he building it?" Misha asked. "There are schools in your kingdom."

"So that we can make sure our children are safe. And we are going to have all manner of classes. I'm surprised that Raul and Simon haven't told you because it is for all of our children. And you could help teach classes," Annabelle said with a big smile.

"What would we teach?" Luca scoffed.

"Well, there are going to be classes in military arts and many types of fighting, horse riding and whatever else our husbands want to set up. Vitomas and I are going to work on art classes for the younger children. Marie is going to teach cooking. Alexander is going to teach woodworking and Laurel is going to teach sewing. Of course there will be all the sciences, mathematics and languages like a regular school," Annabelle said.

"Gala is going to teach about herbs and medicines," Vitomas said. "And the Sanuri is going to teach about The Great Ruler."

"Have you told anyone else about this?" Calen said. "I mean from our family?"

"I guess we thought Raul and Simon would tell you," Annabelle said. "I thought you all knew about it."

"I don't think anyone knows," Luca said as he tried to walk to the table with Anthony and little Sudfad hanging from his arms. "But I think it sounds like a great idea."

"Tomorrow at breakfast you should tell everyone," said Calen. "I know they are going to like the idea, who knows you might even get some volunteers for teachers."

"It's going to be a while before your kids are old enough for some of those classes," Misha said. "But we had been talking about setting up classes for the young Ruala warriors who request to be on our team. We have sort of a training program for them but we had talked about doing a great deal more. I think we could combine our resources and have regular classes, you know reading and writing and the such and classes that teach about fighting demons."

"What are you looking for?" Raphael asked as he sat in bed waiting for Vivian.

"You'll find out," she said with a coy smile. "I am so glad you brought my things from home, it was nice to change my clothes."

"I just emptied your drawers and put everything in the bags, I really didn't look at what I packed."

"You did well," Vivian said as she continued to search in the bags. "I should have gone to the house with you, especially after I heard you were attacked."

"You looked pretty exhausted," Raphael said as he watched his wife. "Gael said it would take us a while to heal and you're the one who gave up your life source."

"Honestly I still am really exhausted and I don't feel my old strength but it is just a matter of time. Found it!" Vivian said with a grin and picked up the bag and walked into the next room and closed the door.

"You were awfully quiet tonight, was it because you don't feel well or do you miss your family?" Raphael called through the closed door.

"You are so perceptive," she called back. "I do miss them," before she completed her sentence Vivian opened the door and walked into the bedroom.

"You look beautiful," Raphael said as Vivian walked into the room wearing a light pink silk nightgown. "I like my surprise."

"Oh this isn't the surprise," Vivian said and giggled. Then she sat down on the bed next to Raphael. "I had this made for you before I got taken; it was in my dresser at the house. She opened a small pouch and pulled out a necklace made of braided strands of gold; the chain was thick and masculine. There was a large rough cut emerald wrapped in strands of gold as a pendant. "There's an inscription on the back of the stone," Vivian said as she handed the gift to Raphael.

"Honey it's beautiful," he said as he took the necklace and read *I love you* that was engraved on a small golden plate affixed on the back of the stone. "And it goes with our wedding rings. Thank you," Raphael leaned forward and kissed Vivian.

"I'll put it on you; turn around," she said. "Glad those demons didn't steal anything. When do you think we can go home?"

"We don't want to take any chances with the children," Raphael said. "So I don't have an answer yet."

"There," Vivian said and walked over to the dresser and picked up a small mirror that she brought back to Raphael. "It looks really nice on you."

"Now I wish I had a gift for you," Raphael said as he looked at his image in the mirror.

"Raphael you are always giving me gifts. I told Emeral that I wanted to get you something but I didn't feel right spending the money. She talked me into getting the gift."

"Honey it's our money now, I told you that."

"I know but you saw how I was raised, we didn't have a lot."

"Your parent's home is warm and loving," Raphael said. "And it was always filled with people who love your family. That means more than fancy things."

"What a wonderful idea," Hannah said the next morning at breakfast; as Vitomas and Annabelle talked about Sudfad's learning center. "When will it be completed? I am willing to help in any way." Gabriel smiled as he listened to Hannah's excitement.

"That goes for both of us," Gabriel said. "We could have some of the Patronus teach classes, I am sure some of them would enjoy it."

"I apologize to everyone," Sudfad said. "Not to pass blame but Raul and Simon said they would tell you."

352

"I think with everything going on it slipped our minds and I am very sorry. After breakfast let's all take a ride and you can see what has been completed so far."

"Do you need any help?" asked Maxwell.

"Yes, there is a lot to be done yet," Alexander said.

"So far there are two main buildings for studies," Sudfad explained. "One will be for the children as they grow and the other will be a university. There is a chapel on the campus that is almost completed. There is a riding arena, a large area for outdoor training and a woodworking shop. Many of the rooms are completed but they need to be painted and furnished."

"Is there a library?" asked Raphael.

"We have a large room designated for that but the shelves aren't completed and we don't have the books yet," Renya said.

"I know a lot of the priests at the Cicero outpost are well educated and a little bored, why don't I contact them to help," Raphael said. "And I will purchase the books for your library."

"We will help with that too," Gabriel said. "And anything else you can think of. As Misha told Vitomas and Annabelle last night we have been talking about a training program for our team members. While everyone is trained to battle humans there is much they have to learn about demons. Are any of the areas close enough to completion that we could set up a classroom?"

"The building that is the farthest along is the one for the children," Sudfad said. "But as you can see most of them are too young to attend yet; so today pick out the rooms you want to use and we will get them ready for you."

"King Tobias sends everyone who he has chosen for the Guardians to the Patronus for training," Edward explained. "I can't say enough about that training, it was excellent. Raphael if you set up classes like the ones I attended I think everyone would benefit."

"Well, I will be the first to sign up," Elan said.

"Bekka and I would love to go too," Cassandra said. "And I will help get the classrooms ready."

"Since there is so much enthusiasm about this project I am just going to throw an idea out to Raphael and Gabriel. For centuries all the Patronus have received their educations and training at the monastery in Philiste. If you think it could benefit your organization you could establish a second training center here." "I will accommodate anything you want. I can certainly build housing for your men," Sudfad said.

"That is most generous of you," said Gabriel. "And it is an exciting idea but Raphael and I would need to contact our leaders before we could commit to that."

"Don't misread what Gabriel is saying," Raphael said. "We are sure that our leaders will be very pleased with the idea and your generosity."

"I know what you are saying," Sudfad said. "Just let me know what you need. And did the girls tell you that the Sanuri will be teaching here also?"

"Now I can guarantee our leaders will approve," Raphael said with a laugh.

"Calen has a real gift for drawing building plans," Gabriel said to Sudfad then turned to Calen. "Interested in drawing up plans for housing for our warriors?"

"Sure," Calen said with a proud smile. "Would it be possible for more members of our tribe to attend this school than just the members of our team? I am sure many warriors would want to come."

"I was thinking the same thing," Koby said.

"They are most welcomed," said Sudfad.

"Mother you and Renya are awfully quiet and the smiles on your faces make me think the two of you are up to something," Luca said with a grin.

"We are just happy with what we are hearing," Emeral said teasingly. "Besides what would make you think Renya and I would be up to anything?"

"Are you kidding?" Calen said loudly. "I still have nightmares about the two of you entering those fighting competitions."

"Yes our sons all stood there with their mouths open and watched the two of you," Maxwell said. "Sudfad and I just stood there enjoying the moment."

Chapter XXIV
Worlds Away

"Don't get me wrong," Claudius continued as he led his army eastward towards Nora. "I know the Angels are good for their word but I still feel uneasy about leaving that village. I just feel like the demons have been waiting for us to depart so they can descend on them."

"I think many of us feel the same way," Sorren said. "Honesty I was surprised at how much alike our tribes are; why I felt like I was with family the whole time we were there."

"They are good people," Raul added. "They had so little but they shared everything they had." Stephan and Thaos chuckled at this remark.

"What is that all about boys?" Sorren asked with a grin.

"Thedes do you want to tell them?" Thaos yelled into the air as Lakin was flying directly over the riders carrying Thedes.

"All they did for us," Thedes said loudly. "Especially Joshua and Iris taking us in like they did; and they wouldn't let us give them anything so we left them a surprise."

"We're waiting," Sorren said.

"You know that big crock that Iris always had full of cookies," Thaos said. "Well, we took the cookies out and stuffed if full of money."

"I wish you would have told us," Simon said. "We would have given some."

"Iris and Joshua treated all our wives like they were their daughters. We appreciated that," Stephan said. "And Iris is a darn good cook, she fed us well."

"I wish you would have told me," Matthew said. "I left money in Joshua's pipe tobacco." This comment made many laugh. "I know it sounds crazy but I wish we could just move that entire village to Lentz."

The hot afternoon sun beat down on Sampson causing him to sweat profusely. Flies buzzed around him, unconsciously he slapped at the insects. Sampson's own movements woke him. Sampson looked around groggily then shot up quickly to a sitting position, which caused him to immediately vomit. The poison from the darts made Sampson violently ill. Once he started vomiting he couldn't stop. His muscles were cramping and his head was pounding. Finally exhausted from vomiting he lay back down in the dirt.

"This is kinda fun," Natasha giggled as she sat with Lila and the Sanuri in a small cave. "Although I don't understand at all how it works." The three were staring at a large portal in one of the walls of the cave. The portal allowed them to watch the group of Quatar Demons that had tried to abduct the women.

"Sanuri I don't know how you are doing this," Lila said in awe.

"It's not me, The Lion is doing this. Before he was sending me images that I could see in my mind, but now he is allowing both of you to see the same things."

"It's much easier to know what to say, when we can see what is going on," said Natasha.

"I am so confused by all this," Lila said. "First how can they hear our voices and secondly how can those demons not know we aren't really with them anymore?"

The Sanuri smiled, "I really can't explain how The Lion is perpetuating that illusion. But I will admit I am in awe also."

"They are travelling pretty fast for being so big and clumsy looking," Natasha said as she watched the portal.

"They have nine days before the thirteenth night of the blood moon," the Sanuri explained. "I suspect they are travelling to Nora, but that is only a guess. They have a lot of distance to cover on foot."

357

"Renya, Emeral," Delilah gushed as she ran into the main parlor of the castle. "Archetenus just bought ten acres of land next to Jared and Zoya. I am so excited I can hardly stand it."

"She's been like this for an hour," Archetenus said with a laugh as he entered the room. Jared, Zoya and Alexander walked in with the happy couple.

"I'm happy for you my dear," Renya said. "Talk to Sudfad because we have a large crew of carpenters on staff, I am sure they could build your house."

"Oh Archetenus did you hear that?" Delilah turned quickly and looked at her husband, who smiled with delight at her happiness.

"When you settle down we need to talk about the house," Archetenus said to Delilah. "I was thinking about asking Calen to draw it up."

"Good idea," Jared said. "He needs something to keep his mind on while Natasha is gone. That poor guy just seems lost."

"I agree," Emeral said. "In fact the sooner you can get him working on your plans the better."

"Oh Zoya did you hear that?" Delilah asked exuberantly. "Honey are you feeling alright you look kind of pale?" Jared was holding Zoya's hand and now quickly turned and looked at his wife.

"I'm not feeling well," Zoya mumbled. "I am sure it will pass. Jared what are you doing?" Zoya asked as Jared picked her up and started for the stairs.

"I am putting you to bed and getting Hannah," Jared said. "And don't think about arguing with me."

"I'll get Hannah," Delilah said and ran out of the room.

"Everything seems so quiet now," Iris said to Joshua as they ate a late afternoon meal. "Of course I miss Vivian and Raphael but I miss the others too. I didn't think I would."

"I miss Elan," Adrone said sadly as he played with the food on his plate."

"It was exciting when everyone was here," Paul said. "I miss them too."

Joshua looked at his two youngest sons and smiled. "Doesn't look like you are going to finish your meal but I will let you have dessert anyway. Adrone why don't you grab some cookies." Adrone smiled and jumped up from the table and ran to the kitchen shelf that held the cookie crock.

"There aren't any cookies," Adrone said as he looked inside the crock, his eyes wide with amazement.

"Sure there are," Iris said as she turned in her chair to face Adrone. "Why, I just baked some yesterday."

"No there aren't," Adrone said adamantly. "But you should see what's in here."

Joshua stood up quickly and walked over to Adrone. Joshua did not want to alarm his family but he was fearful of retribution from Sampson and Hecate. A smile of relief crossed his face as he took the crock from his son and walked over to the kitchen table. Joshua spilled the contents of the crock onto the table. A folded piece of paper and three pouches fell out.

"What is that?" asked Paul.

"I don't know, why don't you open them while I read the letter," Joshua said then proceeded to read the letter out loud so all the family could hear. *This is a small token of our thanks to all of you for taking us all in and making us part of your family.*

Stephan, Thaos and Thedes

P.S. We ate your cookies.

"Joshua look," Iris said as Paul and Adrone emptied the pouches of gold coins onto the table. "I've never seen that much money before."

Hecate nervously paced back and forth in her lair. She wasn't sure why but she was overwhelmed with a feeling of doom. Hecate was a powerful and controlling demon; she rarely felt the way she did now and Hecate believed her feelings were a sign of something to come. Suddenly she stopped pacing, "What if Raum is setting us up?" she thought. "Sampson could be walking into a trap." The more Hecate thought about her conversation with Raum the more she became suspicious of his intentions.

Quickly Hecate set up a circle of black candles on the floor of her bedroom. She sprinkled a mixture of dried goap root and the berries of the palun plant on the floor inside the circle made by the lit candles. Hecate opened up a huge wooden chest that sat on the floor near her bed. She took handfuls of precious stones, jewelry and gold coins from the chest and threw them into a large leather pouch. She ran over to the ring of candles and walked into the center. Hecate turned slowly as she mumbled the language of her home world; in less than two minutes she was gone.

"Hannah hurry," Emeral said as she ran down the hallway and met Hannah and Delilah who were walking towards Zoya's chambers.

"Has something happened?" Hannah asked as she quickened her pace.

"She's unconscious now," Emeral said and now the three women ran into Zoya's chambers.

"Hannah she was talking one minute and passed out the next," Jared said nervously. "I don't know what happened."

"I need the men to leave," Hannah said as she was opening her medical bag. "I am going to examine her."

"Do you need any help?" Emeral asked.

"I might if you would like to stay."

Everyone but Emeral left the room; when the door closed Hannah pulled the covers off from Zoya and started to examine her.

"Emeral, Delilah said that Zoya looked pale then said she wasn't feeling well," Hannah said. "Was there anything else that you can think of?" Emeral thought for a moment.

"I did notice that she was sweating but no one else was. You see they all just walked into the parlor from looking at land."

"See if you can find a nightgown and we will change her," Hannah said. "She has been feeling sick a lot because of the baby but that shouldn't cause her to pass out."

"Well, I don't see any wounds," Emeral said as they changed Zoya into a nightgown.

"She's burning up," Hannah said. "Would you get cold water and towels and if you see Jared ask him if Zoya has been eating."

That night as Claudius and the others sat around their campfires, Stephan started to laugh. "I keep thinking about Sampson; I wonder how long it will take him to figure out where he is."

"Does anyone know where the Angels took him?" Matthew asked.

"Not any of us," Thaos said. "Maybe they went back and told the villagers."

"I just keep thinking about what Hecate looked like in hell," Sorren said with a grin. "Can't imagine Sampson saw that before he married her."

"They say love is blind," Stephan said with a grin and everyone laughed.

"Claudius you're so quiet," Lakin said. "What is troubling you?"

"It's going to take us at least two days of hard riding to get to the Patronus headquarters. And that is without any interruptions," Claudius said as he looked into his cup of whiskey. "That doesn't give us much time to find those hostages or to stop the demons."

"I don't know if the Sanuri told you but the Patronus have been looking for those hostages for weeks," Gael said. "And there is a small contingency of Rualas helping them."

"When we get there we will have to find out where they haven't searched," Sorren said. "And get on it right away."

"Hannah you can go back to your quarters," Jared said. "I will come and get you if anything changes."

"Jared I don't want to disturb you but I want to keep putting cold compresses on Zoya," Hannah said. "I am still not sure what is wrong with her."

"You're not disturbing me; I was gonna sleep in the chair next to her bed. I thought you might want to go home with Gabriel and the kids."

"How about if I go home and put the children to bed then return?"

"That's fine too." As Jared talked there was a knock at the door and he got out of his chair to open it.

"How is Zoya?" Renya asked.

"Better talk to Hannah," Jared said solemnly.

Renya, Vitomas and Annabelle walked into the bedroom. "What happened to her?" Annabelle asked.

"At this point I am ruling things out," Hannah said. "She's not losing the baby and I put crystals on her and there are no signs of demons all of which is good. But she has a horrible fever."

"Has she awakened?" Vitomas asked.

"For brief periods," Hannah said. "And every time she knew where she was at; which is also good."

"Do you think she ate something that made her sick?" asked Annabelle.

362

"Jared and Delilah said she has eaten the same food that they have and actually what we all have been eating," Hannah said. "Besides if it was bad food I would expect her to be vomiting. And I haven't found any signs of wounds or bites. I'll admit I am not sure what is wrong with her."

Hecate had not visited her home world in almost two hundred years. She was from a hell dimension in the World of Sidus; which was in the same solar system as the World of Nunc. Both planets were similar in size and inhabitants the main difference being that the demons owned kingdoms above ground in Sidus. That was because they had conquered most of the humans centuries before. The Solar System of Astrum had three suns that formed a triangle; these suns were surrounded by seven planets. Nunc was the third plant from the suns and Sidus the fifth.

Hundreds of years earlier Hecate had followed her lover Orbus to the World of Nunc. A world with so many potential victims ripe for the taking was intoxicating to the demons. Neither demon had planned to stay in the World of Nunc when they first arrived. Hecate was only in Nunc for six months before she left Orbus for a Tafort Demon.

Orbus did not take Hecate's betrayal well and the two waged war against each other for almost three hundred years. Now hundreds of years and many lovers later both Hecate and Orbus had settled their differences and become friends again. Hecate made her home in Nunc while Orbus enjoyed homes in several other worlds.

Renya was sitting up in bed reading when Sudfad entered their chambers. "Why are you so late? Is anything wrong?"

"No," Sudfad said with a smile as he bent down and kissed his wife. "Elan and Cassandra wanted to meet with me. They love the chapel we are building and would like to have their wedding there when it is completed."

"Wonderful," Renya said with delight. "Perhaps that is how we should open the chapel. Does Emeral know yet?"

"They were going to her chambers after they left my study."

"You'll have to have the workmen make that a priority now," Renya said.

"Already planned to talk to them in the morning," Sudfad said sleepily as he crawled under the covers.

Gabriel walked into the dining room of the Royal Family for breakfast; he was carrying Cere and holding Nicholas' hand. "Has Hannah come down yet?" Gabriel asked of anyone in the room as he helped his children onto their chairs.

"I haven't seen her yet this morning," Renya said as she was cuddling Arianna who was crying. Then as an afterthought Renya added, "I haven't seen Jared either."

"You two stay here; I am going to check on Mama," Gabriel said to his children but before he walked to the door he heard Hannah's voice.

"I am right here," Hannah said wearily as she walked into the dining room.

"Hannah have you been up all night?" Laurel asked. "You look exhausted."

"I just can't figure out what is wrong with Zoya," Hannah said then kissed Gabriel and her children. "Poor Jared looks worse than I do. Marie is taking a tray to him."

"Did you consider that this illness might have something to do with Zoya's abilities as a seer?" Raphael asked as he held a chair out for Vivian to sit on.

"I put crystals on her and they didn't turn black," Hannah said and poured herself a large cup of coffee.

"The mind is a powerful thing," Raphael said. "And with Zoya's abilities to see into other worlds she might be on a journey without a demon trying to take control of her."

"How would I determine such a thing?" Hannah asked with interest.

"She has no signs of injury or illness other than a fever and the fact that she is still sleeping. Can a journey like you are suggesting cause these effects?"

"I have read texts about people taking what they called spiritual journeys, where their bodies appeared unconscious but they were very much alive but in another realm," Raphael said. "As for the fever, perhaps that is associated."

"That sounds like what happened to Gabriel when..." Hannah stopped talking and looked at her children. She did not want the children to hear about what happened to Gabriel. "When Ahriman was trying to get him."

"And Simon and Natasha too," Gabriel said.

"Both Simon and Natasha were burning up when we found them," Dagon said. "And they remained unconscious for a long time."

"But they were all fighting demons," Hannah said. "Other than placing the crystals on them I don't know how to look for other things that may not be physical by nature. I wish Lakin was here."

"Perhaps Emeral and I can be of some help," Maxwell offered. "We don't have the training that Lakin or Gael have but we have a little knowledge."

"I would appreciate any help I can get. It makes me feel helpless when I can't figure out how to help my patients."

"Raphael and I can try to help also," Gabriel said. "I don't want to say a lot in front of the children."

Sampson awoke to a light rain hitting him in the face. The act of sitting up caused him to have great pain in his head and eyes. He felt nauseous and dizzy but did not vomit. He sat very still, holding his head until the feelings passed. As Sampson slowly looked around he did not recognize his surroundings. He tried to clear the fog in his head and remember the last thing he did. Sampson knew he had to be some place but he couldn't remember where or why.

The Angels had erased Sampson's last memory of spying on his village and seeing the Half-Mans. They did this to both protect the villagers and Half-Mans and to send Sampson on a new journey. Minutes passed as Sampson tried to recall his memories, suddenly he grabbed the breast pocket of his vest and felt Hecate's note. He pulled it out and unfolded it but the poisons in his system were still affecting his brain. Sampson was having difficulty focusing his eyes, the words on the paper seemed to dance and mock him. He carefully put the paper back into his pocket and stood up.

Sampson's knees were weak and he felt light headed. He stood motionless for several moments to center his balance, then with great difficulty he walked to his horse, that was grazing a few yards away. The poison the Half-Man's used on their darts was lethal at one third of the dose that Sampson was given. Since his body was still in transition he did not respond to the poison as a normal man but he was still experiencing painful and debilitating side effects.

The poison was affecting Sampson's muscular system which made all movement intensely painful and difficult. Sweat was pouring from Sampson's body and he felt like everything was spinning around him. But he made the short walk to his horse and painfully mounted it. Sampson was not familiar with his surroundings he just knew he had to travel north.

Hecate entered a dark and smoky room in the back of the Traxor; a tavern that was frequented by all manner of demons. Traxor was not the type of place one went to for a relaxing drink and entertainment. Traxor drew certain types of clientele; a consortium so to speak of demons and other beings with talents not often advertised. Hecate changed her appearance as soon as she arrived on her home world. She did not want to be recognized until the appropriate time.

Hecate took on the appearance of a Staffer Demon. She now, was almost eight feet tall with a long tail and double sets of antlers. The antlers were heavy and Hecate had to work on balancing herself as she walked.

Now Hecate stood with her back against the wall, searching the dark and dismal room for a specific face.

As the Royal Family and their guests were finishing breakfast, Simon's twin boys jumped out of their chairs and ran up to Misha. Anthony tugged on Misha's warrior robe and asked, "Misha are you coming to play tonight?"

"Yes," Misha said with a grin and Anthony and Alexander ran out of the dining room.

"Luca can we go too?" Christopher asked.

"I was planning on it," Luca said.

"Hannah, Gabriel can Nicholas and Cerey come with us?" Christopher asked.

"I'm not really sure what you are talking about," Hannah said.

"Misha, Luca and Dagon have been helping us out," Annabelle said. "Our boys really miss their fathers and every night when Calen comes over to play with Lily the others come over and wrestle with the boys. It's been wonderful because the boys don't seem so sad anymore."

"Raul and Simon play a lot with the children," Vitomas explained. "And they would wrestle with the boys every night before we put them to bed."

"It helps that they fix us treats every night," Dagon said with a grin.

Gabriel looked at his children, "Nicholas, Cerey do you want to go?" Both children nodded. Gabriel turned back to Vitomas and Annabelle. "Mind if Hannah and I come along?"

Annabelle and Vitomas looked at each other with embarrassment. "Why, we would love it if any of you came over," Annabelle said. "We just didn't think anyone would want to be around us with all these little kids."

"Do you want to go?" Koby asked Bekka, who smiled and nodded. Then Koby looked across the table. "Elan, Cassandra are you going?"

Elan and Cassandra were both smiling brightly when Elan said, "We might be busy."

"Busy," Koby scoffed. "Doing what?"

"We're getting married as soon as the chapel is completed," Elan said with both pride and excitement. "Sudfad thinks it will be three or four weeks yet."

"Do me a favor," Misha said sarcastically. "If we are all in the wedding, don't let Emeral assign the same girls to us."

"Those were lovely girls," Emeral said with a laugh. "You and Dagon never gave them a chance."

"Speaking of girls," Vivian said as she looked at Misha then Dagon. "Half the girls in my village had crushes on you two and you didn't even respond. Is it because my village is so poor?"

Both Dagon and Misha looked shocked at Vivian's statement. "Are you telling the truth?" asked Dagon.

"Yes she is," Cassandra said. "And a couple of those girls were absolutely beautiful. Isn't that right Elan?"

"Yes," Elan said and smiled. "All those girls kept asking us questions about you. Well, more than you two but since you are both single, well you know."

"Vivian, I really don't know what any of you are talking about," Misha said with indignation. "But I think you should know by now that a person's wealth means nothing to us. We may not have noticed your friends but we certainly did not ignore them because they came from poor families. And I am insulted that you would even ask that question."

"I am sorry if I offended either of you," Vivian said. "It's just that is was obvious to so many of us that those girls were trying to get your attention."

"Well, we are sorry if we offended your friends," Misha said angrily. "But Dagon and I were focused on the demons and the mission."

Many of the people at the table had never seen Misha get angry before but it was clear that Vivian's words greatly insulted him. Dagon decided to break the tension at the table. "Vivian, we all loved your tribe and respect them as warriors. If we insulted anyone it was not our intent."

"I didn't mean for my words to come out the way they did," Vivian said apologetically. "And I am sorry. You are both such wonderful men, it would have been nice if you could have, oh I guess I don't even know what I am trying to say."

"Did it ever occur to anyone that Dagon and I might be happy with our lives?" Misha asked. "Just because most of you decided to get married in the last few years doesn't mean that we have to. Don't try to push your lives on us."

"Well to change the subject," Hannah said as she stood up. "I am going to check on Zoya. If anyone wants to come with me that is fine." Hannah started to walk out of the room then turned and walked back to the table.

"All of you are the family that I never had," Hannah said emotionally. "And I think the reason we have all been able to work together and live together is because we accept each other for the people we are. Misha I agree that Vivian could have chosen her words differently but she loves you and wants you to be happy. Now if being single is what makes you happy, well, I believe we all can accept that. I know you are really angry now but know that we all love you and Dagon for the men you are."

Hannah left the dining room and everyone sat in silence for a few moments before Misha got up from his chair and quickly left the room. "Emeral do you mind watching the children?" Gabriel asked. "I am going to check on Hannah."

"Of course," Emeral said.

"Dagon I really am very sorry," Vivian said. "I really didn't mean to sound as awful as I did. What can I do to make up for it?"

"Vivian I know," Dagon said. "I am not mad at you."

"Why did Misha get so mad?" Vivian asked. "I've never seen him like that before."

All the Ruala warriors looked at each other then at Maxwell. "Well I guess I am delegated," Maxwell said. "Misha is a good man; dedicated to his work like the rest of my sons. He guards his heart closely, I think that is because of the life he had before he came to live with us. Vivian, Misha has always been quite taken with you but he would never act on his feelings because he loves and respects both you and Raphael too much. Perhaps he is just a little more sensitive to the things you say."

Vivian's mouth fell open as she listened to Maxwell speak. "I, I had no idea," Vivian stammered. "Now I feel even worse." Then she looked at Raphael. "Did you know?"

Raphael nodded. "I could tell by the way he looks at you."

"Why didn't you say anything?" Vivian asked with surprise.

"Because you two are such good friends, I didn't know if things would change between you if you knew."

"I feel absolutely horrible," Vivian said as tears came to her eyes. "What should I do? Should I go and talk to him?"

"I had the same situation with Hannah," Luca said. "And as reluctant as I was to talk with her about it, once we did, well it was the best thing we ever did. We became closer friends after our talk and didn't feel awkward any more, which is important because we are working on the same team."

"I am not going to tell you what to do," Raphael said. "But since you asked; I think you should talk to him but not now, wait until he calms down."

Hecate spotted the demon she was looking for. He was sitting at a small table near the back of the crowded room. It wasn't until Hecate walked closer to him that she realized he was sitting with two other demons that she did not recognize.

Hecate turned and walked to the bar and ordered a drink. She sipped her glass of whiskey and watched Otterus, the demon she wanted to speak with. Although Hecate had not been on her home planet long she was wise to the behavior of demons and criminals. As she sipped her drink, Hecate noticed several demons that entered the room and stared at Otterus. These demons split up and each approached Otterus' table from a different direction. Otterus appeared drunk and deep in conversation with his companions, which seemed to distract him from his surroundings.

Hecate was not the only one who noticed this group of demons because they all wore the tattoos of the Thesarles on the left sides of their heads. Thesarles were vicious mercenaries usually employed by the Old Ones or other very powerful demons. Their tattoos were simple and distinctive; two large red dots that sat one on top of the other with a dark blue tear drop below both the dots. The red dots represented blood and the tear drop represented pain.

As Hecate watched the scene before her she was trying to decide if she should warn Otterus. She certainly did not need the wrath of another Old One upon her and at the same time she needed to talk to Otterus. Then Hecate realized that if one of the Old Ones had sent Thesarles after Otterus he might not be as useful as she had hoped. As all of these thoughts ran through her mind; Hecate realized she was walking towards Otterus' table. "He must be really drunk," she thought because Otterus was oblivious to the fact that other demons were moving away from his table.

Hecate flirtatiously put her arm around Otterus and kissed him on the cheek. Then she whispered into his ear, "You are in great danger here." Otterus turned and looked into Hecate's eyes and in that instant the two disappeared from the tavern.

Chapter XXV
Loyalties

Gabriel walked up behind Hannah as she stood near Zoya's bed. "Are you alright?" he asked as he put his hands on her shoulders.

"Yes, I just hate to see them fighting," Hannah said then she looked at Jared, who was sitting in a chair next to the bed. "Jared tell Gabriel what you told me."

"Most of the time Zoya is sleeping peacefully," Jared explained wearily. "But, oh I don't know, maybe ten minutes before you came in here she looked like she was dreaming. She started moving then really tossing and turning, she was mumbling but I couldn't hear what she was saying so I moved closer. The only word I could make out was 'Sanuri'.

"Jared we were just talking that Zoya might be on some type of spiritual journey instead of suffering a medical illness," Gabriel said. "I am going to get Raphael and we will see if we can find out what is going on."

"They didn't pull her into hell like they did me?" Jared asked anxiously.

"Hannah has crystals on Zoya always," Gabriel said as he examined the crystals that had been placed on Zoya's chest. "They would be black if something like that happened and as you can see they appear unchanged." Gabriel left the bedroom.

"Jared did you eat breakfast?" asked Hannah.

"I can't."

"Well, you aren't going to do Zoya any good if you get sick too. Did Marie leave you a tray?"

"I told her to take it back."

"I am going to get you a tray and as your physician I am telling you to eat something."

372

Sampson was bent over as he rode his horse. The aching of his head and the dizziness was disorienting him. His muscles were cramping. "What the hell is happening to me?" Sampson thought as he fought to stay on top of his horse. "Hecate," he called out. "Hecate help me."

Hecate could not hear the cries of her husband because she and Otterus were being chased through a time tunnel. Only extremely powerful demons could instantly move through time and space. Otterus could not do this on his own but he understood what was happening when Hecate removed him from the tavern. She had intended to rematerialize in another location but when the Thesarles followed her; Hecate realized she would be safer in the time stream.

Otterus was quickly sobering up as he realized there were four Thesarles chasing them. "Whoever you are, thanks," he said as Hecate pulled him through the maze.

"Why are they after you?" Hecate asked loudly as she surged forward.

"I don't know."

"I find that hard to believe."

"Really I don't know."

"Well, they must have been sent by one of the Old Ones if they have the ability to follow us, hang on." Hecate started to spin, faster and faster until she was affecting the atmosphere around them. Since Otterus was hanging onto Hecate he was in the heart of the cyclone cloud she was creating and could not see what was happening beyond his field of vision.

"What are you doing?" yelled Otterus.

"Watch and see," Hecate said as she suddenly turned towards the Thesarles who were so focused on the chase that they did not immediately realize they were being attacked.

373

The intense velocity of the wind that Hecate created tore the flesh of the Thesarles demons and flung them, wounded and bleeding to other areas of the time field.

"Who are you?" yelled Otterus.

"You will find out soon enough."

Gabriel, Raphael, Emeral and Maxwell were already in Zoya's room by time Hannah returned with a tray of food for Jared. Both of the High Priests were praying over Zoya as Maxwell and Emeral placed more crystals upon her. Jared stood at the foot of the bed watching the process. His sadness was evident upon his face. Hannah set the tray on a table then walked over to the bed; she stood in silence watching the others.

Both Raphael and Gabriel prayed in unison for almost twenty minutes, then Gabriel stopped praying as Raphael continued. Gabriel sat down on the edge of the bed and started to talk to Zoya.

"Zoya if you can hear my voice move a finger on your right hand," Gabriel said softly. Zoya did not initially respond which filled Jared with fear. But after a few moments Zoya tapped the blanket with her right forefinger.

"Zoya when I ask you questions tap your finger once for yes and twice for no, do you understand?" Gabriel asked. Zoya tapped her finger once. "Is it easier for you to tap your finger than to speak to me?" Zoya tapped her finger once. "Zoya are you ill?" Zoya tapped her finger twice. "Zoya are you on some type of journey?" Zoya tapped her finger once. "Zoya do you know where you are," Gabriel asked. Zoya tapped her finger twice. Raphael continued to pray but lowered his voice so Zoya could hear Gabriel.

"Zoya are you alone?" She tapped her finger twice. "Do you know who you are with?" Zoya tapped her finger once then twice.

"What does that mean?" Jared asked fearfully.

Gabriel did not answer Jared's question but continued to speak to Zoya. "Are you with the Sanuri?"

Zoya hesitated then tapped her finger once. "Did something happen to you and the Sanuri is trying to save you?" Gabriel asked. Zoya tapped her finger twice. "Are you somehow working with the Sanuri?" Zoya tapped her finger once. "Can we help you?" Zoya tapped her finger once then twice.

"I think that means she doesn't know," Maxwell said.

"Are you trying to stop the blood moon ceremonies?" Gabriel asked. Zoya tapped her finger once then she started to moan and to move but she did not open her eyes. Suddenly Zoya grabbed both of Gabriel's wrists and with great strength she placed his hands on either side of her head.

Hecate and Otterus materialized in a cave in a remote area of the planet Sidus. Hecate was familiar with the cave because she used to meet Orbus there when they were first lovers. "Now tell me why those mercenaries were after you," she demanded.

"I really don't owe you an explanation," Otterus said indignantly.

"I just saved your life and now they may come after me; so I believe you do owe me an explanation."

"In my line of work I make many enemies," Otterus said as he stared at Hecate. "I really don't know who sent them. But you are right I owe you a debt."

"I came a great distance to find you. Because I want to hire you but if the mark of death is upon you; it may not be worth my trouble."

"I have expensive tastes."

"And I am wealthy."

"Well, it sounds like we have a good start," Otterus said. "But I like to know the names of the demons I do business with."

"Otterus with the wars among the Old Ones, no one can be trusted now and like you I have made many enemies."

"I am prepared to pay you very well but how do I know I can trust you? And how do I know you will live long enough to get me the information I need?"

"I am most loyal to whoever pays me the most."

"I expected nothing less."

"But it is not every day that a demon risks their life to save mine. I may be many things but I pay my debts. Tell me what I can do for you."

Gabriel was surprised at the strength Zoya had. He placed the palms of his hands on either side of her head and instantly heard the Sanuri's voice. "The Sanuri is talking to me," Gabriel said and Raphael stopped praying. Gabriel sat motionless for minutes as he listened to the Sanuri, then he removed his hands from Zoya's head and turned to the others.

"Jared, first of all Zoya is fine so you don't have to worry. She and the Sanuri are connected on a level that I cannot explain. But they are literally searching the world with their minds to find the victims that have been kidnapped to be sacrificed for the blood moon ceremonies."

"Zoya is doing this willingly. Also Natasha and Lila are fine. The Sanuri is projecting the images of the girls to the demons who tried to kidnap them. So the demons believe they have the girls. The Sanuri is hoping those demons will lead them to some of the people who have been kidnapped. The Sanuri believes these victims are being kept in more than one location."

"All three of the girls say they miss us and not to worry," Gabriel continued. "If the ceremonies of the blood moon are allowed to take place, doors to many different hell dimensions will open and this world will be attacked. The Sanuri says the sacrifices are a crucial element of the ceremonies. Once again the Sanuri is concerned about us having spies close at hand. He says we can tell our group, what I am telling you but the information should go no further."

"How can the Sanuri not know who the spies are?" Hannah asked.

376

"I don't know the answer to that dear," Gabriel replied.

"How long is Zoya going to be like this?" asked Jared.

"I don't think they know," Gabriel said then smiled. "But the Sanuri knows that you have been distressed so he is giving you a gift. Zoya is carrying a son and because of the choices you have made the baby will not be touched by the darkness that once owned you." Hannah put her hand on Jared's shoulder as Gabriel spoke.

"A son," Jared repeated in awe.

"There is more," Gabriel said. "But I think we should call a meeting and I can tell everyone. Jared would you mind if we held the meeting here? Since the Sanuri is connected with Zoya, he is aware of what is occurring in this room."

"That is fine, besides I really don't want to leave her," Jared said.

"Let me tidy it up in here a little," Hannah said. "While you get the others. And we will need more chairs."

The money and jewels that Hecate had brought with her to Sidus were not for payment to Otterus; she gave him the riches to bribe others for information. After Otterus inspected the pouch that Hecate gave him, she took his hand and they disappeared from the cave. They did not see any of the Thesarles as they traveled to the World of Nunc.

"Where are we?" Otterus asked as they materialized in a cavern that was filled with chests of gold coins and jewels.

"That is not important," Hecate said. "Look around you, this is your payment. And if you do your job and I find that I can trust you, well, I have other caverns like this."

"I believe you and I are going to have a long and rewarding future together," Otterus said. His heart was racing from the sight of the treasures. "You still have not told me your name; how do I contact you?"

377

Suddenly a small black box appeared in the palm of Hecate's left hand. "This box contains special sheets of paper, write your message and toss the paper into the air, it will come to me," Hecate explained.

"What if there is an emergency? How quickly will you get the notes?"

"As soon as you write it I will have it. You may take some of this treasure now as a sign of good faith, then I will return you to Sidus."

"Raphael; Vivian, Elan and Cassandra are in Salar," Bekka said as she and Koby entered Zoya's bedroom.

"Thank you," Raphael said as he carried a chair into the room.

Renya and Sudfad were the last to enter the bedroom. As soon as the door was shut, Gabriel told the group what the Sanuri had said.

"So Claudius' army is staying in Nora to battle the demons," Vitomas said sadly. "Any idea when our husbands are coming home?"

"I don't have an answer for you," Gabriel said. "But the Sanuri said that Miranda and Daniel healed all the people we saved from Ogg and most of them are fighting with our army."

"Do they need us to return to Nora?" Misha asked.

"It sounds like the Sanuri has concerns for all of us here," Gabriel said. "Once again he instructed us to tell no one of this information. He believes there are spies very close at hand and that if the ceremonies proceed this will be one of the first areas attacked."

"Did he indicate who might be a spy?" asked Sudfad.

"No, he did not."

"So then we should plan to be attacked, in what a week?" Renya asked.

"Sudfad I am going to send the staff out to buy extra food and medical supplies so we have these things on hand."

"I will have the forts prepare for an attack," Sudfad said then he paused as if he was listening to something that no one else could hear. "As soon as I leave here I am going to call to The Lion."

"So in the meantime we should just pretend that Zoya has some type of illness?" Hannah asked.

"Yes," Gabriel replied.

"Did he say when Natasha and Lila are coming home?" Calen asked.

"No just that they were safe and missed all of you."

"Well, I have to admit that I am feeling rather useless," Edward said. "Isn't there something more that we can be doing? I don't like sitting around waiting to be attacked."

"A man after my own heart," Archetenus said.

"I will call a meeting after I speak with The Lion," said Sudfad.

Hecate transported Otterus to the neighboring planet of Plateen, which was the fourth planet from the three suns and orbited between Nunc and Sidus. Otterus had a variety of hiding places on different planets. He feared the Thesarles would still be searching for him on Sidus.

After Hecate left Otterus she transported back to Sidus; only this time she materialized on the southern continent of the planet. Once again Hecate changed her appearance. She took on the image of a Plyos demon that was characterized by having the appearance of a human woman from the waist upwards and the body of a snake from the waist downwards. She had long red hair that spewed wildly around her head. Hecate entered a tavern called Costros and slithered up to the bar. After getting a glass of wine, she moved to one of the empty tables. It did not take her long to find who she was looking for.

The right wall of the tavern opened into a gambling area; at the Ketos table stood Orbus. Hecate and Orbus had an intensely passionate relationship for decades and an equally passionate break up. Now as Hecate looked upon her former lover, passion surged through her being. As Hecate watched Orbus gamble she was deciding if she should approach him. Suddenly Orbus stopped playing and looked at Hecate, as if he had sensed her presence. He smiled and walked over to her table.

"How did you recognize me?" she asked with a big smile.

"I would know you anywhere," Orbus said. "No matter how you change your appearance. We have always had a connection; you know that. Are you waiting for someone?"

"I just found him," Hecate replied with a suggestive gesture. "Have a seat."

"To what do I owe this visit?"

"I was on Sidus doing business and had this overwhelming urge to see you."

"I've heard you've gotten yourself in a little trouble with some of the Old Ones," Orbus said.

"That's why I came here," Hecate was blatantly flirting with Orbus as she spoke. I came here to hire someone and damn if he wasn't being attacked by Thesarles."

"Let me guess," Orbus said as he grinned at Hecate. "You fought the Thesarles and made yourself more enemies."

"You know me so well."

"Some things never change. But I always loved the fight in you." Orbus took a gulp of his drink. "I have also heard you have taken at least a couple of human husbands."

"I turned a powerful priest; he became a demon for me. And he was a powerful demon but the Sanuri imprisoned him in The Abyss. I just recently took another but some humans, who Angels brought into hell, interfered with his trials. So now Sampson exists between two worlds."

380

"Angels brought humans into hell? Surely you jest."

"These aren't normal humans," Hecate said angrily. "They work on behalf of The Great Ruler and are protected by Angels. They willingly came into Baal's domain and fought his demons and mocked him; and those humans live to boast about it. They work closely with the Sanuri and there are two incredibly powerful high priests among them. Ahriman set a trap for them in Taperia. The humans only numbered a few hundred but they fought legions upon legions of demons and not only won the battle but Ahriman was beaten and imprisoned."

"I had heard such stories but I did not believe them."

"Well believe them. I want revenge against the Sanuri and his army of humans and that is why I am in trouble. I have been compcting against Molach and Ipos for thcm. Thcn I wcnt to Baal and he agreed to put Sampson through the trials. When I realized that Baal was going to let that army of humans kill Sampson I pulled Sampson out of Baal's domain so now Baal is angry with me too."

"Do you know who sent the Thesarles that you fought?"

"No."

"You may have pissed off another Old One. You always liked living dangerously." Orbus said as he stared into Hecate's eyes. "So is that why you came to me; you want help?"

"I came here to hire Otterus. After I battled the Thesarles I hid Otterus in that cave that you and I used to meet in. It brought back a lot of good memories; so I thought I would look you up."

"So this is pleasure?" Orbus asked with a grin.

"Yes."

"What would your human husband say?"

"How will he ever find out?"

Orbus laughed loudly. "Tell me what drew you to him?"

"His soul is as dark as a demon's and he is a wonderful lover. He was a Venator."

"What! You turned a priest and a Venator?"

"You know I always liked a challenge," Hecate said with a coy smile. "I have heard stories about you also. Let's just say you haven't been lonely since I left."

Orbus laughed again. "That is true but I will say I haven't taken a human for my woman yet."

"You should someday; I think you will be greatly surprised. Some of the humans I have known are darker than some demons. And they make love in a manner that is very pleasing."

"Perhaps you should teach me," Orbus said with a grin.

"Hecate," Sampson yelled again. The poison was affecting his eyesight. "Hecate why aren't you answering me?" Sampson screamed just before he lost consciousness and fell from his horse.

Vivian found Misha talking with Koby and Bekka in one of the gardens that surrounded the castle. Koby was the first to see Vivian. "Bekka there is something I want to show you," Koby said and took her hand and led her out of the garden. Bekka was about to protest, when she saw Vivian. Misha now saw Vivian also but did not speak.

"What is this?" Misha asked as Vivian handed him a large tin.

"Elan said it was your favorite candy. I got Dagon candy too. I know it's not much of a gift but I really didn't know what to get you." Vivian said. Misha noticed that Vivian was not speaking with her normal confidence but seemed awkward and uncomfortable.

"You didn't have to get me anything?" Misha said as he took the tin.

"Misha I really didn't mean to insult you or to hurt you. As soon as those words came out of my mouth I realized how they sounded. I don't know why I said them and I just wish I could take it all back. You are more than a friend you are family and I don't want to lose you."

Misha stared at Vivian; he suspected that someone told her about his feelings for her. "Does Raphael know you are here?"

"He knows I was planning on talking to you. I haven't seen him since I returned from Salar. Why? Misha why are you looking at me so strangely? Did I say something else wrong?"

"You know don't you?"

"Yes."

"Did they tell you after I left?"

"Yes Misha and apparently I was the only one who didn't know. Misha can I talk honestly to you?"

Misha stiffened up and glared at Vivian but said, "I hope you always talk honestly with me."

"I never wanted to settle down and get married. That day I saw Raphael at that wedding, it was the strangest thing. I don't even know if I can explain it. The moment I saw him I think I fell in love with him but it was more than that; it was like I found what I was looking for only I didn't know I was looking. My feelings for Raphael scared me and we had conflict and I hurt him at times. But once I accepted my feelings, well, I have never been happier."

"First I don't want you to think that I was choosing between all of you and decided on Raphael. It wasn't a competition. But Misha there is something about you that reminds me so much of me. I care about you a great deal and admire you as both a man and a warrior. What I meant to say this morning is that I would like you and Dagon to be as happy as I am."

"But my words came out ugly," Vivian continued. "And I did not mean to insinuate there was anything wrong with you or your life. I hope you can find it possible to forgive me someday."

Misha did not speak but continued to stare at Vivian coldly. Vivian turned around sadly and walked away. "Vivian come back here," Misha said angrily. Vivian walked up to Misha, expecting him to say something but he just glared at her.

"Misha why did you call me back?" Vivian asked after a few moments.

"I'll be honest I don't know what to say to you, but I don't want it to end like this."

"End, what do you mean end? Are you telling me you don't want to be my friend anymore?"

"Honestly I don't know what I am saying."

Suddenly Vivian's demeanor changed; she went from being apologetic to almost angry. "Misha you have every right to be mad at me but you better not be telling me you're going to quit the team or stop being my friend. We are both adults and we have to find a way to work this out. Do you want to fight?"

"What!" Misha said with a grin.

"We can have a match, you can choose the style. Maybe you will feel better if you swing a few punches at me."

Misha started to laugh; he put his arms around Vivian and pulled her close to him. "Your husband is probably going to get jealous but I am giving you a hug." Vivian put her arms around Misha's torso and hugged him back. "I might take you up on that match just for the fun of it," he said.

"You have dedicated your life to The Great Ruler Sudfad, so why is it so difficult for you to call upon His messengers for help?" The Lion asked.

"I just don't feel worthy to be in your presence," Sudfad said meekly. "But I will try to do better."

"You were wise to call upon me at this time. Ask your questions."

384

"The Sanuri left here without telling anyone, then he has Natasha and Lila helping him and now he has some kind of mental link with Zoya. In all my years I have never seen these kind of actions by the Sanuri which makes me believe that the danger he is trying to stop is great indeed. What do you need of me?"

"There is more than what you have said."

"The Sanuri and I have a very close friendship and although he has contacted others he has not communicated with me or Renya since the demon attack. I am afraid for my friend. I fear he is distancing himself from us because he does not plan to survive this thing."

"Over the years the Sanuri and I have had many conversations about his closeness to you and your family. Many times he wanted to distance himself from you, not because of his demise but to protect you. Think of the Sanuri as a candle in a very dark room. Where ever he goes, others notice. His presence in your home has brought the demons to your doorsteps. He is filled with guilt every time there is an attack upon any of your family."

"He has not spoken of these things," Sudfad said.

"I have told him repeatedly that he has become part of your family and the love you share makes all of you stronger. He has lived many lifetimes and some of them have been very lonely for him. He takes great comfort and joy with your family; he should allow himself some happiness."

"So are my fears for his safety unfounded?"

"No."

"Then what can I do to save my friend?"

"You are the most powerful king in Opots. You have great power and wealth and yet you yearn to be on the battlefield with your sons. Your place is to be at the head of your kingdom."

"I understand my responsibilities," Sudfad said almost indignantly.

"But as you have said I have great power and wealth in this world. And in this last year I have been greatly blessed by being in the presence of two Angels; you and Miranda."

"The Great Ruler is sending me His messengers and His help. So in a sense I may very well be the most powerful King in this world; so why am I sitting in the safety of this castle while my family and friends are risking their lives? If this danger of the blood moon is so great, I should be standing against it. I do not mean disrespect but I will ask you again, what do you need of me?"

Chapter XXVI
Conspiracies

Claudius led his army to within five miles of the Patronus headquarters at Nora before they were attacked. The journey from the Village of Gesmal had been quiet and uneventful which filled many with a sense of anxiety. They all felt as if they were being watched; it was just a matter of time before they were attacked. The dread and anxiousness they felt was well warranted as thousands of Hutas appeared out of nowhere and charged them.

When the army left the Village of Gesmal they traveled east, crossing the River Cheban and passing the Tar Pits of Dan. After they crossed the River Nebu, Claudius led his army northward towards the Patronus headquarters. They traveled on the eastern shore of the River Nebu. Fort Nora and the large City of Nora lay on the western side of this river. While there were other routes that Claudius could have taken most of them led through either the Tange Mines or the Nora Mines, both areas that were prime locations for an ambush.

Initially upon crossing the River Nebu they traveled in a heavily forested area and were prepared for attack. A few miles from the headquarters the forest ended. As the army traveled across farm fields, in the open with little concealment; the Hutas appeared.

In the two days that had passed since Sudfad's meeting with The Lion; Sudfad told only Renya what was said. But per The Lion's instructions Sudfad changed the manner and the location of his morning meetings. The meetings were being held in Zoya's room so the Sanuri would be aware of what was being discussed. It had been almost three days and Zoya was still unconscious.

None of Sudfad's military leaders were invited to the meetings, but the entire core group that was now living in the castle was expected to attend. The Lion advised them as did the Sanuri to trust no one else, so the group was cautious about what was being said in front of staff, soldiers and the children.

The core group that now comprised Sudfad's elite army was: Renya, Vitomas, Annabelle, Laurel, Alexander, Edward, Archetenus, Delilah, Jared, Calen, Luca, Misha, Dagon, Koby, Bekka, Elan, Cassandra, Maxwell, Emeral, Gabriel, Hannah, Raphael and Vivian.

"This is the morning of the sixth day before the blood moon ceremonies," Sudfad said at the meeting. "And we have much to prepare. As I told you before The Lion named each of you to be part of this group, which in a way surprised me since I command the most powerful army in Opots. He said each of you possessed talents that would be invaluable in our efforts to stop the demons from destroying this world. While some of those talents are quite obvious to me, I will admit I am lost on others and that could be because I don't know you as well as I should."

"I understand many of you don't know other members in the group so this morning I am changing the meeting. I have made assignments for each of you but first I would like us to talk among ourselves as to the assignments we feel each other should have because I am sure new information will surface in this exchange of ideas. Then we will review the military strategies you have been working on."

"I am going to ask some difficult questions," Sudfad continued. "My intent is not to humiliate anyone but to get the information that we need quickly. Who among you do not feel that you could led men into battle?"

Vitomas, Annabelle, Delilah, Laurel and Alexander quickly raised their hands. But within moments Cassandra and Bekka also raised their hands.

"Bekka," Koby asked in disbelief. "Why are you raising your hand?"

"Actually I think I can speak for all of us who raised our hands. We are all fighters but not military leaders," Bekka said. "Some of you possess a gift for that; I am not one of those people."

"And that is exactly the information I am looking for," Sudfad said. "You all possess gifts; I have to put them into the appropriate jobs."

388

"As of this morning I am replacing many of my military officers with the people in this room for I fear many of them are spies. While all of you are fighters, some of you have the military training to understand that it is not easy to take over the command of troops and have them follow you into battle."

"Sudfad, while I have the training, my strength is in covert operations," Gabriel said. "But of course I will go where ever you need me."

"I have plans for your team," Sudfad responded. "I want you just to focus on that."

Sampson's eyes popped open and he quickly sat up trying to remember where he was. The poison had worked out of his system. For the first time in almost four days, Sampson was thinking clearly. He had no idea how much time had passed, nor did he remember what happened to him. Sampson knew he was starving and that he had to get to the monastery at Rubar.

"Where the hell did they come from?" Sorren yelled as the army realized it was surrounded by thousands of Hutas on horseback. Each leader took command of his troops and waited for Claudius' orders. Over a thousand Ruala warriors flew over the Hutas, shooting them with arrows.

"Archers Release!" Claudius ordered his soldiers and the order was repeated by the various leaders. Claudius hoped to minimize the numbers of Hutas that they would be fighting hand to hand. "Release!" "Release!" "Release!"

The Hutas did not falter as their comrades were being killed by the volleys of arrows descending upon them. They did not fire back at the Rualas but focused on the army before them. Driven by their demon masters, the Hutas lust for blood blinded them to all else. "Release!" "Release!" "Release!" Claudius yelled.

Neputa now led his small army of Shettee warriors, who anxiously awaited their conflict with the Hutas. Revenge filled their beings as they watched their greatest enemy charging towards them. The Hutas had all but annihilated their race.

The Hutas had raped, tortured and murdered in the name of darkness. And now on this sunny morning the Shettee war cries were once again heard.

"Vitomas and I want to work with Gabriel," Annabelle said loudly. "We have lived among the monsters, we understand them and we both have been trained to fight."

Delilah stood up shyly. "I have not been trained to fight but I too have lived among monsters and I know a great deal about the Insidiae if that is of any help to you. I can also care for the wounded."

"Normally I have three commanding generals at each fort," Sudfad said. "In Salar that is Raul, Simon and myself. Edward and Raphael as of this morning you will assume those positions but understand that all of these positions are temporary. Misha, Archetenus, Maxwell and Emeral you are all now majors."

"Sudfad I do not want to be left out," Renya said sharply.

"I believe your talents will be best used working with Gabriel's team," Sudfad said. "For the next hour I want the military leaders I just mentioned and Gabriel to decide where you can best use the other members."

"Sudfad do you want me on a team?" Hannah asked.

"That is up to you, if you think you can handle both assignments you would be a great asset to Gabriel's team." Sudfad turned to Jared. "Jared you are valuable to me in either the army or Gabriel's team but I will not force you to leave Zoya's side."

"I will work with Gabriel," Jared said. "It might do me some good to focus on something else, since the Sanuri said she is alright."

The roar and stink of battle filled the air as the Hutas had now descended upon Claudius' army. While many battled on horseback; many warriors fought on the ground.

Now that the armies were intertwined the Rualas discontinued their aerial attack and landed to fight beside their comrades. No one stood on the sidelines, all of the leaders fought with their men.

Matthew and Sorren fought back to back as they both had been pulled from their horses. "I was wondering if these were demons at first," Sorren yelled. "But they're dying like men." Sorren lunged forward with his sword and opened a Huta's stomach; as Matthew grabbed at a battleaxe that was coming towards his head. Matthew gripped the forearm of the Huta and pulled him off his horse. As soon as the Huta hit the ground, Matthew ran his sword through the Huta's heart.

Both Stephan and Thaos fought on the ground near Claudius. The three worked as a team, Thaos and Stephan pulled Hutas from their horses and Claudius thrust his sword into the attackers. Thedes fought with his kind. The Shettees had never fought so savagely as years of pent up hatred surged through them.

Simon quickly rode up behind Raul and sliced the head off a Huta who was about to plunge his knife into Raul's back. Raul was pulling a Huta off from one of their soldiers. Raul broke the Huta's neck and cast him aside. As Raul looked down at the blood covered soldier lying on his back, Raul's heart sank for the soldier was a mere boy. Raul quickly looked around him for any other attackers and not seeing any immediate threats he knelt down next to the young private. Raul picked up the boy's head and cradled it in his arm.

"What is your name?" asked Raul.

"Lionel My Lord," as the soldier spoke he was choking on his own blood.

"Lionel you fought well," Raul said as he watched the pools of blood forming around the boy's body.

"My Lord I am going to die," Lionel said as he grasped Raul's hand. "I'm afraid; tell me it will be alright."

Raul could see the light fading from Lionel's eyes. "It will be alright," Raul whispered.

Lionel started to make gurgling sounds then went limp in Raul's arm. Raul stared at the lifeless boy for a moment then with his right hand, he closed both of Lionel's eyes. Raul kissed Lionel on the forehead and gently laid the boy's head down.

Raul stood up and looked around for more adversaries, within seconds a Huta rode up to him. From a standing position Raul jumped up and pulled the Huta off his horse. Raul grasped the Huta's right wrist with great force, preventing the Huta from using the knife that was in his right hand. Raul grabbed one of his own knives and plunged it into the Huta, over and over again. "This is for Lionel," Raul said through clenched teeth.

While the designated leaders determined staffing, Renya, Vitomas, Annabelle and Delilah left the room and returned twenty minutes later each carrying a large tray of either food, dishes or coffee. Koby and Dagon both jumped up and quickly cleared some tables. As the women were setting the trays down, Raphael stood up and addressed Sudfad. "We have made our decisions."

"That was fast," Sudfad said.

"First as soon as this meeting is over I will be contacting the Patronus at the Cicero headquarters. We want to disguise them as Wetprian soldiers and have them infiltrate the ranks. We agree it would be better if we could transport uniforms to them so they will not be recognized, would that be possible?"

"Yes," Sudfad said. "And I very much like that idea."

"Secondly," Raphael continued. "We want to keep Gabriel's team intact. They work exceptionally well together and we think it would be a disservice to pull any of them out to be in the military. The rest of us are willing to carry extra loads if necessary." Sudfad smiled with approval.

Gabriel now stood up, "In addition to my regular team, Renya, Vitomas, Annabelle, Jared, Vivian, Delilah, Laurel and Alexander will work with us. Hannah will divide her duties between medical care and the team. We have been talking and feel we need to draw out some of these spies, we are trying to figure out the best way to do it."

392

"We can help with that." Everyone in the room spun around when they heard Natasha's voice. Calen and Luca ran up to their wives, who were standing in the doorway of the bedroom, and embraced them. The others smiled as they watched the two young couples hugging and kissing each other.

"Honey are you alright?" Luca asked. "I was so worried about you."

"Luca we had so much fun, I am sorry to worry you so," Lila said.

"Fun!" Luca said in disbelief.

Natasha stopped kissing Calen and laughed. "Yes Luca your wife is part of the team now. Really we were safe the entire time but we have so much to tell you. And the Sanuri sent us back with a message." Calen kissed Natasha again. "Calen we have to tell you, it's important."

"Jared, Zoya will be coming back soon," Lila said. "She and the Sanuri were following up on some information they just learned."

Others in the room walked up to Natasha and Lila to hug them. "Really," Natasha said. "We don't want to be rude but the Sanuri gave us information to tell you right away. But we are glad to see everyone."

"Let the girls talk," Sudfad said.

"We have so much to tell you but first the message," Natasha said. "The Sanuri has been listening to your meetings through his connection with Zoya. He is very pleased with the plans you all just made, which by the way Lila and I didn't hear." Natasha realized they had left the bedroom door open. "Lila shut the door."

"There's no one in the hallway," Lila said after she closed the door.

"Philip your Court Physician is dead. He worked for a demon named Daegal. Apparently this demon hires out and works for several masters but they don't realize that," Natasha explained.

"After Philip died, Daegal went all out trying to seduce people who already had access to your castle. Lila stand by the door and make sure no one is listening," Natasha said then waited for Lila to check the hallway again.

"Marie and her sisters are above reproach, although demons have tried to corrupt them, but none of the women realized what was happening. But all six of Marie's cooks are spies but they don't realize they all are. Daegal makes each of them believe they are his only spy. Renya that younger dressmaker of yours, Rose is a spy as are two of your stable hands Jess and Tony."

"Daegal had a bunch of your soldiers abducted and killed and demons are now wearing their bodies. But we don't know the names of these soldiers. I don't think any of them are officers but the general that replaced Raul and Simon is at a crossroads and the Sanuri said he will make the wrong choices so you should replace him."

"Are you talking about Hoff?" asked Sudfad.

"Yes, that is the name," Lila said. "The Sanuri said this blood moon ceremony is really bad. The Old Ones are going to try to open all the hell dimensions and take over this world. The Insidiae have found out what the demons are planning and they are joining the demons. The demons know all of us work for The Great Ruler so they are planning on attacking this castle as soon as the doors to hell start opening."

"And they know about Claudius' army," Natasha said. "Apparently the Angels allowed that army to go into one of the hell dimensions and mock an Old One. So the demons are after them also."

"The Sanuri wants you to make it very public that Lila and I have returned. He wants Renya to throw one of her great parties for us because it will be easier to bring the spies to us then us trying to figure out who they all are. You see, the Sanuri and The Lion are playing this great trick on those demons who tried to take us. Those demons think they still have us, so Daegal is going to send others to find out what is going on."

"The Sanuri doesn't want you to arrest the spies that we told you about," Lila said.

394

"He wants you to use them to draw out the others."

"How will we recognize the spies and demons at Renya's party?" Gabriel asked.

"I can help with that," Zoya said as she sat up in bed. Jared grabbed her and hugged her tightly. "Ask the Angels and they will have the Mark of Satan appear on the foreheads of the spies. But the Sanuri says to use the people you trust because they possess great knowledge and can recognize many of the spies. Sudfad in your prison you have a man named Timothy, he is the son of Fahron of Lentz."

"Yes, he tried to rape Annabelle," Sudfad said with disgust.

"He has sold his soul to a demon in exchange for the demon helping him to escape so he can return to Lentz and kill his family and the families of Claudius and Mathas," Zoya continued. "Timothy spends a lot of time watching his guards and the keys they use. The demons who are impersonating your soldiers will soon be filling up your dungeons with others who work for the demons. The demon will set Timothy free and he will unleash the others, so your men will be attacked from inside of the fort." Zoya now got out of bed and walked towards the others.

"Delilah do you remember the manner in which the Insidiae sent their messages to each other?" Zoya asked. "Apparently they used a special seal that only the Insidiae can recognize."

"Yes, I know what you are talking about," Delilah replied.

"The Sanuri wants you and Annabelle to draw this seal. He says you should work on it right away. Then Sudfad, he wants this seal recreated so you can use it against the Insidiae."

Both Lakin and Gael stopped fighting the Hutas so they could care for the wounded on the battlefield. Each Prince was surrounded by three Ruala warriors who protected the healers from attack. A soldier saw what Lakin was doing and picked up his wounded comrade and tried to run to the healer but the blood running into this soldier's eyes momentarily blinded him and he tripped over a body and fell, landing on top of his wounded friend.

Adrenalin surged through him and the soldier got to his feet and picked up his friend and ran to the three Rualas who guarded Lakin. The soldier stood in front of the Rualas and stared for just a moment, then he handed the limp dead body of his friend to one of the Rualas and fell dead at the warrior's feet.

"Have you ever seen such a thing?" One of the Rualas asked. "That man carried his friend to us," the Ruala stopped talking because he was choked up.

"What are you saying?" Lakin asked. Lakin was trying to stop the bleeding of a soldier on the ground and had his back to the soldier who had approached them.

"Lakin the man had the top of his head cut off."

After Natasha, Lila and Zoya delivered the Sanuri's initial message they told the others about all that had happened since the demon attack on Salar. "Well we guessed it pretty close," Luca said as he held Lila's hand. "We tried to figure out what happened to you from the clues we found."

"The only thing we didn't guess," Gabriel said was the Sanuri showing up and taking you from the demons.

"I wanted to come back for you girls," Emeral said. "But the Sanuri kept saying you would be safe. He must have known all of this was going to happen."

"After this meeting," Renya said. "I am going to; wait; did the Sanuri say when we should have this party?"

"The night before the blood moon," Zoya replied.

"I am going to announce to the kitchen staff that we are hosting a huge celebration in five days," Renya said. "Then ladies, every one of you come into Salar with me. I will have ball gowns made for all of you and we will talk up a storm in front of everyone we meet. Then we will go to the Scribe's to have the banners and invitations made. Those of you who are newly promoted will need to have uniforms made for you. I will give you the name of the tailor and please talk freely in front of him."

Gabriel laughed, "Renya you are a natural at this."

"Gentlemen," Sudfad said. "If any of you need the proper attire for the ball, just go to the tailor's and put it on my account. I am sure you didn't all pack for such an event."

"Thank you," Dagon said.

"After this meeting, I will take you to the supply area were we keep the uniforms and gear for the soldiers. Take everything you will need for the Patronus," Sudfad said.

"We should remove these things without others seeing," Raphael said. "Having the King with us will draw suspicion." Sudfad was quiet for a moment.

"I have an idea," Sudfad said. "Immediately after this meeting I will call Hoff to my office and relieve him of his duties. Raphael and Edward I will want you to be present and to escort him off the premises and to his quarters at the fort. He is to pack his things and leave. While you are doing that, I will go to the fort and ready the men for an inspection from their new acting commanding generals. And I will introduce the majors at that time and announce the companies you will be responsible for. That will be a diversion for Gabriel's team to get the uniforms."

"I know the building," Annabelle said. "I can drive a large covered boca into the fort without being questioned. The others can ride in the back of the boca."

"Excellent!" Sudfad said.

"We'll bring Annabelle back here," Gabriel said. "And I can take the uniforms to the headquarters."

"I don't want you going alone," said Sudfad.

"I'll go with him," Luca said.

"I would think it better that you and Calen spend a little while with your wives," Sudfad replied with a smile.

"Bekka and I will go," Koby volunteered.

"I can go with Gabriel also," Alexander said.

"I'll start working on lists of what we are going to need for the party," Laurel said.

"Before I do anything I have to see Lily," said Natasha.

The Horn of Asher could be heard through the din of battle, announcing the arrival of the Patronus Priests from the Nora headquarters. The Patronus were arriving from the north. Simultaneously General Colter was leading troops from Fort Nora which was to the west of the battlefield. When Colter heard the Horn of Asher he instructed one of his men to blow the Horn of Cass. The sounds of reinforcements did not deter the fighting between the Hutas and the army that Claudius led; if anything it made the Hutas more anxious to fulfill their orders.

The Angels did not want Sampson to suspect he was involved in a plot to undermine the Old Ones; so they moved his body and his horse to an area not far from Hecate's lair. When Sampson awoke that morning he was unaware of his surroundings; but as he rode north towards Rubar he realized where he was.

Sampson tried to recall what had happened to him. He remembered leaving Hecate's lair and he remembered waking up a few times, in great pain. Sampson remembered the sickness the poison induced in him and now he suddenly remembered his unanswered cries to Hecate.

As soon as General Hoff entered Sudfad's study he knew something was wrong. In the room stood Raphael, Edward, Maxwell, Emeral, Archetenus and Misha. Hoff felt they were all looking at him with suspicion.

"General Hoff, you are being relieved of your duties," Sudfad said. "Please hand me your ceremonial sword."

"What! My sword!"

"This is not an honorable release," Sudfad said. "I have been unhappy with your attitude and performance for some time."

"Now it has come to my attention that you have been consorting with demons." Hoff's face turned white and he stood speechless in front of the King.

"Do you deny this allegation?" Sudfad asked.

Hoff remained quiet for several moments. "It is true that demons have approached me but I have not agreed to work with them."

"And I assume you didn't tell me because you haven't yet made up your mind to take up their offer," Sudfad said. "Here is six months' pay," Sudfad added as he handed a pouch of gold coins to Hoff. General Edward and General Raphael will escort you to your quarters, then out of the fort."

"I protest," Hoff yelled.

"You do realize I could have you put to death," Sudfad said. "I would suggest you take the money and run. And while you are running leave Wetpr and never return."

Hecate's own screams of ecstasy drowned out Sampson's screams of pain as she spent days with her former lover Orbus.

"Are you sorry that you left me?" Orbus asked suggestively as they made love.

"You are making me have regrets," Hecate cooed, then giggled.

"Hecate stay with me," Orbus said seriously.

Chapter XXVII
A Lion Roars

The Hutas were defeated but no one felt victorious as they carried the bodies of their comrades off that battlefield that day. Numbed to the horror around them, men and women searched through the bloody and maimed bodies to find their dead. Thousands of people walked that battlefield yet silence reigned; broken only by the painful cries and whimpering of the wounded.

"We will not bury our dead in one mass grave!" Sorren yelled at the remark of a weary soldier. "They will be buried with honor if I have to dig every grave myself."

"Sorren, he didn't mean anything by it," Stephan said as he grasped the shoulder of his friend. "We will dig the graves."

The Patronus priests blessed and prayed over the dead and wounded. Graves were dug. The living took the weapons of the dead to fashion markers for the graves.

Ex-general Hoff did not want Raphael and Edward to escort him back to his quarters. While Edward and Raphael had expected Hoff to be difficult they were not prepared for what they found. The general's quarters were actually a beautiful house built within the walls of Fort Salar. The house was surrounded by gardens and well-trimmed trees.

"I am not a child," Hoff yelled as he stood at the front door of his home.

"I don't think you really want to make a scene," Raphael said quietly. "Please let's just get this over with." Hoff did not move so Edward; reached around him and turned the door knob, the door was locked.

"Give us the key," said Raphael.

Hoff stared at both men defiantly for several moments before he reached inside his pants pocket and produced a key. Hoff turned and unlocked the door but did not walk inside. "You're not staying out here," Edward said.

Hoff led the two men inside of his house and all three stopped at the entrance to the parlor. Empty whiskey bottles and glasses were strewn everywhere. Furniture was knocked over and pictures had been knocked off the walls and lay broken on the floor. "Was there a fight in here?" Edward asked.

"No," Hoff replied gruffly.

"And you wonder why King Sudfad relieved you of your duties," Edward said with disgust. "Pack your things." Hoff did not move. "Don't tell me the rest of the house is worse than this," Edward said. Without speaking Hoff marched up the stairs to his bedroom.

"I have seen this before," Raphael said as they stared at the bloody writings on the walls of Hoff's bedroom. "Hoff you will not be leaving." Raphael turned to Edward. "Go downstairs and get a detail of men to take Hoff to the dungeons."

Before Edward could move, Hoff grabbed a dagger from his belt and quickly turned; welding the blade at Raphael who blocked the attack. Edward grabbed Hoff's right arm in an attempt to disarm him but Hoff pushed Edward aside and lunged at Raphael again. Now Raphael had his sword drawn and he thrust it into Hoff's chest. Hoff stood staring blankly at Raphael then collapsed onto the floor. A wind now filled the room blowing back the hair and clothing of the men.

"Demon be gone," Raphael yelled. "You have no power here. I invoke the Holy Spirit of The Great Ruler to cleanse this place which we claim in the name of The Great Ruler." The wind grew stronger, breaking the windows of the bedroom. Raphael and Edward were having difficulty standing against the evil force. "Great Ruler bring your Spirit in," Raphael yelled. A lion roared; a roar that thundered through the fort and was heard at the castle. A roar that sent the demon back to hell.

Annabelle and Alexander were driving a large covered boca through the gates of Fort Salar when they heard the roar of The Lion. Gabriel, Bekka and Koby were all riding in the back. "Stop!" Gabriel yelled. "A regular lion's roar is not that powerful, that's the Angel. Do you see anything?"

Gabriel peeked his head out of the boca and looked at the surroundings; hundreds of soldiers had stopped in their tracts and were looking around. "Do you know where Raphael and Edward were going?" Gabriel asked.

"I do," Alexander replied and turned the team of horses towards the house that Hoff lived in.

"Hurry," Gabriel said. "The Lion roars when he is protecting men from great danger."

In less than five minutes, Alexander stopped the boca in front of the house, which now looked like it had been attacked. All the windows in the house were broken. The trees and gardens that surrounded the house were dead and void of leaves and flowers. Shutters were falling from windows. "Stay here," Gabriel said as he jumped out of the boca.

"You're not going in there alone," Koby said as he and Bekka also jumped out of the boca.

"Annabelle where are you going?" Alexander yelled to his daughter.

"I want to see what my husband fights against," Annabelle said with determination. Gabriel stopped and looked at her. "Gabriel don't try to stop me. Hannah and Vitomas have fought demons. I am not going to run away."

"Very well but do what I say," Gabriel said as he hurried into the house.

"We're upstairs," Raphael called out when he heard others enter the house.

Gabriel was in the lead, taking the steps two at a time. "The demon is gone," Raphael said as the others walked into Hoff's bedroom. "But look at these walls; doesn't it remind you of Roch's hotel room before he completed his transformation into a demon?"

"Yes but the words are different," Gabriel said as he walked along the wall.

"I am writing them down," Raphael said. "So I can research them. Can you translate any of the words?"

"No," Gabriel said as he looked around the room.

"I want to know where he got the blood," Annabelle said. "Do you think it was from the soldiers that the demons killed?"

"If Hoff was transforming into a demon, then the Sanuri was wrong in what he told us," Edward said as he searched through Hoff's dresser drawers.

"I can't believe the Sanuri would be wrong," Gabriel said. "Was anyone else living here?"

"Bekka and I will start searching the house," Koby said.

"I will help you," said Annabelle.

After the three left the room, Gabriel turned to Raphael and told him what the outside of the house now looked like. "Edward," Raphael said. "I think you just met one of the Old Ones; I just don't know which one we were dealing with."

"Am I the only one here who didn't really understand the significance of the lion's roar?" asked Edward.

"You already know that when Angels come into this world they often take on a form that, well, that we are familiar with," Raphael explained. "As mere men we do not have the power to defeat a demon as powerful as one of the Old Ones without help from the heavens. I called to The Great Ruler and the roar of that lion was the heavens telling me that The Great Ruler was answering my prayer and also telling the demons that you and I were not in this battle alone."

"So that lion is The Lion that I have heard you speak of?" Edward asked. "I know you said a powerful Angel took that form, I don't know why I was surprised to hear a lion's roar. Do you know why he takes the form of a lion?"

"Not exactly," Gabriel said. "We have been told that the Angel that takes that form is the most powerful warrior Angel in the heavens."

"Perhaps he takes it because the lion represents power and strength in this world."

"Edward as you continue to work with us; that is on behalf of The Great Ruler, you will realize there are no simple answers to anything. Our minds are so limited by the forms we are in that honestly there is so much that we are unaware of or just don't understand. I am willing to bet that the fact that Angel takes the form of a lion has many symbolic meanings that we don't yet realize," Raphael explained.

"Have you both met him?" asked Edward.

"Yes," Gabriel said. "And it is an experience that is difficult to explain. We have also met the Angels Miranda and Daniel. All three of these beings speak to us in a language that we can understand. They are not condescending or boastful like the demons. There is a calmness about them. They are so powerful that they don't have to prove it to anyone and their souls are not sullied by egos. The demons are loud, threatening and self-absorbed. But, I don't know how to explain it. It's like the Angels come in on a whisper and in that quietness you are overwhelmed with awe."

After the bodies were buried and the wounded cared for, Raul and Simon introduced General Colter and General Orlan. Raul now reassigned Orlan and the ten thousand troops he led from Claudius' army to Fort Nora, which would be their permanent duty station. Raul, Simon, Colter and Orlan worked out the responsibilities and assignments of the two generals before Colter and Orlan led their men to the fort. Afterwards Claudius' army and the Patronus priests returned to the Patronus headquarters.

The short journey to the headquarters was quiet; there were no sightings of enemies and the troops were exhausted. High Priest Rueben, who was in charge of the Nora Headquarters was well prepared for their guests. Rueben had hired many of the local townspeople to build additional barracks on the site which included a large kitchen and an eating area. Rueben hired staff to cook and to help take care of the wounded. The citizens of Nora were grateful to have the Patronus near their city because the Patronus provided one more level of security for the city.

When Rueben initially sent priests into Nora to announce that the Patronus wanted to hire people, the response was overwhelming. Many people came out and volunteered their services.

"This has really changed even since the last time we were here," Simon said as they rode up to the headquarters. "This looks like a fort now."

"It will be a fort when I am done," Rueben said as he greeted Claudius' army. "I am waiting to see how much land we use for the buildings before I have a wall built around the complex. The wounded can all be taken to that large building on the right," Rueben pointed out. "Straight back are the stables and the pastures. That white building in the center is a kitchen for the troops, food is already prepared and the leaders among you will sleep and eat in the headquarters. I will show you to your rooms. Get some rest, we won't have a meeting until after dinner."

"Don't touch that," Koby yelled as he saw Annabelle about to touch a drawing on the wall of the kitchen. "Sometimes these demon things are alive or have spells on them."

"I forgot," Annabelle said gratefully. "But Koby look at this, I think this picture is hiding something." Koby walked next to Annabelle and looked at a large mural painted on the wall. "First this is a strange place for a mural and the drawing is too big for this space of wall. But look closely. The mural is done in almost a childish scrawl but underneath it is something that is drawn in fine black ink and it appears orderly and detailed."

"You're right," Koby said as he stared at the wall. "Good thing you are an artist because I would never have noticed that." Koby walked to the kitchen door that led into the hallway and yelled for Raphael and Gabriel.

"Did you find something?" Bekka asked as she walked into the kitchen.

"Annabelle did but I don't want her to touch it until Gabriel and Raphael examine it," said Koby.

Edward and the two high priests heard what Koby was saying as they entered the kitchen. Annabelle told them of her observations and pointed out the fine lines of the drawing underneath the mural. "I think I can get this paint off, so we can see what is underneath," Annabelle said. Alexander walked into the house. "Where have you been Father?" Annabelle asked.

"I filled the boca up with uniforms and the rest that the Patronus will need," Alexander said. "What have you got here?"

"We have got bloody writings on the walls of his bedroom," Raphael explained. "We saw similar writings when Roch was transforming into a demon. Hoff attacked us and we killed him, then a powerful demon entered the house but The Lion scared it off. Now Annabelle discovered a drawing under this painting."

"So Hoff was transforming into a demon?" asked Alexander.

"We don't know," Gabriel replied. "We are wondering if someone was staying with him."

"If so, that person may return," Edward said.

Gabriel prayed silently then placed his hand near the mural. "I don't feel an evil presence. I don't believe a spell has been placed upon it." Gabriel now touched the painted mural. "It seems alright."

Annabelle now examined the paint closely. "I believe I can remove this paint but it will take me a while."

"We're not leaving Annabelle here to work on this," Koby said.

"Of course not," Gabriel said as he examined the wall. "Alexander you are the carpenter, what do you make of this?"

"This isn't painted on the original wall," Alexander said as he carefully felt around the painting. "Looks like Hoff hung a plank of wood up here and painted it the same color as the wall then drew on it. I think I can take it down without damaging it, but I will need some tools."

"Tell me what you need," Bekka said." And I will go to your work shop."

"It might be easier for you just to take me there," Alexander said.

"While you are at the castle, tell Sudfad about all this," Gabriel said. "He was planning on having an introductory ceremony with the troops this afternoon."

"They're coming, they're coming," Margarit screamed excitedly as she ran through the front door of the castle of King Mathas. "Mama, Papa come quickly."

Since Claudius' army left Lentz to rescue Angelina and Vivian, the Kingdom of Lentz had been under attack by the Valdees. During this time Mathas had ordered the families of Claudius and Fahron to move into his castle for protection. After the defeat of the Valdees, Mathas received word of the demon attack on Salar and demanded that Claudius' and Fahron's families remain at his castle. Shara, the wife of Sorren and mother of Angelina also stayed at the castle to help take care of her grandchildren.

"They're early," Bella said as she joined others on the front lawn of the castle. King Mathas, Queen Rosa, Bella, Shara, her young sons Nathanial and Peter stood on the lawn watching a small contingency of Ruala warriors flying towards them. Fahron his wife Isadore and their children Chaez and Tabeth soon joined them.

"We were wrapping gifts and didn't hear Margarit," Isadore said. "It's a good thing Fahron heard her."

Bella, Shara and Rosa were all crying by time the Rualas landed. Angelina, Ingr and Nikki ran to their friends and families, hugging and kissing them all.

"We have so much to tell you," Angelina sobbed. "But first," Angelina turned to the Rualas and motioned for them to come forward.

"This is Aegon, Kelr, Ardin, Faber, Jabin, Eran, Kya and Moti. They protected us and brought us home," Angelina said. "This is King Mathas, Queen Rosa, General Fahron and his wife Isadore."

"This is Bella wife of Claudius, Shara wife of Sorren, Princess Margarit, my brothers Nathanial and Peter and Chaez and Tabeth, the son and daughter of Fahron and Isadore." Angelina turned to Mathas. "We have traveled with little rest or food, I told the Rualas they should stay with us for a couple of days."

"Of course," Mathas said happily. "The Enrops told us you were coming, so we prepared a feast. Please everyone come inside."

"We didn't want to leave our husbands but we missed the babies so," Ingr said as she put her arm around Bella.

"They have grown so much," Bella said as she cried tears of joy at having the women home.

"We have letters for all of you in our bags," said Nikki. "I feel like we have been gone forever."

Alexander and Edward cut the mural from the wall, as the others continued searching the house. "I am surprised we haven't found an altar," Gabriel said.

"I can't put my finger on it," Raphael said thoughtfully. "But something isn't right here. We haven't found any books or objects for dark magics. I'm almost wondering if someone wanted us to think Hoff was turning into a demon."

"You mean for a distraction?" Gabriel asked.

"Yes, let's find Sudfad he should be at the fort by now," Raphael said with concern for the King's safety.

Both men walked quickly down the steps. "Koby," Gabriel said. "We're starting to think this might be a distraction, so we are going to find Sudfad. Will you be alright here?"

"Of course," said Koby.

"Do you know what to do if that demon returns?"

"I do," Natasha said with a grin as she walked out of the parlor. "Bekka and Alexander told us what happened so some of us came over."

"Who is here with you?" Gabriel asked as he hugged his sister.

"Calen, Luca, Dagon, Lila, Elan and Cassandra," Natasha replied. "Raphael you and Edward need to leave soon for the ceremony."

"Calen and Luca why don't you stay here with your wives and everyone else come with us," Gabriel said. "We haven't found an altar or any books or anything other than the writing on the wall and the mural. Raphael thinks someone wanted us to think Hoff was turning into a demon."

"We'll keep looking," Luca said. "With this house in the middle of the fort, I am sure he would have to hide an altar."

Angelina, Nikki and Ingr were shocked when they entered the dining room of the castle and found it filled with people, who clapped and yelled when they saw the women. Many of the guests were members of the Nordes Tribe.

"Are those your babies?" Kya asked as Ryan walked through the crowd holding both of Ingr's twins. Ingr started to cry and kissed her babies over and over. Then to Ryan's surprise, Ingr kissed him too.

Nikki's mother walked into the dining room holding Titus and both women hugged each other and the baby.

"Rosa where are my babies?" Angelina asked as she looked around the crowded room.

"Shara is getting them," Rosa said as she put her arm around Angelina. "We put them down for naps so they would be awake for you." Within moments Shara walked into the room carrying baby Alexas and holding Jacob's hand as he walked beside her. Angelina ran to her mother and hugged her children.

"I am sorry I am so emotional mother," Angelina said as the tears ran down her face. "I haven't told the others yet but I am pregnant again and the Sanuri said it's a boy."

"What!" Shara said excitedly.

Shara kissed Angelina on the forehead then addressed the room full of people with an uncharacteristically loud voice. "Attention, I need everyone's attention," Shara shouted. "Angelina has an announcement to make." The room became quiet.

"Oh I must look a sight," Angelina said as she held Alexas. "I am sorry I can't stop crying. Mathas, Rosa you are going to be grandparents again. The Sanuri said I am carrying a future king. Matthew and I have already picked the name. He will be called Mathas Sorren. Both Mathas and Rosa were beaming when they walked up to Angelina and hugged her again. "But Nikki has news too," Angelina said loudly.

The guests quieted down and Nikki told them of Miranda's prophesy for her unborn baby and the name that she and Thaos had picked out for their son. Bella started to cry again and walked up to Nikki and her mother Gladys and hugged both women. "I will be so glad when everyone is home," Bella said.

It didn't take long for Gabriel and the others to find the King. As soon as they walked out of Hoff's house they saw companies of soldiers being marched to the ceremonial grounds. Gabriel and Raphael knew that if the King was not in the fort he soon would be. Gabriel told the Rualas to take to the air and search for terrorists while he, Raphael and Edward walked through the crowd.

"Orbus, really I don't want to keep arguing with you," Hecate said with frustration. "Can't we just go back to making love?" Orbus didn't speak but Hecate saw something in his face that concerned her. "I have known you too long," she said. "There is more than you are telling me. Orbus what is it?"

"Hecate I have heard rumors; I don't know if there is any truth to them. But I can keep you safe, your human husband can't."

"Tell me of these rumors," Hecate said as every muscle in her body stiffened.

"You continuously defy the Old Ones, which sets a bad example," Orbus said. "I have heard several very different rumors, which is why I don't know if they are true."

"Some of the Old Ones want to make an example of you; there is a bounty on your head."

"And the other rumor?" Hecate asked.

"The blood moon ceremonies are close at hand for the World of Nunc. Some of the Old Ones fear you will interfere with their plans to kill the Sanuri and others. I haven't heard any details but they want you out of the picture for a while."

Hecate stared at Orbus as rage surged through her, then she suddenly smiled. "You would risk your life to protect me; perhaps I should give your offer more consideration." Hecate leaned forward and kissed Orbus. "Have you heard how they plan to kill the Sanuri?"

"Only that they have set many traps" Orbus said. "I have not been to Nunc in a very long time, so all I know is what I hear in the taverns."

Hecate reached up and put her hands on either side of Orbus' head. "I am going to put the location of my lair into your head," she said. "Share this information with no one. I am also putting an essence stream into your head so you can contact me immediately from anywhere." Hecate closed her eyes and transferred the information telepathically to Orbus. When she had finished she kissed him, a long passionate kiss. "Now my love I must go," Hecate said. "I have business on Nunc."

Elan and Cassandra saw the King leading a company of soldiers to the fort. Both Rualas quickly landed on the roadway to block Sudfad's passage. Emeral, Maxwell and Misha were flying over Sudfad and his troops and Archetenus and Jared were riding behind the King.

"King Sudfad," Elan said as the King stopped the convoy. "Gabriel and Raphael believe this thing with Hoff might have been a distraction and that you are riding into a trap."

Sudfad stared at Elan for a moment, "I will not back down from demons," Sudfad said.

"But you don't know which of your men you can trust," Elan reminded the King.

Sudfad knew that Elan spoke the truth; the very soldiers he was leading could be demons. "Sudfad closed his eyes for just a moment and whispered, "Lion, I might need some help down here." Then Sudfad looked at Elan and Cassandra. "We will proceed as planned," Sudfad said. "And may The Great Ruler be with us."

"Why are there so many citizens inside of the fort?" Raphael asked Gabriel as they walked through the crowd.

"I was thinking the same thing," Edward said. "Certainly Sudfad has not made an announcement to the city about this ceremony."

Gabriel walked up to a young woman who was getting onto a boca. "Excuse me; do you know why there are so many citizens inside of the fort today?"

"I come here every day because I sell vegetables and eggs to the cooks. There are a number of people who do business with the soldiers every day." Then the woman looked around the complex. "You know there are a lot more people here than usual. If something is going on, I don't know about it."

"Thank you," Gabriel said then silently called to the Enrops. He returned to Edward and Raphael and told them what the woman said. Raphael saw Koby flying overhead and motioned for him to come down.

"We haven't seen anything strange yet," Koby said as he landed next to the three men.

"We think it's the citizens," Gabriel said. "There is no reason for so many of them to be here. I just called to the Enrops to help us." Trumpets sounded to announce the arrival of the King.

"The Enrops are coming," Edward said as he watched a flock flying towards them.

412

"Koby meet them and have them watch for demons and terrorists," Gabriel said. "Edward and Raphael you need to meet Sudfad, I'll watch the crowd." Before Raphael and Edward could leave, Calen, Natasha, Luca and Lila ran up to them.

"There wasn't anything in the house," Calen said. "So we came out to help. Annabelle and Alexander are still in the house working on the mural."

"Why are there so many people here?" asked Natasha.

"We think they may be terrorists," Gabriel said. "Calen watch over Sudfad, if there is an attack pick him up and fly him out of here. Luca you can best serve by flying overhead. The girls can stay with me."

"We have weapons," Natasha told her brother. "Lila knows how to use hers and I am wearing my jacket," Natasha said with a grin. She was referring to her jacket which was lined with sheaths of throwing knives.

"I don't have a good feeling about this," Gabriel said as they watched Sudfad approaching the platform of the ceremonial grounds. Raphael and Edward pushed their way through the crowd to join Sudfad. Gabriel, Natasha and Lila walked closer to the platform. Ruala warriors and Enrops flew overhead. There were less than twenty-five Ruala warriors, not enough to stop a major threat against the King.

Sudfad and the others dismounted. Jared stood close to Sudfad on his right side; while Archetenus took a position on Sudfad's left. Misha, Emeral and Maxwell stood behind Sudfad, because everyone understood that the King was a possible target. "I don't need a protection detail," Sudfad said to his friends.

"We disagree," Maxwell said. "We will come forward as you introduce us."

As Archetenus looked at the thousands of soldiers and citizens standing around them, he whispered, "Miranda we might need some help."

Within an instant Miranda's voice spoke softly inside of Archetenus' ear, "That you do. We are here."

413

"The road you just rode on is now blocked to prevent Sudfad from returning to his castle."

"Can the Rualas take him?"

"A better question would be; what is blocking the road?"

Archetenus smiled, "Ok what is blocking the road?"

"Amulth demons, like the ones that attacked Jared's home," Miranda said. "They are sent courtesy of the Insidiae. But there are more players here than the Insidiae. Tell the others what I have said and that we are here. This is The Lion's mission but he is allowing Daniel and me to help."

Archetenus immediately told the others on the platform what Miranda said. Calen landed so he could hear what Archetenus was saying. Calen flew to Gabriel and told him the Angel's words.

While Sudfad felt relief that the Angels were watching over them he was infuriated that the demons and Insidiae would come into his kingdom and threaten all. In that instant Sudfad decided to change his speech. He turned to his friends, "Do not stand close to me, I don't want the demons to think they are intimidating me. Sudfad took four steps forward and held up his hands until the crowd became silent.

"General Hoff has been relieved of his duties for consorting with demons, as my men took him home, he attacked them and was killed in the fight. The inside of Hoff's quarters are covered with demonic messages. Effective immediately High Priest Raphael and Edward are acting commanding generals of Fort Salar." Raphael and Edward stepped forward. The crowd was silent.

"It has come to my attention that at least two hundred of my loyal soldiers have been murdered and imposters are taking their places. Also effective immediately there are four new majors at this fort, Maxwell, Emeral, Misha and Archetenus. These changes have been made to protect the citizens of this kingdom from the darkness that beats at our door. Failure to follow the orders of Raphael, Edward or the new majors will result in death; for only the imposters would make such opposition."

414

Sudfad took several more steps towards the crowd. "Now for those of you who are not loyal subjects of Wetpr, those of you who are not free men and women because you have sold your souls to darkness. I am aware that the fort is surrounded with demons and that demons are wearing the uniforms of some of my men. You may rule by fear and intimidation in your worlds but you will not rule in my kingdom. Wetpr and my family honor only The Great Ruler. The demons have no power here and they never will."

As Sudfad spoke both soldiers and citizens looked around the crowd nervously. Natasha was watching a man who seemed very confident to her; she motioned to Gabriel that she was going towards the man. When Natasha realized the man was mumbling a spell she pulled a knife out of her jacket and yelled, "Demon," the man turned and her knife entered his throat. Although the body of the man fell to the ground with blood gushing from it, Natasha could see the cloud of the demon leaving it. "Demon be gone, you have no power here," Natasha repeated as she walked towards the dark cloud.

The cloud started to take form and Lila ran to Natasha's side. Both women repeated the phrase, "Demon be gone, you have no power here." As Natasha focused on the demon in front of her she did not realize that her initial scream caused panic among the crowd as innocent citizens ran to escape the fort.

"You cannot leave," Sudfad yelled. The fort is surrounded by demons, stay calm we will destroy them. Edward have the gates closed."

Cassandra shot an arrow into a man who lunged towards Sudfad. A soldier heard the private standing to his right mumbling an incantation and ran his sword through the imposter.

Gabriel tackled a man wearing a hood. When Gabriel pulled the hood off the man's head he was staring into the eyes of hell. "Good to see you priest," the monster said with a laugh.

Daniel's voice whispered into Gabriel's ear, 'Your knife." Gabriel pulled his knife from the sheath on his belt and realize it was glowing from holiness. The monster looked terrified when he saw the blade, which Gabriel thrust into the demon's chest.

"What is going on?" Renya asked as she and Laurel entered the parlor where all the women and children in the house were gathered. "Vivian why are you dressed like that?"

"This is the uniform of a Venator," Vivian replied about her short leather dress. "It is much easier to fight in. An Enrop just brought me a message from Raphael. A trap was set for Sudfad at the fort. There are demons on the road and demons inside of the fort. The Angels have been called. I am to protect you since we don't know which of your soldiers are terrorists. It would be easier for me if you are all gathered in one area."

"My dear," Renya said. "I have been a warrior since before you were born; I will not sit back and let someone else protect this family."

"I will fight too," said Vitomas.

"Laurel take the girls and children upstairs," Renya said. "Vitomas we need weapons." Renya and Vitomas ran down the hallway to Sudfad's study because there was a weapon's room near his desk. Barely had they entered the room before they heard a woman scream.

The scene inside of the fort became chaotic as people's fears overtook them. The gates to the fort were locked to prevent demons from entering and people from leaving. Raphael and Edward were thrown into their new roles. They ordered soldiers to the guard stations on top of the walls surrounding the fort. Soldiers were stationed at the gates prepared for attack. Soldiers and citizens were fighting with each other and the newly promoted majors were fighting with people trying to get near Sudfad.

Sudfad saw the panic and fear and called out to the heavens, "Lion show us the faces of our enemies that we may stop them." With that simple prayer the human masks dissolved exposing the faces of the demons. The humans who were working for demons lost their human appearances and took on the faces of hell. Soldiers and citizens alike momentarily stopped in their tracts as they watched in horror as the demons were unmasked.

"The Great Ruler has revealed our enemies to us," Sudfad yelled. Then he found himself saying, "Those who do not serve darkness, your weapons will destroy the demons before you." Soldiers and citizens realized the blades of their knives and swords were glowing but they did not understand the significance.

"Majors, leave me and take control of your troops," Sudfad yelled.

"I'm staying with you," Jared yelled as he and Sudfad stood back to back on the platform and looked at the multitude of demons charging at them.

"What are you doing? What is that you are putting in the gravy?" Marie demanded as she saw two of her cooks suspiciously pouring the contents of a vial into a large kettle of gravy. Marie commanded a staff of six female cooks, all of whom were in the kitchen. When Marie challenged the two, a third woman wielding a large kitchen knife ran towards Marie, who screamed for help.

Vivian pulled her sword from its sheath as she ran towards the kitchen door which she found locked. Vivian backed up and ran towards the door which she broke with a powerful flying kick. Vivian landed on the floor of the kitchen and instantly went into a forward roll, then to a standing position. The six female spies where not warriors and were initially shocked to see Vivian flying through the door. "Marie they are spies for demons, run from here," Vivian said as she readied her sword.

"What!" Marie yelled angrily. "They are in my kitchen and they work for demons." Instead of running out of the kitchen, Marie ran to a table and grabbed a large frying pan. The woman with the knife once again lunged towards Marie. Vivian thrust her sword through the woman's back. Another woman ran for the back door but Vitomas ran after her and grabbed the woman's hair, using it to pull the woman back into the kitchen.

Renya threw a knife into the chest of a woman who ran towards her with a knife as Vivian cut another woman's head off with one slice of her sword.

Another spy ran towards Renya and Marie hit the woman on the head with her skillet, the woman collapsed onto the floor. Two spies remained, Vitomas had one by the hair while the other held a knife but looked fearfully at Vivian and Renya who were walking towards her.

"You would spy on our family and sell us out to demons," Renya said angrily. "Tell me what are our lives worth?" Renya held her sword to the woman's throat and demanded again. "What are our lives worth!"

"A bag of gold," the woman stuttered.

"You would kill my grandbabies for a bag of gold," Renya yelled and ran her sword through the woman's neck.

"Should I kill this one?" Vitomas asked.

"No," Renya said. "Tie her up and that one that is unconscious; we will give them the truth potion."

Calen, Luca, Dagon, Elan, Bekka, Cassandra and Koby now concentrated on the horde of demons that were charging towards Sudfad and Jared. "Sudfad I will get you out of here," Calen yelled.

"The hell you will," Sudfad yelled back. "This is my fight."

Natasha kept Lila with her as they ran through the crowd stabbing demons. Both women grabbed swords from dead soldier impersonators. As soon as Lila and Natasha grabbed the swords the blades began to glow.

"Gabriel," Lila yelled and grabbed Natasha's sleeve. Natasha turned and saw her brother surrounded by demons. Both women ran to Gabriel. As Natasha ran she pulled a knife out of her jacket. Natasha threw the knife hitting a demon in the throat, then she ran her sword through the back of another demon. Lila didn't hesitate she stabbed a demon in the back, pulled her sword free then swung and cut the demon's head off.

The arrival of the women momentarily distracted the demon directly in front of Gabriel allowing Gabriel to run his sword through the demon's chest. As Gabriel pulled his sword out of the demon he hit another demon hard with his elbow, breaking the demon's nose. Gabriel swung around and thrust his sword through this demon. Natasha and Lila kept stabbing demons until they were close to Gabriel, then the three humans formed a triangle with their backs to each other and fought.

"Stop!" Renya yelled as Petra and Kyra ran into the bloody kitchen. Both children stopped immediately and stared at the scene before them.

"My Lady I caught them putting something in the food," Marie said. "I will have to throw everything out. The meal will be late with just me cooking."

"We'll help you," Petra said then he turned to Renya. "Mama did you kill them?"

"We all fought them," Renya said. "Now you should leave here."

Kyra marched up to Renya. "My Lady, Petra and I have worked very hard. We can fight with swords and staffs let us help."

"They are good," Vitomas commented as she was tying one of the women to a kitchen chair. Vivian was holding the woman still.

"Renya I wasn't much older than them when I started hunting alone," Vivian said.

"I know you practice well," Renya said. "But it is very different to actually use your weapon to kill. Do you think you can do that?"

Petra walked up and put his arm around Kyra. "To protect our families, Kyra and I can do it."

"Very well," Renya said. "Tell your tutor that studies are done for today. Get your weapons and return to the kitchen. You can protect Marie and watch the back door while you help her cook." Petra and Kyra ran out of the kitchen.

"I'll bet those two get married some day," Vitomas said and laughed.

"I know," Renya grinned then she turned to Vivian. "Bring Gala to the castle, she will be safer here and have her bring some truth potions. I will have the soldiers clean up this mess."

"Put me down!" Annabelle screamed as the power of Molach threw her against the kitchen wall of Hoff's home.

"You have an insolent mouth," the mighty demon yelled. "No one talks to me like that."

"And you are nothing but a bunch of hot air that is too scared to fight like a man," Annabelle yelled. The demon dropped Annabelle to the floor then picked her up and slammed her against the wall again. "You are nothing but a pitiful coward," Annabelle yelled contemptuously.

"Annabelle shut up," Alexander yelled to his daughter. Then he turned to the dark cloud in the kitchen. "If you want to hurt someone, hurt me."

"Oh I plan to hurt a lot of people before this day is over and when the Sanuri seeks revenge I will kill him too."

"You can't hurt the Sanuri," Annabelle yelled. "He is too powerful and too smart to fall for your traps."

"Annabelle stop antagonizing the monster," Alexander said as he was afraid the demon would kill his daughter.

"You should teach your daughter to be more respectful of her superiors," Molach yelled.

"Superiors, you're just a scummy demon; you're the lowest form of life," Annabelle yelled. "Father," Annabelle screamed as Molach picked Alexander up and slammed him against the wall. "Are you alright?" Alexander was momentarily dazed. "Miranda, Miranda," Annabelle yelled. "We need help."

Molach released his hold on Annabelle and Alexander and they fell onto the floor as Miranda and Daniel materialized in the kitchen. "And what do we have here?" the demon asked tauntingly.

Annabelle ran to her father and helped him to stand up, then she ran to the Angels, who ignored Molach's remark. Annabelle stared at the Angels excitedly, then she curtsied and stood back up. "Both of you are as beautiful as everyone says. Thank you for coming. This damn demon is trying to trick the Sanuri. I won't let him."

Both Daniel and Miranda smiled. "We know he is setting traps," Daniel said. "Why don't you take your father out of here?"

Annabelle didn't move but stared at both of the Angels in disbelief. "I don't mean to be disrespectful," Annabelle said boldly. "But I will not."

"Why?" Miranda asked with a grin.

"Because almost everyone in my family has fought at your side; I haven't been able to because I am always pregnant. But I am not now and I won't let this windbag hurt the Sanuri. I too made a covenant with The Great Ruler."

Both Angels smiled. "Do you know how to fight?" Daniel asked although he already knew the answer to his question.

"Yes, my husband taught me and he is a very good teacher."

"Do you have a sword?" asked Daniel.

"Not here but at home; shall I go get it?"

"I will loan you mine," Daniel said and a glowing sword appeared in his hands. As Daniel handed the sword to Annabelle, Miranda addressed the demon.

"Molach are you brave enough to fight this child?"

Chapter XXVIII
Brave Hearts

With the faces of the demons exposed, Raphael and Edward were free to organize the soldiers to protect the fort from the army of Amulth that was descending upon them. Earlier that morning Sudfad had given his new officers the information about the companies they now supervised and their new responsibilities. Raphael and Edward assigned Maxwell and Emeral to the battle within the walls of the fort, while Misha and Archetenus were assigned to the impending battle with the Amulth.

Contrary to Gabriel's supposition, most of the civilians in the fort were not demons and while some chose to hide others joined in the battle against the monsters. Flocks of Enrops swarmed the fort and attacked the demons fighting inside of the walls. Emeral cut the head off from a demon that was running towards Sudfad then took to the air so she could look down upon the battlefield and determine where best to deploy her troops.

Emeral's eyes widened when she saw the huge group of demons surrounding Gabriel, Natasha and Lila. Emeral swooped down, without landing and ordered one of her companies to follow her. Although the men were embroiled in battle they followed their new leader. Emeral already had an arrow in her bow before she reached her friends. Her speed and agility had tempered little with age as Emeral showered arrow after arrow into the gang of demons before her soldiers reached them.

Calen and Luca were unaware of the danger their wives were in as they battled the horde of demons that were trying to kill Sudfad and Jared. The King repeatedly refused the Ruala requests to remove him from battle.

Sudfad had chosen wisely in determining his new contingent of officers. Not only were they all leaders with battle experience but battle was second nature to them all. The new generals and majors understood their enemies and had strong strategizing abilities; it did not take them long to form a strong team.

Raphael, Edward, Misha and Archetenus positioned their archers along the walkways at the top of the wall that surrounded the fort. The men heard the rumbling of the earth before they saw the army of Amulth demons that proceeded to surround the fort. Although Raphael and Archetenus were on opposite ends of the fort, they both called out simultaneously to the heavens.

"May The Great Ruler be with us," Misha said in a whisper when he laid eyes upon the sea of demons marching towards them. Misha screamed the Ruala war cry; the battle began.

"You are not afraid little girl?" Molach asked tauntingly as Annabelle reached for Daniel's sword.

"I was raised among demons," Annabelle said as she grasped the sword and felt its light weight. "And all those demons are dead because the Angels watch over us. I have just one question for you," Annabelle said as she firmly grasped her sword. "Are you the demon that has been trying to kill my husband?" Up to this point Annabelle had been deliberately antagonizing the demon because she understood that fear would give him more power. But as Annabelle asked her one question, her demeanor changed; for she planned to fight to save her family.

Hannah had been upstairs with her children and now ran down to the kitchen just as Petra and Kyra were leaving. "What happened here? Are any of you hurt?" Hannah asked as she walked around the bodies.

"Marie caught the spies putting something in our food," Vivian said. "They attacked her when she tried to stop them."

"You can help us with this one," Vitomas said as she and Vivian tried to carry the unconscious woman to a chair.

"Marie hit her pretty hard," Vivian said with a grin. "Not sure if she will wake up."

"What did you hit her with?" Hannah asked as she examined the woman's bloody head.

"My frying pan," Marie said. "She was going after the Queen."

"We are going to give them truth potion," Renya said as she checked the bodies to make sure they were all dead. Renya stood up and drew her sword when a young sergeant ran into the kitchen. He stopped when he saw the bloody bodies.

"My Lady are you alright?"

"Yes, they were spies for demons," Renya replied. "Why did you come?"

"Well, it's kind of hard to explain," the young man said. "But you know how we were all wondering if there were demon spies among us?" He did not wait for Renya to reply. "Minutes ago, all the demons showed us their faces. They seemed as surprised as us; it was like their masks fell off. The soldiers have killed all that we found, but we want you to be warned."

"Thank you," Renya said. "When the men are done fighting have some come in here and dispose of these bodies."

"Yes, My Lady," the sergeant said and bowed then turned and left the kitchen.

"Annabelle," Alexander gasped as he watched his daughter transform. Without telling her, Daniel had blessed Annabelle with holiness as he handed her his sword.

"Apparently Molach isn't brave enough to fight you," Miranda said sarcastically to Annabelle. "Because the great demon is sending his minions." The house shook violently from Molach's anger and dark clouds started to take shape in the kitchen.

"Annabelle always remember that courage and faith can topple the walls of hell," Daniel said as a sword appeared in his hands.

"Please can you get my father out of here?" Annabelle asked. In that instant Alexander appeared in the parlor of Sudfad's castle.

"Archers aim for the ones with the ladders," Raphael yelled as he watched groups of Amulth demons running toward different areas of the walls with wooden ladders.

424

Raphael, Edward, Archetenus and Misha were all standing on the platforms at the top of the wall that surrounded Fort Salar. Each one of the men was in charge of a different quadrant of the wall.

Raphael was at the front of the fort. He had a platoon of men on the ground below him, fortifying the front gates. Archetenus was at the rear of the fort, where there were also gates into the post. Misha commanded the eastern wall while Edward supervised the western wall. The Amulth demons had completely surrounded the large fort. The demonic army was so vast that it covered the land to the horizon.

"Miranda, that help would be appreciated any time," Archetenus said with a grin as he looked over the army below him. Suddenly he realized a demon's head was showing over the top of the wall. Archetenus ran and kicked the demon in the head with such force that it knocked the demon off the ladder. When the demon fell he knocked the next two demons on the ladder to the ground. Archetenus was a giant of a man but it took all his strength to push over that ladder and the multitude of demons on it.

By the time the Amulth demons were climbing the walls of the fort, the battle inside of the walls had ended except for the battle being waged inside of Hoff's house. Emeral and Maxwell reassigned their companies to the walls of the fort. Every civilian who could fight was on the ground, near the gates. Sudfad and Jared quickly ran to the platform on the front wall. Sudfad's eyes widened when he saw the ocean of demons surrounding the fort. "Lion," Sudfad said out loud. "Please help us and protect our families at the castle."

Calen and Luca were horrified when they found their wives and Gabriel for they all had wounds and were covered with blood. "None of them are life threatening," Natasha said as she was tying a piece of her underskirt around Lila's arm which had been cut.

"What is that?" Lila yelled and pointed to Hoff's house which was now crumbling. Bolts of lightning appeared to be coming out of the windows and smoke was coming from the roof.

"Annabelle," Gabriel yelled and ran towards the house with the others behind him.

"It smells like demons," Calen said as they ran inside.

The Angels and Annabelle were still inside of the kitchen fighting, but demons filled the house and attacked Gabriel and the others as soon as they entered. "Annabelle, Annabelle are you alright?" Gabriel screamed as he ran his sword through a demon that had just materialized before him.

"Yes," Annabelle yelled. "The Angels are protecting me."

Luca was the first to fight his way into the kitchen, he had Lila by the hand and they both stopped at the scene before them. Annabelle, Miranda and Daniel were fighting an army of demons. All three were glowing as were their swords. Calen was hanging onto Natasha's hand as he pushed his way into the kitchen while Gabriel was still fighting in the hallway.

"Molach is here," Miranda said. "But we are defeating him. Your help is needed at the walls." Gabriel and the others ran out of the house and to the walls of the fort.

"Miranda are you going to lock Molach in The Abyss?" Annabelle asked as she blocked a sword strike by a demon.

"You know about The Abyss?" asked Miranda.

"Yes, the Sanuri taught us."

"Why would you want him in The Abyss?" Miranda asked.

"Because he wouldn't be able to hurt anyone anymore."

"You would not ask us to kill him?" Daniel asked.

"Well I guess that would be up to you," Annabelle said as she lunged at a demon.

"Annabelle," Daniel said. "It is time for you to return to your father." As soon as Daniel completed his sentence Annabelle materialized in the parlor of her castle.

Sudfad and Raphael suddenly realized that Miranda was standing with them.

426

"We have both called to The Lion but he has not come," Raphael said.

"Have faith," Miranda said. "Daniel is imprisoning Molach as we speak. That information is going through the hell dimensions like a lightning bolt. Soon other Old Ones will be here; that is what The Lion is waiting for." Miranda watched the soldiers fighting with the demons and the thousands of demons that were trying to scale the walls of the fort. "Order your archers to shoot another volley," Miranda said. Both Sudfad and Raphael yelled the command which was then yelled around the wall until all had heard it.

"Release!" Sudfad yelled and thousands of arrows where shot into the air, where they multiplied again and again until their numbers reached hundreds of thousands. The arrows started to flame as they shot downwards towards their targets. Suddenly every ladder propped against the walls of the fort burst into flames. Demons screamed as they jumped from the burning ladders; many demons themselves caught fire.

"Have your archers continue to fire upon them," Miranda said and she turned and started to walk along the platform at the top of the wall. While most soldiers did not speak to her; Miranda's presence brought them comfort and strengthened their courage.

When Annabelle found herself in the parlor she quickly ran to find Renya and Vitomas. She found them in the kitchen with Gala, Vivian, Hannah, Marie, Alexander, Petra and Kyra. The group was standing around two women who were tied to chairs and the floor was covered in blood.

"You're back," Alexander said with relief and grabbed his daughter and hugged her.

"I fought with the Angels," Annabelle said excitedly. Then in the same breath she asked. "What happened here?"

"The spies were putting something in the food," Renya explained. "Marie caught them and they attacked her. Alexander was just telling us about the battle at the fort. It sounds bad."

"Yes, just before the Angels sent me home, Gabriel and some of the others ran into the house and the Angels told them to go to the walls instead," Annabelle said as she looked around the room. "Petra, Kyra you have weapons?"

"Mama said we can help," Petra said proudly.

"Did you find out the name of the demon you were fighting?" Hannah asked.

"The Angels called him Moloch. He was going to kill us so the Sanuri would go after him for revenge, then Moloch planned to kill the Sanuri. That's why I called the Angels and they came, I couldn't believe it."

"Moloch is one of the Old Ones," Hannah said. "They are the most powerful demons."

"Well I think the Angels are putting him in The Abyss right now that is why they sent me home." As Annabelle spoke five soldiers walked into the kitchen.

"My Lady, we have disposed of the bodies as you said. What do you want us to do with these two?" The young sergeant asked.

"Keep them in the chairs but move them to the chambers across from the King's study," Renya replied.

The second spy was conscious now and tried to kick the soldiers as they picked up the chair. Then she spit at one of the men. Marie grabbed her frying skillet and walked up to the woman threateningly. "Settle down or I will hit you again." Marie said soberly. The soldiers grinned as they moved the now compliant woman.

Miranda's words came true as a thick darkness overtook Fort Salar. Some of the Old Ones had come for revenge. Baal, Ipos, Zede and Bentra left their hell dimensions to personally attack this fort filled with humans. The Angels themselves spread the word through the hell dimensions that Moloch had been imprisoned in The Abyss of The Great Ruler. But with the message the Angels flashed the image of the Sanuri.

428

The demons saw no Hengers or other signs of the presence of Angels at the fort.

The Sanuri, this enlightened human, was considered a scourge among demons for he understood the truth. The Sanuri knew that no matter how dark the peoples of the world became in their desires and allegiances to the demons; that one voice, one pure heart could call the Spirit of The Great Ruler in. And this knowledge created great fear in the demons because underneath the boasting, arrogance and ego; beneath the ignorance and cravings; the demons knew, even in the smallest portions of their minds, that they were not as powerful as The Great Ruler.

King Sudfad himself now walked among his troops, as all could sense the battle had taken on new proportions. "Have faith," was his simple message as he walked among the soldiers trying to give them courage. When the darkness surrounded the fort, the Amulth demons stopped their attack as they awaited orders from their leaders. For the Amulth too, were surprised by the arrival of the Old Ones.

Hecate arrived at Fort Salar moments before the Old Ones but once she sensed their presence she left because she wasn't sure if they were after her. Hecate took sanctuary in her lair and like the rest of the dark worlds, waited to hear the results of the battle. Since she had just arrived from Sidus she did not hear the information that Moloch had been imprisoned. Hecate poured herself a large glass of wine and thought about her next moves.

When Renya realized the seriousness of the attacks against the fort, she assumed command of the castle troops in place of her husband. Three thousand soldiers were assigned to the protection of the castle. Renya told the young sergeant to call the troops to a formation and she would address them.

"Renya I mean no disrespect," Vivian said. "But please let me try to talk with Miranda before you address the soldiers."

Renya looked at Vivian with surprise, not because of what Vivian said but because Renya realized she should have had the same thoughts. "I may be the only one here who has not met the Angels," Renya said with sudden realization.

"Perhaps this is my lesson to learn." Renya turned to the sergeant, "Do not call the troops yet but prepare them for an attack." Renya took Vivian's hand and led her to Sudfad's study. As soon as they closed the door to the study Renya said, "My husband calls to The Lion and yet Miranda and Daniel have appeared to so many of you. I am not sure who to call to."

"I may be wrong," Vivian said. "But I get a sense that The Lion is a higher rank than Miranda and Daniel. So as the Queen, perhaps he is the one you should call to."

To Vivian's surprise, Queen Renya got down on her knees and silently prayed for guidance from The Great Ruler. Renya continued to pray until she heard Vivian gasp. Renya looked up and saw a huge lion standing in the study; there was a presence about him that made her want to laugh and weep at the same time.

"Stand up Renya," The Lion said softly. "While you encourage others to call to me you have never before considered doing so; why is that?"

Renya started to stammer as she stood up. "Why, I don't really know, I guess, well, I am not really sure."

"You and Sudfad have worked equally on behalf of The Great Ruler you do not need intermediaries; you should call upon the heavens more often." Then The Lion turned to Vivian. "Vivian it was your faith that brought Renya to this moment but this is her journey. It is time for you to interrogate your prisoners. You will know the questions you need to ask."

As the dank darkness of hell surrounded Fort Salar, lightening started to flash. But this lightening did not come from the heavens downward; it came from the hell dominions upwards. "They are trying to intimidate you," Edward yelled loudly. Archetenus, Misha and Raphael repeated Edward's words.

"Well, they are doing a pretty good job," Lila whispered to Natasha as they peered over the top of the walls of the fort at the ocean of demons surrounding them. The Amulth stood at attention and stared at the fort as they awaited further orders from the Old Ones.

Although the Amulth had been sent to attack the fort by the Insidiae, these demons understood that the wishes of the Old Ones superseded that of the dark lords.

The lull in the battle did not last long. Talmuth, the demonic versions of dragons appeared in the skies as did Durisks, the demonic birds of prey that resembled flying skeletons. These creatures appeared in the sky but did not move; it was as if the Old Ones were showing the humans their arsenal. The ground started to shake and rumble as hordes of Rogetts immerged from their caverns. But these ravenous monsters too, stood in obedience to the Old Ones. "We want the Sanuri," a voice screamed from the darkness.

"Do not tell them that the Sanuri is not here," Miranda told Sudfad.

"You can't have him," yelled Sudfad.

"Then prepare for battle," the voice yelled out.

"I am curious," Sudfad yelled back. "If you are so powerful, why do you hold back? It certainly isn't out of mercy." The voice did not respond. "The answer is that for all of your theatrics and parlor games you have no power here. This fort, this kingdom, these people belong to The Great Ruler and you know you are not as powerful as He is."

As Sudfad spoke a ring of incredible light now surrounded the darkness caused by the demons. The light blinded the demons and their monsters and caused their skins to smoke and burst into flames. An army of Angels, as the world has never seen, immerged from that ring of light; their holiness and brilliance was blinding to the demons. The soldiers started to yell and clap when they saw the Angelic warriors. Loud screeching filled the air as thousands of Blue Hengers appeared in the sky.

"This was a trap," Baal screamed with rage. "I curse you Sudfad and your army of mortals."

A calm and incredibly loud voice filled the battlefield. "If you want to curse someone, try me." And the image of a lion of tremendous proportions appeared on that battlefield.

431

So powerful was The Lion's presence that the Amulth and Rogetts that were standing around him dissolved into piles of dead red snakes. The soldiers and all within the fort became quiet for they too, were overwhelmed with awe.

"Moloch wasn't courageous enough to do battle with a faithful human girl," The Lion mocked. "Tell me are all the Old Ones cowards?" Baal, Ipos, Zede and Bentra started to materialize around The Lion.

Gabriel, Raphael and Sudfad had been standing with Miranda, Gabriel and Raphael both turned and started to run from the platform. "Stop!" Miranda yelled. "Where are you going?"

"To fight with him," Gabriel said. "He is surrounded."

"My dear precious children," Miranda said sweetly. "This time the battle is not yours. You have proven that your faith and courage are more than mere words. This battle is ours." Miranda walked up to Gabriel and kissed him on the forehead and she turned and kissed Raphael on the forehead. Then Miranda's voice rang out across the grounds of the fort. "Misha can we hear that war cry again?" Misha raised his voice and started the war cry and every voice within the fort joined in. Miranda appeared on the ground next to The Lion.

Meanwhile at the castle, Renya walked into the chambers where Vivian and the others were interrogating the female spies. "Are you alright Renya?" Vitomas asked as she saw that Renya looked drained and like she had been crying.

"Yes," Renya said. "It wasn't really what I expected but it was very emotional. The Lion had to leave. What have you learned from these two?"

"A demon named Daegal approached each of the women who helped Marie in the kitchen. Each woman promised to give him information for a bag of gold; this much we already knew. But this morning Daegal gave Freda here a vial of liquid, she claims she didn't know what it was, and ordered her to put it in our food," Vivian explained.

"By this time all six of the women realized they all work for Daegal so while Freda was pouring the liquid in the gravy the others were watching the doors. But Marie pushed into the kitchen and caught them."

Renya walked up to Freda and asked sharply, "Freda you sold her soul to a demon just what did you think was in that vial?"

"I didn't sell my soul," Freda protested.

"You really are a fool," said Renya.

"Sally did we sell our souls?" Freda asked the other spy.

"I didn't think so," Sally said fearfully.

"You didn't answer my question," Renya demanded.

"I thought it was probably poison," admitted Freda.

"That is all I needed to hear," Renya said. Then she turned back to Vivian. "What information did they sell the demon?"

"That's the curious thing," Vitomas said. "Just who was in the castle, what our routines were and about the celebration we are having."

"Didn't the demon want to know more?" Renya asked Freda.

"Not really, he mainly wanted to know if the Sanuri was here."

Vivian and Vitomas both looked at each other. "That she did not tell us," Vivian said.

"Did the demon say why he wanted this information or why he was interested in the Sanuri?" Renya asked as she looked sternly at both of the spies.

"He never really talked to us about himself," Sally said. "He just gave us orders."

"That's true," said Freda.

"Do you know any information about threats to these families or this kingdom that you have not told us?" Renya asked. Sally and Freda looked at each other with confusion.

"Well, the demon asked a lot of questions about your celebration, so I don't know if he plans to attend. But like Sally said, our meetings with him weren't social."

"They don't know how to find or call to the demon," Vivian said. "He always approached them."

"I am drawing a picture from the description they gave us," Annabelle said as she sat at a table with paper and pen.

"They said they don't know of any other spies here," Vitomas said. "The women only recently discovered they were all spies. And today was the first time they put anything in our food. There have been no other assassination attempts."

"Assassination!" Sally said in bewilderment.

"What else do you call it when you try to poison the King and Royal Family?" Renya asked sharply.

"Treason is another good word," Alexander said. Both Sally and Freda now looked at each other as if they suddenly realized the trouble they were in. Annabelle stood up and walked over to the women.

"Tell me what changes I have to make," Annabelle said as she showed her drawing to Sally and Freda.

"That really is a good likeness," Sally said but his eyes need to look more evil.

"I'm not sure how I can draw that," said Annabelle.

"The center of his eyes are yellow," Freda said. "And his lips are thinner, but you pretty much got him."

"Does anyone else have questions?" Renya asked.

"Did he ever talk about our children?" asked Vitomas.

"Not that I know of," Freda said. "Mainly the Sanuri."

"Alexander would you have the soldiers come in here?"

"My Lady what are you going to do with us?" asked Sally.

"Are you going to let us go?" Freda asked.

"Let you go!" Marie yelled as she walked menacingly towards the women. "You tried to kill the Royal Family. Sally you were trying to attack the Queen when I hit you. What do you think they are going to do with you?"

"I don't know," Sally said fearfully.

"Sergeant," Renya said when five soldiers entered the room. "Take these women to the dungeons." Sally and Freda screamed as the soldiers took them out of the castle.

"Were they like that because of the potion?" Renya asked.

"No they are just stupid," Marie said with disgust and walked out of the room.

"Are you going to address the troops?" Vitomas asked Renya.

"The Lion said it was not necessary," Renya explained. "He said we are all safe here and that our husbands and soldiers are all safe at the fort. The Lion said this is a battle between the Angels and the demons." As Renya talked she walked through the room and closed the door. Now only Vitomas, Annabelle, Hannah, Vivian, Gala and Alexander were in the room. "I asked The Lion about the Sanuri's safety because of what Annabelle said Moloch was planning. And The Lion said this battle also served as a distraction to help the Sanuri find the people the demons plan to sacrifice for the blood moon rituals."

"Wouldn't you think the Angels would know where those people are?" asked Hannah.

"I didn't talk to him about that," Renya said.

435

"The Lion said that after this battle there would be a crisis in the hell dimensions that would draw some of the demon's attention from the blood moon ceremonies because they would be too busy attacking each other."

The humans and Rualas stood in awe as they watched the epic battle taking place outside of the fort. Not one demon or any of their monsters entered the fort. At times the spectators could not see because of the blinding white light of the Angels. The screeching of the Hengers and the Durisks was deafening at times.

Lightning was flashing through the dark clouds created by the demons. Tremendous winds started to blow and the ground shook violently at times. Although some inside of the fort had fought with demons themselves; this battle of the immortals was like nothing they had ever seen.

When Baal, Ipos, Zede and Bentra realized they would be fighting with Angels instead of butchering humans they called for reinforcements. While legions of demons responded to the call, many others sat back to see the outcome of the battle because if these Old Ones were destroyed their territories would become available. As soon as the hell dimensions received the news that Moloch had fallen, other demons started to fight over Moloch's domain.

After two glasses of wine, Hecate decided to contact the underworlds. She first said a special spell to mask her location from anyone she would speak with. Hecate had difficulty reaching any of her normal contacts because of the chaos and upheaval in the hell dimensions. Finally someone responded to her call and the information that Hecate received pleased her greatly. They had fallen; all of the Old Ones who had put a price on her head had been beaten by the Angels and imprisoned in The Abyss.

Hecate poured herself another glass of wine and sat down on her sofa; she wanted to relish this moment. Now Hecate considered the possibilities, with Moloch, Baal, Ipos, Bentra and Zede out of the way, there would be new opportunities and new leaders of realms. Perhaps she should make a power move.

As Hecate thought about strategies she suddenly realized there were no Old Ones to stop her from going after the Sanuri and the priests. Hecate laughed out loud; with this battle she had been freed in so many ways.

Then Hecate thought about Sampson, perhaps she should stop him from the mission that Raum had sent him on because she would not need Raum's protection any more. Then Hecate reconsidered; Sampson still needed to complete his trials but if she could conquer a domain she would have enough power to put Sampson through the tests. And if she decided to go to war for a hell region she might need the items that Raum ordered Sampson to get. Hecate could not remember the last time she was this happy.

Long after the battle was over, Sudfad and his new command staff remained at the fort to restore order and to settle the new officers into their offices and assignments. Koby, Bekka, Dagon, Elan and Cassandra escorted Gabriel as he drove a large boca filled with soldier uniforms and gear to the Patronus headquarters at Cicero. Raphael and Gabriel were not sure they still needed the Patronus to infiltrate the ranks of the soldiers since so many demons had been identified and destroyed this day, but after consideration they decided to continue with their original plan.

Calen, Luca, Natasha and Lila, took the large mural from the kitchen in Hoff's house to the castle for further study. The piece of wall was large and heavy. They borrowed a large boca from the fort to transport it to a shed on the castle grounds. Since no one understood what the mural was or if it contained any malignant energy they did not want to bring it inside of the castle.

Sudfad walked through Hoff's house and shook his head at the darkness that had gone undetected. When Sudfad was convinced that Raphael and Gabriel had taken everything they needed to study from the house, Sudfad ordered his soldiers to burn it to the ground. Sudfad ordered his new majors to assign their men to search details; these soldiers would go building to building looking for any sign of demonic activity.

Archetenus was surprised at how at home he felt in his new role. While he had never achieved the rank of major in the Army of Stordt, the military was the only life he had ever known and he was glad to be working in it again. Misha, Maxwell and Emeral were deeply honored by their new assignments because never in the history of the Ruala race had a Ruala commanded human armies.

Edward and Raphael were the natural choices for acting commanding generals and if anyone had doubts before the battle they did not afterwards. These two men were born leaders with minds that formed strategies that others could not at first comprehend. As an added bonus, Raphael and Edward greatly respected each other and their skills and strengths complimented the other's.

Sudfad worked hard and expected the same from those he supervised, but he also demanded that his new staff stop their work and return to the castle for dinner. As weary as everyone was, the table was filled with excited talk as everyone told their versions of the day's events. Marie was asked to join them and tell everyone about the spies. Zoya and Hannah felt more at home because they helped Marie prepare the large dinner, since she no longer had staff. Alexander's story about Annabelle challenging Moloch and fighting with the Angels turned many heads at the table.

"I would wait and tell Simon that story in person," Calen said. "Or he is going to be so worried about you that he won't be able to concentrate."

"Actually I was thinking the same thing," Annabelle said. "But, well, I don't know if you can understand this. But all of us have made covenants with The Great Ruler and everyone but me is having adventures and doing their part. Don't get me wrong I love my babies but I want to do more, does that make any sense?"

"Oh yes it does," Natasha said with a grin.

"Have you told Simon how you feel?" Vivian asked.

"No, he worries so," Annabelle said. "And honestly he and Raul are gone all of the time working on missions."

"Annabelle you have a lot of gifts that help the missions without putting you in danger," Calen said. "My entire family tells me that my fears for Natasha's safety are unfair to her. And while I agree with them, I can't stop being afraid for her. But whether I am right or wrong, Simon and I have gotten to know each other very well and we are a great deal alike. I would expect Simon to be just as afraid for you as I am for Natasha."

Late that night, Raphael walked into his chambers and was surprised to find Vivian awake. He smiled when he saw the fire roaring in the hearth and a tray with a bottle of wine and two glasses setting before it. Vivian was sitting in bed reading. When she stood up the black nightgown she was wearing took Raphael's breath away.

"I was wondering if you were going to work all night," Vivian said as she walked up to her husband and kissed him.

"Gabriel and I were trying to translate the words we saw in Hoff's house," Raphael said as he picked Vivian up and kissed her passionately. She wrapped her legs around his waist and Raphael walked over to their bed. They were lost in their embrace for many minutes before he set her on the bed and took off his clothes. Raphael lay down near his wife and kissed her again and again. "I don't know why but I feel we are going to make a baby tonight," he whispered.

"I'm sorry to wake you," Gabriel said as he slid under the covers next to Hannah.

"No I was waiting up for you, I must have just dozed off," Hannah said and put her arms around Gabriel's neck. She kissed him on the lips, then his chin. Hannah's lips caressed Gabriel's neck and chest.

As Gabriel gently got on top of Hannah he whispered, "I don't know why but I feel we are going to make a baby tonight."

Chapter XXIX
Plyogram

"This is the morning of the fifth day before the blood moon ceremonies," Claudius said at a meeting at the Patronus Headquarters in Nora. "We don't have much time so we have to be wise in how we search."

"I prepared this map for our meeting," Rueben said. "All of the shaded areas are places we have searched, both on the ground and from the air." Rueben stood up as he spoke and pointed to a map he had previously affixed to the wall. "The pins indicate towns and villages where the Hutas have taken hostages. The small nails indicate individual farms, at least the ones that we are aware of that have been attacked by the Hutas and hostages taken. It wasn't until last night when I was putting the pins and nails in this map that I realized the scope of their attacks."

Generals Colter and Orlan had ridden from Fort Nora to attend the meeting. Colter now stood up and walked over to the map. "Unfortunately as you can see, when I brought many of the local farmers and townspeople inside of the fort for safety the Hutas have expanded their radius of attacks. The Kingdom of Gandt has been brutalized, the attacks have extended into northern Stordt and as far west as Ryed."

"But that is assuming the ceremonies are taking place around Nora," Raul said. "I don't know about the Hutas but the powerful demons are cunning; I think they put that mausoleum here so we would focus our efforts in this area. I can't see it but does anyone see a pattern in where the attacks have occurred, because we know they are hiding the victims quickly?"

"They have to be moving them underground," Colter said. "Because the Rualas and Enrops have been searching from the sky. This entire area is mines and tunnels so that would not be difficult to do."

Simon stood up and walked closer to the map. "I agree with Raul, I think the mausoleum is a diversion and I am not the expert at this but when those crazy priests tried to raise Omnibus The Lion came here and stopped them."

"Does that mean holiness has touched that ground, and if so would that be a deterrent for the demons?"

"Good question," Sorren said. "But we all know that sometimes the best way to hide something is to put it in an obvious place. With all the time and effort that has already been put into this search I think we need to rethink this whole thing."

As Raphael and Vivian were entering the Royal Family's dining room for breakfast, Vitomas handed Vivian a large envelope. "Enrops just brought this for you, the flock is feeding. We have a grain area for them behind one of the barns and they will be there for a while. The Enrops know you might want to send a letter back."

"Thank you," Vivian said excitedly. "Raphael it's from Mother and Father. The majority of the household was already seated at the table. Vivian opened the envelope and pulled out two smaller ones. "This is for you and Gabriel," Vivian said as she handed her husband an envelope. "And this is for Elan and Cassandra," Vivian said with a grin. "I can tell my little brothers wrote it."

"Last night we were talking about Adrone and Paul," Elan said. "We miss those little guys."

Vivian looked at Renya and Sudfad, "I have two younger brothers five and seven and they adore Elan and Cassandra, in fact Adrone and Paul wouldn't leave them alone for a moment.

"They are very cute boys," Cassandra said as she read the letter over Elan's shoulder.

Raphael finished reading his letter and handed it to Gabriel. "Joshua said that shortly after we left their village a group of Half-Mans found Sampson spying on the village and shot him with three darts. The poison they use on their darts is strong enough that one dart should kill a man but Sampson was not killed; but he was unconscious."

"You can all read the letter but the Half-Man's got Joshua and Simon and the others. Raul was searching Sampson's pockets and found a list that named and described holy objects."

"They called to the Angels, who said that Sampson was going to rob the monastery at Rubar and bring those objects to the demons to use at the blood moon ceremonies."

Raphael continued, "Duncan wanted to execute his son but Thaos and Simon wanted to use him to trick the demons, which is what they did. Sampson was relocated and the Angels took away his memories of what he saw at the village and being shot by the Half-Mans. When Sampson wakes up he will resume his journey but the objects he takes will have some unexpected surprises for the demons."

"What did he see at the village?" Vivian asked.

"He saw the army packing up to leave," Raphael said. "Miranda and Daniel said that Sampson was waiting for them to leave so he could complete his trials, which means he will kill his brothers."

"Kill his own brothers," Renya gasped. "To become a demon!"

"Sampson is a very evil man," said Vivian.

"Sudfad," Gabriel said as he looked up from the letter. "I had talked to Joshua about the Teivel Clan. Joshua said that two young Venatores just returned to the village. They were hunting in northern Ryed while we were there."

"I am sure he is talking about Thor and Diana," Vivian said. "They are brother and sister and hunt as a team. They are fierce warriors."

"You're right," Gabriel said. "Joshua said that they spent months hunting in the lands owned by the Teivel Clan. Joshua has spoken to Thor and Diana and believe they have a great deal of information that we might find useful. He is wondering if we want to send some Rualas to get them."

"Did you tell Joshua our concerns?" asked Sudfad.

"Of course not," Gabriel said. "But Joshua is a smart man; I think he could read between the lines of some of my questions. We plan to move back into our home after the blood moon ceremonies, I will have someone get Thor and Diana then."

442

"Well, they can certainly stay here too," Sudfad said. "It's not like we don't have the room."

"Cassandra and I were talking," Elan said. "If we are sending warriors to Ryed, well, Vivian do you think your family would come to our wedding? We would like to have Adrone and Paul in the wedding."

Vivian looked at Raphael excitedly. "I am sure they will, oh I would love for them to meet all of you and see where we live. Let's send them a letter today."

Sampson was riding hard and fast to get to Rubar. He had stopped at a small farm just south of the castle of Erebus, for fresh water. It was while Sampson was talking with the farmer that he first realized he had lost several days in his travel. Sampson knew he was unconscious for a while, although he still did not understand what had happened to him.

The Angels had erased Sampson's memory of his last visit to his village and they had transported his body and horse to an area north of the Village of Gesmal. The location that Sampson found himself when he awoke was consistent with a route he would have taken to get to Rubar.

The Angels had also removed the marks on Sampson's skin made by the poison darts. In an attempt to remember what had happened to him, Sampson had examined himself for injuries, but there were none. As Sampson rode north and thought about the maladies that had beset him he became more and more convinced a demon had attacked him. But what demon and why?

Vivian read her letter out loud at the table. Iris had written about the Angels healing everyone in the village. She wrote about the Angels healing the Hutas, the gift a Huta gave to Adrone and the prophesy the Angels said about the Huta race.

Iris wrote about the gifts of gold that their family had received from Matthew, Thaos, Stephan and Thedes. Vivian smiled as she read the end of the letter. "They miss us all but mother says that Adrone wouldn't eat for two days and just kept asking everyone what they thought Elan was doing."

443

"That is so cute," Laurel said.

"Mind you, my brothers never stop eating when I leave the village," Vivian said with a laugh.

"Well, your family sounds wonderful," Renya said. "I am looking forward to meeting them. And of course they are welcomed to stay here too."

"Christopher, Nicholas," Luca said as he turned to the children's table in the dining room. "Vivian has two little brothers who are about your ages; they might come and stay with us."

"When are they coming?" Christopher asked. "Cuz Grandpa Alexander is building us a fort?"

"You're building them a fort?" Hannah asked with surprise.

"Wait until you see it," Laurel said with a proud smile.

"I will admit I got a little carried away," Alexander said. "It's rather large so you may have to put it in the yard but it breaks down into pieces so you can move it."

"Thank you Alexander," Gabriel said. "I will pay you for the work."

"You will do no such thing," Laurel said. "Alexander probably gets more joy out of building these things than the children do playing with them."

"I doubt that," Annabelle said with a laugh. "Our boys love the toys Grandpa makes for them. And he is building a fort for when they get bigger."

"I'll be so glad when we have a baby," Vivian said then she looked at Raphael and smiled. "Last night Raphael said he had a strong feeling that we were making a baby."

Hannah gasped. "Gabriel said those exact same words to me last night." Gabriel and Raphael both looked at each other with surprise.

"Miranda kissed you both on the forehead," Sudfad said and smiled. "I don't believe an Angel's kiss is ever just a kiss."

Hecate slept little the night before as her mind was filled with strategies. She was shrewd, she viewed the politics of the underworld as a game board and she was figuring out anticipated moves. But periodically as Hecate planned her future she would think of either Sampson or Orbus; both had their qualities.

Hecate laughed out loud when she realized she wanted them both and she knew she could play that game for a while. But she also knew that neither Orbus nor Sampson would put up with that behavior and she had a good chance of losing them both. That was one of the qualities Hecate loved in both lovers, that they both had the strength to stand up to her.

Hecate had been a seductress for hundreds of years. She was used to making males of any species putty in her hands. But the males who attracted her were strong. As Hecate continued to think about Sampson and Orbus she realized there were many similarities. Then Hecate suddenly laughed when she also realized that the human had a darker soul than the demon.

Claudius copied what he had seen Sudfad do on many occasions. He stopped the meeting and broke the people into smaller groups. Each group was to brainstorm the problems they had been discussing in the morning meeting.

"I have a question," Thaos asked. "Before we get too far into this, where are the areas that we know with certainty the Angels have been. I don't mean just for visits, I mean areas where they may have destroyed demons with holiness."

"That dark lords compound in Port Friada," Matthew said. "And maybe the battlegrounds we had in northern Ganz when we were trying to save Archetenus and Delilah."

"Rueben do you have another map that we can mark these areas on?" Thaos asked. Ruben left the meeting room and returned a few minutes later with a large map and pens. Thaos walked up to Rueben and helped him affix the map to the wall.

Then Thaos started to mark the locations that Matthew had just mentioned. "The Caves of Sundra," Sorren called out.

"The mountain The Lion blew up here," Raul said as he stood up to mark the map.

"The monastery at Malga," Rueben said.

"Those caves near Roch's castle, where the first transformation was supposed to take place," Simon called out while Raul marked them on the map.

"Salar," Stephan added.

"The Angels said the Village of Gesmal was protected," Lakin said. "And of course the Kingdom of Ogg doesn't exist anymore."

"That hotel in Taperia," Matthew said. "But the rest of that city is filled with evil."

"I don't know if any of you know this," Rueben said. "But centuries ago demons had taken over the monastery at Philiste, The Lion chased them out and King David witnessed all that. Afterwards King David created the Patronus."

"I am thinking there is enough holiness in these places to keep the demons out," Thaos said. "If anyone can think of another place, shout it out and add it to the map."

"Come in," Sudfad called out as he heard a gentle knock on the door to his study.

"I don't mean to take up your time," Delilah said as she shyly entered the study. "I just wanted to thank you for giving Archetenus a position in your military. He is so happy, it's like he is alive again."

"You know the history between Archetenus and Vitomas," Sudfad said as he pushed back in his chair. "Your husband had to prove himself to us and he did. I am glad that he is happy because he is doing an impressive job."

"You know the side of Archetenus that kidnapped Vitomas, well, I have never seen it and I am not just saying that," Delilah said. "He told me that Miranda came to him for years, trying to get him to change. Thank The Great Ruler she did. The Archetenus I know is kind and loving and courageous. I won't take any more of your time; I just wanted to thank you."

Sudfad held his usual morning meeting with his leaders but this day he also held a meeting after the midday meal. This meeting included the women in the house hold and Renya brought Marie into the meeting. "It's only fair that Marie knows what is going on," Renya said as she closed the door behind them. "I have briefed her about the party we will be hosting the night before the blood moon."

Hannah stood up, "We have been talking among ourselves and since we are so threatened by spies now, all of us women will gladly help Marie in the kitchen. We don't feel this is a good time to bring new employees in."

"Thank you," Sudfad said. "Your contributions are appreciated. I have talked with Gabriel and Raphael and we have already sent a letter to the Village of Gesmal inviting Thor, Diana and Vivian's family here. Maxwell will you make arrangements to have Ruala warriors bring them. But I don't want Misha or any of the other Rualas here to leave. I need them all."

"I agree," Maxwell said then he turned to Vivian. "You believe it will be all four of your brothers and your parents; will anyone else want to attend?"

"I believe that Duncan would love to come, but he needs to stay at the village with Sampson on the loose," Vivian said.

"Let me know if the numbers change," Maxwell said. "But I will send a message to the Ice Caves today."

"We know you are all anxious to move back into your homes," Sudfad said. "But until the blood moon ceremonies are completed it is too dangerous for all of you. I have been sending patrols to check on your homes daily and they inform me that everything seems normal."

"But I would feel better if you allowed my soldiers to do thorough searches of your homes before you reenter them."

"I think we all agree on that," Gabriel said.

"Archetenus and Delilah you are more than welcomed to remain here until your home is built," Sudfad added.

"Thank you," Archetenus said. "Calen tells me he is almost finished with the house plans."

"Good," Gabriel said with a huge smile. "Because Raphael and I want some nurseries built in our house." Everyone in the study laughed at this remark.

"May I say something?" Marie asked after the room quieted down. "My Lady has told me about the party and normally we would hire extra staff to serve the food and drinks. I come from a really big family and as you know from hiring two of my sisters, we work hard and are honest, but the others aren't accustomed to fancy things. If you would like I could bring in some more of my sisters for you to meet and decide if you would like them to serve at the party."

"I think that is an excellent idea," Sudfad said. "For anyone who does not know, our nurses Abigail and Gabriella are Marie's sisters as is Kyra, Petra's close friend. And I just want to add, the reason little Kyra is being tutored with Petra is because she fought the men who kidnapped Petra. And apparently inflicted some wounds on them," Sudfad said with a grin. "I offered her a gift for what she did. I will admit I expected her to ask for a pony; she asked for an education," Sudfad said with a proud smile. "I believe that tells you the caliber of Marie's family."

The meeting at the Patronus Headquarters in Nora went late into the night. The people took a few small breaks to eat. Generals Colter and Orlan decided to stay at the headquarters so they could continue working on the issues at hand.

"I wish the Sanuri was here," Raul said. "He is so familiar with ancient prophesies and well, just about everything come to think of it."

"When the Sanuri was here last he spent most of his time in the study," Padre Gilbert said. "I was healing from some wounds and worked with him. Hannah's father left a great many books and scrolls in his library that we were reviewing. The Sanuri said he started wondering what position Hannah's father really held in the Insidiae because he had information that only a high ranking official should have; information identifying members."

"I thought we pretty much emptied that library out," Simon said.

"There's still a lot of books and manuscripts in there," Rueben said.

"Claudius I propose we break for the night," Raul said. "I am going to pour a glass of whiskey and spend some time in that library."

"Actually that sounds like a very good idea," Claudius said. "I believe I will join you. Rueben what time should we reconvene?"

"First thing after breakfast," Rueben said. "There are bottles of wine and whiskey on the kitchen table; please help yourselves."

So many people entered the study to help with research that many additional tables and chairs were brought into that room. "This brings back memories," Raul said. "Simon and I spent a lot of time here when we were hunting those crazy priests."

"I feel like we are missing something that is right under our noses," Prince Gael said out loud. "The demons know where we are going to look so obviously they are going to have the ceremonies in a place we would never consider."

"Do you think another monastery?" asked Thedes.

"That's a possibility," Rueben said. "But it was big news when the Patronus chased the demons out of the monastery at Malga; I think the entire continent heard about it."

"Thedes this is a different subject but have you heard from Ibula?" Lakin asked. "She should be home by now."

449

"I got a letter this morning but I haven't read it yet. I was waiting until after the meetings."

"Thedes," Raul said humorously. "Take a break and read her letter. You must have been thinking about it all day."

"I have been having the same feeling all day that Gael has," Stephan said loudly to the group. "What if the Hutas are taking victims from this area just so we believe the mausoleum is the place? We have no idea if the Hutas have been taking people in other kingdoms. If I was going to perform these ceremonies I would do it in Marba, no one ever goes into Marba because it's all Hutas and demons."

"Or Xepoltr," Lakin said. "The Hutas run that kingdom after they defeated the Shettees."

"They run much of Norkv too," Thaos said.

"But that means they would be transporting their captives over the Safer Mountains," Neputa said.

"Actually we don't know if they aren't just killing them and hiding the bodies," Thaos said. "I mean I am starting to believe this is all one big ruse to keep us on the wrong trail."

"Raul, Simon and Matthew, since you are princes perhaps you should write letters to the kings of all the kingdoms and ask them if Hutas have been abducting people or if anything unusual has been occurring," Claudius suggested.

"That is a good idea," Matthew said. "Rueben do you have paper and pens?"

As the princes were writing letters, Thedes stood up. "Ibula and Tamas made it home safely. The Rualas who escorted them are returning to us. She says the Sanuri has contacted Manu and asked that Rualas fly over the kingdoms of lower Opots including the Waste Lands of Manod."

"So the Sanuri is thinking the same thing we are," Simon said. "Actually I would put money on the Waste Lands; I mean nobody is even familiar with that area."

"We are," Neputa said. "We crossed the Waste Lands searching for our people. We didn't get captured by the Valdees until we had reached the coast."

"Neputa could you draw us a map?" Claudius said. "I have never even seen a map of the Waste Lands."

"The Waste Lands are directly south of us, on the other side of the mountains," General Colter said. "I suppose it is possible they could take their captives over those mountains. But there is no way we could get troops there in four days."

"If we are right, we are going to have to ask Miranda and Daniel for help," Sorren said.

"Gabriel, it's Koby," Koby said as he knocked on Gabriel's bedroom door.

"Come in," Gabriel called out wearily as he sat up in bed. Only the fire from the hearth provided light in the bedroom.

"What time is it?" Hannah asked as she sat up also.

"It's a little after three," Koby said. "I am sorry to wake you but I thought you would want to see this right away. Annabelle has been in that shed all night working on that mural. Bekka and I stayed with her because we didn't want Annabelle out there alone. Well, she got all the paint off that was covering the original drawing and I think you and Raphael really need to see this."

"You're right," Gabriel said as he jumped out of bed. "Have you awakened Raphael yet?"

"No, I am going to do that now," said Koby.

"Don't wake anyone else until we see it," Gabriel said.

"Edward is there; apparently he couldn't sleep and came down to investigate the light he saw in the shed."

"I'm coming too," Hannah said.

451

Gabriel and Hannah met Raphael and Vivian in the front foyer of the castle. "Did Koby tell you anything about this picture?" Vivian asked as the two couples were walking down the front steps of the castle.

"I got the idea it was difficult to explain," said Gabriel.

"Oh my!" Hannah gasped as they walked into the shed and saw the large piece of wall that was propped up against a work bench.

"This is why I wanted you to see it," Koby said. "Do you think this is another demon trick or is this the real thing?"

"It is drawn with black ink," Annabelle said. "Someone did a pretty good job of trying to cover it up. I saw a little ink from behind a paint chip. That is how I found it originally. I was really careful getting the paint off."

"Annabelle you did a great job," Raphael said as he and Gabriel bent down to look at the drawing.

"Hannah would you make some coffee?" Gabriel asked. "I don't think we will be returning to bed. And grab some paper and pen."

"I'll go with you," Bekka said. "Annabelle you have been up all night, do you want me to walk you home?"

"I'm too excited to sleep," Annabelle said as she looked at the drawing. "Do you know what it is?"

"As you can see this is a series of pictures within pictures," Raphael said. "This is called a plyogram. In ancient times kings used to have these drawn up to hide important information in plain sight. I have never seen one used by demons before."

"How do you know it was done by demons?" asked Edward.

"It's divided into thirteen sections and each of those is divided into thirteen sections," Gabriel said. "Thirteen is considered an unholy number."

"Do you think Hoff drew this?" Edward asked as he was staring at the fine detail in the drawings. "Because this looks like an artist did it."

"I was thinking the same thing," Gabriel said. "The bloody writing we found on the walls of Hoff's house was sloppy and uneven. This drawing is meticulous."

"Annabelle, do you think Sudfad would be angry if we woke him at this time of the morning?" Raphael asked.

"No, I think he would want to see this right away."

"I'll get him," Koby said and left the shed.

"Annabelle, were you working on this when Molach came to you?" Gabriel asked.

"Yes, Father and Edward had already cut it out of the wall and placed in the floor. I was removing paint when I smelled this horrible smell, I can't describe it. Then I heard a voice talking but it was in a language I couldn't understand. Well, I knew it was a demon and I started yelling at it to go away. Then the voice starts to yell back at me in my language. I started insulting it and calling it names. The reason I did that is because Simon told me that demons are empowered by fear; so I thought that if I ridiculed it, the demon might become weaker."

"I can't believe he didn't kill you on the spot," Raphael said.

"Oh he started to throw me against the wall when he got really mad. Father kept telling me to shut up. But I kept at the demon and the demon told my father that he should have taught me to show respect to my superiors."

"Well, that made me really mad and I kept taunting it. Then Father tells the demon to hurt him instead of me. That's when the demon said he was going to hurt a lot of people and when the Sanuri came for revenge he would kill him. That's when I called to the Angels. I still can't believe they came."

"So you got the demon so mad that he exposed his plans?" Gabriel asked. "I'll bet the Angels were already close at hand."

453

"When we came into the kitchen the room was filled with demons but do you remember where Moloch's voice was coming from before that?"

Annabelle thought about the question for several moments. "Now that you mention it, the voice seemed to be coming from the wall where the mural was. That is the area the Angels faced when they spoke to him."

"Did Moloch say anything to you about the mural?" Raphael asked.

"No but like I said I didn't understand the words he was saying at first."

"Do you think you could remember some of the words?" Vivian asked. "I'll write them down and try to translate them."

"Actually we are going to need some of the books from our room," Raphael said. "I'll be right back."

"I'll get them," Edward said. "You stay and study this damn thing. Where are the books?"

"I'll go with you," Vivian said. "My husband has a lot of books in our room."

When Matthew, Raul and Simon finished writing the letters to the kings of Opots; flocks of Enrops were called to deliver them. The birds were told to wait for responses from the kings.

"The more I think about it," Stephan said. "I vote for the Waste Lands because no one even thinks about that area."

"In the morning I will have warriors fly over those lands." Lakin said. "I too am thinking the Waste Lands would be the place, because that really would be hiding something in plain sight."

"I don't know about the rest of you, but I would like to do more research before we call Miranda and Daniel," Raul said as he stood up and walked towards the library.

"I agree," Sorren said. "I don't want them to think we can't do the job."

Hannah, Bekka, Sudfad and Renya all entered the shed together. Hannah and Bekka carried trays with pots of coffee, cups, cream and sugar. Renya carried a tray with small plates and pastries. "Koby went to see if Luca or Misha or the others want to see this," Bekka explained. Sudfad walked up to the drawing and stared at it in amazement.

"I have read about plyograms but I have never seen one before," Sudfad said as he kneeled down to inspect the drawing. "This is really fascinating. Oh and don't ever worry about waking me up for something important."

Edward and Vivian walked into the shed, each carrying an armload of thick books. "Your room looks like a library," Edward said kiddingly to Raphael.

"While there is writing as you can see most of this is pictures and symbols," Gabriel said so we are going to have to try and find them in the books. Everyone in the shed, including the King and Queen poured themselves a cup of coffee and grabbed a book.

"Annabelle maybe you should try to get some sleep," Renya suggested.

"I am too excited and besides Natasha said she would help Vitomas watch my children."

"Sudfad when Marie's sisters come today, perhaps we should hire another nurse," Renya said.

Sudfad laughed, "This from the woman who fought me about hiring nurses in the first place. But I do agree, in fact I was thinking the same thing."

By four in the morning, most of the people staying at the castle were now in the shed doing research. Vivian returned to their room three more times to retrieve more books. Hannah made two more pots of coffee then stayed in the castle to start breakfast.

"Good thing this is a big shed," Jared said sarcastically.

"It's one of Alexander's woodworking sheds," Sudfad said. "He has been teaching me the craft, I find it very relaxing."

"I found one," Bekka said excitedly as she held a book close to the plyogram. "It's the picture of the sword with two snakes wrapped around it. It is a symbol of chaos. I don't know why that surprises me I thought it would mean war or something."

"I found the one with the thirteen eyeballs grouped together," Luca said just moments later. "It means the Old Ones are watching; that they have a view. Do you think that means some kind of portal?"

"Annabelle said that Moloch's voice came from the area of the wall where this had been hanging," Raphael said. "And she said the Angels looked at that same spot when they were talking to him. If there was a portal in that house, would it have been destroyed when the house was burned down?"

Chapter XXX
Waste Lands of Manod

Most of the people in the study at the Patronus Headquarters at Nora; either stayed up all night doing research or fell asleep in the study. "I smell coffee," Simon said wearily as he rubbed his eyes. "The words are jumping off this page at me."

Claudius stood up and looked at the exhausted faces that filled the room. "Everyone get some breakfast and some sleep; we will move the meeting from the morning to the afternoon."

"Wait," Padre Gilbert yelled and stood up holding a fragile scroll in his hands. "I might have found something. This is written in Shamac. It's an old language that I studied years ago. It took me a while to translate it. The blood moon's used to have a lot of significance for our ancestors. As you know there are blood moons every year."

"This scroll talks about many old prophesies, some mention a blood moon. The prophesy that the Sanuri found and told us about says that on the thirteenth night of the blood moon, in the year of Zenus the doors will open, the waters will part and the blood spilled will rejuvenate the dead and empower them."

Gilbert continued, "This prophesy also refers to the blood moon in the year of the Zenus. It says that the barren ground will be enriched by the blood sacrifices and the blood will reach the darkest of places feeding the creatures that hide from the light. Then it describes what the sacrificial altar should look like. Each victim will be tied to a large flat stone slab that should be thirteen kenoes in front of the altar. The person's throat should be cut from right to left with a thresiose; I don't know what that is. It says the sky will darken and the earth will move with each sacrifice until all the doors to hell are opened."

"I am going to copy that and send it to Father," Raul said. "And I am going to tell him that we are going to concentrate our search to the Waste Lands of Manod."

After breakfast Archetenus, Misha, Emeral, Maxwell, Raphael and Edward assumed their duties at Fort Salar.

Besides the normal routines, they still had troops searching the fort for signs of demonic activity. Before Maxwell left the castle he sent a message to the Ice Caves, asking warriors to bring Thor and Diana from the Village of Gesmal to the castle in Wetpr. Sudfad wanted to bring these two young warriors to Wetpr as soon as possible because they might have vital information about the Teivel Clan. Maxwell said he would send a second group of warriors to the Village of Gesmal to bring Vivian's family to Wetpr, at a time that was closer to the wedding date of Elan and Cassandra.

Most of the others within the castle returned to the wood shed to try and translate the mysteries of the plyogram. Sudfad sent letters for his sons and General Claudius telling them everything that had occurred in Wetpr and the news about Thor and Diana; but it would be a couple of days before the Enrops would reach Nora.

Mid-morning Vitomas and Annabelle joined Renya and Sudfad in the main parlor of the castle, where they planned to interview some of Marie's relatives. Marie was hired by Sudfad and Renya when she was a young girl. Marie and Renya became close when Sudfad was gone fighting in the wars and Renya was left to raise their only son Raul. It would be nine years before they adopted their second son Simon.

Marie worked hard and never complained. Her dry sense of humor made her a favorite with the entire Royal Family. But it wasn't until the Princesses came to the castle that Marie was seen with new eyes. The savage lives that Vitomas and Annabelle had to endure before meeting their husbands made them grateful for everything in their lives. Both women strongly desired a family and a life without horror. Vitomas and Annabelle fell in love with Marie as soon as they met her and treated her like family.

"How many brothers and sisters do you have?" Annabelle asked Marie when she saw a small line of people in the front foyer of the castle.

"Most people don't believe it," Marie said with a laugh. "Let's just say my parents were very healthy."

It took almost two hours for the Royal Family to interview five of Marie's sisters and two of her brothers. The announcement after the interviews surprised Marie since she thought her siblings were being interviewed for the positions of servers at the upcoming celebration. Sudfad asked Marie and her sisters and brothers to return to the parlor for the determinations of the interviews.

"We have decided to hire all of you to be servers," Sudfad said. "Marie will teach you what you need to know. But I am sure some of you were curious at the questions we asked of you. Amiee and Darlah would you also consider positions as nurses for our grandchildren? You would be working with your sisters Abigail and Gabriella.

"Oh yes," Amiee said excitedly. Darlah did not speak but smiled brightly and nodded her head.

"Good," Sudfad said. "We will have your sisters introduce you to the children and teach you the job after this meeting. Jack and Curtis, we recently lost two of our stable hands. Would you like those jobs?"

The twin teenage boys looked at each other with surprise. "Yes, My Lord, thank you very much," the boys said almost in unison.

"Wonderful, you can start after this meeting," Sudfad continued. "Evelyn, Mildred and Lois would you be interested in filling the positions of cooks? You would be working for Marie."

"Yes, thank you," the women responded.

"Marie we still need to hire more staff for you; please feel free to give me names of any people you want us to consider." Marie was beaming proudly that so many of her brothers and sisters were now employed by the Royal Family.

Claudius called a meeting after the midday meal. "This is the afternoon of the fourth day before the blood moon ceremonies and we are running out of time. Before we went to bed this morning we were in agreement that we should focus our efforts on the Waste Lands of Manod. Has anyone changed their minds or learned new information since then?"

"I am still in agreement," Lakin said as he stood up in the crowded room. "I just wanted to tell you that I sent a message to the Ice Caves before I slept. I told them our suspicions and asked that our warriors fly over the Waste Lands."

"Simon and I sent a long letter to Father briefing him on everything," Raul said.

"And I sent one to Mathas as well," Claudius said. "I have never been in this part of the country before. Does anyone know if there is a pass through the mountains that is directly south of here? And my second question is; does anyone know how long it takes to travel through the mountains?"

"Claudius this isn't answering your questions but it is information you need to know," Neputa said. "I led my men westward from Marba. Once we left Xepoltr and entered the Waste Lands there was no water to be found until we reached the Schenomi Sea. My men were so weakened from our journey that we made easy prey for the Valdees. Besides the dangers of the desert, there are pockets of quick sand and tar pits. The terrain is very rugged and difficult to cross even with horses. Once we get over the mountains it will still be slow going."

"I have tried to obtain every map I can get my hands on since my assignment in Nora," General Colter said. "I have never seen any with a pass through the mountains on this side of Opots, there is the Pass of Duvuk entering the Kingdom of Norkv to the east but that is too far out of our way. No one has reasons to go to the Waste Lands."

"Some of the Rualas that are assigned here have flown over the mountains," High Priest Rueben said. "We could call some of them into the meeting. From what they had told me, the mountains sounded treacherous."

"Let's get a couple of them in here," Claudius suggested and Rueben left the room.

"Annabelle finally decided to get some sleep," Natasha said as she entered the woodshed where people were trying to translate the plyogram.

"She worked hard and did a good job," Gabriel said. "Thank The Great Ruler Annabelle saw that little piece of chipped paint on the wall; none of the rest of us saw anything unusual with that wall."

"So you believe it to be genuine and not a trick?" Natasha asked as she knelt down and examined the artwork.

"The more I work on it the more inclined I am to think it is real," Gabriel said. "We have actually found a lot of the symbols in the texts but it's not like they form sentences so I still don't have a clue what the message is. But so far this is the symbol that concerns me the most," Gabriel pointed to one of several symbols of thirteen eyeballs grouped together. "This mean's the demons are watching but also that they have a view into something. Raphael thinks the symbol is referring to a portal or portals."

"Is that what the blood moon prophesy is referring to when it says the doors of hell will open?" Natasha asked.

"I think so but so far we haven't found a symbol that relates to the blood moon."

Sampson stopped at another farm and forced the farmer to trade horses with him. Sampson was riding hard and his horse needed rest. He thought that if he rode hard all day and into the night, he would be at the monastery by morning.

The wars in the hell regions were without precedent. Five Old Ones destroyed in one day, never in the history of Nunc had such a thing occurred. The Old Ones of Nunc were battling over these new territories and they were being challenged by other ambitious and powerful demons, from Nunc and other worlds.

There were no allegiances and chaos took on a new meaning. But some of the Old Ones did not lose sight of the blood moon ceremonies and their chances to bring their domains to the surface of the World of Nunc.

"I thought I would come for a visit," Orbus said as he materialized in Hecate's lair.

Hecate smiled and poured Orbus a glass of wine. "You are a brave man, my husband could have been here," she said.

"He is a mere mortal," Orbus said in a condescending manner. Instead of taking the glass that Hecate was offering him, Orbus pulled her close to him and kissed her passionately. "When will he return?" Orbus asked then kissed Hecate again before she could answer.

"Not for a couple of days," Hecate said as she pulled away from Orbus. She set the glass of wine on a table and took Orbus' hand and led him to her bed.

Sahil and his trainee Dack entered the meeting. "Rueben told us what you are interested in," Sahil said. "We have flown over the mountains several times but never landed in them. We have seen nothing like a pass through them. The tops of the mountains are all snow and ice and the lower portions of the mountains are treacherous. Twice Dack and I have seen avalanches and we have no idea what set them in motion. I can't imagine you trying to cross them on horseback. And even if you could it would take days possibly weeks."

"Thank you," Claudius said.

"Prince Raul, Prince Simon have you seen Bekka?" Dack asked.

"Yes, she fought with us in Ryed," said Simon.

"How is she doing now? She took Fala's death pretty hard," Dack said.

"We all did," Sahil said soberly.

"Calen told me that Bekka had a really rough time when she first returned but I think everyone is trying to help her. She was doing well when she was with us in Ryed," said Simon.

"Good, thank you," Dack replied.

"Sahil, Dack you two are welcome to stay for the meeting," Lakin said. "We could use your insight into the territory."

Sorren stood up and looked around the room. "I believe we have gotten as far as we can," Sorren said. "It's time we spoke to Miranda and Daniel. We will never cross those mountains in time to stop the ceremonies."

Elan and Cassandra were in the woodshed doing research when Hannah and Vivian entered. The women had been going back and forth between helping in the kitchen and helping with research. With the possibility that they could both be pregnant, Hannah and Vivian became more bonded. Before Hannah and Vivian could sit down, Cassandra and Elan asked them to walk outside.

"We are sorry to take you away from the work," Elan apologized. "We wanted to ask you a couple of questions."

"We can't decide what we want for our wedding," Cassandra said. "We don't want to hurt anyone's feelings. We love both Gabriel and Raphael so much we can't decide which one of them should perform our ceremony. Do you think they would be insulted if we asked them both to do it?"

"Heaven's no," Hannah said with a laugh. "They will be honored and honestly the two of them together; your ceremony will be beautiful."

"Then we will ask them tonight," Elan said with relief. "Now that brings us to another subject and please be honest with us. Cassandra really wants both of you in the wedding, would you consider standing up for her if you walk down the aisle with someone other than your husbands? And do you think Raphael and Gabriel would be upset?"

"First of all it takes a lot for our husbands to become upset," Hannah said. "I would love to be in your wedding and it makes no difference to me who I walk down the aisle with."

"I feel the same way but you are going to tell us that we will be walking with Misha and Dagon aren't you?"

"Yes," Cassandra said. "Will that be a problem?"

"Not for me or Raphael but you should talk to Misha," Vivian said.

"I can walk with Misha if it is difficult for him," Hannah offered. "But I am sure he will want to walk with Vivian."

"We were thinking of having Adrone and Paul walk out with the groomsmen then after Cassandra and all of you walk up to the altar, we were going to have your brothers stand on either side of us and hand us our rings," Elan said with excitement in his voice.

"I think that sounds beautiful," said Hannah.

"My family is going to be so honored," Vivian said then paused. "I just had a thought. We all know how Misha was at Luca's wedding. If he is really opposed to being in the wedding with me. He is your blood. I will sit with the spectators. But Thor and Diana should be here by then. Both of them are very beautiful and Diana is so sweet, perhaps Misha would walk down the aisle with her. I know you don't know her, but it is an idea."

"Lila didn't know the two girls that came from the Ice Caves to be in her wedding," Hannah said.

"Vivian we would really like you to be in our wedding," Cassandra said sweetly. "But thank you for the offer and for being so understanding."

"Do you need us to do something?" Rueben asked.

"No," Matthew said. "At first the Angels appeared to just one of us at a time but lately they have appeared to the entire army so I will call now and if they do not come I will go someplace alone. Miranda, Daniel please come to us," Matthew called out. Gasps were heard throughout the room as the two Angels materialized. Before Matthew could speak, Miranda faced the room full of people, many of whom were priests.

"I see the shock on your faces and I hear the words of your hearts," Miranda said. "One of the reasons that Daniel and I have appeared before you is so that you understand that the heavens hear and see everything. You do not need to be a prince to call upon us. The key is faith."

"And while we may not always materialize as this, we hear your prayers." Miranda looked at Daniel, who now spoke.

"We have been listening to your meetings, you are right to call upon us but before we discuss your research and answer your questions we have much to tell you. Raul, Simon and Matthew your families are fine, so please do not become fearful as I tell you what happened in Wetpr yesterday." The three princes now looked at each other with concern.

"You will receive letters from your families but the Enrops are yet a ways from here," Daniel continued. "While you have been gone, demons had filled the castle of Sudfad and Fort Salar with spies. The Lion exposed them all when the ground opened and the demons attacked. But the spies were replaced. Sudfad and Renya had been warned more than once so Sudfad has assigned Raphael and a man named Edward to act as commanding generals until Raul and Simon return home."

"What happened to Hoff?" Raul asked.

"I will get to him," Daniel said. "Misha, Archetenus, Emeral and Maxwell are acting majors. Sudfad was warned that Hoff had been contacted by demons and was on the crossroads of a decision, a decision he should not have made. When Sudfad relieved Hoff of his duties; he had Raphael and Edward escort Hoff to his home to retrieve his belongings."

"Hoff did not want the two men to enter his house and attacked them. During the fight Hoff was killed. Raphael and Edward found bloody writing on his bedroom walls, similar to what you found in Roch's hotel room in Taperia. While Raphael and Edward were searching Hoff's house, Sudfad had made an announcement to have the soldiers assemble so they could meet their new leaders."

"You should know," Miranda said that prior to Hoff's firing, your family and guests had a meeting that morning, they are working as a team, all of them. Simon, Raul that means your wives also because they don't know who can be trusted. At the morning meeting it was decided to secretly take uniforms and other items from the fort and give them to the Patronus at the Cicero headquarters, so the priests could infiltrate the army."

"Annabelle and Alexander drove a boca to the fort to get the uniforms."

"I am already getting nervous," said Simon.

"You may not like what you will hear but you should be proud of your faithful wife," Miranda said.

Now, Daniel addressed the group again. "Annabelle, Alexander, Koby, Bekka and others went to Hoff's house when they heard what had happened. All of these people were searching the house but only Annabelle, with the eye of an artist, discovered a very important piece of artwork under the paint of a mural."

"Raphael and Edward soon realized that Hoff was meant to be a distraction and they feared Sudfad was in danger. After Sudfad and his new commanders entered the fort; legions upon legions of demons appeared outside of the fort. The Lion exposed the faces of the demons that were disguised as soldiers and citizens of Salar. There was a battle within the walls of the fort and the demons were defeated."

"But while this was occurring," Daniel said. "The spies inside of the castle were exposed and a fight broke out between Renya, Vitomas, Vivian and the spies. Needless to say the spies were no match for those three powerful warriors," Daniel said.

"Vitomas is pregnant," Raul uttered in a whisper.

"Your baby daughter is just fine," Miranda said with a smile.

"We're having a girl?" Raul asked with a big smile. Miranda nodded.

"Annabelle and Alexander remained in Hoff's house as Annabelle tried to expose the picture that was hidden. Moloch himself came to the house to stop her." Simon stopped breathing when he heard this. "For those who may not know; Moloch is one of the Old Ones," Daniel continued. "Your wife remembered what you taught her Simon; that demons are empowered by fear. Annabelle gave Moloch a tongue lashing like he has never heard. She made him so angry he exposed his trap for the Sanuri, then Annabelle instantly called to us."

466

"Simon there is a reason we are telling you what happened; both you and Raul are loving and protective husbands but listen to Annabelle's words to us," Daniel said. "I told Annabelle to take her father and leave and she refused. Annabelle said her entire family has fought at our side except for her, then she reminded us that she too had made promises to The Great Ruler."

"Annabelle took my sword then asked Moloch if he was the demon that had been trying to kill her husband. She fought at our side. We did not allow her to be injured, then we sent her home. Annabelle worked all night to expose the artwork that Moloch was trying to hide." Now Daniel looked around the room into the faces of the men and women who were intently listening to him.

"The Great Ruler makes no mistakes," Daniel continued. "All of you who have made covenants with The Great Ruler, you have the wives, the husbands, the children you were meant to have ; to either support you or to fight with you. The Sanuri has told many of you that The Great Ruler sent you the perfect wives. I hope you realize by now that when The Great Ruler sends you gifts, miracles happen. It is just as important for your family members to uphold the covenants they have made as it is for you."

No one in the room uttered a word so Daniel continued. "I took Moloch and imprisoned him in The Abyss. The Lion immediately sent messages throughout the hell dimensions, but the messages may have made some believe that it was the Sanuri who defeated Moloch. As The Lion had planned it wasn't long before four more Old Ones appeared at the fort."

"Sudfad would not bow before them, then an army of Angels appeared. We fought alongside of The Lion and four more Old Ones were imprisoned by the end of the day. The Angels fought the demons as the people inside of the fort watched. With five Old Ones defeated there is an uproar within the hell dimensions as they war against each other for territory and power."

"Instead of us," Sorren said with a grin.

"This new situation will weaken the blood moon ceremonies," Miranda said. "The demons that were defeated are Baal, Moloch, Ipos, Bentra and Zede."

"Moloch and Ipos are responsible for the mysterious mausoleum and the Huta attacks against all of you and the Village of Gesmal."

"But the blood moon ceremonies will still take place?" Stephan asked.

"Yes but before Daniel goes into that there is something I want to add," Miranda said. "The men and women in this room have shown a level of courage and faith that has never before been seen in the World of Nunc. Many of you volunteered to descend into hell to overthrow tyrants and to save others. While we have been winning battles, this war is long from over and Sudfad needs to have an army as faithful as all of you. That is why we gave them a glimpse of heaven when so many were overwhelmed by the glimpses of hell."

Raphael and Edward had been given separate offices at the fort but they moved all the furniture into the largest office and shared it. The two acting generals had spent the morning and the early part of the afternoon touring the fort, just as they entered their office a private knocked at the door.

"Yes," Edward said.

"My Lords, Major Misha wants you to come at once, his team discovered something."

"Do you know what it is?" Raphael asked the young man.

"No, I was walking by when he yelled to me," the soldier said. "I will take you to him."

"We need to ask Sudfad if these have always been here," Misha said to Raphael and Edward when they came to a site at the very back of the fort where cut wood was stored. "We found four tunnels," Misha said. "None of the soldiers here knew about them."

"How were they concealed?" Edward asked as he looked at the four large holes in the ground.

"Just dirt," Misha said. "They go under the wall and into the trees back there. We walked through them but didn't find anything unusual in the forest."

"I'm surprised the demons didn't use them yesterday," Raphael said as he examined the opening to one of the tunnels.

"I know," Misha said. "That's why I think we should ask Sudfad. There might be a chance these are escape routes."

"Did you find any writing or symbols or anything?" Raphael asked.

"No, and I would have expected something like that if they were dug by demons," Misha added.

"They are so big a man can walk through them," Edward said. "Most tunnels I have seen have to be crawled through. This also means someone spent a lot of time working on them without being noticed. Now we post guards back here."

"You have done well with your research," Daniel said to the group. "Miranda and I did not know where the location was either. When you decided on the Waste Lands of Manod; the location was revealed to us."

"I don't mean to be disrespectful," Sorren said. "But why didn't you know?"

"We all have lessons to learn," Miranda said. "This is your world, we are here to help you and to guide you. Daniel and I have become very involved with you and perhaps we weren't shown the location so we would not overstep our place."

"Can you help us now?" Claudius asked.

"Yes," Daniel said smiling.

"It's good to know we have the right area but it is my understanding that the Waste Lands are massive," Claudius continued. "Do you know the exact location?"

"Yes," Daniel said. "And so does Neputa and his men. They crossed through the area on their way to the sea."

"Then it is in the southern part of the Waste Lands which is a long distance from the mountains," Neputa said.

"Will you help us get there in time to stop the ceremonies?" Claudius asked.

"We have just been waiting for that request," Miranda said. "Yes, most of you would die if you tried to cross the mountains in this area. Now what other questions do you have of us?"

"Will you help us stop the demons?" asked Simon.

"That's the other question we have been waiting for," Daniel said.

Raphael, Misha and Edward waited by the tunnels until the King arrived. "I have never seen these before," Sudfad said. "Misha reward your team for this find." As the men briefed Sudfad about the details of the tunnels a private ran up to the group. The soldier stopped and stood at attention when he saw the King.

"At ease," Edward said. "What is it?"

"Major Emeral has found something, she would like you to come," the soldier said.

The meeting lasted long into the night. Miranda and Daniel promised they would stay with the troops until after the blood moon ceremonies. For Raul, Simon and the others who had worked with Miranda and Daniel before they knew the danger must be great for the Angels to remain among them.

Raul and Simon shared a room at the headquarters. They both were sitting on their small beds drinking whiskey and talking. "I will be right back," Raul said while standing up. Raul walked around the headquarters until he found Miranda and Daniel talking with a group of Rualas.

"When you have a moment Miranda, I have a question for you," Raul said. Miranda stepped away from the group and walked to Raul. "I was wondering, well, I was wondering if it would be alright if we named our daughter Miranda, after you. I don't know if giving a child an Angel's name is inappropriate."

Miranda smiled, a smile that seemed to warm the area around her and Raul. "Daniel and I have taken names of your world because we cannot use our heavenly names. I would be very honored that you would name your daughter after me. But Raul naming your daughter after an Angel, she might not be a normal child."

Raul grinned, "Well if she took after you, Vitomas and I would be very proud." Miranda stepped forward and kissed Raul on the forehead.

Chapter XXXI
Desert of Thresdore

"It's Elan and Cassandra," Elan called through the door to Maxwell and Emeral's chambers. "We know it's late; were you sleeping?" Elan asked when Maxwell opened the door.

"No, actually we were working," Maxwell said. "Come in."

"Is something wrong?" Emeral asked when Elan and Cassandra walked into the sitting room.

"No," Elan said as he and Cassandra sat down. "We know you must think us crazy to be thinking about our wedding on the eve of another battle."

"Not at all," Emeral said with a warm smile.

"This is kind of hard to explain," Cassandra said. "You know how life here is so different from the Ice Caves and, well, Elan and I feel so much a part of your family that, oh this is going to sound so awful. But we really don't want our families to help plan the wedding. Emeral you know my mother; she is so overbearing and Elan and I both feel so close to you two."

"Do you want us to help plan your wedding?" Emeral asked.

"Yes," Cassandra said. "But we know how busy you are, especially now."

"Nonsense we would be happy to," said Emeral.

"And there is more," Elan said. "Emeral we would like you to be the maid of honor and Maxwell we would like you to be our best man."

"This is the morning of the third day before the blood moon ceremonies," Sudfad said at his morning meeting. "Tomorrow night is our party to flush out those working with the demons. How are the preparations going for the party?"

"We have the menu, and servers," Renya said as she stood up to address the group. "Ladies every one of you must go to the seamstress today for your final fittings. We have the food and spirits here that we will serve and Marie is checking everything closely for signs of tampering. We don't want any of the children brought to the party; besides the nurses we will have soldiers guarding them. The invitations have been sent and the banners posted. We are following all of our normal procedures so there will be no suspicions."

"All of us, I mean the women," Natasha said. "Have talked and we will take turns leaving the party to check on our babies, we would do that anyway."

"Gabriel where are you on the plyogram?" Sudfad asked.

"We have identified a substantial number of the symbols but I have not figured out the message," Gabriel answered. "But I do find it curious that we haven't found anything about the blood moon on it."

"Do you believe it to be authentic?" asked Sudfad.

"If it's not it is an amazing replica," replied Gabriel.

"As all of you know, I met with my military leaders before you joined us," Sudfad said. "Yesterday afternoon, Misha's team found four tunnels that led from the forest under the wall and into the back of the fort where the firewood is stored. While there were no symbols or writing in these tunnels they were huge; even Jared could walk in them without bending down which makes me believe they were intended for the Amulth to enter the fort. That area is now guarded around the clock. We all have found it curious that the demons did not use the tunnels when they attacked us recently."

"After the tunnels were discovered," Sudfad continued. "Emeral's group found a demonic altar in the back of one of the blacksmith sheds. It has been destroyed. When the Sanuri warned us about Hoff he said the man had not yet made his decision to work with the demons, which means there are others who perhaps have not yet been identified, so we need to be diligent. Which is why I also have soldiers guarding the woodshed that contains the plyogram."

"Sudfad I wish we could find a better place to study that thing," Gabriel said.

"Well, you can certainly put it in one of the rooms of the castle if you think it is safe to bring in."

"Let me work on it more today," Gabriel said. "I really don't want it out there the night of the party."

"I understand your concerns," Sudfad said. "Now speaking of the party, while you will all appear as guests you will also be policing the grounds. As always there will be soldiers stationed everywhere but I don't trust that we have identified all the spies."

"Now on a second note, I would like to discuss something with all of you. I asked many of you to assume positions in my military because of the extreme threat to our kingdom. I had to have officers I could trust and not one of you waivered at my offer. All of you have worked extremely hard and not one report has been late, which I find astounding. I am extremely pleased with your performances especially in light that none of you had time to be trained in our procedures."

"Archetenus I originally offered you a position of captain, you will retain the rank of major. Raphael and Edward, my sons are often absent because they have been working on many missions. Edward I know you work for King Tobias but I would like you to consider working for me. You can work with Gabriel's team and maintain a position of acting commanding general."

"Raphael I am making you the same offer. And Gabriel I apologize that I did not discuss this with you first but of course your team will have priority. As for Misha, Maxwell and Emeral if you would like to maintain your positions as majors they are yours. Talk among yourselves I don't expect any answers now."

"May I say something?" Emeral said as she stood up. "Sudfad as you know all of our people are trained as warriors. I truly did not realize that I was the only woman in your military until one of the soldiers said something. He was not disrespectful he simply wanted to clarify how he should address me. Your men have followed my orders without dissent; which I find rather surprising."

As Emeral spoke she saw that all of the women in the room were grinning. "Have you ever considered having female soldiers?" Sudfad was visibly surprised at Emeral's suggestion. "Every Ruala women is a warrior in our tribe as they are in Vivian's tribe and the tribe of the Nordes. Every woman in this room is a warrior. Each person brings strengths and weaknesses to an organization and the three tribes I just mentioned are known for their strength and ferocity because the men and women work together. It is just an idea," Emeral said.

Renya stood up and walked over and kissed Emeral on the cheek. "Why did I know that would happen?" Sudfad asked with a grin.

Sampson had been hiding in the trees surrounding the monastery at Rubar for almost twenty minutes. He had not seen anyone on the grounds, which he found curious. He stealthily made his way to the main building of the complex because he was told that the items he needed were on display outside of the main room of worship. Sampson walked into the large well-lit hall without seeing a single person; he was beginning to suspect a trap when he heard someone walking. Sampson hid in the shadows as he watched a young priest enter the room of worship.

Sampson ran up and grabbed the priest from behind, holding a knife to the priest's throat. "I need you to put some things in a bag for me," Sampson growled.

"What sort of things?" the priest asked fearfully.

Sampson had Hecate's list in his hand and shoved it at the priest. "I can't read it," the priest said so Sampson let go of the man. The priest read the list and without turning and looking at his attacker he said, "But I cannot give you these things they are not mine to give."

"Then I will kill you," Sampson snapped.

"That is your choice," the replied priest.

"There is a school across the courtyard," said Sampson. "I will kill the children if you do not help me."

The priest hesitated. "Very well," he said fearfully. "May The Great Ruler be with us all." The priest gathered the items on the list and put them inside of the saddlebags and sacks that Sampson had brought into the building. Sampson pushed the priest into a wall and ran out the door towards the trees.

"You were pretty convincing," Miranda said to Daniel as she materialized in the hall. "He believed it." Daniel waved his hand and the real holy vessels appeared in their normal areas for display.

"We just have to make sure he can make it back to Hecate without interruptions," said Daniel.

"Of course," the Sanuri said to himself as he realized the demons he was following were entering tunnels underneath the Vandrew Mountain Range which separated the Waste Lands of Manod from Kingdoms of Stordt and Ryed. "No one would look in the Waste Lands."

After breakfast the troops at the Nora Headquarters of the Patronus were writing letters and packing. Mid-morning they were going to assemble for their journey to the Waste Lands of Manod. Neputa and his men were completing maps of the Waste Lands. Claudius ordered the Shettees to take the lead once the Angels transported the army over the mountains; since the Shettees were familiar with the area. Fortunately for the troops small flocks of Enrops kept arriving during the morning hours bringing mail; for some of the soldiers it would be their last contact with loved ones.

An hour before the planned departure a large flock of Enrops landed at the Nora Headquarters. These great birds carried mail from the Shettee refugees living in the Ice Caves to their husbands, sons and brothers who had been rescued from the prisons of Ogg.

Princess Ibula had taken the names of every one of the warriors rescued back to the Ice Caves. While many of the refugees were heartbroken to learn their loved ones were not among those rescued, at least they now had closure and all rejoiced for the lives that were saved.

476

Thedes knew what his wife was planning but he did not tell Neputa and the others because he wanted them to be surprised.

For warriors far from home, a letter can be the cord that connects them to their families, their homes and sometimes their sanity. A letter can give them hope, strength and purpose. But for these Shettee warriors who had so long ago lost hope of ever seeing their loved ones, the mountain of letters that now arrived at the headquarters would bring these fierce warriors to tears. Thedes collected the letters and organized them, then he called a meeting.

Everyone who entered the meeting room believed they were going to cover last minute items before their departure; but they were surprised when Thedes, not Claudius called the meeting to order. "I would like my brothers Raul and Simon to join me in the front," Thedes said then he addressed the group. "Prince Raul and Prince Simon are my human brothers."

"My Shettee brothers have postponed the reunions with their families to help us on this very important mission. So my wonderful wife Ibula sent a little of your families here." Thedes bent down and picked up two huge stacks of letters, handing one to Raul and the other to Simon. "Would you please hand these out?" Both Raul and Simon got big smiles on their faces.

"Ibula had a meeting with all of our people and told them about your journey and your rescue," Thedes continued. "And she told them of the difficult decisions you made to delay your reunion with your families. Ibula met personally with each one of your families and asked them to send you something to ease the burdens of your decisions."

The room was silent as everyone watched the Shettee warriors opening their letters. Some warriors could not read the words because of the tears in their eyes and others were shaking so badly they had difficulty opening their small packages. The Shettees too did not speak, for most of them were too overwhelmed to utter words.

Claudius and his army suddenly found themselves in the Desert of Thresdore which was located on the eastern half of the Waste Lands of Manod.

The army was east of the Hills of Thermant and about a four days ride north of the southern coast of the Schenomi Sea. The last thing any of them remembered was forming a group around the Nora Headquarters of the Patronus. Horses and equipment were transported with the soldiers.

"Is everyone accounted for?" Claudius asked of his leaders and waited for them to count their soldiers.

"Does anyone remember what happened?" Claudius asked as his leaders returned to him.

"I just remember Miranda and Daniel talking," Raul said. "Then we were here. From the looks of the sun I don't think we even lost any time."

Neputa gathered his men and they studied their surroundings and a map they had drawn earlier. Claudius and the other leaders joined them. "We believe we are here," Neputa indicated on the map. "Daniel said we had to concentrate on these last three hills on the western side of the desert. Claudius sent Enrops to inspect the hills for any openings or signs of demonic activity.

"We are really out in the open here," Stephan said with disdain. "We need to find a better location."

"Other than the hills, there's nothing but cactus as far as you can see," said Sorren.

"Then we are going to have to hide in the hills," Stephan said.

Prince Gael ordered Ruala warriors to fly over the area as the Enrops searched the three hills.

Sampson was riding hard, back to Hecate's lair. He was concerned that he might not make Raum's deadline. Sampson was not as concerned for his own welfare as he was for Hecate's. Proud that he had accomplished his mission, Sampson also had a nagging feeling that something was not right. It was as if a voice in his head was warning him but Sampson couldn't understand exactly what the voice was saying.

Sampson stopped at another farm and stole a horse and food. He left his exhausted horse with the farmer. Suddenly Sampson thought to himself, "This is too easy, how can this be so easy?" He stopped his horse and dismounted. He took all of the items he and stolen and put them on the ground. Sampson carefully inspected each piece. They looked genuine enough. Sampson stood up and repacked the items as he dismissed his own misgivings. "I must just be tired," he said out loud to himself. "How would anyone even know I was going to the monastery to steal these things?"

"All three of those hills have openings into them, lots of openings like you see in areas where people live in caves," One of the Enrops reported back to Claudius. "None of the hills have vegetation growing on them, which could be a sign of the demons or just the desert."

"Did you see anything suspicious at all?" Sorren asked.

"No but we did not fly into every cave opening."

"We need to hide," Claudius said. "Go back and check out some of those caves." As the flocks of Enrops turned back towards the hills, several Ruala warriors landed. "This is really open terrain," Ratri said. "We didn't see anything suspicious, so whatever we are dealing with must be in the hills."

"Think about it Orbus," Hecate said suggestively as she and Orbus lay in her bed. "We could combine our forces and rule a domain."

"I rather like my life the way it is now," Orbus said and kissed her neck.

"But we wouldn't have to take orders from anyone; we would be giving the orders."

"It is a very dangerous thing you are proposing; first we would have to raise an army," Orbus said. "The wars have already begun; while allegiances keep changing some demons were well prepared for a fight of power. We would be entering late in the game."

"Perhaps we let them battle it out then we come in fresh and take out the winners."

Claudius as well as the others wanted to get their army out of sight because they wanted their attack against the demons to be a surprise. Three Enrops flew to Claudius. "The others are still investigating but it appears those caves were homes for people at one time and they are all connected by tunnels," one of the giant birds said.

"An ancient tribe of cave dwellers must have lived there," Simon said. "Is there room for the horses?"

"Yes," the bird said. "Also we heard water running inside of the hill closest to you."

"And there are no signs of demons?" Claudius asked suspiciously.

"Not yet," the bird replied.

"Perhaps I misunderstood the Angels," Claudius said then he mounted his horse and led the troops towards the closest hill.

After the Angels transported Claudius' army from the Patronus headquarters, Generals Colter and Orlan started their return to Fort Nora. The generals assigned one thousand of their soldiers to stay with the Patronus priests. Orlan was twice Colter's age but both men had a great deal of battle experience. Colter was the primary general at the fort and Orlan was assigned to assist Colter with his duties. Colter and Orlan respected and liked each other and forged a strong team.

On this day as they led troops back to the fort both men had a sense of foreboding which they did not share with each other. Finally Orlan looked over at Colter, who was riding beside him and said in a low voice, "My gut is telling me something just isn't right."

"I have been feeling the same way," Colter said and stopped the troops. "I can't explain it but we need to go back."

480

"We are going to need light in those caves," Claudius said as they rode westward. "But I don't know what we are going to burn; there is no wood around here." Claudius and Sorren rode up to the first cave, while the others stayed some yards back. Both men stopped and stared when they saw a campfire burning and blazing torches attached to the stone walls.

"It wasn't like that before," the Enrop said that was flying over the heads of the two men.

"Miranda, Daniel if you did this for us, thank you; if not I will be leading my men into a trap," Claudius said out loud.

"It is not a trap." Daniel's voice was heard by both Sorren and Claudius.

Sorren turned and yelled, "Leaders first, the Angels are lighting the caves for us." Matthew, Stephan, Thaos, Gael, Neputa, Lakin, Raul, Simon and General Hurch, inspected the caves and determined the areas for their troops. The warriors found cool relief inside of the caves from the hot midday sun. Once everyone was settled inside the caves, teams of soldiers were sent to explore the connecting tunnels.

The cave that Claudius chose had an unobstructed view of the land to the east, north and south. "Before we came here, I was thinking the blood moon ceremonies would be held out in the open, under the moon," Sorren said. "But there is nothing out here, no altars or fire pits, not even any sign of activity. So the ceremonies must be inside of the hills."

"My men searched the top of the hills," Lakin said. "There are no openings or signs of disturbance."

"Wouldn't you think this would be big doings for the demons?" Thaos asked. "I mean in our world when there is a major celebration of any kind, people come from all over and platforms, tables and the such are set up."

"Thaos is right," Simon said.

"So assuming Hutas, demons and maybe the Insidiae are attending this thing, they must be travelling through underground tunnels that probably lead into one of these hills."

"If the Hutas are bringing prisoners here, I will bet there is a tunnel door on the Stordt side of those mountains," Raul said. "Who knows how the demons get here but let's say members of the Insidiae come; they aren't going to cross those mountains. I'll bet if we look we will find tunnel doors on the border of the Waste Lands."

Colter was operating on his instincts alone, or so he thought; he was unaware of how the heavens work. Colter and Orlan turned two thousand troops around and raced back to the Patronus headquarters. Both men became more and more anxious as they rode; their fears were confirmed within minutes when they saw plumes of black smoke rising in the sky. "Sound the horn!" Colter ordered. The sergeant, who had the honor to carry the Horn of Cass, quickly grabbed his instrument and blew the notes that would let his comrades know they were not alone.

It was not the Hutas attacking the Patronus headquarters as Colter and Orlan expected but an army of Amulth. "What the hell are those things?" Orlan yelled.

"Demons," Colter yelled back. "The question is; are they the kind we can kill?" Colter's question was answered as they neared the battleground and saw dead bodies of the demons.

"I'm going left," Orlan yelled and he and one thousand of the troops broke away from the main body of troops. Colter led the remainder of the soldiers to the right; they planned to surround the beasts. The demons were on foot and focused on the buildings of the headquarters.

Both General Orlan and General Colter led their troops into the midst of the demons without slowing down. With swords and battleaxes drawn the soldiers hacked and stabbed the demons, while their horses were trampling them.

The Amulth, the demonic foot soldiers that the Insidiae paid powerful demons to create, were made quite literally from the waste of hell.

The Insidiae wanted soldiers that did not have the freedom of choice as had the humans intended to be demonic vessels. These large, powerful monsters were created to follow orders without question.

The Amulth were not created for independent thinking; they could not think quickly on their feet and adapt to changes in their surrounds. The Amulth maintained their focus on their original target, the men and women inside of the Patronus headquarters. The attack by the demons would have been a massacre had Colter not heeded that voice inside; the voice so many others dismiss.

The dark lord Trebonus screamed with rage as he watched the battle through the eyes of a raven. "Turn around and fight you fools," he yelled over and over as he watched the fierce soldiers of Wetpr destroying the army that Trebonus paid his fortune to create. Trebonus had planned to obtain the favor of the Old Ones by supplying priests to be sacrificed at the blood moon ceremonies. Suddenly Trebonus' view of the battle went black as his ravens mysteriously fell dead to the ground.

"Come in," Sudfad called as there was a knock at the door of his study.

"My Lord," the young sergeant said. "There is a warlock here to see you. I would not allow him inside of the castle; he is in the front courtyard."

"A warlock," Sudfad repeated with amazement. "Did he say his name?"

"His name is Erebus and he wants to speak with you and High Priest Gabriel."

"Bring him in here then go get Gabriel," Sudfad said. Within moments Erebus entered the study. He always had a manner of walking which made him appear to be gliding across the floor; this movement was emphasized by the long red robe that Erebus wore.

"Please have a seat," Sudfad said as he closed the door. "Gabriel will be here shortly. Would you like a drink?"

"Yes," Erebus said as he stared at Sudfad, trying to size him up. Suddenly there was a knock on the door but before Sudfad could answer Vivian burst into the room."

"Sudfad are you alright?" Vivian asked but she never took her eyes off Erebus.

"Every time I come for a visit this young woman tries to kill me," Erebus said with a laugh. "Perhaps one of these days I will let her."

"I am alright Vivian," Sudfad said and grinned. "Erebus has come to speak with me and Gabriel. At lunch didn't you say you were expecting Raphael to come back here this afternoon?"

"Yes, for the fittings."

"Send him in here first," Sudfad said and poured a glass of whiskey for Erebus.

Vivian turned and almost bumped into Gabriel who was entering the study. "I just wanted to make sure Sudfad was alright," Vivian said and walked out of the room.

"We have had many personal attacks against my family as of late," Sudfad explained.

"I know," Erebus replied. "That is partly why I am here."

"They came out of nowhere," High Priest Rueben said to Generals Colter and Orlan. "They must have been waiting until all of you left before they attacked." Rueben wiped blood from his forehead with a towel as he spoke. "Why did you come back?"

"Not sure," Colter said with a grin. "Orlan and I both had bad feelings. Guess we would have felt pretty stupid riding in here if nothing was wrong."

"Well thank The Great Ruler you came," said Rueben.

"Those demons are called Amulth," Colter explained. "Raul told me the Insidiae pay to have them made by other demons; so you know who was behind this attack."

"I wonder if they are trying to get us out of the way before the blood moon ceremonies," Rueben said.

"Or they wanted to make you part of the ceremony," Orlan said sarcastically.

Sudfad returned to his chair behind his desk and looked at Erebus. "Gabriel and I have spoken but I would like to hear from you why you are helping us."

Erebus smiled. "It is simple we have the same enemy. Sudfad like you I am a very wealthy and powerful man but the only thing that ever really mattered to me was my wife Sophie. I hold the Insidiae responsible for her horrible death. The only people who tried to help her were Gabriel and his team and if I would have listened to them; well perhaps Sophie would still be alive," Erebus paused. "Basically I live now only to enact my revenge upon the Insidiae."

Sudfad stared at Erebus then said, "Very well, I believe you."

"Since I have nothing but time on my hands I, shall I say I nose around a great deal? And while there is always fear and chaos in the underworlds, some truly unusual things are happening. I am going to tell you what I have been hearing. I am not asking you to confirm or deny the rumors because honestly it makes no difference to me," Erebus said then took a sip of his whiskey.

"I am sure you have heard of the Prophesy of The Seven Sons and the term Keepers of the Scrolls," Erebus said. Neither Sudfad nor Gabriel spoke. "There are many demons and dark lords who believe that your family and these two high priests fulfill those roles, which is why the attacks are increasing on your families."

"So far you haven't told us anything we don't already know," said Sudfad.

"I have no doubt," Erebus said with a grin. "Until recent events there were two reasons the dark worlds believed you to be the ones prophesies speak of, one because the Sanuri lives among you and two because you are good men. Good men stand out from the rest."

"But after the battle in Taperia, where Sophie was killed and Ahriman destroyed; the demons and dark lords have taken to the ancient texts to try and figure out what is happening. Angels have been fighting with your army, the Rualas and the Army of Lentz and as a consequence dark lords and very powerful demons are falling. Then that human army descended into the sea and destroyed Ogg; which by the way, bravo! Then that very same army descends into Baal's hell region and humiliates him and lives to tell of it. You can imagine the fear and paranoia this has caused among the demons."

"It is my understanding that the demons have a text called Infineotous," Erebus explained. "It is not written in a scroll or book but on stone. It is hidden within a plyogram. The original text was cast upon the demons when they first laid their dirty little hands on this world. Some say it was sent by The Great Ruler and His Angels. Mind you I have never seen it nor do I know where it is but I do know that every demon in the hell regions is trying to get their hands on it."

"Do you know what it says?" asked Gabriel.

"I don't think anyone really knows what it says," Erebus responded. "I have heard some say it holds the balance of power between good and evil in this world. Others have said it foretells in detail the fall of the demons from this world. But even if it says nothing at all, demons are waging wars to get it because they think it will give them the power to stop all of you." As Erebus spoke both Sudfad and Gabriel wondered if the plyogram they had was a copy of the Infineotous.

"Now for more bad news," Erebus said then took another sip of his whiskey. "Like humans, demons are greedy and power hungry. Every time a powerful demon falls, wars are waged to conquer their domains. Five Old Ones falling on the eve of the blood moon ceremonies has torn the underworlds apart which I find humorous. But the Old Ones are so arrogant that they never see what is under their noses. Just before Sophie died she was telling me about the Grand Masters, do you know who they are?"

"They are supposed to be the original humans who called demons to this world," Gabriel said. "Without their permission the demons would never have been able to enter, am I correct?"

"Yes," Erebus continued. "Before Sophie was murdered we were talking about going to the Grand Masters for help. She wanted to get out of the Insidiae but all members take a blood oath and death is the only thing that gets them out of the organization. The Insidiae are a large, well organized group with levels of hierarchy like the military."

"The Insidiae fear the Grand Masters, even more so than some of the Old Ones. The Grand Masters are said to live among the humans but no one knows their true identities. There is one named Emeric, who looks like a young man and apparently gives an entirely new meaning to evil, he and his sister Banaka have been stirring up the Old Ones and the underworld even more than your armies and Angels."

"And you know this is true?" Sudfad asked.

"I have witnessed the results of their actions, which I found curious so I started looking into them. From what I have been able to gather I believe they are doing these things so that the Old Ones are distracted because Emeric is making deals with very powerful demons from other worlds. Other demons have been trying to take over territory in this world for a long time but the united efforts of the Old Ones prevent them."

"Things are changing. Which brings me back to you; I don't know if you realize that demons can travel to hell regions on other worlds and news about what has been happening on Nunc is the talk of the town. If you are powerful enough to destroy the Old Ones here, you pose a threat to any demon considering invading this world."

Erebus continued, "I believe Emeric and Banaka are going to gain even more wealth and power by betraying the Old Ones to other demonic war lords. Your interference in the dark worlds here is costing them money. If I were you I would try to find out as much about Emeric and Banaka as I could. I have never seen either of them but I have descriptions. I don't know if you realize that a human retains the form and appearance they had at the moment they sold their soul to a demon. Apparently Emeric and Banaka were both in their teens at the time. Emeric is said to have a slight frame, short brown hair and green eyes. His sister is slender with long black hair and green eyes."

"And now for my gift to Gabriel for trying to save Sophie. The Grand Masters were given immortality by the Old Ones but they never completed the trials required to become a demon, so they can be killed, but only by cutting off their heads," Erebus said.

Claudius and his men searched the caves and tunnels of the hill, they had taken shelter in. They found no writings or symbolic drawings nor did they find any tunnels that led to an area set up for the ceremonies. Claudius called a meeting to get the results of the searches.

"Well we have eliminated this hill," Claudius said after hearing the reports of his leaders. "Now we will start on the other two. We might as well start on the one closest to us, unless someone has a better idea."

"I'm inclined to wait until tomorrow to search them," Simon said. "Let the men sleep now, then wake them tonight. There is a full moon; perhaps we can get some clues if we watch this area at night."

"I actually like that idea," said Sorren.

"Do any of you remember when Zoya had that vision about the mausoleum?" Raul asked. "That was the vision that Hannah's mother was giving to Zoya. Well, Zoya also had a vision of a temple inside of a mountain and the door would be revealed if the moon light hit a rock formation a certain way."

"I believe she thought that was in Ryed," Sorren said. "I was there, Zoya said there did not appear to be an opening in the mountain but there was a rock formation that is tall and thin and stands by itself hundreds of yards from the mountain."
"Then closer to the mountain is another rock formation that looks like an archway. Zoya says when the moon is full as it comes up it will hit the lone rock and a beam will shoot through the archway and show you the door."

"I will send warriors out now to look for these formations," Gael said.

"Wait," Claudius said. "Let's send Enrops just in case there are eyes watching."

488

Raphael knocked on the door to Sudfad's study then entered; he extended his hand to Erebus. As they shook hands Erebus said with a grin, "Your little friend wanted to kill me again."

"She's my wife now," Raphael said smiling.

"I hope things work out for you," Erebus said with a sadness to his voice.

Gabriel looked at Raphael, "Erebus has brought us some interesting information which I will tell you later so he does not have to repeat everything." Then Gabriel turned to Erebus. "I am curious, you know we are being watched and yet you come here in your brightly colored robe during the day when anyone can see you. You know you are putting yourself in great danger, why?"

Erebus smiled. "After Sophie was killed I took to the bottle and became a sloppy drunk; I could not drink enough to dull my pain. In a fit of drunken rage I went after some of the Insidiae and they almost killed me."

"Gabriel I told you about that because I stopped to see you on my return to Ryed. I learned my lesson; if I truly want revenge I had to change my ways. I drink little now. I have spent the last many months working diligently to increase my powers. It is much easier for the Insidiae to find me than for me to track them down. So yes, I am deliberately putting a target on my back."

"It sounds like you are on a death mission," Sudfad said.

"I died when Sophie did but my body has no rest. I feel like nothing more than a shadow in this world. Dying would be a gift but I am going to take as many Insidiae with me as I can before I go."

Chapter XXXII
Hills of Thermant

Orbus and Hecate spent the day and now into the evening alternating between making passionate love and discussing Hecate's ideas about joining the power struggle for a hell domain.

"So do you know what Raum is going to do with the items he sent your husband after?" asked Orbus.

"No, I do not have the relationship with Raum that I did with Ahriman, Raum does not confide in me." Hecate said. "But they are powerful objects."

"So that is why Sampson has not completed his trials?" Orbus asked. "So he could handle the holy objects?"

"I got him out of Baal's domain before those damn humans could kill him. This other opportunity came up later."

"There are advantages to having humans working for you," Orbus said with a grin.

"That is what I have been telling you," Hecate said and kissed her lover.

"But tell me woman, if I go along with your plans does that mean you have chosen me over Sampson?"

"I am still choosing," Hecate said suggestively.

Claudius and his men lay in wait in the cold desert night. Enrops had discovered the two rock formations that Zoya had described in a vision. These formations were north of the hill that this army had taken shelter in. There were two hills in between the rock formations and Claudius' hide out. Before transporting Claudius' army into the Waste Lands of Manod, Miranda and Daniel instructed them to focus their energies on the last three hills in a ridgeline made up by the Hills of Thermant. From the north, the hill that was the closest to the rock formations was the first of these three hills.

The army left their horses inside of their hideouts, this night Claudius' men were trying to get information because the Angels had told them not to attack the demons until the blood moon ceremonies started. "It's amazing how cold the desert gets at night," Simon whispered to Matthew as the two men hid behind a large rock on the very top of the second hill.

The moon had been in the sky for over two hours. Matthew grabbed Simon's forearm as they saw a beam of light shoot out from the rock formation that looked like an archway. From their hiding place, Simon and Matthew could not see where the beam struck on the north side of the hill in front of them.

Claudius and Sorren saw perfectly where the beam struck; a door appeared but did not open. Ruala warriors were in hiding on top of this hill. Everyone waited anxiously but the door did not open. Within moments the image of the door disappeared and the army spent a very cold night in the desert.

Everyone in the castle of Sudfad rose hours before dawn. For this night would be the party where they hoped to expose some of their enemies and weaken the blood moon ceremonies that would be held the following evening. Sudfad mentioned several times that he was concerned because he had not heard from the Sanuri. Every night Petra included the Sanuri in his prayers, this week Renya and Sudfad did also.

Sudfad did not feel as comfortable around Erebus as did Gabriel and Raphael who had dealt with the sorcerer before. The two high priests viewed Erebus' arrival at the castle as more of a gift than a threat but that did not mean they completely trusted him. The prior day, Gabriel had talked Erebus out of making a public appearance at one of the hotels in Salar and set him up for the night in one of the guest cottages on the royal grounds. Well before the sun was up, Queen Renya was knocking on the door to Erebus' cottage. The sorcerer was more than surprised when he saw the Queen and Hannah standing on his doorstep.

"Please come in," Erebus said politely. "Is anything wrong?"

"No," Renya said as they walked through the door.

"Erebus I don't know if you remember me from Taperia," Hannah said. "But I am Gabriel's wife and this is Queen Renya of Wetpr."

"Of course," Erebus said. "Actually I know who both of you are. If you will give me a few minutes I will make some coffee."

"That is not necessary," Renya said as she walked close to Erebus and looked up into his eyes. Then she smiled and took a seat at the table. "I won't beat around the bush," Renya said. "First of all our husbands do not know we are here. I have never met a sorcerer before and wanted to see you for myself."

Erebus laughed and sat down with the two women at the kitchen table. "First of all My Lady, I am willing to bet you have met sorcerers before but you were not aware of it. While you might say we are not on the same team, you are not my enemies and I see no need for disguises."

"I am glad to hear you say that," Renya said with authority. "While we are a family of warriors, currently our home is filled with children, many of whom are my grandbabies. I want to know if you are a threat to them."

"My Lady," Erebus said with indignation. "I have never hurt a child in my life nor do I intend to. If you have some test I must take to prove this to you, show me."

"Renya did not mean to insult you," Hannah said soothingly. "There have been so many threats against our families that we have cause for concern."

The muscles in Erebus' face relaxed. "I understand, in your place I would do the same thing."

"I will admit you are not as I expected," said Renya.

"I am a practitioner of dark magics," Erebus explained. "While I talk to the dark worlds and monitor them, I am not a demon or a dark lord. Nor have I sold my soul to any demon. I have made a great deal of money because people usually hire me to obtain information for them. Information they can get no other way."

"But you worked for Roch, did you not?" Renya asked.

"It may have appeared that way," Erebus said. "I was hired by Cerephus to help him overthrow Roch. Cerephus had to get me close to Roch, so he talked Roch into hiring me to help him find a cure for the infliction The Lion of The Great Ruler had put upon him. I despised Roch as a man and I curse him as the demon that took my wife from me."

"I find myself believing you," Renya said. "If you are not as you portray yourself, I will personally hold you accountable."

"I am here for revenge," Erebus said. "I have not tried to hide that fact but it is not against any of you. I am going to tell you something that I have not talked of before. I know you have reasons to hate my wife Sophie and good reasons I might add but I would like you to understand the entire story."

"Sophie and I fell in love when we were little more than children. Unbeknownst to either of us at the time, her brother Meekos was a dark lord and a member of the Insidiae. He was jealous of the attention that Sophie gave to me and devised a scheme to separate us. He told us each that the other had found someone else. Now I am giving you the short version, but Meekos was very manipulative and his scheme worked."

Erebus continued, "Sophie and I lived the remainder of our lives as lonely and broken people. Sophie more than me became consumed with anger and joined her brother in the Insidiae. When Cerephus brought me to Roch's castle that was the first time Sophie and I had seen each other for decades. Our love had never died and when we spoke we realized that Meekos had tricked us and denied us the lives we wanted."

"Sophie started to change back to the woman I fell in love with and she tried to get out of the Insidiae. But that organization demands a blood oath; only death would get her out. We were in Taperia trying to figure out how to get her out of that organization when Roch transformed into a demon."

Erebus paused, "Sophie and I had invested all we were into the darkness of this world and when we finally needed help everything that we were connected to, betrayed us. Of all things, it was Gabriel's team, people who work for The Great Ruler who tried to come to our aid. Who would ever imagine such a thing?"

"I have since been in Gabriel's home and now yours and been treated with kindness and respect." Erebus paused again. "Although trust is an issue for all of us, as it should be because we represent two different worlds. I have since released my allegiances to many things, mind you that does not mean I am a follower of The Great Ruler. But I had a debit I had to pay to Gabriel."

Renya stared at Erebus as he spoke; she was trying to read him. "Erebus as you told our husbands we have common enemies. I have an idea that might mutually benefit us but I should speak to Sudfad before I ask you. Please join us in the castle for breakfast; it will be served at six."

"Thank you," Erebus said with surprise and stood up as the Queen and Hannah now stood and turned to leave.

"You did what!" Sudfad said loudly at the morning meeting, which on this day was being held before breakfast.

"Now dear," Renya said calmly. "I wanted to meet the man for myself and Hannah escorted me. I invited him to join us for breakfast."

"What!" Sudfad said and he was visibly angry.

"Sudfad you have every reason to be angry but our visit took a very different path than I had imagined. I was honest with him; I told Erebus I was concerned that he might be a threat to the children. He was initially insulted but he ended up telling us about his and Sophie's lives and how they made the choices they did."

Hannah looked at Vitomas and Annabelle, "I know you have every right to hate Sophie, but the story is rather sad."

"Sudfad and the rest of you," Renya said as she looked at the others in the study. "I am not saying we should suddenly trust this man, I am proposing that we work with him. Gabriel he does seem sincere in his allegiance to you."

"What are you thinking?" Raphael asked.

"I think we should invite him to the party tonight," Renya explained. "He could help us identify members of the Insidiae and think of it. We have people spying on us all of the time; won't it cause confusion when they see Erebus is our guest? The only reason we are having this party is to expose our enemies; I believe Erebus could be a great help with that."

"Sudfad, Renya has a good idea," Gabriel said. Sudfad looked at both Gabriel and Renya and did not speak.

"Let's try this," Hannah offered. "He is coming for breakfast, if anyone feels that he is more of a threat than we feel he is, well, then we won't invite him."

"I will agree to that," Sudfad said. It was obvious to everyone that Sudfad was not happy that Renya and Hannah had visited Erebus.

"Sudfad, I did plan to talk to Erebus later to get information about the Teivel Clan in Ryed," Gabriel said hoping the information would calm Sudfad.

"The reason I am so angry," Sudfad said through clenched teeth. "Is that we know little of this man, other than he is a sorcerer and worked for Roch. Renya and Hannah you could have been killed or greatly injured and none of us would have been able to come to your aid because we didn't know where you were. I know you are both capable women but you were really taking a chance here."

"You are right," Renya said. "I am the one responsible for the visit. But Erebus did not work for Roch; he was hired by Cerephus to assist him in overthrowing Roch. Why don't you let us tell you what Erebus told us?"

Marie led Erebus to the dining room for breakfast; she had a disapproving look on her face that caused many to smile. As soon as Erebus entered the room all of the children got up from their table and ran to him, touching his unusual robe. Erebus stopped walking and allowed the children their indulgence. "Mister, why are you wearing a dress?" Christopher asked sincerely, which made everyone including Erebus laugh.

"It's not a dress it is a robe," said Erebus.

"The Sanuri wears a robe," Christopher continued. "But his is really different."

"I am sure it is," Erebus said.

"What is this?" Nicholas asked as he pointed to an embroidered symbol on the robe. But before Erebus could answer Nicholas turned to Gabriel. "Papa you were drawing this same picture." Gabriel stood up and walked over to Erebus.

"I have been trying to translate something," Gabriel said as he looked closely at the many embroidered symbols that covered the robe. "After breakfast would you mind explaining what these symbols mean?"

"Of course," Erebus said. "I can stay that long."

"Actually we wanted to talk to you about staying here a little longer," Sudfad said. "But we can meet after breakfast, when the children are not with us."

Erebus sat down and looked at the faces around the table, "I recognize many of you from Taperia but I didn't get all of your names."

Just before sunrise, Claudius' army returned to their caves. A flock of Enrops continued to search the area as the men and women ate breakfast and got a few hours of sleep. No one had seen or heard anything of significance other than the beam of moonlight revealing the door in the mountain.

They had only slept for a couple of hours when Raul suddenly woke up; he grabbed his knife and jumped to his feet. "Sanuri when did you get here?" Raul asked with relief.

"You sensed me as soon as I arrived," the Sanuri said with a weary smile. "You wouldn't have any coffee left would you?"

"I'll make a fresh pot," Raul said. "Are you hungry?"

"Starving," the Sanuri replied.

Within moments every person in that cave was awake. "Oh, we are so glad to see you," Sorren said as he stood up and walked over to the Sanuri to shake his hand.

"You have done well," the Sanuri said. "The Lion has told me of your feats and your battles. The Angels were very pleased when you figured out the location of the ceremonies."

"Well we still don't know exactly," Claudius said. "But we found those rock formations that Zoya told you about in a vision. They face the north side of the hill that is two hills north of this one. Last night for just a moment the door to the hill was exposed. We have found nothing else, and the door was only revealed to us for an instant."

"You found more than you know," the Sanuri said. "I have been following demons from Wetpr trying to figure out where they are hiding their victims for sacrifice. It was not until yesterday that I realized the ceremonies would be held here. The demons have been travelling in a series of underground tunnels. I believe the demons have been preparing for this for a long time."

"Father sent us a letter telling about the trick you played on the demons," Simon said. "Do they still believe they have Natasha and Lila?"

"Yes. I was able to follow them to the base of the hill where you saw the door. But that hill is protected by strong magics and I could no longer see them. That is when I sensed your presence here."

"So you just got done following the demons?" Matthew asked.

"Moments before I came here. The Enrops told me which cave you were in."

"Needless to say we have a lot of questions," said Sorren.

"I may not have the answers you seek; I too am struggling with this."

"Daniel and Miranda said they didn't know the ceremonies would take place in the Waste Lands until we came up with the idea," Stephan said.

"How could they not know something that important?"

"I don't have an answer for you," the Sanuri replied.

"They said it was because they have become too close to us," Thaos said. "So I am assuming finding this location and stopping the ceremonies is some kind of test for us."

"I believe the same thing although I have not been told that," the Sanuri said. "We all have our journeys to take."

"Well if we don't figure out this journey a lot of people are going to be killed," Stephan said with frustration. "I really thought the Angels would be more help."

"Did you ask them?" the Sanuri asked.

Gabriel and Raphael moved the plyogram into the castle and locked it inside of a basement safe. The men were torn with whether the need to translate that coded artwork was more important than any threat that Erebus might pose if he was asked to help. Gabriel met with Erebus after breakfast and was told the meaning of three of the symbols drawn on the plyogram, but this knowledge brought Gabriel no closer to understanding the meaning of the ancient message.

The entire household was moving at a chaotic speed trying to finish last minute preparations for the party. Misha, Archetenus, Emeral and Maxwell were assigned to work that evening, all but Misha were assigned to Fort Salar. Misha was put in charge of the troops at Sudfad's castle. But Sudfad wanted Misha inside at the party to watch the guests. Under normal circumstances the commanding generals of the fort would be attending such a grand royal function, so it was determined that Raphael and Edward would be at the party also.

It was customary for the Royal Family to be in a receiving line at the start of the festivities. Since Hannah was the new Court Physician she and Gabriel too would be in the receiving line as would Alexander and Laurel. Jared, Zoya, Delilah, Luca, Lila, Natasha, Calen, Raphael, Vivian, Edward, Dagon, Koby, Bekka, Elan and Cassandra were assigned to mingle with the party goers and to watch for spies and signs of danger.

While all of these people were dressed in the finest of clothes, they all had weapons concealed on them.

It was a joint decision that Erebus would attend as a guest and would wear his customary flamboyant attire. Delilah was the only person in the castle who had met members of the Insidiae and she had met many while held as a captive by Dieter. It was decided that Delilah would be Edwards' escort to the party and it was Edward's main responsibility to keep her safe.

All of the staff working at the party were siblings of Marie's. Marie always took great measures to ensure that every party put on by the Royal Family went flawlessly. But now, she also felt a responsibility for the safety of the family. Marie's brothers and sisters, too would be watching the crowd, while they were not to intervene they were to report any unusual behaviors, no matter how small.

Natasha, Calen, Luca and Lila walked through the front foyer and into the Great Hall, performing one last security check before the guests arrived.

"Well look at him," Natasha said when they found Misha in the Great Hall. He was wearing the dress uniform of the Wetprian military. "Misha you look so handsome," Natasha cooed. "You are going to have every woman at the party after you."

"He always has every woman at the party after him," Calen said teasingly. "Of the family, he's the real pretty boy."

"All the men in your family are incredibly handsome," Lila said and kissed Luca on the cheek.

Misha ignored the teasing. "I really don't like how this is set up," he said as he opened one of the many doors that led to a patio and garden. "We need to have more candles put out here," Misha continued. "The brush is considerably denser than at other areas of the garden and this spot is the closest to the wall." Misha was referring to the large stone wall that surrounded the castle.

"We'll take care of that," Natasha said and she and Lila left the room.

Once the women left, Misha walked closer to his cousins and asked, "Am I the only one who has a really bad feeling about tonight?"

"No," Luca said. "And the girls all want to fight but damn near every one of them is pregnant. I am not feeling good about this at all."

Marie entered the Great Hall, "There are Ruala warriors landing in the courtyard and they are carrying two humans but I don't know who they are."

"Thanks Marie," Misha said as he, Calen and Luca quickly walked past her."

"We didn't expect you for days," Calen said when they saw that the two humans were wearing the leather uniforms of the Venatores.

"We took little rest," one of the Ruala warriors said. "We know tomorrow night are the blood moon ceremonies and when we told Thor and Diana they too wanted to get here as soon as possible."

"Well, we can certainly use the help," Misha said. "Or are you too exhausted?"

"We are Venatores," Thor said as he stepped closer to Misha, Calen and Luca. "Joshua has told us a great deal; we are here to help you, we are here to fight." Thor was a man in his early twenties with white blonde hair and bright blue eyes. He was not only tall but particularly muscular. "I am Thor and this is my little sister Diana." Thor held out his hand to shake with the Rualas. Diana, like Thor was exceptionally beautiful, she too had brilliant blue eyes and long, straight white blonde hair. These attributes in addition to Diana's short leather dress, momentarily took Misha's breath away.

"We are trying to set a trap here by having this party," Calen explained. "If you would be willing to help us, it would be better if you were in disguise."

"But we brought nothing but our hunting clothes," Diana said.

"There are many of us here, we can fix you up with something," Luca said as he looked at the two. "I think Thor is about Gabriel's size and Diana, perhaps Vivian's size?"

"Is Vivian here?" Diana asked. "We are good friends."

Luca escorted Thor and Diana into the castle, while Misha and Calen spoke with the returning Rualas. "You need to get some food and rest," Calen said.

"Thor and Diana haven't had any more food or rest than we have; tell us where you want us," one of the Rualas replied.

"Mother will be down in just a moment," Annabelle said as she joined the other family members in the receiving line. "Have you seen Thor and Diana?" Annabelle gasped. "They don't even look human, they, they look like some ancient gods." Annabelle's comment made the others laugh.

"And they are all business," Gabriel said. "Raphael and Vivian are bringing them up to date on everything."

A few moments later, Laurel joined the receiving line. "Raphael wants Misha to go upstairs," Laurel said. "Do you see him?"

"I do," Gabriel said and stepped out of the receiving line to get Misha. Gabriel returned to his position in line as Misha ran up the steps to the second floor chambers. Trumpets sounded, the grand party began.

Edward and Delilah were sitting at a table that gave them a good view of the receiving line, so that Delilah could point out any members of the Insidiae that she saw. The others choose tables with views of various entrances. The line of guests extended down the front steps of the castle, through the front courtyard and past the main gate of the castle wall and into the street.

Misha entered the chambers that Raphael and Vivian were staying in. "I'm here," Misha called out as he walked into the empty parlor. He laughed when he heard Vivian and Diana talking in the nearby bedroom.

"They are beautiful," Diana said. "But I am not sure I can kick in them."

"If you are going to do that you will just have to slip the shoes off," Vivian said. "Now come on I want you to meet my friend." Misha stood up when both women entered the parlor, Vivian was wearing a black lace dress and Diana a dark sapphire blue silk dress.

"You both look incredibly beautiful," said Misha.

"I don't know if I can walk in these shoes," Diana said and pulled her long skirt up to expose her ankles and the shoes she was wearing. Both Misha and Vivian laughed. "Misha this is my good friend Diana and Diana this is my good friend Misha," Vivian said. Misha stepped forward and took Diana's hand and kissed it. Diana stared at him with surprise.

"Is that what people do here?" Diana asked but she didn't wait for anyone to answer. "Misha I have never worn a dress like this or been at a fancy party, in fact I have never been in a castle before. Both Thor and I feel out of our element."

"That is why we asked you up here," Vivian said. "We don't want Thor and Diana to look conspicuous. As soon as they are done with the receiving line, Annabelle and Vitomas are going to escort Thor throughout the party. We want you to escort Diana."

"Under other circumstances I would jump at the chance to be her date," Misha said. "But what if there are problems?"

"You mean at the party or with me?" Diana asked with embarrassment.

"My dear not with you," Misha said. "I just have a very bad feeling about tonight and expect the worst."

"Misha if there are problems with demons and dark lords I promise you will be glad that I am with you," Diana said with a teasing smile. "My concern is that I don't know how to dance."

"Do you have weapons on you?" Misha asked.

"Of course," Diana said with a grin.

"But I am not going to show you were they are all hidden."

Misha again laughed and said, "Alright." He took Diana's hand and started to walk to the center of the parlor.

"What are you doing?" asked Diana.

"You are getting a dancing lesson," Misha said. "I hope you are a fast learner." Misha moved a few pieces of furniture then he faced Diana. He put her left hand on his waist and put his right hand in the small of her back. Misha held Diana's right hand in his left and said. "You don't have to worry about knowing the steps if you can just relax and let me lead, I can guide us along the dance floor."

Vivian laughed, "Letting you lead may be the problem; Diana is a bit like me."

Like Diana, Thor initially felt very out of place at the fancy party. He had promised Raphael that he would personally protect Vitomas and Annabelle if trouble occurred. Thor was not a shy person but he felt uncomfortable as he began to walk through the crowded Great Hall with a beautiful princess on each arm. But Thor's uneasiness soon melted away as he found both Vitomas and Annabelle to be funny and down to earth, things he had not expected.

"Oh did I step on your foot again?" Diana asked apologetically as she saw Misha wince in pain.

"That's alright, you are getting better," Misha said as he tried to smile.

"I might be able to dance better if I could take these shoes off," she said.

"I have no doubt about that, but it's not that kind of party."

"Is this what all of your parties are like? I have never seen people dressed like this before; they must all be very rich."

"This is what the King's and Queen's parties are like," Misha said. "We aren't as fancy at the house. Our team all lives together in a very large house not far from here."

"Joshua and Iris were telling us about it. Misha you could have knocked me over when I heard that Vivian had taken a husband. I mean if she said it once she said a hundred times she would never marry and give up hunting. So I was anxious to meet Raphael, I knew he had to be special and he is."

"He is a good man and a great warrior."

Diana looked at Misha for a while, as if studying him. "Vivian and I grew up together and we have been best friends since I can remember," Diana said. "So I think I may know sides of her that you do not. She is a great Venator and because she is so powerful and skilled she doesn't give out compliments easily. People really have to earn her praise. Vivian has been telling me about all of you and I have never heard her so impressed with a group of people. She said that you are her closest friend here and then comes Elan. She is so honored to be among you, but Vivian might get mad if she knew I told you; so don't say anything."

"She told you I was her closest friend?"

"Yes, why do you say it like that?"

"Well, we kind of had a little fight not long ago."

"What good friends don't have fights once in a while, but things are fine between you now aren't they?"

"Yes and I am glad. I have a great deal of respect for Vivian; I didn't like it when we weren't getting along."

"Oh look Misha; Annabelle is trying to teach Thor to dance. I hope he is better than I am," Diana said with a big grin on her face.

"You're getting better."

"I don't know how you can say that your feet must be black and blue by now."

504

"You can pay me back by giving me a foot massage later," Misha said with a grin. Diana smiled and looked at him but she wasn't sure if Misha was teasing her.

"Would you like a glass of wine?" he asked as a server was walking through the crowd with a tray of wine glasses.

"Yes, but I better not. I haven't slept or eaten much in the last few days. Can you imagine trying to dance with me if I was drunk too?"

"Honey there are tables upon tables of food, let's get you something to eat." Misha and Diana stopped dancing and Diana took his arm.

"Misha there is a sorcerer," Diana whispered as she let go of his arm and started towards Erebus. Misha quickly grabbed Diana by the waist and pulled her close to him and started dancing again.

"You really are like Vivian," Misha said and grinned. "He is on our side."

"You are not telling me the truth," Diana gasped.

"His wife was murdered by the same people who are trying to kill us. He is here to help us identify some of them."

"And you believe this story?" Diana asked incredulously.

"I was there, at that battle. A demon tore his wife to shreds. Gabriel tried to help her and now Erebus feels he owes Gabriel a debt. That sorcerer may be a lot of bad things but it seems that he really loved his wife. Besides he is not hiding what he is, the people we have to be concerned with could be dressed like lords or ladies or priests or even soldiers."

"Really?" Diana said as she again looked around the room.

"Now if you promise not to attack anyone I will take you over to get some food before you faint from hunger," Misha said with a grin.

Diana laughed. "I like you, you're funny."

Chapter XXXIII
Dancing Among Demons

Claudius and his army slept most of the day since they planned to stay up all night. The men and women ate their dinner as they waited for darkness to consume the desert. "Wouldn't you think there would be some kind of pre-ceremony ceremonies tonight?" Sorren asked.

"Actually there might be," the Sanuri said. "As soon as it gets dark I want to go where you saw the door appear."

"Sorren and I were the closest," Claudius said. "We will take you."

Thedes and a large group of Shettees entered the cave from one of the connecting tunnels. There were so many Shettees that they decided to stand in the tunnel because the cave that Claudius and the others were in was already full. "Sanuri could I speak to you for a moment?" Thedes asked.

"Of course," the Sanuri replied and stood up and walked over to Thedes.

"These are my people who we rescued from Ogg" Thedes said with pride. "Like me before I met the Rualas, they have never heard of you or The Great Ruler, but they did meet Miranda and Daniel. I would like to introduce you."

The Sanuri entered the tunnel and shook hands with each Shettee warrior as Thedes made introductions. "Thedes has told us so much about you," Neputa said. "We owe the existence of our people to you."

"Not to me, but to The Great Ruler," the Sanuri said. "Would you like me to tell you about Him?"

"Misha was talking about his bad feeling, well now I have it," Calen said to Luca and Gabriel. "It is too quiet and I feel like we are being watched." Natasha joined them.

"I just checked on the children," Natasha said. "Everything is fine there. I am going to talk to Erebus; it won't be believable that he is a guest if he looks so isolated."

"That's a good idea," Gabriel said then paused and looked around. "I feel like the hairs on the back of my neck are standing up."

"Do you feel better now?" Misha asked Diana.

"Yes, thank you. I didn't realize how hungry I was until I smelled that food. You still have that bad feeling don't you?" Diana asked as she watched Misha looking around the room. The two had returned to the dance floor. He was leading them around the outside of the large dance area so he could look at the room and the people.

"Yes and it is getting worse. Diana, Thor will be protecting the Princesses; if something happens I will be leaving you."

Diana stopped dancing and looked at Misha disapprovingly. "I promised Vivian I would fight at your side. I don't break my promises."

Misha looked at Diana and grinned. "I like you too. But we should start dancing again." Misha glided across the floor, toward one of the doors that led to a garden. "How long are you and Thor staying?"

"I don't really know," Diana said. "I guess that depends on Gabriel and Raphael, why?"

"Well, if the world doesn't end tomorrow night after the blood moon ceremonies, Elan and Cassandra are getting married next week. Would you go to the wedding and dance with me?"

"I would love to," Diana said excitedly then her demeanor changed. "Will it be fancy like this?"

"Probably."

"Do you think Natasha will let me borrow this dress again?"

"I will buy you a dress."

"You will not Misha, I hardly know you."

"I am taking you to the wedding and I will buy you a dress, that's all there is to it," Misha said with authority and a huge grin. Diana was going to protest but stopped herself from saying anything; instead she scowled at Misha. "Let me guess you are used to getting the last word," Misha said and grinned again.

"Actually I am," Diana said and laughed then changed to a scolding tone of voice. "But you just talked to me like my brother does."

"I certainly don't want you to think of me as a brother," Misha said with such a grin that Diana started to laugh again. Misha twirled Diana when she suddenly stopped and whispered, "The garden."

As darkness enveloped the desert, Claudius and his army crept out of the sanctuary of their caves and positioned themselves on top of and around the two hills that were north of the hill they had been hiding in. As the previous night, it was uneventful until the moon beam exposed the door in the hill. Claudius and Sorren did not realize that the Sanuri had left them until they saw him standing before the door. The moon beam disappeared as did the image of the door.

The Sanuri's voice whispered into the ears of Claudius and Sorren, bring some men and come up here, quietly. Claudius and Sorren took fifty men and climbed the hill, as soon as they reached the Sanuri the door in the hill was again illuminated and now it slowly opened. "We are just going to look around," the Sanuri whispered.

The door opened slowly and revealed a huge well-lit room before them. As they passed through the door, the soldiers felt as if they were entering a palace, so spacious and beautiful was the interior of the hill. The room was nothing more than a large foyer with five hallways leading from it. Claudius and half of the soldiers crept down the first hallway. Sorren led the remainder of the soldiers down the second hallway and the Sanuri walked alone down the third hallway.

Diana grabbed Misha's hand and ran off the dance floor and out of the doors leading to the garden; their exit of the Great Hall was seen by others who now realized there might be intruders. "What did you see?" Misha asked as they ran across the patio.

"Demons," Diana said. "She let go of Misha's hand and quickly bent down and slipped off her shoes. Diana threw one of the shoes with great force towards a bush. They heard a loud thud then a moan. Another demon now came out of the shrubbery towards them and Diana threw the second shoe and impaled it between the eyes of the monster. Lifting her skirt, Diana ran towards a third demon, she flew through the air and kicked him in the throat shattering his larynx. Diana did a forward roll, grabbing one of her sheathed knives in the process.

Two demons ran towards Misha as soon as he and Diana left the patio area and entered the garden. Misha pulled his sword and stabbed the first demon, then he quickly flew over the head of the second demon and stabbed him in the back. When Diana came out of her roll she saw three more demons running towards Misha.

"Misha duck!" Diana screamed and threw a knife at the demon that was about to stab Misha in the back. Fortunately for Misha he heard her orders and ducked. Diana's knife went into the throat of the demon. As Misha ducked down he stabbed the demon in front of him in the groin, then he quickly turned and stabbed the second demon behind him.

Diana grabbed another knife that was in a sheath at the back of her neck. "I'm at your back," she said to Misha as demons were starting to surround them. Within moments Gabriel, Raphael, Calen, Luca, Koby and Bekka joined Misha and Diana. The fight did not last long.

"The other doors," Misha said.

"We have men going out every one of them," Gabriel said as he turned over the bodies of the demons and searched them for information.

"There's a couple more in the bushes," Diana said and led Raphael to the bodies. "Calen, I broke Natasha's shoes," Diana called out as she pulled the heel of one of the shoes out of the forehead of a demon. Diana and Raphael searched the bodies then returned to Gabriel and the others.

"Misha said you just grabbed him and started to run out the door," Gabriel said. "What did you see?"

"Misha was twirling me around so for an instant his eyes were away from the door, I looked up and saw three of the demons looking in at us. When they realized I saw them, they started to run."

Misha grabbed Diana around the waist and pulled her to him, kissing her on the lips. "You are a great fighter," he said. Then Misha turned to the others, "She killed three before I got one."

"But this was very strange," Diana said. "I started out attacking them but all the demons were focused on Misha. I have never had demons not want to fight me because I am a girl. I think they were after him."

"Why would they be after me?" asked Misha.

"They are probably after Gabriel's team," Sudfad said as he walked onto the patio and saw the carnage. "They didn't recognize Diana."

"Diana this is King Sudfad," Gabriel said.

Diana looked flustered and bowed then curtsied. "She's not afraid of the demons but she's nervous around you," Misha said to Sudfad and laughed.

"Where is Vivian?" Raphael asked. "She is supposed to be guarding you and Renya."

"She's alright, she is guarding Renya. But I don't think she is happy about her assignment. I think she wanted to patrol the area."

Raphael looked at Diana, "Vivian might be pregnant so I don't want her fighting unless it is really necessary."

"She must," Diana said then changed her words. "That sorcerer is coming."

"Erebus do you recognize what kind of demons these are?" Sudfad asked.

"They are called Kafas," Erebus said as he bent down to examine one of the bodies. Without looking up Erebus said, "Hand me a knife." Diana was closest to Erebus and gave him one of her knives. Erebus cut locks of hair off several of the demons. Then he stood up and gave Diana her knife while looking at Sudfad. "Give me a few minutes and I will find out who sent them."

"How are you going to do that?" asked Raphael.

"I have some things in my suitcase, I will perform a spell."

"Can I come?" Raphael asked.

"I will be contacting dark spirits that are not likely to respond with an emissary of The Great Ruler in the room. I will go to the cottage and be right back."

"And what if the demons come after you?" Gabriel asked.

"I can go with him, I'm not holy like the rest of you," Diana said.

"And who are you?" Erebus asked as he looked at Diana.

"I am a Venator of the Clan of Gesmal," Diana said with pride.

"I should have known," Erebus said with a smile. Erebus and Diana turned to walk off the patio but Misha grabbed Diana's arm.

"Erebus, will the spirits talk to you if I am flying around your cottage?" asked Misha.

"As long as you aren't inside it should be fine."

"We'll come too," Koby said as he and Bekka walked towards Erebus.

511

"This is like a maze," Stephan whispered to Claudius who put his hand up for Stephan to stop talking. The hallways were made out of white marble. The holders that held lit torches on the walls appeared to be made out of gold, everything was spotlessly clean. This was not at all the environment that Claudius and the others expected to be inhabited by demons. After almost twenty minutes Claudius turned a corner and saw a marble wall at the end of the hallway. He and Stephan closely examined the wall trying to find a secret lever but they found nothing, the group turned around and headed back towards the foyer.

"Erebus I am going to carry you," Koby said and grabbed the sorcerer by the waist and ascended into the air. Koby had expected Erebus to protest but instead the old sorcerer seemed quite thrilled to be flying. Misha picked up Diana and quickly ascended into the air next to Bekka.

"I can't believe you kissed me," Diana whispered to Misha with a disapproving tone to her voice.

"Why?" Misha asked but Diana did not answer. "Are you promised to another?"

Diana sighed and rolled her eyes. "No, it's just that I don't know you. We just met."

"Well that doesn't make a difference," Misha said with a grin. "What matters is whether you liked it or not." Diana didn't respond. "Well did you like it?"

"It was alright," she said with a big grin on her face.

"Well, I guess I will have to do better next time," Misha said as they flew around Erebus' cottage looking for demons. "Now you be careful in there. If you sense anything isn't right, let us know."

"Misha will you quit sounding like my brother, I'm not helpless you know."

"That was absolutely incredible," Erebus said. "Now stay out here and I should have an answer in five minutes."

512

"I am coming with you," Diana said. "There might be demons inside."

Erebus was an unusually tall man and he now looked down at Diana, who was particularly short in stature and smiled. "This little girl is going to protect me?" he asked with a grin.

"I would be careful about who I called a little girl," Diana said then laughed. "Why don't you let me go in first?" Erebus chuckled and stepped aside. A fire in the hearth illuminated the cottage. Diana walked inside and searched the rooms then she returned to the door, "It's empty."

"Remember what I said," Misha said then ascended into the air.

"Yes, Father," Diana called out sarcastically.

Matthew walked directly behind Sorren as they explored the second hallway. This hallway like the one Claudius was searching was made of marble with gold trim and was immaculately clean. After the second turn in the hallway they saw large oil paintings hanging on the walls. Each painting was surrounded by an ornately carved golden frame. Suspicious of the paintings, Matthew looked behind each one for hidden compartments. "These are all scenes of hell," he whispered loudly.

"Well, I suppose that makes sense for demons," Sorren replied in a whisper.

They walked down the well-lit corridor for another ten minutes before it ended at a massive marble wall. "Why would this hallway end like this?" Sorren asked. Sorren and Matthew examined the marble wall while other soldiers examined the side walls and floor; they found nothing and turned back towards the foyer.

Erebus took a large wooden bowl from a shelf and placed it on the table, then he opened one of his suitcases and took out small jars which he placed on the table. Erebus looked over at Diana who was sitting on a chair watching him. "Why aren't you wearing any shoes with a fancy dress like that?"

513

"I used them to kill demons," Diana replied nonchalantly. Erebus roared with laughter. "I don't mean to insult you," she said. "But you sure don't seem very scary for a sorcerer." Again he laughed.

"I guess I am not sure how to take that," Erebus said with a grin as he put the demon hair in the bowl then sprinkled different powders on top of it. "I will be starting the spell now; under no circumstances should you speak." Diana watched as Erebus covered the demon hair with dried herbs, then he poured a liquid in the bowl and smoke started to rise from the concoction. Erebus started to chant and the contents of the bowl burst into flames. He stared at the burning ingredients for several moments then poured a pitcher of water into the bowl. "We can go now," Erebus said to Diana.

As they stood in the doorway of the cottage waiting for the Rualas to land, Diana said, "I thought you were going to talk to ghosts, I'm rather disappointed."

Erebus laughed loudly and when Koby, Bekka and Misha landed, Erebus said, "This little girl is a joy." Then the sorcerer's demeanor changed. "Hecate sent the demons which means they are probably looking for your team."

"We should return to the castle," Koby said and picked up Erebus. Misha again picked up Diana and the five flew to the castle, entering the Great Hall through one of the garden doors. They told Gabriel, Raphael and King Sudfad of Erebus' findings.

"There were no signs of demons anywhere else around the castle," Raphael said. "We were fortunate that Diana saw them when she did." Diana now looked around the room at each door that led to a garden area.

"This makes no sense," Gabriel said. "Misha and Diana were dancing at the far end of the dance floor. The demons would have had to cross the grounds to get to that specific door."

"Were any other members of your team near one of those doors when I saw the demons?" Diana asked.

"Bekka and I were and I believe Dagon and Elan were," Koby said.

"They either wanted Misha or they were sent out to scout the area and make sure you were here," Thor said as he joined the group with Vitomas and Annabelle.

"Diana, Misha did any of the demons get away?" Thor asked.

"Not that I know of," Misha said. "I think we killed them all. But I am going out and alert the troops to expect an attack."

"I'll send Enrops to the fort," said Gabriel.

As Misha was walking through the Great Hall he realized that Diana was following him. "Where do you think you are going?" he asked.

"Vivian told me to stay with you."

"I believe that was for your safety," Misha said. "Stay inside."

"I'm not the one who the demons were after," Diana said with annoyance. "I am coming with you."

"Fine," Misha said and turned towards the door.

"Misha has anyone ever told you..." Diana didn't finish her question. "What is that sound?"

"The Horn of Cass, we are under attack. Now stay here!" Misha yelled and ran out the door.

The Sanuri made his way down the third hallway. He didn't hear any sounds but he could feel the presence of evil all around him. There were no oil paintings hanging on the walls of this hallway but large brightly colored murals were painted on the walls. There was about ten feet of white space between the murals and each painting depicted an image of hell.

The Sanuri realized that every time he walked past a mural his sensation of evil became stronger. The Sanuri stopped and closely examined one of the murals. Nothing in the pictures was moving or pulsating as a demonic alarm but when the Sanuri held his hand close to the mural that portion of the picture began to smoke.

"What is this evil?" the Sanuri thought to himself and moved his hand in a large sweeping motion in front of the mural. Not only did the mural smoke but the Sanuri could smell the stench of hell and hear the cries of the tortured.

The Sanuri stood back from the wall and counted thirteen murals. "Are these some kind of gateways into the hell regions of the Old Ones?" The Sanuri thought to himself. Hearing a sound the Sanuri turned and saw Claudius and Sorren leading their groups down the hall towards him. "Stop!" the Sanuri said loudly and held up his hand. "Come no farther."

Diana ran up the stairs to Vivian's chambers, unfastening Natasha's dress as she ran. She could now hear the sounds of fighting. Quickly Diana changed into her leather dress and sandals then she sheathed her knives and sword. She grabbed a bag of weapons and ran down the stairs.

The Sanuri closed his eyes and started to hum. Loud cracking and groaning could be heard, then one after another the murals started to explode. Claudius ordered his men to back up to the foyer. The Sanuri did not move; the frequency of his humming became higher and higher, causing the murals to explode at a faster pace.

Explosion after explosion echoed through the marble hallways, then suddenly there was silence. Claudius and his men moved forward, stepping over huge slabs of marble. They quickened their pace when the unique stench of hell overwhelmed their nostrils for they recognized the smell. Suddenly the Sanuri's voice was heard in the ears of each man in that hallway. "Do not enter the murals, proceed down the hallway to where you saw me standing."

Sudfad, Raphael and Gabriel had suspected that the demons that were found in the garden might be a distraction. So they were not surprised to hear the sounds of battle outside of the castle; their concern was for the many spies and demons that might be inside.

While Koby, Bekka and the others were with Erebus, Sudfad opened his weapons room and distributed weapons to all those he could trust; which did not include Erebus. When Koby and the others returned from Erebus' cottage they were not informed of Sudfad's suspicions because Sudfad did not want Erebus to overhear the plans.

Now as Diana descended the stairs she saw Vivian and Thor dressed in the outfits of the Venatores fighting with other humans in the Great Hall. Gabriel, Raphael, Koby, Bekka, Dagon, Elan and Cassandra were also fighting with the outlaws sent by the dark lords. To Diana's surprise she saw Sudfad, Renya, Vitomas and Annabelle fighting with swords in their hands.

There were Wetprian soldiers in the Great Hall but some of them were fighting against each other. Diana remembered that Misha had warned her the spies could be dressed as anyone. Diana took all of this in as she jumped over the railing of the staircase and screamed a war cry.

Claudius and the others could hear voices, many, many muffled voices and they began to run. When they reached the area where the Sanuri had last been seen; Claudius stopped. Before them was another world, similar to what they had seen in Baal's hell domain. Except in this world there was a sea of human beings, tied, shackled and being tortured.

"Miranda, Daniel," Matthew yelled as he followed Claudius and Sorren into the hell region where the Sanuri was fighting with demons.

"Help us! Help us!" people screamed as Claudius and his few men jumped through the portal that divided two worldly dimensions.

Somewhere in the distance Sorren heard a lion roar, then explosions, powerful explosions that rocked the hill. But all Sorren could think about were the cries of the victims. He raised his head and screamed the Nordes war cry, then charged into a group of demons.

War cries after war cries filled the air as Raul, Simon and Thaos led the rest of the army into the hill. Miranda's voice guided them as they ran through the foyer and into the third hallway. Without hesitation Shettee, Ruala and human ran through the portal entering Raum's hell domain. The demons were taken by surprise but they too screamed war cries and reinforcements responded.

"Miranda free them," Raul screamed as a giant demon grabbed him and started to pound his head against a wall. Raul gouged the eyes of the demon, dislodging one from its socket. The demon yelled in pain and dropped Raul, who stabbed the demon in the stomach, groin and thigh as he fell.

Simon ran to Sorren who was surrounded by demons. Simon had a sword in each of his hands. He stabbed a demon in the back with his right hand and plunged his other sword into the stomach of a demon that was running towards him. Simon killed five demons before he could get to Sorren. The two warriors stood back to back and fought their attackers.

"Don't take them all," Sorren yelled to Simon. "This group was mine." Simon laughed then raised his right arm to block a blow from a demon.

Demons and members of the Insidiae did not make personal appearances at the party hosted by the King and Queen of Wetpr but instead hired gangs of street thugs to attend the party in disguise. Hecate had paid Daegal well to organize an attack by humans within the castle simultaneously with an attack by demons outside of the castle. Daegal suspected the party might be some kind of trap, so he warned members of the Insidiae not to attend.

Vivian ran to Thor who was fighting with three men. The men were trying to surround the Venator but his movements prevented them from getting behind him.

Vivian held a sword in her right hand and a dagger in her left. She ran her sword through one of Thor's attackers while Thor killed the second attacker. The third attacker looked at both Thor and Vivian then turned and ran. Thor threw a knife which struck the man in the back and killed him.

Gabriel heard Hannah yelling his name and he ran towards the room where all the children and the nurses were hiding. Natasha was already in the nursery fighting with two spies who were dressed as Wetprian soldiers. Petra and Kyra had swords and they too were fighting as more of the attackers ran into the nursery area. Laurel and Alexander were helping the nurses to shield the children.

"The children!" Vitomas screamed when she saw Gabriel running in the direction of the nursery. Renya and Annabelle followed Vitomas. The three women were filled with fear for the safety of the children, but this was not a crippling fear. With their adrenaline surging through their bodies the three women stabbed, kicked and gouged their way through the battling crowd.

Raphael and Sudfad fought back to back as the King was singled out as a target by the attackers. Diana jumped on the back of a man who was about to grab Vivian. Diana snapped the man's neck then jumped back as he fell to the floor. Erebus stood against the wall, watching the fight, then he slipped out of one of the garden doors and into the darkness, Dagon followed him.

When the Horn of Cass was blown, Edward left the party and ran out to the walls of the castle. He commanded the men on the northern and eastern walls while Misha commanded the soldiers on the southern and western walls. No reinforcements came from Fort Salar for they too were under attack.

The demons that attacked the fort and the walls of the castle were the same Kafas demons that Misha and Diana had fought with earlier.

With leathery faces that dated back to the beginning of time, the Kafas were large demons that resembled long haired animals but they walked on two legs. They had large powerful arms and hands that could crush a man's skull. These demons were not from the World of Nunc, a fact Erebus had failed to tell Sudfad and the others.

Elan saw Renya and the Princesses running towards the nursery; he flew over the crowd and kicked a thug in the head who Cassandra was fighting with. "Come," Elan yelled and they too flew towards the nursery. The two Rualas flew over Renya, Vitomas and Annabelle and arrived in the nursery immediately after Gabriel.

Elan flew towards one of the nurses who was trying to prevent a spy from grabbing baby Arianna. Elan swung his sword and the man's head fell off this body, the body remained standing for a few moments before it collapsed onto the floor.

The children were all screaming and Gabriel fought like a mad man when he saw almost twenty men in the nursery being fought off by Hannah, Natasha, Petra and Kyra. Never had Gabriel been so blinded with emotion; later he would hardly remember his killing rampage. Cassandra plunged her sword into the back of one of the men who Natasha was fighting with then immediately turned in the air and sliced the head off from a man who Hannah was hitting with her fists. Hannah had dropped her sword but she refused to let the attackers near her children.

Renya felt terror as never before when she ran into the nursery and saw the men trying to get to the children. "Great Ruler help us," she screamed and ran across the room and stabbed a man who was about to grab Petra. Vitomas and Annabelle only remembered hearing their babies cry, they didn't remember stabbing and kicking the men in front of them.

Lila anxiously stood by the door of her chambers with sword in hand. Luca told her to guard Delilah and Zoya before he and Calen left to warn the fort of an attack. Lila had given the other two woman swords in case any intruders got past her. The sounds of the battle were loud and terrifying and the women prayed.

While Diana, Misha and the others had escorted Erebus to his cottage after the first demon attack, Gabriel sent Calen and Luca to the fort to warn them. But the fort was the first to be attacked; a move that Daegal hoped would prevent reinforcements from helping those battling at the castle.

Once at the fort, Calen and Luca split up. Calen found Emeral and fought at her side, while Luca found Maxwell and fought with him.

"Miranda," Archetenus yelled as he saw the demons were now climbing over the walls of the fort.

Thor was a powerful man who was truly in his element in the heat of battle. He stabbed an attacker in front of him then ducked down and rolled forward, coming back up on his feet he turned and stabbed the man who had been running at his back. From this new view, Thor saw Sudfad and Raphael, who were fighting back to back and were completely surrounded. "Diana the King," Thor screamed and ran towards Sudfad. Diana heard her brother's cry but was fighting hand to hand with an assailant. Bekka flew over them and stabbed the man in the back. Diana pushed his dying body off from her and ran after her brother.

Through the din, Koby heard a woman scream and flew up the stairs towards the room that Lila, Delilah and Zoya were in. He found the door open with a dead man lying in the doorway. Zoya ran and jumped on the back of another attacker who was trying to stab Lila as she pulled her sword out of another body. Koby quickly killed the man who Zoya was on. "Are there any more?" he asked.

"No just the three," Delilah said fearfully.

"Are any of you hurt?" asked Koby.

"I don't think so," Lila said as she looked at the blood on her dress. "It's not my blood."

"Quickly leave here and go into our room, I will guard the hallway," Koby said as the three women ran into the chambers shared by Koby and Bekka. When the women were safe, Koby flew back to the Great Hall.

Dagon flew silently as he followed Erebus; who was running back to his cottage. Sudfad had little trust for Erebus and wanted him watched at all times.

Dagon landed outside of the cottage and peered through a window as Erebus moved quickly throwing items into bowls and talking out loud. After several moments Dagon burst into the cottage. "What are you doing?" he demanded.

Erebus did not stop moving but looked at Dagon and said. "Close the door and be quiet, I am trying to help."

"How do I know you speak the truth?" Dagon asked as he walked towards the table.

"Look at me," Erebus said. "I am not a warrior; that is not where my strength lies. Those demons come from another world but they are not powerful enough to transport themselves. I am cutting off their connection with Hecate; it will greatly weaken them."

"How can I trust you?" Dagon demanded.

"I guess you will just have to kill me if this goes wrong," Erebus said. "Now be quiet." While Erebus was talking he was forming a mixture that resembled bread dough in one of the wooden bowls. He took some of the mixture and roughly formed it into a torso with arms and legs. Then he took some of the hair he had cut off the demons and pressed it into the mixture. Erebus picked up a small piece of cord and rammed it into the back of the form.

Erebus loudly chanted a spell and as he spoke he first waved his left hand over the form five times, then he held the form up into the air and while chanting he pulled the cord from the form's back, then Erebus turned to Dagon. "Stab it with your dagger." Dagon hesitated for a moment then stabbed the form that was now lying on the table. Loud screams were heard from outside of the cottage. "Those are the demons," Erebus said. "I destroyed their connection and you inflicted pain."

As soon as the demon's screams were heard, so too were the screeches of thousands of giant Blue Hengers as they descended from the sky and attacked the demons both at the fort and at the castle.

"What took you so long?" Archetenus asked sarcastically as Miranda appeared next to him on top of the wall surrounding the fort.

"Choices, there are many who had to make choices tonight," Miranda said. "Archetenus don't you know by now there is always so much more than what appears before you?"

"You know I never doubt you Miranda," Archetenus said. "Thank you."

"You doubted me for a very long time; do you remember when your heart was as dark as that of the demons you fight this night?"

"Yes and you just kicked my butt Miranda, but I am so glad you did. Once I started listening to you my life changed and you brought me Delilah and soon our baby."

"I'm glad to hear you say that and I have a gift for you."

"A gift? What sort of gift?"

"You will need to choose more than one name," Miranda said and disappeared. A huge smile consumed Archetenus' face.

So intent was Renya on protecting her grandchildren that she did not realized her left arm was bleeding profusely from a knife wound. Renya picked up Kyra who had been stabbed in the shoulder and screamed for Hannah. Natasha and Hannah were hugging their children and now came to the Queen's aid. Gabriel and Elan killed the last two intruders. "Are any of the babies hurt?" Annabelle screamed hysterically as she ran to her children. Vitomas couldn't stop crying as she first hugged her boys then picked up Ariel.

"Christopher come here," Gabriel said when he realized the boy was standing by himself looking terrified. Christopher flew into Gabriel's arms. "Nicholas, Cerey come to me," Gabriel said as he bent down and hugged all three children.

"We could use some help here," Natasha yelled. "As she was trying to stop the blood that was spurting from Renya's arm." Hannah was working on Kyra and Petra ran back and forth between Renya and Kyra.

"Elan get my medical bag," Hannah yelled. "Cassandra help me put pressure on this wound." Once Cassandra was applying pressure to Kyra's wound, Hannah ran to Renya. Hannah started to tear her underskirt into shreds to put over the wounds. Once Vitomas realized her children were unharmed she ran over to Renya.

As Elan flew through the castle to get Hannah's medical bag he saw that the fighting inside of the castle had ended. Sudfad was ordering teams to search the castle for wounded and for more intruders. Both Sudfad and Raphael were bleeding but their wounds appeared minor. "Sudfad, Renya is hurt, Hannah is with her in the nursery," Elan called out. "I am getting the medical bag." Fear filled every fiber of Sudfad's body as he ran out of the Great Hall and to the nursery.

Raphael ran to Vivian who was bleeding from the mouth, "Honey I am fine, I just got punched in the mouth," she said as Raphael hugged her tightly. "But let me look at your wounds," Vivian said with concern.

"Hannah, I need Hannah," Koby yelled as he found Bekka lying on the floor with blood gushing from her side. Koby opened up Bekka's warrior robe and saw a long cut down her right side. "Hannah," Koby yelled again.

"I'm here," Gala said as she ran to Koby and Bekka. Gala was carrying her medical bag. "Koby please move so I can get to the wound," Gala asked as she knelt next to Bekka. Koby moved to Bekka's left side and held her hand tightly.

Thor and Diana made up one of the teams that were searching the castle. They were going through the rooms on the first floor when they heard Marie scream in the kitchen. As Thor and Diana ran into the kitchen, Marie yelled. "I saw a demon by the back door."

Thor charged out of the back door with Diana behind him. They saw a demon running and took chase, not realizing they were running into an ambush. The screeching of the Hengers was deafening, Thor did not hear his sister's screams as six demons jumped out of the bushes and attacked him from behind. Diana threw a knife and hit one of the demons in the back. She screamed her brother's name again and again as she tried to get to him.

Diana was tackled by a demon that stabbed her in the back. She felt the searing pain, but her fear for her brother was greater than her fear for herself. She rolled onto her back and put her knife into the throat of the demon on top of her. She pushed him off and picked up her sword which she thrust into another demon that was running up to her side. Diana could see the pack of demons trying to take Thor down to the ground. She screamed his name again, then collapsed on the ground, unconscious as a demon prepared to hit her a second time with his club.

Chapter XXXIV
Choices

For every member of Claudius' army who joined the battle in the hell dimension there were three or four demons that joined. The warriors and soldiers were so busy fighting that none of them could free the human prisoners. Men, women and children cried out and screamed as the battle was waged around them. In the days before the Kingdom of Xepoltr fell to the Hutas, Neputa and the other Shettees would never have risked their lives to help another species. Now the plight of these prisoners filled the Shettees with compassion and spurred them on; for they too had been the captives of demons.

Smoke started to rise, although there did not appear to be any fires in the area. The smoke was thick and started to choke and blind the men and women who were attempting such a daring rescue. More of the soldiers and warriors started to fight back to back with their comrades because they had increasing difficulty seeing their foe.

"Damn," Stephan yelled when he lunged forward with his sword. "I can't see, I thought a demon was there." Stephan was fighting back to back with Thaos.

"If you can't see them, you can still smell them," Thaos yelled.

"Old friend, give us sight," the Sanuri prayed as the demons swarmed around him. The smoke became thicker, then everything stopped. Later the Sanuri would explain that time literally stopped in the World of Nunc. The demons, the victims and the rescuers were motionless, their actions suspended in time.

The smoke cleared quickly and while the minds returned to all involved in that battle scene, their bodies seemed frozen. An incredibly powerful blinding light came from the portal entrance into Raum's hell domain. Everyone was blinded. The bodies were no longer suspended in time but all stood in silenced awe and stared at the entrance.

Soon the figures of Angels appeared in the light, Daniel and Miranda stood on either side of The Lion and behind them stood any army of incredible proportions. Clanging sounds were heard but it took several moments for the prisoners to realize their shackles had fallen off them; yet no one moved.

"You are here," The Lion's voice thundered through all of the hell dimensions as he spoke to the demons. "Because people call to you as one voice which never stops. But for all who revel in your darkness these men and women have the courage to stand up to you and say 'No.' They will not bow to you, they will not worship you."

"The choices have been made. This battle is over; you have not won this war this night. The blood moon ceremonies will not take place." With The Lion's words armies of Angels passed through the portal and into the hell domain. And the demons ran back towards their darkness as they tried to escape the holy light. And the demons ran.

"There you are," Sampson said sarcastically as Hecate appeared on the roadway before him. "I have been calling you day and night why have you not answered me?"

Hecate did not answer Sampson's question. "Why has it taken you so long to return? Did you get the items?"

"Yes," Sampson shouted back angrily. "But I was attacked right after I left our lair. I was injured for days and you did not answer my calls."

"How were you attacked?" Hecate asked with her voice softening.

"I don't know, I was poisoned or cursed, I fell from my horse and lay on the ground for days, puking and in great pain."

Hecate stared at Sampson; while his story made no sense to her she felt he was being sincere. "So you did not stop to see other women?"

"No, you are my wife!"

"Come, let's go home. I have much to tell you."

"Miranda should we go after them," Claudius yelled over the din.

"Let them go," The Lion said. "Your role here is done." Miranda, Daniel and The Lion now walked among the rescuers. Then The Lion turned and walked up to the sea of captives, who still had not moved. "I am sending you to the Patronus Headquarters in Nora. You can go where you choose from there. The priests know you are coming and have prepared for you. Go in Peace." Suddenly the captives disappeared. Claudius and the others stared with disbelief.

"So you are not going to allow the blood moon ceremonies to take place?" Claudius asked.

"That is correct," The Lion said. "Your soldiers and warriors are weary and injured. Many will not make the long arduous journey home. For your service, we will transport you."

"Thank you," said Claudius.

Raul looked at The Lion and asked, "What did you mean when you said choices have been made?"

"It's all about choices," The Lion responded.

Hecate and Sampson materialized in her lair. Orbus left when Hecate went for Sampson. Hecate saw that Sampson was looking suspiciously around the room. "Is something wrong my husband?"

"This room smells of sex, as do you," Sampson said angrily and tried to strike Hecate with his right hand. With the power of her thought Hecate knocked Sampson to the floor.

"I do not want to hurt you. Your imagination is running wild. We have much to discuss, my husband. Much has happened while you were gone. And I want to hear more about the infliction that was set upon you."

528

"As we speak a battle is ending in Wetpr," The Lion said. "Your families are alive but there are many wounded. Lakin and Gael would you mind returning to Wetpr to help?"

"Oh course not," said Lakin.

"Sanuri your help is needed there also," The Lion continued. "Raul and Simon your kingdom was overrun with spies, in your absence Sudfad chose among the few he could trust and put them in positions of power in your military. You would be wise to consider leaving some of them in those positions. Your destinies are opening before you. You may have less time for the duties required of generals." The Lion now turned to Claudius, Sorren and Matthew.

"Claudius, Sorren, your kingdom has not been attacked. Your loving families are waiting for your return. But this war is not over; do not let your guards down. Matthew, you too are one of The Seven Sons, you may want to reevaluate your duties."

The news that Raul, Simon and Matthew were three of The Seven Sons of prophesy was new information for many although not surprising. Matthew felt relieved now that the others were aware of his destiny and responsibilities.

"Claudius, Stephan and Thaos, soon an old face will reappear in your lives, do not take this lightly and do not underestimate the power of revenge," The Lion said.

"Mother," Raul yelled as he, Simon and many others materialized in the nursery of the castle.

"Raul," Vitomas screamed but could not run to him because she was putting pressure on Kyra's shoulder. Lakin knelt down next to Hannah.

"I am so glad to see you," Hannah said.

Simon grabbed Annabelle who was running to him, with baby David in her arms. "What happened here?" Simon demanded angrily.

"They went after the children," Gabriel said as he still held Christopher, Nicholas and Cerey.

"Only cowards go after children!" Raul spat. "Who was behind this?" Raul and Simon both knelt down by their mother. Lakin was helping Hannah control the bleeding from Renya's wound.

"Erebus said it was Hecate," said Gabriel.

"Erebus," Simon repeated. "Is he here?"

"Yes," Gabriel said. "There is much to tell you."

Hecate and Sampson talked and made love all night and much of the morning. As Sampson slept Hecate went to her unholy altar and called upon Raum but he did not answer her supplications. Over and over Hecate tried to contact her benefactor but there was no answer. Hecate knew something was wrong, suddenly fear surged through her. "Daegal," she gasped out loud and called to him. But Daegal did not answer her repeated cries. Hecate called out to demons and dark lords but no one answered her. She quickly returned to her bedroom and put a spell upon Sampson that would cause him to sleep.

Late the next afternoon, Vivian walked into Bekka's and Koby's chambers in Gabriel's house. Bekka was sitting up in bed with Koby, Misha, Elan and Cassandra in the room talking with her.

"Misha could I speak with you for a moment?" Vivian asked then turned to Bekka. "I haven't been ignoring you; I have been taking care of the others, I will come here next."

"Vivian I know; so many are hurt. I got the flowers you picked, thank you."

Misha walked out of the bedroom and closed the door. "Can I ask a favor of you?" Vivian asked; it was obvious to Misha that his friend was exhausted.

"Of course, what do you need?"

"Diana is afraid that Thor is dead and we are keeping it from her; she is determined to see him. And Hannah doesn't want her out of bed. Would you carry her, it's not far?"

"Of course, actually I was going to visit her next, "Misha said as they walked out of Koby's and Bekka's chambers."

"Their parents were fierce Venatores and both were killed on a hunt when they were children. Thor raised Diana because they have no other family. Of course other members of our clan helped. They stayed with us a lot." Vivian opened the door to Diana's room and yelled, "I told you to stay in bed!" Diana was trying to get out of bed but her legs were tangled in the blankets.

"Vivian your friend isn't very obedient," Misha said with a grin as he walked over to the bed. "Last night I told her to stay inside so she would be safe."

"Venatores are not trained to be obedient," Diana said with a grin and fell back onto her pillow.

"Misha will carry you to Thor's room," said Vivian.

"Oh thank you," Diana said weakly. "But I have to warn you I am heavier than I look."

Misha laughed, "I think that I can manage." He lifted the covers off from Diana. "Do you have a robe?"

"No, in fact this is Vivian's nightgown," Diana said then her eyes grew wide. "Why, can you see through this?"

Misha smiled as he looked at the pale pink silk nightgown that clung to Diana's body, "Well, not really but it is pretty thin; mind you I'm not complaining."

Diana started to laugh then winced in pain, "Misha don't make me laugh it hurts."

"Diana," Misha said in a stern tone of voice. "This is going to be like dancing, let me lead. You have several wounds and it will probably hurt when I pick you up."

"That's fine but you're talking to me like my brother again." Diana winced and caught her breath as Misha picked her up.

"Are you alright?" Misha asked as Diana weakly leaned her head against his chest.

"Yes, how are your feet?" Diana asked with a grin.

"Black and blue and full of cuts," Misha said smiling. "I still expect that foot massage."

Diana started to laugh, then said sadly, "I won't be able to go to the wedding with you."

"You're not getting out of it that easily," Misha said. "Elan and Cassandra are postponing it a couple of weeks because so many people are injured. We might even have enough time for a few dance lessons." Diana giggled while Vivian opened the door to Thor's room. Hannah had given Thor pain medicine and he was sleeping soundly. Misha gently set Diana on her feet near the bed; immediately Diana's knees started to buckle and she grabbed Misha's warrior's robe.

"I am sorry, I am just so dizzy."

"I'll hang on to you."

Tears flowed down Diana's cheeks as she looked at her brother. "He looks dead."

"He had four knife wounds," Vivian explained. "But Hannah is a great physician and Thor will be fine, but he will also be in bed for a while."

Diana moved away from Misha and took a couple of steps closer to the bed so she could touch Thor's hand. "We were chasing a demon and ran right into an ambush, we should have known better."

"Diana you are getting really pale," Vivian said.

"Maybe I should go back to bed."

Misha picked Diana up and carried her out of the room. Diana was quiet as they walked down the hallway. Misha laid Diana on her bed and covered her with the blankets, then he bent down and kissed her on the forehead.

Diana's eyes were closed but she smiled and said, "I thought you said you would do better the next time you kissed me."

Misha laughed, "I don't think you are in the right condition for that kind of kiss."

"You're not getting out of it that easily," Diana teased.

"Get some rest, I will be back to see you," Misha said and he and Vivian walked out of Diana's room.

"Thank you for doing that," Vivian said. "She really likes you."

"So Vivian, are you trying to match me up with your friend?"

"Is it that obvious?" Vivian asked with a grin.

"Yes."

"Are you mad?"

"No, I like her," Misha said. "She's beautiful and crazy."

"Misha I should tell you that Thor probably won't let her go to the wedding with you. He is really over protective; I don't remember him ever letting her go some place with a man."

"Are you telling me Diana has never had a boyfriend?" Misha asked with disbelief. "I would think all kinds of men would be after her."

"Oh, there are many in our village who want her. "I'm saying that I don't think she has ever held hands or been kissed before. Apparently you kissed her; that was probably her first time."

"Miss me already?" Orbus asked with a grin as Hecate materialized in his lair.

"This is business," Hecate said seriously. "I have spent the last two hours trying to contact just about anyone in the hell regions, is something going on?"

"You mean you don't know?"

"Sampson came home last night; no I don't know, tell me."

"The news is spreading through all of the worlds like a wildfire," Orbus said. "There will be no blood moon ceremonies in Nunc. An army of humans, Shettees and Rualas attacked Raum's hell domain and called the Angels in. The sacrifices have been released and legions of Angels are still battling with demons."

"What!" Hecate said in disbelief and quickly sat down. "And my attack against the Royal Family of Wetpr and those priests?"

"That too failed, but Hecate not only did the Angels intervene but also black magics."

"I don't understand what you are saying?"

"I only know what I have heard," Orbus said. "The humans were holding their own in all of the attacks, then someone with knowledge of black magics interfered and blocked your connection to the Kafas. Were you so immersed in sex that you did not realize that?" Hecate did not answer. "Then thousands of Hengers attacked the demons. Hecate it is useless for you to keep attacking those humans, they are protected by the heavens."

Hannah spent most of the day at Sudfad's castle tending to the wounded. Instead of resting, Sudfad, Simon, Raul, Gabriel, Raphael, Edward, Calen, Luca and the Sanuri were in meetings all day. Dagon was still with Erebus, who remained in his cottage. Natasha, Lila and Vivian were taking care of the wounded who had been moved to Gabriel's home and the children. Koby spent most of his time with Bekka, while Elan, Cassandra and Misha were busy moving their team's belongings from the castle back to Gabriel's house.

Delilah and Zoya helped Gala with the wounded. But Delilah could not stay focused with the happy news that she and Archetenus were going to have twins. Laurel, Alexander, Annabelle and Vitomas were alternating between caring for children and restoring order to the castle. Renya and Kyra were each confined to bed and Petra kept running back and forth between their rooms to tend to them. Archetenus, Maxwell and Emeral returned to duty at the fort.

Hecate was quiet as Orbus' words filled her mind. "I can't believe this, I just can't believe this," she started repeating. Then Hecate paused and her eyes grew wide. "Orbus, Sampson got them, the holy items that Raum wanted; they are in my lair. Think of the power they will give us. We should move forward with our plans to go to war."

Chapter XXXV
Changes

Tears flowed in Lentz as the army Claudius led suddenly appeared in their homes. The members of the Nordes Tribe were returned to their village, except for Sorren, he was reunited with his family at the castle of King Mathas. The families of both Claudius and Fahron were still living in Mathas' castle, so Claudius, Stephan, Matthew and Thaos appeared with Sorren in the King's dining room.

"Why didn't you tell us you were coming home?" Bella cried as she hugged and kissed her husband and sons.

"We didn't know," Claudius said. "We have so much to tell you and honestly you may not believe some of it."

Although it was late, Mathas ordered his cooks to prepare a feast and everyone in the King's castle sat up all night, eating, drinking, talking, laughing and crying.

The Shettees were amazed that they were returned to the homes of their families in the Ice Caves. The Rualas had more experience with Angels and while happy they were not as mystified as the Shettees. King Manu ordered a week of celebrations. The families of Gael and Lakin at first feared the men dead, but were greatly relieved to learn they were at Sudfad's castle caring for the wounded. The wives and children of the Shettees who did not return; also rejoiced in the grand homecoming.

Two days after the return of Claudius' army, battles were still waging in the hell domains between the demons and the Angels. This news also traveled to other worlds, to other hell domains, to other powerful demons. Unbeknownst to Sampson, Hecate and Orbus were monitoring the battles and planning to wage a war. Raum's domain was now available to the most powerful demon that could control it, for Raum had fallen to the Angels and was imprisoned in The Abyss.

"Well, look at this," Natasha said and smiled as Misha carried Diana to the breakfast table.

"I'm going crazy staying in bed," Diana said as Misha set her in a chair.

"You're healing rather quickly," Hannah said as she was pouring coffee into cups. "I think today we will start you walking, but only short distances and you can't over do it."

"I understand," Diana said cheerfully. "When will Thor start walking?"

"Probably not for a couple of weeks, his injuries were much more serious than yours," Hannah replied.

"Will they be walking in time for our wedding?" asked Cassandra.

"I am sure Diana will but I don't know yet about Thor. But even if they are walking they will be weak," Hannah said.

Cassandra looked at Diana, "If Thor is up to it do you think he would walk down the aisle with my sister Melinda?"

Diana smiled, "I think he would be honored to. In fact you should ask him now, it might help him heal."

Cassandra looked at Elan then continued, "Diana we were wondering if you would walk down the aisle with Misha." Diana turned and looked at Misha who was sitting next to her. He smiled and nodded and Diana turned back to Cassandra.

"Oh, I would just love to," Diana said excitedly.

"If you and Thor aren't healed enough by that time, then Misha and Melinda will walk together," Cassandra said.

Misha leaned over and whispered into Diana's ear and she tried not to laugh, "You better be healed by then."

"Diana when you are feeling better I would like you to look over some maps we have of northern Ryed," Gabriel said.

537

"Joshua's first letter about you and Thor made it sound like you found things you weren't expecting. I want to wait until you both are better before we talk business."

"I'll look at the maps today," Diana said. "It will give me something to do. Northern Ryed is a very dangerous place it is filled with criminals, dark lords, witches and demons. And it is as if the Teivel Clan has booby trapped the land. Thor and I were very careful when we hunted because we saw what happened to others who were not."

"There is a big meeting at the castle today which most of us must attend," Gabriel said. "But perhaps afterwards, we could talk a little about your experiences."

"Gabriel if you would like, Thor and I could guide you and your team through that area?" Diana said. "It's the very least we could do for your hospitality."

Raphael and Gabriel looked at each other. "We will take you up on that offer," Raphael said. "It would help us a great deal."

"I can't go because I might be pregnant," Vivian said with disdain.

"We have a rule that if any of our wives are pregnant we are not putting them in increased danger by working on the missions," Raphael said.

"I guess I can understand that," Diana said. "But our Venatores have the choice whether they want to hunt if they are pregnant."

"And a lot of them don't make it back alive," said Raphael.

"When we go on missions," Natasha explained. "We can't let the dark lords and demons see the Rualas because then they will know that believers of The Great Ruler are in the area, so the humans do the direct contact with people. I just had Lily so I can't go, Lila is pregnant and Hannah and Vivian probably are pregnant. If I taught you some of the things you needed to know would you be willing to help Gabriel and the others on the mission?"

"Sure, I think that sounds like fun," Diana said happily. "Who is going on this mission?"

"That hasn't been determined yet," Raphael said. "We should have a better idea after the meeting today."

"I want to go on the mission," said Misha.

"Does that mean you will turn down the position if Sudfad offers it?" Raphael asked.

"I'm not sure; I would really like to do both. Do you think he would let us have time off for the missions?"

"That is a question I have been wondering too," Raphael said.

"Well I have decided," Emeral said. "While it is a great honor to be an officer over an army of humans, and to say nothing about being the only woman in Sudfad's military; I would rather be a grandmother. Our children are still traumatized from that battle and with possibly three more babies on the way; I would rather be here."

"We love having Emeral and Maxwell here," Hannah said with a sweet smile.

"I plan to take the position," Maxwell said. "I'll tell you, it made me feel alive again."

"What are you all talking about?" asked Diana.

"The demons had corrupted so many of Sudfad's staff and military that he put many of our group in his military as temporary officers. He was very pleased with everyone's performance and we believe he is going to offer those people permanent positions in the military," Gabriel explained.

Diana turned to Misha, "You were wearing a military uniform when I met you."

"Yes, I was an acting major. I did enjoy it but I love working on the team."

"You two are awfully quiet," Gabriel said to Calen and Luca.

539

"We're been on the team since the very beginning," Calen said. "Of course we are going on the mission."

Gabriel and Raphael looked at each other, then Gabriel spoke. "Over the last two days we have had many meetings at the castle and partly because The Lion told Simon and Raul their destinies as two of The Seven Sons has priority over their military positions. Sudfad asked about every one of you in this room, well almost everyone, not Hannah, Natasha, Lila and Diana. He wanted to know who would be interested in a military position. So you might want to think about it before the meeting this morning."

"Are you saying he asked about us girls too?" Cassandra asked.

"Yes, you, Bekka and Vivian. But we don't know exactly what he will be offering and to who and I am sure he will give you a little time to think it over," said Gabriel.

"Raphael you didn't tell me that," Vivian said.

"Honestly I didn't want you disappointed if Sudfad didn't ask you. As Emeral said, there aren't any women in Sudfad's military."

"So you would let her be an officer in the military if she wanted?" Natasha asked.

"I think she would be good," Raphael said to almost everyone's surprise. "But I still don't like the idea of her fighting when she is pregnant."

"Vivian I am not trying to talk you out of it," Natasha said. "Everyone knows how much I love working on missions but I will be honest, I never realized taking care of a baby was so much work. I am just telling you so you aren't as blindsided as I was."

"And I pretty much plan to keep her pregnant until we are old and gray," Calen kidded which made everyone at the table laugh.

"You haven't put the babies down since you got home," Ingr said as she bent down and kissed Stephan on the cheek.

Stephan was sitting in a large overstuffed chair in the main parlor of Claudius' castle with his son and daughter on his lap.

"I can't believe how much I missed them and you," Stephan said. "I used to make fun of guys who wanted to get out of the field and go home to their families, now I am one of those guys. But I am glad you girls came home when you did. The battles got so much worse."

"I hated to leave you, but I couldn't stand to be away from the babies any longer," Ingr said. "I swear Bella must have cried for two days after Nikki, Angelina and I came home; she was so worried about us. I hope all of this madness is finally over, Juleta's revenge against our families. It's no way to live, always looking over your shoulder."

Stephan looked at Ingr without speaking. Claudius, Thaos and Stephan had decided not to tell their wives about the warning of The Lion. These men felt that their wives had been through too much to add more worry in their lives.

Vitomas was overjoyed when Raul talked to her about naming their daughter Miranda. But Vitomas became concerned when Raul told her what The Lion had said about his, Simon's and Matthew's destinies unfolding. "Oh Raul I hope this doesn't mean you are going to be gone all of the time. I understand you are doing good but it is so hard on me and the children. Gabriel's team came over every night to wrestle with the boys because the children missed you and Simon so."

"If Simon and I give up our positions in the military perhaps we will be home more. It's hard on Simon and me too. Our children are getting so big, I hate missing out on the little things in their lives. And I can never stop thinking about you."

"I'm going to be fine," Renya said. "I don't know what all of this fuss is about."

"Renya you had a very serious injury I want you to do everything that Hannah tells you," Sudfad said. "Which for now means you stay in bed."

541

"I'm bored," Renya protested.

"You are weak but I know how stubborn you are, so I brought you some work. It is fine if you don't want to do it, I just thought you might find it interesting."

"What sort of work?"

Sudfad picked up a large leather bag that he had sitting on the floor. "This bag is too heavy for you to lift, so I am going to put it on the bed and you can take things out. When the Sanuri was at the Patronus headquarters in Nora this last time, he was looking for information about the blood moon ceremonies. He found these old scrolls which contain valuable information about the Insidiae and the Grand Masters. As you know many of them live under false names."

"These scrolls may provide the first clues as to their real identities." Sudfad was pulling scrolls out of the bag as he spoke. "Remember that Erebus warned us about a couple of the Grand Masters, well he gave me this stack of papers. I have not had time to read them all but they contain all of the information that Sophie told him and later his own research on the Grand Masters and the Insidiae. I hope you can uncover some mysteries here."

"Sudfad this sounds fascinating," Renya said happily. "I will need some paper and pen for my notes.

"Already thought of that," Sudfad said and handed Renya a large leather bound journal with her name printed in gold. The leather contained ornate decorations. Then he handed Renya two beautiful pens and a well of ink.

"Oh Sudfad these are just lovely. Thank you so much."

"Don't overdo it," Sudfad said. "I have to go down to the meeting now."

"Honey we can finish this discussion after the meeting," Simon said as he held Arianna.

"I can't believe the Angels tattled on me," Annabelle said. "Why would they do that?"

"They told us about your encounter with Molach to teach us a lesson."

"And what lesson would that be?" Annabelle said as she took Arianna from Simon.

"That every one of us has journeys to take and basically that Raul and I should stop protecting you and Vitomas so much and let you take your journeys."

"Really," Annabelle said with a big smile. "I really like those Angels."

"I have to get to the meeting," Simon said and kissed Annabelle on the lips. Then he smiled and added, "When I come home we can talk about your journey."

"No need I can tell you now," Annabelle said. "Your mother raised a family, and worked side by side with your father, while upholding her responsibilities as Queen. Vitomas and I want the same thing, we made the same covenants and neither of us plan on breaking our promises to The Great Ruler."

"Thank you for coming," Sudfad said. "I moved the meeting to the family dining room so we would have more space; the Great Hall is still being cleaned after the battle. Please help yourselves to the trays of refreshments; this meeting may take a while."

Raul stood up, "Father may I say something?"

"Of course."

"Before we get started on business, I want to thank all of you for taking care of our families and kingdom while Simon and I were gone. Vitomas told me how many of you even spent time playing with the boys because they missed Simon and me. We truly appreciate what you did."

"I think you two should take your wives on a trip or treat them to something," Dagon said teasingly. "Every night they had a table of treats prepared for us and your kids are great but seven of them plus Lily, I don't think Vitomas and Annabelle ever sleep."

"You're right," Raul said with a smile and looked at his brother. "Simon and I have been talking about taking them on a second honeymoon. And Father is getting anxious to start the meeting."

"Actually what my son said is the basis for this meeting," Sudfad said. "In one of the darkest hours of this kingdom every person in this room, including some of your spouses who are not here, were the only people I could trust. I have the most powerful army in all of Opots and yet no one from my military is represented here."

"Looking among you it is almost ironic and I mean no insult to anyone. Jared and Archetenus once thought to be our enemies have proven themselves over and over in their abilities and their loyalty. Priests, Rualas, Venatores and a major from another kingdom's military. Erebus will be joining us later, I am not saying I trust him, but he does seem to be helping us. Some of you may be too young to remember but there were times when our peoples would never have mingled much less worked together as a team."

Sudfad continued, "This situation has made me see many things with new eyes. I know most of you are expecting me to announce some major changes and I will admit I was planning to do so until the Sanuri and I spoke this morning. In his wisdom, he suggested that I put my concerns on the table and that we try to find solutions together. I want to offer every person in this room a high ranking position in our military. But I do not want to upset the balance of Gabriel's team."

"You are all so talented you can be used in both arenas. This morning I received a message from High Priest Nicholas from the monastery at Philiste. As soon as our training center is completed we will become the second training location for Patronus Priests. I bring this up now, because so many of the soldiers in my military were corrupted by the demons. So my questions are these: how can I best utilize all of you and what do you want?"

"We actually talked among ourselves about this," Raphael said. "Many of us find both positions desirable, but the team is our true love. Would it be possible for some of the people here to do both? For people to be in your military except for the times they are needed on missions?"

Before Sudfad could answer Gabriel stood up and said, "Lately our missions have required a great deal of manpower and resources but that is usually not the case. Every mission is different. We have had many missions that only required a few of us to work them. A great deal of planning goes into every mission so I could give you a count of the people I will need well in advance to aid you in filling positions."

"Where is everyone?" Hannah asked as she walked in the house with bags of food. "Is the meeting still going on?"

"I think so," Lila said as she took some of the bags from Hannah. "Is there more?"

"Oh yes, the boca is almost full. I went shopping after tending to the children at the orphanage, and that always makes me want to buy more for our babies. So there are toys besides food. Where are the children?"

"When they found out that Diana was going to be in her room drawing maps they wanted to draw with her," Lila said.

Natasha entered the kitchen and said, "You have to see this it is so cute." Then Natasha left the kitchen and Hannah and Lila followed her. They walked up the stairs and Natasha opened the door to Diana's room. Diana was sleeping on the bed with her arm around Cerey, who was also sleeping. Christopher and Nicholas were lying on the floor sleeping and they were surrounded with sheets of paper containing pictures they had drawn. Natasha closed the door.

"Guess it was nap time for all of them," Natasha said with a grin.

"I better get back before Sampson wakes up," Hecate said then kissed Orbus passionately.

"Does he know about us?"

"Of course not. He would probably kill us both."

"Is he going to complete his trials to become a demon?"

"I may have to postpone that," Hecate said. "Now that we have those holy items he is the only one who can touch them. And besides with all of the chaos in the underworlds I have to find another benefactor." Hecate smiled and kissed Orbus again. "If we take control of a domain we will be strong enough to be benefactors."

"I've been thinking," Orbus said. "The Angels attacking the hell regions actually works in our favor, because it deters demons from other worlds from going to Nunc, thus eliminating competition."

"Sorry we are late," Gabriel said as his team entered their house. "Something smells good."

"I was about ready to send a message to the castle to see if you would be here for lunch," Hannah said as she walked up to Gabriel and kissed him. "So what happened?"

"Oh lots of changes, we will tell everyone at lunch. Where are the children?"

"Camped out in Diana's room. She said the maps you have of northern Ryed are really bad so she is drawing new maps. The children wanted to draw with her. An hour ago they were all taking naps."

"Diana what are you doing?" Emeral asked in a scolding tone when she saw Diana slowly walking down the stairs with Christopher, Nicholas and Cerey.

"The children said they would tell you if I fell. I don't like being a patient."

"Well you are pretty pale," Maxwell said and quickly walked up the stairs and put his arm around Diana.

"Grandpa, she's teaching us how to draw maps so we can help you," Nicholas said.

"Nicholas give that map to your papa," Diana said as Maxwell helped her down the stairs.

"I can make as many maps as you want," Diana continued. "As you can see my map is very different from yours."

"Nicholas, Cerey we got toys," Christopher yelled when he saw new stuffed animals sitting on the children's chairs.

"Did you walk down here?" Misha asked disapprovingly when he entered the house and saw Diana.

"You're talking to me like my brother again."

"Well maybe somebody has to," Misha scolded. "You're as white as a sheet."

"Where are Vivian and Raphael?" Cassandra asked. "They were right behind us?"

"She's puking," Misha said with a grin. "And Raphael is with her smiling like a fool."

Elan and Koby were helping Bekka down the stairs to the dining room, when Natasha joined them on the stairs with a tray in her hands. "Hannah, Thor is hardly eating anything. He's so weak still I had to feed him."

"What!" cried Diana and tried to quickly turn around but lost her balance. Maxwell caught her.

"Don't get upset," Hannah said to Diana. "I have him on strong pain medication and that behavior is normal, so we have been feeding him more often because he can't eat much at a time."

A few minutes later when everyone but Thor was seated around the table Natasha said, "Ok let's hear the news."

"To our surprise Sudfad let us make a lot of the decisions," Raphael said. "He wants to utilize our talents as best he can. There are going to be five generals assigned to Fort Salar, Sudfad, Raul, Simon, Edward and me and other than Sudfad the rest of us will divide our duties between the team and the military. As you know Emeral wants to stay home with our children but she said she would help out in an emergency."

"Maxwell, Archetenus and Misha have been promoted to colonels; Misha will be the only one of the three to divide his duties between the team and the military. Jared wants to work on the team as do all of the women here but Vivian would like to train with the military at times. Raphael continued, "Calen, Luca, Dagon and Koby are all majors in the military who will divide their time between that and the team.""

"What!" Natasha said loudly to Calen. "You're in the military now?"

"It's not going to change a lot," Calen said. "I will just have other things to do between missions. Besides we all decided this would help us keep an eye on what is going on in the military. We are going to be doing group inspections of the other forts."

"Elan does not feel he has enough experience under his belt to lead soldiers, so he remains on the team but he will be training with the rest of us," Raphael explained.

"Vivian, I thought you would have taken a position in the military," Natasha said.

"I was thinking about it but after having to keep leaving the meeting to puke, I decided against it."

"I'm so proud of you," Lila said and kissed Luca on the cheek.

"I'm proud of all of you," Hannah said. "But you left out Gabriel."

"I am still going to run the team and I want to spend my spare time with my family."

"Now that makes me happy," Hannah said and kissed Gabriel on the lips.

"Sudfad wants to talk to you too," Gabriel said to Hannah. "Tomorrow after you visit your patients, stop into his study."

"Why?" Hannah asked suspiciously. "He doesn't want me in the military does he?" Many at the table laughed at this question.

"No, but after the last couple of battles he realizes you are going to need a medical team. So you can start thinking about what you want. See everything has changed now; until recently the terrorists never attacked Salar. Sudfad says we are going to have to change the way we do business," said Gabriel.

Chapter XXXVI
Families Uniting

Gabriel and his team returned to the castle after telling Hannah, Bekka, Natasha, Lila and Diana about the changes in their job positions. Vivian decided to stay at the house since she wasn't feeling well and Emeral stayed to help with the children. As soon as the team was gone Hannah turned to her friends, "Ladies we are fixing a feast tonight to celebrate everyone's promotions. Emeral would you watch the children while I get more food?"

"Of course and I love that idea."

"Well I think we should get them gifts," Natasha said. "But what should we get them?"

"Some of the soldiers that I supervised had swords and daggers with the military emblem on them. They are very smart looking. The soldiers have the option of carrying them and they purchase them at a store in Salar but I don't know which one."

"Emeral why don't you come with me and we'll stop at the castle and find out the name of the store," Natasha said. "Maybe we could get their names engraved on them."

"I'll watch the children," Diana said. "It's not like I can do anything else."

"I'm not sure you should be doing even that," Hannah said.

"I'll stay with the children and I can start some of the food," Lila offered.

"Oh Emeral, you should make your famous cake," Bekka said. "Everyone loves it so. I want to help with something too."

"I know; Bekka and Diana why don't you help the children make cards for the gifts," Natasha suggested. "They know where the paper and supplies are. Write all of our names on each card and that includes Diana and Thor."

Diana turned red, "But we have no money to put towards the gifts."

"Our families have been very blessed," Hannah said. "Don't worry about the money."

"What should I do?" asked Vivian.

"Go to bed you look worse than I do," Diana said teasingly. "Are you throwing up because of the baby?"

"I think so," Vivian replied.

"Joshua and Iris are going to be so happy. And I am still trying to get used to the idea that my hunting friend is married and now you're having a baby. Wait until Thor hears this."

"Diana since we are having a celebration, would you like something to wear besides my robe?" Natasha asked. "Don't be shy I have a lot of clothes."

"Actually, that would be nice. Perhaps I could wash my hair too."

"I'll help you," Lila said. "Just let me finish clearing the table."

As the Royal Family were finishing their midday meal Annabelle said, "It is so sweet of Sudfad to take his meals in their chambers with Renya."

"It seems so strange not to have them at the table," Vitomas said. "It's I don't know, sad."

Simon looked at Raul and winked. "At the meeting this morning the guys were telling us how hard you two work with all of our children, then taking care of Lily too. Dagon said we should take you on a trip just so you can get some sleep," Simon said.

Both Vitomas and Annabelle laughed. "They were all so good with the boys, we really appreciated them coming by."

"Well, Raul and I were already talking about taking you two on a second honeymoon. There are some beautiful hotels on the ocean in Lentz; we could visit family and see the sights. What do you think?

"You mean without the children?" asked Annabelle.

"Yes."

"But who will care for them?"

"We will," Laurel said with a big smile.

"We should probably wait until David is a little older," Annabelle said.

"Do you want to do this before I have the baby?" asked Vitomas.

"It is up to you two," Raul said. "You let us know when you want to take a trip." Vitomas and Annabelle looked at each other with excitement.

"What is all of this?" Gabriel asked with a grin as the team returned to the house that evening and found the dining table decorated with flowers and gifts.

"You look amazing," Calen said as Natasha walked out of the kitchen in a beautiful dress.

"We are celebrating all of your promotions," Natasha said. "Koby wait a couple of minutes before you get Bekka. Misha will you bring Diana down here?"

"You are so obvious," Misha said with a grin.

"You two are attracted to each other," Natasha said. "Everyone can see that. Just go and get her."

"Yes My Lady," Misha said and left the dining room.

"Dagon put that down; we will tell you when you can open the gifts," Natasha scolded and laughed.

"Natasha sometimes I feel like we are married," Dagon joked.

Hannah, Emeral and Lila all came out of the kitchen carrying trays of food and dressed elegantly. "Emeral made her famous cake," Hannah announced.

"This is a feast then," Maxwell said and started to open bottles of wine.

"Is Vivian feeling any better?" Raphael asked as he looked around the room and didn't see his wife.

"She is getting the children ready," Lila said. "She thought she would need the practice."

"You look really nice," Misha said when he walked into Diana's room and found her sitting in a chair. She was wearing a light blue dress and her hair was curled. "How do you feel?"

"A little tired but excited, this is really fun. Is your family always like this? Everyone is so nice."

"I guess they are. Did you sleep at all or were you helping with the party?"

"Helping."

"I'm going to carry you because you are probably doing too much."

"I can try walking..." Diana said but Misha picked her up before she completed her sentence.

"You know you are a lot heavier than you look," Misha teased.

Diana laughed, "You just wait until I am well."

Misha and Diana met Koby and Bekka on the stairs, "Doesn't she look beautiful?" Koby said of Bekka, who was wearing a light yellow dress.

"Both the girls look beautiful," Misha replied.

"Well don't the two of you look pretty," Maxwell said as he watched the two couples enter the dining room. A few minutes later Vivian walked into the room wearing a beautiful pink dress. She was carrying Cerey who was also wearing a pink dress and walking with Nicholas and Christopher. Both boys were dressed up and carrying baskets full of cards.

"It was harder to get them all dressed than I thought it would be," Vivian said with a laugh. "The boys kept tearing their ties off."

"Hannah is it time?" Christopher asked loudly.

"Yes," Hannah said then she turned to the adults. "The children made each of you a card. Your names are on the envelopes, but you will have to help the children, since they can't read that well yet. You can open your gifts after you read your cards."

"Let's have a toast first," Maxwell said happily. He waited until everyone had wine in their glass then he held his wine glass in the air. "To family."

"To family," they all repeated.

Nicholas and Christopher gave Cerey some cards from their baskets. Cerey in turn handed all of her cards to Maxwell so he gave them to the correct people. Christopher and Nicholas just handed their baskets to people and let them pick out their own cards. "Ok now open your gifts," Christopher said excitedly and ran over to Luca.

The members of the team were pleased with their gifts and cards and each of them thanked the family members.

"It doesn't seem right that Thor's and my names are on the cards," Diana said with embarrassment.

"Oh nonsense dear," Emeral replied. "You're practically part of the family now."

Diana and Misha were sitting next to each other at the table and he leaned down and told her again how pretty she looked. Diana blushed. Just as the family was starting to eat, the front door opened. "We're home," Joao called out.

Cassandra jumped out of her chair and ran up to Joao and Dack as they entered the dining room and hugged and kissed them both. Both men walked up to their close friend Bekka and hugged and kissed her.

"You're wounded," Dack said when he saw how Bekka was holding herself.

"It's nothing, I am so glad to see you."

"It's worse than she is letting on," Koby said. Misha grinned when he saw the look on Koby's face. Koby did not look happy at the attention these two handsome young men were giving Bekka.

Misha's amusement soon ended when he saw how Joao and Dack looked at Diana. "Vivian," Cassandra said. "This is my brother Joao and Dack they are both new members of the team and have been working in Nora. This is Vivian; she is a Venator of the Clan of Gesmal and Raphael's wife."

"Cassandra has written about you," Joao said politely. "It is nice to meet you."

"And this is Diana, she and her brother Thor are also Venatores and both were injured in the recent battle; Thor is upstairs in bed," Cassandra explained. "You know everyone else."

"Are you anyone's wife?" Joao asked with a grin. Immediately Calen and Luca looked at Misha and smiled.

"No," Diana said and blushed. Natasha set two additional place settings while Dagon brought two more chairs into the dining room.

Joao and Dack kept staring at Diana which was making her blush and feel uncomfortable; after a few minutes Joao asked, "Are you going to Cassandra's and Elan's wedding?"

Diana looked at the two young men and smiled sweetly, "Yes with Misha."

Joao looked at Misha and said, "I didn't know, sorry."

Calen got a mischievous look on his face and asked loudly, "Misha is it just a onetime date?" Both Misha and Diana quickly looked at Calen, who was grinning at them.

"Calen quit trying to put people on the spot," Natasha scolded then she looked at Joao. "Except for Vivian the rest of us have only known Diana and Thor for a few days."

Diana could feel tension although she didn't understand what was going on between Misha and Calen. Diana placed her right hand on Misha's left forearm but looked at Joao and Dack as she spoke. "Misha is buying me a dress and teaching me how to dance which is why I am trying hard to get my strength back. The other night when Misha and I were dancing at the party at the castle, I kept stepping on his feet and kicking him because I don't know how to dance. He must have been in pain but he was a good sport about it."

Misha was smiling at Diana as she spoke, as was Emeral. Joao and Dack now understood that Diana was at least somewhat involved with Misha and not interested in them.

"Misha and Diana are walking down the aisle together at our wedding," Elan explained because he too could feel tension at the table.

"Joao you will be walking down the aisle with Vivian because Raphael and Gabriel are performing the ceremony. And Dack you will be walking with Elan's sister Janja," Cassandra explained.

"Before I forget," Natasha said loudly since she wanted to change the subject. "The carpenters came by this afternoon. They want to start work on the nurseries tomorrow is that alright with everyone?"

"Good," Gabriel said and turned to Raphael.

"Perfect timing," Raphael said with a proud smile.

"Good because I already told them to start," Natasha said. "But after breakfast some of you will need to help us move Thor. His room is pretty close to where the work is taking place and Hannah is concerned he won't get his rest."

"Oh course," Luca said. "We should move him to our wing of the house and we should probably move Diana too, so she can get some sleep during the day."

"I'm fine where I am," Diana said. "My room is beautiful."

"No, Luca is right," Hannah said. "You need rest to heal."

"The rooms on either side of my chambers are open," Misha said. "Put them in those rooms, then I can help them." Misha turned to Joao and Dack and said, "Diana isn't supposed to be walking yet and Thor can't get out of bed."

The tension at the dinner table subsided as everyone shared stories about what they had been involved in. "You came back at a good time," Gabriel said to Joao and Dack. "I am planning another mission that will take us to northern Ryed and possibly the west coast of Wetpr. That's why Diana and Thor are here, they spent months hunting in northern Ryed although we haven't had a chance to talk about it yet." Gabriel turned to Hannah, "Any idea of when Thor will be able to join us for meetings?"

"It is really too early to tell, his wounds were very serious." Hannah glanced at Diana as she spoke.

"Diana do you think you will be up to participating in a meeting tomorrow night after dinner?" Gabriel asked.

"Sure," Diana said cheerfully.

"She's going to have to get more rest than she did today," Hannah said. "I can't believe she is still up."

"This has all been so exciting," Diana said. "You see Thor and I don't have any family. Our parents were killed when I was six and he was ten. We've been taking care of each other ever since. But Joshua and Iris took us in a lot, that's why we are such close friends with Vivian. But what I am trying to say is, it has been so much fun to be part of your family for a couple of days, I just wish that Thor was better so he could enjoy it. You are all so nice and I feel like a princess in Natasha's clothes." Everyone at the table was quiet after hearing Diana's words.

"So you are saying you were too excited to sleep today?" Misha asked as he wanted to cut through the silence so Diana wouldn't feel uncomfortable.

"Yes," Diana said and laughed. Then she turned to Emeral. "Could we save a piece of cake for Thor? I have never tasted anything this good before."

"I'll tell you what," Emeral replied. "When Thor is up to eating solid food, I will bake a cake just for him."

"Really?" Diana asked with excitement. "He would really like that; thank you."

Maxwell looked at Emeral and said with a soft smile, "I can hear the wheels spinning in your head. They are a little old to adopt."

"Nonsense," Emeral replied and winked at Maxwell.

"What are you talking about?" asked Diana.

Koby looked at Diana and explained. "Emeral and Maxwell are Calen's blood parents but they took in me, Luca, Dagon and Misha and raised us as their own with their other children. They were living in the Ice Caves but now that they moved here, they have pretty much adopted everyone in this room. And all the children here, except for Lily are adopted, it's kind of what this family does."

"I just checked on Kyra," Sudfad said to Renya as he walked into their bedroom chambers. "Petra is asleep in the chair next to her bed. It is so cute, I covered them both up like you always do."

"You know we could probably put a second bed in that room. Those children are young enough that they shouldn't get embarrassed by that," Renya said.

"I can have that done tomorrow," Sudfad said as he changed his clothes. "I am going to tell you something but don't get mad." Renya put down the papers she was reading and looked somberly at Sudfad. "All the dogs are curled up on the bed with Kyra; I didn't have the heart to make them move."

Renya chuckled, "I suspect those dogs are on the beds more than I realize. I never catch them but I find the hair."

"They are both really good kids," Sudfad said as he got into bed. "Remember what Raul and Simon were like at that age? They were in trouble every day. I don't think it is so bad that Petra sneaks his pets into his room. I mean it really doesn't hurt anything."

Renya smiled, "So you want me to stop scolding him? Alright, tomorrow tell him he can have the pets in his room. I was going to talk to you about Petra and Kyra anyways. Those children helped to defend the other children from the attackers. They did well, but I was wondering if we should talk to them to find out how they are feeling about it. I think it is the first time they have really fought other people."

"I'll talk to them tomorrow and if I botch it up then you can talk to them," Sudfad said with a grin. "How are you coming on your homework assignment?"

"This is absolutely fascinating," Renya said. "This is exactly the kind of project I needed."

"Misha will you take me in to see Thor first?" Diana asked as Misha carried her up the stairs to her bedroom. "I really appreciate you helping me like this but I feel stupid having to be carried around."

Misha grinned. "I'll find a way for you to pay me back."

"Why does that scare me?" Diana joked.

Misha sat down in the one chair next to Thor's bed and pulled Diana onto his lap. Her face was filled with sadness as she looked at her brother. "I haven't seen him awake since the attack," Diana said. "Hannah, Lila and Natasha have been feeding him. I need to get better soon so I can take care of him."

"Then you have to get more rest. Sleep all day tomorrow so you can attend the meeting after dinner."

Diana did not respond to Misha's comment. She continued to stare at her brother and after a few moments she turned and looked at Misha. "What was going on between you and Calen tonight?"

"We are always joking around with each other, it was nothing."

"Well, it seemed like something because everyone got so tense." Diana paused for a moment. "I hope you weren't mad at me for telling Joao and Dack about you giving me dance lessons and buying me a dress, I only told them because it seemed like you were on the spot and I don't even understand why."

"There wasn't anything wrong with what you said, you told them the truth." Misha was watching Diana's face. "You know they are both interested in you, don't you?" Diana didn't say anything. "Diana could you tell that?"

"Misha I am not stupid."

"I am sorry but you confuse me because sometimes you seem so naïve."

"Misha I don't go out to parties like you do and I am sure that Vivian has told you that Thor doesn't let me go out with men. But part of the training to be a Venator is in reading people and your environment. I am sure I probably do seem naïve to you."

"I didn't mean to insult you."

"I do know that Vivian has been trying to match us up and I haven't stopped her. Because it has been fun and you have been really kind to me. But Misha you don't have to spend time with me because you're a good friend of Vivian's. I am pretty sure I am not the type of girl you normally spend time with."

"First of all I am spending time with you because you are a lot of fun to be with and being beautiful doesn't hurt either. And has somebody told you about the women I date?"

"No, but I did understand Calen's comment tonight about a onetime date."

"Ok if you are so good at reading people, tell me what kind of women I am attracted to."

"Only if you promise not to get mad at me."

"Well, that doesn't sound good; now I really want to hear what you think. Should we go to your room in case we get into an argument?"

Diana smiled, "That might be a good idea." Misha tensed up as he carried Diana to her room and set her on the bed. He walked over to the bedroom door and closed it then sat down on the chair next to her bed.

"You look so defensive," Diana said but Misha did not respond. "Misha you are incredibly handsome, you are smart and charming. You are a great warrior; actually you seem to be good at everything you do. I saw how women were watching you at that party and I will bet you have beautiful women throwing themselves at you all of the time. But for all of these good things you have this invisible wall around you and you don't let people close to you."

"I think you have sex with a lot of women but don't let them close enough to get to know you. I see the way you look at Vivian, it's obvious you have feelings for her but I think a part of that is because it is safe to have feelings for her because she belongs to someone else. Just like it is safe to let your guard down a little around me because you know I will be going back to Ryed and we will never see each other again." Misha stared at Diana but didn't speak.

"I thought you were like this because a woman broke your heart but after Koby said how Maxwell and Emeral took all of you in, I think your family betrayed you and you still feel the pain. You look really mad and I am sorry because you are a nice person and I enjoy being with you but you asked me for an honest answer."

Misha glared at Diana, never before had someone seen into his heart and he wasn't sure how to react. Misha stood up and started to pace around the room. "Misha I am sorry you are so mad. Maybe we shouldn't go to the wedding together."

"Are you saying that so you can go with Joao or Dack?" Misha asked angrily.

"No, of course not. Why would you even ask that?"

"Because at first I thought that's what all of this was about."

"Misha you expect everyone to betray you so you twist things around until they do," Diana said angrily and stood up from the bed. "If you and I don't go to the wedding I still won't go with one of the others because it will make you lose face in front of your family and I wouldn't do that to you."

"Do you mean that?"

"Yes," Diana paused. "You don't have to take me," Diana said as sadness crept into her voice.

"I want to take you," Misha said as he walked towards Diana. "You really confuse me, sometimes you almost seem like a child and just now, it was like you opened me up and looked at my soul. No one has ever done that before and I didn't like it. But you were right, at least about most of it."

There was a knock at the door, "Diana do you want me to help you take that dress off?" Natasha asked.

"You can come in," Misha said. "We are just talking."

"Sounded more like you were fighting," Natasha said. "I can come back."

"No," Misha said to Natasha then he looked at Diana. "I could have helped you unbutton it."

"I need more help than that because I can't lift my arms up."

"I don't understand," said Misha.

"You would see her naked if you would help her," Natasha said with a grin. "So why don't you just turn your back for a couple of minutes."

"Thank you so much for letting me wear that," Diana said. "It is so beautiful."

"You're welcome, it looked nice on you. Didn't it Misha?"

Misha laughed, "Yes it did."

"Ok Misha you can turn around now," Natasha said as she walked out of the room. "Now you two be nice to each other."

Misha turned around and saw that Diana was only wearing Vivian's pink nightgown. "Do you want me to go?"

"No," Diana said. "But I think I will get under the covers because I am cold." Diana sat up in bed and Misha sat down on the bed next to her.

"The part you got wrong was about me feeling comfortable with you because you are leaving. Gabriel and Raphael have not said anything yet but I would not be surprised if they ask you and Thor to join the team; which means you would be staying with us."

"Really? Us?"

"You and Thor would be good members, you shouldn't act so surprised. So now that you have me totally confused, tell me how you feel about me."

"You're a smart man I don't think you confuse that easily," Diana said with a grin then her demeanor softened. "I really like you a lot Misha. You're funny and sweet, although a little bossy at times," she said sarcastically.

"I want to make sure you don't like me like a brother."

"No," Diana said emphatically.

"Do you still want to go to the wedding with me?"

"Yes," she whispered.

Misha leaned forward and kissed Diana on the lips, softly at first but their emotions took control and passion filled their hearts. After several minutes Misha said, "I should leave now. You know for a girl who has never gone on a date you sure can kiss." Diana didn't say anything but turned bright red. Misha laughed loudly.

Misha started to stand up but changed his mind and kissed Diana again. This time she giggled then winced with pain as she tried to put her arms around his neck. "We're going to have to get creative," he said with a grin and kissed Diana again. "This time I am really leaving," Misha said and left her room and walked through the house to the new wing and knocked on a door.

"Can I come in?" Misha asked as Maxwell opened the door.

"Of course, is anything wrong son?"

"No, I just wanted to talk."

Chapter XXXVII
Understanding

"How do you like your new room?" Emeral asked Diana as she visited her the next morning. Diana was sitting up in bed drawing a map.

"It is so beautiful," Diana gushed. "I have never seen a house like this before. I just wish Thor would wake up so he could enjoy it."

"You two have had a rough time of it."

"Sometimes; but we always had each other and somehow things always worked out. We owe Vivian's family a lot." Emeral sat down on the edge of Diana's bed and looked at her. "Emeral is something wrong?" Diana asked when she saw the look on Emeral's face.

"Misha came to our room last night after he left you."

"Emeral I hope you aren't mad at me; I didn't mean to hurt his feelings."

"I'm not mad at you my child, in fact I am grateful. Misha told us what you two said to each other. Then he told us about his family. We have three daughters besides the boys and of all our children; Misha was the one who locked his heart. He is a cousin of Calen's and Misha's father was killed in battle, leaving his mother with ten children to care for. Misha is the second from the youngest. He used to come over to play with Calen and Luca and Misha always ate like he wasn't sure where his next meal was coming from."

"One day, he must have been seven, he shows up at our door with a little bag of broken toys. He was filthy and his clothes were torn. He was crying and asked us if he could live with us. Well you can imagine how we felt; in that moment he became our son. He has never told us what happened that he left his family. He never talks to them or even of them; until last night." Emeral paused. Diana touched the older woman's hand because Emeral looked like she was going to cry.

"Maxwell and I just feel awful now, if we would have had any idea how those children were being treated, we would have taken them all. Nada, that's Misha's mother, was a beautiful woman but she was also weak and now I understand she had many demons. Nada fell apart after Adwell was killed and took her fear and rage out on her children. You have to understand the Ice Caves are huge; they are a whole other world. We didn't know what Nada was doing and if we had we would have stopped her."

"What happened?" Diana asked in a whisper.

"I feel like I will be betraying Misha if I tell you all of the horrid details," Emeral said as tears started to flow down her cheeks. As I said Nada was beautiful and had many demons, apparently she brought home many men who also abused her children; she never protected them. Misha is a grown man and last night he cried when he was telling us about his life."

"Does Misha know you are talking to me?"

"No," Emeral said. "I hadn't planned on saying anything and suddenly the words came out."

"Emeral I haven't known any of you long but I do know that everyone in this house loves you so much and holds you and Maxwell in such high esteem. It is awful what happened to Misha and his brothers and sisters, but he was so incredibly lucky to have you and Maxwell become his parents. Vivian has told me a lot about the people here. She is so proud to be part of this family and it was because of you and Maxwell that your children turned out like they did. You should feel proud of the effects you and Maxwell have on others instead of beating yourself up because you couldn't have saved more." Emeral hugged Diana, who hugged her back tightly.

"Diana you are good for Misha but if the two of you develop a relationship, well, I can't promise it will be easy. Until last night I was fearful that Misha would break your heart. Now I don't know what to think because you seem stronger than my son."

"Why are you back so early?" Renya asked as Sudfad walked into their chambers.

"I kept thinking about Petra and Kyra so I ended the meeting early."

"Did you talk to them?"

"Well, they are very happy that the dogs can sleep with them. But they would talk little about the battle. From what they did say it sounded like they were more horrified about their family members being in danger and being hurt than they were about stabbing intruders. I really couldn't get them to open up," Sudfad said with frustration.

"Petra worships the ground you walk on, he might be afraid that he will dissappoint you. Have Raul and Simon talk to them; Kyra and Petra might be more comfortable talking to his brothers."

Sudfad smiled and kissed Renya on the forehead. "I don't know what I would do without you."

"I'm beginning to think I should get injured more often," Renya said teasingly.

"Don't even say that," Sudfad said sternly. "I would rather die than to see you lying there bleeding like that again."

"I think it is easier for me to understand Misha because in some ways he is like Thor. I love Thor more than anyone in this world but I worry about him so."

"What are you two talking about?" Misha asked suspiciously as he stood in the doorway of Diana's room. Both women looked at him and smiled.

"Misha join us," Emeral said. "Diana was just telling me about her brother and their life."

Misha looked at Diana, "Do you want me to hear this?"

"Of course silly." Diana was surprised when Misha kissed her in front of Emeral. He sat down on the bed next to Diana.

"Our parents were fierce Venatores," Diana explained. "Some Venatores stop hunting after they have children but our parents were very dedicated to their positions. They took Thor and me out and started training us when we were really little." Diana paused for a moment. "We weren't with them the night they were killed. They were chasing a demon and ran into an ambush just like Thor and I did. That's why this has been so scary, we should have known better." Diana turned to Misha.

"I was telling your mother about what a wonderful man Thor is. He is brave and smart and kind but I worry about him because he has been so full of anger since our parents died. And it seems like the anger is, I don't know how to explain it, harming him in some way. Joshua and Iris took us into their home right away." Diana looked at Emeral. "Have you met them?"

"No but I have heard a great deal about them and they sound like wonderful people."

"Oh they are," Diana said and turned to Misha.

"I have met them, and you are right."

"Well, they just took us in as more children, like you and Maxwell did with your sons. They were very good to us and wanted us to become part of their family. But Thor would have nothing to do with it. Thor loves Vivian's family but sometimes," Diana lowered her voice and looked at both Emeral and Misha. "Don't either of you ever tell Thor what I am going to tell you. Thor always seemed jealous of Vivian's brothers because they had parents and that was so crazy because Joshua and Iris wanted to be our parents too."

"For years I was trying to figure out why Thor was acting like he was," Diana hesitated. "Thor isn't afraid of anything but I think he didn't want Joshua and Iris to adopt us because he was afraid that they would die too, I know that may sound crazy."

"Actually it makes a lot of sense," Emeral said. "So where did you two live?"

"Thor made me leave Vivian's and we lived off the land. I mean we would still spend time with Vivian's family we just didn't live with them."

568

"One day Vivian tells me that I am turning into Thor. She meant that I was angry all of the time. I got mad at her at first for saying that, but I realized she was right. Vivian asked Joshua to talk to Thor and me and I will never forget what he said. Joshua told us we had no control over the past, that there was no way we could have saved our parents. But he told us we could control our futures by the choices we made; then he said that how we looked at life was a choice. Joshua said he was afraid that Thor and I were letting ourselves become filled with darkness."

"I'll be honest I didn't understand what he was talking about at first and Iris had to explain it to me,"Diana continued. "So right then and there I decided to be grateful for everything in my life instead of dwelling on all of the things that I didn't have or the things that went wrong. And it was amazing, Johsua and Iris were right; as soon as I changed how I looked at things I became happier. That's why I worry about Thor, he understood what Joshua said but he didn't want to change. That's another reason I want him to wake up and meet all of you; I think it would be good for him."

"I think Thor is very lucky to have you as a sister," Emeral said. "And now I am even more anxious to meet Joshua and Iris; you know they are coming here for the wedding don't you?"

"No," Diana said with a big smile.

"Paul and Adrone are going to be in the wedding," Emeral continued. "As far as we know the entire family is coming."

"You'll like them," Diana said then looked at both Emeral and Misha. "Misha knows that Thor never lets me date but he doesn't date either. He hunts and takes care of me; so I was really happy when Cassandra said she wanted him to walk down the aisle with her sister. It would be good for Thor to meet a nice girl." Then Diana got a mischievious look on her face. "Emeral I heard that you like to play matchmaker, do you know any girls for my brother?"

Emeral laughed loudly, "Let me think about that."

"Just don't tell him I asked you to do it," Diana said with a smile.

Emeral turned to Misha, "It just dawned on me; what are you doing home this time of the morning?"

"The meeting at the castle was short so I was thinking about taking Diana shopping."

"For the dress for the wedding," Diana said excitedly. Then she changed her demeanor. "Misha I can't lift my arms enough to try things on without help."

"I realized that last night when Natasha had to help you out of that dress, so I asked Vivian to come but she is really sick again today, so Natasha offered to come along. The two of you wear the same size, you can just pick things out."

"Things? What are you planning on buying?" Diana asked.

Misha laughed, "You bring a huge bag of weapons with you but no clothes. So I was going to buy you a few things."

Diana looked very embarrassed and Emeral realized that Diana didn't own anything besides her one hunting dress. "Misha I can't let you do that, it wouldn't be right."

"Nonesense," Emeral said. "My son has more money than he knows what to do with. In fact it sounds like fun; do you mind if I come along? Perhaps we should pick up a few things for Thor too. Diana do you know what size he wears?"

Diana smiled brightly and said, "I don't know but Raphael gave him some of Gabriel's clothes to wear at the party and they fit him well."

"Honey I am getting worried about you," Raphael said as he sat down on their bed. Vivian was dressed and lying on top of the blankets.

"This is normal and Hannah just gave me something that seems to be helping," Vivian said. "I feel bad because my friends are here and soon my family will be; I hope I am better by then."

"How long can they stay?"

"I don't' know, I didn't ask them, why?"

"Well you are carrying their first grandchild; they might want to stay for a while. I was thinking that we should fix up a chambers for them. After all the carpenters are already here."

Vivian sat up and looked at Raphael. "You mean build some rooms for them?"

"I don't know why we couldn't connect them to our part of the house, like Calen did for his parents."

"Oh Raphael you are the most generous man," Vivian said happily and put her arms around his neck and kissed him.

"Are the bumps in the road hurting your wounds?" Natasha asked Diana as Natasha drove a small boca. Diana sat next to her in the front seat while Emeral and Misha were flying overhead.

"I am so excited I don't even care if it hurts. Emeral is going to buy Thor some things, he will be so happy."

"I don't know if anyone told you but Gabriel raised me from a small girl after our parents died. Raphael isn't my blood brother but he moved in with us and helped Gabriel. So I understand how close you can be to your brother."

"I didn't know that," Diana said, then she paused before speaking again. "How did he react when you met Calen."

Natasha started to laugh. "Gabriel was really protective of me like Thor is with you. Gabriel chased away all the boys but not Calen. But Gabriel and Calen were good friends and had been working on missions for years; I just had never met Calen. But even with all that, Gabriel was still very worried, you see he never wanted the members of the team to get emotionally involved because it could distract them and of course put people in danger."

"Well Calen and I got married three days after we met. I felt bad abandoning Gabriel but within the month he met Hannah and you can see how happy they are."

"There was another couple working with us who got married during that mission too, we had three marriages, it was fun." Diana didn't say anything so Natasha continued, "I want to explain something to you; except for Elan, Joao and Dack all the men of the team have worked together for years. They never thought about marriage because they are so dedicated. Calen and I married after three days, then weeks later Gabriel and Rabe marry. Everyone thought we were crazy to marry so quickly. Then Luca meets Lila and proposes a week later and Raphael and Vivian married quickly. I think all of this change scares some of the others."

"Natasha I did understand the question that Calen asked Misha last night. That is what we were discussing when you came."

Natasah grinned, "Sounded to me like Misha was jealous that you might be interested in Joao or Dack."

"That came up too."

"Diana its not my business but if you and Misha fall in love, don't let Thor stand in your way. I don't think Gabriel ever would have allowed himself to fall in love as long as he was taking care of me."

"Gabriel, Gabriel are you home?" Hannah called excitedly as she ran into the house.

Gabriel quickly came out of his study, "Is something wrong?"

"No, I am so excited I can hardly talk," Hannah said and ran up to Gabriel and kissed him again and again. Gabriel laughed.

"There are two things actually," Hannah said and kissed Gabriel again. "I was sick this morning so I believe I am pregnant." Gabriel picked Hannah up and twirled her in the air.

"Maybe I shouldn't do that if you are sick," he said then kissed his wife as he set her down. "What is the second thing?"

"You know I had a meeting with Sudfad. We talked about a lot of things."

"He asked me how Lakin and I provided medical care for the battles in Nora and Ryed. Gabriel he is not just giving me a staff, he is building a hospital on the grounds. Now of course it may not be used often but we will have it when we have large numbers of injured like we did after the last battle. He wants me to figure out what I want and he suggested that I contact Lakin and get some ideas. Then he will build whatever I say, isn't that the most incredible thing?"

Diana did not find the shopping trip as exciting as over-whelming. Both Misha and Emeral were buying her clothing and other gifts. Diana felt like her head was spinning. Many times Natasha was trying on things to determine if they would fit Diana, everything seemed to be going so fast. Then Misha and Natasha went shopping while Emeral took Diana shopping for things for Thor.

"Emeral you are so nice but I don't understand why you and Misha are buying us so much? We will never wear these fancy things in Ryed."

"Is there any reason the two of you can't stay with us for a while?" Emeral asked.

"I guess I don't know."

"Some of the clothes we bought you are for the next mission. The members of the team often play parts, you know they pretend they are someone else. You need to be dressed for the roles you will play."

"Do you know what Gabriel is going to have me do?"

"Not yet, but you will be prepared," Emeral said and hugged Diana.

Raul and Simon walked into their parent's bedroom chambers and kissed their mother on the cheek. Renya was sitting up in bed reading. "So did you have us do that to get experience for our children?" Raul asked kiddingly.

"Did they talk to you?"

"Yes," said Simon.

"Your Father should be here for this," Renya said.

"He's coming, he just finished his meeting with Hannah," Raul said. "You should have seen her, she was so excited she couldn't talk."

Sudfad entered the chambers and kissed Renya on the cheek. "I just heard what you said about Hannah, she had to come back to my study because she forgot her things," Sudfad said with a laugh. "So how did it go with Petra and Kyra?"

"I think those kids are stronger than you think," Simon said. "Remember Petra saved Padre Bartholomew from the Hutas and he and Kyra both fought his kidnappers. They have the mindsets of warriors, they will protect their familes. But seeing people they love hurt is what is really bothering them. Both the children, especially Petra are filled with guilt because they didn't protect Mother."

"And Petra also feels guilty because he couldn't protect Kyra, which caused an argument between the two of them," Raul said. "I bet they get married some day," Raul added with a grin.

"Both of the significant women in Petra's life were hurt during that battle," Simon said. "His feelings are understandable."

"He is just a boy," Renya said with emotion.

"Vitomas said that when she got to the nursery, Laurel and Alexander where using their bodies to protect the babies and Petra and Kyra were standing in front of them fighting the intruders," Raul said.

"Would you boys bring the children in here so I can talk to them?" Renya asked.

"What are you going to say?" asked Simon.

"I don't know yet but those children can't live with that guilt."

"Is that one of your new dresses?" Hannah asked Diana at dinner. "You look very nice."

"Thank you," Diana said shyly. "You can't believe all of the things that Emeral and Misha bought for me and Thor, I thought I was dreaming."

Maxwell looked at Emeral and smiled, "Are you telling me we are parents again?" he whispered into her ear. Emeral did not answer his question, she squeezed his hand and smiled.

"Vivian," Emeral said. "Diana told me about her life today. She has said such wonderful things about your parents and your family that I am even more excited to meet them."

Diana looked across the table at Vivian, "I told Emeral and Misha everything so they know; I don't care if you tell the others."

Vivian paused for a moment. "My friends have endured great hardships in their lives. I believe to keep their sanity they devoted everything to hunting. They are incredible warriors. But Thor and Diana have very different outlooks on life. When Thor is well enough to join us some of you might find him a little difficult."

"But he is a good man," Diana said. "Gabriel don't worry he will work well for you."

Gabriel looked at Diana, Emeral and Vivian. "Why do I feel like I need to ask for more of an explaination?"

Diana and Vivian looked at each other before Diana said, "My brother changed after our parents were murdered. He just seems filled with anger all the time."

"He has a temper," Vivian said softly.

"Vivian and Diana you are both seasoned warriors and intelligent women. We are very accepting of differences in this house, which makes us strong. But the types of missions we do are very delicate and I must know my people, their strenghts and their weaknesses. If you feel that Thor could in any way pose a danger you must tell me," said Gabriel.

"Gabriel, I think you will just need to talk to him yourself," Vivian said. "Venatores are trained to be independent and to work alone, so it may be difficult for him to work with a team. But he is a great warrior and very smart. I don't know, it could go either way."

"We worked well with the Venatores in your village," Calen said. "We had no problems, they are impressive warriors."

"Except for Sampson," Koby said.

"You met Sampson?" asked Diana.

"He pulled a knife on Raphael before we even got to the village," Vivian said.

"Right after our parents died," Diana hesitated. "Sampson pulled me into the woods. I was only six and didn't understand what was happening. Iris had to tell me later. But I knew I was in danger and I was fighting and screaming. Thor found us. He was only ten, much younger than Sampson. But Thor almost killed Sampson. He just kept beating him. Joshua found us and pulled Thor off Sampson."

"Father just told me about that; I never knew," Vivian said.

"Diana I hope you don't think what Thor did was wrong. Sampson was trying to rape a little girl, he should have been killed," Misha said angrily.

"Sampson grabbed Vivian when she was five," Raphael said with disgust. "Iris fought him off."

"Vivian I didn't know that," Diana said.

"Honestly I didn't remember until Father was telling Raphael."

"I am glad you brought this up," Luca said. "We all saw what Sampson was like. Then he marries the demon Hecate and tries to kill his own brothers to fulfull the tests to become a demon himself. He attacked his village and we found out that attack against us the other night was paid for by Hecate. Don't you think it is time that we thought about going after both of them?"

"Raphael and I have been discussing that," Gabriel said. "Let me brief you about the next mission then we can discuss if we want to do two missions simultaneously or one after the other."

The meeting was nearing the end when Lila flew into the room, "Hannah I need you!" Lila screamed. Hannah and Natasha both jumped up and quickly left the room.

"Is it Thor?" Diana called out but no one answered. She stood up and started to run out of the room.

"What are you doing?" Misha yelled.

"I didn't get stabbed in the legs," Diana said as she ran. Misha followed her. Although Diana was weak from loosing so much blood when she was stabbed, her adrenaline was racing through her. She sped up the stairs to Thor's room where Hannah, Natasha and Lila were trying to control the bleeding in two of Thor's wounds.

"What happened?" Diana asked loudly.

"Your brother woke up and got out of bed," Lila said. "He fell and some of his wounds started to bleed."

"Diana is that you?" Thor asked weakly.

"Thor I am here," Diana said as she ran to the bed. "Hannah is a physician you have to do what she says. We're safe here. These people are wonderful and they have been taking care of us."

"Thor, I am Hannah. We are going to roll you onto your stomach so I can work on the wounds in your back. Are you in a lot of pain? Tell me truthfully."

"Yes," Thor whispered.

Hannah looked at Natasha who ran to a small table and started to mix a powder with water. "Here drink this," Natasha said as she returned to Thor. "It will help with the pain."

"Thor drink it, you can trust them," Diana cried. Thor looked at his sister then drank the liquid.

"Do you need help?" Misha asked.

"You can help us roll him over," Hannah replied. "Then I need you to get Diana out of here."

"Can't I help?" asked Diana.

"Honey we need to concentrate on Thor, it will help us more if you aren't in here," Natasha said warmly.

The medicine that Natasha gave Thor quickly knocked him out. Diana gasped as she watched the others rolling her brother onto his stomach because his sheets were covered with blood. "You should go now," Natasha said as she was repositioning Thor's body.

As Lila ran out of the room she yelled, "I am getting hot water and towels."

"Can't I help?" Diana asked softly.

"Diana we are more help if we are out of their way," Misha said and took Diana's arm but she did not move. "You can come back when they are done." Diana continued to stare at her brother in horror. Misha picked Diana up and carried her downstairs. The meeting had ended and everyone was now milling around the dining room table.

"How is he?" Emeral asked when she saw Misha carrying Diana, who was crying and struggling to get free.

"Koby will you pour her a whiskey?" Misha asked then set Diana down on one of the dining room chairs. Misha held Diana's shoulders to keep her from getting out of the chair but Diana kept struggling. "Diana drink the whiskey," Misha said.

"No," Diana yelled as tears were flowing down her face.

Koby looked at Misha, "Do you want me to make her drink it?"

"No," Emeral said sternly then walked over to Diana. "Honey take a deep breath and tell me what happened." Diana stopped struggling but she was crying too hard to talk.

578

"Diana the boys are trying to help you; here take a sip of this and when you feel up to it tell me what happened with Thor."

Diana took the glass from Koby and sipped the whiskey, then coughed. "This is awful," Diana choked out.

"It will calm you down," Emeral said sweetly.

"Can I have some wine instead?" Luca poured a glass of wine and handed it to Diana. Cassandra entered the dining room and handed Diana a handkerchief. Diana started to relax so Misha released his grip on her shoulders. Diana halted repeatedly as she talked to Emeral, "Thor woke up and tried to get out of bed but he fell. Lila helped him back but he busted open his wounds and everything is covered with blood." Emeral looked at Misha, who gravely shook his head from side to side, to indicate he thought Thor was not going to live.

"Hannah is a wonderful physician, she will take good care of Thor," Emeral said. "Diana I don't think you should be alone tonight." Then Emeral looked at Misha and said in a low voice. "Do you want to stay with her or she can stay with us."

"I'll stay with her," Misha said. Then he looked at his brothers. "Thor is a big man; the girls need help moving him, so someone will need to check on them."

"Joao and I can," Dack said then he lowered his voice and said to Joao. "This is reminding me too much of Fala."

"Who is Fala?" Diana asked as Luca poured more wine into her glass.

"I'll tell you later," Misha said.

Diana looked up at Misha, "I'm better now, you don't have to stay with me."

"You're not getting rid of me that easily," Misha said teasingly and kissed Diana on top of her head.

Bekka sat at the dining room table and tears flowed down her cheeks because memories of Fala's death were flooding her being. Koby put his arm around Bekka and held her as she cried.

"I am going to see if they need anything," Elan said and walked up the stairs.

At Gabriel's request, Vivian took the three children to Nicholas' room. This room was the farthest from the room that Thor was in. No one wanted the children to witness the grim scene. "They aren't sleeping," Vivian said as she joined the others in the dining room. "But they are playing and promised to stay in the room. I did get them into their night clothes." As Vivian spoke she walked up to Diana then knelt next to her friend and put her arms around Diana. The two girls held each other and cried.

Chapter XXXVIII
A Home

No one in Gabriel's house wanted to go to bed until they knew Thor's status. Hannah, Natasha and Lila had been in his room for hours. Most of the people were sitting in the dining room. Gabriel and Raphael were working in Gabriel's study.

"Maxwell I would like to talk to you," Emeral said and stood up and walked into the kitchen. Maxwell followed her and closed the door. "Maxwell I want to adopt those children. Diana is the sweetest child and if Thor lives he will need care. They have no one and all they have ever wanted were parents."

Maxwell put his arms around Emeral because he could see she was becoming emotional. "I expected this," he said warmly. "But I think Misha needs to be a part of this conversation." Emeral nodded and Maxwell opened the kitchen door. "Misha could we speak with you a moment?" he called out. Misha stood up and walked into the kitchen. After the door was closed Diana looked at the others.

"Is Misha in trouble?" Diana asked.

The men all started to grin. "Don't worry, if he is he is used to it," Koby said.

Maxwell shut the kitchen door behind Misha. "Your mother would like to adopt Diana and Thor but we think you should have a say in this since you and Diana have some kind of a relationship."

Misha smiled, "I think that is a very nice thing you are doing. Honestly I suspect Diana and I will be more than friends but I can't tell you for sure."

"Misha what if you two have a romantic relationship and it ends badly?" Emeral asked. "Would it be too uncomfortable to have them in the house?"

"If that happens Diana and I will just have to work something out."

"So we have your blessing?" asked Maxwell.

"Yes and I appreciate you asking me. I think you should talk to Diana now, it might lessen some of her fear for the future. She saw Thor; she knows it's bad."

As soon as Misha returned to the dining room Diana asked, "Misha are you in trouble?"

"Not this time," he said and laughed. "Maxwell and Emeral want to talk to you." Misha looked across the table and winked at his brothers, who started to grin.

"Why are you smiling?" Bekka asked Koby in a whisper.

"Just watch," he replied.

Calen was holding Lily and now stepped into the study. "You two might want to come out here."

"Is something wrong?" Raphael asked.

"No, just watch."

By the time Gabriel and Raphael entered the dining room, Emeral and Maxwell were kneeling in front of Diana. "Emeral and I have been talking and we would like to adopt you and Thor," Maxwell said with a big smile on his face.

Diana stared at both of them in disbelief. "Are you really serious?" she asked.

They both smiled at her and Maxwell said, "Yes." Diana quickly spun around and looked at Misha who was smiling at her.

"I will admit it will be strange dating my sister, but you should say yes."

Diana was wide-eyed. "I can't believe I am hearing this. Vivian did I hear it right?" Diana turned and looked at Vivian who was smiling and crying.

"Yes," Vivian whispered.

Diana turned around and looked at Emeral and Maxwell again. "We realize you will have to talk it over with Thor," Emeral said.

Diana started to cry. "No," she said loudly. "He is always telling me what to do, this time I am telling him. We would love to have you as our parents." Diana threw her arms around Emeral's neck and hugged her tightly. "Thank you so much," Diana said between sobs. "I can't believe we have a family." Emeral hugged Diana and burst into tears as did Bekka and Cassandra. "We will be really good, I promise," Diana said which made everyone laugh.

"If you're too good you won't fit in with the rest of us," Dagon said loudly. This comment too caused laughter.

Diana let go of Emeral and put her arms around Maxwell's neck; hugging him tightly. "Thank you so much," Diana said. Maxwell felt a tear come to his eye.

An hour later, Natasha came down the stairs carrying an armload of bloody linens. She was not surprised to see the dining room filled with people. "Hannah was able to stop the bleeding," Natasha announced. "But he lost a great deal of blood. Thor is going to need someone to watch him around the clock for a while in case he starts bleeding again."

"I'll watch him," Diana said and stood up.

"Diana you are still weak and healing from your wounds, what if you fall asleep?" Natasha asked.

"We will watch him in shifts," Emeral said. "I think two hour shifts are reasonable. I will take the first two shifts."

"Elan and I will take the next two," Cassandra said.

"I will watch him after that," Vivian said, "That should take us to breakfast."

"I will watch him then," Diana said. "But I want to look in on him now."

"Why don't you give Hannah a couple of minutes before you go up there," Natasha said and walked out of the room with the soiled linens.

"You both look exhausted," Emeral said to Hannah and Lila as many of the family members entered Thor's room. Both Hannah's and Lila's clothing were soaked with Thor's blood. Luca was one of the first people to enter the room and he walked directly to Lila and hugged her. "We are going to take turns watching him, so you girls get some sleep," Emeral continued. "I will watch him the next four hours then Elan and Cassandra. Vivian will be after them, then Diana. We haven't figured out the rest of the schedule yet."

"Thank you," Hannah said wearily and put her arm around Gabriel's waist, he had his arm around her shoulders. "But you must wake me if anything seems wrong."

"Do you think he will try to get out of bed again?" Emeral asked.

"He must be so weak I would be surprised," Hannah replied.

"Hannah is he going to live?" Diana asked in a whisper.

"Right now I will say yes, but if he starts to bleed like that again, I just don't know."

Diana walked over to Thor and held his hand; the tears flowed down her face. "He doesn't even know we have a family now."

Diana opened her eyes and saw Misha's face. They were lying on top of the blankets on her bed, both still wearing their clothes from the night before. Misha had his arms around her. She smiled and kissed him gently on the lips. Misha did not wake. Diana kissed him again and again. Without opening his eyes Misha pulled Diana to him and kissed her passionately on the lips. They held their embrace for several minutes then they both stopped, they knew they had to turn their attention to Thor.

"Oh Misha, I wrinkled this beautiful dress," Diana moaned when she stood up.

584

"The wrinkles will come out. Do you want me to unbutton it or are you going to be too embarrassed?"

"You can unbutton me. I'm wearing something under the dress. I think Emeral called it a slip."

Misha laughed and walked up behind Diana and started to unbutton her dress. "This is going to take a few minutes; there are a lot of little buttons."

"Misha thank you so much for everything," Diana said. "I can't believe how nice you have been to me." Misha didn't say anything so Diana continued. "It was nice waking up with you this morning."

"I was thinking the same thing. If you don't hold still I am never getting this dress off from you." Diana giggled at his comment.

"Last night you said we were dating," Diana said. "Are we?"

"Do you want to be?"

"Oh yes," Diana said enthusiastically.

"Then we are dating."

"Good," Diana said then she paused. "Misha don't laugh at me because you know I have never dated anyone before. But does this mean we will be sleeping together, like Koby and Bekka?"

"You mean making love right?"

"Yes."

"That is often part of dating but Koby and Bekka are a few steps past dating, they are living together, like they are married."

Diana was quiet for a moment, "You can tell me I am naïve again; but explain to me what we do if we are dating?"

Misha grinned, "We spend a lot of time together."

"Are we going to make love?"

Misha turned Diana around and looked at her. "Do you want to make love?"

"Not right now because I have to watch Thor but yes."

"You are sure you're ready?"

Diana frowned. "Don't you want to make love to me?"

"Oh, I want to make love to you but with everything going on in your life I want to make sure you know what you are saying."

Diana stared into Misha's eyes as if she was trying to read his soul, then she got a mischievous look on her face and smiled. "I am saying that I think I love you and I want to be with you and I want to make love. Will you stay with me tonight?"

"You are full of surprises," Misha said and kissed Diana on the lips. "Yes I will sleep with you tonight?"

Vivian walked into the dining room for breakfast and kissed Misha on the cheek before taking her seat next to Raphael and kissing him.

"Vivian how is Thor?" Emeral asked.

"He is sleeping, Diana is with him now."

"What was the kiss for?" Misha asked with a grin.

"I have never seen Diana so happy."

"Misha did you two have sex last night?" Emeral asked in a scolding manner, which made the adults at the table laugh.

"No we didn't," Misha replied with a grin.

"She told me what she said to you," Vivian said. "We should probably talk."

"Does she really understand what she said?" asked Misha.

"Oh, I have no doubt she is falling in love with you," Vivian said then paused.

Misha looked at Emeral, "We were talking last night and fell asleep on top of her bed in our clothes, nothing happened. Then this morning she asks me all kinds of questions about dating and living together. Then she tells me she thinks she loves me and she wants me to stay with her tonight and make love."

"Did she really say that?" Bekka asked skeptically.

"That's exactly what she told me," Vivian said. "Misha in many cultures women are forced to marry or are enslaved but in our clan if a woman passes all of the trials of a Venator she has the same rights and powers as a man. Not only can she not be forced into marriage but it is as acceptable for a woman Venator to propose to a man as it is for a man to propose to a woman in your tribe."

"Was she proposing to me?"

"No and I don't know if she will but if she gives you her lamsman that is," Vivian looked at Raphael. "Help me."

"It's the same as an engagement ring," Raphael said. "When Vivian and I agreed to marry I gave her a ring and she gave me her lamsman, which I wear on my ankle."

"You may want to think about this brother," Luca said with a grin.

"Son, if you aren't sure what you want," Maxwell said to Misha. "Perhaps you should get out of the house today, get some fresh air and collect your thoughts. You seem to want to take care of Diana while she is going through this crisis and that might be clouding your thoughts."

"Not that it is any of my business," Natasha said then laughed. "Misha you seem happy too. If your relationship is going too fast, slow it down and give it a chance before you get scared and discard it."

"I agree with Natasha," Hannah said. "I think she is a good match for you."

587

"I'm interested in hearing this," Misha said. "Because honestly she really confuses me sometimes."

"That's part of it," Natasha said. "Misha you are so handsome you have grown up with women throwing themselves at your feet and perhaps acting in the same manner. Diana fights alongside of you, tells you off and yet is so innocent and vulnerable that you want to take care of her. You are treating her like you do us, the women in this family; which is different from how you act around your dates. Calen what do you think?"

"I'm not going to say," Calen said with a smile.

Natasha laughed, "Are you afraid I am going to get mad?"

"No," Calen said. "Because the way you described Diana is exactly how you are."

"My Lord," screamed Marie as she found Erebus lying in the front doorway to the castle. "My Lord, the front door." Within moments Archetenus, Raul, Simon and Sudfad ran to the front foyer.

"What happened?" Simon asked as he turned Erebus onto his back. "He's alive," Simon added but they could all see the blood that had soaked into Erebus' robe.

"Where are the soldiers?" Raul asked as he looked out the front door. "There is no one in sight."

"I was going to set the table and just found him," Marie stammered.

"Vitomas keep the children away," Raul yelled as the family members started to arrive at the dining room for breakfast.

"Put him in bed," Sudfad said to his sons, "I will send someone for Hannah."

Archetenus had left the group to check on the back door of the castle. "I didn't see any soldiers out back either," Archetenus said as he returned to the front foyer. "Something is very wrong."

Suddenly they heard the Horn of Cass being blown, "We're under attack," Sudfad yelled. "Gather all the children and take them upstairs."

Natasha smiled at Calen's comment and leaned over and kissed him on the cheek. "Misha," Calen said jokingly. "Run while you can." As everyone laughed Natasha playfully hit Calen on the arm.

"What is that?" Hannah asked as every man at the table suddenly jumped to their feet.

"It's the Horn of Cass," Raphael said. "Either the fort or the castle is being attacked."

"Lock the doors behind us and don't anyone leave this house until we return," Gabriel yelled as he was running towards the weapon's room.

Diana heard the horn blowing outside, then she heard the commotion downstairs. She ran to the bedroom door and listened then Diana walked to the top of the stairs and yelled, "What is happening?"

"Either the castle or the fort is being attacked," Lila called up to Diana. "Just stay with Thor."

Diana returned to Thor's bedroom and screamed, "Thor!" Then she ran into the hallway. "Hannah, Hannah come quickly."

The Warrior in his holiness

On bended knee does pray

'Lord carry me in battle'

'Lord find a better way'

The Warrior On Bended Knees © 2008

By

Sandra J Yearman

Glossary of Characters

Aaron: an escaped prisoner from Wetpr

Aaryan: a male Grand Master of the Insidiae

Abaddon: an ancient demon/one of the Old Ones

Abella: daughter of Prince Lakin and Princess Zada/Ruala

Abigail: sister of Marie/ nurse for grandchildren of King Sudfad

Adi: son of Elen and Batya/ Ruala

Adrone: youngest son of Joshua and Iris/younger brother of Vivian/Clan of Gesmal

Adwell: Prince/ son of King Zachariah and Queen Noella of New Samona/husband of Nada/father of Misha/ Adwell was killed in battle leaving Nada to raise ten children/Ruala/

Ael: an ancient demon/ one of the Old Ones

Aetes: Shettee warrior

Ahriman: an ancient demon/ one of the Old Ones

Akasha: former king of Ryed/grandfather of Nehmota

Alexander: former servant of King Roch's parents/ father of Annabelle

Alexander: one of the twin sons of Simon and Annabelle

Alexandras: King of Wetpr/brother of Jaretta/uncle of Sudfad and Roch

Alexas Rose: daughter of Matthew and Angelina

Alexis: son of Usman, the leader of the Valdore Tribe

Alice: and her husband find Jorge near death in Nora

Aloeus: Shettee warrior

Amiee: sister of Marie/ nurse for grandchildren of King Sudfad

Amundsen: Commanding General of Fort Friada in the Kingdom of Ganz

Amy: a young girl who was kidnapped by Sal

Ana: Princess/daughter of Zeman and Oda/niece of King Manu of New Samona/Ruala

Anda: one of Chief Romogi's three wives/Huta

Andres: Princess of Ryed/daughter of Oren and Astrel/ has twin sister Jorga

Andrew: jeweler in Salar

Andrus: father of Rabi/Ruala

Angelina: daughter of Sorren, Chief of the Nordes Tribe/female warrior

Annabar: daughter of King Sharonne

Annabelle: handmaid and best friend to Queen Vitomas of the Kingdom of Stordt

Anthony: one of the twin sons of Simon and Annabelle

April: a young girl who was kidnapped by Sal

Arca: Enrop leader who protects King Mathas' family

Arches: a Patronus priest

Archetenus The Brave: Captain in the Taperian Army

Arianna: daughter of Simon and Annabelle

Ariel: daughter of Raul and Vitomas

Armstrong: soldier and scout in the army of Wetpr

Arthur Marcus: father of Hannah

Asher: male Ruala warrior

Asmodeus: an ancient demon/ one of the Old Ones

Astrel: former princess of Ryed/daughter of Akasha and Norah

Atomos: Elder of the Centras and Keeper of the Box of Itifer

Augustus Endleson: a wealthy businessman who owned part of the City of Nora

Baal: an ancient demon/ one of the Old Ones

Babu: Enrop

Bac: male Ruala warrior

Bachnenus: warrior guarding refugees/Shettee

Bali: Enrop leader of the flock that does battle at Juleta's castle

Balius: Shettee warrior/brother of King Neputa

Balin: Prince of Norkv/son of Thaddius and Omara/grandson of Benjeman and Esther

Banacus: General in the army of King Tobias of Puntd

Banaka: a female Grand Master of the Insidiae

Barak: Prince of Norkv/grandson of Benjeman and Esther

Barak: Prince/son of King Neputa and Queen Tiara/Shettee

Barid: Prince of Ogg

Barid: Prince of Ryed/son of Nehmota and Vasart

Bastra: Huta captain

Batina: young female Nordes warrior

Batya: wife of Elen/Ruala

Beatrice Endleson: wife of Augustus

Becca: Princess of Norkv/daughter of Thaddius and Omara/granddaughter of Benjeman and Esther

Behtay: Princess/daughter of Segal and Cahina/niece of King Manu of New Samona/Ruala

Bekka: female Ruala warrior

Bella: wife of Claudius and mother of Stephan

Benedict: Prince of Norkv/son of Benjeman and Esther

Benjeman: vicious rebel leader who overthrew the government of Samona

Benson: a Private in the Wetprian military

Bentra: an ancient demon/ one of the Old Ones

Berta: cook at Racing Horse Tavern

Berta: Queen of Stordt/wife of Micha/grandmother of Roch and Sudfad

Bertha: an elderly woman from Nora

Betty: a woman from Nora

Betu: male Ruala warrior

Bianca: young female Nordes warrior

Black Jack: a regular patron at the Ghost Ship Tavern in Port Friada

Bode: Shettee warrior

Botis: a demon

Brik: son of Prince Lakin and Princess Zada /Ruala

Brina: Princess of Norkv/daughter of Valor and Cai/granddaughter of Benjeman and Esther

Cabal: son of Karzman and Nadia

Cacu: Enrop leader that joined Raul and Simon on a mission

Cade: son of King Pergo and Queen Vinus/ Kingdom of Gandt

Cadi: daughter of Prince Hadar and Princess Paj/ granddaughter of Manu/Ruala

Cael: Shettee boy who is adopted by Thedes and Ibula

Cahina: Princess/ married to Segal son of King Zachariah and Queen Noella of New Samona/Ruala

Cai: Princess of Norkv/wife of Valor who was the son of Benjeman and Esther

Calen: male Ruala warrior/cousin of Luca/son of Maxwell and Emeral/

Calla: female Ruala warrior

Calvin: a desk clerk at The Captain's Retreat Hotel in Port Friada

Campbell: one of the spies at the Castle at Wetpr

Canton: Cisero's second in command

Cara: Princess of Ogg

Carlsman: a Lieutenant in the Army of Lentz

Carson Dormors: a wealthy landowner in the Kingdom of Ganz

Carston: member of the governing body of Nora

Casey: male Ruala warrior/father of Melanie/husband of Tasha

Cassandra: female Ruala warrior

Cassandra: daughter of King Friada and Queen Marla of the Kingdom of Ganz

Cedrick Teivel: a ruthless, powerful man in the Kingdom of Ryed

Celo: Prince of Ryed/son of Oren and Astrel

Cere: daughter of Tristt/Shettee

Cerephus: General in the Taperian Army

Cerey: orphan girl/sister of Nicholas

Ceria: Princess/daughter of Gunnel and Uma/niece of King Manu of New Samona/ sister of Elan/Ruala

Chaez: son of Fahron

Chaladrone: an ancient demon/ one of the Old Ones

Chalice: hired fighter for Dieter

Chalta: daughter of King Pergo and Queen Vinus/ Kingdom of Gandt

Chance: works with the Patronus

Charlene: a woman from Nora

Charles: Father of Cassandra, Joao and Melinda

Charles: hired farmhand of Arthur Marcus

Chief Romogi: leader of the Hutas/ Kingdom of Marba

Christopher: six year old boy who Luca saves from the Hutas/brother of Lila

Ciao: female Ruala warrior

Cisero: a member of the Insidiae

Clair: a woman from Nora

Claudius: General in the Army of Lentz

Cleo: a man who works for Cicero/a vessel

Cobren: Prince of Norkv/son of Grace and Makalo/Grandson of Benjeman and Esther

Compro: Taperian soldier injured at Wall of Dorath

Corina: young female Nordes warrior

Corwin: son of King Fahra and Queen Sitha of Zorta

Crater: a Sergeant in the Wetprian army

Crater: a soldier in the army of Wetpr

Crispus: a guard at King Roch's castle

Crocell: a demon

Cronn: a demon

Cronos: Shettee warrior

Dack: male Ruala warrior

Dacron: former prince of Ryed/is murdered by his younger brother Nehmota for the throne

Dael: an ancient demon/ one of the Old Ones

Dagon: a male Ruala warrior

Dagor: son of King Fahra and Queen Sitha of Zorta

Dai: son of Gael, grandson of Manu/Ruala

Damas: an ancient demon/ one of the Old Ones

Danar: a man created to be a vessel for demons

Daniel: an emissary of The Great Ruler who takes on the disguise of a human man

Danilla: mother of King Mathas

Darius: Prince of Samona/son of Thomas and Rewel/brother of Varden

Darla: young female Nordes warrior

Darlah: sister of Marie/ nurse for grandchildren of King Sudfad

Delilah: wife of Dieter

Delilia: Queen of New Samona/mother of Ibula, Lakin, Gael and Hadar/ wife of King Manu/Ruala

Demanko: a demon

Demetries: a demon

Denise Froush: wife of Martin who is a wealthy ship builder in Port Friada

Denks: a soldier in the army of Wetpr

Denton: one of the spies at the Castle in Wetpr

Derek: friend of Thaos

Derlock: Huta warrior

Diana: a Venator/sister of Thor

Dieter: member of the Insidiae

Dion: Princess of Samona/wife of Yorggi who was the son of Thomas and Rewel/brother of Varden

Dixon: a Taperian soldier

Dominic Petlov: was the senior High Priest at the monastery at Malga before he was murdered

Dorme: Prince of Ogg

Doros: works for High Priest Meekos

Douma: King of Ogg

Dresden: a Sergeant in the Wetprian army

Duncan: Chief of the Clan of Gesmal in Ryed/ husband of Liza

Duran: father of Nikki/Nordes Tribe

Dymas: Shettee warrior

Eachann: Shettee warrior

Edith: wife of Lloyd a banker in Nora

Elan: male Ruala warrior/son of Gunnel and Uma/

Eldridge: works with the Patronus

Elen: son of Andrus and Naomi/ brother of Rabi/ Ruala

Elexas: a female Nordes warrior

Elsa: female Ruala warrior/mother of Mia/wife of Tyron

Emeral: mother of Calen/Ruala

Emeric: a male Grand Master of the Insidiae

Emmet: worker for Gabriel

Emon: a male Grand Master of the Insidiae

Erebus: sorcerer from Ryed

Erwat: a member of the Half-Man's Tribe who helps the Clan of Gesmal

Esser: Prince/son of Segal and Cahina/nephew of King Manu of New Samona/Ruala

Esteban: a member of the Insidiae

Esther: Queen of New Norkv/wife of rebel leader Benjeman

Fabron: Prince of Ogg

Fadil: a male Grand Master of the Insidiae

Fahra: King of Zorta

Fahron: General in the Army of Lentz

Fala: female Ruala warrior

Farnsworth: General in charge of building Fort Serpha in Wetpr

Fatima: Prince of Ryed/ son of Oren and Astrel

Fatronas: an ancient demon/one of the Old Ones

Fengu: Enrop leader who helps Gabriel and his group against Omnibus

Ferguson: a Sergeant in the Army of Lentz

Fraisier: a businessman and member of the Insidiae in Nora

Frank: a villager in Telmark

Fred Stapleton: a farmer in Wetpr

Friada: King of the Kingdom of Ganz

Gabriella: sister of Marie/nurse to grandchildren of King Sudfad

Gad: male Ruala warrior

Gael: Prince/son of King Manu and Queen Delilia/Ruala

Gala: a healer from the Kingdom of Stordt

Galen: male Nordes warrior

Geoff: Prince of Lentz/son of Princess Isabella and Captain Josef

Geoff: Prince of Norkv/son of Benedict and Sasaha/grandson of Benjeman and Esther

George: an advisor for King Fahra of Zorta

George: middle son of Chief Duncan and Liza of the Clan of Gesmal in Ryed

Gita: wife of Hadi/ Ruala

Gladys: member of Nordes Tribe/ mother of Nikki

Glenda: great, great, great grandmother of Gala/ a healer from the Kingdom of Stordt

Grace: Princess of New Norkv/daughter of Benjeman and Esther

Gracie: cook for the Arthur Marcus family

Grady: worker for Gabriel

Great Ruler: God

Gregory Bancar: a wealthy landowner in the Kingdom of Wetpr and member of the Insidiae

Greta: older Ruala woman/friend of Emeral's

Gunnel: Prince/ son of King Zachariah and Queen Noella of New Samona/husband of Uma/father of Elan/Ruala

Gus: owner of Racing Horse Tavern

Haas: a Lieutenant in the Wetprian military

Hadar: Prince/son of King Manu and Queen Delilia/Ruala

Hadi: son of Andrus and Naomi/brother of Rabi/Ruala

Hadu: female Ruala warrior

Hamon: one of the members of the Nordes Tribe who was injured in an attack at Snakes Crossing

Hamond: General of the Taperian Army who declares himself king

Hanger: one of the spies at the Castle at Wetpr

Hannah: physician in Nora/ Roch murdered her sister

Harold: husband of Berta/part owner of the Racing Horse Tavern

Harold: owner of the general store in Nora

Harriet Marcus: mother of Hannah and Laurabelle/wife of Arthur

Hatus: General in the Army of Lentz/on loan to Sudfad

Hecate: a powerful female demon

Hector: fighter hired by Juleta

Hector: Prince of Samona/son of Varden

Henry: and his wife Alice find Jorge in Nora

Henry: husband of Noreen/father of Jacob

Hermanas: second in command to Archetenus at Wall of Dorath

High Priest Aaron: member of the Patronus

High Priest Amos: a member of the Patronus

High Priest Barnabas: most Senior High Priest of the monastery at Leven

High Priest Caleb: member of the Patronus

High Priest Ephraim: a member of the Patronus

High Priest Gabriel: member of the Patronus/demon hunter

High Priest Gideon: a member of the Patronus

High Priest Gregory: member of the Patronus

High Priest Joseph: member of the Patronus, in charge of the Cicero Headquarters

High Priest Josiah: member of the Patronus

High Priest Meekos: priest at the monastery at Malga

High Priest Nicholas: most Senior High Priest of the monastery at Philiste and most Senior High Priest of the Patronus

High Priest Paulas: member of the Patronus

High Priest Phanuel: member of the Patronus

High Priest Philetus: member of the Patronus in charge of Malga Headquarters

High Priest Pravis: priest at the monastery at Malga

High Priest Raphael: a leader of the Patronus

High Priest Rueben: member of the Patronus in charge of Nora Headquarters

High Priest Silas: a member of the Patronus

High Priest Tenebrae: priest at the monastery at Malga

High Priest Timothy: was murdered by Meekos, Pravis and Tenebrae

High Priest Tyrus: a member of the Patronus

High Priest Uriel: member of the Patronus

High Priest Vincent: assigned to the monastery at Malga before he was murdered

High Priest Zophar: priest at monastery at Malga/ trained as a healer

Hobart: a man who works for demons

Hores: son of Chief Romogi and Anda, Kingdom of Marba/Huta

Horta: Prince/son of Gunnel and Uma/nephew of King Manu of New Samona/brother of Elan/Ruala

Hunter: Prince of Samona/son of Varden

Ian: husband of Mia/ brother-in-law of Calen/ Ruala

Ibula: warrior princess and healer of the Ruala Tribe/daughter of King Manu and Queen Delilia/

Iden: warrior guarding refugees/Shettee

Igor: brother of King Sharonne

Imad: a male Grand Master of the Insidiae

Ina: daughter of Mia and Ian/ Ruala

Ingr: female warrior of Nordes Tribe

Inon: one of Cisero's men/a vessel

Ipos: an ancient demon/ one of the Old Ones

Iris: mother of Vivian/wife of Joshua/Clan of Gesmal in Ryed

Irit: daughter of Hadi and Gita/ Ruala

Isabella: Princes of Lentz, sister of Mathas, Renya and Tasha, married to Captain Josef

Isadore: wife of Fahron

Isla: daughter of Prince Lakin and Princess Zada/Ruala

Isla: female warrior of Nordes Tribe

Ivan: youngest son of Chief Duncan and Liza of the Clan of Gesmal in Ryed

Jace: husband of Oda/ brother-in-law of Calen/Ruala

Jack: member of governing body of Nora

Jackson: a private in the Army of Lentz

Jackson: an escaped prisoner from Wetpr

Jacob: boy who Angelina found in the woods

Jacot: son of Prince Lakin and Princess Zada/ grandson of King Manu/Ruala

Jaden: Sergeant in the Army of Lentz

Jago: son of Elen and Batya/ Ruala

Jake: works for Talverson Transport Company in Port Friada

Jakiv: Prince/son of Segal and Cahina/nephew of King Manu of New Samona/Ruala

Jama: Enrop leader who protects Chief Sorren's family

James: Taperian soldier

Janja: Princess/daughter of Gunnel and Uma/niece of King Manu of New Samona/ sister of Elan/Ruala

Jared: hired fighter

Jaretta: King of Stordt/husband of Queen Lillian/ father of Roch and Sudfad

Jarrod: works for Pravis/leads attack on castle in Wetpr

Jarvis: a farmer who is killed by escaped prisoners

Jasmine: young female Nordes warrior

Jasper: a large white dog that Gabriel brings home

Jasper: Prince of Lentz/son of Princess Isabella and Captain Josef

Jatu: Enrop leader who protects Fahron's family

Jeb: friend of Thaos

Jeb: one of Cisero's men

Jela: Queen of Samona/wife of Varden

Jeremy: cousin of Andrew the jeweler in Salar

Jerik: a male Grand Master of the Insidiae

Jess: a soldier of Wetpr

Jillian: Queen of Ogg/wife of King Douma

Jinn: an ancient demon/ one of the Old Ones

Joao: male Ruala warrior

Joey: adopted son of Elan and Cassandra

Jonas: Captain in the Taperian Army

Jorga: Princess of Ryed/daughter of Oren and Astrel/ has twin sister Andres

Jorge: a cook who is kidnapped from Endleson Hotel in Nora

Josef: Captain in the Lentz military/ married to Princess Isabella, sister of King Mathas

Joshua: father of Vivian/husband of Iris/Clan of Gesmal in Ryed

Josie: an escaped prisoner from Wetpr

Juleta: cousin to Raul and Simon/daughter and oldest child of King Mathas and Queen Rosa

Kadin: a member of Valdore Tribe

Kagen: a man who kidnaps and exploits children

Karta: male Ruala warrior

Karzman: leader of Kozach Tribe/ stepfather of Michael

Kasper: Prince/son of Zeman and Oda/nephew of King Manu of New Samona/Ruala

Kata: Princess/daughter of Gunnel and Uma/niece of King Manu of New Samona/ sister of Elan/Ruala

Khryriss: an ancient demon/ one of the Old Ones

Kiana: Princess/daughter of Gunnel and Uma/niece of King Manu of New Samona/ sister of Elan/Ruala

Klass: Lieutenant in the Wetprian Army

Koby: male Ruala warrior

Koh: son of Prince Gael and Princess Mada/grandson of King Manu/Ruala

Kora: Princess/ married to Raphael son of King Zachariah and Queen Noella of New Samona/ mother of Luca/ Raphael and Kora were killed in battle when Luca was a small boy/Ruala

Korth: son of Tristt/Shettee

Kraus: hired fighter and intended vessel, works for Dieter

Kretcher: Commanding General of Fort Polta in Wetpr

Krister: Princess of Samoan/daughter of Thomas and Rewel

Kyra: young sister of Marie/ friend of Petra

Laban: Prince of Samona/son of Yorggi and Dion/grandson of Thomas and Rewel

Lael: daughter of Nina and Rhea/ Ruala

Lakin: Prince/son of King Manu and Queen Delilia/husband of Zada/Ruala

Lala: Princess/daughter of Adwell and Nada/niece of King Manu of New Samona/ sister of Misha/Ruala

Lana: female warrior of the Nordes Tribe

Lana: Princess/daughter of Segal and Cahina/niece of King Manu of New Samona/Ruala

Lani: daughter of Mia and Ian/Ruala

Lara: one of Usman's wives

Larson: a fighter hired by Juleta

Laurabelle: Hannah's sister who was murdered by Roch

Laurel: Annabelle's mother and former servant of King Roch's parents

Lazo: fighter hired by Juleta

Lea: Princess/daughter of Adwell and Nada/niece of King Manu of New Samona/ sister of Misha/Ruala

Leo: Prince of Samona/son of Darius and Rebek/grandson of Thomas and Rewel

Lila: seventeen year old girl who Luca saves from the Hutas/sister of Christopher

Lilian: female warrior of the Nordes Tribe

Lillian: Queen of Stordt/wife of Jaretta/ mother of Roch and Sudfad

Lily: daughter of Calen and Natasha/Ruala and human

Liza: wife of Duncan the Chief of the Clan of Gesmal in Ryed

Lloyd: banker in Nora

Loftus: Commanding General of Fort Styls

Loni: daughter of King Friada and Queen Marla of the Kingdom of Ganz

Louie: works for Talverson Transport Company in Port Friada

Luca: male Ruala warrior

Lucifer: an ancient demon/ one of the Old Ones

Luque: Prince/son of Segal and Cahina/nephew of King Manu of New Samona/Ruala

Mab: a female Grand Master of the Insidiae

Mabon: warrior guarding refugees/Shettee

Mada: Princess /wife of Prince Gael/Ruala

Madam Bular: owner of a dress shop in Port Friada

Maggie: elderly store owner in Salar

Mahon: son of King Neputa

Makalo: Prince of Norkv/husband of Grace who was the daughter of Benjeman and Esther

Malana: daughter of King Neputa

Mali: Princess of Norkv/daughter of Makalo and Grace/granddaughter of Benjeman and Esther

Maligma: an ancient demon/ one of the Old Ones

Malik: member of the Insidiae

Malus: sorcerer from Ryed

Mandrake: Taperian soldier

Manu: King of New Samona/The Chief of the Grand Council made up of Rualas and Shettees/ father of Ibula, Lakin, Gael and Hadar/husband of Delilia

Marcia: friend of Hannah's/ Roch's men murdered her family

Marcus Stephan: son of Stephan and Ingr

Margarit: daughter of King Mathas and Queen Rosa of the Kingdom of Lentz/ cousin of Raul and Simon

Margo: a young girl who was kidnapped by Sal

Margolia: girl from Nora who was sacrificed to a demon

Marie: a cook for King Sudfad and Queen Renya

Markus: a soldier in the Army of Wetpr

Marla: High Priest Meekos' housekeeper

Marla: Queen of the Kingdom of Ganz

Marsha Jarvis: a sixteen year old girl who is raped and killed by Timothy

Martha: a cook for Cerephus

Martha: hotel owner in Telmark

Martin Froush: wealthy ship builder in Port Friada/husband of Denise

Mary: Jared's young wife who was brutally murdered by Hutas

Mata: Igor's wife

Mateo: Chief Healer of the Ruala Tribe

Mathas: King of Lentz/ brother to Queen Renya

Matilda: one of Usman's wives

Matthew: son of King Mathas and Queen Rosa of the Kingdom of Lentz/ cousin of Raul and Simon

Maxwell: father of Calen/ Ruala

Maxwell: infant son of Nina and Rhea/grandson of elder Maxwell/Ruala

Melanie: female Ruala warrior/daughter of Casey and Tasha

Melina: mother of Thaos

Melinda: grandmother of Misha

Melinda: older sister of Cassandra and Joao

Mia: daughter of Maxwell and Emeral/ Ruala

Mia: female Ruala warrior/daughter of Tyron and Elsa

Mica: Princess of Norkv/daughter of Benedict and Sasaha/granddaughter of Benjeman and Esther

Micha: oldest son of Joshua and Iris/older brother of Vivian/Clan of Gesmal

Micha: son of King Sharonne/ grandfather of Sudfad and Roch

Michael: ancient king of Wetpr/father of Queen Sumona

Miranda: emissary of The Great Ruler who takes on the disguise of a human seer

Miriam: a friend of Hannah's/works at Endleson Hotel in Nora

Misha: male Ruala warrior/lieutenant

Molach: a member of the Insidiae

Moloch: an ancient demon/one of the Old Ones

Morris: member of governing body of Nora

Muhar: Shettee warrior

Myla: wife of the owner of the Dragons Inn in Salar

Naal: warrior guarding refugees/Shettee

Nabi: male Ruala warrior

Nada: Princess/ married to Adwell son of King Zachariah and Queen Noella of New Samona/ mother of Misha/ Adwell was killed in battle leaving Nada to raise ten children/Ruala

Nadia: wife of Karzman

Naomi: mother of Rabi/ Ruala

Napo: Enrop leader who protects Claudius' family

Natasha: sister of High Priest Gabriel

Nathaniel: Sorren's oldest son/ Nordes Tribe

Nebula: son of Chief Romogi and Anda/ Kingdom of Marba/Huta

Nehmota: King of Ryed

Nelpus: Shettee warrior

Neputa: leader of the Shettee Tribe when it was conquered by the Hutas

Nestor: a demon that specializes in procuring things for a price

Nica: Enrop leader who protects Sudfad's family

Nicholas: orphan boy /brother of Cerey

Nicolas: Prince of Puntd/son of King Tobias and Queen Tasha

Nieatzae: an ancient demon/ one of the Old Ones

Nikki: female warrior of Nordes Tribe

Nina: daughter of Maxwell and Emeral/Ruala

Nina: youngest daughter of Karzman and Nadia

Nita: Princess/daughter of Adwell and Nada/niece of King Manu of New Samona/ sister of Misha/has twin brother Waed/Ruala

Nobel: former prince of Ryed/son of Akasha and Norah/father of Nehmota

Noella: the first Queen of New Samona/wife of King Zachariah/mother of seven sons/Ruala

Norah: former queen of Ryed/grandmother of Nehmota

Noreen: mother of Jacob/ wife of Henry

Norris: hired fighter and intended vessel, works for Dieter

Nyla: oldest daughter of Karzman and Nadia

Oda: daughter of Maxwell and Emeral/ Ruala

Oda: Princess/ married to Zeman son of King Zachariah and Queen Noella of New Samona/Ruala

Odam: male Ruala warrior

Odell: one of the spies at the Castle at Wetpr

Omar: Prince/son of Zeman and Oda/nephew of King Manu of New Samona/Ruala

Omara: Queen of Norkv/wife of Thaddius who was son of Benjeman and Esther

Omnibus: an ancient demon/ one of the Old Ones

Omoria: former queen of Ryed/wife of Nobel/mother of Nehmota

Opago: an ancient demon/ one of the Old Ones

Orbus: a powerful demon and former lover of the demon Hecate

Orcus: Shettee warrior/brother of King Neputa

Oren: former prince of Gandt who marries princess Astrel of Ryed

Ottillia: Princess of Lenz/daughter of Princess Isabella and Captain Josef

Padre Augustus: a member of the Patronus

Padre Bartholomew: survives the massacre at the monastery at Avaide

Padre Cornelius: a member of the Patronus

Padre Darius: a member of the Patronus

Padre Dibon: a priest at the monastery at Malga

Padre Dominick: priest at monastery at Malga

Padre Edgar: member of the Patronus

Padre Edward: a member of the Patronus

Padre Francis: priest at monastery at Malga

Padre Joram: member of the Patronus

Padre Lucas: a member of the Patronus

Padre Octavos: runs orphanage in Salar

Padre Philip: a member of the Patronus

Padre Philip: a priest at the monastery at Malga

Padre Simpson: priest at the monastery at Malga

Padre Sorben: a member of the Patronus

Padre Stephens: priest at monastery at Malga

Padre Thomas: priest at the monastery at Malga

Padre Tobias: a member of the Patronus

Padre Xavier: priest at monastery at Malga

Paj: Princess/wife of Prince Hadar/Ruala

Pallas: Shettee warrior

Pata: daughter of Chief Romogi and Trina/Huta

Paterson: a Private in the Wetprian military

Paul: third son of Joshua and Iris/younger brother of Vivian/Clan of Gesmal

Paulas: a man who works for Cicero/a vessel

Paulas: Sergeant under Archetenus in Taperian Army

Paullo: works for High Priest Meekos

Pearl: eldest daughter of King Tobias and Queen Tasha of Puntd

Pergo: King of the Kingdom of Gandt

Peter: Sorren's second son/Nordes Tribe

Peters: member of the governing body of Nora

Petorus: an ancient demon/one of the Old Ones

Petra: peasant boy from Ort who saves Padre Bartholomew

Philip: Prince of Puntd/ son of King Tobias and Queen Tasha

Phillip: Court Physician to the Royal Family of Wetpr

Polgate: one of the men who kidnapped Petra

Potomas: warrior guarding refugees/Shettee

Powell: a lieutenant in the Military of Lentz/stationed at Fahron's castle

Prescott: a hired killer

Rabi: male Ruala warrior

Radnor: a male Grand Master of the Insidiae

Rael: Prince of old Samona/husband of Krister who was the daughter of Thomas and Rewel

Rahi: a female Grand Master of the Insidiae

Rakio: Prince/son of Adwell and Nada/nephew of King Manu of New Samona/brother of Misha/Ruala

Rako: a male Ruala warrior

Raphael: Prince/ son of King Zachariah and Queen Noella of New Samona/husband of Kora/Ruala/father of Luca/ Raphael and Kora were killed in battle when Luca was a small boy/Ruala

Ratri: male Ruala warrior

Raul: Prince/son of King Sudfad and Queen Renya of the Kingdom of Wetpr

Raum: an ancient demon/ one of the Old Ones

Rebek: Princess of Samona/wife of Darius, who was the son of Thomas and Rewel

Renya: Queen of Wetpr/ wife of Sudfad

Rewel: Queen of Samona/wife of Thomas/mother of Varden

Rex: a notorious pick pocket in Port Friada

Rhea: husband of Nina/ brother-in-law of Calen/ Ruala

Riftca: male Ruala warrior

Riker: a scout in the Wetprian military

Roch: King of the Kingdom of Stordt/brother of King Sudfad

Rogers: one of the men who kidnapped Petra

Rolif: son of Chief Romogi and Silva/ Kingdom of Marba/Huta

Romale: member of the Insidiae

Romos: an elder of the Centras

Rosa: Queen of Lentz/wife of King Mathas

Rosalie: a dressmaker in Nora/wife of Peters

Ryan: grandson of Jeb/friend of Thaos

Sabot: member of the Insidiae

Sahil: a male Ruala warrior

Sal: a murderous pedophile/also goes by the name Tyrone

Sally: a young girl who was kidnapped by Sal

Samael: a demon as powerful as Ahriman from the hell world of Xibalba

Samara: wife of Tristt/Shettee

Samat: son of Chief Romogi and Silva/ Kingdom of Marba/Huta

Samos: Prince of Norkv/son of Thaddius

Sampson: oldest son of Chief Duncan and Liza of the Clan of Gesmal in Ryed

Sampson: Sergeant in the Taperian Army

Samuel: a high priest at the monastery at Malga who was murdered

Samuel: Prince of the original Samona/grandson of Thomas and Rewel

Samuel: second son of Raul and Vitomas

Sanuri: a holy man/emissary of The Great Ruler/warrior

Sar: an Enrop

Sar: male Ruala warrior

Sara: daughter of Usman

Sarah: baby granddaughter of Mathas and Rosa

Sarah: housekeeper for Claudius and Bella

Saran: daughter of Karzman and Nadia

Sasaha: Princess of the original Samona/granddaughter of Thomas and Rewel

Sasha: young female Nordes warrior

Sasha: female warrior of the Nordes Tribe/wife of Galen

Satan: an ancient demon/ one of the Old Ones

Sattleman: a Sergeant in the Wetprian army

Saunders: a Taperian soldier

Schroeder: man who works for Insidiae leader Dieter

Segal: Prince/ son of King Zachariah and Queen Noella of New Samona/husband of Cahina/Ruala

Seguna: former princess of Ryed/daughter of Akasha and Norah/ committed suicide

Selen: house keeper for Juleta

Shanksaw: mercenary

Shara: wife of Sorren/Nordes Tribe

Sharonne: King of Stordt; great, great, grandfather of King Roch and King Sudfad

Shon: son of King Fahra and Queen Sitha

Shone: Princess/daughter of Zeman and Oda/niece of King Manu of New Samona/Ruala

Sicily Bella: daughter of Stephan and Ingr

Sila: Princess of Ogg

Silva: one of Chief Romogi's three wives/Huta

Simmons: Commanding General of Fort Nir

Simon: adopted son of King Sudfad and Queen Renya of the Kingdom of Wetpr

Sinclair: King of Lentz/father of King Mathas

Sirius: works for High Priest Meekos

Sitha: Queen of Zorta

Smoking Joe: a regular patron at the Ghost Ship Tavern

Sonja: female warrior of the Nordes Tribe

Sophie: cook and servant of King Roch

Sorren: leader of the Nordes Tribe

Sporos: priest turned demon

Stephan: Captain in Army of Lentz/son of Claudius and Bella

Stiller: a fighter hired by Juleta

Stolas: an ancient demon/one of the Old Ones

Stone: hired fighter and intended vessel, works for Dieter

Sudfad: King of the Kingdom of Wetpr and brother to King Roch of Stordt

Sudfad: little Sudfad is grandson of King Sudfad

Sumona: Queen of Wetpr/wife of Alexandras/aunt of Roch and Sudfad

Swenson: one of Shanksaw's hired men

Syrius: a Bakken hired by Juleta

Tabeth: daughter of Fahron

Tabith: son of Tristt/Shettee

Tabitha: Princess of Lentz/daughter of Princess Isabella and Captain Josef of Lentz

Tadeo: Prince/son of Adwell and Nada/nephew of King Manu of New Samona/brother of Misha/Ruala

Tafer: a warlord who drove the Hutas out of the Kingdom of Norkv after years of wars and rebellions

Tahira: a female Grand Master of the Insidiae

Tahira: Princess of Samona/granddaughter of Thomas and Rewel

Tal: son of Oda and Jace/ Ruala

Talmai: Shettee boy who Thedes and Ibula adopt

Tambor: male Ruala warrior

Tamour: General in the Army of Lentz/on loan to Sudfad

Tanner: a Lieutenant in the Wetprian army

Tanner: a Sergeant in the Army of Lentz

Tapster: a demon who works for Meekos

Tarig: a lieutenant in the Huta army

Tarin: son of King Neputa and Queen Tiara/Shettee

Taron: Prince/son of Adwell and Nada/nephew of King Manu of New Samona/brother of Misha/Ruala

Tasha: female Ruala warrior/mother of Melanie/wife of Casey

Tasha: Queen of Puntd/ married to Tobias/ sister of Renya and Mathas

Tate: a Lieutenant in the Wetprian Army

Tatterd: a Sergeant in the Wetprian military

Tavin: son of Prince Lakin and Princess Zada/Ruala

Tega: housekeeper for the cabins of the captains of the Taperian Army

Tegman: soldier of Wetpr

Tehtfote: a Lieutenant for Dieter

Temark: villager of Neva

Thadddius: Prince of the new Kingdom of Norkv/son of Benjeman

Thaddies: member of Nordes Tribe/ father of Ingr

Thanatoes: an ancient demon/ one of the Old Ones

Thaos: a hired fighter

Thatcher: Prince/son of Zeman and Oda/nephew of King Manu of New Samona/Ruala

Thatus: Taperian soldier

The Lion: emissary of The Great Ruler who takes on the appearance of a lion when he is in the world of man

Thedes: warrior guarding refugees/Shettee

Thomas: King of the original Kingdom of Samona/father of Varden

Thomas: second son of Joshua and Iris/older brother of Vivian/Clan of Gesmal

Thomas: the young husband of Zoya who was murdered in Taperia

Thompson: Wetprian soldier

Thor: a Venator/brother of Diana

Thronson: one of Meekos hired killers

Tiara: Queen of Shettee Tribe when it was conquered by Hutas/wife of Neputa

Timothy: son of Fahron

Tina: Mother of Cassandra, Joao and Melinda

Tito: member of Valdore Tribe

Titus Derek: son of Thaos and Nikki

Titus: a lieutenant in the Taperian Army

Tobart: a member of the Nordes Tribe

Tobias: King of Puntd.

Tomas: works for High Priest Pravis

Tome: a businessman and member of the Insidiae in Nora

Tomi: son of Usman the leader of the Valdore Tribe

Toni: young female Nordes warrior

Toomback: Huta warrior

Torance: father of Thaos

Torin: oldest son of Karzman and Nadia

Tratz: one of the men who kidnapped Petra

Travor: Taperian warrior who was injured at the Wall of Dorath

Tresdore: son of King Sharonne

Trevor: Prince/son of Zeman and Oda/nephew of King Manu of New Samona/Ruala

Tria: daughter of Oda and Jace/Ruala

Trina: one of Chief Romogi's three wives/Huta

Trina: Princess/daughter of Zeman and Oda/niece of King Manu of New Samona/Ruala

Trist: a male Ruala warrior

Tristt the Horrible: Shettee warrior

Tye: Prince of Norkv/son of Princess Grace and Prince Makalo

Tyron: male Ruala warrior/father of Mia/husband of Elsa

Tyson: Wetprian soldier

Ulger: a demon

Uma: Princess/ married to Gunnel son of King Zachariah and Queen Noella of New Samona/mother of Elan/Ruala

Umar: Prince/son of Adwell and Nada/nephew of King Manu of New Samona/brother of Misha/Ruala

Uri: son of Nina and Rhea/ Ruala

Usman: leader of the Valdore Tribe

Valerie: young female Nordes warrior

Valor: Prince of the new Kingdom of Norkv/son of Benjeman and Esther

Vandrew: Petra's male tutor

Vania: Princess of Samona/daughter of Yorggi and Dion/granddaughter of Thomas and Rewel

Varden: last king of Samona/he and his family were murdered by rebels

Vardin: one of the men who kidnapped Petra

Vasart: Queen of Ryed/ wife of Nehmota

Vinca: Queen of Stordt, wife of Sharonne

Vincent: Prince of Ryed/son of Nehmota and Vasart

Vinus: Queen of the Kingdom of Gandt

Vitomas: Queen of Stordt

Vivian: a demon hunter from the Clan of Gesmal

Voltar: Prince of Samona/son of Darius and Rebek/grandson of Thomas and Rewel/later becomes King of Wetpr

Vuall: a demon

Waed: Prince/son of Adwell and Nada/nephew of King Manu of New Samona/brother of Misha/has twin sister Nita/Ruala

Wallis: member of governing body of Nora

Wilard: Captain at Fort Polta

Willis: son of King Pergo and Queen Vinus/ Kingdom of Gandt

Xeni: a female Grand Master of the Insidiae

Yara: daughter of Nina and Rhea/Ruala

Yorggi: Prince of Samona/son of Thomas and Rewel/brother of Varden

Yori: son of Usman the leader of the Valdore Tribe

Yuri: Prince/son of Adwell and Nada/nephew of King Manu of New Samona/brother of Misha/Ruala

Zac: one of the men who kidnapped Petra

Zachariah: first King of New Samona/husband of Queen Noella/father of seven sons/Ruala

Zada: Princess/wife of Prince Lakin/Ruala

Zadok: a male Grand Master of the Insidiae

Zede: an ancient demon/ one of the Old Ones

Zehmann: an ancient demon/ one of the Old Ones

Zeman: Prince/ son of King Zachariah and Queen Noella of New Samona/husband of Oda/Ruala

Zieman: a demon

Zorda: Taperian soldier injured in battle at the Wall of Dorath

Zoya: a seer from Taperia

Glossary of Terms

Aboultis: the calling cards of demons

Abyss: a vast void used to imprison demons

Acura: the whispering shadows/are in the inner circle of demons that directly serve the Old Ones

Alferto: a type of grain that is common in Opots

Amark: ancient language of The Great Ruler

Amulth: means filth in the language of demons/these monsters are made out of the waste of tortured souls from the hell dimensions

Anewa: one of seven continents in the World of Nunc

Aplewort: an herb when mixed with water purges poisons from a body

Asherane: ancient tribe that lived in the northern regions of the Kingdom of Lentz

Ashta: a common herb/when the dried leaves are boiled they give off a pleasant scent

Astras: the ancient underground city of the Centras

Beltrad: a species of lower level demons

Blood Moon Prophesy: a demonic prophesy that foretells of a time when the doors to the hell worlds will open

Blood rings: Large red rubies set in silver with markings of the Old Ones

Boca: a covered wagon pulled by horses

Box of Itifer: a gift to the world of man from The Great Ruler; this gift affects the balance of creation

Bozie: a game of skill played by the Nordes Tribe

Cava plant: a poisonous plant that grows freely near bodies of water

Centras: ancient race of creatures who have the responsibility of protecting the Holy Box of Itifer

622

Chalice of Ascension: a gift from The Great Ruler, this gift contains unimaginable powers

Cicero College: in Wetpr, outside of Salar, where Raul, Simon and Hannah attended college

Clan of Gesmal: a tribe of demon hunters who live in the southern region of the Kingdom of Ryed

Crystal pillars: in the Ice Caves of Mordv/are blessed by The Great Ruler and filled with spiritual life force

Czarsta: one of seven continents in the World of Nunc

Demalogs: an inferior species of demons

Demosa: a slow acting poison from the cava plant

Diamond of Cazo: a gift from The Great Ruler, this gift can unleash powers from the center of the world

Durisks: large demonic birds/their elongated beaks contain rows of fangs

Ekel Beast: similar to a deer

Engas: a wild cat that inhabits the Vandrew Mountains

Engor: a small pack animal that lives in trees

Enrop: a large species of bird that can speak many human languages

Farduth: a Shettee necklace that symbolizes a male has completed his rite of passage to become a warrior

Gafet: an ancient Shettee weapon

Gants: large apelike creatures/Watchers of the Caves of Muldun

Gate of Isula: the only opening in the great Wall of Dorath

Gefrey Games: games of sport where men fight each other and great beasts to the death

Grand Masters: the first people to call to the demons and invite them into this world

Half-Mans: a tribe of creatures that are partially human and partially nature. They are three feet tall and walk on two legs but can change their coloring to match their environment.

Hall of Antiquities: a giant hall located in the monastery at Malga/ a sanctuary for holy items and manuscripts

Hall of Light: the Great Hall in the Ice Caves of Mordv

Hengers: giant blue eagles/ birds of war

Highland Pass: the only passage through the Rosu Mountain Range

Holy Scrolls: gifts given to each kingdom by The Great Ruler, these gifts contain powers, wisdom and immortality

Holy Vault: a secret vault under the King's study in the castle in Wetpr designed to protect holy objects

Horn of Asher: a horn used by the Patronus warrior priests to signal each other

Horn of Cass: a horn used by the Wetprian soldiers to signal each other

Horn of Cornwell: a horn used by Dieter's men to signal each other

Horn of Eel: a horn used by the Ruala warriors to communicate with each other

Horn of Esker: a horn used by the Valdore Tribe to communicate with each other

Horn of Ire: a horn carried by the Taperian soldiers to communicate with each other

Horn of Shana: a horn carried by the soldiers of Lentz to communicate with each other

Horn of Tula: a horn used by the members of the Nordes Tribe for communication

Horn of Vamont: a horn used by the Kozach Tribe for communication

Horn of Xepoltr: a horn used by the Shettee warriors to communicate

Huta: a race of humans that is driven by hatred and ideas of racial superiority who live in the Kingdom of Marba

Infineotous Text: a demonic text hidden within a plyogram/contains prophesies of the balance of power between good and evil

Insidiae: means conspirators/a highly organized secret group of humans who have sold their souls to demons

Jacar: giant leech-like creatures

Jacept Plant: a plant that a powerful poison is made from

Kafer: a small crescent shaped knife carried by the Beltrad

Keepers of the Scrolls: the Royal Family of the Kingdom of Wetpr entered into a covenant with The Great Ruler to protect his gifts until a time when they can be safely given back to the world of man

Kozach: a tribe that lives in the far north central regions of the Kingdom of Wetpr

Lamsman: an ankle bracelet worn by Venatores/stones in the bracelet signify great feats they had to accomplish to become a demon hunter

Linges plant: a plant that grows in damp, swampy regions in Opots/the white berries are used to make the drug Melanwhop

Lynswood: an herb that reveals tracks that are concealed by black magic

Mark of Satan: a coiled red snake with green eyes and a yellow tongue

Matu potage: a food staple of the Shettee Tribe

Mayka: one of seven continents in the World of Nunc

Melanwhop: a drug made from the linges plant, causes lethargy and apathy

Mordov: the special place in hell for hypocrites

Motfer: the land of the dead

Nefandus: a secret sect within the Insidiae

Nordes: a tribe of fiercely trained warriors who live in the northern region of the Kingdom of Lentz

Nunc: the world where this story takes place

Old Ones: the original demons that came to the World of Nunc

Opatu bread: a food staple of the Shettee Tribe

Opots: one of seven continents in the World of Nunc/the continent where this story takes place

Oran: a tobisk that is filled with a mixture of ramni oil, buruto powder and meno salts, designed to explode on impact

Patronus: an elite group of men who serve as the protectors of the church

Plyogram: an ancient form of coding information/the information is hidden within pictures

Porto: one of seven continents in the World of Nunc

Prophesy of the Blood Moon: a demonic prophesy that predicts the doors to hell being opened.

Prophesy of Isdod: is contained in the demonic Book of Horror/this prophesy explains the significance of the thirteenth level.

Propilatry: a powerful form of demonic curse

Prostras: an ancient Tribe that once inhabited the Ice Caves of Mordv

Raftifa: ancient bat-like creatures that devour human flesh

Ravens: messengers used by the dark lords

Recupero: a sect within the Insidiae that worships the demon Omnibus

Rogetts: a tribe of humans that have digressed into murderous mutant monsters

Rualas: an ancient tribe of warriors said to be half human and half bird

Salszar: one of seven continents in the World of Nunc

Salts of Envoy: a sleeping potion

Scio: a crystal ball

Scroll of Imari: a gift of The Great Ruler, a scroll that unleashes the power of the Box of Itifer

Seal of Natun: a gift from the Holy Ruler that can open doors to other worlds

Serpents of Satan: can only be called forth by dark lords and demons, large red snakes with green eyes and yellow tongues

Seven Sons Prophesy: an ancient prophesy about seven sons who stand up against the demons and dark lords

Shesone: an ancient fighting style of the Shettee Tribe

Shettee: an ancient tribe of warriors said to be half human and half lion

Solv: a specific prison within the Abyss

Song of the Second Son: an ancient prophesy about an evil that is passed between second sons of a family resulting in a monster that brings terror and darkness to the world of man

Sundra Templer: a gift from The Great Ruler that was stolen by dark lords/an orb with extraordinary powers that can be used in multiple ways such as transporting humans through other worlds

Tabutu: an ancient form of fighting developed by the Asherane Tribe of the Kingdom of Lentz

Talisman: an object with magical or supernatural meaning

Talmuth: giant red dragon-like creatures

Tangers: large wild, grazing animals that travel in herds

Tansof: one of seven continents in the World of Nunc

Telgras: a hell beast that looks like it is half wolf and half panther

Teragon: death terror/a monster created as a result of diabolical acts

Terbot bear: a bear that roams in the northern regions of the Continent of Opots

Tervator: fourteen foot monster that walks like a man with long dark hair over its entire body and bull-like horns protruding from its head

Texts of Semalia: ancient texts about demonic language and rituals

The Book of Horror: a book that is worshipped by demons/contains prophesies

The Celebration of Days: an annual celebration of the Centras

The Hall of Understanding: the building in Astras where the history of the Centras is documented in drawings

The Hunters: another name for the Shettee Tribe

The Lion: a very powerful messenger of The Great Ruler assumes the form of a lion when he walks in the worlds of man

The thirteenth color: not seen in the world of man it is the color of horror/hell

Timbar: ghost dragons/ demons that can fly

Tinchure water: an herbal pain remedy used by the Nordes Tribe

Tincture of the Redeti Plant: Hutas dip the tips of their weapons in this insect infested liquid. The insects lay eggs inside of the victim. When the eggs are mature and hatch, two inch worm-like creatures are produced and will eat the organs of the victim causing a long and painful death

Tobisks: sphere shaped objects, metal and hollow inside that are designed to be launched from a Trebuchet

Trebuchets: wooden machines used to catapult objects

Tygrus: a ship that docked in Port Friada

Unholy altar: altar used to worship demons

Valdees: the tribe that lives in the underwater Kingdom of Ogg

Valdore: a tribe of merciless separatists who live in the extreme northern regions of the Kingdom of Lentz

Venator: means hunter in the old language

Venom of the Atha serpent: one of the poisons that Hutas put on their arrows

Vessel of Darkness: a human created from darkness to hold the essence of a powerful demon

Wall of Dorath: a giant wall that separates the Kingdoms of Norkv and Xepoltr from the Kingdom of Marba

Willimonns: small furry creatures that are hunted for food and sport

Xelope: the oneness of spirit with all that lives

Yellow Mandeze: a song bird common to Opots

Zendoti: demons that are distinguished by the geometrically shaped tuffs of hair that protrude from their heads

Glossary of Maps

The maps are displayed in order of relevance

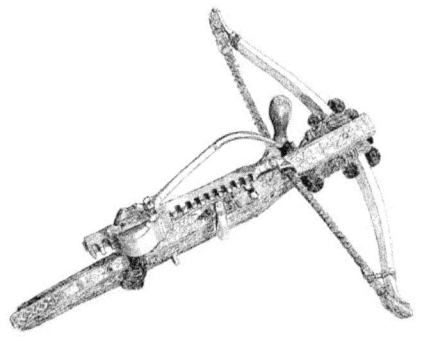

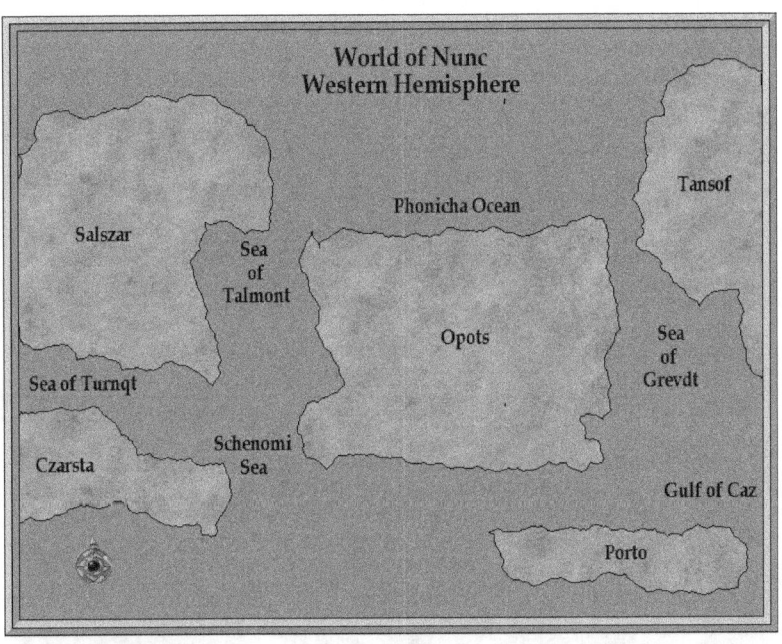

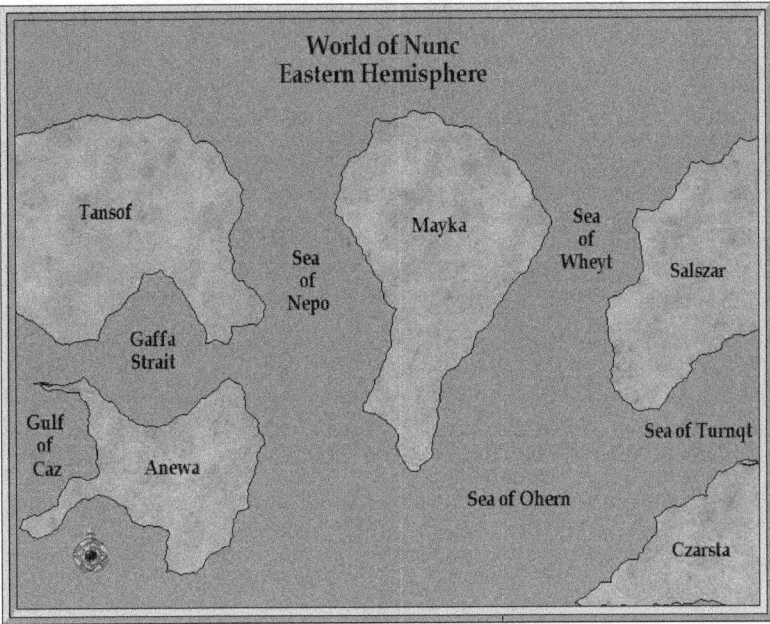

Continent of Opots
With new forts

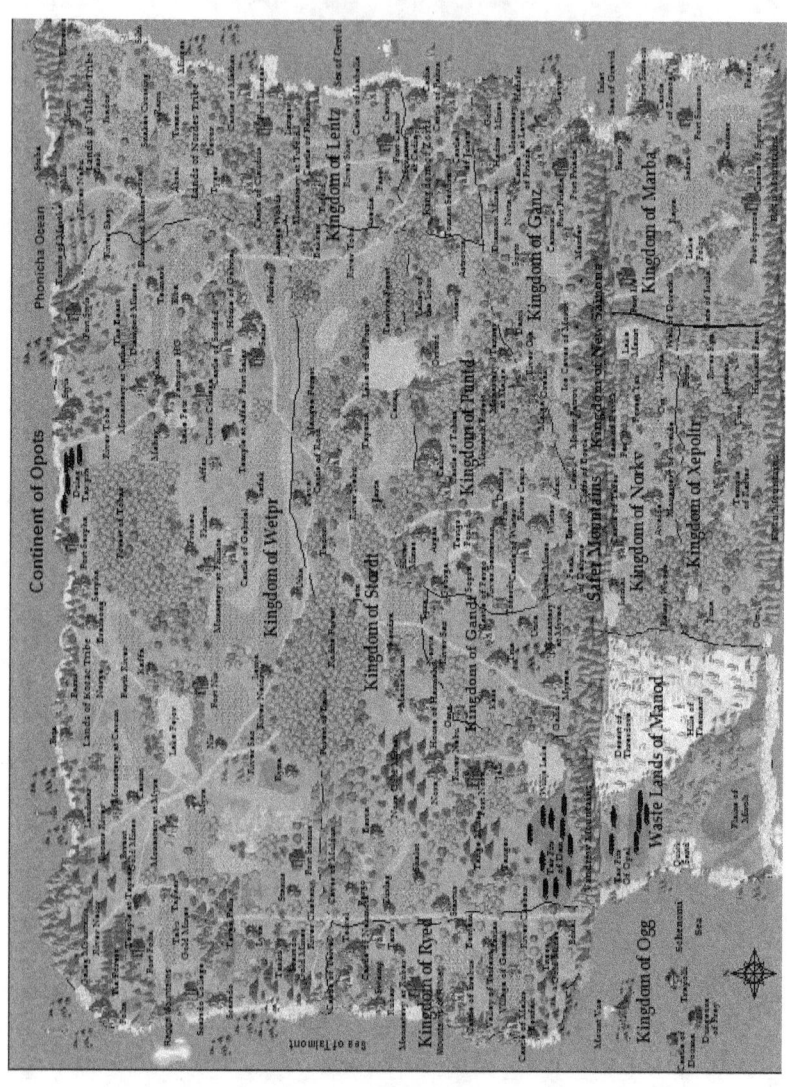

Western Stordt
With Fort Nora

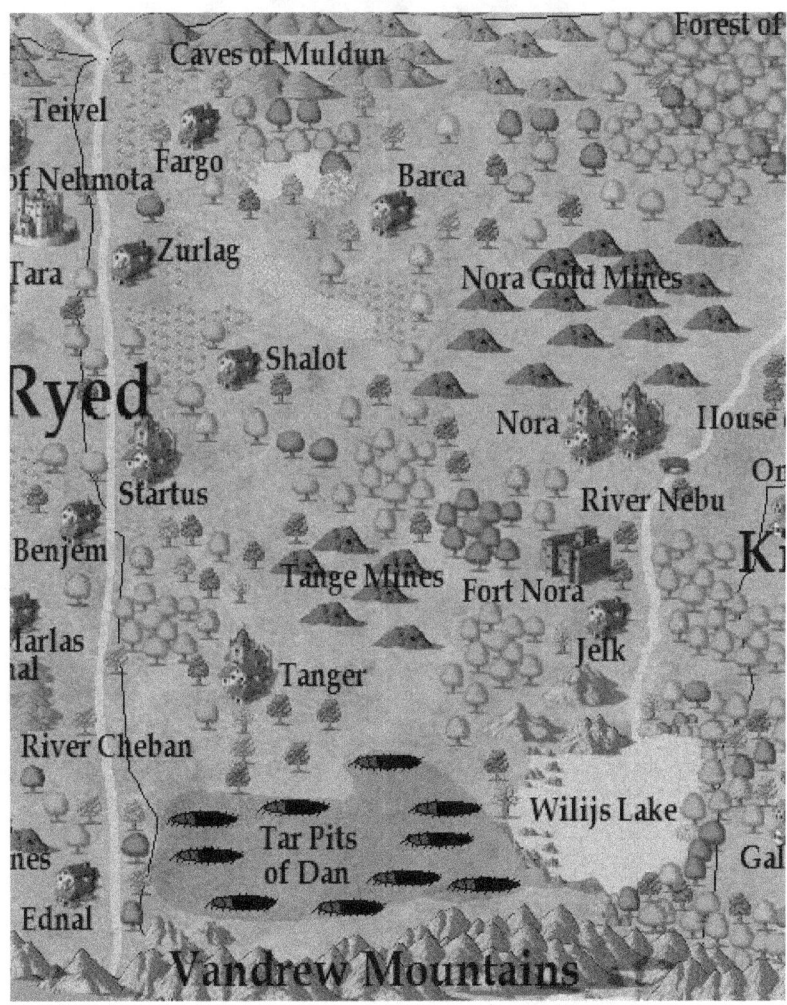

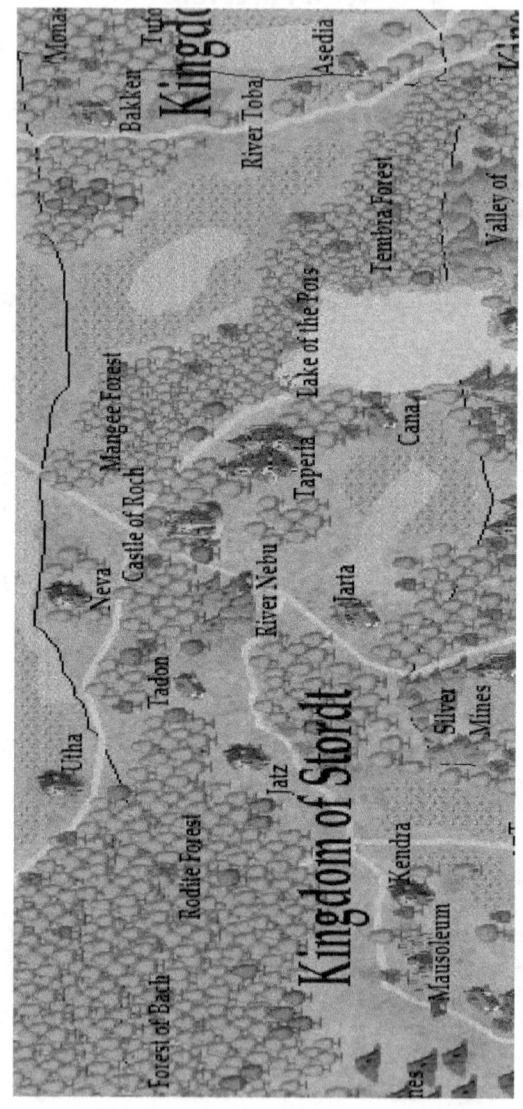

Western Wetpr
With Fort Stanus

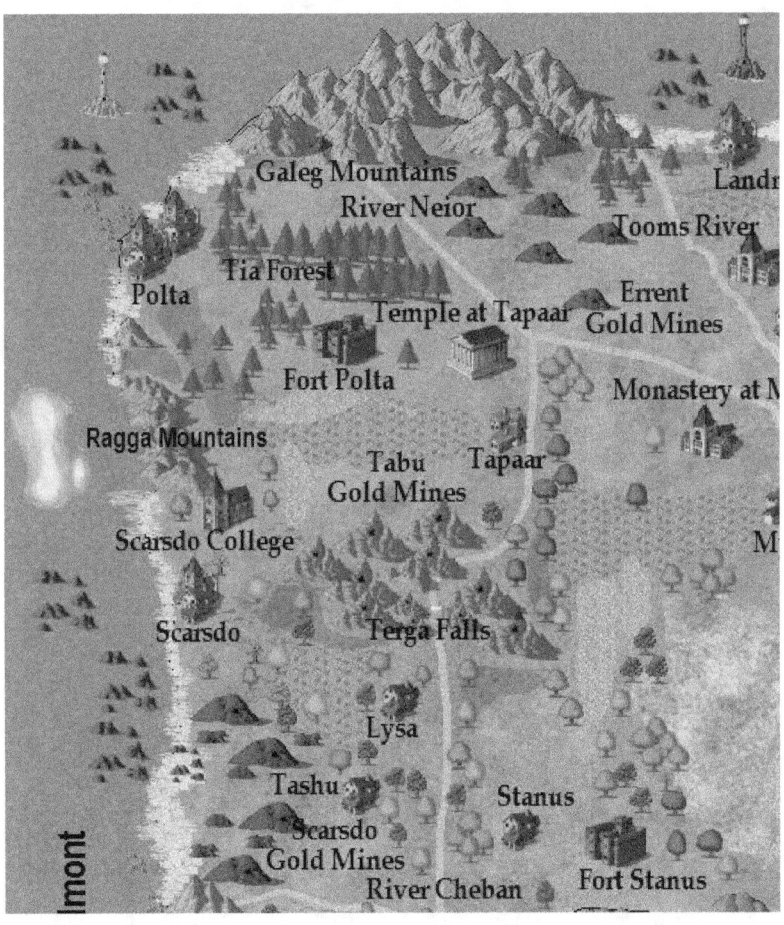

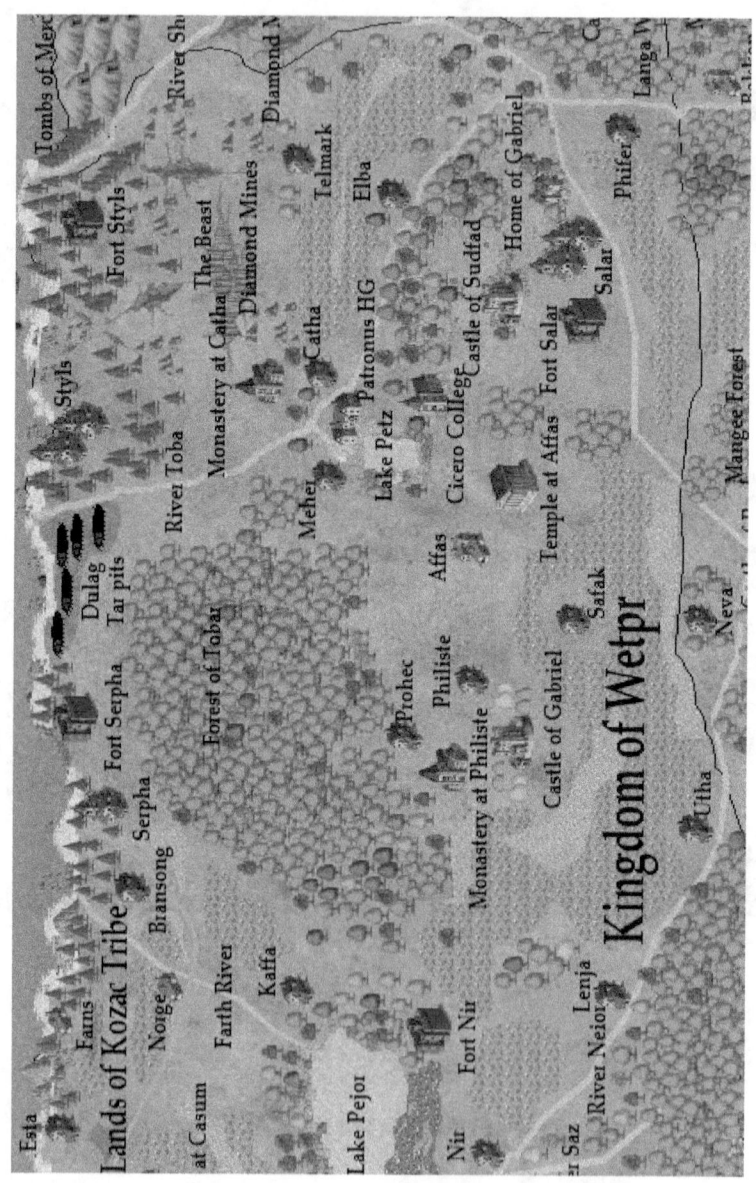

Marba

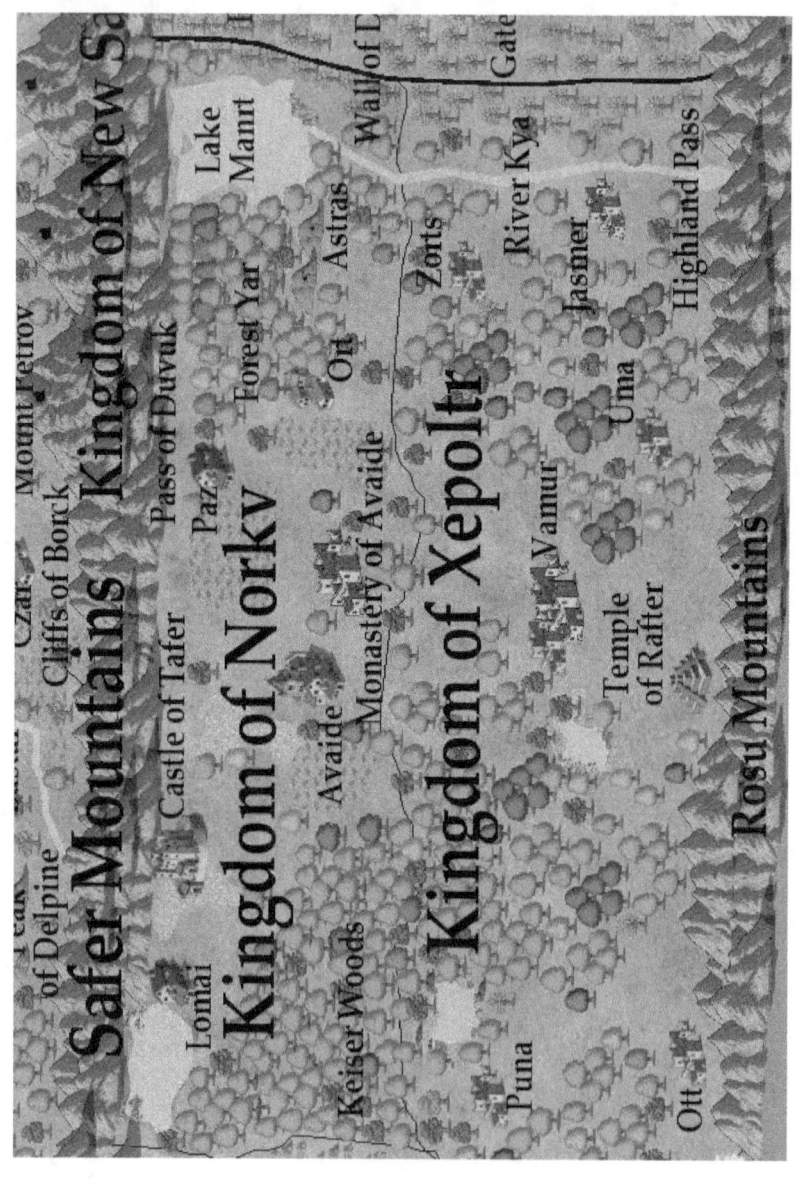

Waste Lands of Manod

Lower Opots

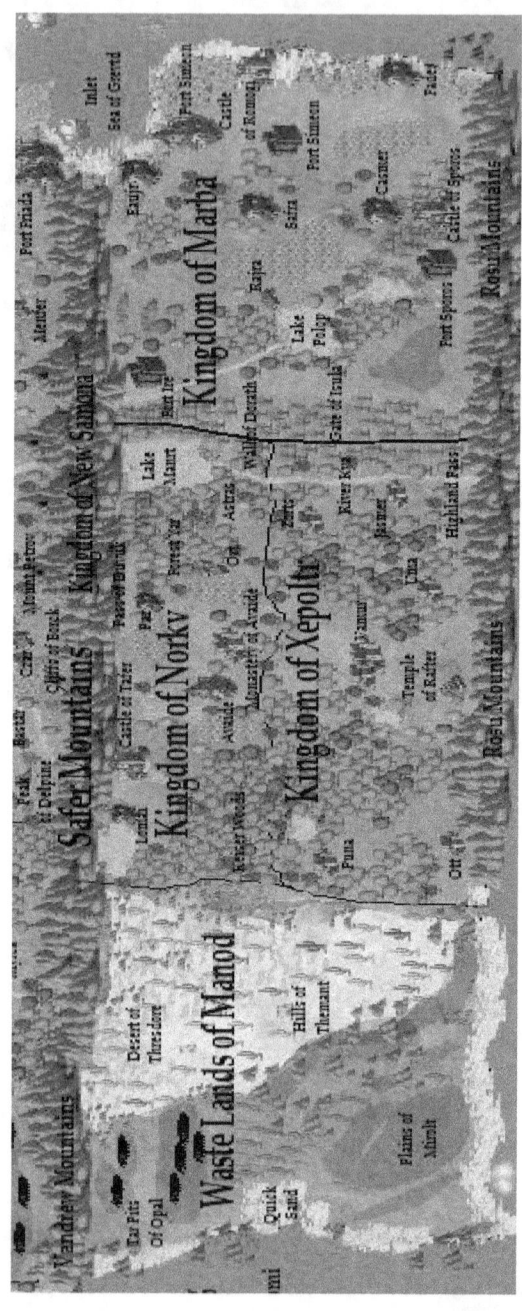

Astrum Solar System

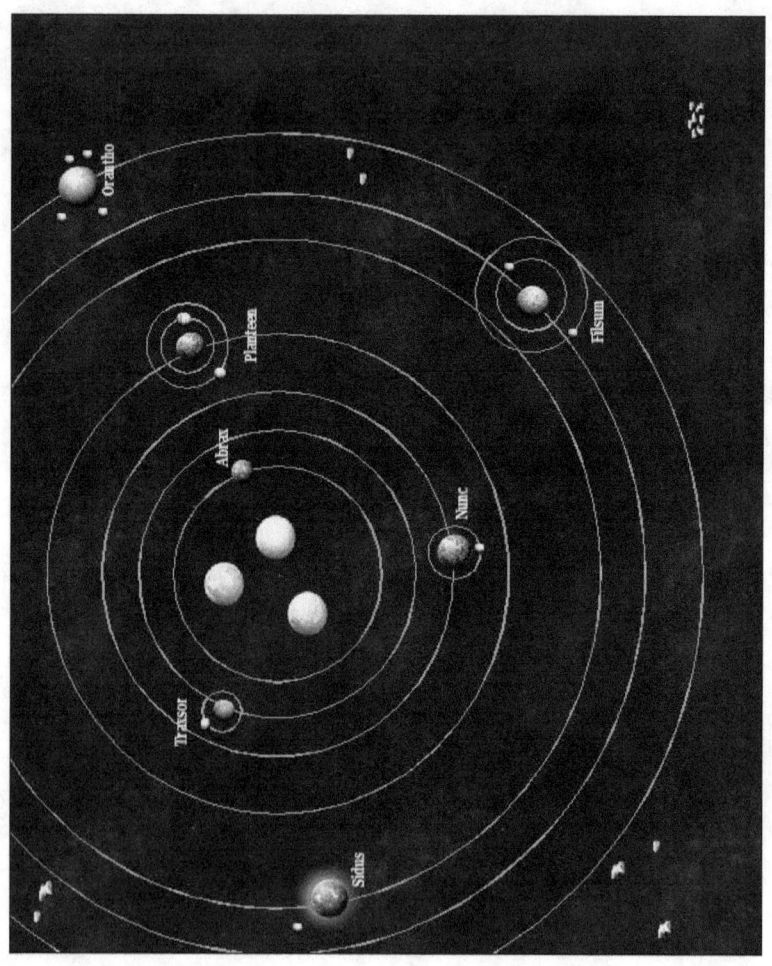